# 1635

## THE PAPAL
## STAKES

# BAEN BOOKS by ERIC FLINT

## The Ring of Fire series:

*1632*
*1633* with David Weber
*1634: The Baltic War* with David Weber
*1634: The Galileo Affair* with Andrew Dennis
*1634: The Bavarian Crisis* with Virginia DeMarce
*1634: The Ram Rebellion* with Virginia DeMarce et al
*1635: The Cannon Law* with Andrew Dennis
*1635: The Dreeson Incident* with Virginia DeMarce
*1635: The Tangled Web* by Virginia DeMarce
*1635: The Eastern Front*
*1635: The Papal Stakes* with Charles E. Gannon
*1636: The Saxon Uprising*
*1636: The Kremlin Games* with Gorg Huff & Paula Goodlett

*Grantville Gazette* ed. by Eric Flint
*Grantville Gazette II* ed. by Eric Flint
*Grantville Gazette III* ed. by Eric Flint
*Grantville Gazette IV* ed. by Eric Flint
*Grantville Gazette V* ed. by Eric Flint
*Grantville Gazette VI* ed. by Eric Flint
*Ring of Fire* ed. by Eric Flint
*Ring of Fire II* ed. by Eric Flint
*Ring of Fire III* ed. by Eric Flint

*Time Spike* with Marilyn Kosmatka

**For a complete list of Baen Books by Eric Flint,
please go to www.baen.com.**

# 1635
## THE PAPAL
## STAKES

# ERIC FLINT
# CHARLES E. GANNON

1635: The Papal Stakes

A Baen Books Original

Baen Publishing Enterprises
P.O. Box 1403
Riverdale, NY 10471
www.baen.com

ISBN: 978-1-4516-3839-4

Cover art by Tom Kidd
Maps by Gorg Huff

First printing, October 2012

Distributed by Simon & Schuster
1230 Avenue of the Americas
New York, NY 10020

Library of Congress Cataloging-in-Publication Data

Flint, Eric.
    1635 : the papal stakes / Eric Flint and Charles E. Gannon.
        p. cm.
    "A Baen book."
    ISBN 978-1-4516-3839-4 (hc)
    1. Urban VII, Pope, 1521–1590—Fiction. 2. Popes—Fiction. 3. Italy—History—17th century—Fiction. 4. Americans—Italy—Fiction. 5. Time travel—Fiction. I. Gannon, Charles E. II. Title.
    PS3556.L548A6186665 2012
    813'.54—dc23

                                                            2012029810

10  9  8  7  6  5  4  3  2  1

Pages by Joy Freeman (www.pagesbyjoy.com)
Printed in the United States of America

Thanks to

—The Editorial Board of the *Grantville Gazette* for many
instances of help and acclimatization, but particularly
Rick Boatright and Walt Boyes.

—John R. D'Angelo of the Fordham University Library.
Without his kind assistance, the Wild Geese would not
have flown from history into my pages; his provision
of countless references and original documents was
invaluable.

—Eric Flint, who invited me to play in this wonderful
sandbox of the past that never was.

—My late father, who would have been astounded to learn
that his insistence on schooling me in the intricacies of
Roman Catholicism and canon law would have ever borne
such strange fruit.


But ultimately, I dedicate this book

—As always, to all the members of my family, who lost me
for so many irreplaceable hours in this real world as I
unfolded this story of a fictional one.

—Charles E. Gannon

# Contents

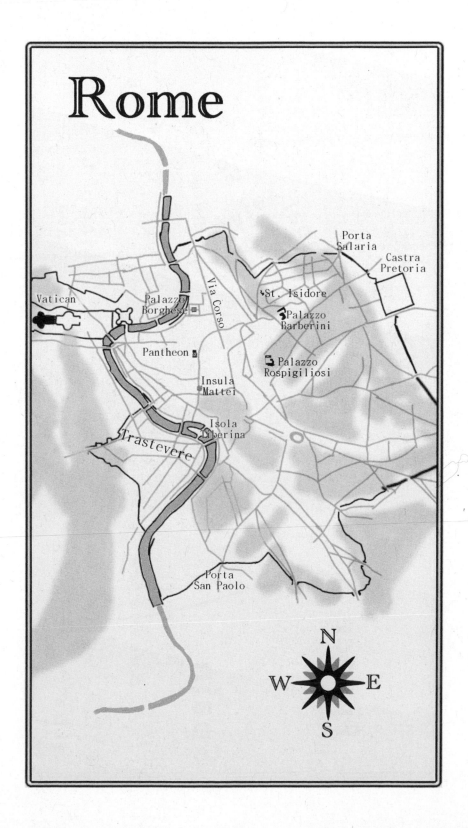

# Rome

Porta
Salaria

Castra
Pretoria

St. Isidore

Vatican

Palazzo
Borghese

Via Corso

Palazzo
Barberini

Pantheon

Palazzo
Rospigiliosi

Insula
Mattei

Isola
Tiberina

Trastevere

Porta
San Paolo

N

W        E

S

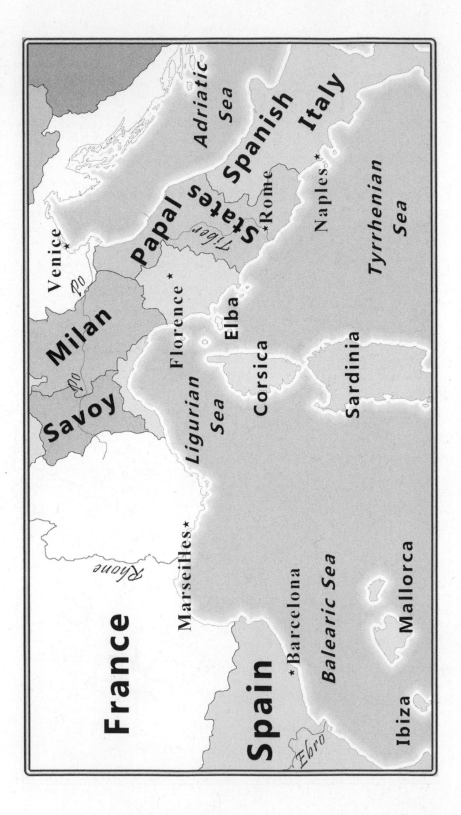

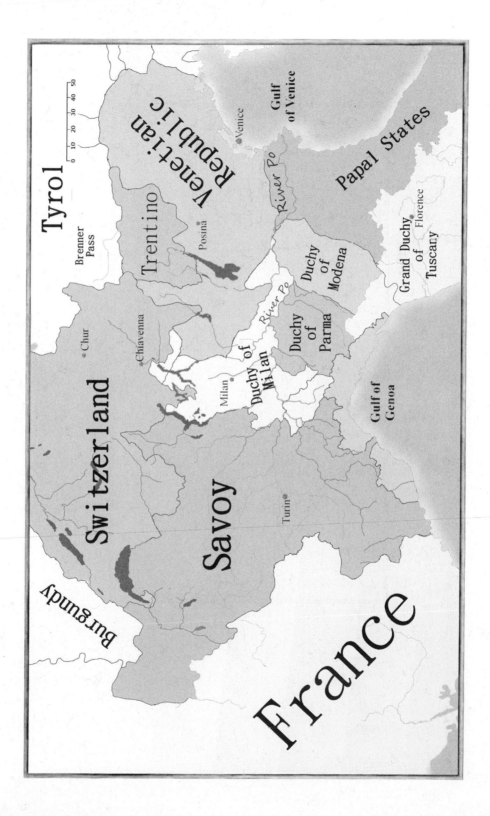

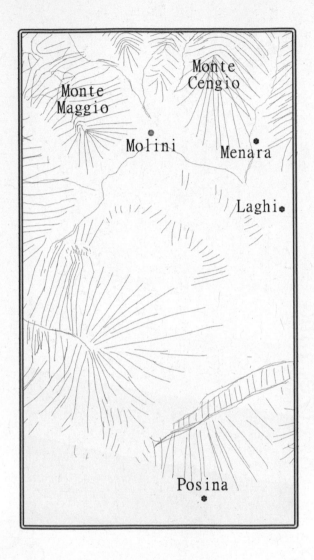

# Part One

## May 1635

The line of the horizon, thin and fine

# Chapter 1

Odo, the young German operating the radio, shook his head. "I'm sorry, Ambassador Nichols, but the signal has been lost."

Sharon Nichols, displaced ambassador to Rome for the United States of Europe, edged so far forward that her ample figure began pushing into Odo's incongruously wiry back. "Did Colonel North confirm that he was moving to the extraction point as quickly as possible?"

Odo shook his head again. "No, Ambassador. The frequency started becoming garbled before I could send those instructions. I shall try to raise Colonel North again."

As the young miller's son from Rudolstadt set about this task, Sharon's husband and de facto chief of intelligence and security, Ruy Sanchez de Casador y Ortiz, placed a hand on her arm. "My love, there is no cause for alarm."

Sharon turned toward him, eyes bright, the smooth curves of her very dark face creased by lines of worry. "We've lost contact with Colonel North, who's supposed to meet our team when it comes out of Chiavenna. A team that just happens to include my father, who told us—*promised* us—that he'd signal us by one PM today with a mission update. That update is already two hours late. So until I know that my father and my friends are with Colonel North's forces and heading back to Grantville, every second of uncertainty is cause for alarm."

She turned back to watch Odo ply the various tricks of his arcane trade.

Ruy raised an eyebrow, but said nothing. In the last few weeks— weeks during which he and Sharon had married, fled Rome, and secreted themselves in this obscure inn near Padua—Ruy had learned that although his new wife had a fiery temperament (both in debate and in bed) she was not given to being testy. She was a large person in every regard: physiognomy, sympathy, forgiveness, and passion. There was nothing narrow about her.

So whereas her rebuff of Ruy's reassurance might have seemed snappish to others, he knew better. He not only had intimate knowledge of Sharon, but insight accrued through three prior marriages and almost six decades of living. No, Sharon Nichols was not being testy; she was wracked by anxiety, exacerbated by the fact that she herself had agreed to send her father and friends into harm's way.

Odo was shaking his head again. "Still no response, Dr. Nichols. And the noise around that frequency is not promising."

"Did Colonel North say where he and his Hibernians were located?"

"They weren't able to report their position, Ambassador. We spent most of our clear air-time trying to establish a mutually secure code."

"What? Why?" Odo seemed to shrivel before Sharon's growing tone and looming torso.

Ruy intervened. "Dearest, the code-checking protocols require absolute precision. If there are any missed symbols, the authentication must be deemed suspect. So with a bad signal it can take many minutes to confirm a secure transmission."

Sharon collected herself. "Odo, when was the last time we had a precise location for Colonel North's unit?"

"Two days ago, Ambassador Nichols. He and his men had just arrived in Silvaplana, having come down out of the Alps by way of the Julier Pass."

"Then, if they've been making steady westward progress, they should be near the extraction zone now. Correct?"

Ruy saved the young radioman from his wife's desperate glare one more time. "Near to the extraction point, perhaps. But we cannot know. They could not head toward it at best speed, my love. What if the extraction was not called for until next week?

Why would two squads of mercenaries—who are known to work exclusively for you Americans—spend a week loitering about the western end of the Val Bregaglia? I doubt even so ingenuous a Spaniard as myself would believe them to simply be on an extended alpine fishing holiday."

Sharon had to smile. But only a little. "Odo. Try again and see if you can raise my da—raise Captain Simpson's group in Chiavenna."

Ruy prayed that someone—anyone—in Chiavenna would respond this time. If they did, it would probably indicate that they had completed their mission in that factious open city and were ready to call for extraction.

But Odo was still struggling with the designated frequencies, all of which sounded like monsoons of static; the legendary vagaries of radio communication to and from Alpine valleys were dominating the day. "No response on any of the primary frequencies, Ambassador. Shifting to check the emergency backup frequencies."

Ruy, seeing his wife's breathing increase, murmured words only she could hear: "My love, you must be calm. Your staff all looks to you; if you panic, they shall surely do so, also."

She closed her eyes. "I know, Ruy. But it's my dad out there, and Rita, and Tom: all the up-time family and friends I have left in this—in your—world. I should never have had them stop in Chiavenna. Never."

Ruy ran what he hoped was a soothing palm down her firm arm until he could hold her hand—low, where no one might see. Feeling his fingers, she clutched hard, almost as a frightened child might have. And in that hungry grasp—so incongruous in his strong wife—Ruy found the answer to an aspect of up-time behavior that had perplexed him for many months.

Despite the advantages in technology and knowledge enjoyed by the up-timers—the twentieth-century Americans who had become time-stranded refugees in seventeenth-century Germany—they often seemed paralyzed into inaction by fear of loss. It was not cowardice, for even the most stalwart up-timers evinced this tendency. So Ruy had been unable to conjecture a common cause for this up-time trait until, just three days ago, during a radio communiqué with his wife, Prime Minister Mike Stearns of the USE had used the phrase "risk aversive." Ruy had understood the term's meaning, but only now—triggered by the clutch of his wife's hand—did its underlying emotional contexts become clear.

In the up-timers' world—that of the rather improbable year 2000 AD that had been home to the even more improbable democratic republic of the United States of America—almost all risk had been reduced dramatically. War, shipping, mining—even flying huge rockets to the moon—had to satisfy safety requirements that were almost comical by Ruy's standards. For people born in his time, great undertakings inevitably involved great risk. The seas routinely swallowed sailors, the mountains buried miners, and pestilences and famine took their toll upon all the children of the Earth, no matter their location or station in life. Life was a gamble, at best.

But not in the twentieth century, evidently. When a child or a mother died during birth, it was deemed an uncommon tragedy. In Ruy's world, the same event was simply a reminder that the attempt to create life often ended in death.

The up-time elimination of risk had even extended to war itself. The Americans' medical knowledge and practices made many mortal wounds survivable. Ruy himself was alive only because of these up-time skills. A lethal belly wound from a sword—he had been horribly outnumbered by those assassins, after all!—had turned out to be simply a morning's challenging surgery for the second, or maybe only third, ranking physician among the three-thousand-plus up-timers.

Ruy looked over at the third-ranked surgeon who had performed the medical miracle to which he owed his continued existence and smiled. Sharon Nichols was a medical prodigy in this world. The surgery that had saved Ruy had been performed before the cream of Venice's medical community, ensuring her immediate stardom as a *Dottoressa* of international renown. But in the world she had come from, she had held a relatively lowly post, furnished with a suitably humble label: she had been an Emergency Medical Technician. But, being the daughter of the greatest doctor now alive—her ex-street thug, ex-Marine Corps father, James—had no doubt given her advantages and experience beyond those normally possessed by other EMTs. Or so Ruy presumed.

However, regardless of their skills, the up-time physicians routinely cursed themselves upon losing a patient, as if they expected the power of the Creator Himself to be manifest every time they treated a patient. And this, Ruy realized as his wife continued to squeeze his hand tightly, was the key to the up-timers' "risk-aversion": they had become utterly unaccustomed to taking the chances that were unavoidable in this "down-time" world. Most of the threats they faced now had been eliminated by the sciences of their future world, so they had to continually remind themselves that they were dwelling in a much more dangerous time—and that adjustment did not come easily to most of them.

As an attitude, it shared common psychological roots with the frustration he had observed among many of the more accomplished up-timers. Although they did not intend to demean down-timers or the technical limitations of the world of 1635, one could often hear Americans mutter deprecations upon its crude tools, interspersed with bitter longing for the devices of the future. Except, of course, that the future they remembered would never come to pass, now. In their world, no American town had ever arrived in the midst of the Thirty Years' War, radically changing its outcome, and the history and technology of Europe along with it. So whatever the coming days held, they would not lead to the future the Americans had come from. Their own arrival had undone the possibility that the world they called home would ever exist.

From out of the radio's washes of static emerged a single, clear click. Ruy felt his wife's hand flex quickly—and then grow still, tense, as two more, longer clicks sounded, followed by a rapid patter of them as the interference diminished to a sound more akin to bacon frying in a distant room.

"Is that them—the group in Chiavenna?"

Odo smiled. "Yes, it's my friend Matthias."

Ruy smiled too, half out of his own gladness, half simply to see his wife's radiant joy and relief. "What is Matthias sending, Odo?" he asked.

"That they are still in Chiavenna. The rest of the group is on their way to the rendezvous point with the cardinal."

Ruy raised an eyebrow. "Well, our courier apparently caught up with the cardinal while he was still traveling along the Spanish Road in the Valtelline. Meaning that the holy father's information was accurate."

"Accurate enough to save the cardinal's life," appended Sharon. "And he might be the only cardinal loyal to the pope who'll be saved, at this rate. Unless, maybe, some of the other cardinals whom Borja has 'disappeared' might still be alive somewhere, waiting for—"

Ruy shook his head. "Kings, like criminals, cover their misdeeds with great finality, my beauteous wife. And Borja is both a king of the church and a criminal of the basest kind. He will not leave any evidence if he can help it."

The room was still. The threat to the lives of the incognito refugees who were with them here outside Padua—Pope Urban VIII, his nephew Cardinal Antonio Barberini, and Father Vitelleschi, the father-general of the Jesuit Order—seemed suddenly very close. Glancing at the countryside outside the room's small window, Ruy found it distressingly easy to imagine it filled with shadowy assassins and informers. The sooner they could get His Holiness on one of the up-timers' wondrous airplanes, the better.

Odo leaned forward as the snarling static returned. "Matthias indicates they have not been detected by the Spanish or Milanese on their journey north, and that they will depart as soon as—" He stopped, moving his head quickly from side to side.

"As soon as what?" Sharon tried to sound calm; Ruy was sad to admit that his beloved was failing miserably.

"I could not make it out; I'm only receiving fragments now. And given the trapdoor codes built into this cipher, I cannot be sure if the letters I think I'm hearing are still accurate. I might have missed a trapdoor character."

"Which changes the code, right?"

"Yes, Ambassador Nichols. But, from the rest of the message, I would say that Captain Simpson's group plans to leave Chiavenna immediately after meeting the cardinal."

Ruy's and Sharon's eyes drifted to the window; the sunlight was no longer yellow, but late-day amber. "That had better be one quick meeting," observed Sharon.

"Do not worry, my love. I'm sure all will go well."

She half turned, looking at him over her thickly graceful shoulder. "Oh? Really? And why would you say that, Ruy?"

Ruy shrugged. "To ease your mind, love."

She touched his arm lightly, then turned back to encourage Odo to check other frequencies.

As Ruy studied his wife's wide, watchful eyes in their fixation upon the radio, he silently conceded that Sharon was, of course, entirely correct: his assurance that "all will go well" was merely hopeful nonsense. The simple truth of the matter was that he *hoped* all would go well.

But of course, it rarely did.

# Chapter 2

The proprietor of the rustic *Crotto Fiume* leaned a bit closer to Tom Simpson and almost crooned: "Are you sure you won't have the soup, signor? It is a local specialty: black cherry and game. A favorite of men who are large like you—who are so, so...*robusto*."

"Oh, puh-leeze," Rita Simpson whisper-groaned down at the tabletop.

As much to taunt his wife as satisfy the culinary curiosity that the stew's description had piqued, Tom assented. "*Si, grazie.*"

"*Brego*," replied the innkeep, cook, and owner—for that was the arrangement in most of these small, informal *crotti*—who bowed himself out to prepare their meals.

As soon as he was gone, Rita leaned against Tom's Herculean bicep. "My *robusto* hero," she cooed, "He can eat with the best of them."

And while it was true that Tom had a healthy appetite, the era into which he had been thrown—the end of the Thirty Years' War—had also trimmed off any small residual fat that might have originated with meals taken in the fast-food eateries and saturated fat emporiums of the very late twentieth century.

Melissa Mailey looked at Tom and seemed less amused. "Did you really have to have the soup?"

"Uh...no, but it sounded good. And I get to see all of you roll your eyes." He leaned back, stretching his immense arms outward from his even more formidable chest and shoulders.

"I'm not rolling my eyes." Melissa's voice was devoid of jocularity. "I'm worried about our rendezvous."

"What? You think the soup takes half a day to cook?"

"No, Tom: I think that we should not spend a second more in towns than we must—not since leaving Lombardy, at any rate. We don't have a lot of friends in these parts."

James Nichols broke open a small loaf of bread, not much bigger than his thumb; it sent up a fragrant puff of steam. "Now, Melissa, we're on neutral ground, here. Chiavenna is an open city."

"Which is a very nebulous term here, James. This isn't simply Casablanca with the Alps instead of the Atlantic, and with snow instead of sand. These folks don't define 'neutral' the way we do, and they've not had much success with co-dominium—excuse me, *tri*-dominium—arrangements like this one."

Diminutive Arcangelo Severi leaned over so that he could see past James' large, prominently veined black hands to the people farther down the table. "The Signora Mailey, she speaks correctly." Two weeks on the road with the group had almost ironed the idiomatic peculiarities out of his English—almost, but not quite. "The Spanish now guard Chiavenna instead of the Milanese? It is a black wolf replacing a gray wolf: same breed, same teeth, just a slightly different coat."

"And the French observers are hardly our friends, either." Melissa tapped her fork for emphasis. "Officially, we are still every bit almost-at-war with them as the Hapsburgs."

"Well, not with the Austrian Hapsburgs, at least," temporized James. "And they also have a guard detachment here, right?"

"Yes, comprised of about a dozen reprobates that the commander down in the Valtelline didn't want rousting Protestants any more." Melissa sniffed. "So he sent them up here, a region where almost six hundred Protestants were massacred only fifteen years ago. Another typically deft move by another typically tactful servitor of Imperial Viennese spleen and incompetence."

Tom smelled a medley of rich foods approaching as the door to the kitchen opened. "Aw, c'mon, Melissa: the Austrian Hapsburgs are a country mile better than the Spanish. And their new 'emperor,' Ferdinand III, is way more open-minded than his parochial pappy. You know as well as I that there have been plenty of positive overtures traded with Vienna in the past year."

"Wonderful," was Melissa's wooden reply, as their meals—cold wheat polenta shot through with small chunks of cheese, boiled potato, spring vegetables, and what looked a lot like salami—emerged from the kitchen. "I'll be charitable and assume our diplomatic nattering with the Austrian Hapsburgs is the promising harbinger it seems to be. But what good does that do us here?"

James smiled sideways. "You sound nervous, hon."

"I am."

"A shame. And you always lose your appetite when you're anxious, so I'll just help you with th—"

James' reach for Melissa's plate was deflected by a prim and well-aimed slap at his hand. "I'm not *that* nervous. But I am dead serious. And I hope that doesn't prove to be an ironically apropos choice of words."

A multi-vocal and multi-lingual exchange that was more of a mélange than their entrees poured out of the kitchen door as a young fellow brought them their drinks. Waves of Italian splashed against two dialects of Lombard, all capped by a gull-like screeching in Romansch. At an adjoining table, two men ceased their mutterings in Savoyard French in an attempt to eavesdrop. They gave up as the babel of languages became too fluid and dense for untangling. At which point, Arcangelo leaned forward, and under the cover of the multi-tongued cacophony, stressed at both Tom and James: "You will do well to heed the words of Signora Mailey. We should have simple food only."

Tom slurped his thick soup with defiant gusto. Nichols smiled and spoke around his mouthful of polenta and cheese: "Relax, Arco: with the exception of the high-protein fodder selected by Captain Kodiak, here"—his merry eyes flicked over at Simpson's immense torso—"we bought the cheapest, least conspicuous meals that would also sustain us for the last leg of our journey."

"*Si*, true, it only cost a few quatrines more, but maybe it would have been better to buy food we can carry, hey? So that when the cardin—eh, when our 'last companion' arrives, we can leave *molto presto*."

Tom chewed a piece of what tasted like smoked venison. "Why in such a rush now, Arco? I would have thought you would have been more nervous on the way up here."

Arcangelo shrugged. "Before yesterday, we were on lake boats with a dozen other foreigners, all bound over the Alps. Some were even traveling without the benefit of a native to guide, and speak for them, such as I have done for you." His smile, gap-toothed, was nonetheless full of quick, light charm. "So: from Garlate, to Lecco, to Como, then up the Mera to the north end of Lago Mezzola, it was a long day, but still, only *one* day. Thirty of your miles, at most. And a boat owned and crewed by Bergamaschi, so except when paying the tolls, when did we even see the Milanese?"

Tom felt the eyes of the other Americans focusing on spare Arco as he spoke, realizing just how much more than a simple native guide he was. He had come to them from their fiscal partners in Venice, the Cavriani family, and that clan's proclivities for subtlety, mild self-deprecation, and invisible shrewdness were rapidly becoming evident in the almost elfin Arcangelo—

—Whose description of their earlier journey continued unabated. "And yesterday, we walked along with scores of others, following the Mera road up here. But we were already in Milanese territory, so no checkpoints, no further tolls. I'm not sure we even saw a soldier."

"We saw two." James Nichols' tone was not confrontational, but quite sure. "One as we got started in the morning, but he was looking north, up the valley, and not along the road. Then another just as we passed the intersection with the Via Valtelline. He was on the crest of a defile, watching the road."

"*Si*, with a few cavalry out of sight in the defile below, I'll wager."

"That's not a bet; that's a certainty. But I must say, Arco, you are starting to seem more like a—well, yet another Cavriani factotum, not a guide."

Arco smiled. "A guide? I never said I was a guide."

"Yes, you did. You just said—"

"I said I was sent to guide you on your journey back to Grantville. *To guide*—that is a job, an activity, not a title. I have never claimed to *be* a guide." Interestingly, as Arco moved into what should have been the trickier lexical ground of argumentation, his English became more self-assured and fluid. No, definitely not a guide after all.

"And so now you're all jittery, Arco? Why?" Rita was, somehow, never so charming as when she was utterly direct. Or so it seemed to her still-infatuated husband.

"Signora Simpson, it is our last, eh, 'fellow-traveler' that worries me. This decision that the ambassadora Nichols sent yesterday—that we should wait for him to meet us in Chiavenna, in this *crotto*—this I do not like."

"Why?" Rita persisted. "The cardi—the friar was intercepted when he arrived in the Valtelline from Austrian territory, before he had even sent word of his return to Rome. As far as Borja and the rest of Philip's papal usurpers know, he's still on Legation business in Vienna."

"Yes, so it would seem. But answer me this: how did the ambassadora know where to find him? And in the middle of his journey through the Alps?"

"She has sources who were intimately—and *officially*—familiar with the friar's estimated progress and itinerary."

In that moment, the full cleverness of Arcangelo Severi was revealed for a split-second: his eyes were as clear and sharp as a mousing cat's. "Yes, I . . . see," he confirmed for himself and everyone else with a tight little nod: he had pronounced "see" as "See." As in "Holy See."

*Damn it, from just that one little tidbit of data—that Sharon has officially reliable sources on the probable actions of the cardinal—Arco figured that we've got Pope Urban stashed near Padua with the rest of the embassy staff that high-tailed it out of Rome when the Spanish invaded. Pretty clever "guide," we've got. Easy to underestimate, too. Which makes him doubly valuable to the Cavriani, I'll bet.* Tom leaned back, the last of the black cherry-and-game soup reflecting up like inky blood from the reservoir of his large spoon. "So, Arco, does knowing the source of the ambassador's knowledge make you a little less worried?"

"No: it makes me a little *more* worried. Well, no—a *lot* more worried."

"What? Why?"

Melissa answered Rita before Arco could even open his mouth. "Because anything one side *does* know, the other side *could* know. Can we assume everyone associated with our former Rome embassy—and our embassy in Venice—is unbribable? And that the papal troops who are no doubt traveling along with the friar are equally virtuous? The bottom line is this: there are too many places where a leak could occur. Our ambassador's very authoritative official source is also far too important to keep his own correspondence. And it's not as if he was in any position to simply drop in on the friar himself to send news of this rendezvous: he had to send a courier."

James Nichols shrugged. "At least the embassy is communicating with us by radio; that's half of the potential intelligence leaks eliminated."

Rita was frowning at Melissa. "So you think that the ca—the friar—could be intercepted before he gets to us?"

"Maybe. Maybe killed outright; it's what Borja reportedly did to sixteen other 'friars' in Rome just a few weeks ago. Or maybe our friar will be apprehended and questioned to see who he was planning to meet here in Chiavenna." Melissa's gaze made a significant circuit of the table.

"Or he might have simply been followed," put in Arco, "which would be the worst. If our foes were that clever—"

The door to the *crotto* creaked open slowly and a soldier sauntered in. A buff coat, a saber, one pistol on his belt, but the bandolier and high boots said "horseman." He wore no colors or livery—typical for armies of the period—and hadn't as much as a colored armband to suggest his allegiance. But, if the message passed on by James' daughter Sharon was accurate, he would be a guard dispatched from the papal troops to provide the friar with an escort over the Austrian Alps and down to Rome.

The trooper's eyes swept the room, rested on the table of locally garbed up-timers for a moment and then narrowed when they reached James Nichols. It was hard to tell if his expression was smile or sneer; perhaps a bit of both. He gestured for a small, rotund man to emerge from behind his shielding bulk. "I've eaten in this *crotto* before, friar. I can vouch for the food and prices"—he turned and started out the door—"but not the company. *Arrivederci*." In exiting, he signaled the need for a hasty departure to a similarly equipped trooper just beyond the door, which he closed after himself with a tug at its rough iron handle.

The friar actually flinched as the heavy timbers slammed home with a drumlike boom. He stood wringing his hands, looking at them. Tom wondered if he was about to start crying.

In that second, Arco was on his feet, face bright, wide smile revealing an impressive collection of teeth that had evidently resisted the normal genetic command to follow a common scheme of alignment. "Friar Luigi, Mamma sends you warm wishes, and hopes for your health. Now, sit with us and share our meal." A bit overcome, the man in the friar's robes allowed Arco to guide him to the table. He looked at the up-timers as if they might make him their next course at dinner.

"Please, Friar," said Tom, "have a seat. And please, I presume you will accept our hospitality, particularly since Brother Michael sends his regards?"

The friar looked up quickly at the mention of "Brother Michael." "Yes . . . yes; I will. I am glad—very glad—for your invitation." Small, clever eyes assessed the proximity of Tom and Rita, quickly determined the implicit relationship to be spousal, and then his eyes shifted to Rita, alone. "Tell your family—particularly Brother Michael—that his hospitality honors me."

The friar who was in fact Cardinal Ginetti was probably not a man of action or courage, but he—like the rest of the cardinals Tom had met—was clever and subtle. Two sentences had been exchanged each way and they had already established each others' identity, that asylum was being offered by Rita's brother Mike Stearns—prime minister of the USE—and that it had been accepted. But for anyone not aware of the precise identity of the group around the table, the exchange would merely have sounded like a meeting that mixed old friends with new acquaintances. *Either way, the contact part of this rendezvous went easily and quickly enough. These little cardinals are pretty smooth operators. Now, time to pay the bill and stroll back to the—*

The door opened: a medium-sized man stepped in, closed it, a broad brimmed hat pulled low, covering the upper half of his face. His clothes were simple, but made for travel; they might be well-worn, but they were not worn out. There was no sign of a weapon on his belt or in the loose folds of his cloak, but his flowing attire would make it entirely possible to carry a large dagger completely undetected. The proprietor came rushing out: the Babelesque debate in the kitchen flooded briefly into the room before he shut the door. "*Signor—mangi*? Food?"

The newcomer nodded, murmured a request, and took a seat at one of the two remaining tables, the one closest to the group. He turned his hunched back toward the up-timers in an apparent effort to afford both parties some modicum of privacy.

It was, even to Tom's untrained eye, all an act. Judging from the long, significant looks he got from both James and Melissa, he was not alone in his assessment. *Well, we never planned on* this, *at least not so quickly after meeting the cardinal. Whoever this guy is, he must have been right on the little friar's tail. Which means Melissa was probably right: someone dropped a dime on our rendezvous with His Eminence. And with this new guy's big ears only a few feet away, we don't have any way to come up with a plan on the sly. He probably speaks the whole gamut of local languages: Italian, Lombard, Savoyard, German, Romansch, maybe Romlisch. And since he obviously knows that we're the folks he's looking for—*James' dark black skin was, to put it lightly, distinctive in Alpine Italy—*this guy was probably chosen, in part, because he speaks English, as well. So how do we—?*

But James was smiling. "ooD-ay oo-yay eak-spay ig-pay atin-lay?"

*Damn, but Doc was smart.* "I an-cay."

Arco, for the first time in Tom's acquaintance of him, looked utterly flummoxed.

Melissa looked like she was swallowing lye with every word she uttered. "Oo-yay av-hay an an-play?"

James nodded. "Tom, ell-tay Arco out-abay oor-yay ick-say other-May."

*Wha—? Oh, I get it.* Tom rose, head hung a little. The *crotto's* newest patron shifted slightly, probably trying to use his ears to gauge what the movement behind him was and it if represented potential danger. Tom drew out the chair at the end of the table next to Arco, who had recovered enough to feign understanding of the pig-latin gibberish flying past him. "Arco—" said Tom with feeling.

Rita's foot tapped against Tom's ankle. *Okay, I guess I was going over the top, already. Hell, my idea of method acting is Arnold Schwarzenegger.* Whom he almost resembled, physically. "Arco, did I tell you how sick my mother is?"

One microsecond of confusion flitted across the young Venetian's face, which then became a study in heartfelt compassion. "Tom, I am so sorry. I had heard she was doing poorly, but I had no idea—"

Under which James muttered. "Ore-may of em-thay in the eet-stray."

Melissa nodded tightly. "No oubt-day."

Tom hung his head as the proprietor brought his newest patron a bowl of the same black-cherry-and-game soup. "She's so sick," Tom sighed mightily. "I should return home at once, but—leaving here is so hard. How can I possibly go?"

That line—consistent with the "sick-mother" act, but also a pertinent question about the tactics of exiting the *crotto*—earned a broad smile from Melissa.

"Om-tay oes-gay irst-fay. I'll et-gay the oor-day. James ext-nay. We eer-clay the eet-stray and un-ray. Okay?"

Tom nodded at Melissa's plan, but made the nod also look like he was simply harmonizing with Arco's consoling pat on the back. "So, how do we start you on your way home, Tom?" Arco asked. But as he spoke, he leaned in James' direction.

James said, "Arco, I believe that fellow behind you just insulted Tom's mother."

Arco's head snapped up straight, as though startled, but his eyes were bright with shrewd amusement. He turned, shocked, in the direction of the apparent patron behind them. "How dare you! Tom, do you know this *suino*? Do you hear what he said about your sick mother?"

Tom looked up from under ominous brows at the same moment the newcomer turned around, stunned; evidently, it had taken him a second to realize that the outburst behind was both aimed at, and about, him.

Arco's outburst flowed on like an alpine cataract. "He calls your mother a—a *puttana del diavolo! Merda!* I will—"

The other patrons looked up, aghast. The fellow's mouth leaked food forgotten in mid-chew and his eyes widened: partly in surprise, partly in fear.

Because Tom was up and moving. With reflexes so fast that they were incongruous in so large a man, he had jumped out of his seat and closed to combat range even as the startled *faux*-patron was rising from his chair. A denial was half out of his mouth, but his lowering brow suggested a dawning realization that he was being suckered.

Or rather, sucker-punched. Tom's right fist came shooting straight out from his shoulder, landing with a sharp crack on his target's somewhat pointy jaw. The much smaller man went straight back, unconscious as he hit the table, sending his own bowl of soup and beer flying up in a cascade of chunks, dark red broth, and foam. "Bastard!" shouted Tom, who, feigning sudden emotional distress, moved quickly for the door, his apparently solicitous companions rising to follow and comfort him.

As he reached the door, Tom snaked the Hockenjoss & Klott

revolver out from under his cloak, cocked it, and nodded Melissa toward the door.

"Tom?" Rita whispered, not noticing that the dark red broth had splashed along the left-hand side of Tom's cloak.

"Yes?"

"You're a lousy actor, darling."

"I know," Tom said as he nodded at Melissa Mailey to yank open the door. "Now, here we go."

# Chapter 3

Tom Simpson leaped out into the cool alpine air, the cap-and-ball revolver ready in a two-handed grip. As he drew a bead on his first target, he saw exactly what he had expected to see.

Four armed men—medium-to-large in height and build—were positioned around the entry to the *crotto*. Because they were in a public street, they were not in combat-ready postures or positions. Neither were their weapons; the tools of their grim trade were concealed in their cloaks, or by their bodies. And while Tom wasn't a great shot, at these ranges—six to twelve feet—he didn't need to be.

Tom started firing, double-tapping as he went. His first target was not the closest of the thugs, but definitely the most dangerous, already raising a double-barreled flintlock fowling piece that had a menacingly short profile. Tom's first shot missed completely but the second .44 caliber bullet punched a red hole in the man's chest. He went down without a sound.

Sidestepping to clear the doorway, the American shifted his aim to the big swordsman who was even now rushing forward, blade rasping out of its sheath and reflecting the failing sunlight. He fired two more shots from the H&K revolver, both of which went higher than he'd aimed. That was the adrenaline at work, making his motions jerkier than he'd intended them to be. Tom understood the reaction and had tried to be ready for it. But "being ready" simply wasn't a substitute for the constant training that special forces and assault troops underwent. He was an artillery officer, not accustomed to fighting at close range with a pistol.

Luckily, the "miss" didn't matter. The first shot struck the thug high on his forehead. The ball gashed open the flesh and ricocheted off the skull, throwing the man's head back—and leaving his trachea exposed to take the second ball full on. He fell backward, out of the fight and mortally wounded.

Tom had only two rounds left. He felt a moment's sharp desire for an automatic pistol with a large clip—and an even sharper desire for a twelve-pounder loaded with canister.

*Doc, you better be out here when you're supposed to be...*

Tom made a split-second decision to fire his remaining two rounds at one assailant rather than trying to take down both men. He simply wasn't a Wild West gunfighter—as demonstrated by the fact that only one of the four shots he'd fired so far had hit precisely where he'd aimed it.

He chose the smaller of the last two, whose double-barreled snaphaunce pistol was almost leveled at him. He fired twice again—and was dry.

The choice to double-tap his third target saved his life. This thug had been the furthest off, and Tom's first shot went a little high and wide: it only grazed the assassin's shoulder. But that had made the target flinch; he discharged both barrels a split-second too early. One round cut a seam in the back of Tom's boot; the other bullet spanged and whined off the center of the flagstone he was straddling.

As it did, Tom's second and final shot vented the bottom of his target's left ribcage. The assassin doubled over and went back with a shuddering moan. But the last of the ambushers was racing in, saber poised to start swinging through a lethal arc. Despite Tom's ex-football-player reflexes, amplified by military training and combat, there was no way he was going to be able to—

Three sharp reports split the air just to Tom's left: James Nichols had finally entered the firefight. His first shot missed entirely and his second shot inflicted a minor flesh wound in the man's side. The wound wasn't fatal. Just a crease, really, that might have broken a rib but hadn't done much more damage. But it stopped the man's charge long enough for the doctor to steady down and fire a third, careful shot. That ball struck the man squarely in the chest and he went down as if he'd been struck by a mallet.

"Damn, getting rusty," muttered the ex-Marine from just behind Tom's shoulder. He grinned suddenly. "Being honest, my street gang training didn't really emphasize marksmanship."

Tom barked a little laugh. Like him, Nichols was no master of the handgun. The doctor had been trained as a sniper when he was in the Marines—with a proper damn rifle, with a proper damn caliber and real by-God telescopic sights.

"Two out of three shots on time and on target are plenty good enough for me, Doc. Let's get moving."

Tom's wife Rita emerged from the *Crotto Fiume,* which was still silent. The muttering and then shouting of the startled clientele would start soon enough, no doubt. "Done making noise out here, honey?" Rita asked. Despite the levity of the words, her voice was shaky.

"I sure hope so," Tom replied. He also hoped his own voice didn't sound as shaky as his wife's—but he was pretty sure it did.

Rita shuddered as she started stepping over the bodies. "I'm never going to get used to situations like this."

"And you shouldn't," put in Melissa Mailey, who emerged from the *crotto,* towing the shocked cardinal. "Accepting bloodshed is a necessary part of being human; failing to notice it means you're becoming less than human. No offense, James," she added with a glance at her Vietnam-veteran life-partner.

"None taken," James murmured as he snatched up the double-barreled fowling piece, searched for ammunition, and kept a swivel-necked watch on both ends of the street. That didn't deter him from some gentle teasing: "Of course, darling wife, your own rhetorical peacenik robes are starting to fray at the edges."

"They've been reduced to threads and lint by living in this century," Melissa responded grimly. Changing the direction and tone of her voice, she urged the cardinal, "Step quickly, Your Eminence; we need to move rapidly now." The small, pudgy man nodded unsteadily, looking rather pathetic in the nondescript friar's garb.

Bringing up the rear—and scattering coins, apologies, and wildly implausible explanations in their wake—Arco Severi closed the door gently and turned toward them, smelling of old garlic and fresh sweat. "*Merda,*" he breathed, "what now?"

"Now," said Tom, snapping up his pistol's barrel assembly so that it closed upon the fresh cylinder he had loaded, "we run."

The small cardinal's voice quavered: "Won't that attract attention?"

"Your Eminence," Tom said through a patient smile while wondering if the cardinal *could* run, "we've fired almost ten shots. We are leaving four attackers dead in the street, and one unconscious in the *crotto*. I think we've probably attracted about as much attention as we possibly could. Speed is our only friend, now."

And setting his actions to match his words, Tom Simpson began running in the direction of the Mera River, trying to put aside the growing feeling that the pine-carpeted alpine peaks that soared up at every point of the compass—except due south—were closing in on, and even over, them.

They stayed close alongside those buildings whose shadows were already long enough to start creeping up the opposite façades. Two blocks shy of reaching the river, Tom turned left, leading them into a small lane that paralleled the main road—the Viale Maloggia—which wound out of town to the northeast. It followed alongside the Mera, which, although merely a shallow gorge at present, had been a white-frothed flume only one month earlier, due to the spring *Schmelzwasser* that had come rushing down out of the swollen mountain cataracts.

As the rest of the group caught up with him—Melissa wheezing almost as much as the cardinal—Tom looked downstream toward the town's center: no reaction from there, yet. Good: with any luck, they might—

"Tom." Melissa's voice was very calm, low-pitched. Which meant disaster on the hoof.

"What is it?"

She pointed down. "That."

Tom and the rest followed her finger: a dark, brown-red stain was collecting near his feet, dripping down from his traveling cloak. As a watch whistle shrilled back near the *crotto*, Rita stepped closer to her husband, her worried eyes scanning his body.

Tom shook his head. "But I'm not hit."

Melissa nodded. "Of course you're not. That's not your blood; that's your soup."

*Soup?* Tom stared at the stain, remembering the flurry of action—and wide spray of soup—that had immediately preceded their exit from the *crotto*. *We're going to be tracked—tracked and killed—because I chose to have the* soup? Had the situation not been so desperate, he would have laughed. His life—and the lives of his wife, his friends, and charges—now hung in the balance because he had chosen to have a bowl of soup.

Tom looked up from the bloodlike spatter on the ground, glanced behind them and then toward the Viale Maloggia. He tore off his cloak and threw it aside: "We've got to run. Fast. Now."

"We just *were* running," complained Melissa, her hand on her side, one corner of her mouth wrinkled in the attempt to suppress what Tom guessed was a wind-stitch.

"We run or we fight."

"So what are we waiting for?" asked Melissa, stretching her long legs northward to run parallel to the bending course of the Mera.

Four minutes of near-sprinting put the sound of the whistles a little farther behind them. As they panted to a halt in front of their *taverna*, the whistles of the town watch stopped abruptly.

"They found the cloak," panted James. "Figuring out where to search next."

"I will get Matthias—"

"I am here," said the young German from one of their windows on the second story. "I just reestablished contact with Padua, and am in the middle of sending an update to—"

Tom shook his head. "Break down the radio, Matthias. Keep the up-time transmitter separate, in your pack. I'll send Arco and the ladies up to help you load our—"

"No need," he assured them as he detached the wire he had hooked to a roof-tile as an antenna. "All our bags are packed. Trail gear only. Everything else I have left under the beds."

"Matthias," gasped Rita, "how did you know to—?"

"Why, Frau Mailey suggested I have our gear ready, in the event that the rendezvous would be—what is your word?—'compromised.'"

James straightened up. "It's great to have a girlfriend who's always thinking."

"Particularly when no one else bothers to. Matthias, are you just about through?"

"Yes; could Herr Severi lend hands?"

Arco was inside before Matthias had completed the request.

Rita looked back down the road. "How long do you figure we've got?"

Tom shrugged. "Could be as much as ten minutes. They'll have to gather together, see how many searchers they've got, and

then eliminate which ways we definitely didn't go. We're near the
northern limits of the town, here, and the lack of walls is a big
help, but if we're not moving soon—"

Matthias and Arco came bustling out the door, the latter adding, "Our account is settled, with a tip to encourage the owner's
tardy mention of our lodging here."

"Excellent. Now, Matthias, dump the batteries in the river."

"What? But Captain Simpson, they are priceless—"

"And make sure the jars break on the rocks. Everything else
that will sink goes in the water as well. We can't afford any extra
weight and I don't want them to learn that we had a radio. Did
you get a general signal out?"

"Yes, sir."

"And were the conditions right for it to be heard in both
Padua and Chur?"

Matthias shrugged as he sent the battery-jars crashing down
among the rocks of the Mera. "It is a good time for a signal . . .
I think."

Tom led them into a sustainable trot. "You *think*?"

Matthias shrugged as he jogged. "You can never know for
sure, Captain."

*Well, that's just great,* thought Tom as he noted the cardinal
already laboring to maintain the pace, and Melissa putting on a
pain-proof, but increasingly pale, face.

*Just great.*

Odo leaned back from the radio, frowning. "No, Ambassador,
it is neither a failure, nor meteorological interference. Matthias
simply went off the air—like that." He snapped his fingers sharply.

Sharon tried to keep the frown off her face. "Was there any
word, any warning that—?"

Her husband put a fine, but very strong, hand on her shoulder.
"Beloved, there was no warning. And nothing you could do that
you have not already done."

"I could have listened to you a week ago, Ruy, when you warned
me against setting up this rendezvous. Getting our five people
over the Alps is tricky enough with Spanish and Milanese troops
watching the alpine approaches from Lake Como to Chiavenna. I
should never have agreed to burdening them with the exfiltration
of Cardinal Ginetti, as well."

"My heart, it is most difficult to refuse a pope, particularly when his reasons are so compelling."

A soft voice from the doorway echoed Ruy's logic. "Indeed, Ambassadora Nichols, the fault—if any ill has befallen your father and your friends—is entirely mine."

Sharon turned, wondering—given the very dark black complexion she had inherited from her father James Nichols—if the flush of heat she could feel in her face produced any visible sign. "Your Holiness, my apologies. I did not know you were standing there."

"Hovering unseen outside doorways is, alas, a bad habit. It also provides much information one would otherwise not have." Pope Urban VIII smiled. "I'm sure this bad habit had more to do with my becoming pope than any worthiness in the eyes of Our Savior." His tone was jocular, but shaded with penitence, also. Urban had been more somber since his rescue from the Castel Sant'Angelo by Ruy and Tom. Or perhaps it was a result of learning that over a dozen cardinals who had been his friends, or at least allies, had been disappeared, and probably killed, by the Spanish invaders, based upon the thinnest of pretexts or, in some cases, outrageous prevarications. Urban seemed to feel their losses keenly, as though their deaths were an indictment of failure on his part.

Which, Sharon realized, was how Maffeo Barberini—now Urban VIII—had been brought up to think in relation to his allies. "Pontiff" had been a late addition to his many titles; first scion and incumbent head of the powerful Barberini family had been roles he inherited upon his birth. He had been trained to think in terms of stratagems against hereditary enemies, and sinecures for loyal vassals—and his ascension to the *cathedra* of the Holy See did not diminish his adherence to that *modus operandi*. Urban VIII, never forgetting his family or friends, had left a legacy (well-recorded in the up-timers' books) of shameless nepotism—for which he was infamous, even among the many early modern popes that had been known for it.

But now, Sharon wondered, did she see some signs of regret? His brother Francesco was among the cardinals who had been slain attempting to flee Rome. His nephew, Antonio, had made good his escape to Sharon's refugee embassy by only the slimmest of margins himself, and would not have succeeded at all had not her husband Ruy chanced upon him while he was trying to find a way to escape the city's walls.

Urban's hands were folded passively on the front of his cassock. "I shall pray for your friends and father, Ambassadora. I owe them all a great debt. And, in the case of Thomas Simpson, I owe him my very life—along with you, Señor Casador y Ortiz. If it was not for your bold rescue of me from Sant'Angelo, the rubble of Hadrian's tomb would surely be my burial mound, now."

Urban extended one hand and placed it briefly upon Ruy's head. Then he turned and left. When Ruy rose, his face was transformed—utterly open, utterly without pretense—rather like a man who remembers, for one brief instant, the innocent hope and faith he had as a young boy. Sharon felt the strangest rush of both tenderness and arousal, seeing him so stripped of his façade for that moment—and then Ruy as she knew him was back: he smoothed aside one wing of his mustaches and turned to her, his dark brown eyes glittering and alert. "We should send word to the exfiltration team in Switzerland," he said.

"Word to—? Yes, of course!" Sharon turned to the waiting radio operator. "Odo, raise the exfiltration team. Let them know that contact has been lost with both the group they are to extract and Colonel North's security detachment. They may have been monitoring and heard it themselves, but it's also possible that the signal didn't get through to Chur."

"And is there any other message for Chur?"

"Yes. The extraction team there is to start for the rendezvous point now."

"Ambassador, it will be night before they arrive. And if they reach the site early, and must loiter—"

"Odo. I understand the risks. To all three groups. But if Dad and the rest are on the run, they probably won't be able to signal again. So we've got to consider the abrupt end of their transmission as a call for extraction." She drew in her breath. "Send the message to Chur—and tell them to move as fast as they can."

# Chapter 4

"So, you see," said Estuban Miro to the other two men, "the USE in general, and the State of Thuringia-Franconia in particular, is most interested in discussing mutual political and fiscal interests with the powers here in Chur."

The more animated of the two men leaned forward eagerly, dark hair framing a pale, deceptively soft-featured face, out of which shone two very dark, but very bright, eyes. "And what— *specifically* what—would those interests be?"

Miro looked into those intense, unblinking eyes and thought: yes, this was the Georg Jenatsch he'd read about in the Grantville library, the man who killed a political rival with a savage axe-blow and then left the corpse pinned to the floorboards.

Well, Miro amended, it hadn't been Jenatsch himself who'd swung the axe that killed the night-shirted Pompeius von Planta as he stood, stunned, in his castle's main bedroom suite. At least, that's what the later histories of the up-timers claimed. Most of them, that is.

Either way, Miro was fairly sure that anyone foolish enough to ask Jenatsch about it now would get their hair parted in a similar fashion. Jenatsch, despite his charming public persona, sent out an aura of mortal determination which radiated a mes- sage best verbalized as: *do not toy with me; I shall kill you, if you do.* This man might well be a patriot, but he was also a creature of immense ambition and ego: no slights were forgotten, no vengeances left untaken.

"Herr Miro, your expression is—whimsical?" Jenatsch's prompt was polite and sounded casual. Indeed, a person less versed in the nuances of negotiations and personalities might have attached no special significance to it. But Miro had maintained the secrecy of being a "hidden-Jew"—a *xueta* from the Balearic island of Mallorca—for ten years while trading with the nobles of Spain and Portugal and around the far rim of the Mediterranean; he did not miss the intent focus behind Jenatsch's inquiry. The Swiss powerbroker knew that whatever thoughts had flitted through Miro's mind a moment ago could provide him with valuable insight into his interlocutor.

But Miro had dealt with far more subtle negotiators than Jenatsch, and waved a dismissive hand. "I was distracted for a moment, trying to decide which of our mutual interests I should present first."

Jenatsch's smile said he knew that Miro was lying. Miro returned a smile that congratulated Jenatsch on the correctness of his perception, and assured him that no further insights were to be gained from this line of inquiry. The third man in the room stared at them with the stolid, unimaginative detachment of a very capable factotum who had absolutely no imagination, and even less awareness of social subtleties.

This third man, a burgomeister who was also the hand-picked representative for the Bishop of Chur, set two meaty fists squarely upon the table. "I presume these mutual interests have something to do with your—unusual—method of transportation, Herr Miro."

"Indeed they do, Herr Ziegler. The airship by which my party traveled here is merely the first of many which will be traversing the Alps to facilitate the USE's business in Venice."

Ziegler's brow lowered a bit. "So. Given Venice's traditional support of Reformists in the Valtelline, this is to be a relationship favoring Protestants? Hardly a surprise, since the Swede is your king."

*Careful, now.* Miro spread his hands. "First, we hope to trade with Tuscany and Rome, as well as Venice. If Rome is difficult to trade with at this moment—well, that is hardly our doing."

Ziegler almost winced: only arch-Catholics—the kind who daily hungered after any excuse to go abroad at night and string up their Protestant neighbors—found Borja's recent occupation and sack of Rome to be anything less than ghastly. Ziegler was not of this extreme papist stripe; indeed, few in the Alps were. But that had not prevented bloody sectarian massacres from creating deep chasms of mistrust in the region, particularly where Miro found himself now: the capital of the Gray Leagues, or Graubünden, of Grisons. Originally a promising social experiment in both democracy and religious tolerance, the last fifteen years had seen the coalition erupt into vicious religious warfare, largely through the machinations of both the Spanish and Austrian Hapsburgs. In the "old history," the one the Americans' books depicted, further wars had been fought here, with the French driving out the Spanish this very year. But in this world, with France and Spain ostensibly at peace, that course of events had been derailed. All parties were now in historical and political terra incognita, and deeply suspicious of all the impending possibilities.

Miro continued his soothing explication. "Also, it would be precipitous to dismiss the religious toleration espoused in the USE as merely a façade. It is quite genuine. Yes, Gustav is a Lutheran, but he is also a wise ruler, wise enough to arrive at the same conclusion the peoples of the Graubünden did centuries ago: that a federated state, with religious toleration guaranteed by law, is the only way to end sectarian strife."

Ziegler did not look fully convinced, but did look at least moderately comforted—enough to go ahead with business, at any rate.

Miro extended another tidbit of polite gratitude. "I would also like to express my thanks for gathering the supplies we requested earlier this month, in anticipation of our visit."

"The lamp oil and pure spirits—you use these to power your 'blimp?'"

"Yes, Colonel Jenatsch, that is correct. However, only a small part of the fuel goes to the actual propulsion. Most is used to generate the hot air that causes the vehicle to rise from the ground."

"So without the fuel—?"

"The vehicle would be useless, immobile." And Miro and Jenatsch exchanged another significant look, which amounted to Jenatsch indirectly signaling that he understood the vulnerabilities of the blimp and the need for Chur's cooperation, and Miro affirming that he had no interest in being evasive or withholding information.

"The under-hanging part where you sit—the gondola?—seems to be rather small to make much difference to commerce. When you arrived today, I counted only ten persons, and it was crowded, at that." Ziegler had removed his fists from the table in order to fold his arms.

Miro nodded. "It is small. And it is useless for cargos that are of great volume or mass. But Herr Ziegler, consider the small items that constitute much of today's commerce: the 'new' commerce as it is being conducted in Amsterdam, and Venice—"

"—and Grantville." Jenatsch's smile was feral.

"—yes, and Grantville. It is a commerce in people, documents, bank notes, specie, books, plans, samples, chemicals, medicines, key ingredients. Imagine being able to issue timely market instructions to a factor in Venice in one or two days. Radio, if you have one, will become a possibility in the coming years—but even coded messages are no guarantee of confidentiality. On the other hand, the blimp is available right now and can transport high-value items a hundred miles in three hours, leaving a safe margin for operational error. I already have the first dozen flight manifests completely booked."

"Will not weather prevent the flying of this blimp?"

"If it is severe enough, yes. Which is why we advertise two or three days per hundred mile journey: that represents a safe average."

"That is also not much faster than a man on a horse." Ziegler looked a bit smug.

"True enough, but that is a good day on a horse, and a very bad average for the blimp. But tell me this, Herr Ziegler: when was the last time a man on a horse made thirty-three miles a day over the Alps? And without the slightest vulnerability to bandits? That's what the blimp assures: absolutely direct travel, completely free of banditry, from city to city—no costly adventures on the road. And it seems that travel through the passes south of here now frequently involves just such adventures."

Ziegler frowned, but not out of anger. Miro had struck a responsive and very pertinent chord. Travel south from Graubünden was no longer a simple proposition. The once modestly populous valleys were now home to as many recent graves as people: accompanying the wars and purgings that had scourged Grisons in the past fifteen years, the plague had swept through the region twice. Thriving towns were now shadows of themselves.

Many smaller villages stood vacant, ruined by the harsh, battering winters. In this comparatively barren environment, bandits increased, but plied a sparse trade, made especially brutal and indiscriminate by the lack of prey.

But the source of this cycle of misery lay in the fact that all the major passes down to Italy funneled through Chiavenna, which was controlled by Graubünden's arch-nemeses: Spain and Milan. Austria had also contributed to the Chur's woes in the 1620s, but had become steadily less energetic in imposing its will upon Grisons. And, at the start of the decade, the inhabitants had been cheered by rumors of French aid.

But, in this world, Richelieu's much-vaunted plan to send the duke of Rohan into the Valtelline—thereby seizing the only overland connection linking Spain to her forces in the Low Countries—failed to materialize. Jenatsch, an ardent supporter of Rohan's campaign and presumed leader of France's allies in Grisons, had watched these plans evaporate like morning mist once the arrival of the up-timers and their strange town from the future became widely known. The Spanish-French animosity diminished and ultimately transmogrified into the uneasy entente that allowed them to cooperate in the destruction of the Dutch fleet off Ostend in 1633. Like all contracts between thieves, their so-called League of Ostend was certain to unravel—sooner, rather than later. But in the meantime, Grisons continued to suffer under foreign interference or direct control.

So, naturally Georg Jenatsch was interested in any new stratagem for freeing his homeland. And for making himself a national hero in the process. Jenatsch's monomania in pursuit of those objectives made him capable of changing his alliance, religion, and even his own traits—as the up-time histories attested. But Miro, meeting this man with whom he had cautiously corresponded for months, was satisfied that he had correctly identified the one character-trait of Jenatsch that was as steady as a lodestone and which made negotiations with him relatively predictable: he was far more famous for his decisiveness than for any deep wells of patience. Jenatsch was not mercurial, but he hadn't the taste for long games or the temperament for waiting upon fickle fate to provide him with a tool to achieve his ends. An active and victorious new international force such as the USE was almost sure to catch and kindle his interest.

And, unsurprisingly, it obviously had. But he was too accomplished a statesman not to stringently critique the deal Miro was proposing. "So let us say that we become a part of your growing network of—do you call them 'airing-domes'?"

"Aero-dromes," supplied Miro mildly.

"Yes, 'aerodromes.' To have such a facility here is clearly advantageous for you: Chur is the most convenient way-point over the Alps. As I understand it, our location is valuable because it is less than one hundred miles from Biberach, on the north shore of the Bodensee, and also less than one hundred miles from Bergamo, in Venetian Lombardy. And so, perhaps more people of note will visit Chur, spend a bit more money. But how does this benefit us beyond that modest increase in trade?" Jenatsch smiled; he knew the answer, of course, but he wasn't going to agree to the deal without suitable promises from Miro. And of course, Ziegler still had to have to have it spelled out for him.

Miro pointed to the opened letter before Jenatsch. "President Piazza's letter outlines the general defense benefits rather comprehensively, I think."

"I would have preferred a few more specifics, as well."

"Please understand, Colonel Jenatsch, we must walk a thin line if we are to ensure that our relationship does not bring you more problems than it solves. Yes, Gustav Adolf has approved using Chur to facilitate our current operations into Italy. And yes, President Piazza has indicated that some of our proceeds from establishing your town as a transport hub would allow us to base a dedicated mercenary company—exclusively contracted to us—in Chur to secure it from foreign intrusions. But a more overt, national alliance would call attention to itself, and your most dangerous foes would not miss its significance."

"That will occur anyhow, as your ability to balloon directly into Italy becomes more clear to the Spanish."

"It is true that they may become annoyed by that, but not so much to mount an attack on you."

"Why not?" Ziegler threw his considerable bulk forward aggressively. "Are you suggesting they will sit idly by while this new trade route opens up?"

"Yes, that is exactly what I am suggesting."

Clearly, this was not the answer Ziegler was expecting; his bulk fell back in surprise. "Why?"

"Because the Spanish—of all the powers of Europe—have shown the least understanding of, or interest in, the new economy that air travel will enable. Their banking methods are hopelessly archaic and filled with exclusions and restrictions that ensure that their nation's power remains firmly in the hands of the hidalgos, the upper classes. They do not know how to grow wealth—and therefore, will not even understand the value of this new route of exchange. Not until it is too late."

That brought a grimly satisfied smile even to Ziegler's face. But this time, it was Jenatsch who held to the prior point like a bulldog: "However, this still means that there will be no direct military alliance between you and us. And, for us, that means no offensive to liberate the communes that are still in Austrian or Spanish hands. So we might be a bit safer, and a bit more wealthy, but still crushed by foreign occupiers in many of our regions."

Miro smiled. "But for how long?"

Jenatsch looked suspicious. "What do you mean? Do you propose that Heaven will deliver us? God alone knows how often and ardently I have prayed for divine deliverance—"

—Miro reflected that Jenatsch might even be telling the truth—

"—but no angels have come to drive out the invaders. So what mysterious power are you suggesting will deliver us?"

"Not a mysterious power: just simple geography. The geography of *realpolitik*."

Jenatsch blinked at the unfamiliar term, even though it was in his native German. "What do you mean?"

Miro pointed to the map on the table, located at their equidistant center. "What do the Hapsburgs call the Valtelline?"

Jenatsch frowned; he clearly did not appreciate any discursive approach that left him feeling as though he was being schooled. "It is the transalpine part of what they dub the Spanish Road. As you well know. From Chiavenna to Tyrol, it is how the thrice-damned Spanish and Austrian Hapsburgs exchange troops and goods. It is also a barrier against similar north-south exchanges for the rest of Europe."

"And which Hapsburg activities has it enabled in the last ten years?"

Jenatsch considered. "The wars in Germany: what the up-timers call the Thirty Years' War. Also, the Spanish campaigns against the Dutch."

"But what has happened to those activities?"

The smile returned to Jenatsch's face; Miro could well imagine that savage expression glaring at him over the glinting edge of an axe.

Miro explicated the obvious for Ziegler's benefit. "Spain's adventurism north of the Alps has all but vanished. In the Low Countries, the infante Fernando increasingly turns his back on Madrid; his brother the king seems no more eager to send new troops to him than the new 'King in the Low Countries' seems to have them. Besides, any further influx of Spanish troops would make his partner in the Provinces, Frederik Hendrik of Orange, exceedingly nervous. Possibly warlike."

"And with that old papist firebrand Ferdinand of Austria dead," Jenatsch said with satisfaction, "his namesake son and successor is pursuing a more moderate course of action."

"Much more moderate. Particularly since his sister married Fernando, who rescued her from a war zone with the assistance of an up-time aircraft. Indeed, after the recent war with Bavaria, one could almost call the relations between the USE and Austria cordial. They are at the very least quiescent. And if Wallenstein can be induced not to encroach southward across the Austrian border from Bohemia, I very much suspect that the worst of the middle European wars are behind us—with the greatest loser being Spain."

Ziegler looked baffled. "Spain? What do you mean? Other than losing a few tercios, how has Spain suffered so greatly?"

Jenatsch's predatory grin was back. "Our visitor is talking about losses in influence, not men or money, Herr Ziegler. This new Austrian king has allowed his relations with Madrid to cool, has tacitly approved Fernando's claim in the Low Countries by allowing his sister to marry him without challenging the legitimacy of the title and land he claims. And this is why Spanish movement through the Valtelline has diminished so greatly in these past two years."

Miro nodded. "You see the rest, of course."

The blank look on Ziegler's face was the antithesis of the cunning insight on Jenatsch's. "Of course. Spain holds its Road in the Valtelline, but feels less need for it. Its value as a conduit is lost; its value as a defensive blockade, interposed between the north and south extents of Europe, diminishes also. With its treasury ever-more overdrawn, Philip of Spain—or rather, Philip's puppet-master and lap-dog, Olivares—will withdraw most of the investment required to retain the Valtelline. And when their alliance with the French finally unravels, as it must—"

"—you will be able to stand aside, and let the weak French and Spanish alpine forces exhaust themselves upon each other."

"At which point, the USE will intervene and help us take back all our lands!" Jenatsch's smile was shadowed; he wasn't in jest, but he knew he had gone too far, intentionally so. He was testing Miro.

Miro smiled. "That last projection is beyond current consideration, Colonel. But the rest of what you envision seems very likely to transpire within the next several years. All you need to do is save your treasure and energy, and await the inevitable. The USE presence in Chur will disincline any trifling adventurism by Spain or France. And you, I'm sure, will give them no reason to do so. In the meantime, we will increase regular overland trade to Chur as well."

Now Ziegler sat up straight again; the discussion had moved back into familiar territory, for him. "How so?"

"I am even now negotiating to establish a proprietary trade link over the Bodensee between Buchhorn and Rorschach."

"And why is this trade route useful to you?" Ziegler's brows were beetled in intense suspicion. "It has been of only marginal interest to the Germans, up until now."

"In addition to various resources and goods common in the Alps but somewhat scarce in Germany, we can provide Graubünden with finished goods from northern Europe without adding on the tariff costs incurred when they pass through Constance or Zurich first. But also, we must have a way of ensuring that there is always enough fuel on hand here in Chur, and a regular schedule of overland portage is the most prudent way to do so."

Ziegler actually rubbed his hands together. Jenatsch at last leaned back, his eyes almost blank, his imagination no doubt racing inward along spider webs of new, interlocking schemes and stratagems. "So Herr Miro," Ziegler exhaled, "which of our alpine goods most interest your—?"

There were two slow knocks on the door, followed by three, staccato raps.

Miro held up an apologetic hand. "With your pardon—" Over his shoulder, he said, "Enter."

Virgilio Franchetti, Miro's senior blimp pilot and builder, stuck his head in the door. "Don Estuban, you asked to be informed when the fuel test was complete."

This was a complete and utter fabrication; the fuel mixture had already been tested and set. This phrase was, instead, a prearranged code to inform Miro that new priority orders had been received over the radio, orders that required immediate action.

Which was simply another way of saying: *there is a new crisis brewing.*

# Chapter 5

Miro stood and nodded to Virgilio. "Thank you, Signor Franchetti." Miro turned to face his hosts. "Gentlemen, I must ask you to excuse me; I have some technical matters to attend to regarding our airship."

"All is well, I trust?" Jenatsch's nose now looked like the beak of a stooping hawk, ready to pounce on important new information.

"I will learn soon enough." Miro smiled. "The first time we arrive in a new location, there is always the matter of fuel quality to be considered."

"Are you saying our oils are inferior?" Ziegler had folded his arms again; preemptive indignation was writ plain across his broad and full-fleshed face.

"Not at all, but each town's are distinctive. Since they are made from different substances, they burn a bit differently. And depending upon how much ethanol—eh, pure spirits—we can find, that also influences how best to mix the fuel so our engines consume it most efficiently."

Mollified, Ziegler's arms relaxed. "I see." Clearly, he did not. Jenatsch on the other hand, seemed to get the gist of it. Miro foresaw that, in the commercial negotiations of the months to come, the two of them would reprise this juxtaposition of ill-concealed incomprehension and silent perception many, many times.

Rising, he nodded to them both. "I thank you for the dinner

and conversation. My factor will meet with yours tomorrow morning, then?"

Ziegler returned his nod. "As we agreed."

Jenatsch's nod was slower. He smiled. "Safe travels in Italy."

Miro managed not to let his surprise show. "*Auf Wiedersehen, mein Herren.*"

Once the door was closed behind them, Franchetti turned to Miro. "How did the small one know that we are about to travel on to Italy?"

"He doesn't know. He guesses it, and was probing to watch our reactions. He was also letting me know that he does not believe your reason for interrupting the meeting."

"That one is too smart." Franchetti began descending the stairs into the commons room of the *Grosse Hart*.

"I'd be far more worried if he took pains to conceal his intelligence from us. If a man like Georg Jenatsch believes you to be a possible enemy, he will make himself unreadable. He will not let you know how smart he is—or what he conjectures."

"So this means—?"

"It suggests—and only that, Virgilio—that he is at least provisionally thinking of us as allies. And, not wanting to be taken lightly, or undervalued, he is showing that he is not a man to be underestimated nor trifled with. Which he would not be doing if he felt fully secure in his current position."

"Is he not the political leader, up here?"

Miro smiled as the noise of the tavern rose to meet them. "He is, as much as anyone can be in this loose federation. And if he can legitimately represent himself as having brokered a new relationship with up-timers—in the form of an agreement with President Piazza of Thuringia-Franconia—it will solidify his claim to that leadership."

Miro walked over to a large corner table, where a handful of locals were frowning over their cards. A newcomer in a mix of up-time and down-time garb grinned predatorily over the top of his own hand. Miro suddenly understood where the American term "cardshark" had come from. "Harry," he said.

Harry Lefferts grinned wider. "Just a minute; I'm fleecing a few more alpine sheep." Those members of his rag-tag special operations group who had accompanied him to the *Grosse Hart*—Gerd, Paul, Felix—smiled also.

"Harry," Miro said quietly, "we don't have a minute."

The betting was concluding. Harry's smile. "Oh? Then I'll be there in half a minute. Just enough time to finish out this one last hand."

Miro shrugged. He looked at the three members of Harry's infamous and effective Wrecking Crew. "Gentlemen, your presence is required immediately." He did not bother to look at Harry again, but exited. Behind him, he heard urgent whispers in the strange part-German, part-English dialect that had been dubbed Amideutsch.

Franchetti fretted. "Why does he do that?"

"Do what?"

"You know what I mean," muttered Franchetti, "defying you. Not disobeying, exactly. But not behaving as he knows he should. As he has behaved on missions before this one."

"Well, I suspect one of the reasons is that he's usually not had to work under supervision. The head of Grantville's intelligence community, Francisco Nasi, told me that Harry follows orders best when he is given great freedom in deciding exactly how to carry them out. But that was not possible this time."

"Si—and the other reason for his insolence?"

Miro looked at his master pilot and blimp builder. "Why, probably because Harry wanted my job, Virgilio."

"What? But he's—he is a *condotierre*, not a man of affairs."

Miro shrugged. "He thinks otherwise." And in his heart of hearts, Miro could hardly blame Lefferts, could even imagine the American's first thoughts when receiving the news that he was not in overall command of the mission: *I am not so much younger than this Miro fellow—who arrived, unknown, in Grantville only a year ago and is now giving me orders. Who meets with Ed Piazza in closed sessions from which I am politely excluded. I have been a good soldier who has succeeded at every task; I have won the acclaim of young emulators all over Europe; I am bold and strong and intelligent. It is I who should have been placed in charge of this mission, not this usurper, this lately-come Estuban Miro.*

But if Harry had thought such things, they had not settled and festered as jealousy. Estuban Miro had smelled the corrosive musk of envy before, and there was none of it wafting about Harry—although he could hardly have blamed the up-timer if there had been.

✧    ✧    ✧

There was, however, the faint odor of schnapps about Harry as he arrived—the last of the Crew to do so—alongside the already inflated blimp. He was passing out some shared winnings as Miro began his update for the rest of the group, amongst whom there was now a quiet figure in a monk's habit, hood pulled low. "Ambassador Nichols' radio message was quite clear; we cannot wait until morning. We must get under way now."

"I thought flying in the later part of the day can be dangerous," commented the only other up-time member of the Wrecking Crew, Sherrilyn Maddox.

Franchetti jumped in. "Here, in the Alps, it is madness. We will probably have calm air when the sun begins to set, but we will not reach the Maloja Pass until nighttime. So we will be flying in the swiftly changing alpine air currents—and without light. Don Estuban, I know Ambassadora Nichols was adamant, but—"

"She was not merely adamant: she gave a direct order, and we will follow it."

The hooded figure nodded silent agreement.

"And do we know why we are being invited to be the guests of honor at a suicide party?" When Harry Lefferts drawled his absurdities that way, even Miro had to smile.

But only fleetingly. "Yes. Contact was lost with Captain Simpson's party. Abruptly."

The cocky expression swept off Harry's face, replaced by fell intensity. "When?"

"About twenty minutes ago. Franchetti was minding the radio at the time, monitoring the traffic between Chiavenna and Padua. Captain Simpson's radio operator was sending out a good signal—and then nothing. Dead air."

Franchetti nodded vigorously. "*Si.* At first I think, 'maybe a sudden weather change between here and Chiavenna.' After all, it *is* the Alps. But then comes the message from Padua. The ambassadora, she had clear reception of the same signal but heard the same thing: the transmission ended sharply, and did not resume. No interference, no increase in static. They went off the air."

Sherrilyn Maddox, Harry's former gym teacher, looked at her ex-student and gritted her teeth. "Shit."

Harry nodded. "So they didn't even give the pick-up signal."

"No: this is what you and Ed call an 'emergency extraction.'"

"Except there may not be anyone at the rendezvous point to extract."

Miro nodded. "That is entirely possible. We do know that Captain Simpson's group made contact with Cardinal Ginetti, but they could have been apprehended while doing so, or shortly thereafter."

"And what's the big deal with this cardinal, again?" asked Harry. "Why's he worth the extra risk?"

"Cardinal Marzio Ginetti is prefect of the Pontifical Household, secretary of the Sacred Consulta, and papal legate to the Austrian Court. Which means that he's a close confidante of the pope."

"And therefore, on Borja's hit list," Sherrilyn supplied with a glance at Harry.

"Thanks for telling me what I already know. I mean, why rescue Ginetti specifically: there have got to be a dozen Italian cardinals in the same situation."

Miro shook his head. "Not any more. As of last week, the suspected total of cardinals that are missing—and probably dead—rose to sixteen. Borja was evidently quite thorough." He looked to the hooded figure, who nodded once.

Juliet Sutherland, the Crew's other female member and a woman of many roles, breathed in sharply: "Bloody hell." She wasn't a Catholic—exactly. But she wasn't anything else, either—exactly. Or so it seemed. Miro couldn't figure her out any more than he could the rest of the Crew—and he had given up trying to do so. Accepting the group's dynamics and identities was a lot easier than trying to understand them.

"Yes: Borja has eliminated the great majority of Urban's most reliable and trusted allies in the Consistory. That's why Ambassador Nichols added Ginetti to our extraction list, and had him rendezvous with Tom Simpson's group in Chiavenna. If the cardinal had actually reached Italy, it is unlikely he would have survived a week. Possibly not even a single day. So, at the pope's behest, a confidential courier intercepted Ginetti during his journey westward along the Valtelline and redirected him to the rendezvous in Chiavenna."

"Which now sounds completely fubarred," Harry finished. "Ten to one the courier wasn't so confidential after all and they put a tail on the padre."

Miro nodded. "That's the most likely scenario. And if Simpson's group survived being discovered, they will be making best speed for the default extraction site, just a few miles west of the Maloja Pass."

Harry grabbed a taut catenary cable and hopped into the dirigible's gondola. "Then what are we waiting for? Let's ride!" He held out a hand for his ponderous backpack.

Miro shook his head. "Light pack only."

"What? Wait a minute, you said—"

"Harry. We thought retrieving Tom Simpson's group would be a leisurely pick up. Franchetti, me, two of your Crew as security, and the rest of you to stay here. But now we—well, *you*—could have a real fight on your hands. That means the whole Crew is going to have to deploy for the rescue. It also means that there won't be enough room for us on the return. And any of us who wait for a day or more in the Val Bregaglia probably won't evade the Spanish long enough to be around for a second pick up. So whoever doesn't get extracted by the blimp will need to immediately press on to reach Ambassador Nichols and her staff in Padua."

"So we're going to Italy on foot."

"I'm afraid so."

Harry shrugged. "Well, that means forty-pound packs, max. Combat load only. And it means leaving a lot of our support equipment back here."

"Yes. But it will follow us down. Eventually."

Harry looked up. "Eventually may not be good enough, given the fuse burning on this mission. Frank Stone's wife Giovanna is now—what? Five months pregnant, almost? I can work a lot of miracles, but jail-breaking a mondo-pregnant lady ain't one of them. So we don't have a lot of time to wait around. So gear that gets to us 'eventually' is gear we're never going to see again. *A capeesh?*"

"Yes, I understand," said Miro, who very nearly did not; the deformed Sicilian dialect that Harry had heard in American gangster movies was barely recognizable as Italian. "But whether or not the gear gets back to us in time, the dirigible must take Ginetti to a safe haven immediately. That means the balloon's next flight after Chur must be to Grantville. So we won't have access to the dirigible—or the equipment—for at least two weeks. Possibly more."

"Well, that's just great." Harry hopped out of the gondola, seized his backpack, started pulling out nonessential items and making a semi-neat pile. "So we go in all teeth and no tail."

"As usual," commented George Sutherland, Juliet's immense husband. "Do we at least know whether the security unit already in the valley has secured the extraction site yet?"

Miro shrugged. "So far, we haven't been able to raise Colonel North. Nor has the ambassador's radioman. Of course, they may be on the move and unable to send or receive."

"So we don't know where anyone else is?" Harry spat. "That's great; just great. This operation hasn't started, and already we're scattered and screwed."

"As usual," added George once again.

"Colonel?"

Thomas North squinted, trying to get a better look at the roofs of Soglio about three miles ahead to the west, and farther down the slope of the Val Bregaglia. "What is it, Hastings?"

"Sir, some of the men are asking to stop and fill their water skins."

"They've drained them? Already? They filled up only a few miles back in Vicosoprano."

"Yes, sir, but it's a hard march."

"My, my. Then perhaps all of them should have, as children, simply accepted the life of leisure and independent wealth that was no doubt their birthright. Ah, but the siren song of the mercenary life was evidently too strong for them to resist." North did not smile while he made this response. "Besides," he added grudgingly, "if they put any more water in their bellies this quickly, we'll lose some of them to cramping. And while I would be delighted to indulge their masochistic impulses, I suspect that we will all be needed at the extraction site. And as quickly as possible."

From the corner of his eyes, North saw Lieutenant Hastings shift from one foot to the other. "Sir, it's not as if we actually heard the extraction code given. We just got a few garbled signals. That's all."

"Yes, Hastings—that's all. But that's why I possess the lofty role and rank of colonel and you are but a lowly lieutenant. Who has been evidently been promoted above the threshold of his ability, I might add."

"Your confidence in me is always inspiring, sir."

"Ah, and now irony, too? I'll make an officer of you yet, Hastings. Tell me, Lieutenant: what information can we be certain of, despite the 'garbled signals' of which our radio operator could make no sense?"

"I beg your pardon?"

North folded the spyglass, handed it to his batman, faced Hastings. "Lieutenant, for the last three weeks, we have been winding our way through Grisons and the Graubünden, not quite showing the USE flag in the region, but making no secret of the fact that they are our exclusive employers. And in all that time, how much radio traffic have we received? Or heard?"

"Three messages to us, sir. Maybe four or five others. Mostly from Ambassador Nichols' dislocated embassy in Padua."

"Yes. At least, we *think* that was the source, since those messages were almost as badly garbled as this last bunch. So given the general scarcity of radio traffic, what do you make of today's flurry of activity?"

"That something important is happening, sir."

North sighed. "Hastings, your hypothesis is almost as inspired as the conjecture that maybe—just maybe—night follows day. Well, you're not to be blamed, of course: you are only a lieutenant, after all. Whereas I am a colonel—a near-divinity. And here is what I divine from the clicks, hissings, and scratchings that have afflicted our radio-set today. First the group we are to extract is on the air with something that sounded like a routine update; it had that tempo. But rather concluding with back and forth housekeeping to fix a time, frequency, and cipher for their next sitrep, the comchatter ended quickly. With, I think, a time being set."

"For rendezvous?"

North felt the weight of command heavy upon his shoulders. "No, Hastings. There would have been a triple confirmation of extraction. The pattern and rhythm of the exchange was all wrong for that." Hastings blinked, said nothing. North pressed on. "Logically, they were establishing a near-future call-back time. Probably because the group in Chiavenna was about to make contact with its newest member, a rather important 'friar.' Then a long wait. Then a brief exchange—and then nothing. There were repeated, unanswered comm-checks from Padua—or so it seemed. Then more coded comm traffic—between Padua and the airborne extraction team at Chur, I'm guessing. Lots of it. So, Hastings, what do you make of it all?"

"That there's trouble with the group in Chiavenna? That something went wrong when they went to the scheduled meet with this friar? And that they are moving to the rendezvous and unable to communicate anything further?"

"Bravo! There's hope for you yet, Lieutenant." North frowned sadly. "Well, actually, there isn't any hope for you, but I can't stand to see you sulk, so I lied. Now, have the squad leaders employ the necessary invective and make the suitable threats so that we can pick up our pace. And I'll let the men stop to piss, but not to drink any more. They'd give away our approach with all that water sloshing in their guts."

# Chapter 6

The north-leaning shadows of the Bregaglia Mountains were starting to crawl across the Mera River; the sun was moving swiftly down toward the alpine peaks in the west, Chiavenna already lost in the gloom at their feet. Tom paused and let Rita move abreast of him. She glanced up—way up—at him, quizzically. "Honey," he whispered to her, "you set the pace. I'm going to the rear. To push 'em along and keep us together."

Rita turned as she strode ahead with a longer gait, inspecting their column. "Yeah, we're starting to straggle out a bit."

*You, wife, have a talent for understatement,* thought Tom as he peripherally saw Melissa and Cardinal Ginetti lagging yet again. Worse yet, the two of them slowed the group down even more by eliciting excesses of solicitousness. James Nichols was capable of a better pace, and, as an ex-Marine, he certainly knew how crucial it was that they maintain one. But the primal call of protecting one's mate trumped training and logic, and Melissa, given her feisty personality, was neither the easiest nor most receptive person when it came to assistance.

The cardinal was simply not cut out for even this modest hike. They were two miles east of Chiavenna, well within the mouth of the Val Bregaglia and passing the thundering cataract of the Acquafraggia, which was perched over them to the north. The upward slope of the narrow valley was modest, here: not more than a five percent gradient. But the road meandered around copses and over meadows, rather than sticking close to the straight, rocky banks of the Mera, which had already narrowed considerably.

Tom had considered leaving the road at the small village of Piuro, but ultimately decided against it. The group needed speed more than stealth, and the open pastures reached all the way from the the river to the steep slopes on the north side of the valley. Although the pastures presented rolling contours to the aesthetically inclined gaze, they looked like an extra aerobic workout to Simpson's utterly practical eye.

Even the winding country lane became more taxing when the river road joined with it shortly beyond Piuro, where the three locals they encountered all stared in surprise at James (and the rest of the group too, for that matter). Now, only ten minutes into the countryside, Melissa and Ginetti were already fighting to keep up—and failing. Tom, his long strides cut in half as he assessed the situation, had now fallen back to the rear of the group.

Melissa looked up, annoyed, a sweaty gray-brown bang hanging down across her severely straight Boston-Brahmin nose. "Yes, Tom, I know: I'm going to get everyone killed."

"Now, Melissa—"

"Don't 'now, Melissa' me, Tom. It's true. James gave up denying it about half a mile ago. Now, he just tries to change the topic."

Ginetti panted out his own opinion "I mean no offense in contradicting you, signora, but it is clear that I am the cause of our troubles, not you. I walk even more slowly. Let us be frank: if I had not met you in Chiavenna, you would have been allowed to pass over the Alps unmolested. As it is, I fear we are lost." Shivering, for he was clearly not a particularly brave man, Ginetti presented his solution in a rush: "If I am to fall into the hands of Borja anyway, at least you might escape. I might be able to draw them off by taking a different course—"

Melissa stopped and stared down at the cardinal. "With respect, Your Eminence, that's ridiculous." Ginetti stopped and stared back; quite possibly, he had not been addressed in such a firmly remonstrative tone since his boyhood. "First, they will not stop following us just because they capture you. *I* wouldn't stop, if I were them. After all, we are murderers in the eyes of Chiavenna's authorities. And if the confidential agent following you—the one

Tom decked in the *crotto*—has played his cards right, he'll be following along, too. After all, if his masters only wanted *your* head, Cardinal Ginetti, they could have collected it long before you reached Chiavenna."

"You overlook that I had four guards. The agent in the *crotto* may not have been courageous enough to—"

"Counting the agent they sent into the *crotto* to keep any eye on you, there were five men following you. So they had you outnumbered. Had they wanted, they could have eliminated one or more of your guards during a night ambush and finished the job on a subsequent day. No, Cardinal, they want us, too. Dead or alive, perhaps, but I suspect they'd prefer alive. We'd be much more useful—and informative—that way." She raised her head, breathed deeply, and accelerated her flagging stride again. "No, we are all in this together. And that means you and I have to step lively, Your Eminence, because escape is our only acceptable option."

James nodded. "And so far, luck is with us."

Tom couldn't figure that one out. "Seems today the only luck we've had has been bad."

"Look, Tom: if the local garrison back in Chiavenna were seasoned pros, they'd have caught up with us by now. Sure, our trail ended at the Mera, but they must know we didn't head west; to do that, we'd have had to double back past the *crotto* itself. And what for? To go straight up a big-ass mountain, through pine forests and toward god knows what? That's not a bad plan; it's no plan at all.

"And I doubt it took them more than ten minutes to figure out that we hadn't crossed to the other side of the Mera; we'd have been seen going over the bridges. Besides, that's the more densely populated side of town: lots of well-trafficked piazzas. Where we don't exactly blend in. Particularly me. And certainly not when we're running for our lives.

"So ten, maybe fifteen minutes after they found your cloak, they would know that we either fled to the north or the south. So maybe they had to split up into two search parties, but any way you slice it, we're lucky we've gotten this far without any sign of—"

Over the stony roar of the plummeting Acquafraggia, Tom thought he heard a faint *prapf!*—and the next moment, he felt a burning stripe across his left buttock. *Damn it,* he thought as he staggered, more from the pain than the grazing rush of the musket ball fired at long range, *hit in the ass again?*

Grinning because he could still find humor in the situation, Tom did not fall, thanks to the ready hand of Matthias, their geekish down-time radio operator. Who asked solicitously, "Can you travel, Herr Kapitan?"

Tom nodded, saw Matthias' relieved smile—and then another musket ball went neatly into the down-timer's right temple. It came out above his left ear in an eruption of bone and brains at the same moment that the weapon's report reached them. Which meant that some of their pursuers were much closer than they had thought.

"Run!" Tom shouted at the top of his lungs. "Everyone! *Now!*"

On the one hand, Miro was glad for the tail wind out of the north. Keeping a good distance from the alp known as the Tscharnoz to the west, Franchetti was catching at least seven miles per hour of free forward speed. That made it possible to throttle back the four thirty-horse-power up-time mower engines propelling the dirigible, and thereby, save a considerable amount of fuel.

The downside of this situation was that it put Miro, along with two-thirds of the passengers, downwind of the motors. Along with the burner, these engines left little doubt as to the origins of their fuel.

"Damn," said Sherrilyn, wrinkling her nose. "Smells like a dead sheep. Being cremated in its own rotting fat."

"Yeah, a sheep that died eating codfish," Harry expanded.

"Who washed it down with the nastiest rotgut ever brewed from Satan's own piss," added Juliet, with a punctuating shriek of disgust and despair.

Donald Ohde shrugged. "Ah . . . I've smelled worse, I have." They all looked at him. "Can't think where, though."

"Matija's drawers," Felix sneered.

"Your obsession with my drawers—and their contents—is ungodly, you sodomite."

Gerd, not to be left out, looked up, sleepy-eyed as ever. "Get a room, you two," he advised. Then he sent a questioning glance toward the up-timers of the Crew. "I think that line is from a movie we have seen, *ja?*"

George Sutherland, one arm around his wife, the other gesturing grandly at the white-fanged Alps surrounding them, exclaimed. "It's a fine day to be flying, here over the very roof of the world, with all my friends." He sucked in a great lungful of the noxious fumes. "And so refreshing, too."

Miro wondered if the banter ever—ever—stopped. Sometimes, it abated, but rarely and not for long. It seemed to be an essential part of the social glue that held the Wrecking Crew together. Which, he supposed, made it a good thing. But he was outside of it, just as he was outside of their circle.

Franchetti shouted at Miro over his shoulder. "Don Estuban, look ahead." He cocked his head toward the horizon. "Do you see it? The Lai di Marmorera?"

Miro squinted. A tiny sliver of deep ultramarine nestled between close-set mountains some miles ahead. He pointed at it over Franchetti's shoulder. "In that valley, you mean?"

"*Si*; we head there. Then south to the Septimer Pass. We have gone more than half the way. Almost two-thirds."

Harry had come to stand alongside Miro. "What are we looking at?"

Miro pointed again. "The Lai di Marmorera. Beyond that lies Bivio and the Septimer Pass."

"Lake Marmorera?" Harry's brow wrinkled, one eyebrow shot up, and in that moment, Miro saw why the young rogue had scored so many amorous victories across the Continent in the past two years. "I thought we were going over something a little bit bigger than that duck pond, something called the . . . eh, the Marmelsee."

"That's it," Sherrilyn howled over the engines. "That's what was here before they used a dam to make it the genuine alpine lake we saw on the Fodor's map."

Harry shook his head. "Okay, but what do the locals call it: Lai de Marmorera or Marmelsee?"

"Both," shouted Miro. "The names change from language to language up here. French, German, Italian. Some rarer languages, too. And dialects mixing them all together."

"Chaos," pronounced Harry. Then with a smile, he said, "Sounds like my kind of place."

Thomas North peered out through the trees; two primitive carts creaked over a low rise to the east and were lost to sight.

He waited a moment, then waved the first squad forward. The men advanced just beyond the edge of the tree line but stayed well within its lengthening shadow. No sign of reaction from the outskirts of Soglio, which was upslope to the north. Behind them, less than thirty yards to the south, was the Mera. Pine-lined at this point in its course, it chattered over rocks down toward the next town: Castasenga.

"It's fortunate we're moving so close to dusk. Easy to stay hidden, this way."

North turned to looked up at the very tall, very broad-shouldered Hastings. "Fortunate for movement, perhaps. Hardly ideal for a rendezvous, though. You have the crossbow ready?"

"Yes, sir."

"And the signal bolts?"

Hastings nodded and watched as the first squad started trotting down slope, slipping beneath the sleeping brows of Soglio. "Shall we follow, sir?"

North, chewing his lower lip lightly, nodded. "Pass the word: weapons out, but no firing except at my orders. We've only got two miles left; let's not cock it up by having someone mistake a squirrel for a Spaniard."

North, up-time 9mm automatic in his right hand, signaled with his left to the second squad. Along with him, they emerged from the black shadows of the woods into the gray shadows beyond its margin and moved quietly down the hill after their comrades.

The approach of hooves told Tom Simpson that he had been right to remain behind and lie in wait; if he didn't slow the Spanish down here, they would overtake the group within the hour. Now, if only he could keep his separation from the others from becoming truly permanent...

Tom eased open both frizzens of the double-barreled fowling piece that, in any self-respecting Western, would have been called a "coach-gun" and checked the powder in the pans. It was still dry, despite the mists generated by the cataract thirty yards farther along the track to the east. Working around to his right, which was also the upslope side of the immense tree that he was sheltered behind, Tom leaned out for a quick peek.

Four horsemen, coming in a one-two-one sequence. Not as dispersed as bred-to-the-saddle cavalrymen would have been, the two in the middle were all but riding abreast. But the arrangement did suggest the competent training that was the norm among Spanish troops, which these were, judging from their helmets.

Tom leaned back behind the tree—no sudden motion now—and took a deep breath. He had been in several memorable gunfights over the past few years. The most recent involved shooting his way out of the Castel Sant'Angelo while rescuing the pope. However, this time he was alone and heavily outnumbered. As the first horseman drew abreast of his position, lazily riding point toward the dull thunder of the alpine cataract, Tom took consolation from the fact that the noise muffled other sounds like a great blanket. This, along with the shadows in which Tom was hidden, amplified the efficacy of his one great advantage: surprise.

Timing the approach of the next two riders by recalling their separation from, and projecting back from the current position of, the first, Tom now leaned slowly around the down-slope side of the tree. The Spanish riders, about twelve yards away, did not see him. He counted through two more seconds, brought his weapon up slowly, waited for the pair to reach a range of about eight yards. When they did, he aimed low, and squeezed the first trigger.

The weapon sounded like a small cannon going off. The far horse, the one on the right-hand side of the road, caught the great mass of the shot in its chest. The creature screamed, went down frontwards, spilling the rider roughly onto the road. The second horse, hit by two, maybe three, balls in the breast and the foreleg, staggered then reared desperately.

Aiming slightly higher, Tom squeezed the other trigger.

The second blast did not seem as loud, probably because he expected it. This charge of shot caught the same, stricken horse in the side as it was wheeling in panic, its rider hauling at the reins in an attempt to control it. The ribcage of the animal rippled under a spatter of bloody eruptions; a similar splatter of red appeared between the rider's hip and kidney. Together, man and beast fell sideways.

Tom did not see them hit the ground. Dropping the shotgun, he leaned back behind the immense tree-trunk and snatched up his waiting cap-and-ball revolver. His back covered against fire from the rearmost rider, he drew a two-handed bead on the point-man, who had pulled his mount around and had his wheel-lock pistol already in hand, looking for the source of the attack.

Tom fired, resteadied, fired, resteadied. Just before he triggered off a third shot, he saw that he had hit the target with his second bullet: the rider flinched as a dull red puff momentarily obscured his right clavicle. Probably aiming at Tom's muzzle flash, he discharged his own weapon in unison with Tom's third shot.

Which cut through the Spaniard's diaphragm and dumped him out of his saddle; his return shot hummed into the upslope forest to Tom's left, snapping twigs as it went.

A moment later, Tom heard the report of another wheel lock. He simultaneously felt and heard a thump deep in the tree behind him. No time to waste.

Tom leaned around the darker, upslope side of the tree, drew a bead on the last horseman, who had already yanked a second pistol from his saddle-brace. Tom fired; the Spaniard fired. They both missed. The horseman reached for his next pistol; Tom fired again. Another miss—but it grazed the horse's flank, causing the creature to rear and the rider to consider the rate of fire he was obviously facing. He pulled his mount around and sped back the way he had come, riding low and forward in the saddle.

Rather than waste a shot, Tom ran into the road, pistol up and ready. The first rider who had gone down was dead: the open eyes, staring almost straight back over his shoulder, bore witness to his snapped neck. The lead rider—the third Tom had shot—was not moving, nor was he making any noise audible over the perpetual rumble of the cataract. Although neither of the point-man's wounds had been instantly fatal, the odds were good that his fall from the horse inflicted a concussion. Which was a lucky bit of mercy, since the gut wound inflicted by Tom's third bullet promised a long and miserable death.

But the second rider Tom had shot, the one who had gone down sideways with his mount, was pinned under his dead horse, groaning and bleeding heavily.

Tom approached, then stopped. For a long second, he could not form any thought other than *this is not how it's supposed to end. This wasn't part of the plan. They were supposed to die. Or, if I was unlucky, flee. But not this.*

The Spaniard had evidently heard Tom's movement; he struggled to turn his head, to see who might be coming. That attempt to turn had evidently required a reflexive twisting of the lower back: the cavalryman screamed in agony.

That shook Tom out of his stupor. He reached the wounded man in two long strides. Careful not to look him in the eyes, the up-timer snugged his revolver's barrel under the soldier's chin and pulled the trigger.

Tom did not hear the report; did not stop to look at the body; did not remember clambering up the slope and on to the game trail by which he had doubled back to set up this ambush. Up until now, he'd always felt like a soldier. Now...he tried not to think of himself as a murderer.

The complement in the gondola had grown very quiet. Alps this big, when seen close up, were no longer scenic, were no longer even majestic: they were ominous gargantuas. The figure in the hooded clerical robe stood very still at the rear of the gondola, watching the towering monsters slide slowly past.

Angling to enter the north of the Sur Valley from the east, Franchetti had swept around the Piz d'Err with about one thousand yards to spare, and well under the level of its 11,080 foot peak. But as he drew closer to the Marmelsee, he seemed to be struggling to maintain a steady course.

"What's wrong?" Miro shouted above the engines.

"Nothing, Don Estuban."

"Virgilio—"

"Well, the air currents are—are hard to predict here. The drafts around these mountains, they can speed up very quickly."

Miro looked up at the next alp in the line of snow-and-stone giants arrayed in a frozen, southward parade; this one was even taller, more jagged. Miro pointed. "And that one is called?"

"Piz Calderas."

Gray horns and fangs protruded from its upper reaches; lower down, where they were, the topography was less forbidding.

"And isn't that one the Matterhorn?" Sherrilyn pointed across the valley and the Marmelsee, where a great monolith of stone was now framed by the rapidly setting sun. She sounded almost giddy; she seemed to be the last passenger whose enjoyment of the trip was undiminished.

Miro smiled. "No. That is Piz Platta."

"What?" Sherrilyn sounded personally affronted. "That's a rip-off! It's a, a...a damned look-alike. A fake."

Miro's smiled widened. "Can God steal a creative property

from himself? A worthy question for Talmudic scholars, though I suspect—"

Franchetti's "Don Estuban!" was uttered in the very same second that the gondola seemed to plummet away from under them. Miro fell to the deck, glad not to be falling further. Franchetti was giving orders to Gerd and Donald, who were his assistant engineers on this trip. Donald opened up the burner, which sent a hoarse, bright roar of flame up into the dirigible. A wave of sultry warmth washed over the gondola. At the same time, Gerd was adjusting the engine pitch for a steep climb.

Between the two adjustments, Miro expected the blimp to shoot higher. Instead, it laboriously crawled upward. Miro rose, crouched behind Franchetti, and smelled the sour stink of sudden, panicked sweat. "Virgilio, what is our situation?"

"I—I am not sure, Don Estuban. One minute I was correcting for side draft. The next a slight updraft, then a gust came down off the peak, hard. It is the air over the lake, near dusk. With the temperatures changing this quickly—"

"—wind directions and speeds are changing just as quickly."

Harry Lefferts spat over the side of the gondola. "Damn it. I knew this was a lousy idea. Flying just before sunset: it's nuts."

Miro watched the steep sides of the Piz Calderas come closer. "Virgilio, is it wise that we—?"

"Don Estuban, the air is calmer here, farther away from the surface of the lake. I think we can probably—"

Then they were shooting upwards, rapidly closing with the Piz Calderas. "What the fuck—?" shouted Sherrilyn.

Miro knew better than to interrogate Franchetti, who was trying to both save their lives and adapt to conditions he had never encountered in the more predictable flying conditions of central Germany. Besides, Miro had a pretty good idea of what the problem was.

They had entered a fierce new westerly draft. Glancing across the valley, Miro guessed it was produced by the funneling effects the two immense alps he saw there: the Piz Platta and its northerly partner, the Piz Arblatsch. Winds from the west were pinched between the peaks and accelerated, as would a stream of water that is forced to flow through a narrow tube. Entering the valley, the airship had been north of the draft. And later, until it struggled up out of the downdrafts over the lake, the balloon had remained under the air current. But rising up had brought them square into the blast, which had not only removed the downdraft effect, but was pushing them sideways, toward a high-altitude impalement upon the snowy spikes of Piz Caldera.

Except not all those lethal projections were clearly snow-marked, Miro realized. "Virgilio—!"

Franchetti saw the daggerlike horn of dark-gray rock that jumped out of the shadows at them. Probably the morning sunlight had melted it clean, allowing it to lurk, camouflaged, in the shadows of dusk. As they sped sideways to meet its disemboweling slice, sure to shred the gondola and drop them thousands of feet to their collective deaths, Miro watched Franchetti struggle to get the airship down and out of the cross-valley draft. And that was when he realized that, instead, they had to—

"Climb!" shouted Miro. "Pitch engines for rapid ascent; throttles wide open!"

"Wha—?"

"Do it!" roared Miro, who leaped over to the burner and opened its choke to full burn.

No longer trying to fight back down into and through the cross-current, the sudden increase in both lift and upward thrust pushed the dirigible suddenly higher with what seemed like a hop. Piz Calderas' granite claw reached out for them—

—and bumped lightly against the bottom of the gondola, before they soared up beyond it. They were still angling toward the higher reaches of Piz Calderas, but without the same powerful side draft. They had also climbed over the most intense core of the winds. Behind Miro, people began to breathe again.

Franchetti turned; his brow was as wet as if he emerged from the lake they were now angling back toward. "Don Estuban, I— thank you. *Merde!* Just thank you." From the other end of the gondola, Miro was pretty sure he could hear the robed passenger murmuring what sounded like a prayer of thanks.

Miro sank back into a seat and then felt something thump against his back. He turned around just as George Sutherland's big, meaty paw landed for a second friendly pat. "Not half bad, Don Estuban, not half bad."

Harry, too, was smiling at him. Indeed, they all were. Miro nodded, smiled back and stared once again across the valley at the alps that had almost killed them.

# Chapter 7

North watched the light dying in the narrow strip of sky that looked down at them from between peaks that soared up and away like walls reaching to Heaven itself. Then he lowered his gaze to peer beyond the edge of their sheltering copse, following the track that descended toward the western extent of the Val Bregaglia.

But before the valley dipped down to where the Mera picked up speed and spread wider and shallower, the wagon track passed before the door of the humble church and cottages that comprised the hamlet of Castagena. Where, evidently, a wedding had run late; a dozen revelers were still milling about. Half seemed to be trying to tidy up the area and hush the other half. Who, for their part, seemed unwilling to realize that the festivities had ended.

North drew a deep breath. "Pass the word: as soon as the last of these bloody merrymakers have cleared off, we travel weapons out and at the trot. We have to move swiftly to the extraction site and establish our defensive perimeter in the dark. Not a simple exercise."

"And still no way to know if there will be anyone there to be extracted."

"Yes, a bit problematic, that."

"How long do we wait at the extraction site, Colonel?"

North gave Hastings a sour look. "Until it's time to leave. How the hell do I know how long we'll have to wait?"

✧    ✧    ✧

Nichols put a hand on Tom Simpson's arm. "Hold up, there. Let me look at that wound, again."

"Doc, we don't have the time—"

"There's a lot of things we don't have the time for. You bleeding to death is on the top of the list. Now stand still."

The rest of the group moved on ahead. Melissa's iron determination had kept her going—that and the decreased pace that Tom had set. Rita and Arco were taking turns all but carrying Ginetti as they made their way upslope around a hamlet that made tiny Piuro look like a bustling metropolis.

Tom looked over his shoulder. "Is it bad?"

"Not bad but messy. And unlucky. This musket ball reopened the grenade wound you picked up while rescuing Urban. I've got no way to stop the bleeding out here."

"Can't you—I don't know—bind it?" Tom felt idiotic even as he said it.

James Nichols' long silence made him feel even more stupid. "Tom, just how would you propose I bind a lateral wound on a single buttock?"

"Okay, dumb idea. Look, we don't have much farther to go. On the far side of the hamlet—Villa, I think they call it—the Mera widens out. There's a light forest hugging the north bank. When we get beyond that forest, we're at the rendezvous point. So listen: you go on ahead and—"

Tom felt James' shoulder muscles, corded with age but still strong, slip under his right armpit and hoist. "Nope. You're coming with us." Tom rose to his feet, wobbled.

"Pain?" asked Nichols.

"Naw, just dizzy."

"That's the blood loss."

"Blood loss? What, do I have an artery in my ass?"

"No, Tom. But you've been pushing yourself over hill and dale for hours now, and even slow bleeding is going to make you light-headed and weak."

"Not a good time for those symptoms," Tom observed, trying to move without Nichols' help, but not succeeding brilliantly.

James Nichols paused, lifted his head to hear over the Gallegione cataract crashing down from the heights ahead and to the north. "No, not a good time at all."

Tom had heard it too: the fraction of a shouted order. In Spanish, and farther back along the wagon track they had been following.

It had become so dark that Miro was uncertain how Franchetti was flying. The last light glimmered off the Lunghinsee, far to the left. The lake was the source of the River Inn, a distinction that conjured images of a broad expanse of water, cascading over rocks in a flume that would eventually reach the sea. But in actuality, the Lunghinsee was a puddle compared to the Marmelsee. It was small, stark, and alien: an absolutely unrippled mirror surface, held in the grip of mountains as barren as those of the moon.

The dirigible dipped sharply; Miro and the other passengers braced themselves, but Franchetti's explanation—shouted over the engines—put them back at ease. "We have gone over the Septimer Pass, which is just above seven thousand, two hundred feet. The last alps of the Oberhalbstein Range are now behind us to the left, the west. We now head down into the Val Bregaglia by turning west at Vicosoprano."

"And we should be at the rendezvous in how long?"

"I cannot say until we see what the winds are like in the valley. But about half an hour. Sooner, if conditions are good."

Miro turned to the Wrecking Crew. "Ready your weapons."

North hissed at Hastings as he went past. "Keep your squad away from the banks of the river; there isn't enough tree-cover there."

Hastings looked dubiously overhead at the stars that were beginning to shine through the dusty-rose and mauve of late dusk.

North grumbled as Hastings opened his mouth to reply. "No, Lieutenant, it's not as dark as you think. Not so dark that buckles and barrels won't catch a bit of light and alert the Spanish. That's why our men's rifles went back in their cases for the nonce. The Spaniard is not always imaginative, but he's a steady, seasoned soldier. If you get lazy, he will teach you the error of your ways: a lesson that might end with you waking up in Heaven. Or in slightly less lofty regions, in your case."

"Yes, sir."

"No heroics, Hastings. When you get to the edge of the woods overlooking the cataract, set up a loose skirmish line that extends upslope thirty yards from the cart-track."

"Sir, this being spring in the Alps, there could be several mountain run-offs, so how can I tell which—?"

"Hastings, this is a genuine cataract. Flows all the way down from the peak of that alp"—He pointed up at the pink-tinted snow-cap of the Piz Gallegione, towering over them just to the north—"so I don't think you're going to miss it. Although, in your case—"

Hastings cleared his throat. "And you'll be in reserve behind us, sir?"

"Yes, but I'll be down two men. They'll be detached to make contact with the airship when it arrives in at the extraction site. And while we're waiting for Captain Simpson's group to arrive, do see if you can keep from getting killed, Lieutenant. It would take an unreasonably long amount of time to train someone to replace you. Given the high caliber of your skills, I estimate it might even require two days. Now go—and remember: even with the countersign, it's going to be difficult distinguishing friend from foe in this light. No eager trigger-fingers."

"Yes, sir." And Hastings was gone, a shadow consumed by shadows.

North looked out over the broad spread of the Mera, smooth and quiet here, though he could make out two pinpricks of yellow light just beyond where the river gathered together and, swollen by the cataract, plunged down once again. Probably oil lamps in upper story windows of Villa, he thought. *But five years ago, my eyes were keen enough that I wouldn't have had to guess. I'm getting old, damn it. Old.*

*Hell, next month, I'll be halfway through my thirties.*

Tom ran, limping, to join the rest of them at the edge of the fuming torrent that swirled down into the Mera at the northeastern edge of Villa.

Rita and Arco, supporting Ginetti on either side, ventured into the swift current, stumbled, righted themselves, and then fell again, going down to their knees.

"Shit," swore Rita, grabbing after the limp cardinal.

"*Merde,*" echoed Arco.

A light came on in a second story window of the largest house in Villa.

*Now,* reflected Tom, *things are likely to get very interesting.*

✧    ✧    ✧

As the airship passed over Castagena, Franchetti started level-
ing out from his descent. The Val Bregaglia was almost flat here,
allowing the Mera to fan out. Miro, hand upon the covered
bull's-eye lantern that was to serve as a landing light, started
looking for the prearranged extraction zone, a meadow just north
of where the river widened—

Melissa, forgetting her own infirmities, jumped over to help
the cardinal back to his feet; James scrambled into the water
after her—

A musket discharged from within the confines of the town.
The ball struck one of the rocks flanking the ford, pieces of stone
spalling upslope. The miss had been well wide of the group that
was struggling over the shallows in the dark, but it was close
enough to be worrisome. Orders were shouted in Spanish. From
back along the upslope path they had followed to get here, a
whistle shrilled in answer.

Tom dropped into a crouch. He exhaled through the sudden
flare of pain that blossomed as his right buttock hyperextended.
The Spanish were coming from two directions. One group had
followed the upslope trail, which put them due west. The other
group—probably the larger of the bodies of troops—had stayed
on the wider, better track that wound through Villa; they were
approaching from the southwest. Probably at a good clip.

Tom pulled out his revolver, checked that the priming caps
were snugly seated. Not long now.

Having just settled his squad within the trees one hundred
yards west of the extraction zone—about a third of the distance
to Villa—North tilted his head to listen. Yes, that was a musket
report, which came across the sluggish water like a sighing *pop!*
"Damn it."

The colonel's batman, Finan, scuttled over. "Sir, what is it?"

"Did you hear that?"

"Hear what, sir?"

North closed his eyes, remembered a particularly apt American exchange, reprised in so many of their movies. "I have good
news and bad news."

"Sir?"

"The good news is that Captain Simpson and his party are still alive, and are, in fact, quite close."

"And the bad news is—?"

"That we're not alone. Send a runner to Hastings: positive target identification before firing. It's going to be close."

As Finan disappeared into the murk, another two shots came faintly over the water.

*Very close indeed.*

Harry Lefferts stood. "Okay, *that* wasn't 'just my imagination.' Did you see the flashes?"

Miro nodded. "At the western end of the wide part of the river, near the Piz Gallegione cataract."

Harry turned. "Listen, we're not going to be able to run over there in time to save them, not if we land here at the extraction site."

Miro nodded again. Lefferts' assessment was inarguably correct. "So where's Colonel North?"

"If he's here, he'll be somewhere between the extraction zone and the anticipated contact point."

Miro peered at the thin woods. "I don't see anything there."

"Of course not. North is good: you won't see him until he wants you to."

"So what do you recommend?"

Harry frowned, considering. "North will stay under cover until we signal. But with a firefight in progress, we'd be stupid to follow the original plan to hover out over the river. And he'd be stupid to give away his position before seeing us. So we have to change the plans. *We* have to send the first signal. We shoot the first whistle-bolt."

Miro met Harry's eyes. He saw eagerness but no *berserkergang*, no indication of a battle lust that might impede judgment. He looked over Lefferts' shoulder at Matija. "Shoot the bolt."

Tom couldn't see the Spanish approaching, but he could hear them. Muttered orders, whispered acknowledgements, occasional rustling and soft footfalls: the sounds of a stealthy platoon advance.

The only other two shots the Spanish had fired were blind misses, meaning that the first shot's proximity had probably been the result of luck, not skill. Probably a Hail-Mary discharge in the general direction of the voices heard at the ford.

Which the last of the group had almost traversed. The cardinal had cleared the rocks on the other side, hanging like a drowned rat between Rita and Arco. Melissa was finally picking her way out of the churning white melt-waters, too—and then she went down, quick and hard, with a most improper and biologically implausible oath.

The timing was unfortunate. James had just turned to start back and help Tom across. Hearing Melissa's sharp cry, Nichols spun and caught her arm before the rush of water could carry her under and away. *Pretty damned spry for a guy in his sixties,* thought Tom. But as James helped Melissa hobble up out of the frothing current, he glanced back over his shoulder. His eyes—desperate and apologetic—met Tom's.

Tom Simpson nodded his understanding and approval; a man's first duty was to his woman. Nichols faded into the trees on the far bank, working as a human crutch for Melissa. It was obvious that her ankle was at least sprained, maybe broken.

Tom looked at his black-powder revolver, wished it was any one of a half dozen up-time weapons he had used in the past three years. But that kind of armament had been deemed both unnecessary and too unsubtle when they set out on this journey. Back in safe, sunny Padua. Back before they were given the additional task of rendezvousing with a renegade cardinal who had the physique of a couch-potato.

Tom hunkered down behind the largest rock he could find, took the cap-and-ball revolver in both hands—and heard a strange bird call over the water. *Wait: was that—?*

North held up his hand. "Was that a—?"

Finan nodded. "Sounded like a long-winded whip-poor-will to me, Colonel."

The signal. The dirigible was here.

"Fire our bolt," he hissed urgently at his batman. "Right now, out over the water."

Lefferts was focused in a way that Miro had never seen before. Now he understood why, despite his swagger and reputation for occasional impulsiveness, Harry had been so successful on operations like these. "Franchetti," the up-timer said, "keep us close to the slope, inside the shadows if you can."

"*Si*, but where am I—?"

"Look dead ahead, due west, just upslope of where the cataract hits the river. You see that small pasture?"

"Near the abandoned farmhouse?"

"Yeah. Can you put down there?"

"Well, yes, but—"

"Do it. Now." Lefferts turned to the rest of his Wrecking Crew. "Well, folks, it might be a hot LZ. Ready for some fun?"

Tom Simpson heard a second strange birdsong—the whistle-bolt countersign—respond promptly to the first and allowed himself a small smile. *Well, I just might get out of this alive, after all . . .*

Four shots sputtered from between the buildings in Villa; two more came from upslope, flashes marking their sources within the tree line. Most of the balls missed by a reasonable margin; one thumped into a decayed tree trunk lying in front of the rock behind which Tom had taken cover.

*But then again, I might not.*

North stood as the runner he sent to the front rank returned. Before the winded fellow could speak, the colonel gave new orders. "Back you go. Tell Lieutenant Hastings that he has a new relief force coming in on his right flank."

"A new relief force? Where from, sir?"

North pointed upward. "From thin air." He motioned for the rest of his squad to get their rifles out of their all-weather hide cases. "Ready on the line," he ordered, as he readied his up-time nine-millimeter pistol.

Franchetti screamed, "Pitch the engines down! Full braking thrust!"

Miro complied, yanking the engine angling bar up sharply. The props rotated into an earth-aimed attitude, slowing the descent. The gondola came to an unsteady halt, a mere four feet off the ground.

Juliet—a short, round woman—looked dubiously at the gap that Lefferts, Gerd, and Sherrilyn had already jumped down.

"C'mon!" hissed Lefferts, before disappearing into the downslope tree line, with the Gallegione cataract roiling and crashing on its downward tumult about thirty yards to his right.

George Sutherland hopped to the ground—lightly for a man of his size—and held up his arms for his wife. "Down you come, dear." He said it as if she were descending from a coach after a ride in the country—which is how she exited the airship.

Franchetti glanced back. "Don Estuban, we should—"

"Yes—yes, Virgilio; take us back to the extraction point."

As Miro and Franchetti swiveled the engines into a down-draft position again, and throttled the burner up, the dirigible rose and swung away from the small meadow.

In the back of the gondola, the one remaining passenger started praying in Latin.

Tom let the first tactical probe get within twenty-five yards before he fired four times, quickly. Of the three approaching Spaniards, two fell: one, howling and writhing; the other, silently and limp. Having finally given away his position, Tom ducked, just in time to hear a ragged crackle of musketry from both the hamlet and the upslope trail. Perhaps a dozen balls spattered Tom's sheltering rock, the rotted log, and the ground nearby. Many more hissed into the white, whirling veils of the cataract and beyond, into the trees.

Tom popped up, saw a thin horizontal line of gun smoke diffusing slowly in his direction. He also saw the last Spaniard advancing on his flank, hunched low, pistol and sword at the ready. Tom fired twice at the skirmisher, turned and jumped into the stream, hopping and struggling his way across. The Spaniard's pistol, and a more distant musket, discharged behind him; either Tom was not hit, or he did not feel it. Either way, he continued his uneven progress across the ford, wondering how long the gun smoke would obscure the vision of the Spanish line, and how long it would take them to reload.

Harry Lefferts was so focused on finding a way to get closer to the cataract that he was completely surprised by the buff-coated man who rose up in front of him. Jerking to a startled halt, Harry squinted into the near-dark: the man's weapon was an immediate giveaway as to whose side he was on.

Harry moved the barrel of the down-time box-magazine Winchester away from his belly. "Wondered where you guys were," Lefferts drawled.

"Waiting for you."

"Oooh, snappy. I like that. You also just about scared me out of my pants." He looked the mercenary up and down. "You're pretty damned good. Wanna work for me?"

The man shrugged. "I like my boss."

"I pay better."

"I doubt it. And I've got a family. Lieutenant Hastings is just down the slope."

"No time to find him. How are you deployed?"

"Loose skirmish line from here to the river to cover Captain Simpson's group as they come up the track." As if to emphasize the harried approach of that group, a clatter of musketry rose above the dull thunder of the cataract.

"Any force closer to the ford?"

"No. None to spare. We've only got two squads."

"You're only one squad, here. Where's the other?"

"Landing zone security and uncommitted reserve."

Harry scowled a little. Frequently, the word "reserve" translated as *the hiding place for cowardly commanders*. "I see Colonel North is sitting this one out."

"That's not how we see it."

"Well, we can debate that over a beer some time. We're going in."

"In? In where?"

Harry pointed in the direction of the recent fusillade. "In there."

"You're going to attack the Spanish?"

Harry smiled and waved for the Wrecking Crew to follow him southwest, angling to follow the upslope limit of the woods. "Not directly."

Tom reached the other side of the ford just as the muskets started sporadically barking at him again. However, from the sound of it, most of the Spanish were giving chase, not stopping to reload. In the dark, any gunfights at ranges greater than ten yards were pretty much pointless.

Feeling solid ground under his feet, Tom up and sprinted forward, following the cart-track. The pain of his reopened wound returned sharply, now reaching up into his lower back. When the shooting had started, adrenaline had swept the discomfort away, but that relieving rush was gone; soon, he'd start limping, stumbling—

He heard movement upslope, some yards beyond the trees linking the track.

Impossible. There had been no way to cross the cataract higher up; how could the Spanish have anyone on his northern flank?

Desperate, and experiencing true panic for the first time in many years, Tom Simpson found another surge of strength which sent him dashing forward along the track.

Lieutenant Hastings watched the man and woman help the little priest stumble past his position, and right behind them, an odd couple indeed: a fit, yet clearly older woman with a useless, dangling foot, being almost dragged along by a fit, but equally aged Moor. And, still farther back along the track, another very large silhouette was emerging from the darkness...

Corporal Eugenio Morca de Torres clambered out of the frothing current, cocked his miquelet musket, aimed after the fleeing figure, then lowered his weapon. *Coño*, the big American was fast, even when wounded. He waved for his men to follow and ran in pursuit.

Harry skidded to a halt, five yards from where the woods ended at the cart-track. He saw a figure running down there, heading towards North's forward skirmish line. A big figure. Tom Simpson. Had to be.

Catching a tree branch to slow himself, George Sutherland readied his up-time shotgun, tracking back along the route of Tom's retreat. Troop sounds—a platoon or more moving quickly—were growing loud enough to rival the cataract back there.

Harry shook his head. "Not yet."

Lieutenant Hastings saw that the approaching figure was the large up-timer, Tom Simpson. He was limping and staggering, now, probably both wounded and exhausted. And behind him, only twenty yards or so, the first of the Spanish were visible. And one, in the lead, was stopping, raising his arms...

...drawing a bead?

Lieutenant Hastings brought up his Winchester and yelled, "Get down, Simpson. Squad, fire at will!"

✧          ✧          ✧

Tom heard the British accent, almost sobbed in relief, and dove forward.

Corporal Torres felt the men on either side of him go down, and discharged his musket in the direction of the small and ominously rapid muzzle flashes. Up-time weapons or copies—no doubt about it. But the range was close, and he had fifty men. And since one of their quarry was obviously a Moor, it seemed only right to cry, "Santiago and at them!" Dropping his spent firearm, Torres sprinted forward. Drawing his sword, he swept it back in readiness…

"Now," said Harry calmly.

Five yards beyond the upslope trees that lined the cart-track, the nine members of the Wrecking Crew unleashed a near-uniform volley from their trademark pump shotguns. With the center of the ragged enemy column now directly abreast of the Crew, the carnage was startling. More than a dozen Spaniards sprawled, their blood black in the early moonlight.

The lethal, hollow-tube sound of the shotguns' cycling actions—the dull *ker-throonk* of rounds being fed back and up from under-barrel magazines—offered a faint counterpoint chorus before they roared again. Other sounds of twentieth-century slaughter added to the waves of sound, echoing off the rocks of the Val Bregaglia several more times before giving way to absolute silence.

# Chapter 8

"Well, I guess that was just about a perfect L-ambush. And improvised on the spot, no less." Harry Lefferts seemed very pleased with himself as he and Sherrilyn emerged from the woods and strolled into the small clearing that had been the dirigible's original extraction zone.

The airship was now resting on the ground; every thirty seconds, Franchetti goosed the burner, sending a long blast of heated air up into the envelope. He turned to Miro and North. "We go soon, *si*? I waste fuel to keep the dirigible in readiness."

Harry looked at the casks of fuel stored at the midsection and ends of the gondola. "I thought you brought extra juice."

"*Si*, but 'extra' is not 'endless.' And flying back could be difficult. We may have to land and take off again—at Bivio, I think. And that will make returning to Chur a very close thing."

"Land again? Before Chur?" Sherrilyn asked, reloading her shotgun. "Why?"

Franchetti shrugged, with a dubious look in Miro's direction. "I am not sure I want to try to go all the way back through the Sur Valley in the dark. It was bad enough in the day."

Cardinal Ginetti got more pale, if that was possible.

Miro nodded and stepped down from the gondola as the Crew hauled out their packs. "I agree with Franchetti: you cannot fly that route at night. The air-currents around the Lai di Marmorera and the Sur are too unpredictable, and you would have to fly to twelve thousand feet to be safely above them. It is too risky. Better to stop at Bivio, at the south entrance to the valley. This part of our mission is to ensure that Captain Simpson's group returns safely to the USE. Having them killed during a daredevil return flight would rather defeat the whole purpose, no?"

Lefferts nodded, smiling. "Well, at least I don't have to take the slow ride back like Ms. Mailey here." Melissa Mailey was limping out of the wood line, supported on either side by members of North's detachment.

The former school teacher responded archly. "A nice, slow ride will suit me just fine, Harry."

Lefferts shrugged, caught the Crews' collective eyes, and tilted his head back in the direction of the cart-track.

As he took his first step in that direction, North asked, "Here now; where do you think you're going?"

Lefferts stopped. "Uh...there's a lot of handy gear back there. Word is, its owners don't have any further use for it, so—"

North shook his head. "Not this time."

"Colonel North, last I checked, you were not acting commander of this operation. He is." Harry pitched his chin in Miro's direction. "And I don't hear him making any noise—"

"Harry Lefferts, you will not loot the dead." Somehow, Melissa Mailey raised herself up to an imperious height, despite being propped up by North's men. "Let's ignore the odious habits of your trade for a moment. Removing gear from that many bodies will take time that we do not have. I doubt this sleepy valley is accustomed to ferocious nighttime firefights, so I'm going to propose the outrageous deduction that news of it will spread quickly. Back to Chiavenna and the Spanish. Who will come here swiftly. So, if we are to leave a false trail that encourages our enemies to conclude that, despite the local reports, this was a relatively mundane ambush—one conducted without the aid of an airship, for instance—then there's no time for looting. Furthermore, those persons who are remaining behind to travel overland to Italy must start on their way immediately. That includes you, if I am not mistaken."

Harry smiled respectfully at his old history teacher's remonstrations. When she was done, he shook his head and sighed. "This is twice, now, I've had to rescue you, Ms. Mailey. And you always spoil the fun. C'mon folks"—he gestured to the Crew—"we need to police our own brass, at least." He and the rest of the Crew left at a trot.

North looked after them, then turned toward Miro. "I do not believe we've met, sir. Colonel Thomas North, Hibernian Mercenary Battalion. I believe it's time to put our respective halves of the operational coin together. What are your further objectives?"

Miro nodded and explained. "Well, as you heard, the dirigible will retrace its path back east to Vicosoprano, then a short hop north over Cassacia. From there, a rising buttonhook westward will put the blimp into the Val Maroz, then north over the Septimer Pass and to a landing on the outskirts of Bivio."

"Will they need to take on extra fuel, there?"

"I suspect so. Besides, Franchetti will not want to fly again before dawn. And I doubt there's enough fuel on board for him to reinflate the balloon and make it the rest of the way to Chur."

"So tomorrow morning he'll have to toddle down into Bivio and try to find—What do you burn in that thing, anyway? Spirits? Oils?"

"Yes, and it uses a lot, very quickly. Luckily, they won't need very much to get from Bivio to Chur. But then again, there probably won't be much fuel to be had in a remote alpine lake town in May."

"I suppose not. Sounds like they'll be lucky to get airborne again after a one day delay."

"I'm guessing two. But from Bivio, it's not even two hours to Chur, more fuel and the route home."

"Which is—?"

"Chur to Biberach, then Nuremberg, then Jena. Probably two or three days between each connection."

"The delay at each point is to be spent getting more fuel?"

"No, we prepositioned enough. But weather and other factors could easily delay the airship that much. Besides, I find that overestimating obstacles is generally a better operational model than underestimating them."

"Agreed. And for those of us who remain behind?"

Miro brought out a map, an exact copy of an up-time document, right down to its "Baedecker" logos. "We are here." He pointed just east of a tiny dot labeled Piuro. "We will head back toward Chiavenna—"

North's eyes widened. "I beg your pardon, did you say 'back toward Chiavenna'?"

"Yes, but I reemphasize: we are heading *toward* Chiavenna, not to it. Instead, we are fast-marching two miles back to the west, to this place marked as Santa Croce."

"Why there?"

"Do you see the southwest line that comes down from Santa Croce?"

"I see a southwest zigzag."

"Yes, well...that is a mountain trail which cuts through to Berzo, here, on the Mera, just south of Chiavenna."

"So we take a nice, long, and rather steep, walk in the woods to avoid delivering ourselves into the hands of the people who would like to make us the central attraction at their next *auto-da-fé*."

"No, I suspect they would reserve that for me, alone. You, they would simply execute. Maybe torture and execute. Hard to say."

"Yes. But why do you presume they would reserve the delights of a personal bonfire as your special reward, Mr. Miro?"

"Because, Mr. North, I am a Jew."

"Ah." The Englishman's eyes were bright. "A so-called 'crypto-Jew'?"

Miro was surprised. "Yes. I was not aware that the writings of twentieth-century historians were among your reading interests."

"I am nothing if not eclectic. Please continue."

Miro decided he liked North, whose sardonic British wit was not entirely out of step with the less arch, but no less ironic, traditions of Talmudic humor. "So we emerge at Berzo, where we will immediately find honest work as the honest security escort of an honest merchant caravan, that just happens to be heading south. And which just happens to be waiting for us in Berzo."

"And how do we come by all these fortuitous—and honest— opportunities?"

"By having one of Europe's most widespread mercantile facilitation families as our trusted partners. More specifically, Cavriani agents are in charge of the caravan waiting in Berzo."

"I see. And then?"

"We travel south along the banks of the Mera until we come to the ferry wharf at the northern edge of the Lago di Mezzola."

"I take it that there, although in the very belly of Milanese control and watchfulness, we will serendipitously discover and book passage aboard an honest barge captained by an honest ferryman."

"Your powers of foresight rival those of the ancient prophets,

Colonel North. Once on Lago di Mezzola, there is little chance that we will even come into contact with any Milanese patrols. The north-south traffic along the lakes there—from Mezzola to Como to Lecco to Garlate—is too valuable for the Milanese to close against all Lombard and Venetian access. So we shall make our way down those interconnected waterways until we disembark at the southern tip of Garlate. There is an 'open-town' custom there, much as has been enforced in Chiavenna since the Spanish and French renounced their squabbles over the Valtelline. From that town, it is a short ride across the border into Venetian Lombardy."

"How many of us are in the party?"

Miro had to double-check the numbers. "You, me, twelve of your men, the nine members of the Wrecking Crew, and our chaplain."

"Our chaplain?"

"Yes," said a new voice. "That would be me."

Melissa Mailey looked up sharply at the sound of that voice, which came from the last, cloaked passenger who was descending from the airship. "Larry?"

Father—now Cardinal—Lawrence Mazzare let the hood of the habit fall back. His smile was thin. "Guilty as charged."

James Nichols, who was helping Tom Simpson gimp toward the airship, almost dropped the wounded ex-halfback. "Good God, Larry, how did you get Stearns to go along with this?"

Mazzare shouldered his own modest pack. "I don't believe in starting arguments I can't win."

James' realization was almost a whisper. "You didn't tell him."

Melissa's jaw dropped, a thing very few of them had ever seen. "Sweet balls," she swore earnestly. "And he will sure as hell have yours, Larry."

Miro got the impression that His Eminence Mazzare's momentary silence was due to the pious suppression of a swarm of scrotal puns and testicular one-liners. "He's welcome to them if I can accomplish what I came for."

"Which is?"

He turned a patient glance on Melissa. "Do you even need to ask? And I'll remind you that not all of the people gathered here have equal measures of information. Most of the security troops don't even know where we're going next. And they certainly have no idea who you were protecting in Padua. Wherever possible, Mike and Sharon Nichols have kept people in the dark on that."

"In which benighted group the good father must regrettably include me," put in North with a tone that was the very model of drollery.

"And it is best to keep it that way for now. What, precisely, have you been told, Colonel North?"

"When President Piazza contacted us, we were already seeing to—erm—'security matters' just south of Nuremberg. He retained us immediately and ordered us to deploy with all haste to Chur, as an escort for a shipment of high quality fuels. Which, unless I miss my retroactive conjecture, were for the airship, here. We were then ordered to move down into the Val Engadine via the Julier pass. We received updates for this extraction mission by radio, on the way. As to what comes next? We were simply told to be 'flexible,' but also to anticipate further field operations without refit or resupply. Which it sounds like we're about to do."

"Yes, you are," answered Mazzare. "And about which you have no speculations?" Miro thought that the up-time cardinal's eyes might have twinkled.

"Speculations? Me?" North seemed positively affronted. "Sir, I am a simple soldier. I have neither the intellect for speculation, nor the taste for it. However, if I did have the intellect—and the taste—for speculation, I would be tempted to conjecture that with one cardinal desperately being extracted from Italy, and another one desperately trying to get into Italy, there is some popish tomfoolery afoot. Additionally, given Cardinal Mazzare's special relationship with the missing-and-possibly-dead Pope Urban, and Cardinal— oh, excuse me—*Friar* Ginetti's long-standing friendship with and service to that very same pontiff, I might surmise that the pope is indeed much more 'missing' than 'dead.' And in consequence of that surmise, I might indulge in a few even more outlandish guesses."

"Such as?"

"Such as this: that the little wet cardinal who's about to take a balloon ride is doing so because he is not only at risk, but may be needed to effectuate the convening of the Cardinals' College outside the boundaries of Rome. And this: that the other cardinal who is now trying to get into Italy is doing so in order to confab with, and maybe attempt to influence the opinions of, the missing pope. For surely, with this jolly monster Borja capering about in what's left of the Holy See, the legitimate pope's next decisions and actions will determine the future of the papacy and Roman Catholicism to a wholly unprecedented degree, even in your own history. But of course, I am but a simple soldier, and do not speculate about such things."

Mazzare smiled. "Of course you don't."

During North's detailed recitation of the speculations in which he had pointedly not indulged, Melissa Mailey's gaze had come to rest on Miro. "You're pretty new to be taking on this kind of initiative, don't you think, Don Estuban?"

"I'm sorry; what do you mean, Ms. Mailey?"

"Coordinating the assets for all the messy work that needs doing in sunny Italy: that alone is a lot of responsibility for a new guy. But bringing Father—Cardinal—Mazzare here without Michael Stearns' express authorization? Well, I just hope you aren't exceeding the bounds of whatever authority you might have been given."

Miro shrugged. "Don Francisco Nasi assured me otherwise. And while President Piazza did not explicitly request that I take Cardinal Mazzare along, he made many noises about separation of church and state, his lack of authority over the ideas and actions of priests, and the fundamental freedom of personal conscience. He then invoked a number of very similar passages from the governing documents of your once-and-future United States. When I bluntly inquired if I was therefore permitted to bring Cardinal Mazzare with us, President Piazza made all the same noises all over again."

"I see," Melissa said with a tight smile. "From the sound of it, I think it's only suitable to welcome you to the club, Don Estuban. Fair warning, though: the membership dues can be pretty steep." She indicated her sprained ankle and winced.

"I am used to high-stakes gambles for worthwhile causes, Ms. Mailey."

Her smile relaxed, became open, almost warm. "Thank you for the rescue, Don Estuban, and good luck in your travels." Then, without missing a beat, she growled at the two mercenaries to make more haste in helping her up into the gondola.

Miro smiled after her, then turned back to North. "So, simple soldier, you've seen my half of the operational coin. What does yours look like?"

By way of answer, North summoned Hastings to him with a crooked finger and started rapping out orders. "Lieutenant, as arranged, I am leaving a reduced squad with you. Retrace our route back eastward through the Val Bregaglia—but with less care for leaving spoor. Give the Spanish a good trail to follow, but nothing too obvious. When you reach the Maloja Pass, muck about meaningfully on the near bank of the Silsersee."

"Uh... why, sir?"

"To make it look like you either had a raft waiting, or found a path along its banks. That should convince your pursuers that you've headed back into the Val Engadine."

Hastings clearly hated saying it again: "Uh... why, sir?"

"Because," North exhaled slowly, "the other end of the Engadine is in Tyrol. Tyrol is, or at least will soon be, part of the United States of Europe. Logically, the Spanish will expect this group of USE nationals to make toward that safe haven. So we'll let the Spaniards chase their own tails a while, and hopefully induce them to overlook the tiny fact that we used a dirigible to get the group out of the region entirely. I suspect they'll be too arrogant to stop and chat with the locals long enough to discover that some of those sheep-sodomizing worthies might have seen a flying sausage cruising about their valley this night. After that, the trail will be too cold to follow, even if they could."

Hastings shrugged. "Very well, sir. But where do *we* go?"

"Isn't it obvious? Once you've left trail sign on the banks of the Silsersee, you double back through Cassacia into the Val Maroz and up over the Septimer Pass. Then via Bivio back to Chur. Where you will await further orders."

As Lieutenant Hastings disappeared, North turned to Miro. "And now you have seen my rather uncomplicated half of the coin. Are we ready to begin our hike? I rather expect the Spanish will send another detachment up here when the first fails to return. Besides, it's almost certain that some of the men in that detachment made their escape and will bring the news even if the local Spanish authorities are lackadaisical. There's no way to be certain of killing everyone in an ambush done in darkness."

"I agree," answered Miro with a nod. "Let's get our people moving then, Colonel."

# Chapter 9

Frank Stone raised himself to look toward the door of his prison cell.

Unfortunately, he forgot about the ring finger he had recently lost from his left hand—an experience which the brutalized nerve endings obviously recalled quite clearly. He hoped that, despite his moan, he had merely sunk back down to the floor. However, the small but strong arms around him, and Giovanna's worried face hovering over his, seemed to suggest that he had fallen. Probably blacked out.

"Shhh...do not move, Frank."

"Is he still there?"

"Our visitor?" She looked back toward the door, where a shadow lurked almost unseen behind the narrowly set bars of the observation panel. "It seems so. Strange: he does not move. Makes no sound."

"So it's probably not Captain Castro y Papas, then."

"No, it cannot be him. He always comes in and talks."

"And checks you out."

"Frank! I am your wife!"

"Hey, as long as you're not interested in him, it's okay by me. He'd have to be blind—or neutered—not to notice you. And if it keeps bringing him back with boiled water and fresh dressings for this"—he raised his hand; the pain made him repent it—"he's welcome to look."

"I think the pure spirits he brings have also helped. Despite the pain, there is only a little infection around the edges of the wounds where—where—"

"—Where my ring finger and wedding ring were. Yeah. That wound could have become pretty nasty."

Giovanna raised her head. Her eyes were not entirely unlike Frank's memory of the up-time Sophia Loren's, and were every bit as fiery. "It could have meant your death: likely, given this sewer in which they have put us. Do they not know who you are? Do they not know that your father is now one of the wealthiest men in Europe? Do they not know—?"

"Honey, whether they know all that or not, I think it's pretty obvious that they don't *care*. Which is kind of what worries me the most."

Giovanna stared (as she often did) at his second-generation flower-child nonchalance. "'Kind of worries you'? Husband, love—it means they are insane! Insane! They care nothing for anything else in the world, or surely they would be treating us, or at least you, differently."

"Well, we're sure not at the top of their priority list," Frank conceded with a grin. "But I don't think we're at the bottom, either."

"No? And why not?"

"Well, we're alive, aren't we?"

Giovanna pouted, not eager to concede the point. "This is true," she said after a time. "But then why—?"

Noise at the door. A key scraped its way into the unoiled lock. The half rusted fixtures squealed and then groaned as the door opened. Two laborers—obviously impressed Romans, judging from the soiled state of their half-ruined clothing and resentful backward glances—entered, bearing two small boxes, the kind used for shipping light cargos.

Giovanna stood. "What have you—?"

"Signora," said the shorter, older one of the pair. "To speak to you means my death. Apologies, but I have a family." He jerked through a very abbreviated bow and backed out, his silent assistant just behind him.

The door closed. Frank was mildly surprised that it didn't burst into self-consuming flame, given the glare that Giovanna had fixed upon it. "Spanish *bastardi*, terrifying even the lowliest—"

"They're moving us."

She stopped, looking at her husband, who was staring down into the boxes. "Moving us? Where? Why? How do you know? What is—?"

"Gia, darling, light of my life, heart of my heart—I can only answer one question at a time."

For whatever mysterious reasons Frank's wife did anything, she now decided the time had come to throw her shapely, olive-toned arms around his neck and snug her small, but even more shapely, body tight against him. This, despite the fact that he was lying down, his broken leg stretched out as straight as possible. The result was a swift, strange mix of bodily pain and bodily pleasure.

"I love you, Frank."

"I love you, too."

"So, here is the first question you must answer: how do you know these old clothes in dingy boxes mean they are moving us? Perhaps they are simply giving us new clothes instead of allowing us to bathe." She wrinkled her nose; in the weeks they had been in this hole, they had twice been given buckets of reeking water to clean themselves. Soap was apparently an unthinkable luxury or not a substance known to their jailers. Probably why, when Giovanna now called them "filthy pigs," it sounded more like a loathsome description than a figurative epithet.

Frank, using his unmauled hand, raised himself up to poke around in the box containing male clothing. "Two hats, shaving bowl—but no razor, of course—nightshirt, and this." He held up a crudely fashioned combination walking-stick and crutch.

Giovanna frowned. "Yes, these are things we do not need here. Some you would simply not wear, such as this nightshirt. Really? In this damp? But Frank, could it not also be that they simply grabbed an armful of the things they have stolen from houses and threw them into a box, thinking we will make whatever good we can of it?"

Frank shook his head and started holding up items from the other, female-themed box. "Nightwear again, a woman's hat, hair combs, and"—he splayed the last object out wide—"a fan? For down here?"

Giovanna's dark eyes focused intently. "Yes. More than chance objects, I think. But why move us now?"

"Hmmm. I wonder if our unseen visitor can tell us." Frank

turned to look for the half-seen shadow beyond the grated aperture in their prison door.

But the shadow was gone.

Cardinal Gaspar de Borja y Velasco heard a faint scuffling behind him. Ferrigno. Of course. As timid as always. Shuffling his shoes to announce his presence. *Must I be served by mice, rather than men?* "What is it, Ferrigno? Come, be quick about it; I am busy."

"Your Eminence, the—the man from Barcelona has arrived."

Borja's eyes crept to the dial set into the roof of the portico just beneath his windows. Hmm. This fellow was more than punctual; he was about ten minutes early. Yet word had it that he had arrived in Rome three days before he had contacted Ferrigno to make an appointment. A strange inconsistency of behavior.

Borja turned, barely noticing Ferrigno's small, spare form. "Show him in, but wait outside. I wish private speech with this man." The cardinal moved to a position behind his desk and affected to stare out the window, half-presenting his back to anyone who would come into his chambers through the main doors.

Time passed. Borja grew impatient. What was keeping this fellow? First, he did not present himself promptly for an audience with his superior, then he was early for his scheduled meeting, now he loitered in the hallway: what inconstant nonsense was this? Turning, Borja resolved to—

Borja blinked. A man—evidently, *the* man—was standing only two feet beyond the front of the cardinal's desk.

Borja sputtered in surprise before he spoke, which compounded the annoyance he already felt. "What do you mean, sneaking up upon me rather than announcing yourself? What are you? An assassin?"

The man shrugged. "Yes."

Borja was too surprised, and also too chilled, to register any new measure of annoyance. This man—sent, he had it on good word, at Duke Olivares' specific behest—had made no sound, was not dressed as a courtier, made no flourishes. He stood, in loose, dark clothing, without any perceivable motion. Like an automaton of some kind, waiting to be set into motion. If amusement, fear, joy, exultation had ever registered in the calm, hazel eyes that were now fixed upon Borja's own, those emotions had left no lingering sign of their passage. Borja swallowed, licked his lips. "And you are, eh, Señor—?"

"Dolor. Pedro Dolor. At your service, Your Eminence."

Pedro Dolor. The Rock of Pain. Yes, Borja could believe that well enough. Almost certainly a *nomme de guerre*, albeit an oddly understated one. Borja considered: he had been prepared for another Quevedo, who had been part playwright, part *bon-vivant*, part *agent provocateur*, part adventurer, part duelist, and wholly a self-satisfied and supercilious popinjay. But what stood before Borja now was not merely a different creature from Quevedo, but his very antithesis. Dolor was all—and only—business, and fell purpose; he radiated it like the reaper no doubt radiated chill.

Borja looked away from those unblinking eyes and out the window; yes, he had wanted a serious, competent man to replace Quevedo. But this? In beseeching God for a new covert facilitator, he had perhaps gone too far in requesting a person of radically different characteristics. *Is this the cross you would have me bear, my Lord? To never have assistants who evince a happy balance of abilities and traits? Must I always endure the challenges of such extremes of temperament?*

Borja squared his shoulders and faced Dolor again. "So, Señor Pedro Dolor. You come well recommended from persons attached to the court at Madrid, and especially by the count-duke Olivares. Yet those recommendations are notably silent insofar as particulars are concerned."

"Particulars, Your Eminence?"

"Yes. Specific examples of your accomplishments."

"Your Eminence will, I am sure, understand that part of the reason His Majesty's confidantes value my service is that I am not only efficient, but discreet. So discreet as to be invisible, one might say. That invisibility is, I suspect, the factor that has earned me most of whatever modest regard I might enjoy."

Borja nodded, stared. Despite the groomed diction of Dolor's explanation, there was no hint of self-satisfied cleverness, not the faintest suggestion of irony or of professional pride. And his explanation was as logical as it was succinct. He was a strange creature indeed to emerge from the underworld shadows cast by certain courtiers at Madrid. Borja resolved to make a few surreptitious inquiries regarding his origins: perhaps that would shed some light on the man's most singular demeanor. "So, have you reviewed your resources?"

"I have, Your Eminence. They are most adequate. And I have taken the liberty of bringing some assets of my own."

"Assets?"

"Reliable persons who specialize in the kind of work I perform, Your Eminence."

"And so you feel capable of meeting the two primary challenges I am setting before you?"

"The matter of securing the hostages is well in-hand. As soon as they are moved—"

"Moved? I gave no authorization for them to be moved!"

"Your Eminence, since arriving in Rome, I have seen how many heavy burdens are daily upon your shoulders. Or do I misperceive?"

Borja raised his chin in what he hoped was a pose of noble resolve and manly forbearance. "You do not misperceive. Continue."

"Therefore, it seemed prudent to begin serving you in the same manner whereby I have rendered service to various persons of the court, some of whom are close to the king. Very close to the king."

*Very close to the king.* Dolor could not have been clearer had he simply said, "I work for Olivares. Regularly." Borja nodded. "Go on. In what special manner do you serve these personages?"

"I minimize their burden of oversight, Your Eminence. Which also makes it far easier to act not only with great discretion, but with few traceable legal connections between myself and my employer. Which—for reasons of both international seemliness and the health of one's soul—is a distance and measure of autonomy my prior clients have been happy to allow me."

Borja nodded and thought, *now I have seen everything. An assassin-philosopher, whose concerns extend to both matters of diplomacy and protecting the souls of his employers from the sins of his deeds.* "So you have ordered this young heretic Stone and his anarchist wife to be moved to a deeper dungeon?"

"Not at all, Your Eminence. Indeed, that would run counter to my plans. Having observed them, I think that a dramatic change is wanted in their circumstances. This is not a kindness, Your Eminence, but a stratagem, which I will explain at length, if you so wish. However, for now, I wish to address your concerns regarding the more challenging matter of assessing if Urban VIII still lives, and if so where, and then, ultimately, reclaiming him to the Holy See so that he may answer for his purported collusion with heretics and sworn enemies of Mother Church."

Borja felt heat in his face. "'Purported' collusion? Do you question his guilt?"

Dolor neither cowered nor became confrontational. "I do not question—nor do I presume—anything, Cardinal Borja. I simply observe that, until you have convened the Consistory to hear the charges, and a court to assess guilt and deliver a verdict, Urban VIII's crimes technically remain 'purported,' do they not?"

Borja tried to look imposing, but feared that he might have only effected a bad-tempered sulkiness. "In time of war, with traitors all about, a man—even a man such as you, Señor Dolor—takes risks when splitting legal hairs in favor of rebels and heretics."

"Now, as always, I refrain from intemperate behaviors or claims."

Borja considered that comment. He could not determine whether Dolor meant it as an oblique accession to the cardinal's warning, or a defense of his original statement. In which lay the comment's disturbingly elegant ambivalence. "So, let us return to the matter of my troublesome predecessor." Borja watched carefully; to call Urban his "predecessor" was a test, for it was not technically accurate, either. But he needed to be sure that Dolor was a loyal operative, not a legal stickler. Indeed, any impulse toward such formal proprieties could become a considerable liability to Borja later on.

But if Dolor nursed any reservations regarding Borja's presumed ascension to the *cathedra*, the agent showed no sign of it. "Urban VIII's location and apprehension—if he is still alive, and not buried beneath the rubble of the Castel Sant'Angelo—is a difficult task. Much hard work will be required. And some luck, also."

"Luck? Are you saying this task is beyond your skills?"

"Your Eminence, I am saying that while no sparrow falls—or hides—without God's awareness, mortal man has no such omniprescience, for he is not omnipresent. And finding a single man is not an easy a task. How many persons have seen Urban VIII—or any pope—close enough to be able to make a positive visual identification? And I am quite sure Urban will no longer be wearing the raiment and accoutrements of his holy office; he will be plainly dressed and adorned. And, if he did escape Rome, I suspect he has had some extraordinary help in remaining hidden."

"Extraordinary help? From whom?"

"From the up-timers and their allies, Your Eminence."

"Have you heard rumors that he is with them, then? Have you already made this much progress?" Borja could not stop himself from leaning forward in sudden, savage hope.

"No, Your Eminence, but it seems a logical deduction. The reports from those troops who were at Hadrian's Tower at the time of the explosion suggest that there may have been one or more up-time weapons used to defend the walls and, later, to clear the path of Urban's presumed escape. But this is hearsay, and many who might have been more reliable witnesses were sent skyward with the stones of the Castel Sant'Angelo, or buried under them."

"So what do we do?"

"We continue our search on all fronts, Your Eminence. Your men continue to excavate the ruins in search of Urban's corpse. At the same time, we search for the missing cardinals—particularly the last of the Barberinis, Urban's nephew Antonio. And also for the members of the USE embassy that left Rome. Finding them is likely to be much easier, and will almost certainly give us a sure path to Urban."

"Very well. Now, my secretary informed me yesterday that you sent word of having uncovered new information regarding this recent fiasco in Chiavenna."

Dolor nodded. "As first suspected, Cardinal Ginetti has escaped, along with the up-timers. He was sighted by an ally in Chur."

"And has it also been confirmed that the rest of the fugitives were originally members of the up-time embassy that was previously here in Rome?"

"Yes, Your Eminence. The Moor who attracted general notice in Chiavenna was the famous up-time doctor, James Nichols. The very large man who figures so prominently in the combat reports matches the many descriptions we have of Admiral Simpson's son Thomas. We have less concrete reports of the women, but their descriptions conform to what we expected: that Simpson's wife Rita and Nichols' aged concubine Melissa Mailey were traveling with them. All four are reported as speaking the up-time dialect of English."

"And there was another with the party, no?"

"At least one, possibly two. The other we know of spoke fluent Italian, but we lack any reliable data on the younger man who remained mostly at their inn. He might have been the one shot through the head just beyond Piuro, or that might have been a fifth person, who could have been part of the embassy staff."

"'Could have been'? Did we not have informers among the embassy staff? Did we not compile a list of its personnel and servants?"

"The Church did, Your Eminence, but that information gathering was carried out by the Jesuits. Who are, of course—"

"Yes, yes; the Roman branch of that order is in Urban's camp more than ever, and are still taking orders from that cadaverous old wolf Vitelleschi. So, since the Jesuits are no longer serving the true Holy See, we do not have a complete list of the embassy staff."

"That is correct."

"Well, very little of this is new information, Señor Dolor. I fail to see why you alerted my secretary that you had new facts pertinent to the events in Chiavenna."

"I come to those now, Your Eminence. The surgeons have completed their post mortem examination of the soldiers slain along the banks of the Mera, just east of the Gallegione cataract."

"And?"

"What the surgeons found corroborates the accounts we received from the handful of survivors. Our soldiers were all killed by up-time bullets or balls, or close copies thereof."

"So the up-time fugitives had help?"

"A great deal of it, apparently. All the survivors report that the speed and regularity of the enemy gunshots were unprecedented."

"Again, indicative of up-time weapons."

"Exactly. And we recovered these—"

Dolor stretched out a hand and laid three objects on the center of Borja's desk. Two were finger-sized brass tubes, sealed or capped on one end. The other was broader, shorter, but again made of brass: rather like a small toy drinking cup for a little girl's doll. "And what are these?"

"These objects are called cartridge casings. These two"—he pointed to the longer ones—"are for a rifle or carbine with a bore size that the up-timers call forty-seventy-two."

"So this is up-time ammunition?"

"Not exactly. Although the design of the ammunition and the guns which fire it are of up-time origin, we are fairly sure that these cartridges are merely copies of the originals. They were made in this world, and use black powder rather than the powerful up-time explosive compounds. This means they generate less power. This would therefore also suggest they were not used in a self-loading gun—which seems to require that extra power—but rather, in one which requires physical manipulation after every shot. Our confidential agents in the USE report that there is one such weapon that is being regularly constructed in this bore-size: it is called a Winchester 1895."

"And what is this squat cartridge casing'?"

"This is even more interesting; this is the casing of a shotgun shell."

Borja scowled at the unfamiliar term.

"It is their term for a fowling piece, Your Eminence, although they often load it with heavier shot, for large game or humans. It seems that after the combat, the force which rescued Simpson's group combed the area to retrieve as many of these spent casings as possible. A prudent step, but in the dark, impossible to perform perfectly." He indicated the three cartridge casings.

Borja nodded, then realized the deeper mystery latent in Dolor's report. "And what made you request the more detailed autopsies, and close surveys of the ambush site, Señor Dolor? Indeed, it seems you had already begun to suspect intervention by USE forces equipped with up-time weapons."

Dolor shrugged. "How else could we have lost so many men in a night engagement which lasted very briefly? And how is it that so few of our men survived long enough to close and bring their swords into play?"

Borja frowned. "A full company of our own troops could exert such a force of musketry, I imagine."

"Yes, Your Eminence. One Spanish company might—*might*—have enough firepower to kill half its number of men in so short a time. But that company would have to boast many other abilities, as well. It would have to be a company that was capable of almost invisible movement, since there was no earlier or subsequent report of any unit moving in the Engadine or the Val Bregaglia. It would have to be a company that—unless it had access to an up-time radio—magically knew when and where to meet Simpson's suddenly fleeing group. It would have to be a company that could vanish into thin air immediately after the ambush, for the trail leading beyond the Silsersee was clearly a false lead. And lastly, it would have to be a company that, in the course of all its actions, left no more signs or spoor than might two squads.

"Your Eminence, we do not possess a company that could do all that. But a few squads of well-equipped up-timers or their trained proxies could do so, particularly if they had already been briefed on Simpson's group, and were following contingency plans to aid it in the event of an unexpected crisis."

Borja rubbed his prominent chin. "So you believe up-time radios were involved, as well?"

"The coordination of our foes precludes any other alternative. How else can we explain Cardinal Ginetti's sudden change of itinerary? How did he know to meet Simpson's group in Chiavenna, and where and when to do so? How else could the rescuing forces know when and where to meet the group, once it was fleeing? But in addition to radios, the up-timers were also equipped with an unusual amount of good luck."

"How so?"

"Your Eminence, I suspect that the troops that rescued Simpson's group were already in the area when they were needed. It takes weeks for the USE to send operatives from Grantville to the Val Bregaglia. So how do we explain the presence of these rescuers in the Val Bregaglia at the very moment they are needed? Not in response to anything we have done; Michael Stearns and his advisor Nasi would have had to dispatch them southward toward the Alps the very minute they learned of our attack upon Rome. But why would they do so? Out of some vague notion that their troops would simply prove useful somehow? To act on such an impulse, Stearns and Nasi would have to be either fortune-tellers or fools—and they are neither."

"So you are saying that the forces that rescued Simpson's party were already en route for another, specific purpose, and they just happened to be on site when needed?"

"It is hard to envision anything else, Your Eminence."

"So why were they there?"

"Discovering the answer to this is a critically important task, upon which I will concentrate all my skills."

"Very well. There remains one other mystery I would have answered, though."

"Yes, Your Eminence?"

"These confidential agents who picked up Ginetti's trail even before he arrived in Chiavenna, and who Simpson and his group killed at the *crotto*—who were they working for? Not us, as first suspected?"

"No, not us. And I fear their actual employers shall never be known. The four bodies left in our possession were searched for identifying papers, or other suggestions of their origin, but there was nothing."

"Yes, but what of the one who survived, the one that Simpson reportedly knocked senseless during an argument in the *crotto*?"

"As feared, he escaped. From the beginning, the authorities leaped to the conclusion that the one survivor was a victim, not part of another plot. Consequently, he was not watched carefully enough. A moment's inattention on the part of his warders and he was gone, back to whoever holds his leash. But I think we can be sure of one thing: if these armed, nameless men were indeed following Ginetti, assassination was not their primary purpose."

"What? Why do you think this?"

"Because they could probably have overcome Ginetti's guards easily enough on the road. A preliminary night ambush at some lonely spot in the Valtelline, and then Ginetti's weakened party would have been easy prey on a subsequent day. No, I believe these confidential agents were not there as killers, but as coursers; they were sent to put pressure on Ginetti, or perhaps, on whomever he was traveling to meet. If some of Ginetti's party had died, I'm sure that would not have bothered their employer. But what the seeming assassins did accomplish—even though they died without inflicting any injury whatsoever—was to create a local furor and propel the up-timers into desperate flight. Which our soldiers responded to. And, as these things usually do, the entire situation soon spiraled out of control, ripe with possibilities for becoming a debilitating international incident."

"A pity we cannot discern more than this. I would like to have interrogated the survivor of these unknown agents."

"Your Eminence, I think you are fortunate that such an interrogation is now beyond our power."

"And how could interrogating the agent of an unknown, but obviously inimical, political entity be detrimental to us? I should think you, who traffics in secrets for a living, should understand that information is the most important tool at our disposal, the sword we wield with rapierlike precision to frustrate our foes' shrewdest gambits and deepest plots."

"Yes, Your Eminence—but just like that rapier, information is a double-edged sword. And if my guess is right, had the agent revealed the identity of his employers, it could have had disastrous effects upon our alliance with the French."

Borja felt his mind spin purposelessly. "The French?" he heard himself say.

"Yes, Your Eminence. For I believe these purported assassins were sent by the French—but not Richelieu. I suspect the assassins were told they were getting orders from Paris, but that the actual hiring agent was a member—or simply a proxy—of the Huguenot radicals, possibly the same ones who were behind the attempt on Urban last year."

"But what would the Huguenots gain by having us believe that the French crown had sent assassins after Ginetti?"

"I believe that was only part of the Huguenots' motivation. Let us consider the events more broadly. In being compelled to foil the presumed assassins, Simpson's party attracts attention to the fact that the USE is sending its nationals home through Milanese, and therefore nominally Spanish, territory. Not exactly a violation of law, but then again, Simpson's party was not traveling openly. They did not declare their identity and presence freely, and were thus traveling without the papers they needed. A wise choice: we would probably have put them in the same dungeon as Signor Stone. At the very least, we would have detained them for an extended period. They represent immense leverage for us.

"Now, had we managed to interrogate the misinformed survivor of these assassins, I suspect they would have told us—erroneously— that they were instruments being wielded by Richelieu's hand, poised in yet another perfidious attempt to kill Michael Stearns' relatives and friends. And in the same instant, we would come to believe that the French cardinal's hand was also trespassing upon our territory, and doing so in a manner that violates the agreement we have with the French in Chiavenna: that they have unrestricted right of passage and trade, but that military and legal matters are to be referred to Milanese authority.

"Of course, Richelieu would legitimately deny his involvement. Naturally, we would not believe him, and would close Chiavenna and the passes to both the French and the USE. The incident would put the League of Ostend in jeopardy and could even lead to separate—maybe even coordinated—USE and French action to reopen the transalpine trade routes. It would certainly give both of them cause to support the interests of both Venice and the Swiss provinces of Grisons in the Val Bregaglia, and the Valtelline as well. And we can no longer count on regional support from our former allies in Tyrol, not since its regent Claudia de Medici has made overtures to seek membership in the USE.

"In short, any successful investigation into the origins of the assassins following Ginetti would have obligated us to pass information to Philip that could have resulted in a disaster for our already overtaxed empire. We were most fortunate, then, that the up-timers—and the confidential agents who were following them—all escaped or died."

A moment after Dolor stopped speaking, Borja felt the world resteady itself around him. That the Earth had such devious minds in it was unsettling to him. Such intelligence ought to be a tool to enable direct, manly action, not serve as the handmaiden to conniving plots and perfidies. But, since that was not the case, he was quite glad that Olivares had sent him Pedro Dolor. "Well, then, it seems that God has smiled upon us in this matter. Or, to indulge in one of the up-timer's sayings, these two wrongs—our failure to apprehend the up-timers and also to retain custody of the last assassin—have made a right. You are dismissed, Señor Dolor."

The man bowed and exited.

As he left, Borja murmured, almost as an afterthought, "*Vaya con Dios.*" He doubted there was any chance of that being the case.

As Pedro Dolor exited Borja's office he was still stifling the urge to rebut the cardinal's penultimate insipidity. No, two wrongs did *not* make a right. In Chiavenna, there had been two signal failures that, this time, just happened to cancel each other out in terms of any larger political damage. It was luck. It was certainly not the sign of insuperable Spanish supremacy, nor the hand of God working in its favor: just blind, dumb luck—of which they were running out as quickly as Philip's treasury was running out of *reales*.

Upon reaching the cavernous vestibule of Villa Borghese, in which Borja had first established his headquarters, and then residence, Dolor was joined by a short, swarthy man. No more than 5' 4" in height, but almost as wide in the shoulders, he emerged from the shadows of one of the many colonnaded galleries. He fell in step with Dolor. "Well?" he asked.

Dolor shrugged. "Borja's cautious but tractable. His unwillingness to get his hands dirty by giving orders that directly violate his vows and Christian piety will make him easy enough to manipulate. That, and his numerous insecurities."

"Another fool in a red robe and hat?"

"No, he's no fool. But he's out of his depth and unwilling to admit he's a murderer. Like most noblemen, he's accustomed to having other people not only do his dirty work, but take the guilt—legal and religious—upon their own backs. He wants to reap the benefits of actions in which he refuses to take a part or take responsibility."

"The way you say that—"

"Yes?"

"It sounds like you know the type well. From personal experience, perhaps."

"It doesn't matter how I know the type. But I know this, too: Borja's dangerous. He'll be careful not to compromise himself by bringing me into his complete confidence, and he'll throw us to the wolves if there's any blame to be taken. So we'll be careful. And I don't need to enter into his confidences to do my job."

*And thereby*, thought Dolor, *to get what I really want.*

# Chapter 10

"So, you'd send us traipsing off to Rome, then?"

"Those are your orders."

"It's a fool's errand—and I'm no fool."

Owen Roe O'Neill suppressed a gasp at John O'Neill's truculent retort to the infanta Isabella Clara Eugenia, Archduchess of the Spanish Low Countries. Owen had known Isabella—his nominal employer and the aunt of King Philip IV of Spain—for thirty years, so he was fairly sure that he knew what was coming. The infanta would tell John O'Neill that if a journey to Rome was indeed a fool's errand, then she had found the perfect man for the job. She would then probably unleash a stream of even less oblique, yet still elegantly vitriolic, barbs at John, third earl of Tyrone. Who would probably understand about one half of them, but would certainly tweak to the fact that he was being insulted. Again.

Owen was wondering if the time had come to risk John's resentment and intercede, but Pieter Rubens did it for him. "Come now, I know what you fear, Conde O'Neill. You fear that with you and Owen gone from your camps, and the earl of Tyrconnell unavailable—"

"—more like deserted—"

"—that Thomas Preston will be the sole acting colonel for the archduchess's four Irish tercios."

"Aye, that's the heart of it, Pieter."

Isabella, still flushed by walking from her nearby chambers to the wood-paneled library in which they were meeting, threw her cherished up-time fountain pen down in impatience. "Oh, not this again. When will you Wild Geese stop your sectarian honkings?"

Irishmen who fled English oppression to serve on the continent as mercenary soldiers were often dubbed "Wild Geese." From most mouths, and at most times, the term enjoyed a cachet of grudging admiration. At other times and from English mouths, not so much.

"We'll keep making noise as long as that *sassenach* Thomas Preston is in regular correspondence with his masters in London, Your Grace." John O'Neill's response was a mutter.

The room's tall double doors opened. King Fernando entered with a dense retinue of guards, his increasingly lovely and curvaceous wife (or so it seemed to Owen) on his arm. All but Isabella rose; being Fernando's aunt, and infirm besides, relieved her of that obligation. Fernando motioned them back into their chairs and seated his wife, but remained standing next to his aunt. "The doors are not as thick as you might believe," he said to no one in particular. "So let me assure you, Conde O'Neill, that Colonel Preston is not an enemy agent. And his cross-Channel contacts do serve a useful purpose."

"Which is?"

Rubens took up the thread smoothly. "There is the minor matter of his being a known correspondent with various moderate parties in London. As a result, he is often tentatively approached by the less-schooled Anglo-Irish spies working for King Charles. This allows us to keep tabs on this lower tier of confidential agents. But more importantly, Colonel Preston is an emergency communications conduit."

"A what?"

John O'Neill did not have his late father's keen mind and rapid wit. Bold, brave, competent, John was a steady enough colonel for his own tercio—but that was, Owen had to admit, the ceiling of the third earl of Tyrone's abilities. Which he made painfully obvious when he repeated, "What do you mean, an emergency communications conduit?"

Rubens' tone was patient, and Owen thought he heard a measure of pity behind it, as well. "Given his part-English heritage,

Colonel Preston serves as an unofficial back-channel through which
we maintain contact with various persons in London, including
high-placed members of the court."

"Which persons?" John asked.

"That varies with the political climate across the Channel,"
Fernando said calmly, "and is not a suitable topic of conversation
in this chamber, at this time."

Even John O'Neill seemed to get that hint.

"At any rate," finished Fernando, "Colonel Preston is to remain
here in overall command of the tercios while you travel to Rome."

Owen cleared his throat; the king looked at him. "Please,
continue your discussion as before. I am not here to hold court."

Owen nodded and turned his eyes back toward Isabella. "Your
Grace, it seems that our party to Rome is rather, well, top-heavy
in senior officers—including one of the last two estranged heirs
to the royal titles of Ireland. This struck us as . . . well, strange."

Isabella sent a small, encouraging smile down at Owen; he
felt as though he'd been patted on the head. "Of late, I have
had much complaint from the senior officers of my Irish tercios
that they are in want of vigorous action. Being an old woman
who hopes to die peacefully in her bed—and until two years
ago, thought that end imminent—I profess no understanding
of this ardor for war. It seems a blight upon the males of our
species and particularly strong in those who come from the
island of your birth, Colonel. So, since you and your young
cousin the conde O'Neill have chafed at the bit of the peace that
now reigns in the Low Countries, this was the first assignment
which promised to sate your appetite for risk and adventure.
I except you from these characterizations, of course, Doctor,"
she concluded, sending a broader, warmer smile farther down
the table.

Sean Connal, surgeon in the Tyrconnell tercio and the third
representative of the Wild Geese, nodded in gratitude and smiled
back. "Thank you, Your Grace. However, I too must ask—Rome?
Now? When it is in chaos?"

"My dear Dr. Connal, that chaos is precisely why you must go
to Rome, and go now. We cannot send a large mission without
drawing undue attention, even if, as Spain's nominal vassal, our
personnel would arouse no suspicion. And since you may have
need of giving orders when there—of commanding Spanish troops

to let you pass, to stand aside, or even to release possible prisoners to you—we cannot send men of lesser rank. And the conde—the earl, in your styling—holds the title of a lineage well-regarded in all Hapsburg territories. That high authority may be much needed where you travel."

Owen wondered if that summary wasn't a bit optimistic. The Spanish respected the Irish of equal rank in most professional regards, but not in social or bureaucratic matters. Equals on a battlefield or in a tavern, perhaps, but not in a ballroom or an audience chamber. But on the other hand, the fame of John's late father, Hugh O'Neill, was particularly conspicuous in Rome, where he was buried along with various family and followers. He, his kinsman Rory O'Donnell, the prior earl of Tyrconnell, and their lieutenants, had journeyed as political supplicants to the Eternal City after fleeing Ireland in 1607. Most never found the means to leave again. Instead, they found the miasmic fevers of Rome and died, almost to a man. Hugh O'Neill outlived them all—but even his facile, ever-plotting mind had ultimately been thwarted by age, infirmity, and exclusion from the chambers of the powerful. He died all but forgotten, living on the charity of his patrons in Rome.

Owen looked over at Johnnie O'Neill: he'd been forgotten, too, most notoriously by his father. That lack of attention had not merely been a sign of his sire's disinterest, but the man's legendarily cold shrewdness: even in childhood, it was obvious that John had not inherited the most illustrious O'Neill's intellect. Just as clearly, however, Johnnie had received a full measure of the man's restlessness and spleen, so as both a youngster and a young man he had wanted action and little else. Now, it was pretty much the only thing at which John excelled; he had not been a patient child and had become a decidedly impatient man.

"There is, of course, another reason we are sending the two of you," continued Isabella.

"Yes, Your Grace?"

"Do not be coy, Owen Roe. Your and the conde's skill with weapons is peerless, and that could become an important factor in the success of your mission."

"I thought Rome was in the hands of our Spanish comrades." This time John's tone was slow and assessing.

"It is."

John thought that over. "I see."

And Owen was glad he said no more; anything else would have been akin to poking a stick into a beehive. Technically, brothers Philip IV of Spain, and Fernando, the former cardinal-infante of the Low Countries, were indissolubly linked as part of the greater Hapsburg hegemony that straddled Europe like a colossus.

Or had. It seemed the colossus had become decrepit in some places and fragmented in others. Ferdinand III of Austria had not taken the steps necessary to become the next emperor of the Holy Roman Empire; that meant he had all but ceded the lands he had lost to the armies of Gustav Adolf. Ferdinand had also stood aside when the same Reformist forces battered down Maximilian of Bavaria, formerly a close ally and an ardent fellow Catholic. Then Philip IV's own brother—Fernando, the cardinal-infante—had received title to the Spanish Low Countries from Isabella, and in short order, had proclaimed himself "King in the Netherlands"— a dubious title, since he was ostensibly subject to another king. Specifically, his brother in Madrid.

The consequences of all this internecine strife had been slow but certain in coming. Spanish *reales* had now ceased to flow into Fernando's coffers. The new king in the Low Countries was thus hard pressed to maintain any tercios—such as the Irish—that were not paid directly by Philip. Madrid's mood was not improved when Maria Anna, sister of Ferdinand III of Austria, eloped with Fernando when he borrowed one of the Swede's up-time airplanes to spirit her back to the Low Countries. The once unified monolith that was Hapsburg power in Europe was undergoing troubling reconfigurations. Consequently, even a person as politically dis- interested as Johnnie O'Neill understood that yesterday's friends might easily transmogrify into tomorrow's enemies.

Sean Connal's youthful baritone rolled the length of the table. "So, Your Graces, I take it that the exact nature of our actions in Rome will be determined by the conditions we find there."

Fernando exchanged an approving look with his wife, who inclined her head to indicate their collective royal pleasure with the young surgeon. "This is nicely put, Doctor; I was not informed you were as deft with words as you are with a scalpel."

"My lady the Queen is as kind as she is eloquent. And generous. I have not yet had the honor of expressing my personal thanks to her for arranging my attendance at several of the medical practica offered by Lady Anne Jefferson. I wish I had a year to study under her tutelage."

"How charming; she used exactly the same turn of phrase when remarking how much she would have liked to keep you on as a student. But it seems other duties must take precedence, now."

"Yes, so it seems. But we have yet to learn what those duties are, other than to journey to Rome. And once there—?"

For a reason Owen could not quite ascertain, the royalty in the room became faintly uncomfortable. Rubens, after waiting a long moment, evidently concluded that this bit of business had been left for him to handle. "We are concerned for the safety of one of your countrymen, Father Luke Wadding. We feel that if all of you were to exhort him to do so, he would agree to depart from the Irish College in Rome."

John's head came up; one of Connal's eyebrows did the same. Owen Roe leaned forward. "Father Wadding is in danger? From whom?"

Rubens looked for help from the Hapsburg end of the table but found none. "Consider the angry crowds in Rome, the violence of the occupation, the disorder. Amidst all that chaos, hunger, and desperation, almost anything could—"

"No." The voice was John's: firm, assured, decisive, like when he was on a battlefield. "Rome would never harm Luke Wadding. I've been there, and have studied"—he stumbled past that dubious claim—"with some of the fathers who are now teaching at the college at St. Isidore's. So let me tell you how the Romans feel toward Father Luke Wadding. When they see him, they don't hail him by any of his titles; to them, he's not 'Guardian of the College,' or 'Procurator,' or 'Reverend Father.' He's just Padre Luca. They say it without bowing, but with smiles as big and bright as rainbows. Which is just how he greets them. There's simply no reason to be worried about his safety in Rome."

"Yet, we are worried," announced Fernando, his face suddenly longer than usual.

"But from whom does he need protection?"

"From my brother's servants."

Now it was Owen's turn to goggle. "What? The *Spanish* would harm Wadding? Your Highness, he studied in Salamanca! He was well-known in Philip's court—"

Isabella leaned forward, her face pained—rather the way it is when a parent must admit they have a destructive or truant child. "My nephew Philip was—unwise—in electing to give Cardinal Borja such wide discretionary powers. In fact, there is rumor that the many of the cardinals who were killed 'resisting lawful arrest' during the attack upon Rome were slain by Borja's agents."

"What were the crimes of these cardinals?"

"What indeed?" answered Isabella, who looked at Owen directly, her face as hard and lined as slate.

Owen gaped for a moment before easing his jaw shut. So they had all been *assassinated*? Upwards of a dozen cardinals? Was Borja mad? And if he was, that could even mean—"What about the pope? Is there word whether he still lives?"

"That is not known. And is yet another topic for us to discuss. However, insofar as Father Wadding's safety is concerned, part of our worry arises from the fact that the Franciscan College at St. Isidore's was built and endowed by Ludovisi money."

Owen shook his head; the family politics of Rome were well beyond the scope of his knowledge.

Queen Maria Anna provided the rest. "The Ludovisi family and its cardinal have a long, friendly affiliation with the Barberinis. And particularly with Maffeo Barberini—Pope Urban VIII."

"Oh," said Owen. "I see."

"Yes," nodded Isabella, confirming the magnitude of both Borja's monstrousness and pettiness. "Now, if it was my nephew the king who was overseeing the situation in Rome, there would be a comparatively even hand guiding the actions of the tercios, inquisitors, and confidential agents. But with Borja in command—"

The whole room had become glum. In the up-timer history books, the name Borja was remembered—in its Italianate form "Borgia"—for treachery and murder, particularly poisoning. That, at least, had been the height of the family's infamy in that world, but here—

"Still," Owen protested, "Wadding is primarily a scholar. And he's a staunch Counter-Reformationist, besides. Surely Borja wouldn't arrest him simply because his college was built with money that came from a friend of the pope."

Isabella inclined her head in agreement. "No, probably not. But there is an added complication."

"There always is," observed Sean Connal with a faint smile.

Isabella darted a glance at him; Owen couldn't tell if she was annoyed or delighted. Probably both, knowing her. "We have it on relatively good authority that in the past year, Pope Urban created a number—an unprecedented number—of cardinals *in pectore.*"

John O'Neill fumbled after the Latin. "*In pec*-what?"

*Oh, Johnnie, Johnnie, you have to do better than that.* Owen furnished the translation. "It's what we call 'close to the chest,' Lord O'Neill. Popes can create cardinals without consulting the Consistory. Because these cardinals are not revealed to anyone else, they are considered hidden, or held 'close to the chest.'" He turned toward Isabella. "So why was Urban creating cardinals *in pectore*? Do you suspect he was preparing for this kind of attack?"

Another smile from the archduchess that might have been a pat on the head. "We do not know, but it seems logical, in retrospect. After all, word has it that he consulted the up-time histories on the future of his papal tenure, and just beyond, very closely."

"And how does all this concern Father Wadding?"

"It turns out that Father Wadding was the first Irish cleric ever to receive votes to be made a cardinal. It did not go through for political reasons. I suspect those same political reasons could make Borja fear Wadding now."

Sean Connal nodded. "That makes sense."

"Not to me it doesn't," John snapped across the table. "I know Wadding, and so must Borja. Father Luke will not lick the boots of heretics, and that's well known by his friends in Madrid—"

"—who are not in Rome to help him," soothed Rubens. "I have had occasion to scan the relevant histories. Wadding did indeed have many admirers among the Spanish Party in the Consistory, who appreciated his eloquent Counter-Reformation writings. But Wadding was also liked by Urban, who supported the expansion of his church, St. Isidore's, and the Irish cause. As you all know. Yet, despite having friends in both circles, he never attracted the support necessary to become a cardinal."

"Bigotry," declared John O'Neill. "The same bigotry that kept the Curia from taking my father seriously when he begged them—"

"No," interrupted Isabella. "The danger to Wadding does not stem from bigotry; it stems from fear."

That stopped O'Neill as surely as if he had run headlong into a brick wall. "Fear? The Spanish cardinals—and Borja—*fear* Father Luke? But—?"

"Your esteemed Father Luke Wadding possesses a further quality that, in both this world and the up-timers', made him anathema to all the papal parties, even though he was much admired by the individuals comprising them."

Sean Connal nodded. "Integrity."

"Yes. History shows that he was famous for speaking his conscience, even when it would have been far more politically prudent to trim his sails in the direction of one political faction or another." Isabella paused. "Cardinal Borja will not trust such a man, particularly not if he suspects that Urban has already made him a cardinal *in pectore.*"

John went back slowly in his seat; the intricate strands of the noose that might be gathering about Luke Wadding's neck were now clear to him.

"Yes," nodded Rubens. "Borja wishes no opposition. He is ensuring that his new Consistory of Cardinals will have no voices that oppose his own. Wadding, if made a cardinal, would never remain silent or accept Borja's atrocities—"

"—making Wadding a natural ally of Urban. Even if he doesn't know it." Owen shook his head.

"Just so. And this brings us to your final task in Rome. It concerns a related, but more—nebulous—objective."

Owen frowned. "And what is that, Your Grace?"

"We would ask you to stay alert for any word on the location or condition of our Holy Father."

"Of course, Your Grace." *But wait, that hardly needs to be made an assignment; we'd be doing it anyhow, given all the chaos in Rome. So why even bring it up as—? Oh. I get it.* Owen pulled himself out of his thoughts and became of aware of the room again.

Isabella, eyes still on his, nodded. "Yes. We want you to seek word of Urban. With exceptional vigor."

"And if we learn of his whereabouts?"

Fernando cleared his throat sharply. "Then, if you feel you can do so without being observed by any persons who report to Cardinal Borja, you are to endeavor to seek an audience with His Holiness the pope and offer to escort him here. For a visit."

Owen wondered if he had heard correctly. "A... a 'visit'? Here?"

Fernando smiled. "Your hearing is, evidently, unimpaired by your many years before the cannons, Colonel."

Owen slumped back in his seat. *Well, Mother o' God and dancing dogs...* "Your Highness, such a visit is hardly a casual day-trip. It's a far journey, from Rome to Brussels. And with some potentially annoyed nations in the way, I might add."

Fernando's smile widened. "You will not be expected—you will not be *allowed*—to convey the pope here yourselves. You are merely to become his guardians, escort him to Venice, and send swift word through the doge. We shall make the necessary arrangements."

"I . . . see. Again, your pardon, but won't that message take weeks to reach you by boat?"

"I do not recall asserting that the message would come to us by boat, Colonel."

And then Owen knew: up-time radio. There were sets operating in Venice, and there were sets in the Lowland as well. Each of the Hapsburgs had their own, it was rumored. And if the USE were to provide additional aid in operating the devices, or even relaying the signals—

"Yes," nodded Fernando. "You see it now. Excellent."

The earl of Tyrone hunched forward. "Any of these missions could become a very perilous business, Your Highness." He paused, studying the many scars on his hands. "If our Spanish allies prove to be uncooperative, we'd find ourselves a bit outnumbered."

Fernando's nod and expression were somber. "Unquestionably. But my aunt has procured some tools that may improve those odds."

"Really?" John sat up, as eager as a boy on Christmas morning.

Isabella looked down the table at Sean Connal, who stood, brandishing a cumbersome looking pistol with a huge cylinder in place of its barrel.

Owen frowned; he had seen this weapon before. "That was the weapon that foiled the assassination attempt at Preston's camp two weeks ago," he recalled aloud.

The surgeon nodded. "Yes, a pepperbox revolver. They are being paid for by Her Grace, the archduchess, and built in accordance with ideas that the earl of Tyrconnell brought back from Grantville."

Owen ignored John's resentful mutter and stared at the pistol instead. It was, without question, the ugliest weapon ever conceived. "It fires five times without reloading, if I recall."

"More likely to kill with its looks than its bullets," grumbled John.

"It's quite effective," Connal observed calmly.

"Hugh O'Donnell can keep his tools and lectures on effectiveness. Me, I'd like a little style, as well."

"Yes," Isabella snapped, "there's the wisdom of my beloved Spain, imbibed in full by her servitors. Let us choose style over progress. Let us all be sure to have the latest boots and saddles—and all well-polished—as we ride down into the merciless maw of history and are consumed at a gulp." A roomful of surprised eyes turned toward her. "It is the journey my brother Philip has embarked upon, with Olivares as his footman to light the way into black oblivion." She snapped a single, gnarled finger down upon the tabletop for emphasis. "Philip has more resources than the rest of the nations of Europe combined, or very nearly so. Does he use it to adopt the up-time radios? No. Their wondrous medicines? No. Their aircraft and steam engines? No. Their weapons? Only those which are modest improvements upon those already in his arsenals. I am sixty-nine and even I—an old, feeble, cantankerous woman—see the need to invest in the changes the Americans have brought. It hardly matters whether we like them; the changes are here permanently. And we will either master, or be mastered by, them."

"Sounds just like her Irish godson," muttered John in an aside to Owen.

Isabella's ears had evidently remained as sharp as her tongue. "Or perhaps the absent earl of Tyrconnell sounds like me. Perhaps it is simply true that great minds think alike." She left unspoken the unflattering comparison she was implying between the missing Hugh O'Donnell and John O'Neill.

But John did not miss the intimation; his lips tightened, became thin. "Ah well, this pistol is wonder of modern weaponry, I'm sure. But where is its much-praised advocate and originator? I've not seen much of the earl of Tyrconnell, these past weeks. Oh wait, now I'm remembering. He left Spanish service, didn't he? Sent back his knight-captain's tabard in the Order of Alcantara, as well as renouncing his Spanish citizenship and position on His Majesty's Council of War. Ah, but he'd have to, wouldn't he? All those honors are a bit hard to keep when you also decide to tell the king who raised you up that, no, you'd rather not be a member of the Royal Bedchamber anymore."

Owen, struck dumb by John's titanically insolent counterattack on the archduchess, held his breath. It was well known that Isabella's godson—Hugh Albert O'Donnell, earl of Tyrconnell—was the brightest beam in her eye and had been ever since he had been made a page in her court more than twenty years ago. But then, less than a month ago, O'Donnell had abruptly quit her service, and, along with two companies of his men, had vanished. The rest of the Irish tercios had awaited the inevitable torrent of angry invective as the spurned rulers of the Spanish Low Countries raged at the disloyalty of their favorite son. But that never happened, and in that strange silence, the Irish Wild Geese had hatched more than a few explanatory speculations, some of which had bordered on the surreal.

But now, here was John, not merely gesturing toward that mystery like the unacknowledged elephant in the middle of the room, but stabbing at it with poison-tipped words. Owen finally dared to look down the table toward Isabella, prepared to witness the end of three decades of her throne's help to the expatriate Irish, sure to be consumed in a blaze of exceedingly justified royal wrath.

But Isabella was calm and collected. Indeed, for an instant, she did not seem a frail old woman in her late sixties; she was the high and Imperial Infanta again, the daughter of Philip II and a *force majeure* when her passions were aroused. Her voice was more terrible for being so level. It was not conveying opinions; it was declaring truths.

"Conde O'Neill, since you have elected to speak with such remarkable candor, I shall follow your example. My godson, the earl of Tyrconnell, traveled to Grantville when none of you would—despite his having recently lost his wife, and only son, in childbirth. He learned many things among the up-timers, and this weapon is one example of that learning. But more importantly, he learned about the collective future of the Wild Geese and their tercios in the Spanish Low Countries. About which you have heard some rumors, I believe.

"The worst of what you have heard is nothing less than the truth. Spain—the Spain in their world, and the Spain in this world—both used you abysmally. I can attest to what the up-time histories claim regarding our motivations in the two decades before this one; you were maintained here in the Low Countries primarily as a threat against the English. You were useful leverage against London, which wanted you kept here to fight against the Provinces, rather than back home, making more trouble in an already restive Ireland. However, many of us also believed that the Spanish crown would eventually make good its debt of honor to you, would help you reclaim your homeland."

"But, in the up-time world, that did not happen." Sean's coda was a whisper.

"Correct, Doctor. The Philip IV of the up-time world never repaid Spain's debt of honor. Rather, starting within a year of this date, he would begin spending your tercios like water in a new war against the French. By 1638, in that other world, four out of every five of you was dead or disabled. The remainders he moved to Spain, and poured into the maw of a Catalan revolt. You died there, John O'Neill. So did my godson."

John apparently did not understand that Isabella was doing more than explaining, or even confessing. Her self-recriminating candor indicated that she, and evidently Fernando, had decided to set a course very different from the one that had led the Wild Geese to their grisly ends in the up-time world. Deaf to that nuance, the earl's face was white as he leaned over the table, fists trembling atop their shimmering reflections in the dark, lacquered wood. "So my father—he died for nothing? After all the loyalty he showed you, all the sacrifice for his faith, for your damned Hapsburg pride—"

Isabella shocked the room by standing and remaining steady as she looked down the table at the earl of Tyrone. "Hugh O'Neill was loyal to himself, first and foremost. You barely knew your father; I did, quite well. He was proud, Machiavellian, brilliantly manipulative, terribly intelligent—but not as intelligent as he thought. Or rather, he had grown accustomed to believing that, almost every time he entered a room, he was the smartest, shrewdest man in it. And that may have been true back in your homeland; I cannot say. But not here on the Continent. His abilities were noteworthy, but they were not unique once he found himself among councilors and captains who routinely navigated the treacherous world of court intrigues and the stratagems of empires. It took him years to realize that Rome was not a wellspring of support for your cause: it was flypaper. The Spanish court and cardinals strung him along with vague promises and hopes—anything rather than having Hugh O'Neill return to the

Low Countries, for once there, he would press the matter of invading Ireland."

"Which was in Spain's interest!" John O'Neill's eyes were those of a man watching the bedrock truths of his world dissolve into gossamer and mist.

Isabella sat down and then smiled; her expression was not condescending, but was perilously close to pitying. "No, Conde O'Neill, that is precisely where you are wrong. The Irish were more useful kept sheathed as a perpetual threat, rather than brandished as an instrument of war. Had you invaded Ireland and won, you would still have become a drain on the Crown's treasury. How would you have held your homeland against English counterattacks without constant, and increasing, Spanish support? All very expensive, my dear Conde O'Neill. But keeping you as a threat in the Low Countries, while also using you as loyal mercenaries whose arch-Roman Catholicism made you perfect instruments against the Protestants of the Provinces? Now that—*that*—was a bargain."

Johnnie's mouth worked uselessly for a moment. "You lied to us." He sounded like a little boy.

Isabella's face changed. "Some of us did—but not all of us. Like me, most of us simply wanted more favorable circumstances before you commenced your quest. So, yes, I spoke against the halfhearted invasion plans my overly optimistic nephew occasionally dangled before you."

"And now, knowing how we've been used, even betrayed, what can we trust in?"

It was Fernando himself who answered that question: "You may trust that I am not my brother." The king in the Low Countries' eyes had become hard. "I give you my word that we shall not forsake you. And plans are afoot to make good the arrears in your pay, with rich garnishments in recognition of your long service. But I cannot promise you a triumphant return to Ireland. Not now, maybe never; I am not Spain."

Owen ran a finger across his lip. Well, at least Fernando wasn't a blatherskite. He was like his aunt, in that way: they both gave you the truth, even when it put them in a hard position.

The king in the Low Countries had not paused. "But the future must wait. Presently, you are the best captains we have to find Urban and to plead with him to accompany you. Not only are you men of title and martial prowess, but your people's respect for the pontiff has ever been exemplary. No true pope has ever feared his Irish flock. They might be impetuous, but they have always been loyal."

"A reputation that might not work in our favor, given Borja's apparent motives in Italy."

Fernando nodded at Sean Connal's observation. "Among Borja and his intimates, this might be true. But among the Spanish rank and file? The Irish are held to be doughty fighters and loyal to Spain, primarily because you are obedient to the Church. The common foot soldier will not reflect upon how, at this moment, loyalty to the Church might mean—for the first time in both your memory and theirs—disloyalty to Spain."

John O'Neill's eyes roved across the Hapsburgs sitting at the head of the table. "So. I'm to accept that the old dream—of Ireland beneath our feet again—is dead."

Maria Anna's voice was gentle. "Let us say that now you are being honestly told that it is a dream that might take generations to realize. If ever."

John nodded. "I've no quarrel with what His Highness has said. Truth be told, I prefer plain speech, hard and true. Better than easy promises of paradise just around the bend. But as I'm earl of my people, then I'd be knowing one more thing: with our pay in arrears, how are my men to keep their families fed? How is it that you propose to pay for our future with you?"

Rubens leaned forward. "That—" he said, glancing at the Hapsburg troika at the head of the table "—is a matter being addressed right now. As I understand it, the projection is that the king in the Netherlands will not only be able to pay you, but exceed—far exceed—your old rate. But it may take a year to achieve this. In the meantime, we will victual your families out of military stocks, if necessary."

"Most reassuring. But how—*how*—will you pay us, next year? Where will the new money come from?" John had never shifted his gaze to Rubens, but kept it on the Hapsburgs.

Isabella sniffed. "Do you really need to know?"

"Aye, I do. You said it yourself: we've been played the fool for twenty years now. Perhaps we were partly to blame, settling for promises without worrying over the details. Well, now I'm worried over the details. Where will you find this money?"

Isabella's eyes narrowed. "Do you believe I would lie to you, that I would sully my honor over such a filthy business as the coin we put into hands that wield swords for hire?"

Owen started. "We are no mean sell-swords, you Grace. Have your Irish tercios ever failed you? Have we ever changed sides? Have we ever been less than exemplary in our valor?"

Isabella's expression softened as her eyes shifted toward Owen. "No, and I repent my harsh words. But let me ask you this in return: although I have not until now been able to speak openly about Spain's use of its Irish Wild Geese, have I ever worked to your detriment?"

"No."

"Not so far." John's voice sounded as surly as he looked.

Isabella's eyes—and words—shifted back over to him sharply. "Then do not insult me by doubting my word that we—the Hapsburgs of *this* land, and *this* time—will make good our promises. Projects *are* in hand that will provide us with coffers deep enough to retain your peerless service for years, for decades, to come."

Owen suppressed a small smile. *Heh—a slap on the wrist and a pat on the head, all in the same sentence.* "Your Grace, one item remains unresolved."

"Yes?"

"What would be the best day for us start for Rome?"

Isabella's smile was wry. "Yesterday, Colonel. Yesterday."

# Part Two

## May–June 1635

The universe, cleft to the core

# Chapter 11

"Ambassadora Nichols!" The embassy runner, Carlo, sprinted inside the house's courtyard from his customary position at the front gate. Sharon Nichols turned, alarmed at Carlo's volume. The modest compound they'd established outside Padua was too small to require that much vocal energy—unless it was to announce trouble. Her concern faded as she noticed Ruy's unruffled calm; he indicated the relaxed postures of the Marine guards standing within the shadow of the main gate's archway. Two of them leaned out a bit, the tilt of their heads suggesting modest interest in some exterior object.

Ruy began striding toward the arch. "It seems we have visitors, my love."

"Seems so." Which could only mean one thing, given her renegade embassy's incognito location in the Paduan countryside—

Harry Lefferts breezed past the Marines and then planted himself at the entry to the courtyard, thumbs in his belt. "Damn," he said, looking around. "This place sucks."

Sharon smiled. "It's good to see you too, Harry." She walked into Lefferts' brief hug as Ruy's left eyebrow rose slightly. She turned, gestured to her husband with almost courtly grace, "Harry, this is my husband, Señor Ruy Sanchez de Casador y Ortiz."

Harry cocked a grin and stuck out a hand. "Heard a lot about you."

"And I about you." Ruy's hand was in the American's with an extra measure of speed and sureness.

"And so our two legendary warriors meet at last. Now, who've you brought with you, Harry?"

"The whole damned Crew." He grinned. "And more than a dozen of the Hibernian Mercenary Battalion."

Sharon craned her neck. "I don't see them."

Ruy put a hand on her arm. "And, for now, you will not, my dear. During the last radio exchange with Señor Lefferts' group, I instructed that they bivouac in the copse by the stream, about two miles west. We do not want to attract more attention than we must."

Harry snorted as he looked at Nichols' husband. "Y'know, you should just call me Harry, because there's no way I'm going to remember that long moniker of yours—Ruy."

Ruy smiled. "As you suggest, 'Harry.' Since your name was appellation enough for one of the most gallant kings of England, then I presume it is sufficient for you."

"Well—just barely." Harry's smile matched Ruy's.

In the meantime, another traveler appeared in the archway. His greeting was in sharp contrast to the casual up-time reunion: the man gave a small bow.

Harry hooked a thumb as the newcomer approached. "This is Don Estuban Miro."

Sharon extended her ample hand and found it being shaken by a longer, fine-boned one which was closer to the color of her own than it was to Harry's. Miro was a man of slightly more than medium height, well-formed and fit but without the aura of "soldier" about him. But as he said, "Pleased to meet you, Ambassador," Sharon was struck by how, upon looking at his face, she spontaneously recalled the bookish phrase "intelligent eyes." Because Miro's certainly were. It was hard to say what made eyes look "intelligent" exactly, and because of that, it was sometimes tempting to think that it was just a literary convention. And it was certainly true that there were some folks who were quite intelligent, but whose eyes gave no clue of it.

But nevertheless, Estuban Miro had intelligent—remarkably intelligent—eyes. She could tell that these were eyes that missed nothing, and yet revealed even less of what went on behind them. Sharon was fairly sure that she, Ruy, and the surroundings, were all being swiftly examined, but she couldn't *see* him doing it.

Ruy's reaction to Miro was quite novel. His own assessing gaze evolved into a sly smile as he extended his hand. "*Viaje largo?*"

There might have been a momentary flash of surprise in Miro's eyes. If so, it was there and gone so quickly that Sharon could not be sure. The smile on the newcomer's face was a match to Ruy's as he responded, "*Com ho saps?*"

Sharon rolled her eyes. "Okay, guys, if you're gonna start in with the Spanish, can you at least translate for those of us who almost flunked it in ninth grade?"

"That is not Spanish." The voice from behind was mellifluous, yet firm. Sharon turned. Three figures in cowled friar's habits had emerged from the small cottage in the courtyard.

"No, not Spanish," Harry agreed with a nod. "But I can't place it. How about you, Father?"

Sharon couldn't resist a half-smile. "Harry, I believe the proper form of address is 'Holy Father.'"

"*Holy* Father?" Harry gawked. "As in, the pope?"

The hooded figure so labeled nodded and drew back his cowl. "The language your friends are speaking is Catalan. I am not well versed in it, but Ruy asked our newcomer if he had had a long journey. And our newcomer asked in return 'How did you know?'—meaning I presume, 'How did you know I was Catalan?'" The face that had been concealed by the hood was well-advanced in years, worldly, patrician, and subtly aristocratic. It was not, in any way, a face that blended well with the garb of a rustic friar. Nor did the gesture of the slightly raised hand and proffered ring.

Miro bowed very low. "Your Holiness," he said.

Urban VIII's brow rose slightly.

Miro provided the explanation with yet another small bow. "Your Eminence, kneeling and kissing your ring would be inappropriate in my case."

Urban's brow became level again and he nodded.

Ruy exclaimed, as if suddenly solving a puzzle. "Ah! So, that's the accent! You are Mallorquin, and a *xueta*."

Miro nodded.

One of Harry's eyebrows climbed. "My-orkeen? A zhoo-wayta? Now does someone want to fill *me* in?" And then, remembering the pope, he removed his hat. "Pleased to meet you, Your Holiness."

Urban's smile was benign and a bit bemused.

Ruy was providing explanations. "Señor Lefferts, in your many travels, I am sure you have heard of Mallorca, the main island of the Balearics. It is several days' sail due east of Barcelona. Their language is mostly Catalan, but a distinct dialect. And the *xuetas*—" Ruy's brow dipped slightly "—are its Jewish population, who were compelled to profess themselves as Catholics. It is awkward to say more about their circumstances in—in the present company."

Urban's smile dimmed, but he nodded. "A tactful close to that unfortunate topic, Señor Casador y Ortiz." He shifted his eyes back to Miro. "And is this all your party that will be staying with us here?" Sharon frowned, wondering. Urban sounded oddly expectant, and a bit wistful, too. What or who was he expecting? This was the full complement that had been approved for—

But a third figure—lean in a dusty habit—advanced through the shadows of the archway. Sharon realized the cleric's gait was familiar a split second before she saw the face. "Larry—Cardinal— Mazzare! What the hell are you doing in Italy?"

"Collecting dust from every road from here to Bergamo, I think." Larry Mazzare, the American village priest that Urban VIII had appointed the cardinal-protector of the United States of Europe, closed the remaining distance with a smile, arms out for the slightly distant embrace that was his wont.

Sharon held him back after a moment, staring at him. "Damn it, Larry. Does Mike know you came down here? No? Oh, hell, Larry. When Stearns hears about this, he's going to have your—"

"Melissa already warned me about my impending castration. But I suspect His Holiness might be willing to intercede on my behalf and explain to Mike that my travel here was necessary. More necessary than a layperson might readily imagine."

Urban VIII came forward. "That is so very true. Lawrence, it is wonderful to see you here. Quite wonderful indeed."

Mazzare kissed the proffered papal ring while the pontiff seemed to restrain himself from putting an approving—and relieved?—hand upon the up-timer's head. As Mazzare straightened, the smile returned to Urban's face—the slightly mischievous version the pontiff reserved for conversations with his intimates. "Evidently, Cardinal Mazzare, my connections to the Heavens rival those of your marvelous radios."

"Unquestionably true, Your Eminence, but why do you remark upon it at this particular moment?"

"Because in my recent devotions, for every one prayer I offered in the hope that you would be prevented from shouldering the perils of journeying to Italy in such troubled times, I confess that I uttered two far more emphatic appeals that you would be able—and blessedly foolish enough—to do so." He took both of Larry's hands in a surge of gladness and what looked very much like profound gratitude.

Sharon suddenly felt as clueless as both Harry Lefferts and Estuban Miro looked. "I'm sorry, Your Eminences, but I'm not sure I'm reading between all the lines here."

Mazzare turned solemn eyes upon her. "Sharon, a pope who sits in the Holy See has the power to control the rate of change within the Church. A pope who has been driven from his seat upon the *cathedra* has no such luxury. He may have to act swiftly, without enough time to deliberate upon the full conse-quence of every decision. But Mother Church is eternal, so no choice is a simple one. And if the pope's utterances are explicitly *ex cathedra*—are canonical proclamations, despite the physical absence of the throne for which they are named—then they are as eternal as the Church itself."

Mazzare turned a gaze that was part searching and part sympa-thetic upon a nodding Urban. "And, unless I am much mistaken, His Eminence must now make a fateful choice on how to proceed from this point. Specifically, who he now embraces as allies, who he does not, and *why*, may dramatically and forever change the Church."

One of the other figures that had emerged from the cottage came closer; it was Muzio Vitelleschi, father-general of the Jesuit order. His thin lips quirked in his tightly trimmed gray-silver beard. "Such insight would have made you a worthy member of the Society of Jesus," he observed in a crisp, clear voice. "But you will help no one if you starve to death, Cardinal Mazzare. Unless I am mistaken, supper is almost ready."

"It is?" asked Sharon of Carlo and two of the embassy's domestic staff who were hovering nearby.

"It most surely is," assured Ruy with a faint wink. "Even if it is not."

"Oh," said Sharon. "Yes. It is. How forgetful of me. Gentlemen, Eminences, please allow me to show you to our dining room. Such as it is."

"And excuse me while I ensure that we are not troubled by any unexpected guests." Ruy was gone with a flourish and a tight about-face toward the gate-guards; the move had the grace and ease of an athlete in his prime. Sharon watched her husband walking for another moment and decided that he was one fine figure of a man. Even from behind. Maybe particularly from behind. Yes, he was one fine—

"Ambassador?" Miro's voice was a gentle reminder, rather than an inquiry.

"Right. Allow me to show you the way..."

Harry ladled what he called "gravy" on top of his second helping of millet polenta and resumed his seat at the kitchen table beside Sherrilyn, who asked, "So what have you learned from the Marines?"

"Not much," he admitted sourly. "Their captain—Taggart—gave me a good run-down on the parts of Rome that visitors don't see."

"Which are the parts where we'll spend most of our time, right up until we rescue Frank and Giovanna."

"Yeah. Particularly Juliet."

Sherrilyn rubbed her knee absently. "Why her?"

"Because if I'm right, we're going to need a lot of local help and intel to make any plan work. And the rest of us shouldn't just sit around nearby, trying to hide, while Juliet's working her magic on the locals. So we'll stay somewhere outside the city."

"Is Juliet really up for this? Is her Italian that good?"

Lefferts stared at his former teacher and short-duration lover—both a long time ago: "You heard her bartering in the market at Brescia. And she can out-Italian the Italians when it comes to volume, plate-throwing rages, and merry-making. They all spend about five minutes arguing with her and then they all love her. What's to worry?"

"That's fine when we're in friendly territory, but in Rome—well, that's enemy territory." Sherrilyn rubbed her knee more assiduously. "They might be a little more suspicious there."

"Suspicious? Of what?"

"Well, Juliet doesn't *look* very Italian, you know."

"Yeah, having functioning eyes, I noticed that right away. But I don't think that matters so much here. Italy's got lots of folks from all over. And Rome is more of a hodge-podge than anyplace else. Besides, you just know that Juliet will concoct a cock-and-bull cover story that will, as always, amaze the natives." He scraped at his plate. "I'm gonna finish up here and compare the domestics' assessments of Rome with Taggart's."

"The workers here are still the same bunch that came with Sharon from the embassy?"

"Yep. She and Ruy kept the whole gang together."

"Why?"

"Security. By the time they got to the first place where they really stopped running,—an inn right outside Padua—all the folks still with Sharon knew, one way or the other, that they had the pope, the father-general of the Jesuits, and the younger Cardinal Barberini traveling with them. Couldn't exactly let that kind of information go wandering off, could you?"

"No, I guess not." Sherrilyn shifted her knee fretfully; the hike down from the Val Bregaglia had played havoc with her old sports injury. "So what, specifically, are you hoping the workers can tell you that Taggart couldn't?"

Harry grinned. "They can fill me in on the *lefferti*—my adoring public."

"Your misguided adolescent Harry-wanna-bes, more like. What are you looking to do, boost your ego?"

"I wouldn't have to if you'd help me reclaim my sense of masculine prowess, Sherrilyn."

"Ah, give it a rest, Harry."

"'It's' been doing nothing *but* resting since we left Grantville." Harry saw her look. "Okay, since Biberach, then. But I only had one night with the burgomeister's daughter. Whereas with you, I could look forward to many—"

"Cut it out, Harry. I'm serious. What are you trying to find about the *lefferti*?"

"Okay, just deflate my ego—and everything else. Look: we're going to need to have the latest word on the street when we get to Rome. The *lefferti* were pretty much poor teenagers who wanted to be toughs, get a little respect, acquire that kind of rogue-do-gooder sexiness that you've always found so appealing in me—"

"Down, dog. You're humping the wrong tree. For real now, Harry; you think the *lefferti* can help?"

Unfazed, Harry started scraping together the last of his polenta while eying the still-steaming pot. "Yeah, for real. The city is occupied right? It's going to have Spanish patrols, command posts, strong points, weak spots, black-market connections with anyone handling provisioning for the invaders: the whole nine yards. We're going to need all that information. And we might need the *lefferti*'s hands and bodies, too."

"What? Harry, the *lefferti* are really just kids—"

"Pretty old kids; some of them are in their twenties. And they're not shrinking violets, either. But I'd only use a few of the older ones in any actual attack. I'm thinking most of the *lefferti* would be far more useful providing us with a diversion." He stood up, stretched, scratched his back. "Well, it's time to debrief the staff."

"And to see if there are any comely wenches among them?"

Harry affected deep emotional injury. "If I do so, it is only because you reject me so continually and completely."

Sherrilyn smiled. "Oh, get the hell out of here," she said to his receding back.

# Chapter 12

As Larry Mazzare had suspected, once grace was said and dinner was served, things became much more informal. Urban waved a freshly cut, steaming piece of bread in the air, distributing the aroma. "There are advantages living out in the countryside. Like this bread. Wonderful. Not so carefully made as the loaves prepared for our discriminating palates in the Vatican. And because of that—wonderful." His eyes seemed to lose a little focus, to veer into a reminiscent trance; it was sometimes easy to forget that popes had once been little boys, too, eagerly awaiting a fresh loaf from a country oven. Of course, for Urban—Maffeo Barberini—that country oven would have been located in a palatial family villa. But still, the pleasures and recollections of childhood had a distinctive sweetness, no matter the socioeconomic strata of the one who possessed them.

Urban's voice brought Mazzare out of his reveries. "You have been very quiet, Lawrence, even for you. Tell me: what is on your mind?"

Mazzare smiled. "Farmhouses and villas, Your Eminence. Of which this is a most unusual specimen. How long since you relocated here from the *taverna* outside Padua?"

Sharon Nichols furnished the answer. "We got here almost two weeks ago. We didn't dare spend much time at that *taverna*." She speared a sliver of roast chicken. "Too much traffic, and we were way too large a party. As soon as we found this place, we paid our tab and hit the road."

"And it looks like you kept almost all the staff with you."

Ruy smoothed one wing of his mustache farther out of the way of his inbound fork of green beans. "Not 'almost all' the staff, Cardinal Mazzare: *all* the staff."

Mazzare nodded. "Yes. Of course."

Ruy matched the cardinal's nod. "The stakes are simply too high. Which is why, of the various choices put before us by the Cavrianis' agent—"

*Ah, that's their local contact, then. Of course.*

"—this house seemed the best."

"The best?" Mazzare looked uncertainly at the dingy walls and the smoke-darkened ceiling and rafters.

Miro set down his knife. "I believe Señor Casador y Ortiz is referring to its innocuousness, rather than its appeal."

Ruy nodded. "Yes. This house was twice emptied by the plagues that swept through Venice late last century. It stood vacant for almost a decade. Then a family tried to 'break the curse'—and all died from yet another malady. From what we heard, I suspect typhus, but the local peasants are now convinced that the hand of divine judgment lies heavy on this roof."

Mazzare looked around. "You must have had a lot of cleaning up to do."

Vitelleschi sounded as if he had bitten into a loaf and found half a wiggling worm in the part he still held. "In service to the pope, I have traveled and dwelt in many places that could not be accurately described as civilized. Amongst them, this house still proved to be the nadir."

Antonio Barberini, the young and rather doughy cardinal who was Urban's nephew, shuddered. "Borja came to Rome and successfully drove us out in a day; we came here and are still trying to evict the roaches and rats."

Mazzare found that his appetite had waned. "So how long do you believe it is safe to stay in this villa? Or is it a farmhouse?"

"I guess we'd call it a hybrid property—and we stay no longer than we have to," Sharon answered. "When you meet with Tom Stone in Venice, Don Estuban, he should have a more remote spot selected for us."

Miro inclined his head. "It shall be my first item of business with him. But would he not already have sent word if he had found something?"

Sharon frowned. "Yes, which has me more than a little worried."

Ruy slipped an arm around her shoulder. "Such matters take time, and cannot be rushed," he soothed. "After all, what would one answer if asked, 'Why such a hurry to find a country villa?' I think we cannot safely respond, 'Ah, well, you see, we must have a house in which to hide a pope.'"

She smiled. So did Urban. Mazzare suspected that the brief lip-crinkling of Vitelleschi was a sign of amusement, also. "At least," Mazzare offered, "it is a little easier to hide in this day and age. The depictions of a person being sought aren't even as good as the 'wanted: dead or alive' handbills that were used in my world in the American West."

"Truly? Even with your wondrous photography?"

"Photographs—or rather printing them out—was too expensive in frontier areas. Besides, even if the likenesses I've seen resembled His Holiness—and they don't—not many people are willing to post them. Italy's ardent Roman Catholics have no desire to turn their pope over to anyone, let alone a brutal usurper like Borja."

"They might, if he offers a reward that piques Italy's equally ardent greed." Vitelleschi's rejoinder was the crisp, arid declamation of a dedicated moralist.

Mazzare shrugged. "Perhaps. Perhaps not." He turned toward Urban. "Either way, Your Holiness, we must announce that you are alive, and we must do so as quickly as possible. Every day we are silent increases the likelihood that Borja can finally break the will of Rome's people, and can bring more of the Consistory's remaining fence-sitters around to supporting him."

Sharon pursed her lips. "I hate to ask this, but might it already be too late? I mean, has the belief in the rightful pope been so badly shaken that the people are already looking elsewhere?"

Vitelleschi's voice was firm with professional conviction. "No, Ambassadora Nichols. For a while, the people will simply be shocked. And then they will be outraged. Only once that rage has passed could it be said that we have waited too long."

"And not having my body to parade will cause a long delay indeed," Urban observed. Then, with his small, trademark smile, he said, "One should not choose a new pope before the old one is dead. After all, two popes at once? If Mother Church is the bride of Christ, we would be inviting our Savior to become a bigamist."

Cardinal Barberini guffawed so suddenly that he almost choked on his chicken; Ruy managed not to laugh, but his smile was almost as wide as his mustache. Miro politely looked elsewhere to conceal whatever expression passed over his face. Vitelleschi looked like an offended schoolmarm determined not to acknowledge the witty quip of a prized, but occasionally mischievous, charge.

Mazzare managed to keep his smile wan. "And that observation also highlights something about Borja's probable intents."

Urban sobered immediately. "You mean, that as in your American West, I am wanted 'dead or alive'?"

Mazzare shook his head regretfully. "I suspect Borja is less interested in the 'alive' option. Given the fate of the cardinals in Rome, I presume he would prefer you were killed attempting to resist the lawful agents of the Church."

"Strange. I would have thought the lawful agents of the Church would still be *my* agents."

Mazzare returned Urban's small smile. "Yes, I would have thought so, too. But we up-timers have a saying: possession is nine-tenths of the law. Borja possesses the Holy See, even though you possess the pontifical title. Unless you were to walk right back in there and order him out, your absence from the Holy City complicates any assertion that its agents are *your* agents."

"Quite right. So, just as it is universally known that Borja now possesses the Vatican, it must become just as widely known that I still possess my life."

Sharon tapped an index finger meditatively against the much-stained tabletop. "I wonder: should we use the Committees of Correspondence to spread news about your survival, and to confirm the rumors of how all the cardinals were killed in cold blood?"

Miro frowned. "If you choose to do so, I recommend you release the information all at once, and through written materials cached at a drop point that the Committee members are informed of later on."

"Why?"

"Because, if Borja now has someone working for him who is more professional than Quevedo, the Committees will be under surveillance. Any direct contact will surely lead assassins to wherever you may hide. Consequently, your contact with the world must be outbound only, and never suspected as coming from your embassy. Any inbound traffic is too perilous to countenance."

Ruy nodded. "Don Estuban could not speak more truly or wisely, my heart. I have some—small experience—with this kind of affair. If Borja is willing to spend enough *reales* to maintain constant surveillance, his agents could snatch up any person arriving at the embassy in Venice, or the Committees, who is suspected of bearing messages from you."

Vitelleschi's eyes were emotionless. "And, as Señor Casador y Ortiz might confirm, Borja's agents will be neither gentle nor patient in the methods they use to extract information from your couriers."

Sharon shuddered. "Okay. No Committees, then. Or a one time news-blast, at most."

"Yes," her husband agreed, "I think it would be wise to limit it to that."

Urban sighed. "Your talk is most prudent, and most upsetting. I can accept a death sentence upon my head, but I have great misgivings about how my presence endangers my best and truest friends, who've aided me, unasked, in this dark hour. My heart tells me—"

"Your heart tells you how to behave as a man, Your Holiness, but you must rely strictly upon your head when deciding how to act as pope." Vitelleschi somehow combined shadings of both compassion and remonstrance in his otherwise dry voice. "Even our friends here—most of whom are not Catholics—still understand the great urgency of keeping you alive, of keeping the papacy from falling into the hands of that monster Borja. And besides, do you really think that if you took flight it would save them? Tell me, Señor Casador y Ortiz: in your experience of such matters, how would Borja's agents alter their search, if they were to somehow learn that His Holiness had departed from your protection?"

"It would have no effect upon them, Your Eminence. Except to make their job easier."

Urban, who was schooled in the intricacies, but not the gruesome particulars, of espionage, leaned forward. "Explain this if you would, my son."

"I am honored to be of service to Your Holiness, but it is my deep shame to possess the needed expertise in these matters."

"Please continue," the pope instructed.

Mazzare felt, rather than saw, some weight seem to rise off Ruy's shoulders, as if it was a burden he had become so accustomed to carrying, that he no longer heeded it. The Spaniard sat straighter, prouder—if that were possible. "Here is what would happen if you left us, Your Holiness. If they were to find this place, but after you departed from it, Borja's agents would torture every individual—no matter their age or sex—for any information as to your possible whereabouts, companions, preparations, anything of relevance. And then they would put everyone to the sword and the house to the torch."

"To conceal their misdeed."

Ruy nodded. "But even if they found and slew you *first*, they would still attempt to determine and annihilate the place from whence you had fled."

"Why this needless barbarity?"

"It is not needless from their perspective, Your Holiness. Consider: you might have left further instructions here, or key correspondence with princes and ministers inimical to Borja. You might have been gathering evidence that would incriminate him, gathering secret support from those cardinals who are not yet willing to decry him publicly. In short, why should Borja believe that all the damage you could do him will die with you? It might well have been left with your intimates, before you struck out on your own. And so he would come here, interrogate, torture, and slay—without exception and without mercy."

The room was very still. Mazzare, like everyone else, was staring at Ruy, whose dark eyes seemed to be seeing inward as well as outward. "I, Ruy Sanchez de Casador y Ortiz swear that this is true." But this time, he uttered his trademark oath quietly, almost like a prayer.

Or a confession.

# Chapter 13

Two days later, Estuban Miro stifled a yawn as he waited for Tom Stone to arrive back at the embassy in Venice. Word had it that the American pharmaceutical magnate had stayed late over on the mainland in Mestre, personally attending to what he had dubbed a "quality control problem" in one of the new jointly owned chemical refineries he had founded in the past half year.

Ironic, since Miro had been in Mestre himself last night. But not wanting to waste the early hours of the day, he had left both Lefferts' Wrecking Crew and North's Hibernians slumbering as he emerged into the predawn glimmer to catch the first available boat from the mainland, which the locals dubbed Terraferma. So he was among the first visitors to arrive on Venetia, that day. And what did he get for all his troubles? A reasonably cushioned chair and a small cup of passable coffee as he waited for the USE's ambassador to Venice to return. Eventually.

Miro stifled another yawn. He'd been working on a sleep deficit for the past two nights. In Padua, he had tried to excuse himself from the dinner table early, pleading his early departure the next morning. Somehow that never happened; every time he started to rise, someone refilled his glass, or asked a question, or embroiled him in a debate. In short, no matter how Miro had tried to get away from that spattered, partially charred, richly served table of good cheer, he couldn't make good his escape. Probably just as well. While it was superficially just a meal with intelligent companions, it had also been a rite of passage.

Among the up-timers, it had been a kind of assessment concluding with a provisional adoption. Mazzare's cordiality had deepened into potential friendship over the course of their joint balloon journey from Jena to Chur, and the up-time cardinal's opinion obviously held great sway with both Sharon and Ruy.

But it had probably been more crucial in securing the benign toleration and cooperation of Father-General Vitelleschi and Cardinal Barberini. Miro had been thoroughly briefed on the former before arriving in Italy. A reputation for stern measures and judgment in his professional life had colored the depictions of Vitelleschi; he was purported to be humorless and vinegary. As Miro had learned, this was a profound misperception. In some ways, he suspected Vitelleschi might have had the most incisive and even blasphemous wit of them all; he just elected not to show it. The younger Barberini had imbibed many of the prejudices of his patrician class: a lack of ease around Jews, a reluctance to have dealings with them. But his uncle's cosmopolitanism had also rubbed off on Antonio Barberini, who, over the course of the evening, warmed to Miro and his wry interjections.

But Urban—he was the hardest of them to figure. *Possibly, because he is most like me,* thought Miro with a smile, thinking how that observation would have scandalized every Catholic in the room. With the probable exception of Urban.

For Urban VIII's was a face and consciousness that had very obviously been washed by many waters, not all of which had been pure or calm. He loved life, enough so that he did not ruin his existence by being desperate to retain it above all other things. Yet he also was intrigued by the possibility of what lay beyond. Urban's speech and attitudes did not reflect a rigid expectation of the shape that Heaven or Hell might take, nor the face of God or the malice of Satan. Before he had become a pope, he had been Maffeo Barberini, head of his powerful family, a creature of his time, versed in arts and letters and the lofty heresies of the Greeks and Romans. No, Pope Urban VIII was not a simple man, and his thoughts and plans clearly moved on many levels simultaneously.

When the dinner group had finally pushed back from the table in search of their beds, Miro was glad to have stayed awake so late; it had been crucial for him to be accepted by these groups with whom he would now be working. But he also dreaded rising the next day, and riding to Venice.

Or rather, to Mestre. The entire traveling party—numbering almost thirty—was hot, dusty, and parched when they reached Mestre just before sundown. It had made no sense to push the horses any harder, and the timing had not been fortuitous. The last boat to the main island was a black shadow receding into the lagoon's red-orange reflection of the sunset sky. That had meant retracing their steps away from the dockside, until they found a predictably over-priced, under-staffed inn in which to spend the night.

A night that had been all too short: five hours after finally settling in, the inn's ostler had jostled Miro awake, as he had requested. Morning ablutions, a quick walk back to the docks, waiting for the first ready boatman—and now, here in the embassy, wondering about the odds of getting a second cup of coffee before—

Tom Stone came up the stairs two at a time, one top-tuft of hair truant from the rest of his somewhat trimmed gray-silver mane. He got to the top of the stairs, saw Miro, frowned, and then his brows rose. "Oh, yeah. Right. You're the guy. Miro. From back home. Sorry I got delayed—uh, detained. I was over in Mestre helping out my partners."

"Yes. I was told. I wasn't waiting long." Miro rose, put out a hand, smiled. "Mr. Stone, I'm Estuban Miro."

"Yeah, yeah. I got the messages about you from Grantville. Great to meet you." The hand-shake was vigorous; unpolished, yes, but very enthusiastic and genuine.

Stone waved off the help of one of the waiting embassy staff, opened the door to his office himself, and apparently presumed Miro would follow without invitation, as if he was simply an acquaintance who had come to call at his home. Miro trailed along. He was impressed at the size of the chamber but doubted Stone had anything to do with the opulent décor incorporating tasteful Renaissance hints and flourishes. Tom flopped down behind the plateau that was his desk and smiled at Miro over the top of it. Then, his hand halfway through waving his visitor toward a seat, Stone reconsidered the arrangements with a frown; he quickly rose up, came around and sat in a chair directly opposite the one Miro was already standing behind.

"No desks today," Stone explained. "At least not with some-one from home. Hey, have a seat; take a load off, Don Estuban. You've come a long way without a lot of rest, from what I hear."

Miro smiled. "That would not be an exaggeration."

"Want some breakfast?"

"Thank you, no; I had a light meal before coming here," Miro lied, hoping that the sudden contradictory growl from his stomach remained inaudible to Stone.

Apparently it did. Tom replied with the strange, neck-bobbing nod that was his wont, and looked uneasily out the window. "I don't mean to rush you, Don Estuban, but—"

"Mr. Stone, there is no need for apologies. If I had family members in the clutches of Borja, I would want to get down to business, too."

Tom smile gratefully. "I'm glad you understand, Don Estuban, really I am. I don't want to seem rude but—well, Frank and Giovanna are on my mind. Pretty much all the time."

Miro noticed the faint blue rings under his host's eyes but said nothing.

"So what's the plan?"

"First, Mr. Stone, have there been any further developments? I haven't received a situation report since Chur."

Stone went back in his seat with a sigh and a grimace. "No. No ransom demands. Not even anyone to talk to. The Spanish ambassador here claims ignorance of Borja's actions. 'Course, he's probably telling the truth; seems all the Spanish big shots in Italy were taken as much by surprise by Borja's actions as was Rome itself."

Miro nodded. "Unfortunately, with no remaining embassy in Rome, we are unable to get any new information on the situation there. Even Don Francisco Nasi's intelligence networks have gone silent. We cannot tell if they have been discovered and eliminated or are merely unable to send messages because of the political and domestic chaos prevailing in the city."

Tom nodded. "So—what's the plan?"

"I don't know."

"Wait a minute. Mike radioed that you were in charge of the rescue operation—"

"I am in charge of the mission sent down here to Italy, but that mission has three separate mandates: protect the pope, recover your son and daughter-in-law, and coordinate with you. I only know the specifics of the objectives I am to be directly involved in. Harry Lefferts is in charge of the rescue operation, and I must remain unaware of his plans."

Tom nodded again. "Yeah, yeah. Compartmentalization of information, right? So even if someone grabs you, you can't tell them anything about any of the other plans."

"That is correct. And that is why you will no longer be hearing from the ex-Roman embassy after it relocates."

"What? Not even by radio?"

"Not routinely. Other than brief, coded status reports at pre-arranged times, radio communications will be of an emergency nature only."

"Why?"

"It is unlikely, but the Spanish may have procured radios. If they have, it is even more unlikely but still possible that they have acquired a working knowledge of signal triangulation. Which could lead them directly to the pope."

"Whoa. Signal triangulation is a bit out of the Spaniards' league, isn't it? Hell, it's out of *our* league, I thought."

"Not quite, and between up-timer defectors and all the down-time radio operators you have trained that have since left your service, the Spanish could easily gather the resources necessary to get an initial sense of the embassy's final hiding place if it sends radio transmissions. Which reminds me; might I have the list of new safe houses compiled by Giuseppe Cavriani?"

Tom took a sealed scroll from his desk and handed it over to Miro. "Just what Nasi asked for: three locations, all vetted and brokered by Giuseppe Cavriani himself. I haven't broken the seal; no one other than he knows the locations."

"Excellent. And the arrival of your large airplane, the Jupiter?"

Tom slouched in his chair and picked distractedly at threads that had come loose from the upholstery on the armrests. "Next few days. Maybe next week."

Miro tried to keep the frown off his face. "I see. Problems?"

"Seems so. That damn Monster's landing gear are turning into maintenance pigs. Or so they tell me."

Miro wasn't quite sure he had parsed all the slang correctly. "I beg your pardon?"

Tom uprooted one of the threads abruptly, seemed to regret

it. "The Monster—which is what most of us call our big, four-engine transport, the Jupiter—has got air-cushion landing gear. It was the only approach that seemed workable when we were building it, and it also allowed us to use any body of water as an airfield. Cool idea, huh?"

"Huh," agreed Miro, trying not to sound confused.

"Yeah, well it was great until this 'ACL gear' started failing maintenance checks. Every time that happened, they had to take it off-line—they had to ground it—and fix the problem. Now, it's grounded more than it's flying. Not that I see why the Monster is needed down here." He cast an appraising glance at Miro.

Miro smiled. "I'm not allowed to talk about that, at this point. Compartmentalization of information, I'm afraid."

Tom grumbled but smiled back. "Yeah, I figured. Although I figure maybe you'll use it to get the pope out of Italy. And I figure that maybe, once Harry springs my kids, it would be a lot easier to fly away from Rome than elude overland or maritime pursuit."

Miro merely nodded. Well, so much for having any major operational surprises up their sleeves. Although, truth be told, if he were the Spanish, he would be expecting these gambits, anyhow.

Tom was still staring at him. "You know, I hear rumors that you have a balloon. That that's how you came over the Alps."

"There are so many rumors, these days, it's hard to know what to believe."

"I got this rumor from some folks here in Venice, folks who are thinking of trying to build one of their own. Seems someone's ex-seaman son has given up sewing sails and has instead been stitching seams for an airship's envelope up in Grantville for the past eight months. Seems the guy paying him is one Don Estuban Miro."

Miro sighed. "It seems that we live in a very small world, indeed."

Tom smiled. "Sorry to pop your balloon, so to speak."

Miro's stomach growled again. So audibly that Tom Stone noticed. Miro waved away any concern. "That was merely distress at your unforgivable pun, not hunger, Mr. Stone."

"Tom."

"Very well. Tom. And I am simply Estuban."

"Great." Tom rang for breakfast before Miro could object—who silently blessed him. "Listen, Estuban, I was thinking. If the Monster doesn't get here on time, or gets gummed up or something...well..."

"Yes?"

"Well, what about your balloon?"

Miro shook his head. "I am sorry, Tom, but no, my balloons are completely insufficient for any of the tasks you are envisioning."

"Whaddya mean? They got you over the Alps, didn't they? You and the Wrecking Crew, who usually come pretty heavily armed."

"Yes, the balloon got us over the Alps, but at a rate of only one hundred miles per day, and only thirty miles per hour."

"What? Why so slow?"

"Tom, these are hot air balloons. They consume fuel at a prodigious rate. Most of our cargo space is fuel tankage for the burner, so that we can keep the air in the envelope hot enough."

"And why so slow?"

"Hot air has much less lift than the other balloons you were familiar with, such as the *Hindenburg* and the others which used hydrogen. So hot air balloons can't afford the weight of a full internal frame. Without that frame, the balloon deforms at higher airspeeds; it begins to flatten at the nose, buckle, veer off course. It is an inherent limit of the technology, Tom. I am sorry."

"Well, can't we build a better balloon? Something like the *Hindenburg*?" Seeing the look on Miro's face, he added, "But smaller, of course."

"I'd like to, Tom. But hydrogen is a dangerous substance. As I'm sure you're aware."

"You're not talking about the flammability issues, are you?"

"Not directly. From what I've read, and from the up-timers I've talked to, the real danger is the brittlization."

Tom nodded. "So, you've done your homework." He considered Miro for a long moment. "I get it. This balloon of yours: this is just Phase One, isn't it?"

Miro tried not to start in surprise. He rarely misgauged people, but he had mistaken the profound informality of Tom's thought processes as diagnostic of the classical "narrow genius." That kind of prodigy who was a wonder in regards to his own field, but disengaged from others. Now Miro saw this was not the case with Tom Stone: there were simply a few areas in which this up-timer was profoundly disinterested—or that he found downright aversive—and so he avoided them. But the idea of ballooning was apparently of interest to him, at least enough to leap ahead and see where Miro was going, what he intended. "Yes, going to hydrogen balloons is indeed my next plan. The hot air balloons are simply the first step. They will get a network of mooring towers and aerodromes established, will acclimate people to the notion of flying. But after that—"

"Sure," said Tom with a lazy, but also canny, smile. "Everyone will want to sail in the clouds: the ultimate, natural trip."

Miro felt, from the emphasis Tom put on the word "trip," that he was not simply referring to a journey. "You sound interested, Tom. Personally."

Tom rocked his feet from side to side. "Yeah. When I was just a kid, I was cruising through the Southwest. Doing my Jack Kerouac thing. Saw a bunch of balloons go up. Drove over. Traded some strictly medicinal cannabis for a ride. Man, oh man." Tom's eyes looked out the window, but were clearly seeing another time and place. "The colors, the shapes, the desert. Like another planet. Didn't need the weed, you know?"

"Uh . . . no, I'm afraid I don't."

Tom blinked out of the recollection, sat a little straighter, grinned sheepishly. "'Course you wouldn't; how could you?" His eyes became very intent. "Listen, Estuban. I've been watching my friends in Grantville build planes, and I've been amazed, just amazed, at what they've been able to do. But no matter how many they build, there's always a need for more air transport. Any kind of air transport, even if it's slow and with limited range. And the people here—you down-timers—can't really get in on the airplane-building action, not for years, anyway. But balloons are simpler, and they can be made here."

"Which is why I built one, Tom. And why I'm building more."

Tom smiled. "See? It's like synchronicity; you were meant to be here, for us to talk about airplanes but wind up talking about balloons. I'm going to talk to the people trying to build them here in Venice, if it's okay with you. Your people have the experience now, but this city has money—lots of money—and resources. And I've got some myself, you know."

Miro smiled. "Yes, I've heard."

Tom nodded. "You and me, Estuban, we're going to help people sail in the clouds. And we're going to rescue lives while we're at it."

"You mean quick responses to medical emergencies?"

"I mean more than that, Estuban. Think of it: my drugs carried on your balloons. We learn of an outbreak of plague, of typhus, and BANG!—" Tom hammered the desktop with the flat of his hand; Miro almost jumped "—we're there, with drugs in hand. If the epidemic is in a single town, we surround it and wipe it out. If it's coming at us like a wall of fire, we land in front of it and build a fire-break of immunity. Estuban, we could save thousands—millions!—of lives before we get to the middle of this century."

Miro nodded. "Yes. But do remember this, Tom: balloons could carry payloads other than life-saving drugs. Much more unwelcome payloads."

Tom's eyes darkened. "Yeah. There's that." He rocked his big feet back and forth again. "I like that you brought that up, Estuban. A guy just in this for the money would have tried to leave that under the rug. Not you. You're okay." The feet rocked one more time and were still. "Listen. After you've sent that scroll on its crooked way to Sharon, you have some business in town, right?"

"I do." Miro's breakfast was borne in by a young man so discreet as to be almost soundless and invisible.

Tom nodded approvingly. "Good. Hang out a bit. See the sights. Lemme think on this balloon business a little. We'll talk soon, okay?"

"Okay," repeated Miro around a mouthful of eggs.

"Hey," remarked Tom, "breakfast! That's a great idea you had." Tom jumped out of his chair, calling after the young attendant who had delivered it.

Miro, mouth still full, was unable to point out that it had been Tom's idea, after all.

# Chapter 14

Harry Lefferts contemplated the largely abandoned shore town to the north, passing quickly now that the *galliot*'s crew had stepped the sail and laid hands to their oars.

Stepping closer, Sherrilyn offered, "Penny—or *pfennig*—for your thoughts?"

Harry nodded at the gray, crumbling buildings and the few fishing boats moored at a single, listing pier, dark with age. "You know what that is?"

"Uh—a hard-luck fishing town?"

"That, oh-former-teacher-of-mine, is Anzio."

For a second, the name didn't register with Sherrilyn. Then she turned and gawked. "You mean, as in the big World War Two battle? That little shit-hole? That's Anzio?"

"Yup," said Harry.

"Robert Mitchum," said Thomas North quietly, from his position farther down the port-side gunwale, almost at the taffrail.

"Huh?" said Sherrilyn.

Harry smiled broadly. "Yeah! That's right! Mitchum starred in the movie. How'd you know that?"

North sent a long sideways look at Lefferts—

—Who remembered. "Right. You're the movie-nut." He turned to Sherrilyn. "If it has a war, or a gun, in it, and it came back in time with us, Sir Thomas North has seen it."

Sherrilyn poked him in the ribs and muttered, "Harry, you want to maybe muzzle yourself on the Ring of Fire references?"

Lefferts smiled. He shrugged off her concern but noticed North look away sharply. "What, you're worried, too?"

North nodded slowly. "Granted we haven't heard any English spoken on this boat. But that means very little, and this is a very small boat."

"God, I'm surrounded by nervous biddies and worriers." Harry smiled.

North shrugged. "Worrying is the very heart of an intelligence officer's job, Harry. Although you will remember that I advised against taking me along in this capacity. Several times."

Harry's smile widened. "Yeah, well, I ignored you."

North was looking over the side again. "Then, in my capacity as your intelligence officer, I strongly urge you to be a little more careful with your references. Or at least the volume with which you utter them."

"Fair enough," said Lefferts. He looked forward over the straining backs of the rowers—most from Rimini, like the ship—at the hazy outline of their destination. A tower, maybe two, a fair number of medium-sized ships at anchor. A lazy little port, far away from Spanish held Ostia and the Rome-wending Tiber River. Lefferts turned toward the rest of the Crew, who, just behind him, were lounging (and in some cases, napping) amongst their duffles and bags. "Okay, everyone, look lively and have your gear at hand. We're coming up on Nettuno."

North found disembarking at Nettuno to be a leisurely affair. The customs inspection was mostly an excuse for an inspector to come aboard with two surprisingly congenial guards and exchange news, gossip, and gripes about The Current State of Affairs. In the time it took for the *galliot*—the *Piccolo Doge*—to have its cargo cleared, several small fishing ketches had come and gone. The passengers—the Crew and North—excited a little more interest, but certainly no suspicion. The customs officer was charmed by Juliet's mastery of both proper Italian and more salty idiom; he didn't even bother to approach the others in the group after she explained that they were all traveling together.

Nonetheless, North breathed a sigh of relief when the inspection party guided the *Doge* to her designated mooring and left.

Lefferts came over and clapped a hand on the Englishman's spare shoulder. "What? Nervous again, Limey? I thought you were a steely-eyed commando type."

"I remain so by remaining alert, Harry."

"If it's all the same to you, I think I'll wait to get to Rome before I commence any heavy-duty worrying."

"You might want to reconsider that decision. Did you notice those two guards?"

"Yeah. What about 'em?"

North lowered his voice. "They were papal troops." Harry frowned, considered.

Sherrilyn merely shrugged. "Last I checked, that means they're on our side."

"Does it?"

"What do you mean?"

North nimbly hopped over the side and came to a sure-footed landing on the modest stone pier. "I mean, what do we really know about the loyalty of papal troops right now?"

"We know it's to Urban," replied Sherrilyn as she grabbed her bags and emulated North's debarkation.

"That's what we saw in Rimini," agreed North. "But here, closer to Rome, and with Nettuno pinned between it and Osuna's Spanish tercios in Naples, I'm not so sure their loyalties will be the same. Or at least, not as fervent."

"Yeah, but these guys didn't look or sound too fervent about being friends with the Spanish, either."

"No, Ms. Maddox, they didn't. They're probably getting leaned on by the Spanish."

"But not constantly. There's not a Spaniard in sight, here."

"Which is why we avoided Ostia and the Tiber. Those wharves are going to be swarming with Borja's forces."

Sherrilyn shrugged. "Right. That's where the trouble is, so we came here instead. What's to worry about?"

"Ms. Maddox, at the best of times, Italy is a hotbed of contending factions. Which in turn spawn a lively network of black marketeers, con artists, turncoats, and informers. They don't have to like Spain to be trouble for us. They only have to like Spanish *reales*."

Harry, who had been watching the exchange like a silent referee, nodded decisively. "Okay, Colonel North, I see your point—and it's a good one. We'll assume that we're under observation at all times. Now, while Juliet finds us a cart and some mounts, why don't you stay here with the equipm—uh, luggage. Although you seem to speak pretty fair Italian, yourself."

"Enough to get in trouble, get a drink, or get—" North stopped and shot a quick glance at Sherrilyn, annoyed at the possibility that he might be blushing.

Harry was smiling broadly, now. "I want to hear the end of that list, North!" And with that, he swaggered off into the narrow streets of Nettuno. Young boys stared admiringly after him; it was that effect that had spawned the *lefferti* trend in the first place. No small number of young women stared after Harry as well, albeit with long, steady gazes that were quite different from the lively displays of boyish emulation.

The strange parade that was the Wrecking Crew disappeared around a corner, Juliet already asking for directions in a shrill Florentine accent.

Three days later, Thomas North found himself in a hazy, oppressive stable. The smell of rotted dung and old hay was so dense and pungent that he imagined he could actually see the stink—a humid miasma of ordure—hanging in the air.

A gust of cool relief washed over him as one of the large doors opened slightly. In slipped Matija and a powerfully built man of medium height, aquiline nose, and lightless black eyes. The man took a second step forward; Matija sealed the door quietly behind them.

Lefferts was already on his feet, hand extended. The smaller man took it slowly, carefully, as if unaccustomed to the greeting. "You're Romulus?" Harry asked.

"It depends. Who are you?"

"I am Vulcan. Live long and prosper."

Near the opposite end of the Crew's rough, sprawling arc, Sherrilyn groaned in what sounded very much like agony.

"What is wrong?" asked Donald Ohde.

"Have you ever seen *Star Trek*?"

"No. Just war movies. I haven't seen many of your old television shows."

"Lucky you." Sherrilyn turned back to Harry. "Really? Did you have to?"

Lefferts shrugged. "Hey, in this world, everyone would naturally guess that a guy code-named Romulus would meet someone called Remus, right? Except us. So that's a good code, I figure."

Thomas, who had occasionally watched the crew of the fictitious *Enterprise* go boldly where no men had gone before, had to admit that Harry was right: it was a smart code, here.

Romulus had watched the entire exchange with little comprehension and less humor. "You have not been followed here?"

"Not that we can tell."

"You took precautions?"

"Yeah. A couple of times, we left one person as a lag-behind watcher. And we have binoculars."

"You have what?"

"Uh . . . they're like a really good telescope. We kept watch behind us, usually as far as a couple of miles back. Nothing."

The man nodded. "Very well. Don Taddeo Barberini sends his personal greeting, and apologizes that he cannot accommodate you in the palazzo itself. It would be—imprudent."

"For all of us," Sherrilyn agreed. "We thank the duke for arranging these lodgings."

"They are humble but will arouse no suspicion, and thus ensure that our rendezvous will remain unseen. Before discussing the situation in Rome, the duke has asked me to confirm that his uncle Maffeo and brother Antonio are still alive."

Lefferts nodded. "Both the pope and the cardinal are healthy and safe."

"The message we received from them seemed genuine, couched in phrases and with references that only they would know. But one can never be too careful." Romulus inclined his head. "The duke also wonders if you would be so kind as to satisfy one other curiosity of his: by what path did you come to Palestrina and what did you see along the way?"

Sherrilyn looked up. "Any particular reason why he wants to know?"

"There is no cause for alarm, signora, but the duke now keeps all his men here in Palestrina. If one ventures out, one might run afoul of a Spanish tithing detachment. Or other potentially dangerous groups."

"Such as?"

Romulus shrugged. "The liveried men of rival houses. With Barberini's fortunes at such low ebb, we must be careful. Our neighbors could transform into wolves. Compared to three months ago, we are easy prey. And of course, who can really trust the papal troops? And now—your journey?"

"Yeah, sure. Colonel North is our intelligence officer, and gives great reports. Tom?" Harry's eyes sparkled mischievously.

North suppressed a sigh. "After making landfall at Nettuno, we traveled by cart and mount to the east, where we picked up the Appian Way at the end of the first day. From there, we followed the Roman Road north until reaching Velletri, where we took the cart path to the northeast. Travel was slow, but that route kept the Alban Hills between ourselves and Rome, which we deemed prudent. That brought us here: three days travel, including this one."

"Any sign of the Spanish?"

"Happily, no, but one of the villages we passed had been visited by a foraging unit from Rome. No one killed, but a few farmers were roughed up when the Spanish impounded all the grain."

Romulus nodded. "This is an increasingly common story. Borja is sending foragers throughout the Lazio, rotating their destination to distribute his policy of public rapine with the greatest possible equity." Although the man did not smile, Thomas was fairly sure he had intended his last comment as a sardonic witticism.

George Sutherland's question came out more akin to a growl. "Is there any resistance to these thieves?"

Romulus turned to look at the immense Englishman. "Very little. None that is serious. Complaints, rather than conflict." The man shrugged. "The farmers and mayors of the Lazio just hope Borja will depart. If he does not, they will need to be in his good graces. It is a most unsatisfactory situation."

"Sounds pretty calm, too." Lefferts was rubbing his jaw.

"Yes. Too calm, for our tastes."

"How so?" asked Sherrilyn.

Romulus's eyes seemed to glint for a moment, despite the dull light of the oil lamps. "Barberini's other uncle—the late cardinal, Francesco—was followed out into the countryside by Borja's thugs, taken prisoner, and then cut down when he 'attempted to escape.' Many of the duke's friends from other families were slaughtered in a similar fashion. Rome grumbles. But does nothing."

Thomas was careful to keep the tone of his inquiry interested, rather than critical. "What would you have Rome do?"

The black eyes flicked over at him. "A good question."

Harry sat on the edge of the cart they had purchased in Nettuno. "I suggest that we do one job at a time. Once we're done getting our friends out of Borja's hands, I'm hoping my boss sends us back to help you with the situation here in Rome. So the faster I get the first job done, the faster I can get to whatever comes next."

Romulus nodded. "I will tell you all that I may about Rome."

Harry nodded. "Good. Let's start with the basics: do you know where Frank Stone and his wife Giovanna are being held?"

"Yes. They were recently moved to the palace now occupied by the Family Altemps. Not the main Palazzo Altemps, you understand." Seeing the unanimous confusion on the faces before him, Romulus attempted to help. "This is the palazzo that was originally built by Scipione Borghese."

That explanation only generated more confusion among the Crew. North sought clarification, "But wouldn't that make it the Palazzo Borghese?"

"No, no; it's—"

"It's what our book calls the Palazzo Rospigliosi," announced Sherrilyn, holding up a book with a bold-colored cover, titled in large letters: *Frommer's Rome.* "Not too far from the actual Palazzo Borghese. Which is Borja's own lair, if our information is correct."

Romulus nodded. "Yes, this is all correct. Your friends were moved to what you call the Palazzo Rospigliosi a little more than a week ago."

"Have any of your people been able to contact them?"

Romulus did not hide his incredulity. "Signor Lefferts—I know your name, since your reputation and style precedes you—we no longer have any informers in such places. Those few that we kept in the staffs of other families, as they certainly kept their own among ours, are no longer safe to contact, even if we could. It is the *lefferti* who keep us apprised of events in the city."

"So," Donald Ohde sounded amused, "Harry's fan club of Lefferts-wanna-bes still exists."

"Yes, but in drastically reduced numbers." Romulus hesitated. "Many were killed in the initial attack. Many more were hunted down."

"Why?"

"They were known to be helping your embassy, at least indirectly."

Harry took the news with, for him, a notable lack of reaction: he seemed oddly still. "I see. And what have they reported about the conditions under which Frank and Giovanna are being held?"

"Not much. Frank was evidently wounded; some injury to one hand is speculated, and he has either lost a leg, or at least temporarily lost the use of it."

"Damn." Lefferts kicked at a tuft of hay. "That complicates things. What about Giovanna?"

"She was not injured, but of course is carrying a child. She is now four to five months pregnant."

"Gotta move fast," Harry muttered to no one.

Romulus stared at him. "'Move fast?' Signor Lefferts, do you have any idea how formidable a structure the Palazzo Rospigliosi is?"

"No."

"It is very formidable. Very large. Many, many halls, rooms, salons." He looked around the stable. "I mean no disrespect, but your group seems very small for the task."

"Maybe. But there are a lot of ways to stage a prison break. And not all of them require a frontal attack with superior numbers. As a matter of fact, that's the kind of strategy we always try to avoid."

"Well, your methods are none of my business, but I must point out: we do not know where in the complex your friends are being held."

"Do you have a map, a floor plan?"

"Not such as you mean. We have only a few crudely mapped sections that former servants have been able to describe from memory. And I would not approach the present servants for additional information, if I were you."

"Why?"

"They might be cat's-paws, bait. Most of the servants live on the premises. This is not uncommon; it aids in the security of any palazzo to minimize traffic from the world beyond its walls. However, if they suspect that any group—rescuers such as yourselves, for instance—is trying to gather current intelligence about its interior—"

"Then they might put a tail on any servants leaving the premises, track them to a meeting with my people, and preemptively hit us before we can hit them."

"Precisely."

"Well," mused Harry, rubbing his chin, "looks like this might be a worthy challenge for the Wrecking Crew, after all."

# Chapter 15

Ferrigno sidled carefully into Cardinal Gaspar de Borja y Velasco's immense office and cleared his throat. "Señor Dolor has arrived. Most punctually. He has brought an associate. Should I have the second man wait outside?"

Borja nodded, and experienced a sensation that he did not recognize for a long moment: a brief pang of fear. Fear? Fear of a subordinate?

But, Borja admitted, Dolor was not the average subordinate. He was not merely unusually efficient and egoless; he was—well, unusual. And the first inquiries Borja had made about him among his senior officers, and those Spanish cardinals who kept close tabs on the coming and goings and changes in Philip's Court, had provided no useful information: a few had heard his name. None knew anything about him.

Dolor was the very antithesis of Quevedo, who had been happiest when everyone knew his name, his deeds, his fame. Francisco de Quevedo y Villega had been an insufferable braggart, relying upon—and endlessly crowing about—his twinned gifts of inspiration and improvisation. Alas, he had had a reasonable foundation upon which to build his flights of self-congratulatory fancy: his 1631 comedy (he usually neglected to mention his co-author Mendoza) *Who Lies Most Thrives Most*, had been concocted in a scant twenty-four hours for Philip IV's Saint John's Day fete,

142

and debuted in the shadow of the Prado. However, Quevedo afterward demonstrated even greater inventiveness in finding opportunities for bringing mention of this triumph into almost every conversation.

Dolor was, in contrast, a nonentity, a shadow—and twice as disconcerting because he was. Borja turned to face the door as the man in question entered. His bow was deep enough to be adequate, but not an iota more. "Your Eminence," he said quietly.

Borja remained seated. "Señor Dolor. You have new information?"

"And activity reports."

"Such as?"

"The doctor assigned to the prisoners indicates that he believes Frank Stone is now well enough to be moved about freely without danger to his leg. We are preparing their next and final point of incarceration now, as well as the special move whereby we will transfer them to that place."

Borja tidied several papers peevishly. "I indulge you in this, Dolor, because of your proven competencies in other regards. I do not see the purpose of all this moving about. We could have left them in their first prison safely enough. It is, after all, the kind of dank hole they deserve, and escape was impossible."

"Escape will be impossible only if we take strong steps to make it so."

"So you tell me. Could we not make this simpler? You may have more men, if you need them. Many more."

"What I need, Your Eminence, is your patience and your continued trust. Stearns will make an attempt to free Stone and his wife. Indeed, I believe some of my new reports tentatively confirm that such plans are afoot."

Borja sat up straighter. "Explain."

"It seems that most of the USE force that aided Simpson's group outside Chiavenna did not withdraw at all, but came south, and entered Venetian territory. We found evidence they used a trail to skirt south around Chiavenna itself and then followed the lakes down in the direction of Bergamo."

"And so you conjecture—?"

"That at least some of those troops intend to come here, Your Eminence."

"Even if that were true, what could such a small group hope to accomplish against a strongly held palace?"

Dolor shrugged. "You heard what happened at the Tower of London?"

Borja frowned. "So you believe that the USE, that Stearns, is foolish enough to send this, this—Harry Lefferts—here? To free Stone's son? That would be madness."

Dolor nodded, but his comment did not gush with ready agreement: "I'm sure the English thought the same thing. But rest assured, Your Eminence, the steps I am taking currently will prevent a repeat of the Tower of London debacle. I am more concerned about the possibility that some of these troops have been sent to the Venetian Republic for purposes of protection, not assault."

"So you still do not believe that Ambassador Nichols and the remainder of her staff will fall back upon their larger embassy in Venice. Why?"

"Because they have not done so yet."

"What? You have confirmed this?"

"I have."

Borja waited for the explanation, then realized Dolor's laconic tendencies would require prompting by a direct request: "How do you know?"

"I have agents in place there. And as of two days ago, there was still no sign of the ambassador or any of her known associates at the Venetian embassy."

"As of two days ago? How did you get this report so quickly? Have you procured radios of your own?"

"No. My Venetian agents located and secured the confidential services of the owners of two dovecotes, one in Venetian territory, one in Bologna. The terminus on the Roman end is a day's ride into the Lazio, but between the two, the birds provide us with coded intelligence that is only two days old."

"Impressive," admitted Borja, who also found Dolor's almost mechanically perfect foresight more than slightly disconcerting. A man like this could become dangerous to whomsoever he chose. The cardinal smoothed his robes and reflected: he would have to be very careful about what he chose to discuss with Pedro Dolor in order to minimize his own future vulnerability. "And so if the remnants of the USE's Rome embassy are not going to Venice, what do you suspect they are doing?"

"I suspect that they are establishing a new secure site. Which is why I suspect many of the USE troops who rescued Simpson are now in Italy: to become the defensive force for Ambassador Nichols and whoever is with her."

Borja did not like the sound of that last clause. "And who do you think might be with her? Urban?"

"It is possible."

"Why? Do you suspect that Urban had a secret arrangement with these Satan-spawned up-timers, that there was prior coordination between them?"

Dolor frowned. "Coordination? No, nothing formally prearranged. Had that been the case, Urban would have been evacuated earlier, probably in conjunction with the embassy's own personnel."

"So why and how would Urban have gone over the border into Venetian territory and joined the ambassador?"

"There are many possible reasons, but this much is clear: if Urban has indeed escaped, where would he go *besides* Venice? Spain has dominion in Naples and Milan. The Lazio is subject to our searches and patrols, and he would be a fool to stay so close to Rome. Tuscany would be the sheerest stupidity; Maffeo Barberini made enemies of the Medicis early in his papacy. Bologna is too diffident and splintered for him to be sure that he will not be betrayed to you. And the Papal States are weak, and the papal troops will not eagerly support a pontiff who cannot pay them and whose status as pope grows ever more questionable."

Borja frowned. "Which leaves us with Venice."

Dolor nodded. "Yes, Venice. Where the USE already has an embassy. Where Frank Stone's father has growing business relationships and influence. Where they would find it particularly easy to land their largest plane—the one that sets down on a cushion of air—directly on the lagoon."

"And so you believe Urban hopes to escape that way?"

"It is the only way out of Italy that Spain's forces cannot block. And the up-timers would be most eager to have Urban VIII further indebted to them."

Borja's affirmation was guttural. "And it would give Urban the excuse he has always wanted to consort freely with them and their heretical Swedish overlord. Urban may have been sitting upon the *cathedra*, but he was always ready to get down on his knees whenever the Swede deigned to dictate policy to Mother Church. But no longer."

If Dolor was moved by the stirring rhetoric, he gave no sign of it. "In short, Your Eminence, we will need to remain watchful in all places, but particularly Venice, while your men continue to dig through the rubble of the Hadrian's Tomb. If, upon turning the last stone, they still find nothing, and my confidential agents have also found nothing, we will need to revisit our course of action in this matter."

"What do you mean?"

"I mean that if Urban was blown into small pieces, how will we ever know that was his fate, rather than an escape? We may have to accept that God has decided to deny us certainty."

"Your point is well-taken, Señor Dolor. But this is my decision: we will search for Urban VIII until his body is found. Or our savior comes again."

"Your Eminence, that could be an expensive proposition. Very expensive."

"I need no schooling in the expense of such operations. But more to the point, I am quite expert in appreciating the methods required to pursue the enemies of Mother Church. And of all possible enemies, the most dangerous are traitors. So if we must keep a day and night watch upon the USE's Venetian embassy, then we must. No matter the cost."

"Constant, close surveillance would probably be detected, and thereby, defeat its own purpose. Happily, I also very much doubt it is required, Your Eminence. Has there ever been an embassy in which there is not at least one individual willing to sell important information for the right price?"

Borja smiled tightly. "Foreign offices are rarely schools of virtue. So, let us presume you are right: that the ambassadora Nichols is sheltering Urban and others of his retinue. Then why have the Americans not already flown down in one of their massive, heretically named Jupiter airplanes?"

Dolor frowned, nodded. "I have wondered the same thing."

"And your conclusions?"

"Let us call them my conjectures. It could be that the Americans intend on doing just that, but either do not have all the desired passengers in hand yet, or are simply keeping them in an undisclosed location until the plane arrives. At which point they see to it that the passengers will arrive in Venice just before the plane departs, in order to make a quick escape."

"You must take preventative steps against such an eventuality."

For the first time, the faintest hint of a smile rippled at the corner of Dolor's mouth.

"Ah. So this is already in hand." Borja smoothed his cassock again. "Do you have other conjectures?"

Dolor pursed his lips for a moment, then said, "Not exactly, but I am troubled by the *number* of USE troops that apparently headed into Italy after the action outside Chiavenna. Why bring in so many security personnel if Ambassadora Nichols' important guests are soon to fly away in an airplane? And why send Simpson and his rather important companions home though a risky transalpine route *first*, rather than waiting for the plane? And why not escort Ginetti down here separately for the same aerial extraction?"

"Perhaps the USE's large aircraft cannot be spared for a trip to Venice."

"I think not, Your Eminence. Even though the largest aircraft are in constant demand throughout the USE, the events here must certainly warrant the speedy redeployment of at least one of their Jupiters."

Borja frowned. "Yes. It is strange, all this running about when they have these wondrous aircraft. There is something missing here. What do you think it is?"

"I do not know, Your Eminence. But I begin to wonder if one of our central assumptions might be flawed."

"What do you mean?"

"Can we be sure that Urban does indeed wish to depart Italy at this time? Even if he means to leave eventually, is there anything he might achieve by delaying that departure?"

Borja scoffed. "You need not trouble yourself with that baseless speculation, Señor Dolor. The man who has forever soiled the papal title 'Urban VIII' remains the back-stabbing, nepotistic, heretic-lover who was born under the name Maffeo Barberini. And you may be sure that his nature will not change: he will forever love his pretty furnishings and his Church-wrecking cronies almost as much as he loves spending money like a drunken sailor. But he loves one thing more—far more—than any of these."

"And what is that, Your Eminence?"

"His contemptible hide. The man is a coward, has always wrung his hands looking for peace and accommodations when it was clearly Mother Church's duty to wage war to protect her interests and her flock. He is a coward and a turncoat and will flee behind his Swedish pimp's skirts at the very first opportunity."

Dolor had raised one eyebrow but said nothing.

Still caught up in his ire, Borja snapped, "Is that all?"

Dolor nodded. "Yes, Your Eminence."

"Very well. Keep me apprised of any new developments. You may go."

As Pedro Dolor emerged from behind the absurdly tall doors of Borja's office, the short man who had accompanied him on his first visit to the Villa Borghese rose from an upholstered chair farther down the hall. When Dolor reached him, the fellow fell in beside his captain, observing, "If Borja is going to converse with everyone as though he is issuing a public declaration, he needs to get thicker doors." Dolor did not answer; they walked on together for a few more steps. "Does he really intend to kill Urban?"

"Borja has reportedly killed sixteen cardinals, although some may only be languishing in hidden dungeons. Either way, he does not seem like a man who stops at half measures."

"Maybe not, but he does seem fond of putting a legal gloss on his atrocities. As I hear it, all those dead red hats were killed resisting arrest. Funny: I didn't think there were that many brave cardinals in the whole Church."

"There never have been and everyone knows it. And of course Borja would prefer Urban VIII dead rather than alive. As you probably heard, he wants to keep searching for him until we find the living man, the dead body, or the returned Christ sitting on top of the Sistine Chapel."

"So do we recruit for a full search of Venetian territory now, and—?"

"No. We don't have any intelligence to act upon yet. We don't even know where to look."

"But you just said that Borja ordered you to—"

"Dakis, when your lord tells you to kill a pig that's ruining his vines, you do his bidding, but you don't consult him about how to do it. Like as not he'd steer you wrong or get you killed. That's why the best lord just gives you the order and leaves you to your business."

"And is Borja such a lord?"

"No, but we'll make sure he behaves like one."

# Chapter 16

"There's the Laguna Veneta."

Klaus nodded at his copilot's announcement. He measured the *Jupiter Two*'s sideways drift again, then began the long, lazy bank that would bring the four-engined aircraft 180 degrees about. When the turn was completed, they would be set up at the head of a landing run that would end near the litter of small islands that sheltered Mestre's far western warren of docks and warehouses.

As they started over the lagoon, well to east of Venice itself, Klaus called for a wind check. Arne was a little slower in making his reports than most junior copilots, but he was never wrong; he would have been typecast as the tortoise in any staged rendition of Aesop's fable of that creature's race with the rabbit. "Two knots from the southeast. Very steady."

"Good." And it was. Landing the Jupiter in Venice was, in some ways, very easy: the lagoon was a large, calm body of water which made it particularly friendly to the immense plane's unusual air-cushion landing gear. But if the winds were running in off the Adriatic as they often did, and were strong, then it was safer touching down from the north approach; a nose wind increased lift and was a little more forgiving with the air-cushion landing gear.

And Klaus Kohlbacher was happy for any little advantage. Having started his aviation career flying on smaller craft with

conventional, wheeled landing gear, he had never taken to the ACLG. Of course, he had always kept his misgivings to himself; there weren't a lot of jobs for pilots, to put it lightly. And being a pilot had become his dream the first time he saw one of the up-timers' wondrous aircraft: to make his living among the clouds as a "knight of the air," as his enthusiastic young nephew put it. So Klaus had resolved never to voice any reservations that might reduce the confidence his employers placed in his abilities.

But sometimes, it had been hard to contain his misgivings about the Jupiter—or more particularly, its landing gear. Flying the aircraft was, admittedly, the aerial equivalent of piloting a river barge; it was ponderous and did not respond well to frequent or abrupt course changes. But the Jupiter was strong and steady and surprisingly reliable for such an ambitious multiengine design. So what if she wasn't a high-spirited and agile Arabian mare? She was a sturdy and strong Percheron.

"Surface conditions?" Klaus asked as their turn brought them around to the south of the island of Venice itself, where galleys and noas and carracks and billow-sailed sloops jockeyed for berthing positions in what, at this altitude, appeared to be a graceful but very slow dance.

"Water surface is smooth," answered Arne. "Nothing more than wind ripples."

Which meant all signs were good for the southern landing approach, which would put them just a few hundred yards away from the shallow ramp leading up to the new hangar and shop facilities. "Excellent. We will be landing from the south. Test the blower motor."

Arne nodded. "Testing blower motor." He checked that subsystem's dials, and threw the starter switch with the choke set wide open.

A faint, thin vibration added itself to the customary thrums, growls, and jiggles of the immense aircraft.

"Blower motor tests as ready; shutting off."

The blower motor, which had started its up-time existence spinning the blades of a lawn mower, slept again; the faint vibration disappeared.

"Confirm bearing for final approach."

"Confirmed."

Klaus nodded and brought the plane out of its long banking

turn, nose pointed north toward the low, rambling wharves of Mestre. As soon as the level indicators settled, he checked the slight leftward drift and started easing the four-engined biplane down toward the blue-green water scudding past below.

Although Tom was the one who had asked for the meeting, he arrived twenty minutes late. Miro rose to greet him.

"Hey, Estuban; you're here early. Or am I late?"

"I don't really know," Miro lied.

"Oh, damn. So I *am* late. Sorry. Seems I'm always running behind now." Tom looked out over the Laguna Veneta, which seemed to gather itself to the foot of the belvedere-crested villa upon which they stood. His eyes got dreamy, the way Miro noticed they did when he hovered on the edge of an up-time reminiscence.

"Y'know," Stone drawled, turning his whole body toward the water, almost as if he were addressing it, "I used to hate wearing watches. Seemed that everywhere you looked, up-time, there was a clock. Telling you how many minutes you have left before you have to do this, or do that, or wake up, or go to sleep. No freedom, man; slaves to the clock. But when we got here—"

He raised his wrist; the up-time watch upon it looked like a strange bracelet with a cheap inset stone of grayed onyx. "This thing used to tell the time, do simple math like a computer, record notes: everything. Funny. I hated it, only wore it occasionally. Mostly to please my boys, since they were the ones who gave it to me. But when I got here—it was like a treasure." He looked at the face of the watch, which Miro knew was made of the unusual up-timer material known as plastic. "But now it's dead. No batteries for it. Never will be, either. And still I wear it. Like a gift from the ancient astronauts; like I'm a cargo-cultist of my own making." He realized even before seeing the carefully blank and patient expression on Miro's face, that he had lost the down-timer in the dense verbal thicket of his own esoteric references. "Sorry. But look, here's lunch"—cheese, loaves, and sausages were arrayed on the table—"and we've got the best seat in the house." He pointed out over the lagoon. "Have you ever seen one of these Monsters land?"

"No."

"Quite a sight, even from this distance. There it is now." Tom pointed to the south, where a cruciform speck was easing from a long sweeping turn into level flight.

They were both silent for a time. Tom looked at his shorter companion and smiled, a bit crookedly. "Aren't you going to ask me?"

"About what?"

"About the balloon project we were talking about."

Miro shrugged. "I presumed that if you wished to discuss the matter, you would bring it up. There is no reason to rush."

"See, Estuban, that's what I like about you. One of the things I like, anyway. You're not like other businessmen. Here in Venice business is all very cordial, all very careful, and always in play. You never talk about anything without talking about business, too. 'And your family, are they well?' sounds like someone just being friendly and concerned, but it's also a way of finding out if you're distracted, if your focus on some upcoming deals is wavering, if you're contemplating pulling back from commerce for a while. But with you, it's different."

Miro shrugged. "I am not Venetian. And I am not here as a businessman. Except opportunistically, peripherally."

"See, they don't have any 'peripheral' business, here. In Venice, you may not even be in business—but you still are. You're a soldier, a judge, a scribe, a navigator? Fine, but that's not just your profession; that's also your basis of barter. Everybody is looking for a little fee if you want access to what or who they know. Seems to be the Venetian way."

Miro smiled. "It does indeed."

"Guess you've dealt with it a lot over the years, huh?"

"Some," Miro understated mightily.

"So about the balloons..."

Klaus watched the airspeed indicator fall slowly, felt the slight increase in leftward drift even before Arne reported: "Wind rising a little; now at three knots. And coming about. More from due south."

Of course. Intermittent siroccos and the Adriatic's own peculiar weather and currents were adding to the fun. Nothing stayed very steady very long over the springtime waters of Venice.

The drift diminished, but the right-rear tailwind was now starting to boost the Monster's airspeed, even as her leftward drift decreased. Just what you want during a landing: shifting winds.

He throttled back the engines a tiny bit, brought the nose up a degree—a little earlier than he'd intended, but he had to counteract the accelerating effects of the tailwind....

Miro watched the speck wobble a little as it seemed to settle itself into a straight run, growing slowly larger as it drew closer to the surface of the water.

"First I had to find out which people might be interested in balloons here in Venice. Turns out there are a lot of them, and all with different reasons for wanting to get involved. It also seems there have been foreign agents here, nosing around."

Miro nodded. "There's a great deal of foreign interest in balloons. Hardly surprising since nations without up-time engines can start a blimp-building program and still hope for a reasonable chance of success."

Tom nodded. "From what I hear, you even helped the authorities in Grantville nab an informant. An industrial spy, as we used to call them."

Miro raised an eyebrow. "And where did you hear that?"

"Oh, the Venetians are pretty well informed. And there were some follow-up inquiries made down here. The authorities thought it was pretty strange that although the spy you found in Grantville was Venetian, and was returning here, he was *not* working for any local factors. That worries them."

"As it should. If either the Mughals or Ottomans were seeking access to balloon technology, they would move it through the Mediterranean. Given the disruption in the rest of Italy, Venice is the most likely conduit. Particularly given its unofficial, arm's-length trade relations with Istanbul."

"Yeah, I think that's what they were fretting over. That, and having too much competition in building the balloons. Although a lot of the locals aren't envisioning airships for transportation, but for coast-watching and mapping."

Miro nodded. "Logical."

"So you saw this coming?"

"It was a distinct possibility. And those activities don't require large, or even powered, dirigibles. Just a stationary one-man rig, tethered to the ground."

"Yeah, that's what they were saying. Given the piracy problems all along the Adriatic, they've already got potential interest and permissions from Ravenna, Rimini, and Ancona and are talking with communities on the Dalmatian coast. I suspect they'd send some out to their island possessions in the Aegean, as well."

Miro nodded. "And I'm glad to see that someone obviously read the letter I wrote them about mapping."

"*You* wrote?"

Miro smiled. "I just sent along some observations. Specifically, that given the low cost of its operation, and its stationary position, a balloon is vastly superior to a plane when serving as a cartographic platform. This is not the case when one has much ground to cover, of course. And given your photography, perhaps this was not so true in your up-time world. However, here, and in terms of constructing a detailed map of a limited region, a man in a balloon will be far more accurate and can easily recheck his measurements."

Tom rubbed his chin. "You know, I was talking to some of my advisers—"

—Which, Miro knew, probably meant his very business-savvy down-time wife, Magda—

"—and they say there could be a lot of money in this cartography business. A very lot of money."

Miro nodded. "Naturally. The Venetians I corresponded with already understood the military advantages of having precise maps with topographic renderings. And it only took a little extrapolation for them to foresee the balloon's wider benefits in regard to surveying, prospecting, land and water management, road development, and engineering. And the uses to which they put the balloons will not only prove their utility, but whet the similar appetites of other nations."

Stone watched the Monster growing larger. "Yeah, before long, everyone is going to want high-quality maps. Of course, the big countries will only buy a few balloons each, with one held back as a prototype for copying. But by then, we'll have sold dozens."

"We?"

"Sure, 'we.' You don't think I'm going to sit on the sidelines, do you? My wife—er, advisor—speculates that we might make even more money by offering tutoring on aerial mapping methods."

"Strange." Miro rubbed his chin. "I was under the impression that you were not overly concerned with making money, Tom."

"I'm not, but how else are we going to fund the first airborne ambulances and antiepidemic airships?" He smiled. "The Venetians like that idea, too."

"I was not aware the Council of Ten had adopted such humanitarian attitudes."

"Oh, they haven't. But they realize that after the first few models are flying, almost every country is going to want at least one of their own. Probably a lot more, over time. And then I showed them your map of how to link the major cities of Europe together with flight legs of less than one hundred miles. Man, their greedy little eyes lit up like sparklers on the Fourth of July. They're pretty eager to have a business meeting. But I put that off. I hope you don't mind."

Miro nodded, understanding. "Of course. First things first. And getting your son and daughter-in-law back is the first thing."

Tom nodded and looked out over the water, clearly working at keeping the worry out of his voice and his eyes. "Yeah. And now that the Monster is here, we should be one giant step closer to achieving that."

The tailwind was holding steady, at least: no significant changes in speed or direction. Klaus made a last inspection of the stretch of water leading to Mestre: cleared of traffic, as arranged earlier, and no sign of large debris, new obstructions, or choppy crosscurrents. Perfect.

"Arne," he said, watching the rpms of the four tachometers, "inflate the bag."

Arne flipped the switch to the blower motor.

In the belly of the Monster, the blower's old lawnmower engine growled into life. But the blades it spun now were those of a big attic fan, designed to move air, not cut grass.

The sudden rush of air pushed the leather "bag" out from the small, front-lipped recess in the Monster's fuselage. Spared the constant wear of flapping in the air-stream by this small windbreak, the tough, heavily-stitched and reinforced leather now extruded from the Monster's belly, and in doing so, revealed that it was not so much a bag as it was a skirt. But, rather than rustling like the fabric of a skirt, it creaked and clunked: the typical sounds of its deployment, heard only faintly in the cockpit.

So neither Klaus nor Arne had any way of discerning the slight change in the skirt's behavior as it entered the air stream. Although frequently restitched and painstakingly watched for wear, the repeated soakings and dryings of constant salt-water landings had cost some of the pleats most of their flexibility. Like the spines of old men forced to jump up to attention, several of the most desiccated pieces of leather resisted. The sustained pressure on the stitchings, which struggled to keep the stiff pleats in trim with the flexible ones, lasted a moment too long: two of the desiccated lacings snapped. That gave the rushing wind a gap, which it exploited ruthlessly; a few more lacings weakened, and a bronze restraining rivet popped free, allowing the tearing to continue, almost up to where the skirt attached to the belly of the Monster.

With no further resistance to the varied buffetings of the air stream, the leather plenum bag, which resembled a half-donut when inflated, now moved freely, flexibly, in the wind. But it was no longer the prim, conventional skirt it was supposed to be; a provocative slit now went from bottom to top at its back....

Arne looked up. "What was that?"

"You mean that little tug?"

"Yes."

Klaus shrugged. "Once a bag has been in use for a few months, they start doing that when you push them out into the air stream."

Arne nodded. "Yes. Okay. This is the leather-wear the instructors talk about?"

Klaus nodded. "It's been taking more and more maintenance hours to keep the bags within safety limits." He didn't add that he had now heard three different ground crews muttering about those limits, wondering if they were really cautious enough.

Arne looked at the airspeed indicators again. "That bump seemed a little longer, though."

Klaus thought so too. "Probably nothing," he said, reassuring himself as much as Arne. "Probably the bag was just a little stiff coming out. That cold alpine headwind on take-off could have made everything a little less flexible."

Arne nodded. Klaus couldn't tell if the young junior copilot was genuinely convinced by this explanation, or was just being polite and agreeable. Like everything engineered at—or beyond—the limits of the currently available materials, the air cushion gear was quirky, finicky. Sometimes it made odd sounds; sometimes it got a little temperamental. But so what? It worked, didn't it?

Klaus cut the airspeed a little more, brought the nose up, watched the water come closer...

Just as the wind indicator dropped to zero.

Suddenly. Just like that. A calm cell, courtesy of the unpredictable marriage of the *sirocco* and the Adriatic.

Without the tail wind, the airspeed dropped: not much, but quickly, and at the penultimate pre-landing moment. To compensate, Klaus juiced the engines, brought the nose up a little more. But he couldn't hold that attitude for long, not with the Monster's long tail stretching so far aft of the air cushion skirt and center of gravity.

"There will be a real bump now," he commented with a thin smile.

"Yes," agreed Arne, just before they made contact.

Or should have. Instead of the breathy flounce of coming down on a fully inflated bag, there was a hiss, a burbling, and a lurch to the left rear. The Monster's tail section veered closer to the water, the left horizontal stabilizer almost grazing the surface.

"Bag failure!" snapped Klaus.

To his credit, Arne reacted without delay, helping maintain trim as Klaus re-gunned the engines, not quite rising off the surface of the water, but not coming to rest on it, either.

"Still dropping on the left," observed Arne.

"Give me a little more thrust from the outer portside engine." Klaus cheated the stick and pedals, giving a little more lift to that side.

Meanwhile, the burbling and complaining beneath them increased.

"Klaus..." began Arne.

"Oh, hell," breathed Tom as the Monster landed, shuddered, pulled up, seemed like its nose was no longer in precise alignment with its direction of travel.

"What has gone wrong?" Miro managed to swallow after he asked the question, realizing how terrible it was to watch a flying machine in such obvious peril. Particularly one as large and powerful as the Monster, which, if it truly crashed—

"Don't know. Wind maybe. But no, it seems calm. Probably that damned air cushion gear."

Miro was surprised at the vehemence with which his normally calm companion invoked the name of the landing gear. "I was not aware you had such misgivings about..."

But Tom wasn't listening; he was watching what might well be a disaster approaching. And if it didn't slow down soon, the disaster might well land straight in their laps.

"Distance to the land ramp?" Klaus did not dare take his eyes off the instruments or his senses away from the delicate balancing act he was maintaining between the pitch and yaw improvisations that kept the Monster moving forward.

"Five hundred yards. Maybe six hundred." Arne's voice was taut.

Klaus knew they weren't going to make it; every time he backed off the engines, let the Monster settle a little more, he could feel more of the skirt shredding, felt the lift diminish from the already crippled leather-bound plenum chamber that was his landing gear. Besides, the underside of the Monster would bottom out on the ramp even if he could get that far, possibly ruining the airframe. But if he cut the speed down far enough for a stop, he'd bite the water, possibly digging in the nose—and again, ruin the aircraft.

He glanced up to take his own bearings, saw the villa that the USE had purchased for the support of its Venetian air operations dead ahead, the smooth water that surrounded it on three points obscured on the left by the weed-choked shallows.

*The weed-choked shallows...*

"Arne, I want three, short, evenly pulsed revs from the starboard engines."

"But Klaus—"

"Just do it."

The roar to the right increased and died as quickly as it had risen. The plane tilted to the left again, but Klaus cheated the controls, kept both the tail and left wingtip from digging in—and the craft had altered its course by five degrees or so to the left, pushed in that direction by the lopsided engine thrust that also helped them maintain altitude and extend the time they were airborne.

Another momentary roar of the engines on the right. Then a third and longer pulse—

"Arne, bring it back!" Klaus shouted, as he struggled to keep the Monster's nose up, its tail out of the water, and its wings level—more or less.

"Klaus, we're almost into the weeds!"

Klaus nodded tightly. "Because that's where we're going. Depth here is about—what?"

"Less than three feet."

Klaus started easing off the engines, started to let the nose down ever so slightly.

"Airspeed looks good," Arne gulped out.

—Just as the remains of the skirt made contact with the water. A high-pitched burbling rose beneath them. Klaus gauged what resistance was left in the compromised plenum chamber, let the Monster travel forward another few seconds, and peripherally watched the passing weeds begin to slow in their rearward rush, enough so that he could start to make out individual fronds and stems.

"Two feet of water, no more," Arne rasped.

Klaus sighed and let the Monster settle down on what was left of her air cushion landing gear, cutting the engines.

For a moment, the leather held—a last moment of increased pressure in the bag as the fuselage came closer to the water's surface—and then it let go with a blast. A wash of sharp slaps and bumps announced its tattered chunks flying up against the fuselage.

Without power, the nose came down more quickly—but at just the same moment, the tail's horizontal stabilizers slid slowly into the water, and the lower wing kissed down as well. Arne killed the blower motor a moment before its spinning blades snarled into contact with the weed-choked swells of their landing zone.

Klaus watched the weeds and rushes collect before his slowing craft like an impenetrable wall—

And then realized that the Monster had come to a stop. And was sinking.

Before stopping at a depth of fifteen inches.

Tom's mouth was still open. "Did you see that?" he murmured at last.

*As if I could have missed it?* "Er ... yes. This catastrophe makes our plans quite—"

"No, no—did you see that piloting? Man, whoever that guy is

deserves a medal. Hell, if Mike or Ed or someone doesn't give him a medal, I'll make one especially for him. That was incredible. That plane should have crashed at least three times. Maybe four."

Miro was perplexed. "But it did. Crash, that is."

Tom turned. "That was not a crash. I mean, yeah, technically, I guess it was. But it was a crash *landing*, and a damned good one. A real crash is—well, you'd know it if you saw it. The pilot loses control, and the plane goes in. There's a big blast from the impact alone, even if there's no explosion. Pieces everywhere. Usually not many survivors. If any."

Miro looked at the plane, sitting in the shallows, half-hidden by the weeds, which were already still again. "Very well. But unless I am much mistaken, that plane is not going to be useable any time soon."

Tom nodded, then looked sideways at Miro. "Eh, Estuban, about that balloon of yours—"

Miro smiled. "I learned, while masquerading as a Christian plying the trade routes of the Mediterranean, that one should always have multiple contingency plans. I have now learned that the same is true when one is an intelligence officer overseeing a field operation."

Tom smiled back, relieved. "So your balloon is already back in Jena?"

"Actually, I had it return to Grantville, where it is now being refitted and loaded. There were personnel there I thought we might have need of. As well as equipment. And now, I suspect, repair parts for the Jupiter."

"How soon can it be back here?"

"That is always weather dependent, but on the average, not more than two weeks' travel time."

Tom nodded. "Now let's hope something doesn't break on your balloon."

"Yes, indeed. Although, it must be said: there is far less to break on a dirigible than an airplane."

"No lie," breathed Tom with a nod, and another glance at the Monster's vertical stabilizer, sticking up from the weeds like a large, dull-colored shark's fin. "I also hear you can burn just about any fuel in your balloons. Including fish oil."

"Yes, although I will not vouch for the downwind appeal of such a ride."

Tom's grin was very wide. "Might as well tell you, I'm pretty much sold on the whole balloon thing. Even given the fact that someone—well, everyone, probably—is going to use it to drop bombs. I thought about that a lot, but I still think airships are going to do more good than harm."

"Often, that is all we can ask for in life."

"Oh, we can ask for more; we just don't get it, usually. So what do these balloons cost to build? About a hundred thousand USE dollars?"

"Yes, but if you're proposing a partnership—"

"I am."

"— then I would rather we do not use your money to build more of the hot-airships."

"No?"

"No. In the next few years, I will make enough of those to meet the first wave of demand. Which will be brisk, but moderate; it takes people time to get used to new ideas."

"And then what?"

"And then we will unveil the next generation of airship, the one which we will finance with your investment." Miro smiled, looked into the sky, and imagined it filling with traffic and commerce in the decades to come. "Because that model will get its lift from hydrogen, not hot air. And that, Tom, *that* will truly change the world."

"This changes everything." Rombaldo de Gonzaga tapped his spotless fingernail upon the worn wooden tabletop like a slow, soft metronome.

Giulio, who was still out of breath from running to their rented house with the news, expelled words between his gasps: "How...so...Rombaldo?"

Rombaldo de Gonzaga suppressed a sigh. It was trying, working with amateurs, but the job in Venice was a large one, needing many hands and feet and eyes. Fortunately, his master back in Rome—a displaced Cypriot named Dakis—had no shortage of *scudare* and *reales* to pass around. "With the USE's plane damaged, they cannot remove Urban anytime soon. Nor will the aircraft be a part of any plans to rescue Stone's son in Rome. That gives us more time. That, in turn, makes our job easier. And Cesare, be sure this news is passed along to the dovecote for immediate relay. They will want this report in Rome as soon as possible."

Cesare Linguanti, a small man who rarely spoke, rose and left, making the smallest of nods toward the largest man at the table.

That man, Valentino—who denied having any other name than that—took a small sip of his wine. Valentino always had a glass of wine in hand: the one glass that he nursed all day long. "The Americans, they will repair the flying machine, if they can. And if Giulio is right, it does not sound as though the failure was catastrophic."

"Yes," nodded Rombaldo. "We will need to mount a watch on the plane, as well as the embassy and the USE's known agents. Indeed, we will need to hire many more men to watch and search. And others to wield weapons, when the target is located and the time comes."

"They will need to be special men," commented Valentino. "Not many Italians are ready to kill a pope."

"There may not be many," answered Rombaldo, "but when the pay is high enough, you'll find men enough." He leaned back with a satisfied smile. "More than enough."

Sharon found Mazzare sitting quietly with Urban. They did that a lot, these days. They didn't seem to say a lot. It was like watching dogs or cats who are new to the same house; as if they know their lives are now entwined, they start spending time together. It was both acclimation and the growth of a new camaraderie, all rolled into one.

They looked up as Sharon entered the trellised shade of the courtyard's arbor. She set her shoulders squarely. "It seems like we're going to be staying a little bit longer, after all. The Monster has crashed."

Mazzare looked up, startled. "Was anyone—?"

"No. They brought it down safely. But they're going to have to replace the landing gear."

"And that will take how long?" asked Urban.

"I'm not exactly sure, Your Holiness. I know a lot more about fixing people than I do about fixing machines. But given the parts and getting the plane out of the water and all the rest—well, I'd be surprised if we were ready any sooner than six or eight weeks."

Urban leaned back and placed his palms firmly on his knees. "Well, that settles the matter."

"What matter?"

"The matter of whether or not I should leave Italy just yet. In my pride, I failed to leave this matter in God's hands. But it seems our Savior has decided to take the decision from me—perhaps to remind me I always had the option of relinquishing it into his care."

Sharon blinked. "Your Holiness, I don't understand."

"I should not leave Italy, at least not yet. Not even if your plane was ready to fly tomorrow. Not until I know where I should go."

"And what will determine where you should go?"

"Why, by learning what I am supposed to do next."

Sharon shook her head. "But how many choices do you really have?"

"That," said Urban with a sly smile, "is what I will learn in the coming weeks—and why I am so glad you came, Lawrence." Urban smiled, rose, and headed back in the direction of the kitchen.

Sharon looked at Larry Mazzare. "What does he mean, that this is 'why he's so glad you came'?"

Mazzare shrugged. "It means—well, it means I'm just glad that Thomas North left his Hibernians behind in Venice, because we're going to need all of them to secure the new safe house that Miro set up for us through the Cavrianis."

Sharon nodded, but pressed the point. "You still haven't answered me: what can Urban do here that he can't do back in the USE?"

Mazzare looked at Sharon. "He can decide whether he should go there at all."

"What? Why?" Sharon was becoming annoyed. Not only did she still not understand what was going on, but her ignorance had her repeating herself.

"Sharon, Urban was driven out of Rome, fled for his life. Everyone in Italy can understand why he's no longer sitting in the Holy See. But if he leaves the country now, that will be his *choice*. And he's worried—rightly—that some people may feel he'd be turning his back on both his duty and the Church."

"But he can't achieve anything here except waiting around for assassins."

"We know that, he knows that, maybe even this whole country knows that. But knowing that a course of action is wise doesn't necessarily make it acceptable. And a pope is both a symbol and a representative of God. Now hear me out: I'm not requiring you to believe that yourself, just to accept that many, many others do believe it. You've heard the expression 'trust in God,' right?"

Sharon put her hands on her generous hips. "Yes. Of course I've heard it. As you know."

"Yes, I do. But you've never heard it the way people here, of this time, hear it. For most of them, that saying isn't a euphemism, isn't simply an exhortation to believe that somewhere, somehow, there might be some divine providence that will make everything all right. Here—in this time—there is nothing vague or ambiguous about trust in God. It's presumed that there is a personal God who sees and judges all actions. And for Roman Catholics, it furthermore means that the pope is God's divinely inspired voice and representative on Earth, and is therefore symbolic of the dignity and righteousness of that godhead."

"So you're saying that if Urban runs, he's indicating that he doesn't have faith that 'God will provide.'"

"That, and he will be doing a great indignity to his holy office."

"Which will make Borja look strong and resolute?"

"Well, he'll still be seen as a monster, and mistaken in his methods, but unimpeachable in his dedication to the primacy of the Church and the dignity of the papal tiara. And in these times, that means a lot. Quite a lot, actually."

"So either Urban stays and gets martyred for no real purpose, since no one has the power to unseat Borja. Or Urban leaves and gets—what? Relieved of his popish duties?"

"Something like that. But I think there's a third choice, and I think that's what Urban is focused on."

"Oh? And what is that?"

"Knowing he has to leave eventually, I think Urban is determined to make his ultimate destination a statement of resolve that outshines the fact of his departure. Urban cannot be seen as retreating; he has to attack Borja, albeit on a different front."

Sharon felt her thoughts twirl helplessly. "Attack Borja? Where? How?"

Larry Mazzare smiled his lip-crinkling smile. "That," he said with a long exhale, "is probably exactly what Urban wants to determine before he leaves Italy."

# Chapter 17

They pulled beyond the ramshackle piers and neglected sidings of Porto before the captain of the Savoyard *barque-longue* brought his long, low ship over to the right bank of the Tiber where barges were clustered. His mixed crew of French, Corsicans, and Savoyards jumped over to the makeshift wharf when they were within four feet, counter-pushed with poles, and dropped hawsers into the narrowing gap between the hull and the siding.

The final payment for passage had been handled when Ostia came into view, with John O'Neill counting out the silvers with the regretful intensity of a miser. So now, gear and pack in hand, Owen Roe O'Neill and his fellow Wild Geese departed the boat with a few halfhearted waves; they got few enough in return. The crew hadn't been unfriendly, but the language overlap had been sketchy. Owen knew enough French to get by, as did Sean Connal. The doctor had quickly become the ship's favorite, mostly because of his craft and his willingness to tend to the small crews' minor ailments.

The crew's standoffishness had no doubt been reinforced by John O'Neill's loud and resentful commentary upon the doctor's plying of his art: not in terms of his efficacy, but generosity. Specifically, the earl of Tyrone made it known that Connal's services should rightly have been offered in trade, to offset the cost of their passage. In fact, that was a fairly customary exchange, but the doctor had provided his services without striking such a bargain. He maintained that it was better to earn a little genuine good will than the price of half a fare. For his part, Owen agreed with the young doctor, but Johnnie O'Neill had made some sharp comments about Connal's undue presumptions of independence, and that the group's current circumstances did not allow them "the largesse of such gestures of *noblesse d'oblige.*" That imperious pronouncement also seemed to exhaust the earl's supply of French phrases.

Connal had merely remained silent, as had the watching crew, who thereafter kept their affairs well separate from those of their Irish passengers. They weren't unfriendly, but distant. Particularly when interacting with John.

Owen hefted his pack higher; well, that was the nature of the man. Certainly not the easiest to serve under, but by no means the worst, either. And now they had to set about finding a barge to take them the rest of the way upriver to Rome.

There was a fair amount of Spanish soldiery about, but their loose ranks were already loading on the gathered barges. Seeing the gear and pennant of the Wild Geese, a few of the Spaniards hailed the Irish, curious as to their land of origin. The answers got a few cheers, a few strange looks, one or two shrugs, but nothing negative, since the Irish mercenaries of the Spanish Low Countries were a well-known military fixture. And after all, they had returned the hails in Spanish. Had the answers been in English, or had their names been of the Anglo-Irish variety, Owen wondered what their reception would have been. Cool, at best, he conjectured.

As the barges carrying the Spaniards pulled slowly away from the wharf, Turlough Eubank returned from the cluster of Italian barges.

"What luck?" asked John.

"None, m'lord. Seems the barge master I spoke to is already waiting on a shipment of grain."

"They could have a long wait."

"No, sir. It's a Tuscan ship, due here any hour."

"And this barge master won't take a few extra coin from us to change his plans?"

"He's under Spanish contract, sir. Provisions for Rome, y'see."

"Hell and be damned, is every bloody ship here under Spanish contract?"

Owen toed a bit of stray oakum with his boot. "Could well be, Johnnie. And if the rumors on our ship had even a passing acquaintance with the truth, Florence is sending down as much grain as the Spanish will buy. At regular rates."

"So now Tuscany is Spain's lap-dog, as well?"

"Maybe. Or maybe cheap Tuscan millet is the price the Spanish are demanding in exchange for another de Medici redcap."

"So Borja's selling cardinalships, now?"

"Ah, Johnnie, it would be strange if he didn't. That's how the game is played down here."

"Well, the game stinks like a steaming melder, it does. Eubank, go check with the last barge. Maybe the Good Lord will smile on some *honest* Catholics, for a change."

"As you say, m'lord. Oh, and Dr. Connal sent word: now that we're on land again, he'll be demonstrating the new pepperbox revolver while we wait."

"Oh, he will, will he?" muttered John, who rose and stalked inland, where half of the men had gathered near a vacant farmhouse set back from the banks of the river. Suppressing a sigh, Owen followed along.

Five red roof tiles were propped up on a chest-high wall that paralleled the derelict farmhouse. Sean leveled the nose-heavy pistol and started firing. The reports were sharp and barely a second between each one. On all but the fourth shot, one of the tiles exploded into a shower of dust and fragments.

Although the range was only ten paces, Owen silently conceded that this was some pretty fair marksmanship. Particularly for a physician.

Apparently, John was not disposed to make the same concession. "I think you missed one, Doctor." John had probably intended his tone to be droll, but it had verged over into smug.

Connal did not turn. Instead, his hands moved quickly, unseating the currently loaded cylinder, swapping in a fresh one from a leather chest-pouch of sorts. He locked it in place with a quick twist of a frontal knob, and expertly popped five percussion caps onto the cylinder's five ignition ports (which, Owen had learned, the up-timers rather provocatively called "nipples"). The doctor thumbed back the hammer even as he raised the weapon, aimed, and fired.

The last tile vanished in a spray of pieces.

"My apologies about that straggler," he said as he turned to face the earl of Tyrone. "I'll be tidier next time."

One or two grunts of amusement from the watching Wild Geese faded quickly enough when John sent an annoyed glance in their direction. "Not so fast reloading as you made it sound, Doctor."

Connal nodded. "You can cut the time down by two-thirds if the percussion caps are already seated on the fresh cylinder. But carrying it that way can result in some misfires; the jostling can unseat or even ruin a cap. Not likely, but possible. Logically, it also creates a small chance of an accidental discharge while you're carrying the cylinder on your person, but that would be quite a fluke."

"And when did you learn to shoot like that, Doctor? Not while you were rehearsing the Hippocratic oath, I'll wager. Indeed, if you shot much better, I'd have to suspect it was the hypocritic oath."

There was a single, half-hearted snicker; the tone of the jest had been a bit more accusatory than it was jocular.

But Connal merely smiled. "Well, contrary to common belief, I was not destined to the medical arts from the crib onwards. Couldn't figure what trade to follow for the longest time—not until I was, oh, at least two years old." Smiles sprang up, as well as one stifled giggle. "Sad to say, but I was a late bloomer." His concluding confession got a few outright laughs—and a darker look from John.

"So you thought you'd be soldiering, then?"

"As I said, I didn't know. But when I was first at university in Leuven, Hugh—er, Lord O'Donnell, came to visit occasionally. Visiting the old alma mater, as it were. Taught me to shoot."

"Why, of course he did. No doubt paid your way at the university, too, I'll wager."

"For the space of one semester, yes, he did."

Which only made O'Neill's face darken again, this time with a scowl. Johnnie didn't like anyone allied with, or in service to O'Donnell much better than he did the "*sassenach*" Irish such as Preston. But his distaste for all things O'Donnell was in many ways the more embarrassing of his two prejudices: antipathy toward the "Old English" Irish had long, nationalistic roots. But his dislike of the O'Donnells stemmed from a much less noble trait: jealousy, plain and simple.

But John's focus on the gun had apparently distracted him from his resentment. "So how does this eye-gouging piece of rubbish work, Doctor? I've seen one or two of these up-time revolvers. They're all pretty complicated pieces of machinery."

"This is much less so," Connal explained. "The weapons to which you refer require exceptionally fine tolerances, since the cylinder holding the charge, or 'cartridge,' must align precisely with the weapon's single barrel."

O'Neill scowled. "But that thing has five barrels. All as one piece."

"Exactly. This means that each of the chambers is designed exactly like a self-contained barrel and breech. They are arranged in a pentagram, as you see."

"There you go: witchcraft for sure."

"Hardly," smiled Connal. "Just as with the up-time revolvers you've seen, when you pull back the weapon's hammer—or, in this case, a larger crossbar—it rotates the cylinder." He demonstrated; the weapon made a monstrous clacking sound as the cylinder turned. "The percussion cap of a new barrel has now moved into the position occupied by the last one. When the trigger is squeezed and the hammer falls, it ignites the charge in the new barrel. You can fire five times before reloading."

Owen nodded. "But I've heard Dutch clockmakers complain that when they try to copy up-time devices like this, they can't make the springs strong enough. How did you avoid that problem here?"

"The gunsmiths used larger, cruder springs, which led, in part, to the cumbersome size of the weapon. The only spring that still has a great deal of resistance upon it is the one that turns the cylinder. And if that breaks—" He manipulated a small knob protruding from the end of the cylinder, as if unlocking it, and then turned the entire unit by hand. "Still quite a lot faster than having to reload after every shot."

John was clearly working at keeping the scowl on his face and his growing interest off. "Sure and it's the seventh wonder of the world, Dr. Connal, but you'll not get me to use one of these monstrosities." But Owen knew otherwise: he could hear the reluctant fascination in the earl of Tyrone's voice.

"That will be as you wish, Lord O'Neill. But you might wish to reconsider. The hammer is large and heavy so that a rider can manipulate it easily, even with a gauntlet on."

"So that's why it has a crossbar all the way across, rather than a single hammer?"

"Exactly. It's easier to get a hold of. And given the springs used, it is easier to cock the weapon with a whole-hand pull on the crossbar."

Owen considered carefully. "Yes, and it would also be useful if you're trying to cock the weapon on horseback. You could even snag the bar on a saddle-hook and push the whole weapon downward to prime the action."

"True enough, but there's a more important advantage to the crossbar. Look at the vertical thumb tab at the center of the bar. What do you see?"

John squinted. "Hmmm. There's a small hole, right where the tab and the bar meet."

"Precisely. Just before it meets the crossbar, the vertical tab splits into two parts, rather like a Y standing on its head. The resulting triangle—the space between the arms of the upside-down Y and the top of the crossbar—is left open. If one aims through that aperture—what the up-timers call a 'peep sight'—you'll see a small bead at the end of the barrel that is ready to fire."

Owen nodded. "So when the bead is on your target, and also in the center of the peep-sight—"

"You are properly aligned."

"And how accurate is it?"

"Like comparable flintlock pistols, its accurate aimed range is just under ten yards. However, if loaded with a charge of four single-aught pellets, the odds of scoring at least one hit on a target at twenty yards is almost fifty percent."

"Useless until you're almost at sword range," griped John, even though he hadn't taken his eyes off the weapon for about a minute.

"Aye, but most useful in trenches. Or in a city," emended Owen. "Particularly with five barrels. So it's a smoothbore then, Doctor?"

"Yes; the bore is almost half an inch. Properly charged—the craftsmen are still experimenting with 'sabots' that the up-timers use to increase the velocity of smaller bullets—a shot from this weapon will routinely penetrate a steel cuirass at ten yards."

Eubank approached from the wharf. John raised his chin. "What's the word, Turlough? Will we be walking to Rome, then?"

"Only if you get seasick sailing upriver on the Tiber. Imagine my shock when the last bargeman said he could take our custom."

"Sounds too good to be true," speculated Owen with a long look at Turlough.

"Well, Colonel, on my mother's grave I swear it's true. But it's none too good."

John cocked his head sideways. "And why would that be?"

Eubank shifted his feet uncomfortably. "Seems the bargeman's most recent passengers left the boat a bit of a mess."

"Ah," exhaled Owen. "Gypsies?"

"*Sassenachs*?" asked John.

"Goats," Eubank replied. "Far too many goats."


Harry Lefferts peeked out from under the hood of his monk's habit as the wagon rocked and then jolted sideways. The yellow-tan dust settled long enough for him to see green fields. In the middle distance, those expanses gave way to vines and olive trees that straggled up a low, rocky ridge. It was the same scenery that Harry had been watching for two days now, ever since they began their westward travel on the Via Prenestina. At the start, near Palestrina, the land had been less flat, so there had been more trees and vines, and occasional expanses of scrub given over to goats.

But other than that, not much to see. One or two of the Wrecking Crew had perked up when they passed near the old Roman aqueducts. Sherrilyn had been particularly enthusiastic. Gerd had counterpointed her exclamations with sharp, snorting snores from the rear of the wagon. Disguised as a motley assortment of clerics, farmers, and teamsters, their load of wheat and rice provided an effective layer of concealment under which they had secreted their equipment and weapons. And those who did not look at all like the locals had to keep themselves more completely concealed most of the time.

In Harry's case, this meant nearly head-to-toe covering around the clock, since, having been the visual as well as behavioral inspiration for Rome's *lefferti*, he was conspicuously recognizable in this region. Which meant that he had come to learn that monks' habits were not comfortable; in addition to being itchy and rough, they were beastly hot. It had taken a while for the slight increase of traffic to register through the heat-drowsy boredom into which Harry had sunk. He leaned back toward the driver's seat and drawled. "Are we there yet?"

He could hear Sherrilyn's grin as she interjected, in a shrill *hausfrau* voice from the other side of the wagon. "Zip it; we'll get there when we get there."

Romulus, who clearly did not understand the up-time reference to admonishing whining kids in the back seat of a car, did not find Sherrilyn's retort humorous. He merely shrugged. "See for yourself."

Harry turned and tipped up the rim of his habit's hood. In the distance, so flat on the land that the Tiber was invisible from this modest height, the greater edifices of eastern Rome rose up through the city's own mid-morning haze like a gang of hunched gray giants. Red tiled roofs tilted this way and that around their bent knees. The road they were on apparently led toward the lap of one of the closer stone edifices. Harry nodded at it. "That's the gate?"

"The Porta Maggiore," muttered Romulus as he pulled the wagon to the side of the road and coaxed the pair of rickety old horses to a halt, "or the Porta di Santa Croce, as some prefer. At any rate, now that I can see it, I have reached the point beyond which I may not be seen." As arranged earlier, he handed the reins and long switch over to Matija.

Harry nodded his thanks to their taciturn guide, and smiled. "Not welcome in Rome?"

"Not until the occupiers leave. I will remain at the appointed place for four days. If I have not heard from you by then, I will return to Palestrina, presuming you have no further need of my services."

"Yeah, we may take a boat straight back."

"Or you may be dead," added Romulus philosophically. "*Arrivederci.*" Hat pulled well down beneath his eyes, the man whose real name they had yet to learn walked back the way they had come.

The wagon rumbled into motion again, setting up a drift of dust that hung in the air for a few seconds. When it settled, Romulus was nowhere to be seen, although the road ran on so straight and far that it seemed to disappear into the infinity of its own vanishing point.

# Chapter 18

John O'Neill was able to keep back the tears until the barge drew round the last bend in the Tiber and he saw the Ponte Emilio, which Romans were now starting to call the Ponte Rotto, or Broken Bridge. It had been broken forever, like most things in Rome, but there was something particularly forlorn about it now. Its single proudly-carved arch, the only one remaining, now led boldly to nowhere. As if cut by the cleaver of a giant, the bridge no longer spanned the Tiber, but stopped in its midst; there was no way to tell whether it commemorated a dream abandoned before completion, or one that had fallen into decay.

John wiped his eyes on his sleeve and wondered at the changes that had come over Rome. He had only spent a few weeks there, and his ostensible reason for going—studies—had been both a threadbare excuse and a dismal failure. But the city had left its mark on him, had whispered to him of empires. And with all the exuberance of youth, he embraced only half of the timeless lesson about empires: that they did indeed rise. The sad truth that empires also fell was of concern only to those who were born to be beaten, who lacked the valor to take what was theirs, who doubted that God was on their side and guiding their sword and scepter.

Luke Wadding, along with the other priest-lecturers at St. Isidore's, had striven, mightily, to temper Johnnie's embrace of such mundane glory and destiny. They offered him visions of the divine Empire of God and Trinity, of the Christian conquest of hearts not bodies, of the power of the cross—and yes, the pen—over that of the sword.

But John O'Neill, third earl of Tyrone, had remained dubious of these pacifistic pieties. For him, the story of God's role in the fate of man lost its appeal after the Old Testament, and did not regain it until the records of the Crusades. His one complaint with military life was that there was entirely too much thinking and talking over what to do, and how to do it, and who might be angered. Soldiering was in the doing of deeds, not the conceiving of them. And, being a soldier born and bred, he knew well enough how and when to act.

But seeing Rome this way—sullen, gray, singed around the edges—left him uncertain how to act or feel. Rome had never been a quiet city, or a clean city, or a kind city. It had been loud and crowded and tempestuous—but it had always been very much alive. The average Roman never stopped long enough to look at the monuments of their past; they were too busy scavenging them for pieces with which they could build their future. John liked that about Romans, and so the ruins had never seemed sad or melancholy.

Until now.

As the barge moved toward the left bank, making easier headway in the lee of the current that accelerated as it swept around the Isola Tiberina on both sides, Owen Roe came to stand by his first cousin, once removed. "Are you feeling quite well, Johnnie?"

John nodded. "My body is fine, but my heart; my heart... My God, look what they've done, Owen. The Spanish bastards. First, playing us as fools for years, and now this. Look at all the burned houses, the broken walls. It will be years—no, decades—in the fixing. Damn us, damn *me*, that I ever served the Spanish. If I could do it over again—"

"Calm now, Johnnie. As Isabella said, not all the Spanish meant to mislead us. Just as I doubt many of the Spaniards arrived in Rome thinking they'd do this—" He glanced in the direction of the decapitated bulk of the Castel Sant'Angelo.

"No, maybe this wasn't what they intended, or even what they wanted, but they did it right enough anyhow, didn't they?"

Owen shook his head as the barge bumped to a stop against a row of hawsers and the warm-weather stink wafted down to them from where the effluent of the Cloaca Maxima dumped the city's wastes into the Tiber. "Can't say that we always made much better distinctions than the Spanish did during our own campaigning, Johnnie. I'm sure enough regretting things we did in the Provinces. Orders notwithstanding. Might well have been the same here."

"Maybe," said John, watching a half-dozen morion-helmeted occupiers stagger off in the direction of the Borgo, bottles of wine dangling loosely in their fingers. "But I'm not exactly sensing an undercurrent of regret." He hopped over the low gunwale of the barge. "Have the men gather their gear and be ready."

"Are we in a rush, John?"

"Aye. We need to find lodging, rest, and then move as soon as possible."

"Why?"

"Why?" John looked around at the sagging skyline of Rome, the almost empty streets. "Because that damned battle-axe Isabella was right about something else: if the Spanish did this to a lovely old city, who knows what they might do to a lovely old priest like Luke Wadding?"

Once the door closed behind the invariably sour doctor, Frank turned to Giovanna. "See? I told you my fever was gone."

Giovanna—small, dark, curvaceous, part-Madonna, part-hellion, and just starting to show—pouted. As only she could. "So. Very well. Maybe he is right."

"He is a doctor," Frank pointed out.

"He is a Spaniard and a tool of the Inquisition," Giovanna countered.

"Okay, so he's one of the bad guys, but he seems pretty conscientious. And besides, I think they want me well enough so they can move us again."

She eyed the valises and chests that had been brought in during the doctor's visit. "Because they gave us some containers in which to put our clothes?"

Frank shrugged. "That. But only partly. I was thinking more of the good doctor's visits. Four in the past week, one of which was yesterday, and then today's. That's not just medical prudence; that's a detailed assessment of our readiness to relocate. That's why he wanted to examine you, too."

"The pig. As if I would let—"

"I don't think the Spanish brought any midwives with them, Gia. And I don't think they're going to permit any contact between us and the locals. They've created what we used to call an information firewall."

Giovanna's wonderful, alluring pout was back. "What does this mean, an 'information firewall'?"

"It means that they are making sure that there's no communication between us and the outside world. I'll bet even the guards are specially selected for this duty: probably bunked apart from the others, so that there's no word of us even in barracks gossip—which frequently winds up repeated in bordellos."

Giovanna's head rose to a condemning (if modest) height upon her shoulders. "And how would you know what transpires in bordellos, husband?"

"I read about it. In books. A long time ago. Before I hit puberty. When I was thinking of becoming a priest." She couldn't help but smile. "Is that okay, then?"

"Just barely," she allowed, and then curled up against him like a cat that has decided to use its favorite person as a private cocoon.

After they had enjoyed that closeness for a few minutes, Frank stirred a bit. "Hey. I'd better start packing."

"You? And what makes you think you are ready to pack chests and valises?"

"Gia, I'm not a cripple—"

"No, but you could be!" She got off him like a cat, too: one fast jump and she was four feet away, glaring down, hands on hips. "You will not put weight on your leg. Not yet. No, do not argue. This is not open to discussion." And with that, she turned her back on him sharply and set about the task of packing their sparse belongings with an energy that would have put a sugar-infused ten-year-old to shame. After a time, once her histrionic ire had abated a bit, she asked over one hurrying shoulder. "Why do you think they are moving us again?"

Frank shrugged and put his arms behind his head. "Not sure."

"Do you think it is to make us harder to find? Are they playing a version of—what have you called it?—the shell game?"

"Yeah, but every time we get moved, it calls attention to us. And why move us during the day?"

"I do not know. Could they mean to advertise our presence in Rome?"

"I don't know." Frank sat up, feeling irritability attach itself to him like a small dog that had affixed itself to his trouser leg. "Damn it, I just don't know anything, sitting here. Which is the worst part of being a prisoner. It's not so much that you can't get out, but that you have no knowledge of what's going on out there—" he waved a hand at a wall "—and no way to let them know that you're in here. Wherever 'here' is. It makes me feel, well—I don't know: helpless."

"Well, you are not helpless. You must be strong, so first you had to regain your health. And you have accomplished that. Almost."

"Yeah, well I'm not as strong as you, yet."

"Of course not. You never will be. I am a woman. Except for your arms and chest, we are in all ways the stronger sex. We can endure far more than you can."

Frank discovered that the way she said it—gaze imperious, head and shoulders back, and therefore, other anatomical highlights thrust forward—had been at least as arousing as it had been informative. Almost before he was aware of it, Frank's body pushed forward its own, suddenly awakened anatomical highlights.

Giovanna noticed the reaction with a smile. "We can endure more of that, too. Much more."

"Don't I know it."

"Stop! Stay where you are! You will not move! Not without your crutches. And if you are very cooperative, I may agree to test your—endurance—tonight. All in the interest of ensuring your return to health, of course."

"Of course." He loved it when she smiled that way: the sweetness of an angel infected by the leer of a demon. And a hotter temper than the two put together. But it wasn't just temper: it was passion. Passion—

"Frank! No! And I mean it! Now, we must think what to do after you have made your recovery."

"What to do?" He looked at the walls. They were clean, with some reasonably comfortable pieces of furniture pushed up against them. But they were still prison walls. "I think it will take us a pretty long time to tunnel out of any prison. Hey, maybe that's why they move us, to make sure we don't make too much progress digging our way out with the soup spoons we've cleverly hidden from our warders . . ."

Giovanna grinned widely and Frank decided, for probably the

third time that day, that he really did love her wide, full, lips. "Very funny, Frank. You do have a way with words." She thought. "Which is probably the next thing you should be doing."

"What?"

"Writing. For the cause."

Frank stared at her. At times, she was very much activist Antonio Marcoli's daughter: passionate, charismatic, and wildly impractical. "Uh...Gia, assuming I could even get writing materials, just how do you expect me to get the word to the waiting masses?"

She ignored his gentle facetiousness, rode over it with a raised chin. "The greatest revolutionary tracts have often been written by person unjustly imprisoned by an oppressive state."

Hmmm...maybe not so impractical, after all. "Okay, but there are problems."

"There always are. We shall overcome them. What are they?"

God, how he loved her. "Well, let's see. There's the whole 'nothing to write with' challenge. And once I've written something, how do we keep it? And if I'm writing revolutionary tracts, I'm not sure that liberal-minded jailers like our Inquisitional pals will do anything other than carefully file it in the nearest live fireplace. And then there's the little matter of *what* to write: I don't think my inner author is very inspired—or even alive."

"See? You have already detected the major impediments to this plan. That is half the battle; now, we only need to solve them."

*Only need to solve them.* As if real-world situations were like Rubik's Cubes; you just fiddle with them long enough and eventually, they work out. Unfortunately, the real world was full of changing conditions and changing minds. And not all problems had solutions. But, he had to admit, the notion of writing a revolutionary tract while cooped up had a kind of romanticism to it—probably because his leg felt better, they were warm and well-fed, and their accommodations were no longer shared with several families of rats. Absent any one of those improvements, and the whole enterprise would probably seem a lot less diverting. But for now, Giovanna had a point: it was something that he *could* do, and he'd read more than once that lethargy was a prisoner's worst enemy. So it would be good to have a project, and this one promised to be challenging enough. If only there was some way to...

"Signor and Signora Stone?"

Frank woke from his daze, found Giovanna, eyes opened wide, pointing at the door. *Castro y Papas*, she mouthed silently.

"Hello?" Frank responded.

"It is I, Don Vincente."

He was actually Don Vincente Jose-Maria de Castro y Papas, captain in the Spanish Army of the Two Sicilies. And not at all a bad guy, considering it was he who had taken Frank prisoner. "Yes?"

"I regret troubling you, Signor Stone, but I must enter."

"Come on in, then."

The Spaniard, a well-formed man hovering at the edge of his thirties, opened and flowed through the door with an elegant efficiency of motion. If Spain's fathers hadn't made him a swords-man, he could probably have become one hell of a dancer. His calm—always calm—brown eyes surveyed the scene. "I see you have already begun to pack. Most excellent. I am sorry for the inconvenience, but we must move you. Yet again."

"Yeah, about that: what's with all the moving? We still like the view from this room."

Castro y Papas glanced briefly at the windowless walls. "Despite the singular charm of the scenery, we must house you elsewhere."

"'House.' What a lovely way of saying 'imprison.'"

Castro y Papas may have blushed a bit; it was hard to tell, given his complexion. "It is good to see you have kept some sense of humor about your situation, Signor Stone. I have not been able to do so."

Frank immediately felt sorry for the captain. He noticed that even Giovanna looked away as the Spaniard's tone conveyed bit-ter regret. And Frank suddenly realized why the regret was so bitter: because, clearly, Don Vincente was not allowed to show any more overt sympathy than he just had. Even that measure of commiseration was probably tantamount to treason. Or maybe heresy. In Borja's army, the line separating the two seemed less than distinct, at times.

"Hey, listen, Captain, I'm sorry if I got a little snarky, there—"

Don Vincente's left eyebrow rose. "'Snarky'—I do not know this word. It is dialect? Scottish, maybe?"

"Uh...maybe. I really don't know where it came from. It was a word we used up-time. It means—oh, I don't know, 'testy' and a little rude, I guess."

"Ah. But 'snarky' sounds more appropriate somehow. Perhaps because it sounds so similar to 'snarl.'"

"You've been a pretty good guy—as oppressive conquerors go, that is."

That brought a smile to Castro y Papas' face. "I endeavor to be the nicest villain that I may be," he explained with the intimation of a flourish. "And I am truly sorry you must be moved again. And that I may not tell you why. In part, because it would be a violation of orders."

"And the other part of your reason?"

"Is that I really do not know why you are being moved. I have only suspicions. I may safely say that your situation, both in terms of immediate security and larger political implications, is being handled at the very highest levels. Directly."

Well, no surprises there. "You mean the same levels that gave orders for you not to accept my surrender when you showed up at my bar with a cannon?"

Castro y Papas considered his response carefully. "I was not present when those orders were issued, but my commander tells me that both directives came from the most senior command echelons here in Rome. But it was fortunate that events transpired such that you were taken prisoner."

"Yeah, I've wondered about that. You, uh, skated pretty close to the line on that one, didn't you?"

"If I understand your idiom correctly, I may only say this: I scrupulously found a way to obey the letter of the law. And yet, miracle of miracles, here you are!" His concluding smile was both mischievous and—what? Vengeful? Vengeance against whom? Against whoever had given him orders that he had openly professed were devoid of honor? Because honor clearly meant a great deal to Captain Vincente Jose-Maria de Castro y Papas.

Behind Castro y Papas, his apparently inseparable sergeant, an independently minded fellow answering to the name of Ezquerra, appeared in the doorway. "I am told that the coaches are here, Captain."

"Coaches?" Frank wondered aloud, conducting a quick survey of their sparse worldly goods. "I'm thinking the two of us and our goods could all fit in a donkey cart, with room to spare for two of your guards."

Castro y Papas smiled. "My sergeant is so indiscreet that I

sometimes think he must be working as a foreign *agent provocateur* and informer within our ranks. Ezquerra, perhaps you would like to share with us the final destination of each of the coaches?"

"I'm sorry; I cannot oblige you in this, Captain."

"And why is that?"

"I was not told the destinations."

"You show entirely too little resourcefulness and energy to work as a spy, Ezquerra. I suspect you shall be no more successful in your new covert endeavors than you are as a sergeant."

Ezquerra almost bowed. "The captain's wisdom is widely renowned. Even unto the end of this street."

Don Vincente was clearly trying very hard to suppress a smile, and Frank discovered—suddenly, impulsively—that he was no longer merely sympathetic to this nice enemy; he actually liked him. Which could be dangerous.

Perhaps Giovanna had felt the same thing, or had simply seen the reaction flow through Frank's features. She shut the last trunk with a sharp crack and announced, "We are ready. If we must go, let us go."

As the coaches lined up in broad daylight, and with full-length blinds and canopies erected to obscure the identities of whoever might be handed up into each vehicle, Don Vincente was conscious that he was grinding his teeth.

Audibly, apparently. Ezquerra coughed lightly. "This must be the best-publicized secret prisoner transfer in Roman history."

Castro y Papas nodded sharply. "Yes. Which I do not like at all."

"Well, who wants to share in a secret that everyone knows?"

"This isn't incompetence, Ezquerra. This is an occasion where Napoleon's axiom does not hold."

"Who is Napoleon?"

"A famous up-time general who advised, 'Never ascribe to malice that which can be explained by incompetence.' Except the flaws of this prisoner transfer are not the product of incompetence: they reek of malice. Or rather, malign plotting. These instructions we were given—to follow at a distance and remain watchful for any attempts to surreptitiously follow the coaches—means that our masters are trailing the hostages like bait in the water. Which could get the two of them—no, the *three* of them—killed."

"By whom? Their own people?"

"Sergeant, how long have you served before the cannon?"

"Almost an hour now, sir. Or perhaps eight years. Honestly, I've lost track; serving under you is such a singularly pleasant experience, that time just seems to fly by."

"So, you have been a soldier for a lifetime and a half. And so you have seen how often casualties are inflicted upon one's own side: inaccurate fire, confusion, poor visibility. The causes are legion, but the lesson is all one: if weapons are used, people die—and the wielders of the weapons rarely, if ever, have complete control over *who* dies."

Castro y Papas jerked his head at the second coach. "They are playing *passe-dix* with the lives of hostages whose safety is their responsibility. One of whom is a woman with child." Don Vincente spat. "It is a stain upon the honor of every one of us who must take part."

Ezquerra shrugged. "Maybe, but would you not agree that it is also a clever plan?"

Castro y Papas sighed. "Perhaps. If the audience for which they intend this show is here to see it."

"And do you think they are?"

Don Vincente sighed. "We shall find out soon enough, perhaps." He snagged the reins of his horse, jumped a foot up into the waiting stirrup, and mounted with fluid ease.

# Chapter 19

Sherrilyn's voice was calm. "The carriages are moving."

"Is Juliet back with her street-urchins?"

"Harry." An English-accented mezzo piped up from below. "I'm right down here in the street."

Thomas North smiled. What ears that woman had! There was no under-the-breath spousal grumbling in big George Sutherland's house, that much was certain....

Juliet added, "—and I am currently surrounded by eager palms that want to be filled."

"With bread?"

"No. With quatrines."

"Robbers."

"They take after their idol, *Harry*."—

—Who smiled. "Okay, give 'em what they want. We can't lose track of Frank and Giovanna, now—whichever carriage they turn out to be in. This could still be our opportunity to grab them."

Thomas suppressed a start of surprise. An opportunity to grab them? There were four carriages, one with the Barberini family crest stained with the brown-maroon of dried blood, all starting out from the front of Palazzo Rospigliosi. All had opaque leather blinds bound in place to cover the windows, and each had a cavalry escort. North failed to see how this was an opportunity to retake the hostages.

Thirty minutes ago, when the first of the carriages and cavalry began pulling up in front of the palazzo, Harry had started issuing preparatory orders for ambushing what he presumed would simply be a well-escorted prisoner transfer. But he had also had the foresight to suggest that Juliet should summon the young minions she had recruited over the past two days, in the event that there was more than one potential target to keep track of. The youngsters had responded swiftly; since many of them were related to *lefferti*—both alive and dead—they were glad and excited to do something that might injure the Spanish.

And it was now obvious that today, Spanish security was not merely going to be the product of strength, but guile: the carriages were arranged to move separately, rather than *en convoy*. Thankfully, Harry was a flexible tactician; he now revised his earlier orders with admirable dispatch. "Sherrilyn, take your team up to the roof; use the flue to relay reports down to me here. The rest of you"—his gaze took in the remaining members of the Wrecking Crew, except Thomas—"get down to the ground floor. And be ready to split up; we may have to follow more than one of those carriages."

By the time Harry was done giving orders, his binoculars were already back up to his eyes. And Lefferts' very next word told North that his own fears regarding the Spanish plans had been vindicated: "Shit."

North was pretty sure of the answer, but asked anyway. "What's happening?"

"Two of the carriages are heading northeast, toward the Quirinale. The other two are heading south; they'll pass right under our window."

"Probably making for the Corso. Harry, if these pairs split up"—*which they will*—"we're not going to be able to chase all of them."

"Damn it," muttered Lefferts. "I just didn't expect them to play 'shell game' with us."

"Yes, a bit unsporting. And even if we could follow them all, there's no way any of the groups doing so would be large enough to mount a successful ambush and retake the hostages."

Harry thought for a moment and then leaned over toward the fireplace, shouting up the flue. "All right: here's the new plan, Sherrilyn. You keep eyes on the targets as long as we can. I'll watch from here, too, but will mostly be coordinating with our guys on the ground floor. Juliet's kids should be able to keep up with the carriages easily enough to see where they all go. Rome's widest streets are still none too wide, so they're not going anywhere too quickly. When we're no longer able to keep track of them from this vantage point, we'll choose the most likely shell under which the Spanish have hidden the hostages and go after that one."

"Carefully," amended North.

"Not so carefully that we're too late to strike, if the opportunity presents itself."

Thomas nodded, but thought: *if it's not* already *too late.*

"Well, spank me hard and call me Sally." Sherrilyn saw her team, Felix Kasza and Donald Ohde, start slightly. She smiled. However profane the men of the Wrecking Crew thought themselves—and they had good reason for that self-image—they were always startled when a provocative new colloquialism came from Sherrilyn.

Donald recovered first. "What's up?"

"Not our odds of grabbing the hostages," Sherrilyn answered. She pointed, keeping her eyes planted on the binoculars. "One coach is going northeast along the Via Recta, but it looks like it's preparing to turn left. Probably to head north along the Strada Felice. Another carriage has gone west. I can't see it just now, but—yeah, there it is, turning right to get on the Corso, heading north."

From down below, Harry's annoyed shout hooted out of the flue at her right elbow. "Sherrilyn, you seein' all this?"

"Yeah, I'm seeing what you're seeing and more."

"What's happened to the two that just passed beneath us?"

Sherrilyn pivoted on her heels, scanned with the binoculars, and caught sight of the boxy carriages swaying into and out of view beyond the buildings to the southwest. "They're still going southwest along the Via Recta—no, wait; one has just veered into a small westbound street."

"What's over there?"

"Nothing. They're probably taking a shortcut to get to the Strada Papale."

"And the other?"

"Looks like they're following along to the end of the Via Recta. Again, nothing much in that direction, unless they're looking to get to the Via dell'Aracoeli. And—wait a minute."

"What?"

Sherrilyn strained her eyes; were those two mounted men, far behind the last carriage, also following it? They just seemed like ordinary travelers from the look of it, but—

No. She caught the glint of a light steel gorget when the one closer to her vantage point turned to look behind and his collar gapped, revealing the neck armor beneath. Now that she knew what to look for, she could see the telltale signs of a plainclothes tail. The overstuffed saddle bags that probably concealed weapons, the buff gloves, the way they sat their horses: they were military.

And they were now looking with increased interest at two of Juliet's child-recruits. Looking at them very attentively as they followed along behind the coach, playacting the part of a lord and lady. The two horsemen urged their mounts into a slightly faster walk, peering at the two nine-year-olds more closely. And mouth suddenly hanging open, Sherrilyn realized why:

*My god, those horsemen are not merely security; they're the watchers for anyone who tries to follow the carriage surreptitiously. They're watching for us.*

"So, we're busted? Totally?" Harry rubbed his chin meditatively.

Sherrilyn nodded. "This shell-game they staged: it was a set-up. To see who, if anyone, would follow."

"Pretty crafty," admitted Harry.

"More than that."

Harry turned to look at North. "What do you mean?"

"I mean this tactic of theirs was damned near oracular in its presumptions. Here we are in Rome, conducting reconnaissance preparatory to a hostage rescue. First they give us exactly what we want to see: the hostages, about to move into the open. But then they throw us what you Americans call a 'curve ball': our objective, although right under our noses, is now moving in one of four possible directions. Thereby baiting us to make a weak attempt to get the hostages now, either by hitting all the coaches, or by striking blind at one or two. At the very least, they figure we might reveal ourselves by following a little too eagerly, a little too closely. All staged so they can either strike us preemptively, or at least get a look at our methods and some of our personnel."

Harry frowned. "Are you saying we've been ratted out?"

"Eh? Oh, you mean an informer from our side?" North shook his head. "No, I very much doubt that."

North felt Sherrilyn's eyes studying him closely as she asked, "Why do you doubt it?"

North had to think that through: his tactical instincts had raced ahead of his deductions. "Any informer who knows enough to betray us would have solid information regarding our numbers and our general appearance. Whoever is behind this shell game ploy would have used that information to craft a more precise plan to lure us into killing range.

"I suspect he anticipates that someone will try to rescue Frank and Giovanna, and that they will logically be sent by the USE. But beyond that, I doubt he has anything more than guesswork, although I wouldn't be surprised if the Wrecking Crew is high on his list of probable rescuers."

"Then he'd have numbers and identities, right there."

"Maybe. But from what I heard during my own travels, Harry, intelligence on the Wrecking Crew is pretty sketchy other than that you are its very visible and distinctive leader. How many members the Crew has, and how consistently you all operate together, is unclear. For instance, people in London are convinced that Julie Sims is a part of the Wrecking Crew, thanks to that sharp shooting during the Tower of London escape."

"A classic, that one." Harry beamed at the walls in happy reminiscence.

"Yes, the talk of Europe. Which unfortunately, may be hurting us now."

"Whaddya mean?"

"Well, commando teams are useful, in large measure, because they are covert. Covert, as in unseen and unknown."

Harry frowned. "I guess I see your point. We're not exactly an unknown quantity."

"Harry, I think it might be worse that that. It's possible that whoever is running the show on the other side of the curtain may have made a study of your methods. Let's ignore your technological edge, for a moment. None of your strikes to date could be pulled off without a great deal of advance reconnaissance. That means you, or your agents, observe a target before you strike, often for a long time. That means you are in your area of operations well before you drop the hammer."

Harry nodded. "And so, the guy running the show for the Spanish today put out Frank and Giovanna as bait, figuring that even if he didn't know where we were, that we'd be somewhere close by, probably watching. Maybe being tempted to do something stupid."

Thomas nodded. "That's the gist of it."

The Crew, sans George and Juliet, had been silent throughout the quick council of war that had been summoned on the rooftop. It was Donald Ohde who looked out over the half-classical, half-ramshackle Roman cityscape. "So do we know anything else?"

Sherrilyn had taken another quick, four-points-peek with her binoculars. "The coaches are moving pretty slowly, except the one that went north on Strada Felice in the direction of the Pincio."

"Toward the old embassy and the Palazzo Barberini," nodded Harry.

"Yeah. They're moving at a pretty good clip. Juliet's kids are not going to keep up with that one. Besides, the farther north they go, the more sparse the crowds and the houses. The kids are going to start sticking out more, particularly when they have to start running to keep up. And they've been told not to be obvious, so I think we have to assume that they'll stop following that coach any minute now."

"Does that coach seem to be in more of a rush than the others?" Thomas could hear the predatory anticipation in Harry's tone.

Sherrilyn shrugged. "Hard to tell. Maybe they are. But it might just be that there's a whole lot less traffic out there. So it might be that those Spanish want to move faster, or simply that they *can* move faster."

Donald Ohde nodded. "And the other coaches?"

"I've lost sight of the two that went south and west."

"Any guess where they might have been headed?"

Sherrilyn consulted her map: a tangled composite of modern and recent cartography. "The first one which turned off the Via Recta could follow along the Strada Papale, or might be making for the Ponte Sisto, and over the river into the Trastevere district. It's a rat-warren over there. The one that went south—that's even harder to say: maybe toward the Forum, maybe toward the new palazzi north of the Jewish ghetto, maybe all the way to Isola Tiberina. Again, a maze."

Harry nodded thoughtfully. "And the closer one that went north?"

Sherrilyn raised her binoculars in that direction. "Still on the Corso, moving slowly."

"And the kids got chased away from that one?"

"Yeah, the outriders seemed to assume that our kids were beggar urchins, trying to trail along and stick out their palms at the quality when they finally got wherever they were going. So we'll have no way to know if that's the one carrying Frank and Giovanna."

Thomas cleared his throat. "I would make one addition to Ms. Maddox's summation. We cannot actually be sure that Frank and Giovanna are in *any* of the coaches. Our informer in the Spanish command indicated that this transfer was taking place, and we have certainly observed movement consistent with a transfer. But how do we know—know for sure—that, in the end, the hostages really have been relocated? Or that they were conveyed to a new prison by one of the four coaches? As far as we know, they could have been sealed in an old barrel being removed for disposal from a rear entrance."

Harry nodded. "Okay. That makes it imperative we get a pair of eyes on each of the wagons we can still see to follow. So we've got to put a new tail back on the northbound wagon. The same goes for the one that's headed for the Pincio along the Strada Felice. We've at least got to have someone trail them in an attempt to determine—even if it's after the fact—where they deposited their passengers. If they've got passengers, that is."

Donald shouldered his gear. "Right. Teams?"

"Juliet stays behind here. The kids will eventually return and make their reports on the southerly wagons, and they'll all want their quatrines. And she'll need to set up some occasional watches on wherever those southbound coaches dropped off their passengers."

"I'll tell the missus." George started down the stairs.

"Not so fast, George; tell her on the way out." Harry turned to Thomas. "You, Sherrilyn, and Felix will follow the coach going north along the Corso. When you find where it has stopped, break off, and head east to rendezvous with us one block west of Palazzo Barberini. The rest of us will fall back on that point as soon as we've finished following the coach heading toward the Pincio along the Strada Felice."

"They've got a long head start on you, and that's quite a walk." Thomas considered the manpower in each group. "Why so many people in your group, Harry?"

"Because"—and Lefferts started shouldering his own gear—"I've got a funny feeling about that coach heading to the Pincio. There isn't a lot up there."

"So?"

"So, they must have anticipated that that one would move faster. And if Frank and Giovanna *are* in one of those coaches, that's the one they'd want to make sure we can't cut off. And oddly enough, the coach heading to the Pincio is the only one of the four that is arguably getting away. I find that—" he turned and smiled like a wolf seeing a lame rabbit "—suspicious. It could be an opportunity, too. If they get a little too cocky, if they think they're safe and out of our reach, well, I want most of the Crew's manpower on hand to take advantage of their mistake."

Thomas nodded. Yes, that all sounded good, and maybe Harry was right. But on the other hand, Lefferts was counting on the kind of slipup that Thomas doubted their opponent would make. Their unknown adversary seemed too methodical to create a situation in which the hostages would be easily snapped up by the opposition.

"We're moving." Harry headed for the stairs. "Now."

"Are you sure this is the place?" Owen asked in a low voice.

John O'Neill looked up at the second story of the unfamiliar house. "I think so, but I'm not sure. When I was here, students stayed back there." He waved farther down the street by which they had approached St. Isidore and its college, which was only a small wing added onto the church's rectory.

O'Neill looked up beyond the steep, flanking steps at the porticoed white façade of the church: two tall openings framed an even taller, wider archway that was in line with the doors. Bordered on three sides by the lush green vegetation of the largely unbuilt Pincio, Luke Wadding's Irish College looked unchanged from when he had visited it, shortly after its opening ten years ago.

Owen's voice was still low, but was now worried, as well. "John, we can't stay here. It's too open, and we're too many not to attract attention. Besides, the place is thick with Spaniards."

John frowned. Thick with Spaniards? Hardly. Well, not so much. But, now that he looked closer, beyond the two at the entry, and the two he'd seen leaning in the shade of the portico's arches, there were several more that appeared occasionally in the windows of the rectory and annex. Not exactly patrols, or at least not strict ones. Just a continuous presence, moving irregularly through the whole complex.

"John—"

"Yeh, yeh. I'm cogitating, Cousin."

"Well, do it quickly, Johnnie. I think we've attracted the attention of the guards at the gate."

"Aye, so we have. Well, there's nothing else for it then. You stay here. Stay in the house, actually."

"In this one just behind us?"

"Of course."

"The door is locked."

"And you're a mighty fellow. Besides, it seems like classes have been suspended. There's been no sign of the students who should be running in and out of here, and no fires or domestics preparing dinner. Just wait until I'm distracting the guards at the church's main gate before you bust into the house."

"You're going to distract guards at the main gate? John, what are you going to do?"

"Use the only kind of power these Spanish are likely to understand. Synnot, McEgan: with me."

"What? John—"

But John was already walking briskly across the Strada Felice, approaching St. Isidore's along a small side-road from the west. The two morioned Spaniards at the gate exchanged long looks. One of them took a step forward, a hand raised. "Non si può." The Spanish guard's Italian was ragged. "Chiesa chiusa."

"Hablo español bien."

The Spanish looked at each other again, clearly surprised.

Keeping to their language, John continued: "Besides, I doubt St. Isidore's is closed to me."

"And who are you?"

John produced his travel papers and a copy of his commission. "I am Lord John O'Neill, the third earl of Tyrone, Colonel of tercio O'Neill under Archduchess Isabella of the Spanish Low Countries. Etcetera etcetera etcetera. But most important, I am an old friend and student of Padre Luca. Whom I wish to see."

Again the Spanish looked at each other. One more time, John thought, and it wouldn't even make for a good comedy routine, anymore. "Is he expecting you?" one of them finally asked.

"I don't really know," John lied with a smile. "A letter was sent, but delivery is a little uncertain these days." He gestured at the skyline; the tattered silhouettes of burnt buildings, and their pervasive smell, were unmistakable.

The Spanish nodded. "Yes. This is true. If the conde will be pleased to wait for one moment, I shall sent word to Father Luke tha—"

John brushed past the man, putting on haughtiness like a heavy cloak. "I will announce myself. I have not traveled so far, through such filth, to wait like a boy on the doorstep."

He could hear the rapid conference fading behind him, and then one set of footfalls growing louder. "Lord, Conde Tyrone—please. We have orders. We cannot allow you to pass us without—"

"Well, then, don't allow me to pass you. Come along. Announce me as I arrive, if you must." Clearly not what the Spaniard was going to suggest, but perhaps a course of action he could accept, rather than contradicting or denying a noble a second time.

True to form, the Spanish trooper strode briskly ahead. Behind, John heard the other one exclaim, after them, "Roberto, no! You cannot take him in—" And, soft and almost inaudible behind that exclamation, John heard the pop of a flimsy lock being broken. Which meant that Owen and the rest of the Wild Geese were now in the abandoned dormitory, having done so while the last guard's back and attention were turned away.

O'Neill reached the stairs that led up to St. Isidore's entrance and started up, suddenly feeling ten years younger, possibly because of the memories of the place, but more likely because he was breaking rules and taking chances.

Sherrilyn, her short hair tied back and hat pulled low, turned right off the Via di Condotti. She was not following the coach itself, but had insinuated herself into the clutter of reintegrating traffic the vehicle left in its wake, trying to ignore the growing pain in her knee. And as soon as she swung around the corner, and assessed the carriage's status on the northbound stretch of the Via di Ripetta, she resisted the urge to dodge right back. That was too obvious, so she crouched down, as if searching for a dropped coin. Then she stood, making sure her back was now to the carriage, and limped back around the corner.

And almost ran into Thomas North in the process. Who looked down at her knee. "Have you injured yourself, Ms. Maddox?"

"Just an old sports injury. I'm fine. Here's the situation: the coach has drawn up in front of the Villa Borghese. If anyone was riding in it, we've come too late to see."

"And you are so pale because—?"

"Because the whole damned street is filled with Spanish troops, checking people. Checking everyone who stands still long enough to be checked, from the look of it."

"And not from any pain in your knee?"

"Listen, shut about about my knee. I'm fine."

Felix Kasza licked his lips. "With all the Spanish in the next street over, I am thinking it is time to leave, then?"

North nodded. "I'd say so. As I recall the first briefing with Romulus, it was believed that Frank and Giovanna's first prison was close to the Villa Borghese, wasn't it, Ms. Maddox?"

"Yep," she answered, "they were penned right under Borja's very feet, some thought. Are you thinking they've been brought back there?"

Thomas North frowned as they started to amble casually away from the corner. "No. I don't think so."

"Why?"

"It just doesn't feel right, not the sort of thing our opponent would do. Ask me 'why' again later; my brain may have caught up with my instincts, by then."


"What gives, Harry?" The outdated up-time expression sounded comically awkward coming from Matija. "Those three fellows just walked right past the guards and into St. Isidore's Church."

Harry pocketed the small field glasses. "Not quite, Matija. The leader got stopped by the two guards at the gate, spoke with them a bit. Then he breezed past them."

Gerd smiled. "And one of them ran after him like a little *bub*, trying to make him stop."

"Hmmm. I don't think it was quite that clear cut. Looks like the two Spanish guards wanted to stop him, didn't have the authority to do so, and now one of them is 'escorting' him in."

"Leaving only one guard at the gate," Matija pointed out.

"Yeah, but there are others near the entrance to the church, and a few more stalking around inside the buildings attached to it." Harry considered his surroundings: his team was in a side street, one block north of the Piazza Barberini, across from the

Capuchin monastery. Beyond that dour building there was a scattering of marginally inhabited cottages, and then St. Isidore's, all of which had their backs to the extensive fields that radiated southward from the Villa Ludovisi.

Donald Ohde made a clucking sound with his tongue. "Okay, Harry, what are you thinking?"

"Well, a couple of things. First, I'd like to find out who that guy was, dropping by for a visit just now. This location is off the beaten path for the high and mighty, up here at the green margins of the Pincio. Clearly, he had rank, but just as clearly, the guards didn't know him. That's an odd combination, out here."

"You thinking he's somehow connected with the mastermind who ran the shell-game with the carriages?"

"Could be. Don't know why else they'd get high-ranking but unfamiliar visitors out here just before dusk."

"Okay, but if he's got that kind of rank, why'd he come on foot?"

"Yeah, I've been wondering about that. And the gear of those three guys didn't look right, either. I mean, it could be Spanish, but it's not like what we've seen down here. Their leader seemed to carry a heavier sword than the Spanish use, these days."

"Yeah, and his pal with the very red hair and very pale skin didn't look like any Spaniard I've ever seen. None of them did, in fact."

"Which makes it all the more interesting. And possibly, very significant. After all, just because the Spanish have a criminal mastermind working for them now doesn't mean they hired from in-house. Their evil genius could be foreign talent."

"True enough," drawled Ohde. "After all, look at us."

"You look; my eyeballs have already had their quota of ugly for today."

"Yeah, we love you, too, Harry."

"I think the phrase you're looking for is 'abjectly adore.' But enough sweet talk; I'm thinking that we couldn't have asked for a better tactical situation."

"How do you mean?"

"One guard is off the gate. If we move fast, we can get in."

"What?" Ohde sounded surprised. "Get in? How?"

"Gerd is going to walk past the church, eyeball it a little, just enough to get the last guard's attention. That's when the rest of us slip between the cottages north of the monastery and angle around behind the back of St. Isidore's. From there, we slip into the rear of the annex and take a look around."

Donald Ohde was frowning. "I guess the real question I should be asking is, 'why?'"

"To see if there's any sign that this where they're keeping Frank and Giovanna."

"Here? With this low security?"

"Yeah, low security—which invites us to assume that the Spanish *couldn't* be hiding them here, right? Our opposition might use that kind of ruse: make the real prison look weak—*so* weak that we would dismiss it as a possible site. So we're going to check it out. If it's a dry hole, we withdraw and rendezvous with Sherrilyn's group when they're done chasing after the carriage heading up toward the villa Borghese. And maybe, when we're inside the church, we might see something that tells us whether Mr. Non-Spanish Boss-man is just a random visitor, or someone who was involved in setting up the trap they laid for us today."

"And if he is?"

"Then we're in a perfect position to follow him when he leaves the church. And we'll take that opportunity to show him the hospitality of a small room without windows until we get some answers from him."

Big George Sutherland shrugged and pointed out, "Harry, that Boss-Man also walked like a seasoned soldier, and had the gear to go with the gait. It might not be so easy to compel him, and his bodyguards, to accept your invitation."

Lefferts smiled up at George. "Yeah, it's harder to grab eggs when you can't break 'em. But we're no slouches ourselves. And with any luck, the whole Crew will be together by the time Boss-man decides to head off into the sunset."

"Which might be soon," observed Matija, looking up at the rapidly dimming western skyline.

"Good point. So let's move. Gerd, I think it's about time for you to take a stroll past the church..."

# Chapter 20

Father Luke Wadding entered the rectory in a rush. Spare, soft-eyed, and already white-haired, his face seemed to radiate equal measures of surprise and delight. "My dear Tyrone, how good to see you! Had I known—"

John waved aside the pleasantries. "Father Luke, we're not going to have to go through another long period before you start calling me 'John' again, are we?"

Father Wadding—counselor to popes, rector of the Irish College at St. Isidore's, famous theologian, and lightning rod for Church matters touching upon Ireland's exiles—blushed. John smiled. Padre Luca was indeed unchanged: just as humble and accessible and plain in his manners as he'd ever been. "Very well—John. And Father Hickey is going to be delighted to see you, I know."

John felt a sudden pull in his chest, fought down a lump in his throat. "He's still here? I was worried that maybe—"

"Still here; couldn't get rid of him if I tried. Not that I ever would. Now, John, do have a seat. Tell me how things are in the Low Countries, and how—"

John stared at the waiting chairs, then at the two Spanish guards. "Er, Father..." He shifted languages. "I will speak in Spanish so your protectors understand this clearly. I am here on Fernando's business, concerning sensitive interests of Spain.

196

But I am unable to speak of these matters except in private. So I would be grateful if your men would be willing to wait here while you and I retire to a more private venue."

"Alas, unless we were to sit on the edge of my own bed, this is as private a place as I can offer. But here now,"—Wadding looked at his guards—"surely you know of the earl of Tyrone, of the Irish Wild Geese? With him here, I have nothing to fear. In his presence, I am guarded as though by my own nephew. So kindly wait in the church; I shall be quite safe."

These two Spanish guards also exchanged long looks. John almost rolled his eyes. *Oh, please, please, sweet Jayzus; not another pair who specialize in eyeball dancing . . .*

The older of the two guards began to stammer out, "P-Padre Luca, we d-d-do not wish to d-displease you, but—"

"Your orders are to ensure that I am guarded by the might of Spain at all times, yes?"

The stammerer nodded.

Wadding gestured toward John and then Synnot and McEgan. "Well, here I am: protected by the might of Spain. Indeed, by one of its most famous warriors and two of his best soldiers. So, your orders are fulfilled. If you wish, bring your lieutenant and I will explain the matter yet again."

The two guards looked at each other, traded shrugs, and filed out.

John smiled after them. The moment they were beyond earshot, he gestured quickly at Synnot. "Watch the door. Tell me if someone's coming. If they are, stall them. We're not to be disturbed. McEgan, down to the kitchen with you. Tell them there's word that the cistern behind the apse has been defiled, maybe poisoned."

"Why the kitchen?"

"Because they cook with that water, and because the cook sends meals to guards at their posts. So he'll know where they are, and when he sends word of the cistern, that will pull many, maybe most, of the guards off their rotations. Which is just what we want: no unnecessary obstructions on our way out."

Wadding was openmouthed when John turned back to him. Then the priest's mouth shut and brows lowered. "John O'Neill, what errant nonsense are you up to now?"

"Not nonsense at all, Father. You need to come with me. Now."

"I do not, and I will not."

"Father, tell me something: why are you up to your neck in Spanish soldiers?"

For the first time in John's knowledge of him, Wadding looked away from an incipient staring match. "Cardinal Borja expressed apprehension about my safety."

"More likely he's worried about how you jeopardize his."

"John, perhaps you are succumbing to the Roman fever. Or maybe standing close to cannons for fifteen years has damaged more than just your hearing. Because a bit of clearheaded logic will tell you that there's no way on earth that I could jeopardize Cardinal Borja."

"Oh, you can, Father; you can jeopardize him on Earth, and in Heaven too, unless we're wrong in our guess."

"Who's 'we'? And what guess?"

"Jesus on the Cross, but you always were a great one for turning ev'ryting into words and more words, Father."

"And you were ever a blasphemer. A bad habit you've not managed to break, I see. And I'll hear your confession for it. But first I'll hear answers to my questions. Who is making these absurd claims about the threat I pose to Cardinal Borja?"

John settled his temper. Father Luke was as mild as a kitten—until you raised his ire. And if you did raise it? Well, John had repulsed siege assaults that hadn't been quite *that* fierce. "Father Luke, you have many friends who are cardinals, am I right?"

"Well...yes."

"And how many of them have you seen since Philip's troops arrived in Rome?"

Wadding darkened. But then he smiled.

"Have I said something funny, Father?"

"No. But ten years ago, you hadn't the patience for irony. Or indirect argument. Very well, John. You make a point. As a rule, I'd not judge the actions of a cardinal, particularly when there's so much wild rumor abroad. But it's plain there's been abuse of power, here."

"Plain? *Plain?* Yes, Father: plain to a blind man at the bottom of an oubliette, even."

Wadding closed his eyes. "John, these are evil times, no question. But what would you have me do?"

"What I asked you to do at the first: come with us. Now. It's the right thing. And it's the safe thing, before Borja realizes he can't trust you either."

"Can't trust me? Even if he couldn't, why should he care? Why would—?"

"Because if the pope made you a cardinal *in pectore*, then you'll have a vote on the Consistory. And Isabella knows you well enough to know you'll vote your conscience if it comes down to having to choose between Urban and Borja."

John had never witnessed Luke Wadding speechless. Somehow, it was even more unnerving than being the object of his wrath—an experience with which John had a reasonable familiarity. When Wadding spoke, it was as though he were in a daze. "So, that's the 'they' to whom you've been referring: the infanta and her nephew, the king in the Low Countries."

"Yes. And they're not alone in their opinion regarding Borja's intentions."

Wadding closed his eyes. "So they must suspect that Borja is guilty of much of what he's been accused of, here."

"Much. Perhaps all."

Wadding opened his eyes. "For Borja to have done what you accuse him of would mean he is insane. I know the man; he is not insane."

"Father, I'm not here to argue his sanity, or anything else, for that matter: I am charged to bring you out of Rome."

Wadding stood. "And I may not leave. There are issues that have not been considered: students and clergy who are in my care, and scholarly matters, as well. There are also archives here, crucial to the history of Mother Church, which could be lost if—"

"Damn it, Father Wadding, you are coming with me, if I have to take you out of here at gunpoint—"

"Well now," drawled a new voice, also in English, "you might not want to make threats when you're at gunpoint yourself."

John started, jumped up, hand halfway to his sword when he saw a wide, but unusually thin-walled, black muzzle aimed straight at his eyes. And the face behind it seemed to match descriptions he'd heard of the much-storied and infamous—

"Harry Lefferts, or I'm a caffler!"

Harry stared at the unfamiliar term, couldn't suppress the slight pulse of gratification that went through him at being recognized, and raised his gun meaningfully. "Well, I'm not saying yes or no, but who the hell are you, and why are you threatening this priest?"

The fellow Harry was questioning—the foreign Boss-man who had breezed past the guards at the gate—did not seem particularly daunted by the barrel that tracked with him. "Where are my men? If you've done them ill, I swear by Christ Almighty, I'll—"

The priest was on his feet. "Enough blasphemy, John O'Neill, or I'll strike you here and now."

Harry and Donald exchanged glances, eyebrows climbing high, before the priest turned on them. "And I do not recall inviting you gentlemen into the rectory. And I'm thinking that you did not simply walk past my guards, or the earl's."

Boss-man was an earl? Named O'Neill? The earl of Tyrone? But what the hell was he doing in Rome? Wasn't he supposed to be commanding a tercio for—?

"My men: where are they?" said O'Neill. It wasn't a request. Even though the earl of Tyrone was looking down the barrel of a twelve-gauge shotgun, it was still a demand.

Harry waggled the gun a bit. "Do you know what this is?"

"Aye. And do you know how much shite you're standing in this very moment?"

Lefferts smiled. "You have a point there. We hadn't planned on stopping in, certainly not for this long. But when all the good father's guards went rushing outside to the cistern, it was easy enough to slip in, sneak through the pantry, and find our way here."

"Where you hoped to discover what?"

"Our friends. Or someone who might know something about them. Like you, maybe, Earl of Tyrone. So tell me, are you the mastermind in charge of intelligence operations for Borja, by any chance?"

That query produced the most unusual—and uncomfortable— reactions yet. Wadding tried, unsuccessfully, to conceal his surprised smile; John O'Neill, seeing it, flushed hot red. For a moment, the tense, armed stand-off in the room became secondary to what felt to Harry like an up-time reality TV moment, where one family member revealed the other's faults in front of total strangers. *So John O'Neill isn't a mental giant or a spymaster. Brave, though: damned brave. Well, no reason to leave him embarrassed, Harry—*

"Okay, I get the picture: you're not the guy we're looking for. Which is more than fine by me. Hell, too much thinking spoils a man of action, eh, Your Earlship?"

The change this brought over O'Neill was nothing short of miraculous. The pugilistic stance and pugnacious expression evaporated. "Right enough. Now look, I've got little time as it is, and Father Wadding here needs to come with me for his own good, so I'd best—"

"Whoa, whoa. Slow down there. Last I heard, the good Father doesn't want to go with you."

"Perhaps," said another voice, accented similarly to John O'Neill's "but you'll not be involved in the decision one way or the other. And be very careful as you turn—you and all your men."

Harry obeyed, turning carefully. He discovered that no less than six soldiers, in buff coats and capelline helmets similar to the earl's, had eased silently into the rectory's antechamber. They had evidently entered through the doorway leading out into the small arboretum that was tucked against the building's north side. They were all carrying what looked like primitive, oversized pepperbox revolvers; about half of them were aimed at him. And Harry thought:

*Well, this sucks.*

Owen Rowe O'Neill tried to make sense of what he was seeing: one of John's escorts—big Synnot, no less—had been disarmed by the newcomers, hastily bound, and left behind like a sack of potatoes in the antechamber. These newcomers were obviously not Spanish, but then again, they were not obviously anything. They were deployed like soldiers, or raiders, but they evinced no uniformity of equipage whatsoever. Except, that is, the up-time weapons they were all holding. And these firearms were not the exorbitantly priced and notoriously unreliable copies that were as obvious as they were rare. These up-time guns were the real business, from the look of them. But that implied—*no, no time for hypothesizing.*

"You." Owen jabbed the muzzle of his pepperbox at the youngish fellow who seemed to be the leader of the newcomers. "Why are you here? Be quick in answering; the guards will be back soon enough."

"They are here already, Señor," amended a new voice, in English, but with a heavy Spanish accent. "Drop your weapons. All of you."

Owen and his Wild Geese turned. Standing wide-legged and with a clear field of fire upon both groups of intruders, was a young Spanish officer flanked by two guards, all with guns out and ready. They had evidently followed along right behind Owen and his men over the front grounds and through the small arboretum.

Owen calculated. If he rushed the Spanish, his own men would certainly have time to take cover and then their pepperboxes would carry the day, at this range. If he was less suicidally minded, Owen might live by dropping flat, but then some of his own men would surely get cut down, possibly leaving the newcomers in charge of the situation. And if he waited—

Spaniard lifted his snaplock pistol impatiently: "Señores, I will have either your weapons, or you, on the ground—now. Juan, inform Sergeant Juarez that we have discovered a plot to—"

A hint of movement—a tall, stealthy figure—flitted up to the rear of the young Spanish officer, who must have seen the quick shift of focus in Owen's eyes; he spun.

Or tried to. Behind the triad of Spaniards, the wraithlike form resolved into a man, up-time pistol already hovering at the rear of one guard's head. There was sharp report, then, as the gun re-angled slightly, another report. The first man had barely started falling as the second bullet exited the young officer's skull just above his ear, a jet of blood tracing the projectile's trajectory.

The second guard, his rifle turning through a longer arc, had almost completed spinning about when another weapon spoke twice from farther down the arboretum's path. The last of the three Spaniards doubled up around the first slug, and slumped over limply when hit by the second.

The unseen gunman emerged from the concealment of the arboretum's vines. But no, Owen realized: it wasn't a gun man.

It was a gun woman. The realization of which made Owen's jaw sag.

Sherrilyn almost grinned when she saw the look on the faces of the pepperbox-armed gang that had sneaked in just ahead of them. "Keep those hands up, mister," she said to the one who had been talking. "Same goes for your pals."

"Eh?" he answered.

Thomas North pushed past the still-stunned down-time leader, nine-millimeter pistol secured in both hands as he moved quickly to link up with the rest of the Crew and Harry—

—Who sounded genuinely grateful. "Well, Thomas, you sure are a sight for sore—"

"Make your apologies, later, Harry. Right now, we—"

"Hey, I wasn't apologiz—!"

"Well, you should be. First things first: what the bloody hell is going on here?"

Sherrilyn waved Felix and Gerd—whom they'd met just south of the rendezvous site—toward the guns of the nine buff-coated intruders: Irishmen, from the sound of them. As the two of them collected the weapons and held the Irish at gunpoint, Sherrilyn joined the group clustered around the door into the rectory.

Things had gone deadly quiet as soon as Thomas had opened his mouth. The other Irish fellow in the rectory—medium-sized, built square and deep in the chest, but light in the hips and legs—was looking at Thomas as if he had just devoured a newborn infant. "Feckin' *sassenach*. Of course. Here with some up-time mercenaries to assassinate Father Luke, using the chaos of the moment to sneak in and kill 'im."

For a moment, the whole Wrecking Crew was speechless. "What?" Sherrilyn finally squawked, "What the hell is he talking about?"

But the Irishman wasn't finished. "Well, yeh bastards, you've put your foot in it now. Drop your weapons or I'll call the rest of the Spanish on you so fast that—"

Harry didn't shout often, but when he did, it was a sharp, cutting baritone: "Shut up! Those gunshots have called the Spanish better than you could have. Now, the way I figure it, we've got maybe ten seconds. So hear this: I don't know what the hell a *sassenach* is, but I'm here on orders from the USE. And I'm not here to kill the priest. Hell, I don't even know who he is. But you want him out? Fine by me. Because right now, if we don't work together, we're all going to die together."

The irate Irish earl frowned more deeply but looked less homicidal. On the other hand, at the arctic rate his mood was changing—

"Agreed!" barked the other Irish leader, the taller one who had been in Sherrilyn's sights. "We work together, leave together, sort it out afterwards."

"Done," said Harry—

—Just as the first of the Spanish came charging in through the same doorway that Harry had used, the one that led back to the staff quarters and the kitchen in St. Isidore's annex.

# Chapter 21

John O'Neill, still half-blind with rage and distrust, had taken a step closer to the *sassenach*—who turned away, and leveled his up-time pistol at the oncoming Spanish. Two ear-splitting snaps—reports, but so unlike the hoarse, throaty roars of muzzle-loaders—dropped the first Spaniard who came through the door, a middle-aged man with a sergeant's sash. The three with him brought up their own pieces, but the wide-barreled carbines of Lefferts and one of his men were already trained on the doorway. Their discharge was thunderous, painful within the close, walled space—and John checked to be sure that the weapons had not, in fact, exploded.

But the effects were clear enough: the cuirass of the first Spanish soldier was riddled by holes, and, as he went backward, a wide spray of blood preceded his fall. One of the two behind him must have picked up a ball, as well; his left arm buckling as the impact pulled him in that direction, the Spaniard's own piece discharged, sending a lead ball spalling off the antechamber floor, through a window and whining out into the arboretum.

The discharge of the second up-time weapon—another of these slim yet monstrously powerful musketoons—followed an eye blink behind the first. It made a red ruin of the wounded soldier's head and arms, and must have clipped the third in the leg; he dropped with a moan. That sound was cut short by a single shot from the woman—the *woman?*—with Lefferts' band; the Spaniard crumpled backward.

John knew he should act, should do something productive, but for the moment, all he could do was think: *A woman?* John had heard the rumors, but refused to believe them. *A woman? Traveling with soldiers—no, raiders—in the field? How did they all—?*

Noise. It came from just beyond the side-door of the rectory, the one that led out into the small garden that was tucked into a small niche between buildings of the annex. The Spanish would have had to climb a wall to get there this quickly, but—

"Lefferts, Owen—here!" John was moving as he snapped the order, leaping to the side of the door, drawing his sword in the same motion.

The door burst open even as he landed beside it. He saw a pistol in his face, snapped his wrist to convert his sword's unsheathing into an abbreviated back-handed cut. Blood sprayed into his face at the same moment that thunder and powder-grit exploded against his reflex-shut eyes, and sent a bolt of searing lightning across the top of his right ear.

Which no longer worked.

He noticed.

As he fell.

Backward.

And landed with a crash that he felt rather than heard, but it jarred him out of his daze.

Just in time to gasp as someone fell on top of him. Weapons were discharging above and around John as he pushed the person—well, the body—off of him. Judging from its half-severed hand, it was the corpse of the Spaniard—the captain of the guard, from the look of his blood-spattered gear—who had almost shot him in the face. But John's sword slice had not been what had killed the hidalgo: three perfectly round holes in his cuirass were clearly the cause of death. And the only person near enough to have done the shooting was the woman, who was already stepping sideways to get a better angle out into the garden. Staggering forward one step, John surveyed the situation out there, saw a knot of swordsmen entangled just beyond the door, and smiled.

At last: the perfectly uncomplicated and spine-tingling rush of combat. *Oh, how I've missed it* he thought, as he headed for the melee with great, bounding strides....

✧　　　✧　　　✧

*At least that bigoted Irish bastard isn't dead; there would've been hell to pay for that,* reflected Thomas as he swapped magazines and took stock of the situation.

In addition to the three Spaniards he and Sherrilyn had gunned down, four more had been killed coming in from the kitchen and pantry area, and three more by the rectory's garden door where—for some idiotic reason—the earl and a few of his bog-hoppers had gone outdoors to have a little sword fight. But Matija and Sherrilyn were moving in that direction, too, and they'd be sure to make a quick end of that little machismo-induced melee. Of greater concern was the doorway that led from the rectory anteroom into the short corridor leading to the apse of the church. That was where most of the on-duty guards would no doubt fall-back, make a plan...

Which would involve a flanking maneuver. Probably making use of the same arboretum through which North had entered, since it was easily accessed from the front of the church. But that flanking move would be a feint only. The widest, yet shortest approach route was through the anteroom corridor linking to the apse—

"Harry—"

"Yeah, I know. You take Felix and George, as well as any Irish that aren't needed in the rectory, and cover the corridor to the church. Donald, Gerd, and I will set up a cross fire in the arboretum; they'll be coming that way, too."

Thomas waved to George. "You heard Harry; on me, Sutherland. And you—" he turned to a particularly well-groomed Irishman who had just recovered his pepperbox revolver "—how are you with a sword?"

"I'm better with a scalpel."

Thomas stared, then realized, judging from the easy, elegant diction, that this "bog-hopper" was telling the truth. "Then get in the rear, Doctor, and order your two mates here to cover this door. Swords and pistols, and stand to the side until I say; they'll come hard, when they do. George, Felix, either side of the door. Shotguns out, pistols ready. Doctor, do be good enough to watch the door leading back into the main annex. If you detect any—"

Shotguns started firing rapidly out in the arboretum; the fast-paced *BOOM-thra-thunk-BOOM-thra-thrunk* sequence was consistent with a rapid pumping of double-aught rounds downrange.

Thomas edged close to the apse-hallway door, cheated it open a sliver—

And saw the double-doors at the apse-end of the corridor swing wide, the Spanish bursting through them three abreast, swordsmen in the lead, musketeers behind.

He let them come half the twenty feet. Then he pulled open the antechamber door. Too far into their charge and too far away from cover to settle in for a gun battle, the Spanish came harder, the musketeers shouting for clearance, hoping to get a shot.

Thomas leveled his pistol and said, "Now!" He aimed at the point man, but did not fire. Felix and George leaned around the door jamb and started pumping shotgun rounds into the Spanish at a range of eight feet.

The first rank went down as a wave of tattered and bloody corpses, revealing the second rank, one or two of whom had taken minor wounds from the .33 caliber balls that that slipped between the bodies in front of them. At their center—and now clearly revealed for Thomas—was the target he expected to find: the career NCO, a little salt mixed into the pepper of his campaigner's beard. That career soldier had realized any spot in the first rank was suicide, but had also known he had to be present to press home the charge. He had to get in among the enemy with both a sword and tactical acumen that had been honed by decades of experience. He, the seasoned Spanish sergeant, was arguably the most potent weapon of the epoch, having been forged along a bloody trail that stretched from Madrid to Maastricht to Macau and back again.

Thomas, with an easy but firm grip on the nine-millimeter, let the tip of the bead rise up into the v-notch of the rear sight, saw the sternum line of the sergeant's cuirass aligned there as well, and squeezed the trigger. And again, for good measure.

The sergeant went down.

*Sic transit gloria mundi est*, reflected Thomas.

As the next rank closed in, Thomas stepped back and the Irish jumped up, pepperboxes thundering. Still giving ground, Thomas started targeting the musketeers between the heads and shoulders of the Wild Geese.

The Irish—credit to be given where credit was due—seemed to intuit the overall strategy. After littering the doorway with Spaniards, they too backed up to let the last of them rush into the antechamber.

Felix and George's reloaded shotguns thundered into that press from either side. The space was suddenly choked with falling bodies, helmets, weapons, and blood. A nuisance, really, Thomas conceded as he found an opening and fired two quick rounds at one of the musketeers hanging back at the church doors—

—Who fell. Two of his comrades ducked behind the walls of the apse; an equal number snapped off return shots. One musket ball hit the doorjamb, another hit one of the last Spaniards still standing.

"Cover! Back!" ordered Thomas, obeying his own command.

George, Felix, and the Irish tucked back out of sight in the antechamber, although not before one of them took a ball in the upper leg, and another was clipped along his left calf.

Harry's voice came from behind. "Thomas, hold them here."

He turned and nodded at the American who was leaning in through the arboretum doorway. Harry returned the nod, motioned for Ohde to stay in a covering position and led Gerd forward at a crouched sprint, sticking close to the side of the church and making for its entrance. A reciprocal flanking action: just as Thomas would have done himself.

"Now what?" asked the Irish surgeon from where he was staunching the one Irishman's thigh-wound.

"Now, we play peek-a-boo with the musketeers." Thomas leaned out, took a shot at nothing. Ducked back. Then he edged the rim of his helmet out beyond the doorjamb.

Two musket blasts responded, one of which sent a ball whining into the rectory itself, eliciting a mighty, if indistinct, oath from one of the Irish who had evidently finished amusing themselves playing at swords in the garden.

Thomas studied the litter of Spanish equipment at his feet, saw an undischarged musket, toed it to one of the Irish pistoleers in the antechamber. "Shoot it," he said.

"At what?" the Irishman asked, puzzled.

"At the Spaniards in the apse."

He took a quick squint around the corner. "Can't see 'em."

"You don't have to. Just shoot in their general direction. Keep them busy."

"Why?"

"You'll see. Well, more like 'you'll hear.' Now be a good fellow and shoot at nothing, please."

The Irishman shrugged, sensibly did not expose more than

the barrel and his right eye, fired, and hit the lintel of the door into the apse.

"See," asked Thomas, "now how hard was that?"

"Harder to understand than do—sir," came the answer. "What the bollocks good is it to—?"

The sudden multiple shotgun discharges within the church sounded like a short, intense bombardment by light artillery. *Wonderful acoustics in these Italian churches,* reflected Thomas, as he stepped out into the line of fire. He considered whether or not it would be prudent to swap magazines again. He became aware of someone staring at him: the Irishman with the discharged Spanish musket.

"So all we were doing—"

"—was keeping the musketeers in the apse focused on us, yes. And making sure there was plenty of noise covering the approach of our counterflankers. The Spanish had no way of knowing that all their own flankers had been cut down so quickly by Harry in the arboretum. So we just had to keep them from glancing back at what they thought was their secure flank—the front door of the church—long enough for Harry to make his counterflanking strike there. Now, relieve the doctor at the annex door; he has two wounded men to tend to." North headed back toward the rectory.

John managed to stand up a little straighter when the *sassenach* came back into the rectory. Father Wadding had grown very quiet, staring round at the bodies littering his sanctum sanctorum. Owen approached, asked, "Father, I'm sorry to have to ask, but is this all of them?"

"What do you mean?"

Owen bit his lip before continuing. "Is this the full lot of the guards? Are there any more?"

Father Luke stood suddenly, and John saw that the infamous Wadding ire had ignited. His dark eyes seemed to stab into Owen. "Why do you want to know, Owen Roe? Haven't you slaked your thirst for blood just yet?"

Owen looked away. He was afraid that if Wadding saw the look in his eyes the priest would know that he'd already given the order to have any surviving enemy soldiers slain. He'd disliked giving that order, but hadn't seen any choice. They simply couldn't afford to leave any eyewitnesses behind.

It was a moot point, in any event. From their actions, it was obvious that Lefferts had given his own people the same order. "Father," he said, quietly, "we didn't want this to happen. But it has. And now we must leave. But we can't know how to do that most safely until we know if there are any guards left."

"Ah, so you need to know how many you have yet to hunt down? Well, there might be some hiding under the altar. It'd be a fine place for the crowning glory—or should that be gory?—of this unholy bloodbath. This is a church, blast you, a church! It is sacred, a sanctuary for all who come within its walls. And you have—"

The up-timer woman spoke. "Father Wadding. You are certainly right. And I think we should hear everything you have to say. But if there are any guards left, they could be running for help. From what we've seen of this area, the Spanish have a lot of troops billeted just north of here, in the Villa Ludovisi. If that's right, they will have heard the shooting and will come to investigate, sooner or later. I'm betting on sooner. But if someone runs from here to tell them what happened, their response time will become 'right now.' So please, for the sake of our survival, let me put this to you: other than the ones you see here in the rectory, we've accounted for about thirty more guards. Is that the full complement?"

Wadding's shoulders slumped. "I believe so. Most of them, for a certainty—but I do not keep close track of their numbers. And there are always some coming and going, delivering messages, taking a day or two of leave, or taking an hour or two to pursue other—pleasures."

Harry entered, hearing the end of the report. "I think some soldiers and one or two cooks may have run off right at the start of the fight, but they won't be able to report anything specific that would identify us. I kept Paul stationed out back, watching for leakers who did see something and who might head toward the Ludovisi place. He's still there, and waved all clear. As long as we get out of here quickly, we should be all right."

John remembered to wipe his sword—on a Spaniard—before sheathing it.

"You would so defile the dead, you young scut?"

John stared at Wadding, and remembered the resentment he'd often felt for the man before. "I'm thinking I'd rather you go back to calling me 'Don John,' from here on in, Father. And I'm not in the mood for one of your pious lectures. Where are the domestics, and the other clergy?"

Wadding had drawn up to his full height. "We only had two servants working here, now. And only one was in today. Who no doubt had the good sense to flee when the firing started. And no, he will not go to the Ludovisi Villa; he lost half his family to the Spanish. He will want—need—to avoid questioning upon the events of this day.

"I sent the students and the other priests to Gondolpho, where the Pontifical Irish College has a house for religious retreats. Only Father Hickey remains here with me."

"Who is, I think, approaching," reported Connal, from the antechamber.

Sure enough, Anthony Hickey hobbled into the rectory. Although only two years older than Wadding, the years did not rest lightly upon the priest. Arthritis had already struck permanent, gnarling blows against Hickey's knees and hands, and his lank white hair fit all too well with his much-lined face.

But John hardly saw all that. This was Father Anthony, the priest who had always been more sympathetic than strict, more paternal than profound. Yes, he was an excellent scholar, but he had been better still as a surrogate uncle to the young heir of the great and impossibly detached Hugh O'Neill. A father who had never had time for or interest in this son, who some had snickered was "Johnnie-come-lately... and -slowly." A father who, in the eight years he lived in Rome, never once summoned the boy to his home, and hardly ever wrote him a letter from the time that he was deposited with Archduchess Isabella at age seven.

John felt his command persona fall away, and did not care in the least that it had: "Father Anthony," he said. And opened his arms.

The frail priest doddered toward him. But somehow, when he got there, despite John's slightly greater height and much greater mass, it seemed that it was Father Anthony who enveloped the earl in a great, fond hug, rather than the other way around. After a few moments, John realized that the room had become very still. "Father Anthony," he repeated; his eyes stung a bit.

"Ah, Johnnie," breathed the priest. "You've not changed." He looked around at the bodies for the first time. "What a hash," he breathed. "Johnnie, did you have to?"

John hung his head. "It was them or us, Father. Not what we wanted. We thought to nick the two of you out of here with a piece of paper and a wink, as it were. But—" He looked at Lefferts, who looked away. "—but things didn't work out that way. No evil intended by anyone, Father, but it happened nonetheless."

"Man always runs afoul of man's plans." The priest nodded, looked at the group, smiled at Owen, with whom he had a passing acquaintance, and the other Wild Geese in the room. But the smile dropped away when his eyes found the Wrecking Crew, first resting upon Harry, then Sherrilyn, then Thomas, then George, and then back to Harry. "Johnnie, who are these—persons?"

"Eh—chance met fellow-travelers, Father."

"Travelers? Why 'travelers'?"

"Because we're leaving now, Father. All of us. You too."

"With them?"

"With all our friends," John amended, earning a small smile from Harry.

Anthony looked at the Wrecking Crew yet again, and, alarmed, looked back at his old pupil and unofficial charge. "They're friends, are they? So are you consorting with the Devil, now, Johnnie?"

John sighed. "I just may be, Father; I just may be."

# Chapter 22

The up-timer security precautions surrounding access to their aircraft facilities in Mestre had been challenging to navigate, Valentino admitted, but time and luck had been on his boss Rombaldo's side.

As Valentino tugged his uniform coat straight, he conceded that the up-timers had an almost impossible job maintaining tight security around their flying machines, simply because the complicated vehicles needed so many mechanics and support crew. In addition, there was a constant running back and forth by special artisans who manufactured precision replacement parts, including screws and bearings. With all that traffic, flawless base security was an impossibility.

But as it turned out, there had been an even easier way into the USE's waterside airplane repair and refitting complex in Mestre. Although the aviators themselves oversaw most of the primary engine and structural repairs, they had almost a dozen assistants. Classified into two strata, mechanics and junior mechanics, it was they who did the physical hammering and lifting and replacing and tightening and loosening. All under the watchful eyes of the two aviator-mechanics.

However, in just the past week, one of the senior mechanics had announced his departure. He had apparently been offered a position with a firm determined to build airships; they needed a person with extensive knowledge of, and experience with, up-time engines. In addition to even better pay, it was the chance of a lifetime: the mechanic, a down-timer, was now going to work as a senior, hands-on motor expert.

Predictably, one of the junior mechanics was be bumped up to fill this hole, and that in turn put a hole in the roster of the junior mechanics. With the Jupiter's support staff thus down one man, the aviators had interviewed a number of the more experienced technical assistants: a glorified term for the even larger work crew that fetched parts, maintained regular supplies, and ensured the safe storage of fuels and lubricants. The inevitable result: one of these was promoted to become a new junior mechanic. And this meant that someone had to be brought in to become a new technical assistant, which was itself understood to be an apprenticeship position. Which, for Rombaldo, had been the operational equivalent of finding a diamond under his pillow.

Having comparatively modest entry requirements, the position of technical assistant had been a perfect fit for any one of a dozen persons a local underworld chief had markers on. In the juridical parlance favored by the shady lawyer retained by this underworld chief, these were persons who were susceptible to extortion, due to their prior misdeeds—the evidence of which was now in the underworld chief's hands, thanks to some tips by the shady lawyer. Rombaldo had purchased the marker on one of these compromised individuals: a rakishly handsome thirty-year-old precision tool-maker who had indulged in a rather torrid affair with a slightly older woman, a fading beauty who had married well above her station. To a brother-in-law of one of Venice's august Council of Ten, no less.

The arrangement was simplicity itself. The tool man—a nickname which became a predictable source of bawdy humor, given the nature of his indiscretions—would apply for the position of technical assistant. If successful, he would then follow a few simple instructions. He would, on completing his assignment for Rombaldo, receive the incriminating evidence on him back into his hands. No doubt he would burn those damning (and deliciously indiscreet) letters as soon as he received then. And would just as surely rush to reassure, and possibly reembrace, the nervous Venetian trophy-wife, who would once more be secure in the unassailable esteem—and legally-filed will—of her elderly spouse.

Rombaldo had been forced to purchase the tool man's letters for the exorbitant sum of three hundred lire. However, it was a crucial resource and worth the great price, much like any other valuable commodity.

And so, thought Valentino, to business. He looked over at one of Rombaldo's better local hires, a cheery fellow named Ignatio who enjoyed a good joke and the occasional torture of hijacked house pets. Valentino nodded approval of Ignatio's matching uniform. Arguably, it looked even better on this new henchman, who had served briefly in the militia. Ignatio had not joined those ranks out of civic-mindedness, of course; it had been for the quite lucrative black market contacts he made there.

Valentino glanced at their papers, fakes which had been quite challenging for Cesare, Rombaldo's forger, to duplicate. The up-timers had evidently employed a few rather clever tricks in the crafting of them, but Cesare had painstakingly overcome the difficulties. Valentino now passed the fruits of those labors to Ignatio. He stared at them. Valentino shrugged. "Our lives could depend on these papers. I thought you might like to check yours, at least."

Ignatio shook his head. He smiled, but also blushed. "No need. I can't read."

"Oh," answered Valentino, who pocketed the papers and suppressed his admiration for Ignatio's honesty—all the more because he concealed his own illiteracy with shamed diligence. He led them out of their rented room, down the stairs, and toward the door that would put them upon the streets of Mestre.

And in plain sight of the up-timers' aircraft repair compound.

Valentino arrived at the gate, hand upon sword, a firm, almost grim look plastered on his face. The face that stared back at him was fair, sunburnt, topped by auburn hair scorched into red-gold by the Italian sun. The uniform of a USE Marine from the embassy detachment was unmistakable. Two of his comrades cradled carbine versions of their army's standard flintlock; the posture was not threatening, but their weapons could easily be swung into a ready position.

"Business?" asked the one at the gate.

"Extra guards for the compound," Valentino answered in Italian. "Sent by the Arsenal."

The freckled nose of the guard quirked a bit at the stream of clearly unfamiliar words. "*Arsenal? Garda?* You help USE?"

Valentino nodded twice, severely. "*Si. Garda.* USE."

The gate guard nodded. "Papers."

Valentino presented them, saw the other two guards studying him. And he thought: *Now I'll find out if I got enough of the bloodstains out of this shirt. Pity that it took a knife in the neck to kill the real guard sent by the Arsenal: messy business.*

But in a country full of stained clothing, whatever telltale marks there might have been on Valentino's uniform excited no particular interest by the guards. The one with the brown-red hair opened the gate, returned their papers, pointed ahead and then made a leftward hooking gesture with his hand. "Take the third left. *Dritto. Sinistra.*"

With an abbreviated salute, Valentino entered the compound, Ignatio close behind him.

"So you understand your duty?" the Marine asked Valentino, speaking with a faint German accent.

"Yes. We walk the parmenter—"

"Perimeter."

"*Si,* yes, 'perimeter.' One of us inside, one of us outside. I walk in this direction, like the arms of a clock; my man goes against the clock's direction. Yes?"

"Yes. So why don't you start your firs—wait a minute; here comes the last of the fuel. Stand here for a moment. Guard the other barrels." The Marine left to speak with a startlingly handsome man who was pulling a safety-railed handcart loaded with six casks that, even at this distance, gave off a distinct petroleum smell. It was equally obvious, from the descriptions Valentino had been given, that the glorified fuel stevedore was none other than the Tool Man.

The other Marine inside the building wandered over to Valentino and his partner. "So you're from the Arsenal, eh?" he asked, a good-natured smile creeping on to his ruddy face. This one spoke with less of an accent; was either Scottish or Irish, Valentino guessed.

"*Si,* Arsenal."

"Drinking mate of mine serves the same masters, richt enuf. Would you know Roberto Giacomo? Fine husky lad about yea tall?"

"No *capito*; no understand." Valentino lied. Just what he needed:

some overly friendly pigeon who happened to know someone in the Arsenal.

"Well, I can try my Italian," said Mr. Friendly in a fair approximation of the Venetian dialect. Wonderful. The buffoon was a linguist on top of it. This was just getting better and better. And Ignatio was becoming visibly anxious, which in his case meant an increasing likelihood that he was going to do something singularly violent and stupid.

"*Per favore*," called the first Marine from over by the fuel casks, "help us? *Per favore?*"

Valentino almost thanked the man for providing an excuse to get away from his chatty fellow guard. The Venetian thug stepped lively to the hand-cart and helped to keep it from tipping as the German-accented Marine and the Tool Man turned it. He then laid a thoroughly unnecessary steadying hand on the cart's rail as they wheeled it over alongside the other three, similarly loaded trolleys; he was happy to be doing anything other than fending off friendly inquiries about Arsenal troopers from the Scotsman.

"That finishes it," affirmed the senior German marine with a curt nod. Turning back to Valentino, he said, "Now then; ve shall measure the time of your watch from—"

Tool Man coughed lightly. "Sir."

"Yes?"

"The fuel: you must sign to confirm receipt of it. And you, too," he said, speaking over the shoulder of the German to the Scottish Marine, who approached readily enough.

The German Marine was looking at the proffered papers with a frown. "I have signed these papers before," he declared. "When you brought the first handcart. Surely you remember? When you knocked on the door, ve—"

The Scotsman was now leaning over to stare at the papers himself, his back fully exposed. Valentino looked over at Ignatio and nodded.

The knife in Valentino's forearm scabbard slid down quickly and smoothly into his palm. He hopped, light as a dancer, to a position directly behind the German. The trick to this maneuver, he had found over the years, was to do everything at once, rather than in sequence.

So he simultaneously grabbed a fistful of the Marine's medium length hair with his left hand and pulled sharply backward, even as his right hand came up and drew the plain, quillonless blade sharply across the German's arched neck.

Blood sprayed out over Tool Man, who gasped and stumbled back against the trolley, eyes bulging. The German tried to struggle, but at the end of the neck-slicing sweep, Valentino gave a quick, well-practiced flip of his wrist; the point of the knife dug in just before it cleared the ear, clipping the carotid artery. The blood spray, which had already started diminishing, briefly surged again before the German lost strength, swayed, and fell over in the rapidly widening red pool.

Which was when Valentino realized that Ignatio was having some unexpected trouble: the Scotsman had apparently spent some time wearing armor in the field, and had retained some of those old habits. A light gorget, unseen beneath his collar, had intercepted enough of Ignatio's identical slash so that the resulting wound was serious, but not immediately debilitating. Now the big Scot had Ignatio's knife-hand in one powerful, meaty paw, and was steadily moving his own right out of his assassin's weaker grasp. Toward his pistol.

Valentino assessed, measured, leaped and struck out straight from his shoulder with his own blade.

It entered the Scotsman's back at a right angle to, and left of, the spine, just under the scapula. It plunged in so hard and fast and level that the edge of the handle almost pushed into the wound.

The Scot quaked once, a groan dying out of his chest as he swayed, and then fell forward, heart pierced from behind.

Ignatio's grateful smile annoyed Valentino, who snapped, "Quick! Close and lock the main door!"

Ignatio complied quickly. In the meantime, Valentino stripped off his Arsenal uniform and glanced at Tool Man. "You have the change of clothes for us?"

"Yes, right here."

"Good. Lay them out on the floor. Quickly."

"Yes, but what do we—?"

"There is no 'we,' here. *I* tell you what you do. First, break open the smallest of the fuel casks and spread the contents around. Stave in a few of the others."

Ignatio had returned, a grin on his face. "Now what?"

"Strip. Wipe off any blood. Then get into those clothes."

"Which are—?"

"Which are what porters wear here in the compound, as well as some of the technical assistants."

"And then?"

"And then watch the door." Valentino turned to Tool Man, saw that he was almost done spilling out the first container of gasoline into a wide puddle. "You."

"Yes?"

"There is another way out of here, yes?"

"Yes, a side door. Over there. Only big enough for one person."

"Does it lead to the alley I saw between this warehouse and the next?"

"Yes."

"Excellent. That is how we are leaving."

Tool Man looked suddenly relieved. "Thank you."

"Why?" asked Valentino, as he pulled a pre-cut fuse out of his discarded pants pocket and snatched up the Scotsman's pistol.

"I—I thought you were going to kill me."

"What? Why?"

"Because I saw your faces. I did not think you would let me live."

"Old wives' tales," scoffed Valentino. "If we went around doing that, we couldn't very well successfully blackmail people to help us, could we?"

Tool Man looked even more relieved.

Valentino used the narrow end of the pistol's ramrod to unseat and tear up the currently loaded charge. Once it was loose enough, he shook it out upon the floor. "Ignatio?"

"Yes?"

"Is our way still clear?"

"Yes."

"We're leaving by the side door. But we won't start running until the chaos starts. Then, we'll just be a few more workers rushing to get out the gates."

"Hey, yeah. That's smart!"

Valentino managed not to roll his eyes. He made sure there was ample powder in the pistol's pan, closed the frizzen, cocked the hammer. "Here," he said to Tool Man, "take the other end of this fuse. Now, walk away, toward the fuel, pulling it out straight."

Tool Man complied.

"Now, lay the fuse down along the floor. Make sure the last two inches are in the puddle of fuel."

Again, Tool Man did as he was told.

"No, no," said Valentino with a shake of his head, "you've done it wrong." He walked over, kneeled down, made sure an extra half inch was immersed in the gasoline. "There, that's right. Do you see the difference?"

Tool Man nodded.

"And don't forget," Valentino added as he stood up, "we need to keep those false papers you brought."

"Why?"

"Best you don't know." Valentino pointed. "You left them on the trolley, there."

Tool Man turned around to look at the indicated spot. As he did, Valentino slid out his dagger again and jabbed it into the back of Tool Man's neck, just below the base of the skull. As the first spasm went like a wave down the body, Valentino re-angled the last bit of his thrust higher, pushing the point so it went up under the skull's occipital shelf.

Tool Man fell over, quaking.

Valentino wiped his knife on the body. "You know," he observed sagely, "a lot of those old wives' tales are true." He rose, walked to the dry end of the slow-burning fuse and kneeled down, calling to Ignatio. "Are we still clear?"

"No one in sight."

"Then get out the side door and stay in the shadows. Now."

As Ignatio complied, Valentino scooped the powder from the pistol's extracted charge into a small pile, mounded up over the dry end of the fuse. Then he leaned the pistol over toward it, so the frizzen was almost in contact with the loose powder.

He heard the side door open and Ignatio's footfalls recede through it.

Valentino squeezed the trigger. Without a charge in the barrel, the weapon simply made a hoarse *FARAFF!* when the striker hit the powder in the pan, which flared out and down to touch of the powder atop the fuse.

Valentino stood there long enough to make sure the fuse had caught. Then he turned and sprinted for the side door.

Tom Stone handed another cup of coffee toward Miro, who only shook his head, eyes upon the disaster taking place across the lagoon.

The embassy's veranda afforded them an excellent view of the black plume of burning petroleum. Of course, everyone in Venice could see that. But from the veranda, they were also able to discern the fierce, bright flickers at its base. Meaning that, since the flames were visible from this distance of almost three miles, it was, in actuality, nothing less than a full-blown conflagration. In leaden silence, they continued to sip coffee and contemplate the unfolding of the infernal spectacle before them.

As Tom put his cup back upon the table, a mushroom cloud of seething, yellow-orange flame roiled up, momentarily obscuring the dense black smoke. But even as it threw its defiance at the sky, the fiery fist curled over on itself and died.

"That would be last of the gas still in containers," Tom observed calmly.

Miro nodded, waiting, counting the seconds. Just as he reached fifteen, a low roar reached them. It peaked as a kind of hoarse imitation of a siege gun volley, and then dwindled back down to nothing.

The gulls, attention focused on the scraps that might be available from the humans on the veranda, continued wheeling in their disinterested arcs.

"Well, I'd say we're pretty much screwed," Tom commented, sipping at his third cup of coffee.

"We haven't seen the flare signaling 'plane lost,' though."

"Not yet. But there's no knowing if the fire will reach the plane itself. If they followed my instructions, they moved the fuel to the warehouses furthest away from the hangar. But a fire like that—" He put down his coffee and rubbed his eyes with both hands. "Estuban, given the message Harry Lefferts sent yesterday, I have to admit: I'm getting pretty worried. I should never have let Frank go to Rome."

Miro spoke softly. "Unless I am much mistaken, you could no more have compelled him to remain here than you could have brought yourself to issue such an ultimatum. You may have chosen to craft your family along atypical lines, Tom, but since you love and respect each other, they must have been *good* lines."

"Yeah. Maybe. But right now, those lines are all pointing at the same destination: disaster."

"No, I do not think so."

Tom looked over, eyes controlled—probably trying hard not

to indulge in false hopes, Miro guessed. "Really? You mean we have some good news, for a change?"

"My balloon will get here within the week. Certainly before the Wrecking Crew returns from Rome."

"Empty handed," Tom amended glumly.

"Not quite. They don't have Frank and Giovanna, but they gathered essential information, which all indicates that they will need extra resources for the job. Extra resources which are coming in on the balloon."

"Yeah, Estuban, but not all of the resources you wanted; the repair parts for the Monster took precedence. Now we're not going to be able to get it airborne until we get some more fuel down here. Which means another balloon ride."

Miro nodded. "Yes, Tom. I know. I wish we had another balloon."

"You and me both. Listen: I'm not annoyed at you, Estuban. You've been a life-saver in all this. Where would we be at this point if we didn't have your balloon?"

Miro shrugged. "In a few years from now, we wouldn't have to be depending on a single balloon. Or, even if we were, we wouldn't be restricted to such small payloads."

Tom shrugged, somewhat distracted. "Well, even the hydrogen design is no bigger than the one you're using currently."

"True. But size is not what determines payload."

Tom nodded, snapping out of what Miro guessed was the trance of an increasingly worried parent. "Sorry; yeah, of course. With more than three times the lift of hot-air, hydrogen is going to really boost how much mass even a balloon of the same size can carry. And since you don't have to carry fuel for a burner that keeps the air in the envelope heated, you free up a huge amount of the carrying capacity—volume as well as mass—for cargo. About nine tons useful payload instead of the current limit of just under one ton, if I remember the design specs."

Miro smiled. "I see you've been doing some extra reading."

"Always do, before I get involved in money stuff."

"A smart investor always considers the investment carefully."

"Well, yeah, that too. But that's not really what I meant." Tom's big feet started their customary rocking. "Making money is just not that important. Money comes, money goes, and it's bullshit when it's around. Makes people sick in their heart and their head.

But right now, it seems there's no choice but to live with it. So if I'm going to get involved in something where I have to worry about how much money I am going to contribute, and what it's going to be used for, I look really carefully at what I'm buying. I mean, is the project worth all that worry? Is it going to make that big a difference?" Tom's feet stopped imitating a pair of big, matched metronomes. "Your balloons are worth it. Until I had read through the specs of the hydrogen airship, I didn't realize just how much they're worth it. And I've got to have a concrete understanding of those details before I can bring myself around to getting involved on the money side of a project. Because if I didn't, then when all the shit about costing and pricing and amortization of assets begins—and it always does—then I'd get disgusted and walk away. What keeps me committed to a project is what it's about, what it's achieving. The money stuff—win, lose, or draw—just makes me want to run the other direction."

Miro shook his head and smiled. "Tom, did you ever read the Talmud?"

"Uh, some. Not much. Long time ago. Why?"

"Because although you could not sound less like it, some of your opinions about money—about everything worldly, for that matter—are very reminiscent of its wisdom." Miro sighed, as he looked at the black plume that no longer had any visible flames at its base. "I'm relatively sure that my childhood rabbi would find as much to disapprove of in me as he would find salutary in you. No doubt he would suggest that God destined our paths to cross so you could improve my materialistic soul."

Tom scoffed. "Well, first off, you're not the materialist you think you are. I see your eyes when you talk about those balloons. I know a dreamer when I see one, man. I've been looking in the mirror a long time, you know." Tom grinned sheepishly. "And if you were all about money, you wouldn't be down here on this 'at cost' gig, overseeing the rescue of my son and the safety of the pope."

"And a shining success I've made in both cases," Miro grumbled.

"Okay, Estuban, now let's not talk pity-party shit, okay? If anything, *I* was the one in a god-damned rush to get Harry to Rome; you were the one who wanted to wait for a few more resources, in case the job was 'more problematic.' Your very words. Your only problem is that you listened to a distraught father and let Harry flex his authority muscles, instead of laying down the law. But you're the new guy, and Harry has a lot of successes, so basic human dynamics got in the way. And your instincts about those dynamics were not bad ones, either. Besides, I'm sure Ed Piazza and Don Francisco gave you a few sermons on being a team player, and the problems of having authority over people who really didn't know you, and who had a pretty good track record of getting things done on their own. Probably said something like, 'don't think of yourself as a leader; think of yourself as a coordinator.'"

Miro kept his face blank; actually, Piazza had used the term "facilitator" rather than "coordinator," but in every other particular, Tom Stone's rendition of Miro's sessions with Grantville's intelligence cadre was eerily accurate.

"And as regards the pope, you're doing the best job anyone can. You've got more security forces inbound, and the safe house will be ready in a week. And that"—he pointed at the pillar of smoke—"probably couldn't have been stopped. Again, you called the event before it occurred. 'Too big and too much traffic to be secured properly.' That's what you said when we walked around the compound after the crash, figuring out how to protect the plane from Borja's saboteurs."

"Being right doesn't help if you aren't effective, too."

"Man, you sound like some kind of business school hardass, now. Listen: you want to beat yourself up? Fine. But do it on your own time, and know—*know*—that it's all bullshit. You did what you could. You protected the plane. They got the gas." Tom shrugged. "They've got professionals, too. Which is another prophetic point you made the day you got here: just because you can't see the enemy, doesn't mean they're not here."

Miro nodded. "And have been here for weeks, probably. This was simply the first time they had to tip their hands. If they hadn't acted, we'd have had the plane working again within a few weeks and removed the pope. Or could have quickly extracted the Wrecking Crew a day's sail beyond Ostia after a successful rescue in Rome. Now, without a plane, we're the ones racing against the clock, not them."

Tom nodded back at Miro. "But, thank the Great Pumpkin, we've still got your balloon, because if we didn't, it would be 'game over, man.' So—" Tom leaned forward, fists resting gently on his knees "—what's the new plan?"

# Part Three

## June 1635

A thousand screams the heavens smote

# Chapter 23

Thomas North watched the dark shape of the boat emerge from the morning mist that lay upon the Laguna Veneta like a carpet of gray cotton. "They're here," North called over his shoulder. The sounds of meal-taking in the small pilgrim's refectory behind him diminished, succeeded by the clatter of plates being collected and removed for washing.

Sherrilyn came to stand beside him. "Can you see who it is?"

"I can barely make out the boat." Thomas smiled. "But if you're willing to make a wager—"

"With a sneaky bastard like you? Never."

Thomas grinned, remembering how, just five days earlier, she had actually out-bluffed the redoubtable Harry Lefferts during a marathon session of five-card stud. Despite the excellent sailing characteristics of their lateen-rigged boat, they had nonetheless spent half a day lying becalmed just south of Bari, waiting for a favorable wind that would bring them to the eastern side of the Adriatic and the northerly current that predominated there. Toward the end of that game, she'd taken the hand on a busted flush, eliciting groans and howls from Gerd, and Paul, the only other members of the Wrecking Crew to leave Rome. These sounds of distress had so alarmed the crew of their small Dalmatian *gajeta* that the first mate had rushed over to see who'd been injured.

The card-playing had also been an icebreaker for increasing

interaction with the Irish Wild Geese. However, with the exception of Wadding, who had apparently learned the rules simply by watching a few hands, they became more perplexed as the play progressed. The earl of Tyrone had pronounced the game as a debased variant of *primero* and turned his back upon it. Owen Roe—a bit more congenial than his young earl, and far more even-tempered—unsuccessfully tried to understand it as a new form of the English game *brag*. The other Irish might have found some interest in the game, but, between being poorer than indigent church mice, and more interested in chatting up the up-timers, their focus strayed from the rules and the cards.

After that, the stormy Adriatic had kept them busy, scudding too close to the Dalmatian coast, beacons warning them away from headlands at the last safe minute on more than one occasion. Thomas suspected it was more the extraordinary competence of the crew—a mix of Croats, Ragusans, and Italians—that had saved them in these instances: their knowledge of the coast was uncanny, even at night.

The Venetian lagoon had marked the abrupt end of the crew's collective navigational knowledge, but one of the Italians had shipped out from piers on the Lido on two prior occasions, and so was able to guide them to their destination: San Francesco del Deserto, a small islet just north of St. Erasmo. There had been some debate over that choice; Harry and North had wanted to head straight in to Venice itself, simply because they knew of no other way to contact Tom Stone and the embassy. Wadding, in his typically quiet way, had pointed out that if Borja was indeed guilty of all that he seemed guilty of, then the main island would be watched by his confidential agents and should be avoided. Thomas had been pleased, but not entirely surprised, at Wadding's revised opinion of the political realities in contemporary Italy. The boat ride had provided ample opportunity to disabuse good Father Luke of his rather optimistic hopes that Borja's worst atrocities were, in fact, simply malign propaganda.

Once apprised of the trail of evidence that connected the assassinations, disappearances, and almost capricious slaughter of civilians to Borja's decrees, Wadding's nimble and nuanced mind quickly became an invaluable asset. Their current billet was a case in point: only Wadding had known about the small Franciscan monastery on the islet of San Francesco del Deserto. It was a place that had few visitors, and all of those came for purposes of hermitage or induction. It had no commerce, the monks acquiring their scant needs from the smaller, rustic islands nearby. A perfect place to arrive in Venice and yet remain unobserved and quite comfortable.

Bog hoppers or not, North admitted, the Irish were masters of surreptitious activity; they had little choice, given the stern occupation under which they struggled. Not that North would ever say so aloud, but he was of the opinion that his own countrymen had really gone too far in the subjugation of Ireland, and that there was now no way to reverse the situation, much less undo the damage. Of course, the Irish weren't exactly shining exemplars of Christian charity and restraint, either. North suspected that when the parable of "turn the other cheek" was read out in Irish churches, the priests half-leaned out of their pulpits and whispered *sotto voce* behind a confidential hand, "except when the barstard is a feckin' *sassenach*, o' course." Such were the contextualized pieties of the Emerald Isle.

But also, such were its lessons in subtlety. At Wadding's instruction, a sealed message had gone out yesterday at dawn, entrusted to the order's youngest novice, who was traveling to nearby St. Erasmo for provisions. While there, he had sought and found a slightly younger childhood friend who was also an aspirant to the order. A brief chat after morning prayer, a blessing, and a lira, and that young aspirant was on his way to the main island to pass the ciphered message on to the couriers' collective that handled afternoon deliveries to the USE embassy.

And apparently, the message had reached the desired parties. Hopefully, it had also avoided detection by Borja's many agents. But even if they had intercepted the communiqué, it would do them little good. The cipher was a disposable code, and was only one of the ways in which the monks had protected the message. Only a priest familiar with the legends of St. Francis, who had reputedly made a hermitage on the islet where they were hiding, would understand the allusive and symbolic cant in which it was written.

But even if Borja's agents somehow managed to decipher all of that, they would only have learned that Ambassador Stone and Don Estuban were requested to travel to San Francesco del Deserto this morning. How they would get there was a matter left to those summoned. They had no doubt employed a variety of precautions, probably involving a rendezvous of boats in the predawn, to defeat interception. And if Borja's minions decided to land on the islet itself and attack—

Thomas turned around; Owen Roe O'Neill was inspecting his pepperbox revolver. Standing by his side, the earl of Tyrone was scowling at the weapon, muttering that a sword was the proper weapon of a warrior and a man. Harry Lefferts had just finished reassembling the shotgun he'd field-stripped after racing through his breakfast. More than half a dozen of the Irish, seasoned in the Low Countries campaigns despite their scant years, lounged about the kitchen door. Dangerous men in a fight, they huddled there like so many young boys, hoping for the favor of an extra roll or rasher of bacon from the indulgent friar-cook. Surveying this array of both mechanical and human weapons, Thomas North couldn't help smiling at the thought of what a bunch of assassins would encounter if they were foolish enough to attack this island. A fitting line from one of the up-time movies he had memorized suggested itself: "Go ahead; make my day."

"Well, are you coming—*sassenach*?"

Thomas North looked up and found Owen Roe O'Neill looking at him. With a smile. "That would be 'Lord Sassenach' to you, *cultchie*."

"And that would be 'Lord Cultchie' to you, Lord Sassenach."

North couldn't help smiling back. "It seems we have come to an agreement on the mutually odious nature of our relationship."

"So it seems. Now, are you coming, or are you planning on sneaking off and stealing the sacramental wine when no one's about?"

"You mean they leave it unlocked?"

"Only because they don't know about you. Come along, then."

Miro leaned back when North had finished giving his report. He looked at Tom Stone, who waved the four USE Marines out of the room to join the four already outside. He looked down the table at the O'Neills. John looked back, expressionless. Owen waited a moment for his earl to act, and then nodded at the Wild Geese, who joined the Marines. Miro nodded his thanks to Owen, who nodded back. John looked sideways at his much older cousin, annoyed.

Tom Stone cleared his throat. "I'm sorry to clear the room, but we're going to start talking plans. Seems like the moment to minimize the number of people hearing them."

John O'Neill crossed his arms. "I can trust my men. To the death."

"I believe that, Lord O'Neill, but tell me this: do they ever get drunk? Talk in their cups? Do they keep track of who's new in a shared billet and who isn't? Do they remember that every innkeep, serving girl, farrier, stable hand, prostitute might be a potential informer? Because only people who can maintain that kind of highly suspicious frame of mind should be in this room."

Which made Miro reflect, and not for the first time, that perhaps the earl of Tyrone himself should not be present. But such an exclusion was a diplomatic impossibility.

John seemed a bit mollified by Tom Stone's explanation, but not much. It was Wadding who found a way out of the growing silence. "Ambassador Stone, we are grateful that you agreed to meet us here on such short notice. It seems we have a number of mutual objectives, and I thought it wise for us to confer on how we might best combine our resources to achieve them."

Tom Stone glanced at Miro, thereby signaling that, as the ambassador, he was handing off the meeting to the acting chief of local field operations. Miro knew that Tom didn't much like ambassador-ing, particularly not under these conditions. But protocol demanded his presence. John O'Neill, one of the two exiled princes of Ireland, had asked to meet him, and besides, any conversation that involved rescue plans for his son and daughter-in-law was a conversation Stone had insisted on being a part of, damn it.

Miro leaned forward. "Father Wadding, as I understand it, you *were* the objective of the Colonels O'Neill."

"Technically, yes—but in actuality, that mission was just a stalking horse."

"You mean, if the O'Neills were apprehended in Rome, they could honestly claim that they had been sent after you, without alerting Cardinal Borja to the fact that they were also attempting to rescue the pope."

"That is correct. A venal sin concealing a mortal sin, as it were."

"I see. Now, about the mortal sin to which you refer—"

The earl of Tyrone leaned forward aggressively. "Just say plain: do you have Urban in your care or not?"

Wadding looked at the earl, made a gesture of patience, possibly also indirect admonishment; there was clearly history between those two.

Miro looked at John O'Neill directly and answered, "Yes; the pope is under our protection."

The Irish in the room stopped as though frozen. The Wrecking Crew's representatives weren't much less surprised.

Wadding was obviously the trained negotiator among the Irish; he was the first who recovered enough to ask, "Not that we are ungrateful for your extraordinary candor—but why did you tell us?"

"Because, unless I am very much mistaken, you had already guessed as much."

Owen hid a smile; John's expression softened; Wadding looked at Miro as if he had discovered a fascinating clue to a puzzle. "And how did you surmise this?"

"By having a long acquaintance with human nature, Father Wadding. From what Colonel North has reported, this doctor of yours who stayed behind—Sean Connal, the representative of the earl of Tyrconnell—spent the days before you left Rome asking the Wrecking Crew to join him in speculating upon Urban's whereabouts and fate. An innocent enough question, and perfectly reasonable, since it is on everyone's minds and lips. But the Wrecking Crew's command staff noticed that Dr. Connal did not as frequently engage them on this same topic."

"From which you draw what conclusion?" asked Owen with wonder in his voice.

"Why, that Dr. Connal quickly discerned who in the Wrecking Crew *could* keep a secret and who couldn't. So he concentrated his attention and efforts upon the Crew's rank-and-file members, where he surely discovered the telltale signs of persons who suspected far more than they were willing to reveal. He no doubt communicated their identities to you three before you left him behind in Rome.

"That way, on your sea voyage from Rome to Venice, you had ample opportunity to continue those discussions with these more susceptible members of the Wrecking Crew. It hardly mattered that their speculations were neither specific nor detailed—because they arose, in large part, from wondering about the orders they were receiving and the indirect clues they were sensing from their commanders. Of course, they still felt the need to deny any relevant knowledge—but every time they squirmed, that meant you were possibly hitting close to the mark you were seeking: inferential data on the status and whereabouts of Urban himself."

John and Owen exchanged very long looks. Wadding smiled slightly. "Don Estuban, you do indeed seem an astute observer of human nature, but were these projections the *sole* source of your deduction?"

"Not at all, merely the hub of the wheel, so to speak. It also made sense that you would naturally begin to wonder about our 'possession' of the pope on your own. After all, if the pope's whereabouts and fate were unknown, then why would the USE deploy its most renowned team of commandos merely to rescue an ambassador's son? I mean no offense, Mr. Ambassador, but the fate of the pope has immense and even global implications. It is only logical that the USE would devote its best rescue team to the task of locating and retrieving him, if such action was necessary; the demise of Urban VIII would mean the ascendancy of Borja. That would be disastrous for our interests, as well as those of our allies."

Miro pointed at the O'Neills. "So after the two of you encountered the famous Harry Lefferts and his band in Rome, determined to rescue Frank Stone, you had to eventually conclude, 'If the USE can spare the Wrecking Crew to retrieve young Stone and his wife, they must already know that the pope is either dead or safe.' And safe would naturally mean 'under USE protection,' at this point."

Owen and John exchanged yet another long look. Wadding rubbed his rather pointy chin.

"So," Miro concluded, "remaining coy about the pope's status would only be an insult to your intelligence. And that would undercut our ability to exchange information freely and plan for joint operations. For, as I understand it, Lord O'Neill, you have said it might be in the interests of your employers and your own countrymen to help us rescue young Mr. Stone and his wife."

"Could be," John answered, with a sly smile at Harry, who answered with one of his own. And in that moment, Miro saw that making allies via realpolitik was only half of the earl's motivation for offering assistance; he, too, had fallen victim to the Harry Lefferts Charisma Effect. Not like an abjectly adoring schoolboy worshiping a sports hero; more like a peer who had met a kindred-spirit that was also a freer spirit, one who lived a life of action and adventure unconstrained by the responsibilities of a prince. But that would only be part of John O'Neill's motivation—

"Could be that lending a hand to you is also the only way for me to fulfill my main mission, as well." John explained. "Now, I'll confirm something that *you've* probably deduced: we are charged to bring the pope to the Low Countries, to Fernando and Isabella. And I'm betting you won't go along with that, not right away. But good will starts somewhere, am I right? And besides, unless I make you happy, you're not going to consent to have two of my men appointed as Urban's personal bodyguards."

Miro blinked. "I assure you, Lord O'Neill, the pope has a sizable security contingent. And it will be expanding very soon again."

"I thought no less. But I am not talking about mere soldiers. I am talking about personal bodyguards. My men will go wherever he does, ready to fight and die to keep His Holiness safe at all times. That's the kind of protection we were charged to provide. I would satisfy those orders—at least in part and in spirit—by providing two of my men for that service."

Miro looked at the earl of Tyrone, saw that this decision had come as much from his heart as his head. Miro instinctively understood that this was an important moment, a test of sorts. "Yes. Agreed," he announced firmly.

The earl's broad, and frankly surprised, smile made him look almost boyish. "Well, perhaps we're going to get along famously, after all."

"It would also be helpful," mentioned Owen Roe, "to relay this news to the Low Countries. We had thought to send signals through the Venetian network, but if you were to be so helpful as to use your radio to—"

"Colonel O'Neill, your arrival here"—Miro made sure his glance included Wadding—"was already communicated to Magdeburg and Grantville last night. I suspect it has been passed on to King Fernando. We will append the rest later today. Along with a formal request that Fernando grant you permission to aid us in retrieving the hostages."

"And you will include a report on the welfare of the pope?"

"That," answered Miro through a long exhale "is unfortunately not within my purview. However, not only will I urge that the king in the Low Countries is informed of Urban's status, but I suspect that my superiors are already similarly minded."

Thomas North cleared his throat histrionically. Miro smiled at him. "Just jump in, Colonel North."

"Thank you, Don Estuban. Although I sympathize with the desire to inform select persons of the continued well-being of the pope, I feel duty-bound to point out that there is no way to be absolutely sure that, once transmitted, the message will remain—er, fully secure within its intended circle of distribution."

*My, Thomas, what big intel-speak words you use. Probably either heard them in a movie, or read them in an up-time political thriller.* But, on the other hand, North clearly had a head for genuine intelligence and counterintelligence operations. "I agree with you, Colonel North, but I think the damage done by such a leak will not significantly impact our other plans. Soon Borja will have fully excavated the rubble of the Castel Sant'Angelo. We know they will not find Urban's body there, nor any traces of one. They may find, however, spent shotgun shells, but again, no sign of a shotgun or the person who might have wielded it. They will deduce that Urban was rescued by agents of the USE. So, even if Fernando's court in Brussels leaks the intelligence, it will only tell Philip's spymasters what they would very soon have learned for themselves.

"Consequently, I think that sharing the information with our new allies' liege as a sign of the growing trust between us and the Low Countries is far more important than a few extra days of secrecy. Just as I wanted to make it clear to our new Irish friends that we are willing to help them fulfill their bodyguard assignment, at least until the pope decides to leave Italy."

Wadding leaned forward, surprised. "Don Estuban, do I correctly infer that the pope's continued presence in Italy is not merely because he is waiting for you to repair your plane?"

"That is correct, Father. Pope Urban is weighing all his options, and their consequences, very carefully."

"I would be grateful to sequester myself with his Holiness to offer any services I might in the course of his deliberations."

Miro smiled. "Easily granted, also—since that was the pope's wish, as well."

"The pope? Requested me?"

"Just as soon as he got the message that you had arrived here."

Wadding, imperturbable up until this moment, suddenly seemed impatient to leave. "Upon concluding our business, I shall pack immediately."

"Patience, Father; joining the pope is not easily done, and it is a one-way trip. You will not be able to leave him until such time as he departs Italy. Any traffic to or from his safe house is just what Borja's agents will be watching for."

Harry leaned forward. "Let's steer back to the really time-critical issue: the rescue. Just before we left Rome, we learned from informers that the Spanish have relocated Frank and Giovanna to the Palazzo Mattei."

Tom Stone squinted. "The what? Where's that? Never heard of it."

Wadding answered. "It is a fairly recent construction, just east of the Ghetto and the Tiber. It is a large complex of palaces and houses that takes up a whole block: an *insula*, as the Romans call it. However, whether you plan to rescue your friends by stealth or by a trial at arms, it will not be easy in such a large place. At the very least, you will need more men to attempt it."

"Which," resumed Harry, as if on cue, "is why I'd like to pull a few Marines from the embassy, so that we've got enough—"

Miro shook his head. "No, Harry, we can't do that. At no time would it be advisable for us to use our Marines, but now, with Borja's agents watching us and looking for Urban, it's out of the question."

Harry jerked a thumb in Thomas North's direction. "Then what about some of his guys?" North looked startled, seemed ready to bristle.

Miro jumped in. "Again, Harry, I just can't—"

"Look. I hear you've got a regular balloon service working here. So how about I take, say, three or four of the Hibernian Company, and you bring down their replacements on the balloon?"

Miro didn't like the sound of that for a number of reasons. First, he wanted to keep the security forces as dense as possible around Urban. Second, it was clear that North and Harry had just recently buried a methodological hatchet over the operational cause of their first meeting with Wadding and the Wild Geese. North had been annoyed that Harry had been, to use his words, "cowboying" when he entered St. Isidore's, and Harry had retorted that if it hadn't been for his initiative, they wouldn't have their new allies at all.

But on the other hand, in this matter, Harry was inarguably right: he just didn't have enough trained manpower for the rescue. And the Wild Geese, while a significant addition, were not the full answer on their own. Besides, Miro had kept four of the Hibernians here in Venice, rather than with the pope, just in case something came up. Something like this.

Miro spread his hands wide upon the table. "Very well, Harry. I will authorize the release of four Hibernians to assist with the rescue operations. However, I am placing them directly under Colonel North's personal command."

Harry nodded. "Sure. But, fair warning: on these jobs, formations sometimes get a little messy. It's hard to keep coloring inside the lines when things get exciting, if you know what I mean."

"I understand that during combat operations, the command structure may need to be fluid."

"That's all I'm asking." Harry beamed. Thomas North, conversely, looked much less than pleased. Well, they'd have plenty of time to iron out any persisting difficulties later on . . .

"We also have to head back to Rome quickly," Harry continued.

"Why?" asked the earl of Tyrone; his tone was one of curiosity, not umbrage.

Tom Stone raised his chin. "My daughter-in-law is due sometime in October. I know down-time women are pretty tough customers; I've seen plenty of proof of that. On the other hand, we're not talking about normal circumstances. I figure a rescue could get pretty kinetic: running, jumping, ducking, climbing, crawling. That's not what any doctor ever ordered for the third trimester."

Harry nodded. "Yep, and the longer we wait, the bigger a problem Giovanna's speed and mobility limitation becomes. So, since we've got the extra troops we need right here in Venice, and since the crew and ship that brought us here were pretty trustworthy—"

Miro shook his head. "We'll retain them, but they are not the ones who will convey you to Rome; that will be done by a special ship and crew that you will meet at Ravenna. We will send your current ship after you, as a back-up."

Thomas North tapped the table restively. "Ravenna isn't really a port, Don Estuban."

"No, it's inland a bit, but ships stop at the fishing village close to it. The vessel we've engaged is a *barca-longa*, single-decked and with especially reliable crew. They are part ex-Arsenal, part Napolitano expatriates. They've got a reasonable proportion of military experience, no love of the Spanish, and a bit of experience in the 'small trade' business."

"Black market?" translated Harry. "Outstanding."

John O'Neill raised an eyebrow. "You like traveling with tinkers and thieves, do you, Harry?"

"Hell, I travel with you, don't I?" But Harry's smile made the jibe a jest between comrades.

"Seriously," Harry answered, "that new ship sounds perfect, Estuban. Those guys will have exactly the skills we'll need, including being Italians without any connections to Rome."

Miro nodded. "And since half of their generous pay is contingent upon your healthy return to Venice, your safety and interests will become their interests. They will be alert to subtle treacheries that might elude the notice of non-natives. Now, have you had a chance to look at the communiqués we received from the team you left behind in Rome?"

"Briefly," responded Harry with a shrug. "Looks like Mr. Donald Ohde is becoming a pretty fair hand with a radio."

"Yes. He reports that they've found sufficient vantage points for observing the Palazzo Mattei. And Juliet is developing quite a following among the local youngsters."

"Well, a little cash buys a lot of good will in lower-class Rome, right now. Things are pretty sparse, there. So by the time we arrive—using a different entry method—she should have a good observation network set up. Watching the palazzo's provisioning deliveries as well as their guard rotations will give us the real numbers of the troops we're facing. Also, with Juliet talking to the servants, we should manage to get a good map of the internal layout."

"That last factor is what concerns me, Harry. Donald's messages indicated that there weren't many servants to speak with, as though the domestics are being kept in the Palazzo Mattei at all times. If that is the case, how will you get a workable floor plan?"

"Oh, Juliet will find someone who can draw us a map, I'm sure."

Owen frowned. "And why are you so sure?"

Harry shrugged. "Because there's always a loose end, like a former scullery maid who had to leave employment when she got pregnant, and who can now use a few lire in exchange for a few lines drawn on a piece of paper. Never fails: there's no way to sew up all the folks who know what the inside of a building looks like. And Juliet always finds them. Always. It's her super-power, you know."

"Eh...yes, of course."

"Her what?" inquired Wadding.

"I'll explain it later, Father," Sherrilyn assured him. She turned toward Miro. "Juliet's also busy rebuilding the ranks of the *lefferti*, from what I understand."

"Yes, although that was already half-accomplished by the time you arrived. Juliet's been learning that, due to their martyrdom in the early days of the occupation, being one of the *lefferti* became a symbol of underground resistance among Rome's younger men. So there are a lot of new *lefferti* already available. They are also more political now. Not more *informed* about politics, but certainly more motivated by political issues such as the Spanish occupation of Rome. And, increasingly, Madrid's control over Naples and Sicily." Miro looked around the table, noted the new frown on North's face. "Colonel? Something to add?"

"Something to ponder. Specifically, how much of our future plans we should share with the prince of Palestrina and with Romulus? Do we let them know when we've returned to Rome? It would be good to have the extra support, and an alternate escape route or safe haven if a maritime extraction goes pear-shaped. But..."

Miro nodded appreciatively. "Yes: 'but.'"

Harry sat up straighter. "'But' what? You can't believe Romulus is a turncoat."

Thomas shook his head. "You're right; I think we can trust Romulus. Whoever the hell he is. But can we trust everyone in the chain linking us to him? And him to Don Taddeo Barberini? And all of the duke's advisors?"

Owen's frown was thoughtful. "Is some past event feeding your suspicion, Thomas?"

"'Suspicion' is too strong a word. Let's just say I entertain the possibility that it wasn't mere chance that we were conveniently on hand to witness the shell-game that Borja's spymaster staged on the streets of Rome, using the two prisoners as the pea. Indeed, if word had come from Palestrina that we were in country—"

Harry nodded. "—then Borja's henchman would have had enough time to set up what we saw, hoping we'd tip our hand reacting to it. But since we stayed out of direct contact with the duke during our one-night stay in Palestrina, the opposing spymaster's informers couldn't get any detailed intel on us. Just that some group was bound for Rome and probably for the purpose of rescuing the Stones."

Sherrilyn considered. "And so Borja's folks quickly came up with a plan to bait us into doing something stupid."

"I'm not sure that plan was developed quickly, Ms. Maddox." North studied his own, steepled, fingers. "The complexity of the operation we saw in Rome, and the surety with which it was mounted, make me suspect that our 'opposite number' had the whole ruse in readiness. As I remarked in Rome, it is hardly a stroke of genius to expect that the famous Wrecking Crew might be sent to rescue the prisoners. So he only had to wait for one of his wide net of informers to provide him with credible intelligence that we were in the area. And if his informer was indeed somewhere inside the household of the prince of Palestrina, Taddeo Barberini, it tells our opponent something else, now that I think of it."

Miro blinked. "Of course; it suggests—doesn't prove, but certainly suggests—that Urban *is* alive."

"What?" John O'Neill looked from one to the other. "Why?"

It was Wadding who answered. "Because Taddeo Barberini is another of Pope Urban's nephews. So if the pope was dead, or even if his location was unknown, how reasonably could Harry and the USE presume he would cooperate? But the USE operatives did go to his domain, and Taddeo did cooperate. That suggests that the USE and the duke have some other, common cause— which would logically be the safety of the duke's uncle, the pope. Which would in turn dispose Taddeo Barberini to assist a USE rescue team when it arrived near Rome."

"He might be motivated by revenge, too; his oldest brother, Cardinal Francesco Barberini, was cut down like a dog." John sounded both defensive and truculent.

"Yes, my lord," Wadding replied mildly, "that could be his motivation. But I am familiar enough with the reputation of Taddeo Barberini to know that, like the other nobles of the Lazio, he will not endanger what power and possessions he has left simply to indulge a thirst for personal vengeance. He is too shrewd for that. Indeed, he might have personally preferred to remain wholly uninvolved in the Wrecking Crew's rescue attempt; any hint that he helped Borja's enemies could incite disastrous reprisals. No, I suspect Borja would read this as I would: Taddeo Barberini felt obligated to aid and abet representatives of the USE because they have, and control the fate of, his uncle the pope."

Owen let out a long-held breath. "So, Father, you believe that Borja already knows that the pope is alive and in USE custody?"

"As Colonel North observes, the aid the Wrecking Crew received from Palestrina does not *prove* anything about the pope's fate. However, it suggests certain probabilities, among which the holy father's continued survival in a USE sanctuary ranks very high indeed."

Sherrilyn looked grim. "So the assassination clock has started ticking for the pope."

Miro turned toward her. "The clock is being wound, but I don't think the countdown has begun yet. If Borja's agents cannot find an eyewitness to indicate that the pope is alive—and we have taken measures to prevent that—then they must build their case for his survival upon telltale bits of data and evidence. Like this one. They have no doubt come to provisionally believe that Urban is alive and in hiding with us, but when all the evidence is circumstantial, you must accumulate a great deal of it before you are satisfied you have proven your hypothesis."

Harry leaned forward. "Estuban, leaving aside hypotheses for a second, I'd like to touch on a few facts. Fact: I brought Gerd back with us because he'd like to get his hands on some lively chemical substances, if you catch my drift."

"I suspected as much. Ambassador Stone?"

Tom smiled. "Sounds like my boys. They experimented with a lot of exothermic substances when they were younger."

Harry smiled back. "So I recall. So can Gerd have the run of your warehouse?"

"Well, it's not like we've got a munitions stockpile. But I'll set him up with a list of what's on hand. He can choose from the menu."

Harry nodded. "Great. Thanks. Estuban, how much more gear can you bring in on your balloon?"

"Nothing, not before you leave again for Rome. The balloon is already en route with repair parts for the Monster. It's also carrying fuel and a few more Hibernians, who will now simply replace the ones you are taking to Rome. After that, the balloon's next cargo run from Grantville has to be gasoline for the Monster. We'll fit in some extra cadre as well, but that's a full load, too."

"Cadre? How many? And who?"

"I'm not sure how many seats will be available on that flight, but, with all the Hibernians deployed to protect Pope Urban, and with Colonel North attached to the Wrecking Crew for the duration, I've decided to bring down the ranking Hibernian officer in Chur, Lieutenant Hastings, to help command the papal protection detail."

Harry nodded. "Okay. What about radios? We left one behind with the team in Rome, so now we've only got our backup. Is there another we can pull from stores?"

"Yes, and I have more on the way."

"Any of them voice-grade?"

"Surely you jest. Morse code works just fine."

"Yeah, fine—and slow. And hard."

"Well, the other sets are far too big and fragile for you to be able to transmit on the move. Besides, a slow radio connection is at most an operational nuisance, not a crisis."

"We'll also need money."

"That's already been drawn and is waiting for you. We're only providing Roman and Tuscan coins. That way, the money's origin won't draw any attention, or tip off anyone looking for a USE operations team based out of Venice."

The room remained silent for three seconds. Miro wasn't about to wait until someone thought of something else; there was simply too much work still to do. He stood. "Very well, I believe that takes care of the primary business. I will remain in Venice until the fuel arrives." He looked at Harry. "By that time, with any luck, you will have rescued the Stones and be on your way back here. Father Wadding, you will be escorted to the pope with all dispatch, but please forego leaving this island until then. Anyone who arrives in Venice and associates with us will almost certainly acquire a tail who works for Borja. Lord and Colonel O'Neill, if you would be so good as to accompany me now, we will compose a joint communiqué to your lieges in the Low Countries, and see to any refitting needs you might have." He stood. "Gentlemen and Ms. Maddox, Ambassador Stone and I are compelled to depart within the hour, so my last words to you must be these: good luck and godspeed."

# Chapter 24

Frank Stone looked out the window and down into the smallish courtyard below. Fairly new in construction, it was well maintained, with deep, porticoed balconies at the back. At the front, a modest gate led to the streets, which, if he craned his neck, Frank could see disappear into Rome's Jewish Ghetto.

"It's nice having a view," he commented.

"It would be nicer if the view was nicer," Giovanna retorted, but, smiling, came over and put her arms around him. Her growing bump now made itself felt whenever she hugged him. "Nicer still if I was tall enough to see it." Then, distracted, she turned back toward their bedroom. They had two rooms now, a fine bed, windows, and meals fit for nobility. Well, minor nobility, at least. Indeed, Frank could still smell the remains of lunch: a light stew, mixed greens, and—

"I wonder if there's any vinegar left?" said Giovanna in a suddenly distracted voice.

Frank relaxed his arms, let her move out of his hug and into the other room, her fine nose almost twitching in search of piquant delights. Frank smiled; then, remembering her latest pregnancy cravings, almost retched: the vinegar on the potatoes had been quite reasonable—but mixed straight into the pear preserves?

From the next room, he heard the irregular clatter of his wife

243

rooting through the crockery, a pause and then a satisfied, "There you are. Now, where is the cheese?"

Frank felt his stomach spasm, and he looked out the window again. Not much to see, down in the courtyard. And then he noticed: not only were there no servants running about, and no porters lugging their various burdens, there weren't even any guards. "Hey, Giovanna, have you seen any guards today?"

"No, Frank," came the response, muffled by what was obviously a very full mouth. "I didn't see any yesterday, either. At least, not in the courtyard."

"Maybe it's a sign that there are negotiations under way for our release. You know, make us happier campers before they return us?"

"Perhaps."

"And maybe that's why we've got the view. Maybe it's not just so we can see out, but so some of our folks can see us. See that we're healthy, happy: all that good stuff that my dad would want assurances about. And I don't think he'd trust their say-so. He'd want our representatives to see it with their own eyes."

"Perhaps."

"Well, whatever the reason, it sure is a dramatic change from our prior circumstances. And as changes go, it sure is nice."

"Hmm," was Giovanna's subvocal response, which terminated in a gulp. "Too nice, maybe." A pause, then an almost comically diminutive belch. "I do not trust it."

Frank smiled. "Honey, you don't trust anything."

"And you, my love, trust too many things, too much."

There was a knock on the door.

"Speaking of which—" Giovanna let her voice trail off.

"Signor Stone?" called a voice from the hall. "Are you still interested in the walk I have arranged?"

"Yes, I am. Just a moment." Leaning heavily on his cane, Frank poled over to the iron-bound door and tugged it open. Captain Vincente Jose-Maria de Castro y Papas was ready with a bow and flourish that was actually fairly understated, considering some of the extravagant courtly salutes that Frank had witnessed among Spanish officers.

Frank looked behind the captain. "No Sergeant Ezquerra?"

"Ah, it pains me to report that the lout is up to his excessive eyebrows in paperwork."

"Why does it pain you?"

"Because Ezquerra cannot read."

Frank guffawed once. "Damn. I sure walked into that one."

"Pardon?"

"Uh . . . I stepped right into your joke-trap."

"Ah, yes. You are kind to pretend amusement at my so-called witticisms. And to inquire after the sergeant."

"As men go, my Frank is the model of kindness," Giovanna said from the other room. "Indeed, he is too kind. I, however, am not."

The captain looked at Frank cautiously. "I will presume, then, that Signora Stone still does not wish to accompany us on our stroll?"

Giovanna had appeared, hands on hips. "You presume correctly, Captain. Now go. The longer you wait here, the longer it is until I get my husband back."

"I assure you, I will return him back here quickly, and certainly at the first sign of fatigue."

Giovanna retreated into the other room. "What a charming lie, Captain. Enjoy your stroll." The sounds of eating resumed.

As the door closed behind them, the captain observed, "The signora has an excellent appetite."

"I heard that!" came her voice from the other side of the door.

Castro y Papas' eyebrows raised.

Frank smiled. "Her appetite is pretty good, but her hearing is *amazing*."

The larger, central courtyard of the main Palazzo Mattei—the Palazzo Giove—was imposing, with serried ranks of flowers bisecting the quadrangles fitted between the various buildings. They walked in silence for many minutes, the faint hum of bees and flies stilling and then resuming as they passed each of the garden's colorful, and carefully tended, beds.

"Vincente—may I call you that?"

"Yes, or course. And shall I call you Frank?"

Stone nodded. "Thanks for suggesting this walk."

"It is my pleasure."

"Is it? I mean, don't get me wrong; it's nice, but it's not exactly regular duty for Spanish officers, is it?"

Vincente smiled. "No. It is not. But it is pleasant. And you may be sure of this, Frank: I will not lie. Not even in little things."

"Then just why is it that we two are taking a stroll in the garden?"

Vincente sighed. "Because, as your lovely and very intelligent wife has already surmised, I am to encourage you to trust me."

"Can you really tell me that?"

Vincente raised an eyebrow. "I just did, didn't I?"

"Well, yes, but—"

The captain snickered. "Ah, Frank, you are so earnest. It is a charming trait, really. Indeed, I think if we share too many such walks, the machinations of my superiors may reverse themselves."

"What do you mean?"

"Why, that I will come to like and trust *you*, Frank. Which it is never wise for a captor to do. He who imposes his will must never feel empathy or sympathy for those upon whom that will is imposed."

"That sounds more like training for a slaveholder, than a soldier."

Vincente nodded. "That is because, in our service, it is often the same thing, particularly in the New World. If it is true that the Spanish Empire is the largest the globe has ever seen—and that *is* true—it is also true that we are the least welcome in more of the places that our flag flies than any empire before us."

"Which bothers you."

Vincente shrugged. "Somewhat. Conquest is our way of life. It may not have always been thus, but it is now. And it is the way of the world, as well: the law of nature. The strong always dominate the weak. But I wonder about—well, the limits of imposing dominion."

Frank paused to admire a bush filled with bright vermillion flowers. "Actually, in our up-time world, I think we pretty much learned that it's a slippery slope. Once you get started—once you say to yourself, 'I'm stronger, so it's my right to take what I want'—there's really no stopping yourself. Before long, you're taking everything that isn't nailed down. And then, even the things that are. Because where do you stop? Once you have dominion over other peoples who never wanted you on their land in the first place, you've got to be ready to kill to keep what you've taken. Which means killing people who just want to stay in their own homes, keep their own goods, speak their own languages, and live their own lives without answering to a conqueror. Oppression is an all-or-nothing deal, when you get right down to it, because soon enough, even mercy becomes a luxury a conqueror can't afford. Mercy only enables further rebellion, defiance, hope. And so there you are: master of the world, but the price you have to pay for it is every bit of mercy, justice, and honor that was ever in your soul."

It looked like Vincente had flinched at each of the three words Frank had stressed: mercy, justice, and honor. After five more steps the Spanish captain commented, "I think this walk has become a bit less nice."

Frank shrugged. "Sorry, but that's the truth as I see it."

The captain shook his head. "I was not complaining. 'Nice' walks are pleasant, but they are—well, eminently forgettable, no? One looks at the flowers, listens to the birds, blinks up at the sun, and says, 'Ah! How pretty!' Fine enough, and wonderful for children. But I would have my walks be times for thinking, for speaking frankly, for exploring the ground that lies between us—both the similarities and the differences. A 'nice' walk I would enjoy and forget. I will not forget this walk."

Frank smiled. "You know, you're a pretty okay guy, Vincente—for a domineering creep, that is."

"'Creep'?"

"Uh . . . a creep is a jerk."

"'Jerk'? I thought this word described a motion."

"Oh. Yeah. Uh . . . oaf."

"Ah! Heh. Heh heh. I am not so okay as you think. You should pay more heed to your clever wife."

"Oh, I pay plenty of attention to her. But my dad taught me something long ago that I've found is usually true—true almost as often as anything is, when it comes to human nature."

"So? And what is this paternal wisdom?"

"That people live down to, or up to, your expectations of them. If you believe people are fundamentally good, many, even most, of them strive to be so. And if you think everyone's a, a—"

"—a creep?" supplied Vincente.

"Yeah—a creep—then they tend in that direction."

"That sounds very idealistic."

"Well, that's my dad for you. And here's the realism part, I guess. His caveat to this was that it's always a lot harder—a *lot* harder—to believe the best of people. After all, we're constantly hurting each other, being selfish, being—well, creeps. But if you persist in believing that people are better than that, a lot of them turn out to be. And they remember your faith in them, and repay it. Many times over."

Vincente was very silent for a long time. "That," he said slowly, "is either the most foolish philosophy I have ever heard, or the most dangerous."

Frank stopped. "Dangerous?"

"Yes, of course it is dangerous. Is it not obvious? Kings, captains, and domineering creeps like myself rule through fear. We compel obedience through fear of our reprisals, fear of our discipline, fear of our disapproval. Your philosophy would undermine the instigation of such fear. Oh, there will always be plenty of brutes willing to resort to the lash and the oubliette, but one cannot run an empire with brutes. They lack the brains and the nuance for command. Higher faculties are required among the cadre, who must have a more evolved understanding of, and instinct for, the nature of the human heart. And that would be the hole in the dike of the dominators, no? For happily, persons gifted in human perception also tend to have souls that possess the same weaknesses they perceive and exploit in others. How would such domineering souls fare, faced with masses of the oppressed who still insist upon appealing to their best natures?"

"Dude, you are *so* channeling Gandhi, now."

"I do not understand what those words mean, and your smile is worrisome of itself, Frank. But, I must ask: if this philosophy is so powerful in your world, then why was your time wracked by wars that make ours look like mere squabbles?"

"That," Frank admitted, "is truly the bitch of the situation."

"Eh . . . you are allowing that yours is a flawed philosophy?"

"Let's say I'm admitting that we were still working on it." They'd neared the end of their circuit of the gardens and were angling toward the door that led back to Frank's room.

Castro y Papas was clearly trying to find a tactful way to carry forward the discussion. "I mean no offense, but if in your world you were still working on achieving a society based on this philosophy, after centuries of effort, might that not indicate that its goal is illusory, is impossible?"

Frank shrugged. "Maybe. So does that mean you are saying that Christ was a liar?"

Castro y Papas missed a step, stood straight, offended. "What?"

"You heard me. What about turn the other cheek, only throwing the first stone if you're without sin, the last being first and vice versa, rich men having to wiggle through the eye of a needle to reach the pearly gates? Is that all just so much crap? Because that's pretty much the same message as the one my dad drummed into us, when you get right down to it."

The captain did not move. Then he opened the door out of the garden, and stared at Frank. "This was not a nice walk," he mumbled, "not a nice walk at all. Shall we do it again, same time tomorrow?"

When Dolor entered, Borja greeted him familiarly, offering him a seat. Dolor simply shook his head, and stood, hands clasped behind his back. And Borja felt the anxiety that this apparently emotionless man always aroused in him. In a world where men were influenced by their wants or fears, how do you influence a man who has none of either?

"Our plans for the hostages are now complete, Your Eminence. All is in readiness."

"Yes, yes, but my concern is not over the hostages. They are a minor detail. I must have a resolution in the matter of Urban; I need action, if action is required."

"So. You are now satisfied that there is no body in the ruins?"

Borja looked away. "Not yet."

"Really? My sources tell me you have finished your search. Indeed, they tell me that you ended the search just before the last rubble from the explosion was to be removed.

"And of course, there is another piece of interesting circumstantial evidence: The body of Quevedo."

"And how does Quevedo's miserable corpse bear upon the matter of whether Urban was rescued or remains within the rubble?"

"The manner of his death strongly suggests the former."

"What do you mean, 'the manner of his death'?"

"Your Eminence, I took the liberty of examining the body. Whoever killed him bested him in a sword fight."

"So you are implying—"

"Who but the Ambassadora's husband would have had the weapon and the skill and the proximity to inflict such a mortal wound?"

"But," protested Borja, "but he is old."

"If it is the Catalan we suspect, then I would not presume that age predicts infirmity. And there is corroborating evidence."

Dolor reached out his hand and placed several spent shotgun

shells on the table. "I had two of my men carefully continue the excavation of the general area where Quevedo's body was discovered. These small objects had, of course, been ignored during the main excavations, lost in mounds of small stone and debris. But this leaves little doubt: Urban was rescued. Successfully. And Quevedo evidently died trying to prevent it. What I am less than certain about is why, just when the dig seemed on the verge of providing concrete evidence, you elected not to complete it."

Borja said nothing. How much had Dolor guessed? "You have your own conjectures on the matter, naturally."

"Only one, Your Eminence. Not that it would apply to you. And it is purely hypothetical, of course."

"Of course. Pray share it."

"It seems to me that if one were to consider the current mood among the remaining cardinals of the Church with a jaded eye, their desire to see Urban stripped of his pontifical robes is less ardent than one might have hoped."

Borja said nothing. He also carefully controlled his impulse to fold his fingers into white-knuckled fists of rage. The cowards! Who would have thought that half the Consistory would fail to follow his lead in calling Urban to account for his malfeasance and his willing collaboration with the enemies of the church? Their indifference was tantamount to treason.

But Dolor had not even paused. "In such a political climate, where strong action against Urban is far less certain to be supported, it is perhaps increasingly desirable that the pope not be discovered. Not alive, that is. Better for the Church and its true servitors that he should remain missing, or be discovered after his demise. This would be most helpful in quelling any uncertainties about succession. And it would help the Church to rebuild its unity without any lingering—impediments."

Borja swallowed. "An interesting theory. Complete fantasy, of course."

"Of course. But at any rate, it also shows how the apparent rescue plans being crafted by agents of the USE to retrieve Señor Stone and his wife do, ultimately, connect back to the search for Urban."

"Oh? How so?"

"Let me show you." Dolor reached out his hand again. More spent shotgun casings clattered down on the table. Mixed in with them were almost a dozen smaller, and precisely machined, cartridges. Just looking at them, Borja could feel the encroachment of the up-time Earth: it was there in the eerie, perfect symmetry of their shapes.

Borja nodded. "From St. Isidore's, I presume."

"Precisely."

"But I do not understand. The USE agents must have known that the hostages were not there. Why would they take such a risk, and reveal themselves as they have, at St. Isidore's?" He gestured toward the latest crop of casings.

"I have been wondering the same thing. I have concluded that they were not alone at St. Isidore's, and that whatever other group they met—either by design or chance, either beforehand or at the Church itself—were the ones who actually commenced the attack."

"Why do you think there was another group involved?"

"Several reasons, again deduced from a close study of the bodies. Several of our guards were killed by sword wounds. Very heavy rapiers, or possibly sabers. This is not consistent with the USE raiders known as the Wrecking Crew; they vastly prefer up-time firearms. It is where their primary advantage and expertise lies. So did matters become so dire that they had to resort to swords, or did the swords belong to someone else?

"Additionally, almost half of our troops who apparently tried rushing the antechamber by way of the corridor from St. Isidore's apse were killed by these." Dolor dumped another load of metal on the table, but this was a collection of very contemporary, albeit very deformed, bullets.

"This is, once again, definitely not consistent with the weapons the Wrecking Crew uses. And since they had little to gain by absconding with the two priests, Wadding and Hickey, I must conclude that the Wrecking Crew were not the catalyst for what occurred at St. Isidore's. They were merely facilitators."

"But for whom? And why?"

"I have no basis for conjecture; there are too many unknowns. But there is one last, tantalizing fact: the entirety of the combat was conducted within the street-side buildings, or in the interior grounds. How did the attackers get there, then? No guards were killed at the gate, or even in the portico; indeed, it seems as if those guard posts were abandoned. Yet it makes absolutely no sense that the members of the Wrecking Crew would have been allowed past the guard at the gate, or admitted beyond the portico at the top of the main stairs. It is as if the enemy forces were first detected when they had already gotten inside the rectory. Then, all the guards contracted on that point and were defeated in detail."

Borja waved his hand in irritated disgust. "Señor Dolor, I cannot begin to tell you how very tired I am of these up-time-led brigands slaughtering our men and suffering no losses in return."

"I quite sympathize, Your Eminence. But strangely, I believe this may now be working to our advantage."

"What? How?"

"Overconfidence, Your Eminence. If the Wrecking Crew was involved in the events outside Chiavenna, and has now stormed a church in the middle of a Spanish-held city, I suspect they are quite pleased with themselves. So pleased that perhaps they will begin to assume that they are undefeatable. If so, that is exactly the species of pride that goeth before a fall."

Borja smiled. "Yes, so it is written. And your new plan for securing the hostages—?"

"—is crafted to take advantage of that first deadly sin, Your Eminence: pride."

"Very good. But I still do not see how knowing that the Wrecking Crew is tasked to effect the rescue of the hostages helps us in our attempt to—'locate' Urban."

"Your Eminence, if we can trick the Wrecking Crew into making a mistake, we might be able to take prisoners who know where Urban has been sequestered."

Borja spread his hands out on his desk, unconsciously mimicking a gesture he had seen cats indulge in when crippled prey lay between their paws. "Then the sooner they make their attempt, the better. For all our plans."

# Chapter 25

Old Mazarini brought out Antonio Barberini's bags as he joined the group gathered in the courtyard. There was an ironic appropriateness to the timing of their departure, thought the young cardinal. *It is just as we are leaving that the late-spring flowers are finally coming into full bloom, that the first berries are ripening enough for the table. A table which will be empty once again tonight and who knows for how many weeks, months, years to come.*

It was a melancholy thought, young Cardinal Barberini conceded, one he would not have had two months ago. Two months before this day, Antonio Barberini was fussing over the arrangement of newly acquired paintings in his family's grand palazzo, just south of the Pincio. Now—

He looked around the courtyard. The Marines and Hibernians were checking the belly-straps on the pack-mules, ensuring the right marching order for optimal security, awaiting final orders. The children, families, scattered menials who had made the journey with them were waiting in preassigned groups, somewhat anxious but not nervous or terrified: not like those first, terrible days fleeing from Rome.

Antonio turned back to look down the inviting paths of the country arbor. No overly precise cutting and trimming, here. This was a working garden, a place that fed people, sheltered them, gave them a place for quiet conversation, reflection, repose—all while providing scents that lulled one into a doze as surely as the warm sun that shot through the filigree of leaves and vines.

Barberini smiled. Who would have thought it—least of all him!—that worldly, cosmopolitan, refined, even effeminate and spoiled (it was said by some) Antonio Barberini would come to so love a country garden? So love it that what he imagined he would miss most about Rome—the luxury of his apartments and salons and life in Palazzo Barberini—never troubled him once. Instead, he felt strangely, even gladly, distant from that life of opulence and glory—or more accurately, vainglory. His existence there had been aesthetically refined, very pleasing to the senses—but could one call an environment filled solely with inanimate objects truly beautiful? Were paintings and poses in marble greater than the things they represented?

Two months ago, he might have assayed an argument in support of that claim, suggesting that art was not merely the preservation, but the amplification, of the perfection of form. But now he knew differently. This place—the children playing foolish games that parents did not notice, the bees buzzing in the arbor, the strong flanks of loyal horses, and the faces of stern men sworn to protect lives they had come to know and value—this was beauty. And there was no way to freeze or capture it, let alone amplify it; it was as great a beauty as life itself—and just as inevitably fleeting. And if it was to endure at all, it would not do so as frozen physical forms, but in the memory of a human heart.

In this case, in the awakening heart of Cardinal Antonio Barberini.

"So you will miss it, too, Nephew?"

Antonio started, found his uncle the pope standing behind him, dressed in clothes that marked him as nothing more than a moderately well-to-do townsman.

Urban gestured behind them. "This farmhouse, I mean."

"Yes, Uncle, I will miss it. Very much."

Urban VIII stared around with the same wistful look on his face that Antonio imagined was on his own. "It is strange, is it not, how we humans strive to refine ourselves, to build new achievements upon those past, to accrue piles of ducats, attain fame, create a powerful family, even build an empire—only to find our true happiness in the quiet of a shady garden and solid peasant food?"

Antonio, listening to the tone, detected reverie, not discovery. "So this has happened to you before, Uncle. This kind of rustic self-discovery."

Urban smiled, nodded. "Oh, yes, my boy. Often. But it changes every time. The first time, I was not much older than you are now. It came as a great surprise. And it taught me much. Now, it comes as a reminder. A blessed reminder of what really matters. Of our place in the universe. For very soon, I will need to make decisions that touch upon the difference between the world we encounter with our head, and the world we touch with our heart. And I must seek a way to reconcile the two." He turned to Antonio and smiled. "With your help, of course."

"Of course, Your Holiness. But I doubt that I alone will be able to—"

"Oh, it will not be you alone, Antonio. We will have many friends to help us, including some who will meet us upon the road to our new home."

"Which is where, Uncle?"

A new voice intruded: "In an area called Molini. It's a small mountain valley northwest of Laghi, up in the hills between the Treno-Adige river valley on the west and the Asiago plateau to the east."

The Barberinis turned to look at Larry Mazzare. "It sounds remote," commented the pope.

"That is a profound understatement, Your Holiness."

"Ah. Excellent for our purposes, then. And I suppose it has been the subject of your occasional private discussions with the ambassadora and her husband?" Urban's eyes twinkled, but Antonio heard the probe, and the implicit remonstrance: *You wouldn't keep secrets from your pope, now, would you, Lawrence?*

Cardinal Mazzare did not exactly look sheepish, but he no longer looked as relaxed as he had a second ago. He had his mouth open to make what promised to be one of his carefully measured replies—

—when another voice came from out of the arbor. "No, Your Holiness. I would not ask Father Mazzare to withhold information from you." It was the ambassadora, who was—herself, no less!—carrying a sizable traveling bag in either hand. "But I did ask him to delay doing so until we were under way. I would appreciate it if you did not share the information with anyone else. Anyone. I repeat: I would really appreciate it." The extraordinary emphasis that the ambassadora put on the word *appreciate* made it sound like something just shy of an order, the violation of which would entail dire consequences.

"Of course, Ambassadora Nichols. We do not wish to jeopardize anyone's safety."

The ambassadora smiled; it was genuine, if a bit rueful. "I am very glad to hear that, Your Holiness, because it is your safety that we are ensuring with the secrecy. I doubt very much Cardinal Borja would be quite so interested in the rest of us."

It wasn't exactly a remonstration, but it was as pointed a reminder as Antonio had ever heard uttered to his uncle.

Urban only smiled. "The ambassadora's candor is refreshing. And apt. I do understand the situation. Quite well. Tell me: is there any further word on the saboteurs of the airplane in Venice?"

Emerging from the arbor behind the ambassadora, and carrying enough personal weaponry to equip at least two squads of soldiers, Ruy Sanchez de Casador y Ortiz dusted pollen off the shoulders of his buff coat. "No word, Your Holiness. Not that we expected it. Borja's dogs are well-trained. And after Quevedo, it seems he has chosen a far more capable kennel-master. This one is dangerous, Your Eminences; he strikes seldom, but carefully. And now he is waiting, no doubt, for some clue that will reveal our location."

"But this has been prevented by your prudence."

"As much as possible, Your Holiness."

Urban raised an eyebrow. "And what measure has remained beyond your remarkable abilities at ensuring Our security?"

The Ambassadora stood very straight. "Unfortunately, your own request, Your Holiness. Specifically, that Father Wadding be sent to join us. I understand that it is an urgent matter for the good of the Church, but from a security standpoint, it is a bad move. I will freely admit that I was against it. I mean no disrespect to the well-being of the Church or to Your Holiness' wishes, but quite frankly, it risks both of those things."

Urban nodded. "And who prevailed upon you to permit it, then?"

The Ambassadora smiled at the two men—Ruy and Mazzare—who stood flanking her. "These two idealists. They both seem to understand the necessity of Father Wadding's presence more than I do."

Urban's eyebrows raised. "Indeed? I am not surprised that Lawrence did; it is simply a logical extension of the same wisdom and love of Mother Church that brought him down here despite the perils of the journey and the destination. But you," he said, turning his attention upon Ruy, "Señor Casador y Ortiz, I was not aware that the intricacies of theology and canon law were among your very many wonderful talents."

The Spaniard inclined his head. "Your Holiness, I fear I would find myself well schooled by the average cockroach in such lofty matters. But the Irish priest is well known in Spain. He studied at Salamanca, and went on to a lofty position there before being a presence in Philip's own court. He is known for his wit, his kindness, but above all, his piety and integrity. And he is among the most respected of his order. Should you therefore intend to hear counsel from the many voices and perspectives of the Church, he would seem a likely choice: a respected and famous Franciscan known for his long and warm relationship with Spain's clergy and court. With Father Wadding as part of your deliberative council, no man may say that you surrounded yourself only with voices that echoed your own thoughts and preferences."

The young fellow named Carlo came running up. "Ambassadora, the master of horse, he tells me we are ready to leave. We only wait upon you and the blessed fathers."

"We are coming, Carlo. Go run through the houses now; bring anything you find that has been left behind. Then come back to me."

"Yes, Ambassadora Nichols." And Carlo was off as if shot from a cannon.

But the ambassadora was looking at her husband, who was staring at the line of horses, mules, and carts. "What is it, Ruy? Something wrong?"

"Something we cannot fix. Not yet."

The ambassadora shrugged. "We only have the soldiers we have. Don Estuban radioed that more are on the way."

Ruy sighed. "I hope they will be enough."

Antonio looked between the frowning faces around him. "Well, what of the Marines from the embassy? If more soldiers are needed, cannot they—?"

But the Spaniard was shaking his head. "It would not be advisable, Your Eminence."

"Are they not loyal?"

"Indeed. Almost to a fault. But they are most certainly under observation. If any number of them were to depart the embassy, they would be followed. Discreetly. Perhaps at the distance of a day's journey."

"Then they could lose those who are trailing them, no?"

Ruy sighed again. "I wish it were so simple, Your Eminence, but no, not if the men following are capable. Four mounted Marines must camp, must cook, must get provisions, and may need to seek lodgings; they will be seen. And the embassy's Marines are almost all men of Scotland or the Germanies. In dress and appearance alone, they attract notice, but when they open their mouths to speak Italian—" Ruy's summation was an expressive roll of his eyes.

"Then how will Father Wadding be brought to us at all?"

"First, he has not visited the embassy, and so can not be followed from there. Second, just this morning, I believe, he has commenced the first leg of his journey: westward via boat, up the Po River. Neither he nor his companions will leave that boat, nor moor it at a pier or dock, until they are at least fifty miles west of Venice. Upon coming ashore, they will immediately travel northward, overland. When they have made rendezvous with us, Father Wadding's escorts shall return by horseback. With any luck at all, this will put them well outside the observation of Borja's Venetian agents."

Antonio clapped his hands. "So there is nothing to lead them to us. Indeed, your precautions are so complete that it seems impossible that they shall *ever* find us!"

But the Spaniard was shaking his head. "No, Your Eminence; we are merely ensuring that Borja's agents will be much delayed in finding us. But they will not fail to ultimately learn our location. Our objective is to make it so difficult that, by the time they do locate us, we shall have departed our new safe house for a place of permanent safety, far beyond their reach. But determined assassins such as Borja's will not rest. If led by a patient, thorough man, they know that it is only a matter of time before some clue falls into their ever-watchful, waiting hands."

Antonio, cursed with a vivid imagination and visual inventiveness, could suddenly see outlines of those waiting assassin-hands flexing fitfully, impatiently, within the shadows of the farmhouse's familiar doorways, arbor, sheds. "Perhaps we should repair to our mounts now," he suggested, licking his suddenly dry lips.

Rombaldo de Gonzaga almost spilled his very expensive coffee when Giulio came sprinting into his private chambers, as flushed and excited as ever. "The fisherman reports movement near the island monastery, Rombaldo."

Hmm. Sooner than he had expected. The up-time commandos and their allies had only arrived in Venice—well, at San Francesco del Deserto—a few days ago. And now they were already on the move again. "What movement?"

"The fisherman we have watching the island says that early this morning, the Dalmatian *gajeta* that brought them here set out to the south. I do not know more than that. But the fisherman sent his assistant to follow that boat, thinking its departure might have been meant to draw him away."

"And?"

"And he was evidently correct. Only two hours later, a rowboat was brought out from the cover of bushes and several persons left the island."

"Where did they go?"

"They met and transferred to a ketch of shallow draft in open water of the lagoon. The ketch made for the west; the rowboat returned to the island."

Rombaldo thought carefully. The *gajeta* was probably not merely a decoy; the smart move would be to give it a legitimate task, as well. But it was also harder to follow. He didn't have enough boats at his disposal to track multiple targets. So there was probably little he could accomplish other than sending a prompt report back to Dakis that the Wrecking Crew was apparently on the move again.

"The *gajeta* was heading south, you said?"

"Yes, Rombaldo."

So. South. Well, that didn't reveal much. Except that it seemed unlikely that the Wrecking Crew was going to reinforce whatever security was safeguarding Urban. So, as expected, they were probably returning to Rome. But why not go directly out of the lagoon into the Adriatic? It would have been harder to follow them, then....

Unless, of course, they intended to change boats before they got to Rome. A prudent step, but difficult to arrange on such short notice. Unless, that is, the change was going to take place fairly close to Venice, someplace the USE planners could inform quickly by sending a mounted messenger or a fast boat ahead, farther down the coast. Hmmm—farther down the coast... "Giulio, first message. To all our agents farther down the coast, particularly in Ravenna and Rimini. They should be watching for this *gajeta*. It might rendezvous with another boat. Probably a slightly larger one. There's a bonus for any report that reaches me within twelve hours of the sighting."

"Yes, Rombaldo. Anything else?"

Well, of course there was something else; they had to determine what the second boat, the ketch, was up to. A rowboat leaves the island of the Franciscans and transfers its passengers to the small, shallow-hulled ketch. Which heads due west. Now that, Rombaldo reasoned, might have something to do with his target, the pope.

Might he be stashed someplace on the west shore of the lagoon? No. Too close. Although very unexpected, it was also too bold a move; a little bit of bad luck and the pope's life would be forfeit. No matter how much security Urban had, it was better for him to be well-hidden than well-defended. That meant he'd be found in a modest compound, not a bristling fortress. And anything less than a fortress was something that Rombaldo could overwhelm with sheer numbers, if it was close to Venice. But the farther away the pope's sanctuary was from Venice, the more ground Rombaldo's men had to search and the more scattered they became while doing so. That, in turn, made it increasingly unlikely that whatever band of searching assassins found Urban would also be large enough to overcome his current protection.

So, by process of elimination, the enemy's smart move was not to gamble on sequestering the pope close to Venice, because he would not only be easier to find, but because Borja's hired men could be more easily and swiftly summoned to converge upon, and overwhelm, such a target.

Meaning that Urban was out in the countryside. Maybe up in the mountains, by now. Logically they would want a remote area; a city is full of eyes, and you have no way of knowing which pair is looking for you. On the other hand, an isolated farm or villa—probably one abandoned or infrequently visited—would be perfect. No one had business going to such a place, which meant that any approach would be immediately noticed and engaged.

So, if the boat was carrying someone or something to the pope, then its westward course across the lagoon should logically be bringing it closer to that kind of remote sanctuary.

So they were making for the Po. It was the only logical answer. The boat moving westward—small, with a shallow draft—would be ideal for a long upriver journey, eliminating much of the need to fret over navigating shallows. And it would, of course, be hard to follow. Particularly if they had set in enough provisions for their entire journey, thereby obviating the need to put in at any of the towns along the banks of the Po.

But logically, once they left the boat, whoever was on it would wish to move quickly. Meaning they would need to either purchase mounts, or, more likely, have them already waiting in a prearranged point. And from there, they would almost certainly head farther north. Farther west was pointless; it put them even deeper into the much-trafficked east-west agricultural and commercial belt that followed the Po River valley all the way out to Lombardy. Farther south put them beyond the protection of Venice's borders and just that much closer to Rome's reach. On the other hand, Venice had some truly remote areas in its northern territories, where the land rose up—first as hills and then small mountains—to meet the Alps.

So: "Next message, Giulio. We need our agents in Mestre and Vicenza to spread out along the Po. We need at least one in each of the towns on the north shore that have stables of reasonable size. They are to seek the ketch and watch for its passengers to transfer to mounts. They will do so quickly; they will not spend a night in the town."

"Rombaldo, this will take some time to arrange. By the time the messages are sent, received, and the agents change position—"

"Yes, Giulio, I'm well aware of this. Which means, unfortunately, that our agents might arrive after the boat for which they are searching. So they cannot simply go to the villages and sit by the side of the Po, staring, hoping to see a ketch. They will need to make surreptitious inquiries about recent arrivals, mounts that were recently purchased or stabled there, strangers passing through—some of whom will certainly not be Italians. And yes, it will take time, but we are not in a hurry. Thoroughness, not hastiness, is our best ally right now."

"It shall be as you say, Rombaldo. And if the ketch's passengers are located, should our men ambush th—?"

"Absolutely not. They are to follow, observe, and report. That is all. These travelers are not our targets; they are our guides. We would be fools to slay them before they lead us to our ultimate objective." He waved Giulio out. Then, as an afterthought, he added, "Also, be sure to give the fisherman three extra lire. He showed cleverness and initiative."

Giulio stopped and cocked his head. Rombaldo almost laughed; the scrawny Paduan looked like a quizzical spaniel. He asked, "A bonus for the fisherman, Rombaldo?"

"Yes. Why? What were you expecting?"

"Well, that we'd cover our tracks like always. That we'd kill him."

Rombaldo frowned. "Kill him? Good grief, no." Then he shrugged, "Well, at least not yet."

It was not at all fair, Ruy Sanchez de Casador y Ortiz decided. Not fair at all.

He looked over the ears of his horse and saw his beautiful wife reach down to give yet another child a turn riding behind her. In the time that he had known her, Sharon had become only a passably capable equestrienne. But otherwise, each passing day seemed a divine ordination upon the further growth of her other, peerless gifts. For Ruy, every moment of existence also allowed him to see more clearly how she was the very acme of charm, wit, kindness, beauty, and—and—

—yes. And. That. Ruy sighed. Three days upon the road and two evenings spent in the even less comfortable fields had taken their toll on Ruy's naturally ebullient spirit. Not because of the onset of saddle sores, or the monotonous food, or the omnipresent dust that coated body, mouth, and nostrils. Being a veteran of innumerable campaigns, he no longer noticed such discomforts. No, Ruy resented the absence of a bed. And privacy. Specifically, the bed and privacy that he and his bride of less than two months had enjoyed at the farmhouse.

It had not been a wonderful bed; it was cranky and had needed a thorough dosing of DDT before it was vermin-free. And it creaked. A great deal. But that was part of what he missed. Say what one might, a creaking bed was rather like an orchestral accompaniment, and Sharon Nichols had shown, in the past weeks, that she was a virtuoso performer.

It just wasn't fair, Ruy concluded.

"A *real* for your thoughts?"

Ruy looked up from his funk, smiling, simply because the sound of Sharon's voice always made him happy. "You might not approve," Ruy warned her.

"Try me," she said with a smile that was more than half-leer.

Ruy glanced behind. The pope sat his horse comfortably and loose-limbed; Vitelleschi sat his like a long-necked scarecrow without joints.

"You might approve, my heart, but I sincerely doubt that the pope would."

"Oh, I don't know. I don't think Urban VIII is a prude. But Vitelleschi—brrrr. I suspect he thinks holding hands is the equivalent of fornication."

"Hmf," moped Ruy. "Well, I certainly don't."

"No," she agreed with a smile, "you certainly don't."

"Heart of my heart, it is more than a man should be asked to bear, this abstinence. To touch your beauty, to experience your vigor, it brands a man's soul. It creates a hunger that knows no surfeit. It afflicts me with fantasies and daydreams of delights that are bestowed by an angel with the impulses of a demon."

"In short, you miss the bed."

"Ah, the bed," Ruy sighed, shaking his head. "I remember it almost as if it were yesterday."

"It was. Well, the day before yesterday."

"Is it so? Then why does it already feel like a century of centuries?"

"Ruy, don't herniate your flattery muscles, now. And besides, being on the road is a source of adventure, of new opportunities, new places—new beds." She poked him, her lips curving slightly.

His eyes widened, then narrowed to match the salacious smile that he could feel growing on his face. "It may be true that variety is the spice of life, but I was not done savoring all the many flavors of the farmhouse. And its bed. Which lifted you just high enough, when you lay full upon it, that I was perfectly positioned to—"

"Ruy. You are not going to talk about that here."

"Ah, so now *you* fear that Urban will overhear?"

"That. And I need to keep my head on my business."

Ruy effected an epic sulk. "I *am* your business."

"You most certainly are, you old goat. You are the business I want to get down to. Which is precisely why I'm going to ride ahead of you now."

"To separate yourself from me? I am wounded, wounded unto death."

"Really? Wounded to death? You? *All* of you?" Her challenging gaze drifted south of his belt for just a second; he quite literally rose to the challenge.

As she turned away, Ruy protested to the listening skies. "I am lost, utterly lost. My heart is owned by a cruel temptress who has no pity upon my desperate condition."

Looking back, Sharon smiled. The sensuous curve of her lips seemed reprised in her shoulders, her arms, her hips, her bust. "So your condition is desperate?"

"Despite enduring a thousand battles and a hundred wounds, never have I been in more pain. I, Ruy Sanchez de Casador y Ortiz, swear that it is true."

She raised her chin in a histrionic huff. "I'll bet you say that to all the girls." And with a twitch of her tail that matched her spurred mare's, she moved farther ahead.

Smiling more broadly, Ruy spurred his own charger, keeping up with her. But he was careful not to draw abreast of, or pass, her. No, he must not pass her.

Because he liked the view from back here. Very, very much.

# Chapter 26

The room stank of chronically unwashed bodies and the proximity of Rome's Jewish Ghetto, from which rubbish was removed infrequently. At best.

Tom watched Juliet finish her wine. She placed the sturdy flagon down upon the table and, despite her almost parodically curvy bulk, she belched demurely. Then she stood up and whistled, once, shrilly, followed by her cry of "Benito?"

From out of the milling crowd of young men in the front room, a tall gangly adolescent with a bad facial gash and missing one ear loped over. His face was a study of dedication bordering on adoration: "Yes, Signora Sutherland?"

"Time to send all the young bucks along to their billets now, lad. Get Giovanna's relatives to help you."

"Her brother Fabrizio, he's here. But her cousin Dino is upstairs, fetching—you know, 'him.'"

Thomas North smiled tightly. *Him, indeed.* But it was true enough that Harry's fame in Rome was such that the mere mention of his name and rumor of his appearance could create problems. Fortunately, this was working in their favor, now. Since they had removed Wadding weeks ago, there had been an imaginary "Harry Lefferts sighting" almost every other day. The authorities had apparently pursued these rumors vigorously at first. Now, they simply ignored them. Which was good; although the returned Wrecking Crew took meticulous care not to interact or even be seen by locals, even at night, they could not afford a slip-up. Whoever worked for Borja was looking for them; no reason to help the bastard do his job.

Juliet was rolling her eyes over Benito's report. "Yes, of course, Dino is spending an extra minute basking in the glow of the Great Man. So get Piero to help you, instead."

"*Si*, Signora, we shall have the room clear in thirty seconds. No more."

"You have them trained pretty well," North observed when the youngster had left.

"No training required, Lord North." Why she, alone of the Wrecking Crew, insisted on retaining the use of his title was beyond him. But he wasn't going to attempt dissuading her. He had learned that Juliet Sutherland was not merely determined, she was a *force majeure*. In this case, her resolve was quiet, rather than loud and brash, but no less tenacious. She was probably going to call Thomas "Lord North" until the day he—or she—died.

"What do you mean, 'no training required'?" North sipped at his well-watered wine.

"Well, I'm exaggerating a bit. But just a bit. The only boys who *will* do the work we require are poor. And the only ones who *can* do the work are not so poor that they're too weak to watch, run, report. Which means I've been recruiting scamps who've already spent a few years watching houses and following people, working as lookouts for petty thieves, smugglers, pimps: you name it."

"Sounds a savory crew."

"Sounds a desperate crew," replied Juliet with a touch of heat. "I'm familiar enough with their circumstances, m'lord. Grew up none too different, truth be told."

"Sorry," offered North.

"Ah, nothing to be sorry for, m'lord. I suppose these aren't the kind of skills you ever had much cause to become familiar with, what with you taking your lessons by the hearth in the ancestral manse."

"*Touché*," North offered with a smile. "Although that doesn't quite describe the circumstances of my youth. We had a great deal more title than money, and I was not the oldest son. Nor the favorite."

"Probably why you don't take on airs, then. Knew there was a reason I liked you. Not all quality is quality, if you take my meaning. But you are, right enough."

North hardly knew what to say. "Thank you," was what came out. It sounded ridiculous.

"Well, if you must thank me for something, you can express your appreciation for my expertise as a recruitrix of unsavory crews. Not things you learn in a book, of course, but on the street. You have to be able to tell the ones who are hungry from those who are desperate. Desperate waifs are no good to us; unfortunately, they'll serve or sell anyone for a farthing because they don't believe that anything good will last.

"You also have to be able to tell the ones who are just hard enough from the ones who don't have enough hardness in 'em—they'll freeze or bolt—and also from the ones who are *too* hard—they'll sell you out or blackmail you, if they get the chance."

"I wasn't aware there were such nuances in the recruiting of children."

"Well, why would you be? None of your own, and no interest in 'em."

"Well, you don't have any of your own. Although, given your interest, I'm rather surprised you don't."

"What? Me? Children? Christ on the gibbet, don't even say the words!"

"But why not?"

"Why not? Why not? I should trade away all this"—she ran her hands down her formidable flanks—"for a bump and a baby? I've got a husband to keep, Lord North, which means a figure to keep as well."

North tried not to goggle, or laugh, or sputter in bafflement. She seemed serious. "I hadn't thought about that," he managed to get out.

"I suppose not. But as I was saying, part of the trick of recruiting these lovable scuts is knowing the age at which they are no longer so lovable, and more scoundrel than scut."

"And what age is that?"

"Varies by the child. Boys stay innocent longer, but get mean faster. It's a tricky business, because the oldest are the most valuable, overall, but also the rarest. But we're fortunate having access to the *lefferti*; they all have younger brothers who want nothing so much as to join those scurrilous ranks, themselves. And so, we let slip the implication that our *piccoli lefferti* will help us strike a blow against the Spanish bastards who killed one, more, or all of their family. And yes, it's that bad, in some cases. So, before I'm done talking to the little fellows, they're as loyal as puppies and can't do enough to help us." She sighed contentedly. "I've done my finest work here in Rome. 'S a pity it has to end, tomorrow or the next day."

"What determines which day we start the final party?"

"When Frank and Giovanna's guards give us the kind of incident that will allow us to stir up the local mobs."

"And how can we even predict when such a thing might occur?"

"Predict? Lord North, I see you do not understand what it means to be a professional in my line of work. We are not waiting for a chance event. We are simply waiting for the right moment to make it happen. In a time and a place of our choosing."

"Which is," added the unmistakable voice of Harry Lefferts, "the key to our tactical successes: to always strike at a time and a place of our choosing. Which we are now ready to do." Leading the way down the stairs, he was followed by the rest of the Wrecking Crew, the Wild Geese, and North's four Hibernians. It was quite the parade, North conceded.

Harry took a seat next to Thomas, pulled out a chair obviously intended for John O'Neill, and let the rest file in and find places as they could.

"Okay," said Harry, grinning from ear to ear, as the earl of Tyrone took his seat. "We're done with preparation, and we're done revising and refining the plan. So here it is."

He unfolded a map of the target. Some of it boasted precise floor plans, some more was rather vague, and a whole lot of it was blank. "This is the *insula* Mattei: the palace complex belonging to the Mattei family. It is comprised of three separate parts. The good news is that this big sucker"—Harry ran his hand around the periphery of the immense quadrangle that dominated the center and eastern side of the map—"is not where Frank and Giovanna are being held. We don't have the manpower to go room to room in the main palazzo, the Palazzo Giove Mattei. Even with complete surprise and all our firepower running nonstop, we'd still get nickel-and-dimed to death."

Owen Roe O'Neill was frowning. "So the entirety of the *insula* has been taken over by the Spanish to house two hostages?"

Harry shrugged. "We don't really know. Our intelligence on high-society isn't too good. It could be that the Mattei family is on the outs with Borja, that some of their neighbors used the invasion as a pretext to settle some old scores and run them off, or they could be clustered up in the main Palazzo, giving the Spanish the run of the yard and keeping their heads down. Because so far, we haven't seen anyone who answers to the descriptions of the Mattei clan in the whole place."

"That's kind of odd," commented Sherrilyn.

"Given how smart the guy we're playing against seems to be, maybe it's not so much odd as it is inspired. He's not letting anyone out to tell stories about what's going on inside. No servants go shopping; no new ones come in. Food is delivered. The only domestics they let out are the water-bearers, who get what they need at the dolphin-fountain here"—Harry pointed to a small piazza just below the northwest corner of the map—"while under close guard."

"So we haven't had any inside reports at all?" Donald Ohde rubbed his chin and did not look happy.

"Not recent ones, but plenty of older ones." Juliet leaned forward on dimpled elbows. "That's how we got the floor plans. I learned which of the locals hereabout had worked in the *palazzi* over the years. Got 'em to talking about what it was like inside. Even got a few of them arguing over the details."

"But has our observation given us a sense of patrol rosters? Duty stations?" Thomas tried to keep the worry out of his voice.

"Well, in a manner of speaking, yes, we do have information on that. And it's some of the best news of all."

"Oh?"

Harry smiled. "I think the Borja's troops have bitten off a little more than they can chew. Our small army of casual, underage watchers agree with our older hands: the Spanish are playing the single-file repeating Indian trick all throughout the *insula* Mattei."

"They're playing what?" asked John O'Neill.

"It's an old story from up-time," Sherrilyn explained. "In order to make themselves look more numerous, one war-band of North American natives marched just beyond the edge of a ridge, all in one big circle, each one passing by the crest again and again. To the folks in the fort they had surrounded, it looked like there were thousands of Indians out in the hills, when in fact there were only a few hundred, at most."

John nodded, understanding, but evidently not too pleased that the explanation had come from Sherrilyn. North couldn't tell if the earl was disappointed because the story had not come from Golden Harry, or because O'Neill hated—hated—anything that reminded him that some members of the Wrecking Crew were female. Whatever the reason behind it, Sherrilyn saw John's reaction, and clearly didn't like it very much. She sat back, arms folded, and eyes hard.

"So," the earl mused, "they're short of men, given the size of the area they have to defend."

"It sure looks like it," drawled Harry. "We see the same guys too often, standing triple watches, moving from post to post. If you were just watching casually, it looks like there's a fair amount of activity in the complex, but when you start following the faces, it turns out to be a sham. All of which is in line with what our informers close to Borja and his officers have told the *lefferti*."

Juliet raised her chins. "Which also matches what my little darlings have reported in terms of food deliveries: far less than the apparent garrison would eat. Only about one third as much."

"And from what I've seen through my binoculars," added George, "most of them are not the top-notch Spanish troops."

"How do you know?" asked Owen.

"Well, in part, their weapons. Philip's best have genuine flintlock muskets, now. A lot have snaplocks; the rest have wheel locks or the better matchlocks. But most of the lads in this complex are still carrying arquebuses and matchlocks that came back from the New World with Columbus.

"And if they had enough troops, I'm pretty sure they'd use that big belvedere on top of the main palazzo as more than a sometimes-lookout."

"What else should they use it for?" asked Sean Connal, genuinely perplexed.

"A strongpoint from which to defend all the roofs," George responded.

Most of the Irish stared, more confused than before.

Harry stood. "See, it's like this. All of these buildings are roofed, yeah? And some of them here on the north, and here on the west are pretty close to buildings on the opposite side of the street. Close enough that a group of attackers on these roofs over here"—he pointed to the roofs to the north of the complex—"could lay a ladder over the gap and cross to the roofs of the Palazzo Mattei. Now maybe I'm just paranoid, but I wouldn't want to give my opponent free access to my roof. Particularly not if my opponent was as smart as, say—" Harry smiled "—Harry Lefferts."

"Why am I beginning to suspect that we're going to pull another roof job?" asked Matija sourly.

"Now, would I plan anything as crazy as that?"

"Of course you would, Harry. You're you."

"Well, so I am—but we'll get to that later. For now, here's the other lucky break we're catching: Frank and Giovanna are being kept here, in this small palazzo just below the *insula's* northwest corner. It's called the Palazzo Giacomo. They're in a room overlooking this combo entrance and courtyard, which does not communicate directly with any of the courtyards of the big palace. And we can see the windows of their rooms just fine from the roof of a three-story building near the gate into the Ghetto. Which means that we'll have eyes, and a scoped weapon, on the primary area of operations at all times."

John O'Neill was nodding like he actually understood all of what Harry had explained. In reality, North conjectured, the earl understood that a bold plan had been conceived and that they were within days of executing it. And that seemed to excite him quite a bit.

Harry hunkered close to the map. "Okay, so here's the mission plan. Most of our assault forces will begin hidden in this boarding house to the north of the *insula* Mattei and in these sheds. Two of the Hibernians—who will be the long-range support—will be secreted here, just inside the Ghetto walls."

"The Ghetto walls?" Donald Ohde sounded dubious. "But the guards there—"

Juliet smiled. "You know, I never cease to be amazed how very bribable guards are when you suggest that you want them to wander away from the Ghetto Gate so you can sneak in and torment a few Jews." Her smiled broadened. "So I don't think we'll have to worry about moving in and around the Ghetto. And if one of the guards has a twinge of conscience, well...we'll have people there who can take of that, too." She stared meaningfully at all the readied pistols and swords in the room.

"Okay," resumed Harry, "once we're in position, Juliet will start the party with a diversion. We'll be creating an incident at the well in the next few days, an incident which will lead to some peaceful, but loud and large, rioting outside the doors of the main Palazzo Mattei.

"Once that diversion has drawn in the attention and spare troops of the palazzo, our team in the north will go into action. They'll already be up on the roofs across from the smallest and northern-most of the three palaces, the Palazzo Paganica. They'll push ladders across the gap, scoot over, and from there, will have the run of all the roofs of the *insula* Mattei."

"And if they have a guard watching from the main palace's roof-top belvedere?" asked Sean Connal.

"Well, then I'll just have to use my scoped rifle to close his eyes. Permanently."

"Ah," the doctor responded. "You are another great long-range marksman, like your famous Julie Sims?"

"Doc, at these ranges I could shoot like Elmer Fudd and still bag all the pesky Spanish wabbits that I spy with my little eye."

"I beg your pardon?"

"I'll fill you in later, Doc. Back to the action. So the Wrecking Crew is the roof team. Gerd will make his way to the southeast corner of the main palazzo, find the driest beams under the roof-tiles there, and give them the gift of fire. Nothing that will burn the whole joint down, but enough to get a little attention pulled over that way.

"By that time, the rest of the Crew should have identified and staked out the sections of the roof next to where they're holding Frank and Giovanna."

Gerd smiled. "And then I blow it in."

Harry smiled back. "Yeah. Gerd has been working on tamping and directional demolitions. You can't control these micro-petards too much, but you can manage them enough for our purposes. Once the hole is in the roof, the Wrecking Crew goes in, led by Sherrilyn. They will secure the room next to Frank and Giovanna's."

"And that's when we join the party, right?" John O'Neill's eyes were bright, eager.

"Yep. By this time, the rioters will be making a storm of noise outside the gate leading into the courtyard of the main Palazzo Giove Mattei. Under the cover of that ruckus, you'll emerge from the buildings we've rented around the fountain's piazza, charge and take the gate into the Palazzo Giacomo's courtyard, using those nice new revolvers of yours."

John O'Neill's face fell a bit at the mention of the revolvers, but not much.

"If you need to blow the lock, you'll have a small charge with you for that purpose. Once you're inside, your job is simple: kill everyone who tries to fight back. You are shock troops, and given your weapons and training, that kind of in-close combat should be just your cup of tea.

"As the Palazzo Giacomo's courtyard is being secured by the earl, Sherrilyn's roof team will take advantage of the fact that most of the prisoners' guards will have rushed to the windows overlooking the entry; they'll breach the room where Frank and Giovanna are being held and eliminate the guards. Then they'll send the two love birds scampering down into the waiting wings of our Wild Geese. Then they all run like hell out of the courtyard."

"And us?" Donald Ohde's eyes had not left the rooftop section of the map.

"If Sherrilyn thinks it looks safe to follow Frank and Giovanna down the ladder, then that's what you'll do. That would have us all pulling out together, in the same direction. Easier for the withdrawal to the boats. We want to avoid having separated units trying to make rendezvous, at night; something will go wrong. Hell, it always does.

"But if the Spanish still have too many troops in the courtyard of the Palazzo Giacomo, then Sherrilyn's group will just retrace its steps: up to the roof and back over the ladders to the roof you came from. They're not going to have anyone up there to stop you; there's no real access to the roof except for from the belvedere. And if someone does go up there and starts giving you trouble—well, that's when I get to play the role of your long-range guardian angel. Again. But I kinda doubt that's going to happen. They seem to have almost no tactical awareness of their roof. George here has been watching it for weeks. The Spanish use the belvedere to sight-see and get some sun, not a security position.

"Just to keep Borja's boys extra busy, we'll let the *lefferti* have a little fun at the end: they'll throw a few molotov cocktails. Made out of olive oil. Or cod oil, if they want to add gas warfare to the mix. Then they'll scoot and fade, all going their separate ways."

Owen was still looking at the map and frowning. "And how do we escape?"

"Always important, the get-away. So: we withdraw hugging the wall of the Ghetto until we can turn and head over the Ponte Fabricio, the eastern bridge leading to the Isola Tiberina. We cross that little island, go over its western bridge, the Ponte Cestio, into the Trastevere and head a few blocks south to the extraction boats. They'll be waiting around this bend in the Tiber, just beyond where the Cloaca Maxima dumps the city's sewage into the river. Not a popular area, which should lower the chances of random detection. And from there, we just go with the flow, down to the sea."

"All the way to the sea, in light boats?"

"No. We'll transfer to a single, larger boat before we get to open water. We'll ultimately rendezvous with the same *barcalonga* that brought us here from Venice. But as to the name of the first boat and where along the Tiber we're going to meet it—well, in case anyone here is captured, we're gonna keep that information restricted to the folks who really need to know it."

Sherrilyn looked at the maps. "The plan sounds okay. Well, pretty good, actually, if the assumptions about the number of Spanish troops are correct."

Harry shrugged. "Sherrilyn, even if we're off by twenty, thirty percent, it's not going to matter. Look at the ways we're getting in and out. No matter how many guys they have, they won't see us on the way in. And if they try to swarm us, or chase us on the way out? We have multiple escape routes, and to follow us on any of them, they've got to go through bottlenecks. Bottlenecks that our own people are covering with a huge firepower advantage. With our own guns, and the Hibernians' lever-actions, it will be a turkey shoot if they try coming after us. But I can't see them getting their heads out of their asses that fast. So I really don't think it's going to become a turkey shoot; it's just going to be a piece of cake."

John O'Neill's eyes darted across the maps. "Harry Lefferts, you have the very balls of the Devil himself, but a bold heart after my own liking. This—" he announced to his Wild Geese "—now *this* is a gambit worthy of heroes and bard-songs." They all nodded, one or two with an enthusiasm that matched John's. Several of the others, Owen and Sean among them, barely moved their heads; they kept looking at the maps and frowning. North noted which of the other Wild Geese, and his own Hibernians, evinced those reservations: these were persons with minds like his own, and probably key group leaders if the operation went pear-shaped, for some reason—

"So, Doubting Thomas," drawled Harry, "I see that look. What's bugging you about the plan?"

*Careful now, Tom.* "Nothing specific, Harry. Taken separately, the assumptions and steps are all sensible, and emphasize our strengths."

"So?"

"I'm simply mindful that, as dance-steps go, the ones you have us moving through are very interdependent, and come in quick sequence."

"Meaning?"

"Meaning that we'd better not stumble. Not once. And the Spanish had better not change the music in the middle of the dance."

Harry nodded. "Yeah. We can definitely do without any surprises, but that's why I've got two of your Hibernians in reserve, for a base of supporting fire that we can redirect like a fire brigade. The attack plan doesn't depend on our full offensive superiority; I've held that card back as our ace in the hole. If the Spanish do try to change the music somehow, we'll change it right back."

*If you can*, thought Thomas but said nothing.

"And I've given a lot of thought to quick extraction, as well," continued Harry. "We'll want a small force watching the boats. That same force could also work as a kind of free safety to smack down any other Spanish units that might try to block our escape route. But Sherrilyn has made a pretty good survey of the area: Borja doesn't have any garrisons nearby. He's keeping most of his forces concentrated near the Holy City, and the rest billeted in a couple of dispersed, satellite locations. The nearest of those is ten minutes away, assuming they are moving at a flat-out run the whole time. Meaning we should have twenty minutes before anyone else could reasonably hear the noise, get a team together, and come join the party. And if this operation takes more than seven minutes from the first shots, then we are all under-performing in a big way. The fact of the matter is the Crew has often tackled bigger jobs with fewer resources, so I'm thinking we have a nice safety margin in place for this op."

North nodded. "Very well, then. Who's in charge of the boat and extraction overwatch team?"

"You are, Thomas."

*Oh, now wait a minute—* "I see. And what led you to that decision, Harry?" North tried very hard to keep any tone of challenge out of his voice.

"Okay, now, Tom; simmer down. Yeah, I'd feel that way too. But someone has to be watching our backs and keeping the exit open. You're careful and you've got a nose for when things are going wrong or getting tight, and that's exactly the kind of instincts we'll need in a free safety."

"And which you need even more on the line, so that you'll get the earliest possible whiff of trouble."

Lefferts smiled. "Right you are. Which is why Owen is going to be up front with us." He nodded at the colonel of the Wild Geese. "He's the oldest and wisest among us. And he's also one hell of a toe-to-toe fighter, as I'd heard and have now seen."

Owen smiled at the compliment. Thomas bit his lip. Owen was not particularly cautious, just more so than John. Which wasn't hard to achieve. But as a *sassenach,* there was no way for North to win an appeal to swap roles with Owen, or even broach the topic without arousing suspicions of bigotry. Or accusations of petty displeasure over being excluded from the attack force. Besides, Harry's plan was actually thorough and clever—but still, Thomas had misgivings, the nagging sense that they were missing something. Or maybe that was just his own sour grapes at being consigned to the rearguard. North's throat felt like sandpaper as he made himself ask, "How many and which people are on my extraction team?"

"Five, other than yourself. Two of your own Hibernians for security. Doc Connal in case we're coming back with casualties, one *lefferti* for interacting with any locals, and one of Juliet's little fellas to run messages and sneak around, keeping an eye out."

It was said that Caesar had conquered Gaul with less. "Fine," Thomas replied.

"Any other concerns?" Harry leaned forward to pour himself a little wine.

The voice that answered was a surprise to all. "Well, I've a personal concern, Harry." It was John O'Neill.

"Really? Wassamatter, John?"

"Oh, nothing with the plan. More a concern with one of the skills I'll be needing. I'm not a reliable hand with these pepperbox revolvers, yet. Haven't had the benefit of any truly competent training in it, I'm afraid."

Beside North, Sean Connal reddened briefly, then eased back in his seat with a small sigh and a rapid return of his normal color. A few of the Wild Geese looked at the doctor: if they had expected to see him finally, finally, lose his patience and make some cutting (if oblique) rejoinder to John's outrageous implication, they were surprised by the young man's continued calm.

If Harry caught any of that suppressed inter-Irish friction, he gave no sign of it. "Aw, no worries, John. Give me five minutes of your time and you'll be an old hand with the clunky bastard." He extended his palm; John O'Neill put his pepperbox upon it. "Now, John, let's get to the heart of the problem, which I'm guessing is reloading."

John smiled and watched, but not comfortably, North noticed. He hoped the earl would take the time to practice what he was learning. Practice it until he could wield the pepperbox as easily as his sword, could load, unload, reload in his sleep.

But North rather doubted that would happen.

As Harry repaired to a larger table where he could provide a detailed explanation of the rules of poker to the Wild Geese, John made to follow him. Owen slipped close to his much younger cousin.

"John, do you really think Harry's plan is in trim with our own orders?"

"What do you mean?"

"John, Fernando and Isabella made it clear that they were none too pleased with us acting in concert with the Wrecking Crew and the USE at all. But they understood the necessity, both of the moment and in the larger scope of the Low Countries' future relations with the up-timers. It's not the time for any of us to look like ingrates. But Isabella particularly stressed that we stay mostly in positions to support the attack, not be at the forefront of it ourselves. And that's just where we've been put: leading the charge into the Palazzo Giacomo's courtyard."

John looked like he was going to spit in disgust. "I'll not have my hands tied by that nervous old biddy's apron-strings. Our courage is needed—wanted—here."

"Our courage may be, but our faces are not. Think on it, John:

what happens if one of us is killed or captured, particularly you, or me? Borja—and through him, Philip—could learn that we were here."

"So what of it?" John restively loosened his sword in its scabbard, as he looked over at the poker lesson that was starting. "Philip's abandoned us. It's high time that we abandon him."

*Always spleen first, brain last, with you, isn't it, Johnnie?* "Yes—maybe that's how it is for *us*. But Fernando and Isabella still receive some *reales* from Philip. It's a tense situation between the two courts, and there's a conflict of interest, but still no hostility between the king of Spain and the new king in the Low Countries. Not yet. But if our involvement here were to come to light—"

"It won't," snapped John. "It may be a bold plan, but it's a good plan. Even the *sassenach* said so."

*Yes, he did—but I can see he has the same indefinite misgivings that I do,* Owen thought, but said instead, "And so it is a good plan, but, given our employers' explicit concerns, we shouldn't be assigned to the main assault force."

John turned, the lack of expression on his face all the more chilling because that bluff countenance was typically open and immediate in transmitting the state of the earl of Tyrone's somewhat tempestuous heart. "Owen, if you've grown too old to be comfortable leading men in a headlong charge, then maybe it's time for you to put down your sword and pick up a pen. As our quartermaster, or the like."

Owen hardly knew how to respond. If those words had come from any other man on the face of the Earth, it would have meant a challenge and one of their deaths. He exhaled slowly, carefully, "I'm to be following orders, not the path of a coward, Lord O'Neill."

"Suit yourself. Maybe there's no cowardice in you. So, who's to blame? I guess it's Isabella and Fernando who haven't the nerve to stand tall and fight openly for what they believe. No stain upon your honor or good name, then—not even for continuing to obey people who've admitted that, for almost thirty years, they've used us worse than a tinker's forgotten dog. There. Feel better, now?" And he swaggered off, making sure for the second time that his sword was loose in its scabbard.

# Chapter 27

The tall, lanky man entered the small stables quickly, refastening the baldric of his hanger as he turned towards the stalls lining the right wing of the building.

And came to an abrupt stop. There was a medium-sized man—well, an older gentleman, from what little he could see beyond the large traveling cloak—standing directly in his way. Moving to pass him, the tall lanky man made a hasty apology. "Pardon; I must pass—"

And then he stopped again and took a closer look.

"Yes," said the older man. "It's me. You are not the only one who can effect a disguise."

The tall man leaped forward, sword singing a single metallic tone as it came swiftly out of its scabbard in a fast, fierce, back-handed down slash—

Which the older man nimbly hopped back from, sweeping off the traveling cloak with his left hand, while he drew a rapier. His age-wrinkled eyes narrowed, measuring. "Matadors should never accept bony bulls, but it seems I have no choice." He smiled. "*Toro!*" he whispered.

The tall man feinted a stab, then went for a short forehand cut that the rapier intercepted, not so much blocking it as redirecting it. Which elicited a grin from the tall man; this old fool of a Catalan was not so skilled as Rombaldo had told him. The parry, while effective, had left the younger man's weapon with plenty of momentum—

—which he redirected toward his target yet again: he rolled his wrist, the hanger's path of deflection sweeping into an s-shape that brought it right around into a forceful back cut.

But the old Catalan seemed to have anticipated this. Rather than giving or standing his ground, he came closer—an even more foolish tactic, given that the rapier's advantage was in distance, not proximity. But instead of working with his steel, the Catalan brought up the traveling cloak, its folds wrapping around his attacker's hanger early in its swing. Almost like a matador, the older man gave way before the cut and twisted the cloak as soon as the hanger's edge bit it.

For a long moment, the tall man was utterly disoriented, trying to cut through the cloak and keep a solid grip on his sword at the same time. All the while, the old Spaniard was sweeping around with him like a counterweight, the cloak joining them, a common center of rotation. But then the Spaniard, rather than stepping ever wider in their accelerating, lethal gavotte, planted his front foot, rotated at the hip, and held fast.

The tall man, suddenly swirling faster than his opponent, tried to compensate, tugging, stumbling a bit. He felt his wrist twisting, and took a quick extra step to help stop and ground himself without falling over. And in that moment, with his sword arm committed to balancing himself rather than holding his weapon ready, the Spaniard struck.

He must have been waiting for that near-stumble; the smaller man's rapier—which he had drawn back when he planted his front foot—jetted forward, but not directly at the tall man's midriff. Instead, it shot out on an intercept trajectory: though the thrust seemed slightly ahead of its target when it began, the taller man's forward stumble brought him into alignment with it, the blade transfixing him just two inches under the sternum.

The tall man's half-stagger became a full stagger, and in the second it took him to reorient himself, he felt the blade go in again, just beneath and outside the lower right extreme of his groin. He felt a hot spurting there, felt an onset of vertigo, and then noticed—almost calmly—the tip of the rapier disappearing under his own chin. He smelled hay—quite strongly—and thought he might be falling...

❖    ❖    ❖

A second after Rombaldo's agent fell to the floor of the stable, two of the Hibernians came in. "Don Ruy," one of them muttered, worried, "I thought you said you would call us when—"

Ruy Sanchez de Casador y Ortiz shrugged. "There was no time, and there was no need. But I note and appreciate your concern." He could not resist smoothing the left wing of his mustache, which had become slightly displaced by the brief swordplay. "You have seen to the other one?"

"Yes, sir. He was writing a message, as you suspected. And there is a boy already waiting in the tavern to receive it, apparently."

"Then we do not have very long. When the messenger boy eventually inquires if his services are actually required, the inn-keep will no doubt check the message-writer's room and find his body. Did you remove the message itself?"

"Yes."

"Excellent. Now, let us hide this one under the straw and leave. It will take some time to catch up with the rest of our group, and my wife will no doubt be getting worried about me."

Sharon looked down for the third time. The toe of Ruy's left boot was spotless, still somewhat moist from a recent cleaning, but just past the ankle, slightly behind where Ruy would be able to see it, was a telltale smear of blood. The smallest bit, not even enough to shed a drop upon the floor. But as an EMT, Sharon Nichols had seen plenty of blood, enough so that she didn't miss it when her eyes roved across it, no matter the backdrop.

Sharon remained silent. Not only was she reluctant to interrupt Ruy's report to the clerics gathered round the modest fire; she wasn't sure she wanted to start down a path of questions that could not help but bring the other, ominous side of her husband into high relief. He had been a Spanish soldier on at least three, perhaps four, continents over the course of more than thirty years. That was a job which, within a year or two, either hardened a man to unthinkable cruelties, or drove him away. And her charming, sexy, amusing, effervescent Ruy—*Feelthy Sanchez* as she had dubbed him during his first amorous advances—was not one of the ones who had fled the ranks, but had gone on to successes and triumphs in them.

How many innocents had he been ordered to kill? Because after all, that was often the duty of soldiers in this time, particularly Spanish soldiers. How many more had he slain during his varied service as a confidential agent for several of Spain's cardinals and diplomats? The gentle, passionate, loving hands of Ruy were always immaculately clean when they touched her, yet, at moments like this, they also seemed indelibly stained with the blood of multitudes. Many of those notional corpses, which she now imagined littering the road behind him, had no doubt deserved to die. But not all. Possibly not even most. Sharon closed her eyes and did not open them again until they were raised beyond where she could see the faintly stained boot that bore witness to the prior life and deeds of Ruy Sanchez de Casador y Ortiz.

Who was explaining, "So the ambassadora and I decided not to alert anyone else to the fact that the two men who arrived with Father Wadding and his escorts were, in fact, enemy agents in disguise. We needed enough time to surreptitiously organize a tracking party, while also ensuring that sufficient security forces remained behind with the main group."

Antonio Barberini still seemed amazed at the entire course of events. "But when did you suspect these two of being disguised agents?"

Wadding coughed lightly. Vitelleschi might have smiled, or it might have been a momentary facial tic.

Ruy shrugged. "Father Wadding told me of his suspicions as soon as he arrived."

Barberini swiveled to stare at the Irish priest. "You? *You* knew they were assassins, Father Wadding?"

"You needn't sound so stunned, Nephew," chided Urban through a smile. "A priest who comes from, and has constant involvement in the affairs of, occupied Ireland is no stranger to duplicity and subterfuges."

Wadding shrugged. "Our one horse threw a shoe after our second day journeying north from the Po. Threw it while we were overnighting in a stable, no less. The subsequent appearance of two mule-drivers who'd just lost a contract seemed an even more providential event than our Lord is wont to orchestrate."

"They did not betray themselves in their actions?"

"Not directly, but there were intimations that they were not what they seemed."

"Such as?" Mazzare's interest was keen, clinical.

"Such as their enthusiasm for their work as mule-drivers, and for conversation with us. I mean no slight to mule-drivers as a class, but I have not found them to be exemplars of industry and motivation. They have much the same pace and personality as the creatures they tend, I find.

"That was not the case with these two. They were lively, alert, and not so much familiar with the animals as they were determined to make a good job of it. And whereas most teamsters and ostlers are of a taciturn nature, these two were quite talkative and inquisitive—except with each other. I found them an odd example of their trade."

"And on this alone you ordered their deaths?" Barberini's stare at Ruy was now tinged by horror.

"No, Your Eminence. There was more. When we offered them a commission to continue on with us—pure theater, of course—they declined, saying they had to return in great haste to the Po. Another impending job, according to them. Yet they had never inquired of Father Wadding or his party how long the job of escorting them was going to take; they were simply happy to take their daily wage as it came. But now, suddenly, they had urgent business back by the Po? No, we knew what they were. But just to be sure, on an occasion when one was sharing wine with me and the other was relieving himself in the bushes, I had Taggart check their bags." Ruy spread his hands atop his knees. "Mule-drivers are much skilled in stick, staff, and cudgel; they wield them every day as the media whereby they impart their tender encouragements to the lagging creatures in their team. What Taggart found instead were: one well-hidden hanger, two *couteaux-brèche*, two eight-inch daggers, and a garrote. These are not the weapons of mule-drivers, Your Eminence, of this you may be certain."

"So you suspect they saw Father Wadding arrive on the northern bank of the Po, trailed him, lamed his one horse, and then serendipitously arrived as the solution to his sudden lack of sufficient transportation?"

"Exactly. And when they pleaded the necessity of returning to the same town on the Po, we simply followed. Albeit at some distance; assassins are, themselves, inherently untrusting souls."

The silence that usurped the final piece of Ruy's narrative—how that surreptitious pursuit had ended—was long, and not entirely comfortable.

"So," exhaled Cardinal Barberini, "it seems the danger has been averted. Narrowly, perhaps, but averted."

"Yes, Your Eminence," agreed Ruy in a voice that was full of unspoken caveats. "For now."

Barberini looked like he might have an episode of incontinence, despite his comparatively tender age. "What do you mean, 'for now'?"

Ruy shrugged. "By eliminating these blackguards shortly after they began their return journey to report to their master, Borja's spymaster here in the Republic will have considerable difficulty picking up our trail. Had the two been able to send word that they had encountered us, and where, then he would have been able to resume his search from where we sit now, which is far too close to our ultimate destination."

Barberini spread his hands as if beseeching Providence itself for fair treatment. "But since that information was not relayed, Borja's spymaster will not know where to search at all; his assassins will have to return to watching for signs or connections at the Venetian embassy."

Vitelleschi shook his head. He looked at Ruy, who nodded that he was happy to let the vinegary Jesuit point out the flaw in Antonio's reasoning. "Cardinal Barberini, this would only be true if the man 'running' these agents was so foolish as to keep no track of which of his teams were deployed to which towns upon the banks of the Po. When this team is the only one that fails to return, the enemy spymaster will logically deduce two things: that this was the team that encountered Father Wadding and his escort. And that we discovered their true purpose and eliminated them. Meaning he knows at least where along the Po to resume his search."

"Oh," said Antonio.

"And when he begins expanding his search from there, his men will eventually come across a small town, several days farther north, in which they will no doubt hear tales of a recent double-murder: a pair of strangers—mule-drivers—who were killed for no reason, and for which there are no suspects. That is the trail-blaze which we unavoidably left behind us, marking our path."

Barberini turned to Ruy again. "That is why you tracked them for several days before dispatching them: to put that trail blaze closer to the Po. The next agents will now have a larger area to search, and will have to start farther away from us."

"Yes."

Barberini nodded. "Now I understand. I had wondered—" Barberini stopped, abashed.

Sharon's voice was like slate, even in her own ears. "Wondered why we didn't slit their throats here, Your Eminence? Well, now you know." *But you'll never know about the hushed argument over doing it at all—really the first dispute Ruy and I have ever had. He was right, damn it; we couldn't give the assassins any more of our trail than we could help revealing. But I'm no good at staring at the ceiling, alone in my bed, wondering if he'll live to come back to it. A man his age, playing hide-and-go-seek-and-destroy with assassins on the back roads of rural Italy. I knew I was not cut out to be a cop's wife; how the hell did I think I'd be able to handle being married to—?*

"My heart?"

The voice was Ruy's: gentle, rich, shaping the words like a gift meant especially for her ears. And the doubt fled, and she knew why she would have married him all over again this very moment. "Yes, Ruy?"

"You seem distracted?"

"I was just thinking about how—how lucky we are. And how safe. Thanks to you."

Ruy's eyes widened a little bit; Sharon had not been reticent or oblique about her aversion to his plan. He smiled slowly, warmly at her.

"Lucky, yes," agreed Barberini moodily, "but not lucky enough. Or safe enough. As you point out, Father Vitelleschi, these murderous rogues will most assuredly draw closer to us once again."

"Which we anticipate," said Ruy, rising to his feet so quickly and decisively that, in a man of less poise, it would have seemed that he had leaped to his feet. "And because we can anticipate where along the banks of the Po they will pick up their search, we have trailed some false lures on the roads and along the river."

Six days later, Father Wadding was riding a little bit ahead of Larry Mazzare; as usual, sticking as close as he could to the pope and his nephew. Oddly, Vitelleschi had been spending more of his time drifting back to ride alongside Mazzare. He didn't say anything; he just rode in a silence that, over the days, had become companionable.

But as they entered a small defile nestled in between the green peaks of the Vincentine PreAlps, with the sun rapidly heading towards its hiding place behind Monte Campomolon, Urban seemed to explain something to Wadding that surprised the Irishman. After a few moments, he slowed his nag so that it ultimately dropped back to put him alongside Vitelleschi. After several long, silent minutes, he cleared his throat. "Father Vitelleschi, if I understand the pope correctly, I have you to thank for ensuring that the Franciscans have maintained their control over St. Isidore's, in Rome."

Vitelleschi looked at him sharply. "Father Wadding, I regret to say that your gratitude seems to be misplaced. The decision regarding the legitimacy of Cardinal Ludovisi's will was not in my purview."

Mazzare dropped one eyebrow, raised the other. "Would someone care to fill me in on what's being discussed?"

Wadding nodded. "Certainly, Your Eminence. St. Isidore's benefactor, Cardinal Ludovico Ludovisi, went to be with our eternal Father in 1632. He had long been a friend of the Franciscans, and had been created a cardinal as Defender of Ireland. Given the signal successes of our Irish College, we rather presumed that he would leave a sustaining legacy for St. Isidore. He evidently did, but the will attributed to him transfers the control of the church and colleges to the Jesuits."

"Am I to take it that this dispute has been in process for three years, now?" asked Mazzare.

"Just so," affirmed Vitelleschi. "But the Franciscans, represented in the person of Father Wadding, vigorously contested the legitimacy of this part of the will—"

"Which we did in concert with Cardinal Ludovisi's younger brother, I will point out," Wadding was quick to add.

"It is as Father Wadding says," Vitelleschi nodded as approving of the narrow, winding valley road ahead of them. "At any rate, it was the Sacred Roman Rota that had taken the matter under consideration, not me."

"Yes, Father Vitelleschi, but you were the one who, just a few months after Galileo's trial, encouraged the Jesuit fathers charged with defending the legitimacy of the will to reassess their case. To reassess it 'in great detail.' I believe those were your very words, were they not?"

Vitelleschi's brow descended slightly. "Were we back in Rome, I would set aside some time to discover which of my colleagues have taken injudicious liberties in sharing the content of our private discussions."

"So it's true then: you delayed the process?" When Vitelleschi's only response was an almost imperceptible shrug, Mazzare pressed further. "Why did you delay the proceedings?"

"Because of you."

Mazzare blinked. "Me? How could that be? I have never even heard anything about—"

"Your Eminence, I do not mean 'you' in the sense of your very person, but in what you represent. Change. Up-time change. In the weeks following Galileo's acquittal, His Holiness began contemplating how the arrival of up-time documents—most particularly those canonical texts you sent us before the trial, Cardinal Mazzare—would change the path of the Church. How your people's perspectives on religious freedom would change what you called the Thirty Years' War. He rightly anticipated that the Austrian branch of the Hapsburgs would begin to drift away from the Spanish, and that the shifting of those veritable mountains of Roman Catholic strength would send earthquakes throughout the Christian world." Vitelleschi suffered what might have been another tic or a suppressed spasm of sardonic amusement. "He did not foresee, however, that the epicenter of the first shocks would originate in Rome itself. But in your case, Father Wadding, he wanted to change history for the better: in the up-time world, you were pushed out of St. Isidore's earlier this year. He thought that was not only unfair, but unwise."

"Unwise?" echoed Wadding.

"Unwise," confirmed a new voice. Urban had let his own mount slow enough to be proximal to their own. "Father Wadding, you, along with the late Father MacCaghwell, are among the best Franciscan minds of our times. But more important, you are also a person of high integrity. I will need that integrity very much as we arrive at our refuge, for now I may think and deliberate with you."

"I am honored, Your Holiness, but why do you specifically want a Franciscan as an interlocutor?"

"Oh, I do not want only a Franciscan, Father Wadding. I need a Jesuit, too."

Vitelleschi looked at a distant bird; Mazzare could not tell if he was squinting or scowling.

"And I need a priest who has lived in a world where Mother Church has benefited from an additional three-and-a-half centuries of our Savior's guiding wisdom and the Holy Spirit's guiding grace." Urban looked at Larry and smiled. "One might indeed claim that you possess a truly unique Charism, Cardinal Mazzare."

Mazzare was silent for a long time. Yes, this is what he had felt coming. He had felt it back in Magdeburg as news of Borja's violation of Rome began coming in over the radio, as the communications from the Holy See made it clear that it was not merely a political takeover, it was the imposition of a theological junta. Nothing less than an attempt to change both the pope and the direction of the Church by means of a *coup d'etat.*

And what had been the issue that had started this sequence of dominoes tumbling, that had allowed an army to be put at Borja's disposal—and with so little control that, even if he had exceeded his mandate from Madrid, there was now no way to stop him?

The threat was as profound as it was uncomplicated: true, sweeping, politically-protected and -enforced religious tolerance. At this moment in history, this was the dagger at the neck of the Church. And for its reciprocal part, that Church was not merely confident in its identity as the one true faith, but convinced of its duty to impose God-ordained correctness upon the rest of the world by force of arms and *auto-da-fé*, if need be. Indeed, all too many of its princes were not merely ready, but eager, to resort to those brutal methods.

And standing squarely against such a doctrine and such actions was not only the general religious toleration that prevailed among the up-timers, but the specific, and deeply contradictory, canonical pronouncements found among the Church records that had come back in time with Larry Mazzare's library, *ex cathedra* directives that had emerged from—

Mazzare turned back toward the pope. "This is about Vatican Two, isn't it?"

Urban's smile was slow, appreciative. "Ah, Lawrence, I knew you would see it. Which is only right"—Urban's eyes almost twinkled—"since you were so troublesome as to bring up the whole matter in the first place."

"Vatican Two?" Wadding shaped the words almost as though

he were employing a memory trick. "That was the up-time con-
vocation to begin the reintegration of all their Christian sects,
supposedly presided over by Mother Church, was it not?"

"It was," the pope answered.

"And in which general religious tolerance was made canonical
doctrine," added Vitelleschi.

"I was not aware the pontiff ever reiterated the exhortations
of that council *ex cathedra*," Wadding murmured.

"Ah, see? And this is why I needed you, Father Wadding.
Why I needed all of you." Urban sat very straight in his saddle.
"For a variety of now-urgent reasons, we must decide upon the
canonical status here—in *this* world—of the decrees and doctrines
that proceeded from the Holy See in Cardinal Mazzare's world."

Wadding sputtered. "Your Holiness? At the very least, is not
a different world a different world?"

Mazzare smiled at Wadding. "Are you suggesting that there is
more than one God, with one Will?"

"Your Eminences!" Urban actually laughed. He made a palms-
down gesture as if he was calming obstreperous children. "You
shall have time enough to compare these opinions. Indeed, over
the next few weeks, I will ask you to be their champions."

Mazzare felt slightly disoriented. "Your Holiness?"

"Yes, of course. You, Cardinal Mazzare, can hardly be tasked
to speak for any position other than the positive, in this matter.
The Mother Church of your world, whose extremely tolerant practices you have made manifest here, has not only its best advocate
in you, but I doubt you could bring yourself to earnestly argue
that its canonical pronouncements should have no standing in
*this* world."

Mazzare simply said, "I fear you are correct, Your Holiness."

Urban nodded. "And Father Wadding will be the *advocatus
diaboli*."

The Irishman looked stunned. "Your Holiness? Me?"

"Certainly. Who better?"

"Many would do far better than I. For instance, Father Vitelleschi's familiarity with the theological conundrums of integrating
the perspectives of the up-time Church far outstrip my humble—"

"Father Wadding, your humility, while genuine, is also quite
misguided. You were the veritable spearhead—theological, rhetorical, and spiritual—in the final canonical determination of

Mother Church's doctrine regarding our Savior's Virgin Birth. And I know you have maintained a lively interest in the theological documents and implications of the arrival of the up-timers."

Wadding looked a bit pained. "Your Holiness, what you say is true. But I fear that what I have learned has not left me comfortable with their presence in our world, or congenial to what they call their Roman Catholic faith, so changed is it from our own."

"Which is precisely why you are to argue against one of its great changes: the radical inter-faith tolerance that did not merely arise from Vatican Two, but was its very *raison d'être*."

Wadding looked even more uncomfortable. "Might I point out, Your Holiness, that just thirty-five years ago, Giordano Bruno was burned at the stake for espousing the kind of radical toleration that the up-timers practice, and for claiming—as they also do—that many of His most wondrous miracles are in fact, merely laws of nature?"

"You most certainly may point that out, Father Wadding. Indeed, I expect you to do so. That will be part of your job, in the coming weeks. But it will also be important to remain mindful that the scientific assertions that brought such trouble to Galileo have now, in fact, been proven correct. And not just by the documents of the up-timers, but by our own observers, who now know what to look for, and how." Urban folded his hands upon the front of his saddle, the reins held tightly beneath them. "Father, we have entered into a time when we must reconsider many matters in which we thought our knowledge was absolute. And this will, I suspect, take us down wholly unprecedented pathways of investigation and debate. Over which Father Vitelleschi will prevail as judge and arbiter."

"Not you, Your Holiness?" Wadding sounded baffled.

"No, not me."

"What role, then, do you intend to play in the proceedings?"

"I intend," said Urban with a sly smile, "to watch, listen, and be edified." Seeing the look of surprise, even dismay, upon the faces of the other clerics, Urban lifted a hand, striking a pose that painters often used in portraying Socratic scholars at work among their students. "Our Heavenly Father has, since the arrival of the up-timers, set us upon a fateful road that now forks in two opposite directions. And the respective choices are as terribly distinct, and as terribly portentous, as those that faced our Lord and Savior on the night he was betrayed and contended with his human frailties in the garden at Gethsemane."

Wadding lifted his chin by the smallest of margins. "But there is this difference, Your Holiness: Christ could not err. His was a crisis of the heart, not of holiness, not of grace."

"That is profoundly true—and so I am glad that you are with me to offer counsel. For you must now each argue for one of the two forking paths that lie before us."

"You mean, toward Vatican Two, or away," murmured Wadding, so distracted that he forgot to add the Pontiff's honorific.

"Yes. And let us take another lesson from our Savior's terrible night of trial, for Christ's behavior always stands as a model for our own. He asked for the bitter cup to pass, if it might. This shows us, beyond any argument, that despite the horrors approaching, Our Savior's head was clear. He knew what lay before Him, if He chose to stay in that garden. He knew the prudent, mundane choice, but demonstrated His grace in rejecting it in favor of the wise—the divine—choice.

"So, let us see the same distinction in our own quandary as we approach this fork in our own road. And let us do so by setting aside, just for one moment, our constant mandate that we must always, to the best of our frail abilities, be agents of divine grace. Let us instead, simply reason as practical men as we confront this question: Is there any doubt about the wisest alliance for us to make?"

All of them shook their heads in the negative. Even Wadding.

"Just so. We are certain of the political prudence of allying with the USE and the forces of change exemplified in that land, as well as in the Netherlands and, increasingly, even Austria. We are no less sure of this than Christ knew that the most prudent act was to flee the garden of Gethsemane.

"But, also like him, we have a crisis of the heart as well. However, whereas our Savior's grace is perfect, ours is terribly imperfect. So, flawed as we are in matters of grace, we can only discern the most prudent mundane option with certainty. But what if terrestrial prudence is not, in this case, aligned with what is right and holy? What if, to walk in grace, we must walk in perilous ways, as did Christ that night, and the martyrs thereafter? Is it right—is it God's will—that we should place the safe-keeping of Peter's Church in the hands of those who many of us still call heretics, but who sincerely deem themselves Reformed?"

"We must not." Wadding's voice shook with emotion.

"I am not so certain of *either* path at this particular fork in the road, Father Wadding. But I am sure of this: if, at the end of our deliberations, we retain any doubt that the prudent choice is also the *right* choice, the *holy* choice, then we must construe that doubt to be our Heavenly father whispering the word 'caution' into our ears."

Mazzare nodded, worried but hearing many layers in Urban's musings. "His Holiness has the wisdom of the early Church fathers. But I must ask this question, too: where does the Prince of the Church go if not to a haven made safe by powers which now espouse toleration? Which, indeed, only possess those powers of protection because of the unity made possible by that toleration?"

"An excellent question, my son. But again, that is merely a matter of prudence. And as the unworthy inheritor of Peter's See, I am bound to put questions of grace before prudence, when and if they are separate concerns. As they most certainly are in this case."

They turned a corner in the winding lane, the wooded mountains grown so steep and so close that it was hard to imagine why the pines did not tumble down upon them. And at that road's end, there was a small country villa, boasting a modest enclosed garden and humble, scattered vineyards.

"See," said Urban, turning and pointing at the rustic building with a smile, "Gethsemane awaits us."

# Chapter 28

Harry Lefferts leaned away from the Remington 700's scope and sighed, "I love it when a plan comes together." His two *lefferti* assistants—hiding behind the low wall of the makeshift belvedere that was perched atop the one three-story building that bordered the Jewish Ghetto—nodded, fierce grins on their faces. Whether or not they understood the full details of the plan was really beside the point; they were ardent groupies and were pumped up, thrilled to be chosen as tactical runners for their idol.

One of them was Giovanna Marcoli's brother Fabrizio. Just beyond them, a gangly youth was scanning a tight cluster of rooftops about one-hundred-twenty yards away. "What are you seeing, Benito?"

"Little" Ben, whose growth rate put kudzu to shame, shrugged his narrow, stripling shoulders. "The usual," he answered, moving the binoculars up higher, so they rested well above the still-healing gash on his cheek.

"Any movement on the roof?"

"None. Never is."

"Good. Keep an eye on it."

"Don't I always?" Benito had never been awed by Harry.

Which only increased Harry's fondness for Benito. The kid was a character, a real original, but, because he was only fourteen, others hadn't noticed that just yet. It was a situation that Harry himself had experienced in adolescence and could recall with great clarity. He swung the Remington's scope down to the Palazzo Giove's main entrance and smiled to see the growing crowd of protesters, brandishing handles of every kind. The handles had been harvested from discarded tools, old doors, and shattered pots. The crowd was waving them in time to a chant that, at this range, Harry could not make out. But knowing Juliet, Harry was sure that it was saucy, inspired, and cutting.

He smiled to see her—prominent at the center of the mob— shaking her own pitcher handle at the tall, sealed doors, evidently lost in her role. But she was the consummate performer, able to give herself over fully to her persona of the moment, and yet maintain some part of her mind at a distance, observing, watching, measuring both the effect upon the audience, and the evolving situation around her.

She'd set the current events in motion six hours ago. In the blistering heat of the late mid-day sun, Juliet had waited patiently in the shadows with her water jug, as she had for three days. Three uneventful days when the palazzos of the *insula* Mattei had not drawn water, at least not from this fountain, which was located just across the street from the Palazzo Giacomo, and within twenty yards of where Frank and Giovanna were held captive.

But on this day, at last, two women had emerged from the tall doors of the main palazzo and moved north to the fountain, under the constant and proximal guard of two Spaniards.

Just as the two women started filling their yoke-linked buckets, Juliet had burst excitedly from her hiding place, quickly summoning other women to her with a tale of woe. Juliet had considered and discarded a number of tear-jerking narrative variants: she desperately needed water to soothe a child who had just burned herself at the hearth; to help a young cousin going into labor; to cleanse the wound of a young brother convalescing from wounds suffered during the Spanish attack. But with the increase in heat, the multiplication of mosquitoes, and the proximity of the river and the Ghetto, she had selected a story sure to generate maximum sympathy by playing on the fears of everyone else in the neighborhood: she needed water to combat the Roman fever of her elderly father.

Juliet had chosen her psyops story well; half a dozen other women were close behind her by the time she reached the fountain. Where she was waved off by the Spaniards. Hands on hips, red in the face, she expostulated, pleaded, screamed, gesticulated. The Spaniards ignored her. Indignant, but wary behind her apparent excess of passion, she defied them and stuck her jug into the fountain. In doing so, she came quite close to the *insula* Mattei's designated water-bearers, who were, of course, prohibited all contact with the outside world.

The closest Spaniard pushed her back, just missing her sizable bosom in so doing. But that didn't stop Juliet from claiming a sexual violation of her person, in addition to decrying the callous barbarity of the Spanish invaders. And, determined creature that she was, she surged her bulk back to the fountain, determined to fill her jug with water.

The other Spaniard looked lazily at her for a moment: Harry, watching through binoculars, had held his breath. He knew that look: annoyance coupled with utter disregard for human life. Anything could happen. The Spaniard pulled his sword—a short, straight blade not too different from a basket-hilted gladius—and swung it.

Juliet, mouth open, had frozen in surprise, fear, caution—Harry couldn't tell which—and watched as the flat of the blade smashed her jug to pieces. Leaving her holding the handle.

That was when Harry witnessed Juliet's genius at work, the moment of inspiration writ large across her broad face as she stared down at the fragment of jug which she was still grasping. With a shriek like a wounded Fury, she thrust the handle aloft, and began denouncing the Spanish brutes who were condemning her father to death because they would not share a fountain, not even for the five seconds it took to fill the jug they had destroyed. Thereby further ensuring the death of her father, because how could she now carry enough water?

What followed was a particularly Roman scene: despite the rapid propagation and intensification of her lament for a father dying due to the inhuman cruelty of the Spaniards, not one person interrupted Juliet's agonized tirade to determine the location of the stricken parent, or departed to find other containers for use as soon as the Spanish withdrew. Instead, the emotions and outrage swelled along with the crowd, burgeoning out of all proportion to the offense.

But that was Juliet's genius, to have understood exactly what kind of offense would have enough common resonance with the downtrodden masses to whip them up into the near-rebellious frenzy she had generated by three o'clock. At which point, the crowd had been ready to march on the Palazzo Mattei. But Juliet had redirected that fury, and marshaled what were now very much her forces, crafting a far more organized—and usefully timed—riot in front of the haughty gates of Palazzo Giove Mattei.

Which was now under way. The motif of the broken handle had, as Juliet had known it would, struck a chord with the less-affluent workers who were predominant in the neighborhoods near the Tiber. Now, as dusk was approaching, the anger of the mob was building, the chants becoming more fierce.

*Yes*, Harry thought, *I certainly do love it when a plan comes together.* He looked down the scope again; there'd be ample light for at least another twenty minutes, by which time they'd be done with the job and heading back to the boats. He played the scope across the crowd; roofs occasionally obstructed his view, particularly of anything that might be situated in the immediate lee of any given building. But, thanks to the piazza surrounding the fountain, the arched doorway into the target building, the Palazzo Giacomo Mattei, was in clear view. And over that arch, he could see into the courtyard beyond.

There was a dim light in the windows of Frank's rooms. The two-tiered loggia just beyond them, at the rear of the courtyard, was dark. A good sign: probably no guards there, as usual.

Harry cheated the scope up to the rooftop belvedere of the Palazzo Giove: one guy, staring over the lip down at the crowd in the street below. Nothing to worry about, but Harry would take him out first: an easy shot at only one hundred twenty-five yards.

He roved the scope across the interlocked roofs of the three palazzos of the squarish *insula*, checking for traps as he went. First the Giove, which dominated the southern and eastern halves of the compound; then the Giacomo on the west; and finally the Paganica on the northwest corner. Harry saw nothing new and no movement. As usual.

Satisfied, Harry turned to one of the *lefferti*. "Now, give the signal."

The young fellow nodded and leaned out the rear of their own crude belvedere; he uncovered a bull's eye lantern briefly. He resealed it, waited two seconds, uncovered it again. Repeated the process a third time and waited.

In the house across the street and just beyond the walls of the

Ghetto, a light came on in the second story window closest to the now-unguarded gate known as the *Porto Giuda*.

Sherrilyn Maddox stayed well within the jagged hole in the roof of the gutted church that overlooked the Palazzo Paganica. She saw a light appear in the second story window of the Ghetto-hugging house that she had been watching for the last fifteen minutes. She turned to face the dark behind her. "We're on," she hissed at the rest of the Wrecking Crew, whom she could barely make out. "Push those ladders over the street and get them snug on the roof of the Palazzo Paganica. Felix, Paul, you're the lightest, so you go over first and secure them in place. Then Gerd, you start on your way; you have a lot of roofs to scramble across."

"Yes, but they are flat, so they are easy."

Sherrilyn smiled. "If you say so. Let's move."

Owen Roe O'Neill tapped the earl of Tyrone on his thick, sturdy shoulder and pointed to the yellow glow in the signal window. "First light," he muttered.

John nodded, and turned to his assault team: all the Wild Geese and a half dozen of the oldest *lefferti*. They had spent most of the day in this street-accessed storeroom, located just north of the fountain where Juliet had begun the Broken Handle Riot. "Weapons ready, lads. And stand to stretch your legs. Starting in five minutes, we'll be running and fighting without rest until we've left Rome behind us."

The knock on the door was not the dinner Frank had been expecting; it was Don Vincente Jose-Maria de Castro y Papas. In armor.

"Signor Stone." His voice was very different from when they went on their now habitual garden walks. "It truly pains me to disturb you and your radiant wife at this late hour, but I am afraid I must intrude."

"Vincente, what is—?"

Giovanna must have heard something he had missed. "Frank, my love, do not ask questions; let him in. And come here, to me."

Frank looked at Don Vincente, who would not look him in the eye. Standing aside, Frank asked, "What's wrong? Is—?"

"All is well, Signor Stone. A mild disturbance in the street."

"Sounds more like a riot, to me," Giovanna offered from the doorway of their bedroom, her dark eyes lightless but tracking Vincente around the room as he inspected it for—for what?

"Is it? A riot, that is?" Frank asked.

"What? Yes, yes it seems so."

"A shortage of food? A new round of executions?" Giovanna had folded her arms and stood planted in the space between the rooms. "A toddler trampled under the hoofs of Spanish horses?"

Don Vincente did not look at her directly as he retracted the wick of the room's oil lamp, dimming the light. "A scuffle over drawing water from the fountain. A minor nuisance. It will pass quickly."

"Yes, no need to worry about Italians, eh? An easily routed rabble."

Now Don Vincente looked at her. "Signora, of this, be sure: I have never said, or thought, such a thing. Only a fool discounts the anger and resolve of patriots seeking to liberate their homeland."

If that did not mollify Giovanna, it was at least so blunt an admission that it momentarily took the wind out of her sails.

Frank however, had a new topic of conversation he wanted to pursue. "So Don Vincente, I wonder if you could explain something."

"Certainly, Signor Stone."

"If the riot is just a minor nuisance that will pass quickly, why are you here?"

Vincente looked up at him and sighed. "Because those are my orders."

In the hall just outside their suite, Frank heard movement: men in equipment, jostling lightly against each other. He looked in that direction; Sergeant Ezquerra was now standing in the doorway, hand on the hilt of his sword. That worthy shrugged when both he and Giovanna looked at him, and the accompanying smile was so brittle that Frank thought his face might break into a shower of terra-cotta pieces.

Frank turned back toward Vincente, pointed. "And he has the same orders? Along with the dozen or so others I can hear behind him?"

"Yes."

"And just how many more of your men are waiting even farther beyond the hall outside my room?"

"That," said Vincente, averting his eyes uncomfortably, "I cannot tell you."

"You don't know?"

"I am not allowed to say."

Frank stared at him until Vincente met his eyes again. "It's not just a riot, is it?"

Vincente looked sad. "Of course not."

Harry watched as Sherrilyn and the others reached the roof of Palazzo Giacomo Mattei, just east of the room in which Frank and Giovanna were being held. As soon as they got in position, they crouched low, Matija shrugging off a haversack: Gerd's demolition gear.

Harry swung his scope right, to the south and the east, and saw, at a considerably greater distance, Gerd's spare outline, returning from his first assignment. He was moving spiderlike across the roofs, keeping to the shortest path that would bring him back to Sherrilyn's vertical entry team. Behind him, a wisp of smoke was now visible: the diversionary fire he had started near the southeast corner of the *insula*, the point furthest away from the northwest corner occupied by the palazzos Paganica and Giacomo. Harry cheated the scope a little farther south to the rooftop belvedere on the Palazzo Giove: empty, now. Maybe one of the folks in the crowd had heaved a few rocks at the observer he had seen there earlier. At any rate, the coast was clear.

Harry turned toward the *lefferto* with the light and nodded. Once again, the young fellow commenced signaling with his bull's eye lantern.

John O'Neill saw the second signal window illuminate on the second floor of the tall building beside the Porto Giuda. He pushed open the storeroom door, revealing the fountain that dominated the small square. He jerked his head toward the street and the arched entrance of the Palazzo Giacomo's courtyard. "On me, at the trot," he ordered, and then led the way, as he always did. But this time he went forth with his sword still in its scabbard; there was no need to make clear their intents until they reached the entrance, only fifteen yards away.

Frank, staring out the slightly open window himself, began assessing the scene in the courtyard more carefully, seeing if there were any hints to be gleaned as to what, other than the riot, might be going on nearby. Given the long, slanting shadows of dusk, it was almost impossible to see beyond the arches that dominated both levels of the two-tiered loggia that faced opposite the street entry.

Almost impossible. But now that he looked carefully, he could see faint silhouettes hidden behind the supporting pillars of the upper gallery's arches. Silhouettes of large men. In helmets. With weapons. Then Frank noticed movement: a window's louvered shutters rotated slightly, briefly revealing a dim light in the room behind it. And in the moment before that light was extinguished, Frank saw, quite distinctly, the barrel of a very long gun, set on a pedestal, aiming out into the darkness at a slight elevation. Holding his breath, Frank followed the muzzle's invisible trajectory out over the top of the courtyard wall and then between nearby roofs, at which point it was impossible to determine its precise path. But there were only a few two-story buildings out in that direction, and only one that was three stories, topped by a shabby belvedere, at the edge of the Ghetto. Where he saw, faintly, a tiny twitch of movement: maybe a nodding head, backlit by the setting sun. Or maybe silhouetted by the flash of a mostly shaded lamp...

Before he could think the better of doing so, Frank turned toward Vincente; cold pierced the pit of his stomach even as his brow suddenly burned with panic and rage. "You bastard—!"

Sherrilyn scanned the *insula's* roofs nervously; she wished the riot could be a little more—well, quiet. Eyes were not enough when trying to make a covert entry; you needed your ears as well. And the tides of raucous protest at the main gate was rendering her ears useless.

Gerd was almost done placing the entry charges so that they would—hopefully—send most of their force downward. The tests he had run weeks before had yielded limited success; hopefully, this time would be no worse than those. With any luck, it would be a bit better.

Gerd played out the fast-burning fuse as he low-scrambled back to where the rest of the Crew was waiting, behind a low roof-peak, just six yards from his crude demolition charge.

"Ready?" asked Sherrilyn, rubbing her knee.

"*Ja*, we can start the fireworks," smiled Gerd, who sat up a

little higher to reinspect his handiwork, to make sure he hadn't missed anything.

Owen pulled out his pepperbox revolver as almost a dozen more *lefferti,* led by Frank Stone's friend Piero, emerged from a building on the opposite side of the fountain's piazza and swung in behind the leading wedge of Wild Geese. From an adjoining wain-shed, another half dozen *lefferti* burst out onto the street, but they turned sharply to the right, sprinting southward toward the riot outside the massive gates of the Palazzo Giove.

Owen reached, and sidled up alongside, the much smaller double-doors that led into the courtyard of the Palazzo Giacomo and nodded to David Synnot. The Ulsterman, standing six foot two and heavy-thewed, was carrying a maul.

Since the guards, if they were highly motivated, might be looking out the vision port in the door, Synnot wasted no time. He planted his feet wide, reared back with the maul, and then swung it forward in a fast, overhand arc.

"Knock, knock," John O'Neill snarled wickedly, just before its iron head landed.

Frank saw Vincente's jaw tighten, and then his eyes shot towards the gateway into the courtyard, where a thundering crash sent the doors themselves flying into pieces. Without turning toward Ezquerra, the Spanish captain ordered: "Ready my gun."

The splintering smash of Synnot's maul even drowned out the ongoing protest for a moment. Along with John, Owen shouldered open the tattered remains of the doors. Into that gap rushed Turlough Eubanks and Gerald O'Sullivan, swords out in their right hands, pepperboxes in their left, cuirasses glimmering faintly in the last light of day.

The fight for the door was over as soon as it had begun. The two guards, disheveled and nursing the dregs of nonregulation libations, were cut down swiftly. John grinned, sped past Owen, and then waved in the *lefferti,* who were tasked to secure the ground floor level of the two-tiered loggia at the opposite end of the courtyard. So far, so good: it was all proving to be just as easy as Harry had foreseen. . . .

Owen lagged a step. It was *too* easy, too clean. He scanned

the two gate guards; oddly, neither affected the coiffure stylings popular among the Spanish. No beards either, but ill-shaven, and a bit thin; one had distinct hollows in his cheeks. And where was the inevitable detritus that collected around such a low-trouble watch post? There should have been a smattering of garbage, or the little conveniences that guards brought to their posts: stools, rain-capes, a deck of cards . . .

That was when Owen heard the gunfire start up on the roof, and it didn't sound like one of the Wrecking Crew's weapons.

Sherrilyn saw the flash near the base of the main palazzo's rooftop belvedere a split second before she heard the sharp report—and before Gerd dropped forward like a bag of rocks. He slid a yard down the shallow slope of the roof, upsetting tiles as he went.

"Damnit, Gerd! Gerd!"

But even before Sherrilyn got to his side, she knew Gerd was dead; the bullet had hit him just left of the sternum, and the blood was welling up out of him like a slow spring.

"Bastards," growled Sherrilyn, thumbing the safety off her rifle and popping a round at the site of the flash. "Follow my fire," she shouted to the rest of the Crew, "and suppress."

As another bullet whined overhead, and the Crew's shotguns roared in response, Sherrilyn Maddox lit the fuse of Gerd's demolition charge. Then she scrambled, low and fast, to rejoin the Crew, hoping against hope that the second shot from the belvedere meant there were only two shooters concealed there.

Because if there were more, she might be taking her final breaths and last steps.

Frank looked down into the courtyard; all those men pouring through the shattered gate were coming to rescue him. Whoever they were. And they were going to get slaughtered by the well-prepared Spanish. Slaughtered. But what could he do—?

Frank snatched the oil lamp off the table with his right hand, yanked open the shutters with his left, and threw.

The lamp traced a guttering arc that carried it neatly over the low wall of the arcaded upper gallery; it shattered just to the right of the window with the open louvers.

# Chapter 29

Harry saw Gerd slide down the roof, Sherrilyn going over to him. But where had the shot—?

"Muzzle flash: base of the belvedere on the main roof," snapped Fabrizio Marcoli from directly behind him.

So the Spanish had their own shooter on the roof? What the hell—? Harry tracked over with the rifle, asked, "Do I have a shot?"

"No shot. He's on the far side of the belvedere," Fabrizio announced. Harry saw that Fabrizio was right—and then started to wonder how the Spanish had not only known to put a sniper in the belvedere, but to put him on the side away from Harry's own position—

Back in the courtyard of the Palazzo Giacomo, a faint arc of light traced itself against the gathering darkness. Harry rapidly tracked over to the left, just in time to see an oil lamp, or maybe a molotov cocktail, flare angrily on the second-story gallery. And were those silhouettes up there? With weapons?

Harry was staring so hard at the shadowy figures that he almost missed the small, bright wink of light from behind the louvered shutters of the window closest to the impact point of the oil lamp—

Harry ducked, realizing: *Holy shit; they have us spotted and ranged.*

And he heard, an instant after the distant report of the gun, Fabrizio grunt and fall.

Harry spun, hair raising up. *No. No no no—*

Fabrizio was stretched out his full length, coughing, eyes rolling listlessly. A bullet-hole just under his heart was leaking out his life faster than any up-time surgeon could have staunched; in any century, this kind of sucking chest wound was a death sentence. A quick one, perhaps, but that was the coldest of all possible comfort.

Harry closed his eyes and felt his molars grinding together. He'd come here to rescue Giovanna—and he'd just gotten her brother killed.

Captain Vincente Jose-Maria de Castro y Papas was fast— terribly fast. He crossed to Frank in a single step, grabbed him with both hands and hurled him bodily away from the window. Airborne for at least five feet, Frank crashed into, and slumped down along, the opposite wall.

"Beast!" Giovanna screamed at the Spaniard as she dashed to her stunned husband's side. "Murderer!"

Don Vincente had stepped back from the window. "Signora Stone, I may have just saved his life—"

That's when the gunfire started in the courtyard, and an explosion slammed the roof in the adjacent room, quaking half the plaster off the ceiling.

Harry swung back up into his firing position, slammed the Remington into his right shoulder, and jerked his scope over to the courtyard. As he did, he saw the tail end of another small flash, right next to where the first one had been, but now half-obscured by the leaping oil flames.

Before Harry could react, he felt a red-hot poker lance into his right shoulder, just above the clavicle, and push out the other side with the force of a sledge-hammer. Lefferts went off his stool, but kept his grip on the rifle. *Damned if I'm going to jar the scope out of alignment now,* he thought.

He threw himself upright without delay and snugged the gun tight—agonizingly tight—into his savaged right shoulder. He dropped the crosshairs on some movement he saw through the louvers and fired. At that precise moment, the dark arches lining both the second and ground floor galleries of the courtyard's loggia were raggedly illuminated by a volley of murderous fire.

John O'Neill was so stunned by the sudden wave of fire—*an ambush! we are betrayed!*—that he almost didn't feel the two-headed battering ram that slammed through his cuirass and stuck his chest, almost penetrating the buff coat beneath. As he fell backwards, he was vaguely aware that the *lefferti* in front of him were going down in windrows. He felt the overlapping mental and physical shocks combine and verge toward confusion—and then he turned off his mind. He thought only so much as was necessary to get moving, a trait taught by years on battlefields. He started to roll up into a crouch, checking his pistol, and the situation.

Which was not good: three of the Wild Geese who had charged in with him were down. But like him, two were unwounded and rising, thanks to their cuirasses and buff coats. The third man, Fitzgerald, was having a hard time getting to his feet, trailing a useless left arm. His bicep had been torn through, and was probably still attached only because the Spaniards were using loads of multiple, lighter balls. Lethal against the unarmored troops they had evidently been expecting, but much less so against layered armor.

But as O'Neill swayed upright, he saw the real horror of what such double loads could do. The unarmored *lefferti*, who had been given the presumably easy job of securing the bottom level of the loggia, had caught the brunt of the volley; a dozen were strewn across the width of the courtyard, motionless. Three more were rising unsteadily, their clothes tattered and blood-smeared from multiple wounds.

So John O'Neill did what he did best. Tossing his pistol over to his left hand and drawing his sword with the right, he screamed, "At them!" and led the charge toward the loggia.

Sherrilyn looked over the shallow roof peak as the terra-cotta tile fragments blasted skyward by Gerd's demolition charge ceased to rain down. The explosion had blown open a hole, but not as big as they had hoped or planned. Two at a time could get down into the room below, at most. "Matija, Donald, suppressive fire. The rest of you, follow me."

She scuttled over to the edge of the still-smoking hole—and almost fell in when her weight prompted a little more of the ruined structure to collapse. "Damn it, this is going to be tough. George, Paul, you're going to lower Felix and me down for a look-see."

Paul frowned. "I thought we were just going to jump down and—"

"Nope. We've had too many surprises already. So we take it one step at a time from here on; it might just save our lives." She got her foot in the rope loop that had been prepared for this eventuality, pulled her .357 Smith and Wesson revolver and looked over at the waiting Felix—who had the team's CQC entry weapon, a sawed-off 12 gauge, ready. She nodded to George Sutherland, who held the rope in his massive hands. "Okay: down we go."

As John O'Neill charged, Owen winced. But whether the earl of Tyrone called for a charge by chance or design, it had been the right call. The Spanish had obviously fired all barrels, trusting to inflict so many casualties in that first terrible sheet of flame and lead that the intruders would break. John's charge took them by surprise, and although he had only half a dozen Wild Geese following him, they were in armor and were closing with sword and pistol against musketeers caught in the act of reloading. Owen listened to the battle he could not see; from the sound of it, the lightly armored Spanish were tossing aside their firearms and going for their much smaller swords. So unless they had overwhelming numerical superiority, the battle for the lower level of the loggia promised to be a very one-sided fight. But the upper gallery—

Owen elevated and aimed his pepperbox, securing it with his left hand as Lefferts and North both had counseled. "Fire on the second level, lads. Make 'em corpses or keep 'em busy."

Owen's timing was indeed fortuitous. The Spanish musketeers on the second floor had finally sorted themselves out after dodging the oil flames and reloading. They now rose and brought their weapons to bear—but they had not expected four revolvers aimed up at them. The flurry of pistol fire dropped three of the Spaniards—and then another two went down an instant later. A pair of lagging, distant reports announced that the Hibernian riflemen back at the signal building had brought their own weapons into play.

For the moment, the tide seemed to be swinging back in their favor—but Owen put aside the seductive thrill of pushing ahead with the attack. *The Spanish expected us, knew we were coming. If we get the initiative, we should use it to run. As quickly as possible...*

With bits of roofing tiles crumbling down around them, Sherrilyn and Felix dipped down into the room adjacent to Frank's, separated from it by one thin wall. They had a scant moment to survey the shattered finery before two Spanish soldiers swept around the doorway, firing pistols as they came. Another two stayed back, sheltering behind the doorway and discharging their pieces as well.

It was like some insane video game, Sherrilyn thought as she pounded rounds out of the .357 magnum and wished she had stuck with the nine-millimeter this time: magazine size *was* an entry team's best friend. She saw the first two Spaniards go down, felt a bullet sing past her ear. She fired through the wall at the third Spaniard sheltering behind it; he dropped screaming into the open doorway, clutching a ruined groin. Felix and the last of the defenders traded shots. The Spaniard went backwards, but so did Felix. Sherrilyn grabbed him, kept him on his rope, yelled: "Pull us up! *Now!*"

John O'Neill came back out from under the roof of the loggia's lower tier, his sword drenched red. He saw that Owen had killed no small number of the musketeers on the second level. And that he was forcing the rest to keep their heads down, for the nonce. So now—

Having heard the expected breaching charge go off on the roof in the midst of his attack, John looked up expectantly at Frank's window. Just beyond it there was the sound of gunfire—a lot of it—then silence. Ah, so the Wrecking Crew had gotten inside. Excellent. No time to waste. "Fitzgerald," he shouted, "with me," and ran over to the foot of the window from which he expected a rope ladder, and then the hostages, to descend. Any second now.

The irate mob in front of the Palazzo Giove hushed suddenly, hearing the fusillade of gunfire just up the street, as well as one or two reports nearly overhead, evidently coming from the belvedere.

Juliet frowned; even though she wasn't seeing the battle with her own eyes, the pace sounded wrong. The firing should have been very much one-sided, and not so much of it, but now—

The tall doors of the Palazzo Mattei di Giove seemed to emit a metallic bark: the immense lock had been undone. And then the doors themselves seemed to fly inward on their hinges, so quickly that—

*This is planned*, Juliet thought, and jumped aside, nimble despite her size.

A split-second later, the doors were fully open, revealing a darkened courtyard...Which suddenly belched out a wall of flame and thunder as a waiting platoon's musket volley drove straight into the core of the crowd.

For a moment there was no further sound. It was as though, surprised or outraged or both, the world was holding its breath. Then the screaming started: a chorus of agony from shattered bodies lying upon each other, mingled gore spreading across them.

As Juliet moved farther away from the gateway, she heard the sound of hooves, hammering down in a thunder against the court-yard's flagstones. The riders—armored, swords drawn, pistols ready in fore-saddle braces, crested morions pulled low—swept out of the Palazzo Giove, ignoring the crowd to the south of the doorway, and smashing through the stragglers to their right, to the north.

Six, Juliet counted: no, eight. And behind them, firing occasionally to rout those who did not flee fast enough, were foot soldiers. Who also turned north as one body.

Toward the fountain and the shattered gateway into the embattled courtyard of the Palazzo Giacomo.

*They knew we were coming,* Juliet realized, *knew it all along. And they fooled us; they fooled* me.

Suddenly gripped by terror—more because she had been out-witted than in response to the peril at her heels—she turned and ran for her life.

Sherrilyn handed Felix off to Donald as they got back behind the roof peak. Matija, bleeding from a through-and-through gunshot wound in the upper left arm, hooked a thumb at the belvedere. "I think we got one. Their fire has dropped off."

Donald almost fell when Felix lost all strength in his legs and collapsed. And Sherrilyn could see why: what she had first thought

was a belly wound had actually been a little higher than that. The bullet might have clipped the lower periphery of the right lung.

"What now?" Ohde asked as Paul came over to support Felix.

Sherrilyn shook her head. "We're pulling out."

Matija was dumbfounded: "We're—?"

"Look, if we stay on the roof, we'll still get sniped at. Harry's got no angle on their shooters in the belvedere, so no help there. The hole Gerd's package blew in the roof is too small and the Spanish are all over it, so we can't get in fast enough, even if we wanted to. And it sounds like the courtyard has become a shooting gallery, with the bad guys doing almost half the shooting. So we've got only one option left: we run like hell."

And they did.

John O'Neill, looking up, saw no immediate progress at Frank Stone's window. His gaze turned to the empty pepperbox revolver in his hand, and he realized the moment of truth had come: reloading. Under pressure. In combat.

However, the weapon *had* made a fine mess of the Spanish who had been in the loggia. Particularly since the Wild Geese had loaded their first cylinders with double shot. The two Spaniards who survived the subsequent swordplay—the ones closest to the door—had darted through and barred it.

So, staring at the pepperbox as if he might bend it to his will, John O'Neill began the reloading process. He snapped the locking cap into the "off" position, thumbed the hinge release and broke the weapon open. Well, not so bad so far...

Don Vincente reentered the room and nodded to the hall behind. "Ezquerra, I think they have abandoned their attempt to come through the roof. But oversee the guards in the adjacent room. And mind: the up-timer weapons shoot through these walls. With great effect."

Ezquerra, suddenly neither lethargic nor incompetent, nodded, but paused. "Don Vincente, if I am no longer by your side—"

Vincente held out his hand.

The sergeant gave him a well-oiled leather case of some length.

Vincente nodded his thanks and moved slowly in the direction of the window.

✧    ✧    ✧

John O'Neill slid a new cylinder out of its pouch and tapped off the wooden band that kept the preseated percussion caps snugly in their places. Then he started sliding the cylinder down the axial arm.

Next to him, Gerald Fitzgerald nodded upward. "Movement overhead, Lord O'Neill. Near the window. But it doesn't look like—"

A long muzzle flash jetted from between one of the ground floor windows' shutters. As if side-kicked by the accompanying roar, Fitzgerald fell over with a groan, the shot having punched clean through his buckled cuirass and the buff coat beneath.

John, with the practicality born of long battlefield experience, accepted that Gerald was dead and there was nothing to be done but to reload before the Spanish bastard did.

With the cylinder securely seated on the arm, he snapped it back up into position. Almost ready. And if the first fellow who appeared at the window overhead wasn't Frank, John would have a nice surprise waiting for him....

Don Vincente had opened the leather case and removed an up-time shotgun.

Frank gaped. "That shotgun. That's *mine*. From the bar."

"Yes." Vincente cycled the action expertly.

Frank pushed Giovanna away, while squirming back against the wall and holding up his hands. "Hey, now wait a minute—"

But Vincente did not bring it up or even aim it in his general direction. Instead, he walked briskly to the window.

As Owen helped up the last of the *lefferti*, he looked backward through the courtyard gate into the piazza. The once-bold rioters were fleeing past, running for their lives, no doubt driven off by the huge volley he had just heard from farther down the street. Damn it, there was no doubt left: the rescue attempt had been expected and was a failure. Now the only question was if they could escape before it became a full-fledged disaster.

Unfortunately, Owen had been hearing telltale signs that such a dire outcome might indeed be imminent. The discharges of the Wrecking Crew's up-time arms were no longer coming from inside the Palazzo Giacomo, nor even near their planned entry-point on the roof; instead, they were dwindling, going back the way they had come.

Owen, knowing he'd get an argument he didn't have the time for, turned to tell John the fight was over, and that he'd bodily drag the earl to safety, if he had to.

That was when Owen saw that the window above John O'Neill was opening. "John!" Owen shouted, and sprinted in his direction.

John replied with an annoyed "What?" *Damn it, why does Owen have to start fussing at me while I'm loading this contraption? I just have to snap down the—there, locked. And loaded.* As Harry always liked to say.

Finished, and feeling a great sense of pride, John swung the weapon upward—just in case the movement Gerald had seen at the window was something other than a prelude to the escape of Frank and Giovanna...

A figure was already in the window above. From which bright thunder roared down at the earl of Tyrone, the same kind of thunder that Harry's shotgun made.

Driven down to his knees by a torrent of crushing, searing hammers that cut through his body in a dozen places, John O'Neill almost fell, but pulled himself upright again. He raised the pepperbox—

Another yellow-flaring thunder-bolt struck him down from above; the brief burst of excruciating pain it caused became sudden numbness.

*So,* John thought as he collapsed forward, *that fellow in the window wasn't Frank, after all.*

Owen felt his throat constrict as he saw one of the last two princes of Ireland smashed to the ground by a second full load of double-aught buckshot from overhead. He emptied three chambers at the window—just as the dim figure there jerked back sharply.

Owen arrived at John's side, already shouting orders. "Synnot, get over here. The rest of you, cover us." With Synnot's help, Owen got the mumbling, bleeding John O'Neill up off the ground. "We're leaving," he ordered through his tears. "Everyone: fighting withdrawal."

Harry, blood coating his burning shoulder, noticed that the stock of the Remington was sticky and wet. As was his shirt. And the table upon which the rifle was resting. And the sandbags upon which it was stabilized. "Signor Lefferts, you not look so good," said Benito.

Harry nodded, waved him toward the signal building. "Go over there. Tell them, 'lights out.' Send runners to order withdrawal." After a moment, he gestured at the one remaining *lefferto*. "You go with him." There was no point risking another youngster's life by keeping him up here, since he didn't really need spotters anymore.

As the two young men's feet pounded down the stairs, Harry swayed back into the firing position, gritting his teeth as he set the stock into his brutalized shoulder. Through the scope, he could see Juliet running with the rest of the fleeing rioters but, being heavily built, she was quickly falling to the rear of the crowd.

Juliet was pumping her legs as fast as she could when there was a blast behind her. She went down, her left buttock apparently aflame. But no, it was just a pistol-shot through the thick of the flesh. Flesh, she allowed, of which she had plenty to spare. She struggled back to her feet, her lungs burning almost as badly as her rear end, and tried to resume running.

Sherrilyn, the last to cross the ladder, jumped off its last rung, turned, and pushed it down into the street. Covering her, Donald fired his shotgun at the distant belvedere, jacked another round into the chamber, jerked his head at the knotted line running down the front of the church. "You first," he said.

"No: it's my—"

"Sherrilyn, you've been first in and last out the whole way. Now give it a rest: git." He fired another round at the belvedere; a short scream suggested that his shot had found its mark.

Sherrilyn started down the rope, feeling like some target at the country fair: *Step right up and try your luck! Shoot the teacher off the rope! Three tries a dollar!*

George, just below her, had stopped in mid-descent, looking— no, staring—down the street that ran the length of the western edge of the *insula* Mattei. The cords stood out on his suddenly flushed neck as he screamed, "Juliet! *Juliet!*"

Sherrilyn turned, looked up the street, caught sight of a Spanish horseman, the scattering rioters, the litter of bodies, the distant but approaching Spanish infantry—and somehow, framed by it all, she saw the Spanish cavalryman who had shot Juliet gather his horse carefully and then spur it straight at her. He was smiling as he came. Smiling. Smiling as he rode her under, the hooves crushing and splitting and breaking the body that they churned through and over. And when she was a crumbled, barely moving lump of bloody flesh behind him, he turned in the saddle to look at her. And he was still smiling.

"JULIET!" screamed George, who slid down another ten feet, leaped from the rope, and landed off-center. He tumbled, came up like a gymnast and, loping badly, still sprinted in the direction of his stricken wife, screaming, again, "Juliet!"

Owen came out of the courtyard at a sprint, right behind the wounded Piero. He turned as he exited, grabbing a handful of what was left of the doors and pulled them shut: felt the thud as two musket balls hit them a moment later.

Owen turned—and found himself facing a cavalry charge.

*Jayzus!* "Fire what you have!" he shouted to the clustered Wild Geese. He raised his pistol and started squeezing off rounds. The sustained barrage from their pepperbox revolvers slowed the charge, the riders clearly baffled to encounter so steady a volume of fire from such a small group. But they came on, even so.

The next ten seconds seemed longer than most days Owen had lived through. Caught in a whirl of horses, blazing guns, and falling bodies, there was no time to give orders or even think. Owen dodged, fired, lost his grip on John, fired again, which sent a horse tumbling toward him. He scrambled away, saw a Spaniard loom out of the smoke and chaos, pistol raised, hammer falling. A flash, a boom—and Synnot, who was still close beside him, carrying John with one arm, went down with a bullet through his forehead. Owen brought his own gun to bear, fired back, and missed. But even so, the Spaniard spilled out of his saddle, albeit in the opposite direction from what Owen would have expected.

It made no sense, but Owen had no time to be puzzled; having spent the last three shots in the cylinder, he let the pistol fall on its lanyard, ready to draw steel. But, through the smoke, he saw the last three Spanish cavalrymen had already reversed, leaving five of their number behind. Only now did Owen register the more distant shots he had missed hearing during the melee, and which probably explained the mysterious demise of the last Spaniard he had faced. The rifles of the Hibernians and Harry had come to their aid like angels—angels of death, of course, but angels nonetheless.

He turned, looked for John, and discovered him pinned beneath a horse, inarguably dead. Probably had been from the first shotgun blast that had ripped down through his body. Only sheer animal vitality had kept him going after that.

Owen reached out, took a firm hold on the earl's traveling cloak, just below the embroidered pattern of the Tyrones, and yanked hard. And again. On the third try, it came free, and clutching it as he waved his remaining men into their retreat, Owen wondered *for whom have I taken this cloak? Who is left of the line of the O'Neills who might justly receive it? And if there are none such, then what good is it at all?*

For more than a man named John O'Neill had died in Rome that night. Half the hopes of Ireland had expired with him.

Harry sighed, glad to have saved Owen—anyone—out of all this mess. He had just started thumbing fresh rounds into his empty rifle when the figure of a dark-cloaked man—not much more than a speck, since Lefferts was not using the scope— emerged from the ranks of the of the Spanish foot and walked up behind Juliet. For a moment, he stood very still, watching her drag her broken body away. Then, looking first toward George, who had been tackled by the rest of the Wrecking Crew, and next, vaguely in the direction of Harry himself, he took a step forward. The man drew a revolver, large enough to be the one that Lefferts had seen in Frank's bar, and shot Juliet in the back of the head.

Then the dark-cloaked man stepped back into the ranks of his soldiers. For they were clearly his soldiers; they parted before, and then closed around, him like a sable tide making way for whatever power had conjured it in the first place.

Even as George screamed wordlessly at the now-steadily approaching Spanish infantry, Sherrilyn grabbed both his cheeks, hard, and pulled his face down to look at her. "We need you," she shouted.

If it wasn't for the two Hibernians with the lever actions, she was pretty sure they'd all be dead by now. But those long-range rounds had struck down so many of the foot soldiers' lead rank that they had scattered into the lee of the buildings for cover. Facing this fire immediately after watching their cavalry cut apart by the revolvers of the Wild Geese, the renowned Spanish infantry had apparently decided against making any headlong rushes. Yet.

"George, listen. You have to carry Felix," she lied. "You're the only one strong enough. He needs you."

"Juliet needs me, she—"

"No. She doesn't. Not anymore. Here's Felix: carry him."

Harry stared at the ruin of the plan that he thought, at first, had come together. But instead, it had come apart. The Wild Geese were leapfrogging to the rear in fire teams of three. Sherrilyn had hoisted Felix onto George's back, who seemed bowed, like a tired draft horse about to drop in its traces. Piero was keeping what was left of the *lefferti* moving together along the streets that lay between the Spanish and the Crew's main line of retreat, thereby serving as a flanking screen.

The boy that Harry had sent with Benito to spread the withdrawal orders came pounding back up the stairs. "Signor Lefferts?"

"Yes?"

"You must go."

"Yeah, I was just about to stroll on home. Where's Benito?"

The boy made a face. "He got shot. Not killed, though. Not yet, anyway."

Harry's jaws tightened.

"Any orders?" the boy asked.

"Orders? For who?"

"Why, for me, sir."

"Yes. Here are my orders: run like hell. Then get lost. And don't get found."

Thomas North looked over at Sean Connal for the fourth time in as many minutes. "That's too much gunfire," he opined. "Too much, for too long."

"So you've said. And so I've agreed."

North stood. "Then I'm retasking this force to provide a base of covering fire for a retreat."

"We need a diversion. If Borja has any forces waiting here in the Trastevere, we'll need to draw them away from the Crew's path of retreat. We'll also need to keep them busy long enough so that they miss detecting and following these boats—or we will never get out of Italy alive."

"Excellent points. I hope you have an equally excellent plan."

"It just so happens I do." North turned to the one *lefferto* who had been left with them. "You. Are there abandoned houses in the north side of Trastevere?"

"*Si*. Many. I know of one near the Via Aurelia—"

"Fine. Now take this. It is an explosive. You understand that? No? Hmm, let's try a new approach: this box goes BOOM! Now do you understand? Excellent. Take this to the house you mentioned. Light this fuse, like so. And then run away as fast as you can. Do not stop until you hear the boom. Then find a hiding spot, get rid of all your *lefferto* rubbish, and walk away."

"Why? I am proud to be a *lefferto* and I will not—"

"You will be dead if you do not do as I tell you. The attack has failed. The Spanish will find many dead *lefferti*. They will search very hard for the rest. Do not be stupid. Get rid of the *lefferti* clothes and doodads and do not look back. Go into hiding for a week, at least. Can you do this?"

"*Si*. I—"

"Excellent. Go. Now. Dr. Connal?"

"Yes?"

"You stay here with the boats." North held up a hand. "No complaints. Someone has to guard our ride home." He turned to his own men. "You two come with me. I suspect our rifles will be needed to help Captain Lefferts with his fighting withdrawal. Which, if my ears don't deceive me, is rapidly approaching." He scooped up one of his favorite up-time toys—an SKS semiautomatic carbine—and ran toward the Ponte Cestia at a crouch.

For one terrifying moment, as new gunfire crackled out over the Tiber behind him, Harry Lefferts feared that the Spanish had boxed him in. That they had somehow known he planned to withdraw by boat after traversing the Isola Tiberina and had therefore put a blocking force at the bridge.

But the steady fire was coming from Thomas North's anchor watch. The Limey had apparently pulled his team forward. As Harry reached the Ponte Fabricia, he dropped to a knee and reloaded his Remington for the third time. He looked up intermittently to wave the rest of the Wrecking Crew past him, then the Hibernians, and then the Wild Geese. By the time Owen Roe came along, bringing up the rear, having expended the last of his ready pepperbox cylinders, the Spanish had started closing the distance. They were getting bold again.

Despite the fading light, the early moon showed Harry a good target at just over fifty yards: a foot soldier whose slightly heavier and more weapon-festooned outline suggested a senior sergeant, marshalling the advancing troops. Harry raised his rifle, ignored the incendiary throbbing in his shoulder, let the crosshairs float down to settle on the silhouette and squeezed the trigger. He did not wait to see the result; he simply turned and ran.

As he passed North and his men, there was a loud explosion in the distance, somewhere in the north of Trastevere, from the sound of it.

Harry continued to run until he reached the boats. Thomas North and his two Hibernians were already close behind him by the time he got there. They jumped over the sides together. Waiting hands grabbed them while others—white with clutching poles and oars—pushed the shallow-bottomed punts off and out into the swifter current. As the oars started to creak in the locks and the boats picked up speed, Harry looked back over his boats and the city.

In his own boat, Owen Roe O'Neill sat in the thwarts, empty-eyed, clutching the bullet-tattered cloak that had belonged to the earl of Tyrone. George Sutherland was alternately weeping and laughing. Matija, the bleeding from his arm wound staunched, watched with dull eyes as Dr. Connal moved away from Felix and sat next to Harry.

"Let me look at that shoulder, Captain Lefferts."

"I'm just Harry, Doc. And I can wait. Finish up with Felix, first."

"I have finished. He's dead, Harry."

The pain as the doctor started cleaning the shoulder wound was welcome. Resisting that pain made it easier to resist the deeper, sharper agonies that were cutting down into his soul. Gerd. Juliet. Felix. John O'Neill. Several of the Wild Geese. Most of the survivors wounded. And scores of rioters and *lefferti* littering the streets of Rome. Their jaunty hats trampled. Their *faux* sunglasses shattered.

Harry reached into his chest pocket and drew out his own sunglasses. They were the ones that had given birth to, and had become the trademark of, the myth of Harry Lefferts: commando, ne'er do well, adventurer. And above all, a man who could not be beaten. He looked at his own, distorted reflection in the glasses, ghostly in the fading light. Unbeatable. Uber cool. Yeah, right.

Harry snapped the glasses in two and threw them into the Tiber.

# Part Four

## June–July 1635

And plunged in terror down the sky

# Chapter 30

Cardinal Gaspar de Borja y Velasco actually clapped his hands once in sharp, exultant glee. "Señor Dolor, this is excellent news. And we owe our victory, it seems, to your excellent stratagems. Which you must explain to me: how were you able to defeat the Wrecking Crew when no one else in Europe seemed capable of doing so?"

Dolor shrugged. "By giving them what they expected to see. In every particular."

Borja frowned. "More detail, please, señor: I am not a military man."

*Truer words were never spoken—particularly by you, red hat.* "Your Eminence, you may use simple traps to catch simple beasts; a bit of food left dangling over a pit will capture most unwary predators. But Lefferts and his Crew were not unwary predators; like foxes, they were inherently wary of traps and ploys—having used so many themselves.

"So, in setting this trap, I was mindful that we had to create the illusion of a reasonable defense, but with a few subtle flaws that they could exploit."

"Such as?"

"Such as their belief that we had only a third of the troops that we actually had stationed in the *insula* Mattei. To create that illusion, we had to mimic—in every detail—what an undermanned

321

garrison would do. In this case, that involved denying casual access to the interior of the *insula*, thereby concealing our supposedly scant numbers. But careful observers would detect other hints of insufficient forces: our victualing from sutlers was sufficient for only one-third of our men. To make that possible, we had to stock the *insula* weeks beforehand with enough food and drink to supply the other two-thirds of our men for three months. So the Wrecking Crew drastically underestimated our true strength."

"Also, the second story of the courtyard of the Palazzo Giacomo Mattei was the only site in the entire *insula* where it would be reasonable to house prisoners, and yet have them visible to the outside. Had Lefferts not been able to see his targets ahead of time, he would either have had to cancel or mount a general assault."

"Which we would have crushed," Borja asserted with chin raised.

"Yes, but with much greater cost to us, Your Eminence. It was essential to make Lefferts confident that he would be able to succeed with finesse, rather than brute strength. I do not think a brute strength approach would have worked in any event, but we could be sure of this: if the Wrecking Crew had resolved themselves to the idea that they could only succeed through direct, massive destruction, they would have been far more dangerous to us. Look what they did to the Tower of London. So I gave them a scenario in which it seemed reasonable—quite reasonable, in fact—to believe that they could achieve their objective by finesse. This is particularly attractive to the up-timers, who show marked concern with the amount of peripheral damage—and therefore, civilian casualties—they might inflict."

"They are contemptibly stupid," put in Borja.

*They are excessively moral—a distinction you will certainly not perceive, Borja.* "Whatever the reason, preventing unnecessary casualties is a routine component of their *modus operandi*, Your Eminence. And we counted upon it here. Sure enough, perhaps a week before Lefferts' attack, we began to notice careful movement within and around the belvedere. We set up long-barreled wheel-lock rifles in the shuttered rooms of the courtyard's loggia, each weapon mounted in weighted braces and held fast by vises. This ensured that their aim points remained constant unless we changed them."

"You used them almost as if they were artillery pieces."

"Your Eminence understands perfectly. From prior tests, we knew exactly the elevation and charge required to hit the belvedere, and had some reasonable wind indicators that the enemy would not notice. Unfortunately, one of our snipers was also killed."

"Truly?"

Dolor shrugged. "Every gun flashes when fired—and if you are looking straight down the barrel when it flashes, it is only logical that its operator's head is leaned over that barrel. So, if one aims a bit above the muzzle flash—" Dolor saw a shudder move through the cardinal. "As I said, the up-time tools are not to be underestimated. Nor are their operators; they are superbly trained and very disciplined."

"It sounds as though you admire them, Señor Dolor. I hope I do not need to remind you that—"

*What could be more tiresome than the pious indignation of a hypocritical cleric?* "I am not a man much given to admiration of anyone or anything, Your Eminence. But I recognize capability when I see it. And I acknowledge it freely. That same clarity of perception, of understanding all the strengths and weaknesses of my enemy, was what delivered them into your hands last night, Cardinal Borja."

Borja fell silent, eyes bright but not friendly. Dolor wondered: had he let some of his carefully controlled impatience edge into his tone? Or had the insufferable red hat simply bristled at being interrupted, even if only to reassure him?

"It seems your dispassionate methods are effective," was Borja's only response. "And yet it was still not enough to kill Lefferts. Are you sure it was he in the belvedere?"

Dolor shrugged. "It is hard to be sure of anything one does not personally witness, Your Eminence. But all conjecture points towards it. From the neighboring Jews we have already subjected to questioning, they had agreed to rent the roof of this tower to a man answering Lefferts' description, although they were originally approached by *lefferti*—"

"Verminous traitors," supplied Borja.

Dolor did not understand how Romans working against the occupiers of their own city could reasonably be branded as "traitors," but he pressed on. "However, even without those confessions, the belvedere was a logical location for Lefferts. From there he was able to send the signals that started the attack, initiated supporting fire from other persons with up-time rifles, and indicated it was time to withdraw."

Borja waited a moment before his next comment, which sounded more like an accusation. "So, Lefferts escaped, although he is probably wounded. Indeed, I find it hard to understand why any of them escaped at all, Señor Dolor. Why did your wonderful plans not succeed in this particular?"

Dolor shrugged. "Because the attackers were smart enough not to depend upon any local resources when they infiltrated back into Rome. According to our informers, the Wrecking Crew did not inform Duke Taddeo Barberini's court at Palestrina of their return, much less request assistance from that quarter. Nor did they depend upon *lefferti* to get them into Rome, for even if the *lefferti* are loyal, they would have had to make arrangements with other Romans, some of whom would surely have been on our payroll. Instead, Lefferts entered Rome in such a way that he did not need to inform anyone else ahead of time, and his group immediately went into hiding with the *lefferti*. This meant we had no information as to their whereabouts beforehand, nor any way to determine how they planned to exit the city after the attack. I surmised it would be by boat, but that did not help us very much. Without more precise information, we would have had to have set far more pickets along the Tiber—which would have shown the Wrecking Crew that we were expecting them.

"They also had a force armed with up-time weapons covering their withdrawal over the Ponte Fabricio, as well as diversionary explosions in Trastevere. Taken together, this significantly delayed and confused our pursuing forces. As I said, Your Eminence, even in defeat, the up-timers and their handpicked allies are not to be underestimated: they are far more accustomed to this style of warfare."

"Warfare? This is not warfare; it is simply sophisticated raiding. They are highly evolved bandits, no more."

"So it might appear to us, who associate war with serried ranks and massed musketry. But, as chaotic as their 'small unit tactics' might seem, they are informed by an even more complicated military science than that which underlies our tercios. There is extraordinary order and planning behind the seemingly frenetic activity of their operations."

Borja emitted an unconvinced *harrumpf.* "Skilled or no, I hear you have some trophies to show me."

Dolor nodded and crooked a finger at the tall doors, which

were slightly ajar. The doors opened fully in response to Dolor's gesture, and Dakis led two of his largest men into the room. The pair of them were burdened with heavy canvas sacks.

Borja's eyes were bright again. "Show me," he commanded.

At a nod from Dolor, they lifted the heads out of the bags one at a time. Ferrigno, scribbling down the record of this meeting, made a faint retching noise.

Dolor pointed. "This is the one named Gerd; we do not have a last name for him. He was apparently the member of the Wrecking Crew who emplaced the explosive charge to breach the roof, as well as set a diversionary fire. This next one is the female operative named Juliet Sutherland."

"She is most disfigured."

"She was ridden under by our cavalry."

"She deserved no less. And the very young one?"

"He is a *lefferto*. One of the many we killed. But his death is particularly significant."

"And why is that?"

"Because, if the *lefferti* we captured are correct, this *lefferto*'s name is Fabrizio Marcoli."

Borja waited. "So?"

*Quite a mind for details, red hat.* "Marcoli is Giovanna Stone's maiden name; this is her brother."

Borja's eyes positively sparkled; his smile was wide, ravenous. "This is the most delicious sign of divine justice, yet. Go on; show me the last one."

Dolor complied. "This last head is evidently that of an Irish mercenary, working for the up-timers." Dolor watched Borja closely for his reaction.

There wasn't much to see. "Irish? Working for the up-timers? Although I suppose anything is possible with such uncivilized sell-swords, it seems odd."

*It is indeed odd, you buffoon,* thought Dolor, glad for Borja's lack of perspicacity. *And because you show no greater interest in his head, I will be able to leave the greater mystery attached to this fellow unremarked—for now.* Which was not the course that Dakis had wanted to take in the matter of the Irish corpses: not at all.

When they first walked among the bodies marking the site of the see-saw battle for control of the Palazzo Giacomo's courtyard, Dakis spied the different armor, swords, and unusual pistols found upon three of the enemy dead. Their cuirasses and sabers bore signs of Spanish manufacture, but not in the local style; it was more akin to the fashion employed by the armorers who equipped the tercios in the Low Countries. And although the revolvers were not up-time devices, they were clearly up-time inspired. Were these three fellows—who looked anything but Spanish—mercenaries, or was the relationship something else, Dolor wondered. However, it was when they finally extricated the third fellow, the one who had been trapped beneath the horse, that Pedro Dolor's perceptions altered—and he saw, with strange certainty, how this corpse would change his life.

This corpse was the key he had been waiting for, the tool of vengeance that fate always provides to those who are only patient enough. This man's armor was chased with designs, his clothes of unusually good quality, and his sword set with several jewels. He wore a fine tartan sash with a coat of arms, prominently featuring a red hand, raised as if to command the beholder to halt. Dolor frowned; where had he seen this symbol? He tried every memory trick he knew to tease the connection up out of the gray void of uncertainty, but the answer would not come to him as he stood over the bullet-riddled corpse.

"What have we here?" Dakis wondered as he came to stand alongside his commander.

"A great prize, Dakis. Check his right hand."

"For what?"

"A signet ring."

Dakis did, looked up surprised. "There is one. Shall I—?"

"No. Leave it just as is. We will need to preserve this body—or at least the head and hands—as best we may."

Dakis stood. "Why? Does Borja have some particular interest in this—?"

"Borja is not to learn anything about this body, other than that we found it with the other two who were similarly equipped. But he is to be told nothing of how this body's equipment and accoutrements differed from the others'."

Dakis blinked. "Is that wise, Pedro?"

"It is essential, Dakis. Now, make quiet inquiries among the wounded *lefferti*; promise them clemency if they speak true and quickly as to the origin of these men. I need to know if they are Scottish or Irish."

"Does it really matter, Pedro?"

"It most certainly does, Dakis; it most certainly does."

Dolor forced himself to forget those first twilit moments when he realized that the bullet-ridden corpse might provide him with the political leverage he had long sought, might put his greatest ambition within his grasp. Standing before Borja now, he had to continue before the cardinal noticed any distraction in his demeanor. "There were two more of these Irishmen, Your Eminence. Do you wish to inspect either of the other bodies? Also, there are many *lefferti* and no small number of common townsfolk who were—"

"No, I have seen enough." The cardinal reclined like a cat after a belly-filling meal. "So, your success buys you full discretionary powers, Señor Dolor: what next?"

"Now, we move the prisoners again."

Borja sat up; he clearly had not expected this response. "We move them again? After Lefferts' rescue has been successfully repulsed? Surely we can now resort to normal methods of imprisonment."

"Surely not—not here in Rome, at any rate. As this attack shows, Rome is too comfortably within the operating envelope of the USE and Grantville. And obviously, both the Jews and *lefferti* helped them considerably."

"And so, they will be chastised. Strenuously."

"If you must, you must," commented Dolor with a shrug, "but it would be better to merely threaten the Jews with chastisement, while offering them a better option."

"Which is?"

"Collaboration. To work for us as double agents if they are approached by the up-timers again. If you were to take a few select hostages from the major families of the Ghetto—well-treated, of course—that should serve to ensure the loyalty of the rest."

Borja stroked his vulpine chin. "So do you really think the up-timers might be so foolish as to strike again?"

"If the prisoners remain in Rome long enough, then yes. Which means that next time, they will need to strike at you, too."

Borja's response was surprisingly high-pitched for a full grown man. "They would strike at *me*?"

"Of course, Your Eminence. The up-timers are well aware that they no longer possess the advantage of surprise, and have seen that we are on guard for their tricks. So, failing at finesse, they will resort to brute force."

"We have many tercios to dissuade them from such action, Señor Dolor."

"Those tercios are less of a disincentive to up-timers than to our other adversaries, Your Eminence, owing to their style of warfare. The up-timers rely on speed and small, intensely destructive units, not set-piece field engagements. However, to mount a major rescue attempt now would require them to not only destroy or paralyze our units, but to do the same to our command centers—possibly by using immensely powerful, timed bombs. With you and the generals who assist you dead, our units might remain in their barracks, waiting for orders that never come."

And now, it was time to play one of his trump cards in today's game of *scare the cardinal*. "The agents of the USE might even be able to stir up a popular revolt to preoccupy our military assets in advance of such a strike, and so obscure their own actions. Such a plan might be welcomed by many communes of the Lazio. After all, we are not welcome here, and Duke Barberini has many friends in the hills that ring this city."

Borja seemed alarmed. "Do you think such a disastrous course of events to be likely?"

Dolor smiled within: it was important not to overplay one's hand. "No, I do not think it likely. However, I am less sure of our enemy's next move, now. It was relatively easy to predict that they would employ their famed Harry Lefferts in a rescue attempt: the up-timers were as dazzled by his myth as the gullible Roman boys who emulated him."

"So, you believe we have seen the last of Lefferts?"

"As a commander? For now, probably. But Harry Lefferts is still a dangerous weapon in service of the USE, whose leaders will now realize that in this scenario, it was not Lefferts who failed; it was his methods. Which means they will appoint a very different commander for their next rescue attempt."

"Ah. You mean someone more like you."

Dolor was not often surprised. But he had not yet thought through the probable nature of his next adversary, and he certainly had not expected such an insight to come from a rash pope-intendant. However, Borja's spontaneous assertion had a certain elegant logic to it. "I suspect so, yes. At any rate, I do not expect their next captain to walk so blindly into a trap, no matter how well I lay it."

"So our best option is—what?"

"To move Stone and his wife to a more distant location, as quickly as possible." Seeing Borja about to sputter objections, Dolor extrapolated: "At this moment, we still hold the initiative. The up-timers are still fleeing, probably back to Venice, licking their wounds as they go. So this is the perfect time for us to move their objective. By the time they have recovered enough to begin reassessing the situation, the prisoners will be gone without a trace. We, of course, will maintain the charade that they are still being held in the *insula* Mattei. But I do not expect that ruse to buy us much extra time."

Borja was still not placated. "And so now we must ship these two wretches off somewhere?" His tone became archly facetious. "Where would you propose to send them? To Madrid? Perhaps to be held in a chamber adjoining Philip's own?"

Dolor shook his head. "No. The chamber next to the king would not be secure enough." Seeing Borja's dumbfounded stare, he shrugged. "A king has courtiers. Where there are courtiers, there are debtors. And where there are debtors, there are men who can be bought, extorted, or both. No, Your Eminence. I have someplace much better in mind. A place that will hard for the USE to find, impossible to assault, and so far away from here that you need not worry about becoming a target of their next attack."

That last trump card won Dolor the prize he had hoped to gain. Borja waved airily. "Very well. It seems there are sound reasons for moving them. But before we drop the subject of the prisoners, show me the head of the Roman again."

Dolor nodded to the man holding the appropriate bag. The face of Giovanna Stone's brother Fabrizio rose back up out of the blood-spattered canvas that housed it.

As Borja smiled, the color drained from Ferrigno's face. Almost as white as the paper upon which he was scribbling, Borja's small secretary jumped up and withdrew several steps. Dolor raised an eyebrow but said nothing.

Borja was staring at Fabrizio Marcoli's head and sad, staring eyes. "Given young Stone's meddling during the attack, I wonder if the head of his wife's brother is a providential asset."

Dolor frowned. "I am sorry, Your Eminence, but I do not understand what you mean."

"Surely you must, Señor Dolor, being a man who understands

the need for absolute discipline and obedience. Punishing Stone himself might bring edification through pain, but not so much through terror. And for a man such as Stone, the greatest terror will not be in anticipating further injury to himself, but to those he loves." Borja's smile became positively feral. "For instance, if we were to show this head to his wife, or better yet, present it to her in just one more covered dish brought in with breakfast—"

Dolor shook his head. "Think of the shock, Your Eminence; women have miscarried with far less provocation. Far less." Borja was frowning, considering—but still not fully dissuaded. "And if the unborn child were lost we would have less political leverage against the USE. Also, the prisoners might become suicidally hostile instead of grudgingly cooperative. Right now, they are still concerned with protecting their unborn child. If they lose that child—particularly due to any action of ours—they might welcome death."

Borja sighed and looked disappointed. "Yes, yes, I suppose what you say is wise. We shall not harrow the little she-devil as she deserves. But then you must take other steps to ensure that Stone has learned his lesson. Thoroughly." The cardinal's eyes were bright, eager.

Dolor nodded, accepting this lesser of two inadvisable evils. "It shall be as you say, Your Eminence." He looked over at Ferrigno, who was literally trembling against the wall. Dolor gestured at him with a jerk of his head. "Your Eminence, is he a scribe or not?"

Borja followed the gesture, frowned, and snapped at Ferrigno as he might have spoken to a dog. "What are you doing over there, Ferrigno? Sit here, at my desk, and see to your duties." He turned back to Dolor as the spare scribe shuffled toward the other chair facing Borja's. "We are almost done, though, are we not?"

"Almost. I am grateful for the time Your Eminence has lavished on my review of what we have discovered about both the external and internal enemies who made possible the USE's attack."

Borja started to nod, stopped. "Internal enemies? You mean, the *lefferti* and the Jews?"

"No, Your Eminence. Although they are native to Rome, they are also our obvious enemies, and so, are external threats. I am speaking of traitors within our very ranks."

Alongside Dolor, Ferrigno was scribbling furiously. Borja's jaw swung open momentarily before he barked: "Traitors? What do you mean?"

"I mean," said Dolor, reaching out a hand and placing it gently but firmly upon the back of Ferrigno's wrist, "that my men observed a peculiar phenomenon shortly after every one of my meetings with you. They found that Signor Ferrigno was wont to pile scrap papers near the kitchen furnace."

"For disposal. Secure disposal," Ferrigno gulped out.

"Not secure enough, evidently. It seems that on each of these days, one of the boys who works in the stables invariably came into the kitchen for a snack. And being a tidy sort, he always wrapped the food in some handy paper. Oddly enough, the paper that was always handiest was that which had been discarded by Signor Ferrigno." Dolor felt the narrow wrist beneath his hand grow very cold.

Borja's face had grown bright red; his eyes were wide. "And there is more?"

Dolor nodded. "Oddly enough, the stable boy always had work to deliver to a saddler in the Ghetto, an immense fellow named Isaac, who, it is rumored, also had the USE embassy as a client before all the recent unpleasantness. But that is ultimately not as interesting as another piece of information: Isaac has another client who invariably showed up at his shop less than twenty-four hours after the stable boy had dropped off the leather-work from this villa. Isaac's other client is a fellow named Piero—and has been identified by several of the surviving *lefferti* as one of their senior and most trusted members."

Borja could not speak; he seemed ready to burst. Ferrigno appeared to have aged ten years within the past two minutes; it seemed impossible to imagine how such a small, spare man could have become more withered and bowed, but he had.

Dolor finished. "This is why the agents of the Wrecking Crew were able to immediately discern that we had Stone and his wife at the *insula* Mattei: they had inside information. The *insula* had no outgoing servants, and we did not parade the prisoners in plain view for several weeks. How then did they already know to have us under observation? We noticed their surreptitious observers easily enough, but it took weeks to trace it back to Signor Ferrigno; he made use of routine connections between this villa and the world beyond to pass his intelligence, and he himself seemed a most unlikely candidate."

But Borja's wrath now seemed to focus on Dolor. "And you

did not see fit to inform me at each stage? You lied to me," he hissed. "From the start. You misinformed me about the troop strength at the *insula* Mattei, you—"

"Your Eminence, when I first arrived, did I not ask for your patience and trust? Here you are reaping the benefits of that trust. I spoke lies to your face, yes, but they were not intended for your ears, Your Eminence. They were intended for your scribe's." Ferrigno's skin trembled beneath Dolor's palm.

Borja acknowledged Dolor's explanation with a testy nod, and then stared at little Ferrigno. "Execution is not enough," he asserted after three seconds. "A man may come to grips with the fear of death, but not the fear of agony. Particularly not long, excruciating, varied, hopeless agony that will end in not merely death, but witnessing the dismemberment of one's own body, the uncoiling and dissection of one's own guts."

Ferrigno gulped back vomit; Dolor's nose told him that the scribe had soiled himself.

Borja noticed as well and sniffed in disgust. "Señor Dolor, you have much experience in this area: what would you recommend?"

Dolor shrugged; he knew he could not press too hard if he wanted to change Borja's mind. "I do not recommend torture as punishment. Even when the objective is to gather information, torture is only advisable when there is reason to suspect it will be effective."

Borja looked disappointed. "I would not have thought you squeamish, Señor Dolor."

"I am not squeamish, Your Eminence; among my many faults, this one certainly cannot be reasonably attributed to me. But if one acquires a reputation for torture, it often instills desperate courage in his remaining adversaries. An enemy who knows that capture means mortal torture often chooses certain death of the battlefield. That way, we lose more men. I prefer my reputation to be one of efficiency and undefeatability; I want my adversaries to despair of besting me, but not to fear capture. That way, they may despair of hope and yet safely surrender, rather than fear torture and sell themselves dearly."

Borja looked at Dolor strangely. "There is some wisdom in what you say," the cardinal conceded finally, "but it is the wisdom of the streets, of your particular 'calling.' The wisdom of Mother Church tells us that if we spare the rod upon the back of one treacherous, homicidal child, we shall surely spoil many of the other untainted innocents. Mother Church uses the carrot when practicable—but in this case, we have only the stick."

Dolor nodded. "What kind of stick do you instruct us to use in this case, Your Eminence?"

Ferrigno moaned slightly.

Borja considered. "The greatest terror would come from not knowing what kind of agony to expect, and in what sequence." He stared at Ferrigno, attempted to keep a flickering grin from troubling the left corner of his mouth. "Why select just one stick, Señor Dolor? Be creative. Indulge yourself."

# Chapter 31

Estuban Miro peered into the dark. By the light of the half moon, he could make out the fishing ketch that the embassy Marines had boarded only minutes earlier. According to the morse code message sent by their Aldis-rigged bull's-eye lantern, the boat's single enemy operative had surrendered without a struggle.

Miro sighed; it was unfortunate that they had been compelled to remove the observer that Borja's local spymaster had sent to watch the island of San Francesco del Deserto. In intelligence operations, the only thing better than knowing oneself to be unobserved (a rare, and usually unprovable, circumstance) was to know where the enemy observers were. Such had been the case with this particular fisherman. Ever since Harry Lefferts' rescue team had departed for Rome several weeks ago, this wiry fellow had been casting his nets in the vicinity of the island's Franciscan monastery: sometimes to the east, sometimes to the west; sometimes closer, sometimes farther. But always close enough to keep an eye on any comings and goings. Which, since the rescue team's last meeting there, had been entirely routine.

Miro's response to this observer had been merely to observe in return. Using a well-concealed spyglass, the friars gladly complied with his request that they watch the ketch's positions and maneuverings and keep meticulous record of them. Meanwhile, a few distant friends of the Cavrianis started taking intermittent

334

strolls past the pier where the fisherman tied up and off-loaded his day-end catch; they discovered that he was pulling in scarcely enough to feed his own family, these days. However, he did not seem disposed to try fishing in a new spot, nor did he seem particularly worried about his presumably diminished income. Rather, in just the last two weeks, he had paid for a new stepsail and other useful bits of small-craft chandlery. Taken together, these indicators were almost all the proof Miro needed to confirm that the fisherman was indeed an enemy pawn. However, just to be sure, and in an attempt to detect if the fisherman himself was being watched by Borja's Venetian spymaster, Miro had his own growing network of agents keep track of the seemingly trivial exchanges and activities of the fellow's day. They observed where he got his breakfast loaf, who came to check his day-end catch, which boats (if any) he approached during the course of his profitless net castings. Ten days of constant, but distant, watching had produced no leads; if the fisherman was exchanging information with his handler, there was no obvious sign of it. Which presented Miro with two possibilities: either communication did not occur unless the fisherman had something to report, or that the communication was conducted more subtly than could be detected by the maximally discreet methods of observation employed by his agents.

Miro would now have the answer to that mystery within a few hours. From the look of him, the wiry Venetian was not going to be resolute enough to resist the sustained interrogation that he would experience in a safe-house near the embassy. Not that he would be hurt—he wouldn't; Miro's personal tastes and Tom's explicit instructions eliminated the option of torture. But the fisherman didn't know that and did not look to be particularly courageous. *So few of us are, when we are well-caught and alone,* Miro mused, remembering close calls with the Ottomans, back during his days as a merchant sailing the Mediterranean.

"Don Estuban," said the master of the small, yawl-rigged *scialuppa* that had been provided by the Cavrianis for the night's work, "shall we approach the mooring, now?"

Miro held up a hand and waited. After a few moments, he saw more dit-dah flashing in the darkness to the west: K-E-N-N-E-L. So: the chase was indeed over. That codeword signified that the chase boats and Marines were now ready to return to their

berths and billets, respectively. It was also a shorthand indicator of the concluding situation report: "known enemy observers
apprehended; no others detected." Personally, Miro had been hoping for the code sign "RABBIT." That would have indicated that
the fisherman—FOX—had been caught, and additional, suspected
observers were being pursued, possibly resulting in a clean sweep
of the opposition's monitoring assets.

But that tidy outcome had not occurred. On the one hand,
Borja's spymaster in Venice might not have enough resources to
put more than one man on the job of watching the island. Even
if he had two men, he would then have to choose between keeping the island under almost constant observation, or having the
second man watch what happened to the first. So even if Miro's
adversary had a second man, where was he? At home, sleeping
before his next, solo shift—or was he out here right now, somewhere in the dark, lying low in a rowboat, watching as the first
watcher was scooped up by Miro's agents?

Estuban sighed. *Such are the uncertainties of this business.*
Annoying, but they kept the game interesting. "Paulo," he said
over his shoulder to the master of the small boat.

"Yes, Don Estuban?"

"Take us in to the monastery. Briskly."

In retrospect, Miro wished he had told Paulo to tarry a bit,
despite the fact that it gave any possible, unseen observers just
that much more opportunity to spot their lightless, black-sailed
boat. As it was, they arrived before the skiff that was inbound
from the *galliot* that had retrieved what they now knew to be
Harry's unsuccessful rescue party.

But that was all anyone knew: they were returning without
Frank and Giovanna. That much had been presumed when the
team started missing their radio checks. There was brief fear that
they had all been destroyed or captured, but about a week ago,
one of Nasi's Roman agents—formerly a resident of the Ghetto and
now fleeing for his life—had delivered the news of the repulsed
attack upon the Palazzi Mattei. Though the man had few details,
it was quite clear that most of the rescue party had escaped.

Consequently, Miro was still hoping for the best when there
was a knock on the door of the same conference room in which
they had all met weeks before. Miro signaled for the two Marine

guards to open the door and leave, and felt the old priest, Father Anthony Hickey, rise slowly beside him.

Miro instantly realized the operation had been not merely a failure, but a disaster, because the first face in the doorway—Harry's—was utterly devoid of emotion or expression. It would have been a sobering expression to behold on any face, but on Harry's habitually animated features, it was as though he was wearing a death mask. He gave Miro a shallow nod and seated himself at the far end of the table.

A step behind Harry was Owen Roe O'Neill, who bore a light bundle in his arms. His eyes met Hickey's, and what looked like days of preparation for this difficult moment became rigid resolve: lips stiff, the Irish colonel held out the bundle to the old cleric.

Hickey did not need words to understand the message. He hobbled forward, palsied hands coming up to touch the tightly folded but bullet-rent cloak that Owen held before him. The Franciscan's already-well-lined face collapsed, blinded by the great round tears that ran down his cheeks. He unsteadily patted John O'Neill's patched tartan, family broach, and absent face with tentative hands that he finally raised to cover his red-rimmed eyes. He never made a sound.

From what Miro had heard, Hickey may have been the first person who came to accept that young John O'Neill was never going to grow up to be a statesman, or even a great captain. But, under other circumstances, the priest had hinted, he might have been a good enough man. Yes, he had been a wild wayward boy who did not like books or following rules, but even in his early twenties, John O'Neill had loved listening to stories, and if he had a big temper it was in part a measure of the size of his heart. And Hickey knew these things because it was he who had read the now deceased earl of Tyrone the stories, and had cherished that big heart, possibly above all others.

The monastery's prior, standing nearby, took his brother by the elbow and gently guided him from the room. Owen Roe wandered toward a seat as Sherrilyn and Thomas North entered and did the same.

Miro looked round at the stiff, carefully controlled faces. "So, John O'Neill—?"

The pause was pregnant; Owen opened his mouth uncertainly—but Harry interrupted in a voice both hoarse and raw. "John

didn't make it. A lot of us didn't." He held out a sheaf of papers.
"Here's my after-action report. But I can bottom line it for you: I
fucked up. And no, I'm not selling you any 'my watch, my fault'
bullshit, Miro. Borja's guy in Rome suckered me, and once we
were in his trap, he cut us to pieces. The sorry-ass details—"
Harry waved at the papers "—are all there. End of report."

He glowered at Miro and leaned far back in his chair, arms
folded, shoulders slouched.

Miro, for the first time in many years, had no idea of what
to do or say next. He looked at Thomas North. "How many—?"

North looked cautiously down the table at hollow-eyed Harry's
hundred-yard stare and made an almost imperceptible negational
gesture. "Our casualties are in the report, I believe. But there's
one thing that Harry refused to include."

"And what is that?"

"That Captain Lefferts made no errors in planning or execution. He designed and executed the operation in a most capable
manner."

Miro saw the color rush into and then out of Harry's face;
for a moment he wondered if the up-timer was going to roar or
vomit—but he did neither. Miro let his eyes slide over toward
Owen Roe O'Neill. "Colonel, do you agree with Colonel North's
assessment?"

The veteran Irish commander—who had spent more years before
the cannon than any of the rest of them had been alive—nodded
firmly, but it was slightly less emphatic affirmation than North's
had been.

Miro, hating what he had to do in order to bring the horrible
necessity of this inquiry to a swift and final end, forced himself
to ask, "Colonel O'Neill, you seem to have some reservations in
regard to Captain Lefferts' plan or actions?"

"No, Don Estuban," the Irishman's voice was firm, even stri-
dent, "not at all."

"Then—?"

O'Neill shrugged. "Harry—we—had no way of knowing that
we were walking into a trap. Harry took every precaution, and
more besides. But Borja's man was good—damned good—and we
were too spread out for a fast, orderly escape."

Miro frowned. "What do you mean?"

O'Neill glanced an apology at Harry who might or might

not have heard a word that had been spoken since delivering his damning self-report. "Don Estuban, I've taken towns and defended them for almost three decades now—more, if you count the years I served as a runner and an orderly. And here's a nasty fact of fighting in cities, in castles, or in other tight quarters: you get separated too easily. You can't blow a trumpet and sound a general retreat—particularly when you're skulking around in handfuls here, and there. When disaster strikes—and sometimes it does, no matter what you do—it is often impossible to let all of your men know in time. And then—" Owen Roe's eyes lost focus and Miro had the distinct impression that he was seeing smoking cityscapes from all around the Low Countries "—then your boys start disappearing. Sometimes you see what happens to them, but more often you don't. Bad sight-lines, the tumult of the guns and voices, drifting smoke, blind corners: it's utter chaos. You don't know who you've lost until you regroup at the edge of the town, where you may find that every other man who charged in under your colors is gone, never to be found."

Miro felt a chill run up his spine. "And this—this separation and confusion—was this the ill fortune that exacted such a heavy toll in Rome?"

Owen Roe looked up, eyes sharp. "Oh, there was no ill fortune about it, Don Estuban. It was all part of our enemy's plan. We couldn't approach him unless we came at him in small, separate groups; he made sure of that, and he used it against us."

Miro heard a flat, heavy undertone of remorse. "And you foresaw this, Colonel O'Neill?"

For the first time since meeting him, Miro noticed Owen Roe's gaze waver a bit. "No—no, it wasn't anything I foresaw. I'm not sure anyone could have. It's just—just a matter of learned instinct, y'might say. On battlefields, every plan is always trying to go wrong on you from the outset. It's what Colonel North tells me the up-timers call 'Murphy's Law.' Assaulting a tricky, twisty place like the *insula* Mattei just made us especially susceptible to failures or surprises—and the canny barstard we were facing built a gauntlet loaded with both."

Miro nodded, having heard his indirect answer in Owen Roe's equivocating response: Harry had probably been a little overly optimistic about the operation, and when things went wrong, he discovered that it was not due to chance, but enemy intent.

Which made the consequences much worse than they would have been if the culprit *had* been chance. On the plus side, Harry had escaped with the great majority of the rescue party intact: no small feat, that. But on the negative side, the civilian losses were heavy—and were probably hanging about Lefferts' neck and spirits like a millstone. Well, nothing to be done about that here. The only useful response was to move forward.

Miro straightened and gazed at all of them in turn. "So. This means that we have a new mission to consider, and I need all your energies and attention focused on putting together the best plan possible."

Sherrilyn frowned. "A *new* mission?"

Miro shrugged. "Actually, no; it is the same mission—to rescue Frank and Giovanna—but it will be more difficult, now."

Sherrilyn's eyes were wide. "More difficult? Really? You think?"

Miro heard her tone growing arch, thought of interrupting the coming tirade, but realized that he shouldn't. She needed to let it out. They'd all been fleeing alongside their troops for more than a week, unable to give voice to their own anger and frustration.

Sherrilyn grabbed the opportunity with uncommon ferocity. "Let me tell you just how much more difficult a rescue is going to be this time, Don Estuban Miro. We lost six combat effectives—and friends—in that fight, and most of the survivors are wounded. George is whipsawing between grief and a fugue state. The cadre of our Roman sympathizers has been gutted: Piero is on the run, and Giovanna's brother Fabrizio was killed. Benito, the kid she and Frank all but adopted, was almost killed as well, although luckily we were able to get him out alive." She took a deep, shaky breath. "Best estimates tell us that another thirty *lefferti* were either killed or immobilized, and close to forty of the rioters were shot or trampled to death. So, yes, Don Estuban, I suspect we're going to find it a little harder to mount another rescue attempt in Rome from now on."

Sherrilyn finished leaning across the table, face white, eyes wide. It was Harry who reached out and touched her arm lightly for a moment. Sherrilyn leaned back, sighing. "I'm sorry, Estuban. But—"

He waved a hand that dismissed any concern. "I understand. And I sympathize. And I have another sad addition to your list." All three looked at him. "One of Don Francisco Nasi's agents—who was apparently instrumental in passing inside information along to the *lefferti*—fled Rome. That is how we knew you were coming back at all. But he had other news."

Harry's eyes were grim. "The Ghetto?"

Miro nodded. "Over a hundred killed outright or tortured to death. However, for now, we must look beyond the human costs. As Sherrilyn rightly pointed out, the losses sustained during this first rescue attempt—both in terms of personnel and infrastructure—compel us to completely reconceive our operations. And our first problems are not tactical, but logistical."

Thomas sighed. "They always are."

"So it seems. First, the most pressing logistical need we had in Italy—getting enough gasoline to Venice so that we can fly Pope Urban to safety—is no longer at the top of our list. Now, instead, we have to ship in more security for him."

Owen seemed surprised, maybe a bit indignant. "And why is the pope not flying to safety immediately?"

"There are two equally good answers to that question. First, the repairs to the Monster will not be completed for another three weeks, so getting the gasoline here sooner than that does us no good. Consequently, it becomes more important to ship in further reinforcements for the papal protection detail; the more time Borja's agents have, the more likely they are to locate Urban and attack."

Sherrilyn frowned. "Jeez, Estuban, the roster I've seen for Urban's security detail makes me think that he has more than enough guards already. There's almost twenty in the Marine detachment assigned to the embassy, and two of the Wild Geese. And then there's Ruy, who's worth about ten more, all by himself."

Miro nodded. "Yes, that is sufficient to maintain immediate, bodily security. But if those forces are to have any advance warning that Borja's agents are surveying their facilities preparatory to attack, they will need pickets. The current security complement is not large enough to keep watch over a reasonable perimeter *and* provide terminal defense. And now it seems we may need to provide that defense for quite some time to come."

They all heard his leading tone. "C'mon," Sherrilyn said finally, "don't be coy, Estuban. Just spit it out: what's the new fly in the ointment?"

Miro sighed. "The pope is not willing to leave Italy. At least, not yet."

"*What?*" Sherrilyn blurted. "Why the hell not?"

It was Owen who answered. "Miss Maddox, I am only guessing, but I suspect that Pope Urban is weighing the consequences of seeking asylum with the USE."

"Oh, so we're good enough to save his life when he's on the run, without a friend to his name, but when it actually comes to voluntarily associating with us—"

"Miss Maddox, please. I suspect that Urban the man and Urban the pope are of very different minds on this matter. Urban the man is not insensible to gratitude; he has risked scandal in the Church by showing up-timers as much favor and trust as he has. When you come right down to it, your involvement in Galileo's trial is probably what set Borja, at the head of the Spanish cardinals, on his current course of action."

"Which brings up the matter of Urban the pope. Can a pope seek sanctuary in a Protestant land?"

Harry frowned, then murmured, "The USE strictly—aggressively—enforces freedom of religion."

Owen nodded. "True enough, and an amazement to us all. But the simple fact is that the USE still has Gustav Adolf at its head. He is not merely a Protestant, but the symbol of its successful wars against the Church. He's left plenty of its sons strewn lifeless across the face of Europe—and their families aren't likely to forget who killed them." Owen held up a hand to still Thomas' incipient retort. "I'm not arguing the right or wrong of the war or its combatants, Thomas; I'm simply stating facts as they'll be seen by most Catholics, who have never met up-timers, visited your town, or served alongside you. We—they—are creatures of this world, and bear the stamp of this century's religious warfare and persecutions. So Pope Urban must choose his next steps very carefully."

Sherrilyn crossed her arms and frowned. "Okay," she said. "I get that. But you've gotta admit that, pope or no pope, this is one royal pain in the ass."

Owen cocked an eyebrow. "If you would change your terminology to 'a divine pain in the ass,' I would happily agree with you."

The smile between them was quick but genuine: no hard feelings, and another issue set to rest—for now.

But Owen wasn't done. "Don Estuban, I trust you will send word of my unit's—losses—to Fernando's court in the Low Countries?"

Miro nodded. "I shall. Although I am reluctant to do so; I worry that you might be ordered to commit the rest of your unit to the pope's security detachment. Although I have no reason to hope or ask it, I would much rather you remain part of our rescue operations."

"I have thought the same thing, Don Estuban. I see only one sure way to avoid receiving new orders to guard the pope: to be gone before they get here."

Miro managed not to smile. *Here's a man after my own heart.* "I quite concur, Colonel. And I am very grateful that you are still willing to be a part of our rescue operations. There is, of course, nothing to obligate you to do so."

Before Owen could respond, Sherrilyn had slapped her hand down on the table. "In fact, there's every reason *not* to try another rescue—with simple sanity heading the list of those reasons. Estuban, are you really serious? Do you really think we can, or should, try to spring Frank and Giovanna again? Hell, they'll be waiting for us this time."

"Sherrilyn, as you so eloquently point out, they were waiting for us *this* time. They were probably far more certain that we would try at least once than they are that we will try again."

"And how does that do us any good? They kicked our asses around the block, Estuban; what makes you think they won't do it again?"

"I can't answer that until we see what the Spanish do next. But we can be sure of this: we need to stay close to Frank and Giovanna, if we're going to be able to act effectively. We no longer have a radio operator in Rome, we no longer have an observation network via the *lefferti* or Nasi's former agents, and we can no longer trust nor should we further impose upon the Jews of the Ghetto. In short, we have to gather our own information, now."

"Which is simply another way of saying that we're all alone, from here on," Sherrilyn mumbled. "Damn, the odds just keep getting better and better, don't they?"

Miro folded his hands and looked her straight in the eyes. "Until we get on site and see things with our own eyes, we really can't assess what the odds of success are. For the second matter, we are talking about Tom Stone's son and daughter-in-law. By electing to come on this mission, you implicitly promised him to get those children back; I explicitly promised him the same. Since you started as a volunteer, it is your business if you go with us on a second rescue mission. But I will. Alone if I must."

"You will not go alone," Owen announced.

Miro looked down the table, surprised. "Colonel, your continued commitment to the rescue mission is very welcome indeed. I suspect it will prove crucial. But this intensity of resolve—why? This is not your fight, after all."

Owen Roe O'Neill ran a surprisingly fine-boned hand through silvering red hair. "I'm not about to give an answer that would allow a *sassenach* to accuse me of typical Irish romanticism." He checked for, and saw, the friendly smile on Thomas's face before he continued. "So let's leave it at this: you've the right of this fight, plain and simple. Besides, that bastard red hat who's dangling these two newlyweds like butterflies over a furnace needs to be shown that there are limits to what even a would-be pope may do. I've suffered through enough scenes of Spanish 'justice'—legal and clerical—in my time. I'll not stand by and watch more of it meted out to innocents. Enough is enough."

Thomas was repressing a grin. "Owen, my partner Liam Donovan is a bog-hopper like you, so I'm quite accustomed to the way you Irish use your supposed romanticism to conceal shrewd underlying practicality. What else is driving you?"

Owen grinned sheepishly. "Caught as red-handed as only an O'Neill can be. Very well, here it is: you're the future." He looked around at their surprised glances. "Come now, I've told true, so you've no right to act as though you're puzzled. You know exactly what I mean: up-time ideas and ways are remaking the world around us. Hugh O'Donnell—the earl of Tyrconnell over Sean Connal—visited your Grantville and saw it plain enough. He brought back new tactical training, the idea for the pepperbox revolver, and proof that Madrid was using the Wild Geese as a pawn in a greater game—a pawn they were ready to sacrifice, former promises of honor and repatriation notwithstanding. Hugh O'Donnell woke us up—those who were willing to listen."

Owen sighed. "I wasn't among that number, not at first. But you know the saying: the late-come convert is the most ardent believer. I've not only seen what you can do, but who you are, what you value. My oath is to Isabella of the Low Countries, but here and now, I'm casting my lot in with you. There: is that plain-spoken enough?"

Miro did not know what to say; he merely nodded.

Thomas was smiling, however. "It's said that the support of honorable men is the greatest adornment of any cause. You have just become the diamond at the pinnacle of our cause's tiara, Colonel O'Neill."

Harry surprised them by speaking in a clear, firm voice. "I'm glad everyone is getting along so well, because we've got a hell of a task in front of us, now. And Estuban is right; we can't let up and we can't fail. Our promise to Tom is one factor. The pope's personal and political attitude toward us is another. Remember, Urban married Frank and Gia. That probably makes them extra-valuable to Borja as prisoners; for him, toying with the two of them is like pissing in the pope's own recently consecrated well. And no doubt Urban knows that and feels an additional responsibility to them. Either way, he's going to judge us—our moral character, that is—partly upon our determination to do the right thing by Frank and Giovanna. If we walk away, he'll have reason to wonder if we're really as good as our word. But if we press on, no matter the difficulties—"

"—then he knows that when we talk the talk, we'll walk the walk," concluded Sherrilyn with a nod. "Okay; suicide mission or not, I'm in."

Miro shook his head. "I do not believe in suicide missions. We have many hurdles before us, yes, but I refuse to see them as insurmountable."

Thomas frowned. "Maybe they are not insurmountable, but some of them are unalterable. Time, for one. Unless I am much mistaken, we cannot wait for further reinforcements or specialty equipment via balloon from Grantville; that would mean a two week delay. Given the young Mrs. Stone's delicate condition, we cannot risk that. We must leave immediately."

Miro nodded somberly. "That is regrettably true."

Sherrilyn frowned. "That is regrettably our epitaph. As I count it, Owen has only six men left who aren't already guarding the pope, and that includes the doctor. Thomas here has his four Hibernians. And the Crew is at half strength: there's me, Harry, Donald, Matija, and Paul. George can't be brought into the field, not yet. So, even though I was only a gym teacher, I'm still pretty sure that it all adds up to seventeen people. So tell me: how is taking seventeen persons to rescue Frank and Giovanna from a well-defended Spanish prison not suicide?"

Miro smiled. "The balloon arriving tomorrow will be bringing some answers to that question, Sherrilyn."

"They'd better be great answers."

"The first is that you can increase the size of our contingent by six: that's how many additional Hibernians will be arriving."

"Bloody good of you to let me know how you've decided to use more of my troops," Thomas commented with one raised eyebrow.

"You'll need to work that out with your partner, Liam Donovan—who negotiated a very good rate with Ed Piazza, I'm told. These six men were originally slated for the papal protection detail, but I think we have to divert them to this operation, now."

Harry nodded. "Yeah. We need the manpower. Particularly men who are familiar and equipped with lever action rifles and revolvers. We'll need that volume of fire to offset our small numbers."

"Damned straight," agreed Sherrilyn. "And what's the other good news?"

"Well, although there weren't any other combat personnel ready to travel, we did know that we would need the very best equipment for our modest forces—"

"You had them stop in Chur and pick up the rest of the Crew's gear?" Sherrilyn leaned forward eagerly.

"That, and more. While we were sharing the long road from the Val Bregaglia to Padua last month, Colonel North was good enough to review the various categories and models of 'ready equipment' he knows to be in reserve at Grantville—since so much of it is the object of his professional lusts. I was surprised to note that there was one weapon system he coveted that was still readily available to us in considerable numbers, so I decided to request ten copies of it, on the notion that you would all consider it a useful addition to our resources."

Sherrilyn frowned. "What are you waiting for, Estuban: a drum roll? What did you whistle up for us?"

"Ten SKS's. And, according to the people in Grantville, enough magazines and 7.62 x 39 millimeter ammunition to, I quote them, 'fight the Viet Nam war all over again.'"

Sherrilyn actually pumped her fist up and down in time with her very extended, "Yyy-esssss!"

Thomas North smiled and nodded. "Well done, Estuban, very well done."

Owen stared. "A little explanation might be helpful for the down-time bog-hopper," he put in.

North grinned. "Sorry. The SKS is a semiautomatic carbine. It uses the same round as a famous Russian assault rifle, the AK-47, which was the SKS's successor."

"The SKS is a great weapon," emphasized Harry, with more animation than he had evinced so far. "Reliable, handy, accurate out to one hundred and seventy yards, reasonably effective out to four hundred, and it fires a pretty damned lethal round. Best of all, you can fire ten times—as fast as you can squeeze the trigger—before you need to reload with a stripper clip. Or, in the case of the 'M' series, with a thirty-round magazine."

North took up the paean of praise for the SKS. "I won mine in a poker game at the Thuringen Gardens just before I was incarcerated. A most excellent weapon. A man with an SKS is easily worth ten with muskets. Probably more. Now, Estuban, about my Hibernians: did you happen to—?"

Miro smiled. "The six who will arrive tomorrow were trained on the weapon the week before they left. From what I am told, they adapted to it rather quickly."

Thomas smiled around the table. "You know, I am actually beginning to feel that this mission might not be suicide, after all. But now I'm a bit worried about the safety of the pope; by shifting these troops to our rescue mission, it means at least two weeks will pass before his security detail is reinforced."

Miro spread his hands. "It can't be helped. But the odds are in our favor, there. Borja's agents would have to be very lucky to discover Urban's hiding place within that short a period of time. And if the signals from Grantville are right, the new reinforcements should be there in only ten, maybe eleven, days."

Sherrilyn frowned. "Wait a minute; how is that possible? I mean, if every day from now until then was perfect flying weather, you might get a round trip completed in that time, but—" Miro tried to keep the smile off his face, but she saw it. "Wait a minute—we have another balloon?"

"We do now. The second one constructed—and finished only two weeks ago—was just leased by Ed Piazza for 'official emergency use.' Franchetti's nephew has been preparing it for service, familiarizing himself with its particulars." He turned to Thomas. "It is picking up Lieutenant Hastings and a few more of your Hibernians at Chur, but, in order to keep the pope's location a secret, they are debarking at Campofontana."

"Where?" asked Harry, Sherrilyn, and Owen simultaneously.

Miro answered. "A small town, up in the foothills of the Lessenia Mountains."

"That doesn't help me much," commented Sherrilyn.

It was Thomas who provided more information. "I believe Campofontana is just south of the Little Dolomites. It's all Hemingway country, up there."

"Huh?" said Sherrilyn.

"You know: *A Farewell to Arms*. The campaign in the Italian Alps. A bit slow reading for my tastes, but memorable."

Miro nodded. "The terrain there is rather forbidding. Landing at Campofontana should keep the arrival of the reinforcements away from any of Borja's observers, although it will mean a somewhat long walk to Urban's safe house. However, they should get there long before any assassins do. The next cargo will be the gasoline for the Monster."

"Fetched by the balloon that will arrive in Venice tomorrow?" asked Harry.

Miro smiled. "No. That balloon will soon be committed to other operations."

"Such as?"

"Such as ours."

Sherrilyn screwed up her face. "We're taking the balloon with us to Rome? Who's going to fly it?"

"Virgilio Franchetti has agreed to assist in the rescue, and he is an excellent pilot."

"Yeah, but what if something happens to him? Then we're stuck."

"No, you're not."

"Why?"

"Because I can also fly the balloon—more or less. You see, I'm coming with you."

# Chapter 32

Thomas was not sure that he had heard correctly. "I beg your pardon: you are coming with us?"

Miro nodded. "That is correct."

North stilled a very annoyed internal voice. *Just when it looks we're reassembling a team of seasoned professionals, the pencil-pusher decides to become a field agent. How bloody typical.* "Estuban," he said in his very best, and carefully groomed, tone, "are you sure this is wise?"

Miro smiled. "No, I am not."

*Well, that's a relief. Partially.* "Then why, may I ask, have you decided to become part of a field operation?"

"First, to solve the problem that Sherrilyn indirectly raised: I am the only extra pilot for the balloon, albeit not a very good one. But second, and far more important, if we lose Frank and Giovanna's trail, you are going to need the advice of someone who knows every city, and almost every coastal mile, of the Mediterranean."

Tom considered the profound merits of that argument.

Merits that Sherrilyn did not immediately see, evidently. "Why do you say we might lose their trail? Do you think the Spanish might move them?"

"Absolutely. I expect them to."

"Good grief, why?"

"Because I would."

"No offense, Estuban, but that's kind of crazy. That's—"

"That's called breaking contact," Harry pointed out quietly. "It's SOP for good intelligence work. Particularly in a situation like this one. The Spanish know we're working against the clock. So if they can force us to waste time just finding Frank and Gia all over again, it's unlikely we'd have enough time left to be able to mount a second operation. And if we did, it's likely to be a rush-job, and therefore, prone to disaster. No, the guy working for Borja now has either read our playbook, or has been schooled in the down-time equivalents."

"So even though they kicked our asses—?"

"—their best strategy is to move Frank and Giovanna. Quickly." Harry shrugged. "I suspect they've already shipped the two of them out of Rome; best to move them right after they beat us. They know our local networks are so shattered or shuttered that they probably won't detect the activity, for now."

Owen frowned. "Then how do we find their trail at all? No one will have any word of where they've gone, or even when they left."

Thomas scratched his left ear. "That might not necessarily be true, Owen. Do you remember the first boat we transferred to when we were fleeing Rome?"

"You mean the *scialuppa* that we rendezvoused with farther down the Tiber?"

"Yes, that one. Well, when we left them for the *barca-longa* that brought us back here, we—that is to say Harry and I—put them on retainer."

Owen smiled. "Did you now?"

North smiled back. "Yes. Harry and I wound up getting their whole, sad story as we were heading down toward Anzio. Seems they are fishermen out of Piombino, near the Tuscan border, and can't make a fair quatrine. The Spanish sutlers wait on the docks and impound their catch the moment the mooring lines are fast. So they're making more money by having us pay them to sit still, than having the Spanish only pay a quatrine for a *scudo* worth of fish."

"And do you think they'll be reliable?" Sherrilyn sounded dubious.

"As much as family can make them; their master is the brother-in-law of the senior remaining *lefferto.*"

"And who would that be?" Owen asked.

Harry's voice was dark. "Piero. You know him. Wounded at the attack and, if he's smart, far away from Rome. He was pretty sure that Borja's people would be looking for him. Real hard. And I agreed."

Miro leaned his chin into his hand. "Why him?"

"Because Piero was one of the two main sources from which the *lefferti* were getting inside information on what was going on in Borja's villa. And I'll bet anything that Borja's new spymaster identified those informers, and then used them to feed us the disinformation that corroborated my belief that the Spanish were undermanned at the *insula* Mattei. And once the attack was over, and the Spanish had those informers in their torture chambers, the remaining *lefferti* were as good as dead if they didn't run like hell."

Miro nodded. "Unquestionably. Now, about this Piero. He has agents watching the traffic along the Tiber?"

"Yes. Relatives, in fact. And he can pass news to the master of the *scialuppa* that took us up the Tiber, who could at least follow them for a day or two and get a basic idea of their course. So if anyone is removed from the *insula* Mattei, we'll know about it, and have some sense of which way they were sent."

"Which is another reason why we need to leave immediately," added Owen. "If there is no more intelligence than that on their movement, we will lose their trail pretty quickly. The Mediterranean is a big place, after all."

Miro smiled; Thomas was tempted to characterize the expression as "sneaky." "Yes, it's big, Colonel, but the number of places where the Spanish might keep two such prisoners for an extended amount of time is actually fairly limited. I agree that we must leave at once, but if the *scialuppa* can trail them for even one day, I think I'll be able to narrow down their probable destinations to a fairly small list."

"So you don't think they're going to stick them on some desert island somewhere with a platoon of guards?" Sherrilyn sounded disappointed.

"Absolutely not. First, the Mediterranean is thick with pirates. The Spanish cannot risk keeping the prisoners in anything other than a stronghold. And with a pregnant woman, they must have access to midwives or Hebrew physicians." Miro's smile went from "sneaky" to positively "wicked." "And that alone narrows the list quite a bit."

Sherrilyn nodded, her bangs bobbing. "Okay, Don Estuban, then what's our plan?"

Miro shrugged. "To depart quickly and remain flexible."

Sherrilyn blinked when it was clear that Miro was done speaking. "And that's it? That's the plan?"

North shrugged. "Don Estuban is right: we don't have enough specifics to even begin to know what we might need to do, let alone where or when. Our only option is to gather up any sufficiently portable resources that might conceivably give us an edge and get moving as quickly as possible. I suspect we can get a lot of what we'd want from the airplane facility in Mestre: extra communications gear, tools, wire, maybe even a spare engine for the balloon, if that's where they are kept." He turned to Miro. "Is there any reason we can't leave tomorrow?"

"One," Miro answered. "I had the Monster's gas tanks tapped for the remaining gasoline in them. The amount of energy gasoline produces in the balloon's engines, versus other fuels, makes it too valuable to leave behind. It would give us one 'high performance' flight with the dirigible. And we might need one, before we are done."

North heard something more than general prudence behind Miro's last comment. "You foresee something in particular, Estuban?"

Miro shrugged. "Once the rescue is over, we may need to move Giovanna Stone very quickly. If it takes a long time to find the two of them, or if the escape is a narrowly managed affair with the Spanish in hot pursuit, she might not have much time left in her pregnancy." Miro frowned. "Add to that the possibilities of bad seas, a shipwreck, or running from the Spanish on land if we are compelled to abandon ship and take our chances ashore. A pregnant woman either can't or shouldn't be asked to do any of those things. So, once we have her in our possession, we may need to put Giovanna and Frank in the balloon and send them home—or at least to a safe, well-staffed birthing place."

Owen was nodding. "Sensible. Will the gasoline be on hand in time for us to leave in thirty-six hours?"

"It should be," answered Miro. "We are loading it on the *barcalonga*, which will carry most of the team. The overflow personnel will be traveling in the same *gajeta* that brought you back from Rome the first time."

"Once we rendezvous with the Italian fishing boat, you're going to have to assign an admiral, too," commented Sherrilyn. "But none of us have much experience with high-seas mayhem."

Thomas had never seen Miro's eyes go so flat or serious. "I do."

Sherrilyn cocked her head. "Don Estuban, I know you have a lot of experience on the seas, but shouldn't we have someone with—?"

"Miss Maddox. You apparently think that being a merchant in the Mediterranean is an enterprise that does not involve combat. I must tell you that you are mistaken. Quite mistaken." Thomas believed him.

Evidently Sherrilyn did too; she shut up.

North stood. "Very well, then. With your permission, Estuban, I am going to brief our troops. And please do not take it amiss that I resume calling you 'Don Estuban' in front of them; we'll want that measure of public formality, I think."

"I quite agree. Gentlemen, Miss Maddox, I thank you for your willingness to move again so quickly. A good night's sleep is in order for us all. I doubt we'll have many of them from here on out. Captain Lefferts, one last moment of your time, if you please."

Sherrilyn was strolling—well, limping—along the length of the monastery's arcade when she heard Harry calling after her. She turned, saw him approaching, waited—

—and wondered: why had Miro kept him after the meeting was over? And why was he coming to talk to her now? Suddenly, she was more afraid of the possibility of his talking than she was of his long silences.

Which he had a lot of, these days. The formerly talkative *bon vivant* Harry Lefferts had undergone a startling transition since the debacle in Rome. Whereas in the wake of such a reversal, self-indulgent men might have become snappish or sulky, Harry had simply become very silent. On the journey home, he spoke when necessary and otherwise kept his thoughts and his company to himself, distancing himself from all others equally, even his long-time friends on the Wrecking Crew.

So, as he drew up to Sherrilyn, she was uncertain about what he might say. Which was, it turned out, wholly unexpected. "How's your knee, Sherrilyn?"

"My knee? You mean—? Hey, hold on. I'm just fine; a little tired, that's all. Old sports injuries do that, you know."

Harry nodded. "I know. I also saw how you were running by the time we were retreating from the Palazzi Mattei. I don't want any one of us taking unwise risks—any of us. Well, those of us who are left."

Sherrilyn swallowed her arch but threadbare denials about her very real knee problems; she intuited that Harry's self-recriminations were not merely conversational, but prefatory to some urgent message. "Okay; what's going down, Harry?"

"Me. I'm going down on the chain of command."

"What?" Sherrilyn felt her face grow hot. "What is that bastard Miro doi—?"

"Sherrilyn."

Her name—which Harry uttered with a kind of flat-toned finality—stopped her. "What?"

"Sherrilyn, it wasn't just Miro's idea. It's mine, too."

Sherrilyn searched his face, looked for a hint of prevarication, for any sign that this was a cosmetic lie intended to save Estuban Miro from her wrath. But she saw no such sign. "Harry," she said—and then didn't know what else to say.

He picked up the conversation. "Look, first off: how much of the Wrecking Crew is left? You, me, George, Donald, Matija, and Paul. And we can't take George anywhere with us right now. So we're down to barely half of our strength. And most of us are nursing some kind of injury." He looked at her knee but kept on his topic. "So, let's be honest: we may have big—decisive— contributions we can make to this next rescue attempt, but we don't have the power as a unit to remain the primary players."

"The hell we don't," Sherrilyn snarled in a denial that she knew was simply the triumph of loyalty over common sense.

Harry looked at her and smiled—a small, patient smile that she had never seen on his face before—and shook his head. "Sherrilyn, think it through. Command should pass to the guy who's going to be bringing the decisive hammer to the party."

"North."

"Yeah, and he's good. Let's be honest, Sherrilyn: he's commanded real units—military units—all his adult life. And Rome, and whatever comes next, is likely to be primarily a military operation. The Crew—hell, it's always been hard to fit us into a team-player mold, when you get right down to it. We've always worked on our own: in fast, hit hard, out fast. Rome wasn't like that—not as much as I wanted it to be, and that's part of what got us torn up. North wouldn't have made my mistakes."

"Yeah? Well, he wouldn't have made a bold plan, either. Hell, if we had to wait for Nervous Nelly North, we'd probably still be sitting in Rome, eating pasta, wondering what to do."

Harry smiled. "Sherrilyn, you know that's bunk. North just thinks more like a military commander than a commando. Frankly, if he had been in charge, I'm pretty sure he'd have given me complete autonomy with the Crew. He understands how to blend really good soldiers like his with high-power commando operatives like us. I thought I knew how to, also—but I didn't. Not well enough."

Sherrilyn rose up. "Okay, so maybe you've got something left to learn. Big deal: you'll learn it. Starting now."

Harry nodded. "Yeah, but this time, I'm not going to risk any more lives by learning on the job. Besides, Sherrilyn, let's be honest; the Crew is never going to be the same again. And not just because of the casualties we took, but because someone found a way to mess with our act, to trip us up and knock us down."

Sherrilyn shook her head sharply. "You don't do self-pity very well, Harry."

"This isn't self-pity, Sherrilyn. I'm dead serious. Look: as long as we were tear-assing around Europe, blind-siding the locals and dancing off before they could get their paws on us, we were golden. The Wrecking Crew was like a rock band; we did what we wanted, spent everything we earned, lived like kings, had groupies, roadies, you name it."

He looked sideways at the stars peeking over the roofs of the monastery. "But, also like a rock band, our glory ride had to come to an end. There's always a point where you hit the wall, your moment is over: you've reached your limit and now you're on the downslide. Problem was, we didn't get to learn that gradually, the way most bands do; we didn't see a string of gigs going more and more sour as the opposition got smarter and smarter. We caught it in our faces, all at once. The situation—and the guy—in Rome was deadly serious shit; I wasn't ready for it."

"Okay," Sherrilyn answered with a sharp nod. "So you weren't ready for it. Neither was North. Hell, none of us were. And how could we be? So maybe you're right: maybe you need to watch and learn a bit before you sit in the big chair on that big an operation again. But so what? They say that if you don't fail, you don't learn. So here's your learning opportunity. And one of the things you'd better damned well learn from this, Harry Lefferts, is that, sometimes, you're going to be beaten—and it isn't the end of the world. It means you've met an enemy who taught you a hard lesson—and your job is to learn that lesson and step up the game so that *you* are schooling *him*, next time."

Harry smiled at her. "You give one hell of a pep talk, teach. Break 'em down and build 'em up—all in one minute. Pretty impressive."

Sherrilyn shrugged. "Had plenty of experience at it."

"Yeah, you did. And you always provided a good example—both in victory and defeat."

Sherrilyn narrowed her eyes. "I heard that emphasis on 'defeat,' Harry. Don't try to get slick with me. You got some bad news for me, you just come out and say it."

Harry shrugged. "Okay, Sherrilyn. Here's the deal: you're not coming back out with us. You're going up-country to make sure they have some up-time expertise helping out with the papal security detail."

Sherrilyn felt her jaw drop. "You're benching me? Now?"

"Sherrilyn, I'll ask again: how's your knee? Or do I have to ask you to run a set of high hurdles and then we can both see how much you're limping? Listen, we've all got some hard facts to deal with today. This one is yours: you are as kick-ass capable as you ever were, Sherrilyn, but your knee is giving out. Having you scramble around on tile roofs, climbing ropes, bouncing around on a pitching ship's deck: it's not safe. Not to you, and not to the people depending on you."

Sherrilyn was all ready to tell Harry how wrong he was—but realized that she didn't actually have a rebuttal: she had no way to refute the incontrovertible evidence of her own swollen knee and gimping gait. She limped out from under the last groined vault of the arcade, stared up into the night sky, and sighed. "Yeah, okay—you're right, Harry. But it still sucks—sucks that this could be the end of the Wrecking Crew."

Harry joined her, looking up at the low clouds that had started scudding overhead. "Yeah, that part sucks all right. But we had a great run while it lasted."

Sherrilyn looked over at his fine profile and resolved not to get maudlin. "Yeah," she said. "The best. The very best."

# Chapter 33

Captain Vincente Jose-Maria de Castro y Papas drew up to his full height and stared down at the other man. "This is unconscionable. I will not do it."

"You will, Captain, and you will do it personally. There can be no delay; it must be done before we set sail this afternoon."

Castro y Papas stopped himself from refusing directly. The man he knew only as Dolor had no official place in the military command structure, but, as had Quevedo, enjoyed broad authority. Borja had even instructed all but three of his generals to obey this joyless, black-cloaked reaper without hesitation. So, disobeying Dolor would simply be a way to end his career, and maybe life, given Borja's taste for vigorous punishment of any infractions that could be interpreted as treasonous.

Castro y Papas tried a different tack. "This punishment is not merely pointless; it will further harden them against us."

Dolor shook his fine, close-cropped head. "It will remind them that we are to be feared, and will prevent them from aiding our enemies ever again. And besides, it is Cardinal Borja's explicit order." He stared up at Castro y Papas with calm disinterest, as if the outcome of their conversation was already obvious, and he was simply listening to the other out of courtesy.

His final impulse—to ask, "And why have I been selected to inflict the punishment?"—the captain successfully stifled. The question would not change anything, and besides, it was more his responsibility than anyone else's. But more importantly, if he asked that question, there was the chance that the duty would indeed pass to someone else, someone who had neither the skill nor the interest in restricting the severity of damage inflicted.

Without responding to Dolor, Castro y Papas turned on his heel and harshly ordered one of his own guards—who were now outnumbered by Dolor's retainers—to open the door to the prisoner's room.

He walked in quickly, careful not to make eye contact. "You," he spoke toward the window where he had seen the prisoner brooding a few minutes earlier. "You should not have involved yourself when the rescuers came, and certainly not by attacking the soldiers of His Imperial Majesty King Philip IV with an incendiary device. Now stand up."

Frank Stone did, frowning. "Hey, if anyone's going to be testy around here, I think I'm the one who has the best reason to—"

"Frank!" warned Giovanna sharply.

Castro y Papas grimaced. *Damn it, but that one can read me like a book. Well, there's no point in waiting*—He looked up long enough to firmly fix Frank Stone's position, and then threw the first punch.

It landed as Castro y Papas had intended: squarely on the surprised up-timer's chin. As Frank fell backward and his wife emitted a shriek, the Spaniard saw Stone's eyes get wobbly. Perfect; he was dazed, but not unconscious. This way, he'd feel less pain, but still be awake, which meant that Dolor and his dogs couldn't force Castro y Papas to inflict a second, more complete beating at some later date.

But no, Dolor and his men were not dogs; judging from the barking laughs from behind, they were hyenas. Castro y Papas turned, saw Dolor's little Cretan adjutant, Dakis, leaning against the doorjamb, settled in to enjoy the spectacle. With him and the others watching, there would be no way to end this quickly, so Castro y Papas would have to be very careful.

As he turned back to his loathsome task, he discovered Giovanna Stone staring at him, her eyes as murderous as any he had ever seen in almost fifteen years of soldiering. And he did not blame her in the least. He held her eyes one second longer as he reached down for her swooning husband with his left hand—and carefully shook the signet ring on his right hand so that it rotated on his finger, the immense imprinting head swiveling safely back inside his readying fist.

Her eyes darted to that fist, noting the change. Then she looked at him again, her mouth closed and her chin elevated. She understood, seemed all but ready to nod at him—and not to give the leering animals near the door the pleasure of her further screams.

Castro y Papas closed his eyes, threw his next punch obliquely into Frank's belly, and began calculating the minimum number of face or bone blows that would be required to make the beating look convincing to his savagely eager audience.

The country house that was the only large building of the sprawling farming establishment called Molini was emerging from beneath the soot and dust of long neglect. The Cavrianis' report to Sharon indicated that the last residents had been the elderly remnants of a cantankerous clan that had not repopulated itself very vigorously, and drove off those few offspring that might have one day inherited the remote, self-styled "commune." Some said the last of Molini's antediluvian inhabitants had abandoned it voluntarily; others said they were carted away in their senescent (if combative) infirmity. However, this much was clear: it had stood empty for the preceding nine months, and had fallen into disrepair over the preceding decade.

With the nearest neighbors almost four miles away, no one had any business coming to visit Molini. But if anyone had, they would have noticed dramatic changes. The gardens were being tended once again, walkways were repaired and swept, and what had appeared to be an angular compost heap against the back wall had been replaced with a new pile of kitchen firewood.

After finishing the first full meal cooked in that refurbished kitchen—wild boar stuffed with turnips, wild carrots, and chives— Sharon and Ruy sought the comfort of the smaller, more intimate hearth of the master suite's sitting room. It was not their private retreat, however, despite the fact that their bedroom was contiguous with it. Although the house was quite large, it was still small for their entire contingent: all the rooms fit for sleeping were accommodating at least six people. The only exceptions were the rooms reserved for the Ruy and Sharon, Vitelleschi and Antonio

Barberini, and Wadding and Larry Mazzare, the last eliciting no small number of muttered comments about strange bedfellows, indeed. Only the pope had a private room. Or did in theory, anyway: of the two Wild Geese—Patrick Fleming and Anthony McEgan—one always kept watch over Urban at all times.

So Sharon and Ruy were not surprised when the entirety of the clerical contingent filed into the sitting room adjoining their quarters. But Sharon quickly understood that this was not to be simply another session of the post-prandial companionship that was rapidly becoming a tradition in this space: Urban and Wadding compelled the two Wild Geese to remain outside the room. Then Urban moved over to take the chair closest to the fire; even with summer coming on, the nighttime temperatures of the Italian PreAlps were still bracing. The others found seats and looked at Vitelleschi expectantly.

Ruy glanced at Sharon and then, together, they faced the newcomers. "Your Eminences," Ruy began, "do you require the private use of this chamber for—?"

Urban shook his head. "No, my son, you and your charming bride are welcome to remain here as long as you wish. Although our discourse might bore you."

From the mischievous twinkle in the pope's eye, Sharon seriously doubted that would be the case.

As he often did, Vitelleschi began addressing his fellow clerics without preamble. "As per His Holiness' instructions, I shall preside over the debates between Cardinals Mazzare and Wadding. Cardinal Barberini shall serve as recording secretary. And I reiterate his Holiness' strict instructions that the discussants are not to address arguments to him during our sessions, nor are they to present him with appeals outside of them. He is an observer only.

"The first item to be addressed is whether it can reasonably be asserted that Grantville is an infernal construct. If it is deemed possible, then logically, our discussions will end there."

Ruy poked Sharon's arm gently. "You do not seem demonic to me, my heart. At least, not when we are in public..."

Sharon poked Ruy far more energetically in the ribs. "Stop it, Ruy. You'll get us in trouble." They both turned and saw Vitelleschi glowering at them with a face as pinched and disapproving as a stereotypical spinster schoolmarm.

"However," he resumed archly, "if it is decided that Grantville's appearance cannot be reasonably ascribed to satanic machinations, then we must consider how up-time papal opinions, councils, and decrees bear upon our own Church. In particular, we must establish the theological and canonical provenance of the up-time papal council most frequently referred to as Vatican Two."

"Damn," breathed Sharon, "this sure beats tuning in to the late, late show."

"Eh?" whispered Ruy.

"Shhh. I'll explain later."

"If you are suggesting that we have box seats for the greatest religious drama of the age, I quite agree."

Vitelleschi had not paused. "Finally, we will use the collective outcome of these discussions to inform our final, crucial consideration: whether or not His Holiness should seek shelter and aid from the United States of Europe. In short, we must discover whether that act of mundane prudence is also an act that follows the Will of God.

"We have few documents at our disposal from which to draw citations, so we cannot observe the procedures and protocols of a court of canon law. However, that may prove a blessing in disguise; we have need of swift decisions. Picking at the fine construances of words—half of which come to us through translations of dubious accuracy—would be no ally to our need for alacrity.

"Instead, Cardinals Mazzare and Wadding will write—as briefs—their best recollections of the relevant facts or citations upon which they will base their remarks in each session. But there will be no prepared statements. This must be a living discussion among men, not a paper duel between lawyers."

Wadding leaned forward toward Urban. "And when we have finished all our discussions, and you, Your Holiness, have concluded your deliberations, shall the right or wrong of these matters be asserted *ex cathedra*?"

"I certainly hope to do so," answered Urban.

"Your Holiness," pressed Wadding, "whatever we might say, your final statements remain the *sine qua non* that give this entire discursive process meaning. Mother Church has only one pope, one voice, that speaks God's Will to us. And we must hear that Will clearly."

Ruy leaned and murmured toward his wife, "The Irish priest is a most relentless advocate of traditionalism, I suspect."

"Sure sounds like it," Sharon muttered.

Urban considered Wadding's eager face. "My dear brother in Christ," the pope said with a small smile, "how can I know the answer to your question before we hear and compare the wisdom you and Cardinal Mazzare may bring us? Only then can I responsibly decide how, and when, and with what finality, I shall speak upon the matters we will discuss here. And so I may not answer your question as you wish, Cardinal Wadding—at least, not yet. And now," he said turning to face Ruy and Sharon, "what questions do you two have?"

"Us?" Sharon hated it when her voice came out like a squeak.

"Of course. This is your parlor we are commandeering, after all."

"Holy Father," said Ruy, who somehow rose into a bow, "*mi casa, su casa,* so you are not commandeering this room: it is already yours. I am quite sure I speak for Ambassadora Nichols as well, in this regard."

Urban laughed. "Noble Ruy, I see why you would have had no success in Madrid; you are far too earnest and gracious to be a true courtier. But allow me to speak with greater specificity: do you and the ambassadora have any questions regarding your role in our deliberations?"

Ruy was speechless. Sharon mastered her voice into a husky alto before she asked, "We have a role?"

Urban nodded. "Most assuredly."

"This is—most irregular," Ruy murmured.

Wadding made a sound of gruff affirmation.

Urban elected not to notice it. "Yes, it is irregular. As is this entire messy process. So who will notice a little more mud mixed into the mud, eh? But in all seriousness, my children, I wish you to be present, to hear what transpires in this room as we decide the course of Mother Church. And, at the end of each discourse, I encourage you to ask questions."

Sharon could hardly believe her ears, but managed to maintain a curious caution. "Why? Why would you want us to ask questions, Your Holiness?"

He smiled. "For the reason you just did, my dear: you up-timers hold very little sacred, I've noted. Many say this marks you as heretics and demons. But I believe it is the inevitable cost of holding *truth* sacred above all other things—in which your values recall those in Paul's first letter to the Corinthians."

"Your Holiness," objected Wadding, "while the up-timers might revere 'truth,' that is not quite synonymous with Paul's injunction to embrace 'faith, hope and love.' None of those are 'truth.'"

"No, but truth is often the wellspring of each of those graces, even of faith," replied Urban. "Consider: faith is not the fundamental human virtue whereby unbelievers may come to salvation, Cardinal Wadding, for if it was, the kingdom of God would have no way to grow, to admit new converts. A man or a woman born outside of faith cannot conjure it from a void: for faith to take root and grow in them, it must fall upon a mind fertile with a love of truth, of hungering after the answers of the universe, and hope for a better world. Which, those same minds will later come to realize, are all manifest in His Word."

Urban had never taken his eyes from Sharon and Ruy. "In you," he resumed, "I see many symbols of this. I see in you symbols of our two worlds. Of an aging man whose origins are associated with the slaveholders' whip. Of a young woman associated with slavery's shackles. Of different times and cultures and continents. But all, somehow, joined together in bliss and balance." Urban leaned back and folded his hands. "I came to manhood hearing many men whisper—even in the hallways of the Curia—that the age of miracles was at least fifteen centuries past. But now, toward the close of my life, a town has arrived from what it claims to be the future, challenging everything we know and believe about our world. So I must ask myself: what of the two of you? You might just be a pair of unusual newlyweds, chance-met on a shared road of desperation. But I cannot in good conscience discount the possibility that He has set you here as a symbol of how peoples in contention may ultimately become partners in contentment—despite their apparent differences. You give me much to think about. And I would be a fool to forbid you to ask questions. Who knows?" He smiled mischievously. "You may be the Savior's own mouthpieces."

Sharon thought about her capacity for colorful profanity and felt an invisible blush rise up through her cheeks.

Urban patted her on the knee, rose and turned to his informal canon court. "In the meantime, Cardinals Wadding and Mazzare will prepare to address us on the probability that Grantville was sent here by Satan—a most stimulating conjecture!"

Motioning for the others to follow, he strode from the room.

Larry Mazzare was the last to leave; he turned and smiled faintly. "I'll try to fend off the exorcists, Sharon," he said.

"You do that," she breathed fervently.

He waved and left. Sharon and Ruy sat. They did not speak for almost a full minute. It was Ruy who broke the silence with a hushed observation. "Sharon, my love, I believe we have just witnessed the beginning of a new era."

"What do you mean?"

"I mean that the head of the Roman Church is, at this most dark and crucial moment, not only allowing but soliciting the input of laypersons. In your books, I have encountered a word—transparency. Originally it was strictly a physical noun, meaning a clear plate or sheet. But in the last documents of your era, it also emerged as a concept, was even used as an adjective. Indeed, among some of your governments and corporations, it became a, a—how do you say it? A 'boss-word?'"

"A buzz word."

"Yes. A buzz word. And that word—transparency—does, I believe, describe how Urban means to change the Church's culture: he is trying to make its processes more open. Oh, of course he has other, pragmatic reasons for having us at these discussions: we can verify, for posterity, the things they will say and decide, here. But if that was his only motivation, he could find other alternatives—or simply do what most popes have done: ignored the opinions and questions of the laity. But not this time, apparently."

Sharon stared into the hearth. "So maybe something good will come out of this papal mess: a more honest, open Church."

Ruy shrugged. "It is rightly said that every disaster that lays a temple low is also an opportunity to build a better, sturdier, loftier one. It may be such here. And Urban—unless I very much mis-read my popes—is just the pontiff to lay those new cornerstones."

Sherrilyn stepped out from the small upland copse when the dirigible came into view, flying only one hundred feet over the slopes that sheltered the hamlet of Campofontana, just four miles to the south. She waved slowly, holding a bright white bandana in one hand, a bright red one in the other.

Even at this distance, she heard the dull buzz of the motors modulate into a lower pitch, and watched as the dirigible came around, nosing down in her direction. Sherrilyn heard her escorts back in the wood, two of Tom Stone's embassy Marines, exchange mutters in Amideutsch. She motioned for them to stay back; it was unlikely that anyone else was nearby, but just in case one of Borja's operatives had trailed them up here—well, wasn't it Napoleon who had said that Providence was always on the side of the last reserve?

The dirigible was nearly at ground level now, and she could see that it was almost filled with crates, a few more Hibernians, and duffles full of what was probably their gear and spare ammo.

At the front of the blimp, next to the pilot, a very tall, broad-shouldered man with sandy blond hair and gray eyes was looking down at her calmly. "Ms. Maddox?"

"Yes; is that you, Hastings?"

"Yes, ma'am. We're secure here?"

"Best I can tell. I got here two days early, then set some hidden observation posts to watch for anyone who might have been tailing us. *Nada.*"

"Very well, I'll have my men and gear unloaded in a trice."

Sherrilyn nodded her approval. "Good. And did you bring your most comfortable boots?"

"Er...yes. Why?"

"Because, Lieutenant Hastings, we've got some heavy hiking ahead of us."

# Chapter 34

Thomas North walked to the rail and stared at the collection of age-blackened huts that was this century's pitiful incarnation of Anzio. He pitched his voice so the other person in the *barca-longa*'s stern could hear him above the wind and spray. "You ready, Harry?"

"For what?" The up-timer sounded distracted, as if being roused from immersion in a book.

"For making contact with Aurelio, captain of the Piombinese *scialuppa* we left here."

"Yeah, sure. I'm ready. We just need to find Piero first. Then we'll be set."

North stared at Harry. "Not a lot of fun, this return."

Harry pushed away from the rail. "Nope, not a bit. But there's no time or use for a pity party, Thomas. The way I figure it, I could get down on myself—but if I did, then I'd be wasting time and energy I should be dedicating to our mission. To making all the sacrifices in Rome worthwhile, in the end."

North nodded. "Well said, Harry. It's good to have you here."

Harry shrugged, offering a lopsided smile that was a close cousin to a grimace. "Good to be here, boss. Now let's find Piero so we can start rescuing Frank and Gia."

Piero, with a patch on his right eye and his leg stiff out in front of him, was doing a fair job of imitating a piracy-cashiered

366

sailor, loitering about the waterfront. The tavern in which he resided was small, owned by a distant relative, and located at the midpoint of an eastward-meandering coastal cart-track that joined Anzio on the west to the much larger commercial port of Nettuno on the east. "It was difficult to find me, I take it," Piero said, putting down the goblet of wine that he frequently handled, but rarely sipped from.

"Difficult enough," Miro commented. "You have hidden yourself quite well."

"May have even overdone it," North commented gruffly.

"Your complaints are music to my ears, testimony to my ability to evade Borja's hounds."

Harry looked up. "It's good to see you're alive, Piero. Now, about Frank and Giovanna—?"

Piero nodded. "They departed Rome seven days ago; their ship sailed from Ostia a day later."

Harry looked at Miro. "Damn. They weren't wasting any time."

"No, apparently not. And these rumors we've been hearing about the Ghetto—?"

Piero winced and took a genuine swallow of the wine as Sean Connal started removing the wrappings on his leg; unlike the patch on his eye, these wrappings concealed a genuine injury. "The rumors are true. At least one hundred and fifty killed, as retribution for our attack on the *insula* Mattei."

Harry jumped up—his chair falling over, drinks spilling—and he stalked out of the inn, head low.

Piero looked around the group. "Surely he does not blame himself for—?"

"Let's stick to the information, Piero," suggested North. "Every minute we're here increases the risk to you."

"*Si*, this I know. So: Borja's new lieutenant was apparently watching our informers for weeks before the attack. Meaning that, now, we have no network left in Rome. And we *lefferti*— well, there are no more *lefferti*. Now we are just desperate men, trying to go about our business and remain unnoticed. But we did get one last, useful message out from our informant inside Borja's villa—who was, by the way, a distant relative of mine."

Miro concluded that the relations among Italian families were even more extensive and intricate than among the *marranos*, or crypto-Jews, of Spain. "Yes?"

"Although Borja's secretaries relentlessly screened each others' communiqués to prevent any mention of Frank and Giovanna's ultimate destination, there was one detail they overlooked: the routing of the dispatch pouch that was sent with their ship. My relative—Luigi Ferrigno—managed to slip a copy of the routing order out of the villa just before he was caught." Piero took another long swallow of wine, looked down at his now-exposed leg, which was healing nicely.

"Piero," Miro prompted, "the dispatches in the pouch: where were they addressed?"

"To the viceroy of Mallorca and the commander of a fort called San Carlos."

Judging from North's quick sideways glance, he had apparently expected Miro to be surprised—but was himself surprised when Estuban received the news calmly.

"Did you suspect this?" North asked.

Miro shrugged. "It was a distinct possibility. Mallorca is as far as you can get from Italy if you're traveling toward Spain, and is not easily accessible from the coast of any other nation."

"But why not put Frank and Gia in Spain itself?" North wondered.

Miro shook his head. "No. Borja would not do that. And Philip would not want it. As it stands now, Frank and Giovanna are the products of Borja's actions. If they arrive at the Spanish mainland, Philip becomes directly involved and responsible for them. I suspect he wants to maintain as much distance from Borja as possible, wants to retain the option of denouncing his own cardinal as a rogue who exceeded his mandate and whose excesses must be corrected.

"In turn, Borja knows that Philip's patience is wearing thin. Our informers told us, up until they were discovered, that Borja had received scant acknowledgement from Madrid and all of it had been notably terse. So on the one hand, Borja will not want to put Philip in an awkward position where he must either decide, once and for all, to either support Borja or renounce him. On the other hand, whatever uses Borja has for his prisoners would be lost to him if they were to fall under a greater power's control. Mallorca, as a nominally Catalan possession, has a far more circuitous connection to Madrid, and furthermore, has a number of facilities that are not under the direct control of crown authorities."

"And do you have an idea where the two of them might be imprisoned?" North asked narrowly.

"Only a suspicion, a 'hunch,' as the up-timers say. Now, Piero, did the note indicate if there were any other messages in the dispatch pouch? Other destinations?"

"No, Don Estuban; all the mail was for Palma de Mallorca."

Miro nodded. "So they will make directly for the Balearics. Meaning the ships are fully provisioned for the journey and do not need to put in at other ports along the way. This way, they will leave no word of their passing in other cities, nor will they ever be found lying at anchor near a populous area in which attackers such as ourselves might gather covertly."

North leaned back, arms folded. "So what do we do? Chasing them seems to be out of the question."

Miro nodded again. "We would never catch them. And we could not best them in a fight with our sad little vessels. Nor, even if we won, could we guarantee the safety of the prisoners."

North raised an eyebrow. "By process of elimination, then, it seems like we are bound for Mallorca."

Miro smiled. "At least you will have an expert guide, once we arrive there."

North nodded. "Yes, but to what end? Once we get there, what do we do?"

"Well, it seems like the basic plan of rescuing Frank and Giovanna from their prison cell is still the objective."

"Yes, but how? We'll have fewer men available for operations than our full muster, you realize. Boats in a combat environment need anchor watches; that will drain some of our manpower. If, before our actual attack, we must land our gear and operate from a forward ground base, we'll need to leave pickets there: more manpower lost. And we are starting with under twenty-five combat effectives, all packed so tightly into two boats that it would take half a day to unload the gear we'd need for a serious fight. And that long again just to get all the various components of the airship out and ready for assembly and inflation. If we wind up using the balloon at all, that is."

Piero shrugged. "It sounds like you need another boat."

Miro shrugged. "Yes, but another boat would mean needing another crew. And the larger our operation gets, the more unwieldy it becomes."

"Still," said North, "Piero makes a good point: we need more operational redundancy, more hulls in which to store our gear and spread out our personnel. We'll be more responsive and flexible that way."

"Very well," relented Miro, "but there are not many places for us to get boats, Thomas. I do not think Borja will let us have any of his. Nor do I think the Spanish Viceroy of Naples, Osuna, would be any more generous. The same problem applies to Genoa, with Spain's Milanese factors watching over their shoulders. Which leaves Tuscany."

Piero shook his head. "You will not want to buy from Tuscany, Don Estuban. Their ships are all moving grain to the Spanish, or are fishing to supply the tercios if they have better contracts than that which was offered to Aurelio and his crew. Besides, the Medicis of Tuscany have old family grudges which might keep them from offering you favorable terms—or keeping your deal with them quiet."

North frowned. "Family grudges? Against who?"

Miro sighed and leaned back. "Against the Barberinis—the pope's family. Yes, I forgot that. There is bad blood there. Early in his papacy, Urban VIII became involved in a struggle for the lands of the duke of Urbino, when the last legitimate issue of that line died without heir. A lot of persons felt the Medicis had the better claim, but Urban wanted to add those holdings to the papal tracts—which he did. It was a most unpleasant business, as I recall."

"So where *does* one get a boat around these parts?" asked North testily as Harry came back inside.

"Speaking about boats," Lefferts said, "it looks like Aurelio's boat is coming around the point now. But there seem to be a bunch of guys down at the pier, already waiting for him."

Piero shrugged. "They are all Piombinese. All fishermen."

Harry stared. "All of them? Damn, there must be a lot of fish around Anzio this season."

Piero shook his head. "No. Not at all. The waters are fished out, just now. All to feed the Spanish."

"Then what are they all doing here?"

"Sharing in the money you are paying Aurelio."

Harry pointed down the shore. "All those guys? Hell, we're not paying Aurelio enough to handle all those guys. They'd be lucky getting a quatrine a day, each."

"Less, probably. But that's more than they would make back in Piombino."

"So they didn't come here to fish, really."

Piero tilted his hand back and forth. "They all fish, but about once every three days. It's a communal enterprise, you see."

Harry looked out the door at Aurelio's now-moored *scialuppa*, the waiting throng, and cocked his head, considering. "Hey, Estuban, so if we need boats, how about Aurelio and his gang? They've got a ship, they're seamen, and they are already on our payroll."

North frowned. "Well, that is certainly the half full glass you are seeing, Harry. What I see when I look out that door are fishermen, not seamen *per se*, without training for, or experience in, combat. And yet they are so numerous that they could not fit in their own boat all at once."

Miro rubbed his chin. "What you say is true, Thomas. But, operationally speaking, we are beggars, not choosers. So, Harry, would you be kind enough to ask Aurelio to come in here for a chat? And please bring the radioman to the inn, I need him to set up his equipment and establish contact with Ambassador Nichols as quickly as possible. I have some questions for one of her staff..."

The eager jabbering that had first arisen when Aurelio went back out to his gathered crew and announced the offer of employment fell suddenly silent.

"And that," speculated Miro, "indicates that Aurelio has just informed them of our stipulation that none of them will step on inhabited land again until we return to Italy."

North drummed his fingers on the tabletop. "With any luck, that requirement will chase some of them away. There are too many of them—more than we can use, Estuban."

Miro looked at the Englishman with raised eyebrows. "I seem to recall you being the one calling for more personnel."

"Blast it, yes, but with a suitable increase in hull space, as well. Look at them, Estuban; they'll be packed tighter than rats in the bilge. We've no use for all of them."

But Miro smiled. "At this moment, perhaps not. But as you say, we need both more crew and more ships. The crew materialized first; we must not fail to add them to our resources while we may. And at least it relieves the problem of losing so many of combat personnel to mundane tasks. These Piombinese will furnish the hands and backs that shall bear all the burdens of seamanship, lading, and night watches."

North scowled at the milling Piombinesi, who seemed more somber now, but whose numbers had not decreased at all. "True enough, but as you are fond of pointing out, we have a very limited budget, and those"—he nodded at the fishermen—"are an awful lot of new mouths to feed and palms to pay. And while it may seem like serendipity to find this much crew, they'll bleed us dry while we try to add another hull to our resources. Which may prove a far more difficult lack to remedy."

Harry smiled, lopsidedly. "Yeah, there is that, isn't there?"

A respectful tapping on the doorjamb announced Aurelio's reapproach. He leaned into the common room, hat in hand. "Signori?"

"Yes, Aurelio?"

"The men, they come to a decision. All will go."

"No surprise, there," muttered North.

"Excellent," Miro said, loud enough to obscure Thomas' *sotto voce* grumpiness, "Tell the men we shall set sail for Piombino itself."

Aurelio looked baffled. "Why there, Signor Miro?"

"We need to acquire another boat, and given your contacts in—"

Aurelio shook his head. "No, Signor, this is no good idea. Piombino's boats are all working for the Spanish, or have been taken by them."

"Taken?"

"*Si.* Well, the Spanish, he say he 'bought' the boat. But if a man give you a few coins and take your boat without asking, has he 'bought' it? What would you say the Spanish is doing, when he do this?"

North affected a hoarse, throaty voice and a semi-Sicilian accent: "To quote yuh Godfaddah, I'd say dat he is making you an offer you cannot refuse."

Harry snickered. Miro guessed that North was imitating some up-time media icon—probably from an up-time gangster movie—but understood no more than that.

Aurelio understood the general import clearly enough, however. "*Si.* The one Piombinese who refused the offer got a sword through his belly. So, no sailing to Piombino. No ships for you there, and too many Spanish. Besides, the trip, it is more dangerous, now."

"Dangerous now? Why?"

Aurelio's brows darkened. "Pirates," he spat. "An Algerine."

North rolled his eyes. "Well, we get the full gamut here, don't we? From Spanish highway robbery to Moorish high seas brigandry. I can see why people come to the Italian coast for vacations."

Miro hardly noticed the Englishman's sarcasm. "What kind of ship is she, Aurelio? How is she working?"

"She is a xebec, Signor Miro, and a big one. A crew of seventy, at least. And she is trouble for everyone because she is not working much at all, anymore." Aurelio spread his hands. "The Algerians, they like hunting big ships, big prizes. Merchants mostly. But now, with Borja in Rome, and supply convoys going back and forth to Barcelona—"

Miro nodded. "Of course. The Spanish have impounded all the local shipping, and keep it in convoy. Madrid has probably hired some privateers, as well, working at piracy suppression."

"Sì. So the Algerine, she has to stay farther north than she would like, and must hunt for smaller prey." Aurelio looked resentful. "She even hunts for the smallest fishing boats, now. Whatever she can find."

"And where has this xebec been sighted?"

Aurelio shrugged. "All around the Tuscan archipelago: Elba, Pianosa, Monte Cristo—"

Miro turned to North and Lefferts. "You see? Providence provides."

"No," said North.

"Colonel North, how can you, of all persons, complain?" Miro met his scowl with a cheery smile. "You challenged serendipity to provide us with a ship to hold our too-numerous seamen, and here it is, furnished by the hand of Fate, or God—whichever suits your philosophy. Indeed, one of your Christian priests might counsel you to accept this Algerine xebec as proving the truth of their exhortation 'Ask, and ye shall receive.'"

North grimaced. "Hmph. Now I am only interested in proving the truth of the one religious axiom that pertains to trading volleys with pirates."

"And what axiom is that?"

"That, verily, it is better to give than to receive. Pass me that wine, damn you; I need a drink."

Donald Ohde, the team's unofficial radio operator, popped his head back in the door. "I've got the embassy standing by on the radio, Don Estuban. Don Ruy himself is on the line, wondering what you need."

Miro rose. "Did you tell him that we are bound for Mallorca?"

"Yep."

Miro smiled. "Then I will ask my Catalan friend what he might know about a most significant fortification on the island, the one known as the Castell de Bellver..."

# Chapter 35

Captain Castro y Papas knew that Señor Dolor was approaching him from behind, but not because he could hear the man's boots on the deck. Dolor was, fittingly, as quiet as death, but the sailors working the sails and rigging hushed at his approach. As they always did. Some made warding signs when they thought he wasn't looking. Castro y Papas was quite sure that Dolor saw it all, and more besides.

"Captain," said the smaller man as he came to stand beside Don Vincente at the rail.

"Señor," Castro y Papas acknowledged with as flat a tone as he could manage.

If Dolor noticed, or cared, that the response was markedly unwelcoming, he gave no sign of it. "Have your duties ever brought you to Mallorca before?"

Don Vincente shook his head.

"A pleasant island," commented Dolor, "and Palma is a handsome city."

"I hadn't noticed," Castro y Papas lied. He had been admiring the view as their *frigata* rode the north Saharan wind known as the *Llebeig* into Palma's broad bay. Flanked by eastern beaches on the right, and scrub-covered uplands on the left, their entry brought them abreast of Fort San Carlos, still under construction. Before them lay Palma itself, walls mounting up into an impressive skyline. The immense Gothic cathedral on the east offered its flank squarely to the bay, and pointed toward the rambling Almudaina palace that straddled the midpoint of the walls. The western end of the city seemed to slope down and away from that edifice, which mixed Arab, Spanish, and modern architectural elements into an aesthetic whole that, defying all logic, pleased the eye.

Close against the walls and just back from the shores that ran away to both the east and west city were wide, white arms that waved tirelessly, all doing so at the same speed. Those flanking clusters of well-wishers were windmills, turning in the steady wind that now freshened the ship's sails and brought them closer to the Moorish pier, reaching out toward them like a weathered gray finger.

Dolor looked up into the cloudless light blue sky. "Odd," he commented, "that you see no beauty in such a view. I would have thought you a man receptive to the romance of so striking a vista."

"Perhaps the mood is not upon me just now."

"Perhaps. At any rate, we are passing your new duty station, Captain." Dolor pointed to the west shore. Set upon a knoblike hill barely a mile beyond the walls of Palma, a collection of round towers dominated the scrub-mottled uplands that overlooked the bay. "That is the Castell de Bellver. Formerly the palace of the king of Mallorca, it declined to a mere fortress, and now is descending in stature yet again—to that of a prison."

Don Vincente studied the building that seemed to be perched watchfully over the western approaches to Palma. One tower, noticeably taller and a bit narrower than the other three, pointed like a white finger into the sky.

Dolor must have noticed his companion's attention to that particular feature. "That is the lazarette. The final bastion of the fortress. Which, I might add, has never been taken by general assault. Nor have any prisoners ever escaped from it."

Castro y Papas could see why, readily enough. The main body of the fortress seemed to be a squat tower itself, now that he had a closer view of it; it rose only two tall stories above the ravelins and ramparts that had been cut into the hilltop around it. At each true compass point of the circular main walls sat one of the structure's four towers. The lazarette served as the north pointer, and therefore, sat back somewhat from the bay. With the pennons fluttering from the pinnacles of each tower, it looked much more like a white-pink fairy-tale castle than a prison. Don Vincente felt a tinge of pity for so fine a structure, built as the residence of kings, but now a gaol. "It no longer contributes to the defense of the city?"

Dolor shrugged. "Somewhat. There are cannons in the ramparts about its base and a few still on its roof. But as you can see, its design reflects the wisdom of the ages before cannon. The same is true for the substance of its walls."

"What do you mean?"

Dolor swept his finger along the rough uplands of the west bank. "You will note all the faint white outcroppings, like stumps of teeth along the ridgelines? All sun-bleached sandstone. From which the Castell de Bellver itself was built, quarried from mines in the very hill upon which it sits."

Don Vincente nodded. "So, if such soft stone was ever subject to bombardment by modern cannon—"

Dolor shrugged. "It would be a shattered ruin within an hour."

"How many in its garrison?"

"At last report, approximately fifty within the walls, about that many again manning the ravelins and barbican outside. These will be increased now, of course. Although that change will not be welcome to the Castell's governor."

"Governor? Not commander?"

"No. Bellver's situation is unique." Dolor's lip quirked in what might have been dark humor or genuine annoyance. "Sometime in the fifteenth century, it became the possession of the Carthusian Monks of Valdemossa. Although it is not staffed by them, they assign the Castell its governor, who has control over the garrison."

The way Dolor had put emphasis on the word "garrison" prompted Don Vincente's next question. "The garrison is not very proficient?"

Dolor shrugged. "It is staffed almost completely by Mallorcans. Yes, they are technically soldiers of the Crown, but almost none of them have ever left the island, or been trained and blooded with a real tercio. They are local soldiery. Mostly trustworthy, but not very dependable in a fight, I'm afraid."

"Hence, your resolve to increase the contingent there."

"Yes. By drawing troops from the garrison at San Carlos. Only twenty or so, but that will not please the governor. Not at all."

"I would have expected that he would have seen a larger detachment as an honor, a signification of greater authority."

"No, because the new troops will not be under his command. They will be on detached duty to the Castell, and under your direct authority."

"You put me in a most enviable position, Señor Dolor."

"I do what is necessary, as shall you. You will use the real soldiery from the fort to improve the readiness of Bellver's current garrison. Your men will train with, and provide examples for, the governor's."

"In theory."

"It is your responsibility to make this theory a reality, and quickly, Captain Castro y Papas. If agents of the USE plan on striking again, they will do so with all alacrity; if they wait much longer, they will be endangering the pregnancy of Stone's wife." Dolor moved away from the rail.

"And you, Señor Dolor? Where will you be?"

Dolor stopped and turned to look at the captain. "Wherever I am most needed. I will be at the Castell intermittently. If I am not there, my assistant, Dakis, is likely to be. But I cannot gather and oversee intelligence reports in a hilltop fortress two miles southwest of the viceroy's palace; I must be where ships and roads bring messages. So I will mostly be in Palma."

"How pleasant."

Dolor's eyes held no hint of present or past emotions; Don Vincente believed it conceivable the man had never had any. "I do not tarry in Palma because it is pleasant; I do so because I have only a month to put things in order here. My instructions are to see to the proper incarceration and security of the prisoners and then return to Rome."

"And who will be placed in charge of the situation upon your departure?"

"You, Don Castro y Papas, if you prove reliable and motivated enough. If not, I am sure that some mud-caked, understaffed tercio guarding one of the Holy Roman Empire's surrounded Rhine principalities could make fine use of your skills."

Dolor turned and moved unhurriedly toward the pinnace that was being readied for the first shore party. Don Vincente glared after him.

He almost missed the faint movement sidling up to his right.

"What is it, Ezquerra?" asked the captain without bothering to look over. "Have you come to complain of another bout of sea-sickness?"

The career sergeant shrugged. "I cannot tell if it is seasickness, or simple nausea from being too close to Dolor."

"The man is discomfiting, no question."

"He is abnormal in every particular, Captain—which I can say without fear of punishment in his case, since he holds no military rank."

Don Vincente looked after the black silhouette of Dolor. "Do not assume too much about Señor Dolor, Ezquerra—particularly regarding his ability to do you ill. He may not hold any official rank, he may be abnormal, annoying, and yes, even revolting, but bear this in mind: he is dangerous." Captain Vincente Jose-Maria de Castro y Papas studied the silhouette's easy, economical motions carefully. "Very dangerous."

Frank felt as much as heard the portcullis ram home behind him; it jarred the stones under his feet.

Or, to be more accurate, it jarred the finely cut pink sandstone paving that was arrayed not in a typically crude grid fashion, but in a pattern of faint yet perfect concentric rings. The circular motif was reprised in the almost delicate arches that marked the inner orbit of the stacked, porticoed galleries. Frank stared up through the identical levels, finding them both familiar and alien—and then he knew why: it reminded him of the leaning tower of Pisa, except inside out. And a lot wider. And more squat. But still—

"Señor and Señora Stone, you will come this way."

The sergeant who had spoken to them was a grizzled fellow, at least fifty, and well-scarred. He was as different from the young, diffident gate guards as a mastiff was distinct from dachshunds. He also seemed very annoyed.

Which annoyed Frank, in turn. "Hey, sorry I'm not moving fast enough for you, Sergeant Rock, but getting repeatedly blasted and beaten by you and your buddies hasn't done a lot for my basic fitness level."

The sergeant studied Frank's slight limp. "You will live. Now hurry, or I will have to report your lack of compliance to my superior."

"You mean, the governor?"

"No, Señor Stone. I am not one of the regular guards at Castell de Bellver." Sergeant Rock looked like he had wanted to spit when he uttered the words "regular guards." "I am Sergeant Alarico Garza, here from His Majesty's Fort San Carlos, and I now report to Captain Vincente Jose-Maria de Castro y Papas. With whom, I am told, you have some acquaintance."

"Yeah, you could say that."

Garza frowned. "You are not fond of the captain? I was told that you were on friendly terms."

"Oh, yeah; he's a great friend. Best guy to have around if you're hoping to be betrayed, ambushed, or knocked around. And tell him that if he gets anywhere near me again, I just might have to give his fist another beating with my face."

For a moment, Sergeant Rock was puzzled; then, with great effort, he stifled a grin. Then he simply extended a guiding hand toward the stairway to the second tier gallery.

As Frank hobbled up the stairs, the sergeant hung farther back, giving the couple some room and time to inspect their surroundings.

Which were, frankly, an architectural marvel of extraordinary grace and beauty. When they reached the top step and came out into the open air so that their voices would not echo back to the sergeant, Giovanna grasped Frank's arm a little tighter. "Frank, it is not wise to speak ill of Captain Castro y Papas."

"Why? Because he might beat me up? Oh, wait a minute. He already did that. And for no reason."

"Frank," hissed Giovanna. "I have not seen you so stubborn. Can you not believe what I told you about Castro y Papas?"

"You expect me to believe he was doing me a favor when he beat the crap out of me?"

She sighed. "Frank, one of the reasons I love you is that you are so good a man, you do not readily see or understand the evil that runs deep in so many others." She looked at him squarely, making sure they were still far enough ahead of the sergeant to be beyond earshot. "Captain Castro y Papas beat you because if he didn't, someone else would have. Maybe one of the new guards brought by that vile little hyena, Dakis. Or maybe Dakis was hoping to do it himself; he looks the type. And of this you may be assured, dear Frank: had one of them beaten you, the injuries you have been affecting since Rome would be quite genuine."

The sergeant called their attention to another staircase leading up. As they began ascending it, Frank let his head droop as
he considered Gia's arguments. When they reached the roof—a
broad, ringlike expanse that sprouted towers from each compass
point—he looked at her. "You really think that's what was going
on? That he had no choice?"

Up here, the wind blew fresh from the bay; his wife's fine,
lustrous hair caught it and flew up like shining raven wings.
"Oh, the captain had a choice, husband. I suspect he would have
been allowed to wash his hands of the indignity of what he was
instructed to do. But then he could not have protected you, Frank.
I tell you this not because I have changed my opinion of Castro
y Papas—I have not—but because you are my husband and I will
not lie to you: he may be our enemy, but I must concede that, in
this, he was being your friend. As strange as that might seem."

"Well, yeah—it seems pretty strange," Frank agreed as he
considered the architecture of the Castell from top to bottom. "I
hate to say it, Gia, but it's kind of hard to see anyone breaking
us out of here. Not even Harry could pull that off."

She nodded. "It is a strong fortress."

Frank assessed the defenses, feeling like he was living a lost
chapter from *The Lord of the Rings*. "A hilltop location that you
can only reach by an overgrown goat-trail. An outlying perimeter of ravelins and an outer gate house, all set well away from
other habitations. A dry moat around the Castell itself, with a
drawbridge and portcullis."

Gia frowned. "Yes, as I said, a strong fortress—but not impreg-
nable. The cart-driver told us that during the peasant revolt last
century, the rebels took the whole Castell—including the lazarette."

"Yeah, but why? Because they had someone on the inside. And
those rebels had a much easier job than a bunch of rescuers will."

"Why? Because there were so many more of the rebels?"

"Well, that too. But the real difference is in timing, Gia."

She frowned.

Frank pointed to the outer gatehouse, then the barbican, then
the drawbridge, then the portcullis, then the single narrow stair-
cases that provided sole access to each successive level. "Look at
all those different chokepoints. Each one is going to cost rescuers
time and bodies. And generally, if you need to go quickly, you
lose more bodies. But however fast they go, Gia, they won't be

able to get to us before our jailors do. So what does the endgame look like?"

She nodded. "The last of the rescuers break through the final barrier and find us held by the Spanish, with cocked guns at our heads."

"Exactly. A hopeless standoff. The rescuers can't move without destroying the very people they came to rescue. And by that time, other Spanish forces will be inbound, cutting off any chance of retreat." He shook his head. "There may be no getting out of here, Gia." He took her hands. "I'm sorry I got you into all this. I never expected—"

"You will be silent, Frank Stone, before you say anything more profoundly stupid than you already have. I am here because I love you, and if asked to choose my future a thousand times over, each time, I would choose this one I share with you. So, that is settled. All that remains is for you to get to work."

"To work?"

"On your book, Frank. Just because you are imprisoned does not mean you cannot fight back; indeed, this is when it is most important to do so. And in you, beloved husband, I have seen the promise that indeed, the pen will be far mightier than the sword. Have you made any progress with the book?"

"Well, some."

"Must I guess, or will you deign to tell me?"

"Sure. It's just that I'm—well, I'm kind of embarrassed. I'm not really a writer, you know—"

"Frank, any one is a writer who chooses to be. To be a good writer, well, that is a different matter. But if you can simply write as you speak, you will be a good writer. Possibly much more than merely good. But tell me: what idea has been emerging?"

"Well, it's kind of a parody and an homage all in one."

"Good, good: a work with many layers, with allusion to other masterpieces."

"Uh...yeah. And it's set in a time of warfare and struggle between good and evil."

"Excellent. It is a heroic tale, borrowing its scope from the Greeks and Romans. And the main characters? Who are they?"

"Well...they're hobbits."

Gia blinked, then frowned. "They are who?"

"Not who: what. They're hobbits. They're kind of little people with hairy feet who live in holes in the ground and..." He saw her look. "You don't like it."

Gia floundered for a reply. "Well...it is not Homer or Virgil," she stuttered lamely.

"No. But, well, now that I think of it, yeah, it is. Kind of. See, these hobbits are part of a long saga called *The Lord of the Rings*. It's filled with noble lords and ancient demons and all that kind of stuff, but the real heroes are the hobbits because—well, because they're just the little people who live through war. Like all us little people who have to figure out ways to survive, but also keep goodness alive in our hearts, while the world around us is plunged into war, and dominated by evil."

Gia's smile had returned; it was now wider than ever. "My genius Frank; a book for the working classes. And one which will brighten the eyes of children, even as it calls forth tears of sorrow and fellow-feeling from strong men with great hearts." She flung her arms around his neck. "My genius. And look what you have for your daily inspiration: look!" She pointed out over the eastern ramparts where they had come to stand.

For a moment, they forgot the perils and uncertainties of their existence as prisoners. Gulls wheeled about the blue dome of the sky; upon the glimmering bay, lateen-rigged boats—tiny at this distance—scudded to and from, milling about the skirts of the ochre-stoned edifices with which Palma faced the sea. From this height, and distance, any blemishes were invisible: the world was a panorama of story-book perfection.

"Wow," said Frank after a full minute.

"*Bella*," breathed Giovanna.

"Come," said Sergeant Rock, behind them.

They turned; he pointed over a walled walkway to the north-ernmost tower, a thinner spire that rose up three stories above the roof, two above the tops of the other towers. "Your room is there, in the lazarette. You will be pleased to know that it was once the bedchamber of the kings of Mallorca."

"And what became of the kings of Mallorca?" asked Frank.

"They resisted the dominion of Madrid; they are no more."

"Sounds like a warning, not a history lesson."

The sergeant shrugged. "You may consider it to be both. You will come. Now."

# Chapter 36

Vitelleschi rose, standing before the hearth. "The issue before us tonight is that of Grantville's origins: are they satanic or natural? It is crucial that we have high confidence in our answer to this question. The documents of Grantville, and what they claim about both the physical and theological realities of our own world, must have their provenance established. Collectively, they are either the most cunning of all lies, or the most revolutionary of all truths. If true, they may contain inspirations from a loving god, who is reaching a hand from the up-time world into this one."

"And if they are satanic lies," added Wadding, "then they are invitations to oblivion."

"Yes," Vitelleschi agreed with a nod, "it is one or the other, it seems. For if the up-time corpus is one immense conceit, then to give it credence is to eat the fruit of saplings grown from the seeds of Eden's forbidden tree. Cardinal Wadding, you will begin our proceedings."

Wadding nodded, stood—and surprised Sharon by looking at her directly. "I begin with an apology to our host, Ambassador Nichols. Ambassador, my task puts me in a bitter position. I must now repay your protection and hospitality by calling into question the godliness of your very origins and existence. This is not the way Irish guests are taught to honor their hosts." His smile was genuinely regretful, but brief; he turned to face the other clerics.

"And in fact, my apology to the ambassadora leads to my first task: to correct the wild arguments of those who claim that Grantville's citizens are merely a cohort of duplicitous demons which might at any moment cast off their fleshy disguises and reveal their true, infernal natures. This laughably simplistic perception indicates a dangerously insufficient conception of infernal genius. Consider: is it likely that so juvenile a deception would be the best that the Prince of Lies could craft? Has Satan not been the author of mischief so subtle that even God's own angelic servants were corrupted by his poisonous fabulations?"

"I presume you perceive a more suitably insidious plot, Cardinal Wadding?" Vitelleschi inquired.

"Yes. If the Prince of Lies has the power and freedom to construct a town and its inhabitants out of the formless elements, he would populate it with creatures that genuinely believed the memories he breathed into them along with the spark of apparent life. For it is truly said that the most convincing purveyors of lies are those who do not know that they are, indeed, lies.

"Pertinently, I call your attention to Cardinal Mazzare's own radical embrace of toleration for all religions, and his denunciation of war, particularly those waged to combat heresy. I do not doubt Cardinal Mazzare's sincerity when he attests that these were also the teachings of his future Church. But, if he is an unwitting satanic construct, he would naturally believe in these tenets no less intensely than he would believe that his life in the twentieth century was actual, rather than a fabulation implanted in his mind.

"Surely the danger latent in following the doctrinal laxities of Cardinal Mazzare's supposed future are clear to all. The presumption that warfare is an intolerable and that life is sacred above all other things not only places excessive value on our terrestrial existence, but might also be the telltale clue that these tenets are a Trojan horse, not a holy gift. Certainly, the promise of peace would be eagerly embraced by the war-plagued multitudes of this century—but for precisely that reason, we must study this apparent gift most carefully before we take it within the walls of our faith."

Wadding raised a cautionary index finger. "Is there not the brimstone scent of perfidious elegance about this 'gift'? Imagine what it could engender: toleration so great that it becomes indiscriminate; sympathy so profound that it overrides moral judgment. In the name of peace, we might succumb to requests to relax our vigilance, might fail to teach subsequent generations to strictly observe the sacraments and proclaim their faith in the One True Church. If, then, our faith decays into pallid passivity, we would be responsible for the damnation of untold millions, now and in future generations. For upon those multitudes—all unbaptized, unblessed by the grace of the holy sacraments they have forgotten—Satan would smile benignly from behind a hundred façades of serene peace, reveling in how our lack of moral courage today provided him with the opportunity to devour the souls of all the children of men, for all time.

"And how would this chain of events begin? Why, by following the lesson that Cardinal Mazzare seems to have brought from his future: to work uncritically toward the intertwined values of peace and religious tolerance. And what first, fateful step are we now contemplating which would logically take us in that direction? Nothing less than having the Head of the Church Militant, the only living link with Heaven, place himself in the hands of the greatest scourge upon the True Church, Gustav Adolf of Sweden."

Vitelleschi raised a hand. "Cardinal Wadding, in your zeal, you seem to be losing sight of our process here: one issue at a time. The matter of taking refuge with the Swede shall be considered at a later date. Cardinal Mazzare, you have been singularly silent; is there nothing you wish to say in response to Cardinal Wadding?"

Larry rose. "Has Cardinal Wadding finished making his case?"

Wadding stared at Larry. Sharon saw a hint of trepidation flicker through his otherwise steady gaze. "I am mostly done."

Larry started to sit. "I will wait until you are fully done."

Vitelleschi held up his hand again. "Cardinal Mazzare, I find your reluctance to respond to Cardinal Wadding's points more worrisome than his overzealous exposition of them."

Mazzare spread his hands. "Father-General Vitelleschi, I have not interrupted Cardinal Wadding's arguments out of a sense of both propriety and order. If I were to immediately rebut every assertion with which I disagree, we would still be debating his first point, I fear."

Vitelleschi's thin, wrinkled lips puckered. Urban lifted his hand, apparently to scratch his nose, but the light in his eyes told what he was really doing: hiding the smile he had been unable to suppress.

"So," continued Larry, "I will wait until Cardinal Wadding has finished explicating the primary points of his case. And I will humbly hope that he will show the same patience and forbearance when I present mine."

Wadding's face momentarily became sour.

Ruy turned to Sharon, using that change of position to conceal his own smile. "Your up-time parish priest is quite clever; he has outflanked one of the preeminent debaters of this day."

"What do you mean?" asked Sharon.

"I mean he has used Wadding's own argumentational mannerisms to influence the criteria upon which they will both be judged. Because if the Irish cardinal now interrupts Cardinal Mazzare, it is the Irishman who will be seen as the lesser debater."

Sharon, who congratulated herself on having a good grasp of the principles of argument, grudgingly conceded that she just didn't have the formal training in it to perceive the finer points that well-educated down-timers did. "Okay, I'll bite; why would interrupting show Wadding to be the lesser debater?"

"Because, my love, Cardinal Mazzare has subtly thrown down the gauntlet of true rhetorical sophistication. He is implying that his argument, if presented in toto, will be stronger than Wadding's. After all, he felt no need to interrupt Wadding. So now, if Wadding interrupts Mazzare, it implies that the Irishman's argument is fundamentally weaker, since only he needs to disrupt his adversary's presentation. And so, it is more likely that Mazzare can now make his case without disruption. Masterful."

Sharon nodded, staring at Ruy. "Wow," she said. "Maybe you should be the ambassador, not me."

"What a novel idea—having a Spaniard as the representative of the USE."

"You know what I mean."

"Yes, I do. And I still disagree. I may be well-versed in my century's traditions of debate, my heart, but I do not have your patience, nor your fine mix of practicality and compassion."

Vitelleschi was staring at Wadding. "Cardinal Wadding, will you be able to extend to Cardinal Mazzare the same discursive courtesy he has extended to you?"

Wadding had the wary look of an old fox that knew himself to be in the vicinity of an unseen trap. "I cannot presently see any reason why I would need to interrupt my colleague." Wadding's caveat—"presently"—was not lost on any of his listeners, judging from the collection of raised eyebrows.

Mazzare nodded at his Irish colleague and turned to the rest of the clerics. "I must begin by pointing out that Father Vitelleschi's charge to me—to prove Grantville's origins beyond a 'reasonable doubt'—places the burden of proof upon the accused, not the accuser. That I need only prove it beyond a 'reasonable' doubt, while helpful, is still problematic: there is no criterion for distinguishing what is reasonable from that which is unreasonable. And this is a most urgent definitional requirement since I must adduce positive, rather than negative, proofs."

Vitelleschi frowned. "I am unfamiliar with your terms. What is the difference between a negative proof and a positive proof?"

"Father-General, in my world, there was a philosopher named Karl Popper who averred that the only true proof was negative proof. By this, he meant it is possible to conclusively *disprove* an assertion, but almost impossible to conclusively *prove* one.

"Allow me to furnish an example: I propose the hypothesis that all stones float. It is easy enough to conclusively prove that hypothesis wrong. We walk to the nearest body of water and cast in stones. As soon as the first stone sinks, the assertion is disproven. This is negative proof.

"I then follow with a seemingly logical extension of the first hypothesis: I propose that all rocks will sink. We perform the same test, and achieve the same result. But we have not conclusively proven this second hypothesis, even though it seems to demonstrate the exact same property of all rocks: that they sink."

Vitelleschi nodded. "Of course; the first can be easily disproven by a single test, but the second can only be proven by an impossibly omniscient observer who would have to be present every time a rock is cast into water. Consequently, the hypothesis—however strong and unexceptioned—cannot be considered *proven* as a truly universal law of nature."

"Just so, Father-General. And in the case of investigating the origins of Grantville, this distinction is not a sophistry, but a crucial caveat. Specifically, there is simply no way to conclusively demonstrate that Grantville's origins are entirely mundane, because the task ultimately requires positive proof, not negative proof. Which means that some doubt will always remain. Therefore, insofar as I must eliminate all 'reasonable doubt,' you might say that I do not start from a clean slate, but begin with an unavoidable deficit."

Vitelleschi nodded carefully. "Perhaps so. But what may be done?"

"Simply this: in an issue where all logic and likelihood points in a single direction, let us agree that this constitutes the removal of reasonable doubt. So, if the viability of one of my arguments—or Cardinal Wadding's—depends upon rejecting most of what we hold true about our Church, or goes against the deductive cut of Occam's razor, I would humbly ask that those arguments not be validated. Let us not stand the world on its side to explain how a fly may remain affixed to a vertical wall."

Vitelleschi's face was utterly rigid, which Sharon swiftly and surely interpreted: he was resolved not to show the degree to which Mazzare's reasoning and erudition had pleased him. "Your point is well taken, Cardinal Mazzare. Please begin."

Mazzare bowed slightly. "Logically, if a person asserts that Grantville was constructed by Satan, they must also believe that the Devil either has the power to create life—meaning, the power to create its up-time inhabitants—or he has the power to shape us from either demons or the souls of the damned. In the latter case, Satan must also have the power to replace each soul's genuine memories with false ones. This violates all canonical theology, which holds that Satan does not possess such sweeping powers.

"But of course, if either of these circumstances proves to be true, it not only demolishes some foundations of canonical theology, but obligates you to kill all of Grantville's original inhabitants. Logically, that same campaign of demon-extermination must be extended to include all the offspring of the hundreds of unions that have now taken place between them and down-timers. Your reflex toward mercy might prompt you to spare such unwitting half-demons, but scripture leaves no room for debate: 'ye shall not suffer them to live among ye.'"

Sharon exchanged wide-eyed looks with Ruy. Larry was certainly gambling big with that point, because if he lost...

Mazzare was already moving on. "Let us turn to the material aspects of Grantville, and in particular, its library. You are all familiar with its detailed information on advanced mathematics, science, and engineering.

"However, for every tome of information and insight, there are a thousand utterly banal records buried in every filing cabinet in the town. Now, the Devil may be renowned for being as wise as the serpent, able to wait long years for the final corruption of his prey, but constructing this edifice of flawlessly consistent paperwork would require the patience and demeanor of a slow-witted stockroom clerk. So I ask, according to your own representations of Satan's nature, how and when did he acquire the virtues of humility and patience necessary to construct a conceit so intricately seamless, and yet so numbingly dull? That is almost as great a mystery as the one cited more often: how could data from Grantville be of infernal origin, since it has already promoted both edification and peace in these dark times, and promises to be of greater assistance with each passing year? Would a Prince of Darkness include such beneficences in his construct?"

"Most assuredly, he would." Wadding interjected.

Vitelleschi's left eyebrow raised. "Why, Cardinal Wadding?"

"For the same reason he would give the fabricated persons of Grantville belief in their memories: to make the underlying conceit all the more convincing. The arch-fiend would indeed foresee that many of us presume that there can be no goodness or grace in his creations. Consequently, he would, on the contrary, embed small elements of just such goodness and grace in order to create the perfect illusion that the town was *not* a creation of his."

"And how do you respond to this, Cardinal Mazzare?" asked Vitelleschi.

"I think that Cardinal Wadding must propose this alternative in order to preserve the narrow thread of deduction by which his original argument hangs. For Grantville to be a creation of the Devil, any virtues associated with it must be a stalking horse to conceal deeper layers of perfidy. Of course, one must then wonder why Satan created a town where the young women are clad so scandalously, to down-time eyes. I can hear the *apologia* already: this perplexing mixture of virtue and vice creates an optimally convincing reality by adding an authentic touch of confounding inconsistency.

"However, a cursory study of the library's record of the social and historical trends of up-time America will provide you with simple, culturally consistent explanations. And while you are there, you should also look up the term 'conspiracy theorists.' Their presumptions of a world controlled by *sub rosa* star-chambers resonate with the satanic plots being proposed here today. Both ignore the common-sense limit of every conspiracy: the more ponderous its originating casuistries and implausibilities, the more likely it is to collapse under its own weight. May I resume my own presentation, Father-General?"

Vitelleschi nodded.

"Cardinal Wadding's argument also necessarily presumes that God not only permits Satan an uncanonical measure of power, but that he is permitted equally unprecedented knowledge of both natural phenomena and the future. After all, in our library, down-timers have found precise forewarnings of floods and epidemics, have learned methods to test the fossil record of earlier days, have schooled themselves in novel chemical reactions and natural proper-ties, have found lost cities, discovered unknown islands, reclaimed lost languages, located unsuspected resources. All these revelations must, according to Cardinal Wadding and others, be prophecies and sorcery pouring forth from the bowels of Hell itself.

"Allow me to unsheathe Occam's razor. How do we reconcile these presumptions with the Church's doctrine that, just as Satan is unable to create genuine life *ex nihilo*, that there are also lim-its upon both his knowledge and how much of it he may share? For if he is not so limited, then why has he not used a 'ruse' like Grantville before?

"The only one logical answer—that until now, such a 'ruse' was not a winning strategy—only leads to an even more thorny question: what has changed? Why *is* the 'ruse' of Grantville a winning strat-egy now? Indeed, how can it be, since discussions about Grantville almost always stimulate speculation upon Satan's literal presence in this world. This *benefits* the Church; for a century, priests have wor-ried that the increase in secularism will cause the laity to forget the reality of the Devil. That trend has dramatically reversed—thanks to the Devil himself, if we are to believe Cardinal Wadding.

"In conclusion, to accept Grantville as a diabolical creation, one must be willing to overturn all the Church's canonical and traditional understandings of the powers and prerogatives of both God and the Devil."

Ruy blew out an appreciative breath. "Cardinal Mazzare is quite a formidable philosopher. To say nothing of subtle. Are you sure he is not a Jesuit?"

Larry had evidently overhead Ruy's more-than-*sotto voce* aside to his wife; Mazzare smiled as he said to Vitelleschi, "Father-General, I have one personal observation." He turned in a circle, making eye-contact with his various listeners. "I see before me a pope who paid one up-timer the supreme compliment of officiating at his wedding. I see a seasoned Spanish veteran who has married an up-timer himself. I see a father-general who kindly encouraged an up-timer—me—to address the papal court convened on the matter of Galileo. I see a young cardinal who generously invited an up-time ambassador into his Roman palace, and who has since been happy to find that hospitality repaid in this desperate hour. And I see one last cardinal"—he turned and smiled at Wadding—"who began today's proceedings with an apology for calling into question the humanity—the *presumed* humanity—of his host, that same ambassador."

"And your point is?" muttered Vitelleschi gruffly, evidently discomfited by Larry's reference to his well-concealed kindness.

Mazzare indicated the entirety of his audience. "My point is that none of the down-timers in this room—religious or otherwise— would have behaved as they did if they deeply, truly believed that the beings they were blessing, hosting, marrying, entreating, or thanking were demons or the damned in disguise. I know the moral fiber of the persons in this room as well as I know anything, and none of them would be so remiss in their duty to God, nor so hypocritical, that they would willingly consort with agents of Hell. In short, whatever you may say, suspect, or argue here, your actions have already rendered the verdict of your instincts: that we up-timers are frail, flawed humans no different from you except that we are now orphans in time."

The room was quiet for a long moment, then Wadding coughed politely. "Presuming all this to be true, it still does not preclude the possibility that Grantville may have merely been *brought* to this time and place by the power of Satan."

Mazzare shrugged. "This is true. But the distinction in that alternative is very great indeed, Cardinal Wadding. For if we were only *transported* here by Satan, then we are not his constructs at all; we truly are from the future, and the contents of Grantville are an authentic record of it."

"It is also possible," persisted Wadding, "that the instincts of every down-timer in this room have been misled, that Satan *has* created the perfect illusion."

Mazzare smiled again. "If the cream of the Church's intellect, as well as the common people, can be so completely duped, then the real miracle is that Satan has not used that skill to triumph long before now. To cite an axiom of my time, you can fool all of the people some of the time, and can fool some of the people all of the time, but you can't fool all of the people all of the time. If Satan had such powers of deception, there would never have been any hope for humanity."

Vitelleschi waited. When no debate ignited, he lifted his palms, inviting "Any who have questions may ask them."

Sharon was surprised when Ruy stood. "Learned Eminences, will you allow a poor, ignorant soldier to ask a question?"

Vitelleschi raised an eyebrow. "First, you are none of the things you say, Don Ruy. And second, I did say *any* who have questions. So ask."

"Your Eminences, Father-General, you may certainly presume I have made my own determination that Grantville is not a creation of Satan."

He looked back briefly at Sharon, who was shocked by the sudden gravity of his smile. *So this is what Ruy looks like when he is very, very serious.*

"And yet," he continued, "I am not without my reservations. Cardinal Mazzare, you raised the issue of the knowledge that has come to us from Grantville. I have read many of your books. One author—a Swiss by the name of Nietzsche—has, in particular, troubled me."

Larry's eyes became very grave. "I'm not surprised."

"In particular, I am worried by his famous assertion that 'God is dead.' I understand that he was not literally claiming that divinity had recently expired, but rather, that God had never existed, except in the human imagination: that the idea of God was how early man explained the inexplicable phenomena that surrounded him."

Mazzare nodded. "That is as good a summary as I've ever heard, Ruy."

"His Eminence flatters an old soldier's stunted powers of insight. However, it also seems that this philosopher claimed that Man's increasing knowledge and command of natural phenomena caused 'God's death.' So I ask you: are we not seeing the beginning of that same process in this world? In short, how long before the majority of down-timers make a chorus with this Nietzsche, saying also that 'God is dead'?"

Larry Mazzare smiled slowly, fondly, at Ruy. "Ruy Sanchez, you are indeed a wily old soldier. And I freely admit that what you fear could transpire. But it was coming, anyhow; had we not arrived and changed your history, your outcome would have matched our own.

"But I believe that our arrival may have, in fact, changed that. I think that this world may do better than ours did in handling this challenge to faith. The trial came upon us up-timers slowly, and faith decayed inside us over the centuries, like a citadel falling to a long, slow siege. But here, where this century's eyes of undiminished faith are abruptly shown the natural wonders unveiled by Grantville's science, I think it likely that those same eyes will see that God is more alive than ever. How much more astounding is the wonder of God's design when we see the elegant beauty of His handiwork in the microscopic structures of a leaf, a snowflake?"

Ruy nodded. "I have thought—and hoped—this too. Now, we look into a stagnant puddle and discover a teeming universe of animalcules. We look up and discover not a closed system, but an infinity so vast that its size defies the human mind."

Wadding frowned mightily. "Yes, and the same science that reveals these wonders is also the enabler of oblivion, of 'atomic weapons,' as I believe you called them, Cardinal Mazzare. What dark fruit of human hubris could be more pleasing to Satan, whose imprisonment in Hell fills him with burning envy of, and hatred for, the clean, fertile world of our Creator? How elegant and delicious a victory for him if he can tempt man to build weapons that can destroy this lesser Eden, can reduce God's gift to ashes and ruin."

Larry Mazzare nodded soberly. "I could not agree with you more, Cardinal Wadding. But science, and the technology that arises from it, is neither good nor evil. It is a lens, whereby the intents and hopes—both noble and petty—of its human wielders are magnified. Therefore, atomic weaponry also poses humankind the ultimate test of self-control, of the triumph of peace and grace over wrath and sin."

Ruy's eyes did not leave Mazzare. "As you yourselves successfully demonstrated toward the end of your twentieth century."

Wadding frowned. "Don Ruy, that was but one crisis averted. The problem with such power, such weapons, is that one mistake is a final mistake. They are like the apple in Eden; they wait, eternally, for human frailty to induce a momentary lapse of reason or resolve—for that is all it takes to undo eternity: a momentary lapse."

"True, Your Eminence," nodded Ruy. "But I learned in my catechisms—and again, reading the resolutions that arose out of the Council of Trent—that the Lord our God never permits Satan to tempt or deceive us past our individual capacity to resist. It is a central tenet of the concept of free will, is it not?"

Larry Mazzare could not keep the sudden, bright smile off his face. "Ruy Sanchez de Casador y Ortiz, I think it is you who should be doing my job. What do you think, Cardinal Wadding?"

Who was, strangely enough, smiling also. "I think an old soldier has just reminded an old priest how important the simplest truths of our faith are. I am in your debt, Don Ruy."

Vitelleschi nodded primly. "Are the arguments and questions concluded? Very well. My recommendation to His Holiness are as follow: Cardinal Wadding's warning that the Devil might have transported the town of Grantville to our time cannot be wholly discounted. However, I find that the arguments supporting the assertion that the whole town is a satanic creation to be well beyond the bounds of credibility. As Cardinal Mazzare points out, the magnitude of such a manifestation as Grantville, both physical and intellectual, far exceed those limits that we understand God to place upon satanic action. Cardinal Mazzare also argues—convincingly—that the arch-fiend stands to lose more from such a florid display of his power than he stands to gain. This does not constitute proof positive, but it does answer all reasonable doubts. Consequently, I hereby inform our Holy Father, Pope Urban VIII, that I can find no valid grounds for declaring Grantville a satanic construct."

Urban nodded once. "I humbly thank both advocates for their spirited and learned address of the issue." He raised his chin. "Father-General Vitelleschi, we shall proceed with the further inquiries as soon as it is convenient for you and our esteemed advocates. And I hope that our lay auditors"—he shot an impish glance in the direction of Ruy and Sharon—"shall be able to attend all our sessions, since it seems that, as ever, God sends his most important reminders through the most unexpected messengers."

Ruy bowed deep thanks and sat.

When Urban looked away, Sharon grabbed his arm and kissed the side of Ruy's still-serious face.

"To what do I owe the ambrosial drop of Heaven upon my cheek?" he asked.

"Well, why do you think, you wonderful fool?" Sharon hugged his arm. "Because you done good, honey; you done good."

Giulio burst into the room loudly, as was his wont. "Rombaldo!"

"Yes, Giulio?"

"Valentino's group—they have found our agents. Or rather, their bodies."

Unfortunate that they were dead, but the two had been missing for too long for any other outcome to be probable. "Where did Valentino find them?"

Giulio rushed over to the map on the table; the pins denoting search teams were scattered across Venice and Lombardy. He stared intently for a moment and then jabbed a finger: "Here, in this town just south of Vicenza."

"How were they killed?"

"By sword or knife."

"How long ago?"

"At least a week, maybe more. The town fathers were keeping the whole affair quiet until they could figure out how to proceed."

Meaning that the town fathers had prudently held off reporting a killing that did not seem random, and yet had unclear motivations. In their experience, that would signify a covert conflict between greater powers, a conflict in which they did not want to become involved.

"Very well. Have the other nearby teams converge upon this spot. Send word by our fastest riders: they have ten days to rendezvous with Valentino at this site."

"And after that?"

"After that, Giulio, we let slip the leash and let our hounds run a pope to ground."

"*Under* ground, that is," quipped Giulio broadly, "six feet under ground, to be exact."

Rombaldo forced himself to smile. "Yes. Now, send the word; every minute we lose increases the chance that he will escape."

# Chapter 37

Estuban Miro turned and saw that the xebec had closed to within three hundred fifty yards. "Soon now," he said loudly, over the chop of the oars and the rush of the *scialuppa*'s bow-wake.

In the stern, Harry Lefferts nodded. "It's going to be close," he shouted back, squinting into the sun.

Miro followed his gaze. They were drawing close to the island of Monte Cristo, which, according to Harry, was completely different from the one made famous by the book of some up-time French author. The real Monte Cristo rose out of the Tyrrhenian Sea like a rough pyramid of scrub-covered granite. He saw no dramatic castles in sight; the only structures on the island were the ruins of the monastery of San Mamilliano, in which they had established their base-camp two days ago.

Some of the Piombinesi, who were now adjusting the *scialuppa*'s battered lateen sail, had been somewhat familiar with the island. It was technically part of the extended principality of Piombino, although it remained abandoned and almost entirely unvisited, except by ships in such desperate need of fresh water that their captains were willing to brave chance encounters with pirates who frequented it for the same reason. Two of the Piombinesi had been fairly well-acquainted with its small inlets, particularly the one toward which they were heading now: Cala Maestra.

"The fun is going to start soon," drawled Harry who had turned to inspect the xebec.

Miro nodded. Masses of pirates swarmed on her deck; threats and curses in half a dozen languages reached hoarsely over the waves. They shook cutlasses, scimitars, and a remarkably diverse assortment of firearms in the direction of the small fishing boat, and several of their number were busily setting swivel guns into pintle mounts on the port-side rail. "How many do you estimate, Harry?"

Lefferts, blessed with 20/15 vision, squinted again. "They're milling around so much it's hard to be sure, but I think our first estimate through the binoculars was pretty accurate. There are about twenty manning the sails and lines, about three times that number ready and eager to dig out our hearts with the points of their swords."

One of the Piombinese rowers obviously understood enough English to get the gist of Harry's remark; he retched, and then leaned more urgently to his oar. The man beside him on the bench—one of the four crewmen they'd taken on from the *barca-longa*—poked him with an elbow and motioned for him to maintain a steady stroke.

Harry came forward, leaned closer to Miro so he did not have to raise his voice above the wind and water. "Good thing you brought some of the other crew with us."

Miro shrugged. "It is common practice in convoys, particularly when some ships have crew that have never faced pirates before. You mix some men with experience in with those; the example of the veterans steadies the beginners. Or so one hopes." He smiled at Harry.

Harry was staring at his oilcloth-wrapped SKS, stowed out of sight beneath the stern-most thwart. "Well, so far, your voice of Mediterranean experience has been pretty much on target, Estuban." He jutted a chin at the xebec. "You called their course to within a few degrees, once we picked up their trail at Elba."

Miro shrugged again. "No profound foresight was required. The wild tales we heard in the wharf-side taverna at Marciano Marina had one element in common: when the two Spanish *galliots* met the Algerine off Elba, the pirate did not run, but gave them a brief fight. There are only two reasons pirates fight: because their prey is very weak, or because they want—or need—something very badly. Between them, the *galliots* were probably carrying at least one hundred twenty Spanish soldiers, yet not an ounce of treasure.

And Elba has been so frequently raided by Algerines these past five years, that it doesn't have anything left that's worth taking."

Harry nodded. "Except fresh water. And when the Spanish drove them farther west into the Tuscan archipelago, they had to head to the last watering hole at Isola Pianosa. Where they got chased away again, just like our Piombinesi guessed."

Miro shrugged. "Chased away—or interrupted. There's enough of a garrison on Pianosa that a quick run to shore to fill a few dozen skins was probably all the pirates could risk. Which meant that they needed to head somewhere else to really fill their water barrels."

"And there we are off Pianosa, waiting for them to do just that." Harry nodded appreciatively. "Estuban, I think your plan will work out fine if we manage to do just one more thing."

"What's that?"

Lefferts grinned. "Survive." He returned to the stern, running his hand along a tarp-shrouded bulk covering the aft port quarter of the small fishing boat.

Miro nodded to himself. So far, so good. The pirates, unable to fully replenish their water casks at Pianosa, had done what they often did: they set out to follow the prevailing wind twenty miles southeast to Monte Cristo. But even as they rounded Pianosa's westernmost headland, Punta Libeccio, to begin their journey, they discovered that Dame Fortune was finally smiling upon them; just five miles out, and lying directly along their intended course to the springs on Monte Cristo, was a fishing boat.

Miro had thought he might have to brisk the *scialuppa*'s sails about on the horizon, just to be sure of getting their attention. But the pirates had needed no such enticements; the Algerine had come on with a will, all three lateen sails swelling out, as if straining to reach the little fishing boat ahead of the rest of the xebec.

To whet their appetite for the kill, and to make their speedy closing of the ship-to-ship gap seem natural, Miro had instructed his crew to undo two sets of the lacings that held the *scialuppa*'s own lateen-rigged sail to its gaff. That modification nicely mimicked the look and effect of damage to the triangular sail, which even now flapped fitfully up near the gaff tip, spilling wind.

The Algerine had maneuvered as anticipated. Enjoying the windward position, she used some of her superior speed to move out from a stern chase and set herself up on the fishing boat's starboard aft quarter. This allowed the Algerine to shepherd the *scialuppa* closer against Monte Cristo, on their port side. And if the fishing boat now tried fleeing into the open water to starboard, she'd be putting herself directly in the path of the faster xebec, which would be sure to cut her off.

Miro watched the range close, reassessed their course, and said, as Harry came back from peering under the tarp at the rear of the boat, "They mean to chase us into Cala Maestra. I'm sure of it, given the way they're starting to crowd us now."

"Well, sure, Estuban; they know these waters, too."

Miro smiled. "If they didn't, I'm not sure how well this plan would work." He noticed that the Piombinesi amongst the rowers were starting to push the pace against the resistance of the crew from the *barca-longa*. "Steady pace, not too hard," Miro ordered calmly. "You'll have need of your strength in a bit."

Harry, distracted by a rough mechanical sputter from beneath the tarp hanging over the aft port quarter, now looked back up the mast to where the halyard attached to the boom. "So is our rigged rigging ready?"

"Indeed it is," answered Miro, who, making sure his back was completely to the Algerine, slipped his binoculars out of their case and focused on where the inlet's high, hump-backed southern headland—Punta Maestra—rose up out of the water. The naked weather-worn rocks at its lower fringe quickly disappeared beneath the scrub growth that steadily increased in density up the slope. He tracked the lenses farther up the side of the headland, carefully studying every shrub and rock-cast shadow until he found what he was looking for at its crest: a pair of binocular lenses looking back at him.

"Does Don Estuban see us, Colonel?" asked Orazio Porfino, a young relative of the Piombinese captain Aurelio. In this case, a relative from a very distant branch of their tortuously intertwined family trees.

"I imagine so," responded Thomas North, "since he's smiling, now. Are we ready, Mr. Porfino?"

"Yes sir, all ready."

Thomas grunted. Perhaps they were ready. And perhaps, if he looked up, he'd see a winged pig fly past. But scanning down the slope, he could see nothing amiss—which meant that he saw nothing other than shrubs, rocks, and shadows. He raised his binoculars to quickly scan the lesser slope on the opposite, northern side of the Cala Maestra inlet. Nothing to be seen there, either. Hmm. Well, so far, no one had cocked up the plan. But then again, the day was young.

North leaned backward carefully, staying well within the shadow of the long pillow of rock which crested the signal point of the headland and which he had made his command post. Thomas' slight change in position afforded him a view into the much smaller inlet that flanked the Punta Maestra on its south side, the Cala Santa Maria inlet. The water was a lighter blue, since the inlet was shallower and narrower—but was still large enough to conceal the crowded *barca-longa*, and the more normally crewed *gajeta* just behind her.

Looking up at him from the *barca-longa* was a very white face with very red hair and beard: Owen Roe O'Neill, watching for the next signal. Around Owen were all the present members of the Wrecking Crew—save Harry—and Owen's own Wild Geese. The running crew were well supplemented with Piombinese fishermen, all gesticulating, talking—but, with a look from Dr. Connal, they fell silent, shushing each other fiercely. All of which North saw as a mime-show; from this distance, the only sounds were the waves and the wind moaning softly through the scrub.

Owen's face never looked away.

North nodded and looked over his shoulder at the approaching *scialuppa* and the xebec angling in from the open water, which either meant to push the smaller boat upon the rocks or into the Cala Maestra inlet. He looked back down toward the *barca-longa*, speaking over his shoulder to his adjutant: "Four minutes or less, now, Mr. Porfino. Show Colonel O'Neill two green pennons."

"Yes, sir," and the young Piombinese did as he was told.

Owen nodded, gave a sharp order. In the bows of the *barca-longa*, one white and one black pennon were raised in answer.

"Message received and understood," translated Orazio.

"Very well. Is everything else in readiness, Mr. Porfino?"

"Yes, sir. Our sniper just signaled from his blind across the Cala Maestra; he's waiting for our signals, sir."

North nodded his acknowledgement and raised his binoculars to take one last look at Miro and Lefferts.

✧　　✧　　✧

Miro replaced his binoculars in their case, and turned. The pirate was only two hundred yards off, now, and gaining rapidly.

"Signor Miro," said the senior sailor at the tiller, "we have no choice; the Algerine will push us on the rocks if we do not veer to port, toward Cala Maestra."

As it to encourage compliance with that navigational imperative, Miro heard two pops above the chop of oars and the rustle of the faltering sail. Puffs of smoke marked the sounds' origins on the xebec's long stern overhang; a moment later, two splashes marred the swells approximately ten yards starboard of the *scialuppa*'s stern.

"They're firing," commented a fisherman/rower redundantly, sweat starting out on his lip. Next to him, one of the veteran crew from the *barca-longa* rolled his eyes and simply hunched lower over his oar. Within moments, the other Piombinese fishermen were all aping the actions of the combat-experienced sailors of the Adriatic, except that their eyes were still wide and desperate. But they'd hold together for another few minutes—which was all that was required.

Orazio's voice was tense. "The *scialuppa* is entering the inlet now, sir. The xebec is a minute behind, no more."

North nodded sharply. "Time to show Colonel O'Neill the red flag, Mr. Porfino. Let's get our bull charging toward the ring." He raised his up-time starter's whistle, clamped it between his teeth and watched the xebec bear down upon the *scialuppa*.

"Colonel O'Neill! A red—"

"I see it, Turlough. Captain, get us moving. Best speed."

As two halyards creaked in unison and the yards tilted to catch what breeze they could, the oars, six on each board, rose to readiness, and then, at the order of the coxswain, dipped down and cut deep into the gentle swells of the Cala Santa Maria inlet.

The *barca-longa* surged against the current and wind, and began making northwest for the southern tip of the Punta Maestra headland.

Three musket balls whined off the rocky slope that marked the Cala Maestra inlet's northern extent. Another one went through the sail, not more than two feet over their ducked heads. Miro checked the rear: Harry was smiling forward at him, hands ready on the tarp. "Steersman," shouted Miro above the oars, wind, and flap of the luffing sail, "as the rowers bring us into the Cala Maestra, keep us within five yards of the rocks on the northern side."

"What? Why?"

"Hugging the side of the inlet will conceal us for a few seconds."

Just then the sail began to luff less, sagging instead as they passed into the lee of the northern slope and the wind began to die. *Well, nothing to lose and no time to waste*, thought Miro, who reached up, yelled "Watch out!" and tugged on the lead line of the closer of the two knots belaying the yard's halyard.

With the knot undone, the yard suddenly had four feet of slack; it fell swiftly, stopping within five feet of the deck. The lateen fell in folds, mostly over the bow. A loud cheer went up from the xebec just as the *scialuppa*'s course took it out of the pirate's line of sight.

"Oars, all speed; get us distance!" Miro shouted. "Pilot, prepare to bring us about to leave the same way we came in." He looked aft toward Lefferts. "Harry, it's all your show, now. Pull the tarp and wait for my signal."

As Miro's small boat surged forward, North watched the xebec add oars to full sails and angle toward Cala Maestra as well. But the Algerine's course had her set to enter the inlet about forty yards south of where the *scialuppa* had run in, thereby keeping to the deeper water. As she came within eighty yards of the foot of the Punta Maestra, she heeled over hard to port, clearly meaning to come about as tightly as possible in order to bear down upon the *scialuppa* and cut off her retreat by straddling the mouth of the inlet.

Along the length of the ship's deck, just inboard from the rowers, sure-footed pirates leaned against the turn of the graceful xebec, unable to aim their weapons yet, but ready for the first opportunity. An equal number of them swarmed around the two away-boats that were waiting where the Algerine's waists narrowed into its bow. Casting the lashing aside and preparing to lift the boats over the gunwale, the pirates' hurried, eager actions set their belted swords and pistols swinging.

North saw it all, but only peripherally; he watched, measured the range as the xebec presented its starboard waist full to the slope of the Punta Maestra as it reached the apex of its intended 180 degree turn, and prepared to start back toward the wide part of the inlet's mouth—

"Mr. Porfino," North snapped, "raise the red standard." Then, clenching the neck of the whistle firmly in his teeth, Thomas North blew out a long, rolling shrill.

Coming abreast of the tip of the Punta Maestra headland from the south, Owen Roe O'Neill's sharp ears picked out the sound of North's signal a fraction of a second before anyone else. "There it is! Best speed from the oars. Spikes and hooks at the ready. Boarders, covers off your pieces and blades two inches drawn; we're but a minute away."

And then the sound of firing began.

The lower slopes of the Punta Maestra seemed to roll a wave of thunder at the xebec as it showed them her starboard waist. Thomas North's ten Hibernians, still concealed in the scrub and well-covered by rock outcroppings, began raking the deck of the Algerine at ranges varying from eighty to one hundred and ten yards. The steady *crack-klikka-crack-klikka-crack* of eight black-powder lever-action rifles accompanied faster, sharper reports from two SKS-Ms, each fitted with thirty-round AK 47 magazines.

Both the black powder .40-72 cartridges and the Soviet 7.62 x 39 mm rounds were at their optimum range, and although more rounds missed their targets than hit, there were far, far more bullets in the air than there were pirates to fire at. The pirates did not go down in windrows, but they went down constantly, and within the first five seconds, some started to break for cover, abandoning the lines, the sails, the oars. Even seasoned corsairs, who had learned to brace themselves to withstand at least one murderous blast of grapeshot before leaping over an adversary's gunwales, had little preparation for the unrelenting fire they faced now.

The xebec continued to come about, albeit unevenly—but then the tightness of her turn widened out into lazy arc; the heavy fellow manning the tiller fell away from the handle as three bullets drilled through his thick torso and speckled the deck behind him with blood.

However, the pirates were numerous, and as bad as their

casualties were, there were still more than two score of them, knots of whom were already trying to fight back. Most forgot the *scialuppa* in their eagerness to return fire against the new enemies on the slopes of Punta Maestra, but not all: four made for the portside rail, armed with wheel locks and long-barreled miquelet muskets.

*Damn it*, thought North, who let his binoculars fall loose on their lanyard and snatched up his own SKS, hoping he'd find the range in time....

Harry pulled the tarp off the reconstituted outboard motor that had been borrowed from their dirigible's array of makeshift up-time engines and opened the choke a bit; the engine coughed, then roared, and plumed water up behind the *scialuppa*. "Coming about," he shouted as he angled the engine's handle to starboard.

The prow of the *scialuppa* started coming around steadily to port. But the rowers continued to pull hard, and Harry could feel that their muscles were providing them with additional, and very welcome, speed. Although relatively powerful, the compact outboard motor had been intended to propel dinghies and rowboats, not something as large as a *scialuppa*. They were coming about—faster and more tightly than their enemy could have reasonably expected—but it wasn't going to be fast enough; Harry saw a quartet of pirate marksmen gathering at the xebec's portside rail, which overlooked the open expanse of the Cala Maestra. And the *scialuppa* was the only target in that direction. The range was long—almost a hundred yards—but still...

As the *barca-longa* came around the headland and her lookout could see into the Cala Maestra inlet, the ship's limp lateen sails finally crossed the line of the wind and swelled tentatively. Owen started scrambling forward; they were still hauling as close to the wind as possible, but they'd only accelerate briskly once they began to turn into the inlet, which would bring the northerly wind off their prow and over their portside bow.

"Keep pulling boys, for all you're worth," he shouted as he went along the benches. Eyes forward, he saw the stern of the xebec heave into view around the stony shoulder of the Punta Maestra and thought, *now we've got you, pinned from behind and beside, and not enough room or time to turn out.*

Or maybe they did have enough room and time—or at least, that must have been what the two pirates who leaped to take hold of the tiller believed. They heaved the xebec's rudder back into a tight turn to port. One, glancing over his shoulder, saw the *barca-longa* and screamed something in a swift liquid language that Owen had never heard. But the meaning was clear enough: musket-bearing pirates began streaming toward the protuberant stern overhang that followed the xebec like an elaborately carved afterthought.

"Wrecking Crew," Owen shouted back over the heads of the boarding party in the bows. "you have targets. Clear their poop deck."

Thomas realized, even as he raised the SKS, that if he fired he might well kill his own people. As luck would have it, his own line of fire to the four pirate marksmen taking aim at the *scialuppa* extended onward to the deck of that smaller boat. Miro and Lefferts' men would be safely out of the way in three, maybe four seconds, but that might be too late. Besides, what the hell was the sniper waiting fo—?

From forty yards up the opposed slope of the inlet's northern headland, there was a flash and a viciously sharp report. One of the four pirates at the rail bucked backward a step, then went down, thereby obscuring the high spinal exit wound and the dark blood that was beginning to spread across both sides of his back like a pair of painted wings.

*About time our marksman got into the act*, groused North silently, wishing that it was Lefferts up on the slope: *best sniper among us, by a country mile*. But, being armed with Harry's scoped up-time Remington, the Hibernian who had been given the job was still very well equipped to take down any pirates who might pose an unanticipated threat to the team or its operations. But there were still three pirate musketeers—

—Who fired in a volley even as the sniper's second shot cracked and echoed between the granite walls of the inlet. Another pirate went down, clutching his shoulder. But so had someone in the *scialuppa*. North thought about his binoculars. *If they got either Miro or Harry*—

But he swept up the SKS instead; first things first, now that the *scialuppa* was out of his downrange field of fire. North squeezed the trigger, saw the round send splinters up from the deck a few feet behind the musketeers. *Damn Chinese export ammo; even for Combloc 7.62, it shoots like a rainbow.* As North raised the weapon slightly and let the bead rise a little too high in the sight, then squeezed the trigger again.

Blood spattered outward from the lower back of the pirate on the left. He clutched the rail, his legs sagged, then his knees went—at the same moment that North had finished riding the SKS's recoil back down and cheated over to the right to bring the last corsair into his sights.

His weapon barked in unison with the sniper's Remington; hit from front and back, the last of the four pirate marksmen spun and toppled to the deck.

Thomas grabbed for his binoculars, swept them after the *scialuppa*, looking for—

"Estuban? Estuban?" shouted Harry, his buttocks half off the stern thwart.

Miro's rather round, close-cropped head poked up out of the tangle of sails in the bows, just visible over the back of the slain oarsman.

"I wasn't the unlucky one, Harry; I'm fine. You just keep bringing us around."

"We're around already, heading toward open water."

"Good. Excellent, in fact."

"Yeah. Now, want a piece of advice?"

"Certainly. What is it?"

Harry smiled. "Keep your *own* head down, too, fool!"

As half a dozen pirates swarmed back out across the xebec's stern overhang to fire down into the *barca-longa* that was almost upon them, Donald Ohde, Paul Maczka, and Matija Grabnar raised their shotguns and began the firing-and-pumping sequence that was, more than anything, the combat trademark of the Wrecking Crew. And whereas the high velocity bullets of their other weapons often inflicted surprisingly subtle entry wounds, the twelve-gauge pumps, furnished with double-aught buckshot, left little to the imagination.

Owen had not seen this kind of carnage, this closely, before. As he watched, the left half of one pirate's head simply shredded away in a cloud of red chunks; another lost the fingers of his pistol hand, and the eye that had been peering along the barrel; another's chest rippled outward in a red crescent, a moment before blood and flesh sprayed out of the exit wound on his back, splashing in a wide arc upon the limp sail hanging on the mizzenmast.

"Clear!" shouted Donald.

Owen didn't have time for even one encouraging word. "Get us up tight against her aft quarter!" he shouted over his shoulder at the oarsmen as he edged out onto the prow, from whence he gave new orders: "Hooks and spikes. Weapons ready." He checked the pepperbox in his right hand and drew back the boarding spike in his left.

"You're not boarding amidships?" Donald's voice was doubtful, even above the noise.

"No time," Owen yelled back, swinging and sinking his spike into the hull as the *barca-longa* finally bumped against xebec. "Besides, we'd be between North's riflemen and the pirates. Not a place I want to be. Now, hooks and lines forward; make us fast, and then—when the *sassenach* starts the music—up we go!"

North frowned as he saw O'Neill ready to board the xebec along its starboard aft quarter. It was one of the most dangerous places to board, and comparatively easy to repel. The pirates understood that better than anyone; those who could began flooding back to the stern, weapons ready, savage cries rising up. After having been on the receiving end of so much death and destruction, they were clearly in the mood to begin to reverse the situation.

But, for whatever reason, Owen Roe, while ready, seemed to be holding his men back a bit. They had made fast a pair of grappling lines, but were taking time to gather and ready themselves, almost as if—

North smiled. Owen Roe was a wily bastard of a bog-hopper, after all. Yes, the pirates were indeed rushing to the stern to repel boarders. In fact, so many of the surviving corsairs were rushing in that direction, that they were actually beginning to get in each others' way, bunching up—

"Fire teams!" North roared down the hill. "Supporting fire for our boarders. Now!"

✧    ✧    ✧

Owen Roe O'Neill watched as one of the *barca-longa*'s crew perched on the bows jumped high and swung a tethered boarding hook overhand to sink it into the deck of the xebec's overhang. But as he did, a flat-faced pirate pushed forward; his meaty paw held a hatchet, which was already flashing down.

Owen's crewman watched as the flashing blade severed both the tether and his wrist; only a moment later did he scream and fall into the water. Muskets sputtered from behind him; the *barca-longa*'s own crew was lending a hand. The offending pirate staggered back, a ball creasing his shoulder, but nothing more.

Owen gritted his teeth. He heard the pirates massing near the lip of the stern overhang, just beyond where his people could see—and from which vantage point the pirates had a profound advantage over any number of boarders. *Well, hurry up then, you bloody* Sassenach; *can't you see the target I've made for y—?*

A dark round object, leaking smoke and sparks, went over Owen's head, curving down lazily toward the crowd in the bow of the *barca-longa*.

"Grenade!" Owen yelled—and watched as, with near balletic grace, Paul Maczka of the Wrecking Crew reached up and batted it aside in mid air: the weapon landed in the water with a plop.

And then the fusillade from Punta Maestra began.

"About feckin' time," muttered O'Neill. Then shouting to his boarders: "Go!"

North, intent on saving every round of true up-time ammunition that he could, did not contribute to the fire that rolled out from the rocky slopes below him and drove down into the mass of pirates, packed tightly into the stern of the xebec. The first ripple of fire was, by pure chance, more of a ragged volley that caused a peppering of dark red bursts across the crowded pirate torsos. As those hit fell bleeding to the deck of the xebec, some tried finding cover, others turned and tried to run away from the press on the poop deck.

The sharp report of the sniper's Remington 700 interrupted the flight of the first three that tried to flee back amidships; the ones behind them either dove to the deck or over the rail. Nerve and numbers riven, the pirates fell back from the stern, some now turning about in confusion, uncertain of where to go or what to do.

✧    ✧    ✧

Owen heard the decrease in the Hibernians' rate of fire, the desperate footfalls crisscrossing the poop deck above them without rhyme or reason and knew down in his belly that this was the moment he'd been waiting for. "On me, you *cultchies!*" he roared at the Wild Geese behind him, and jumped high from the prow of the *barca-longa* in the same moment that he caught the rail with a swing of his grappling hook and heaved himself upward.

He half fell on, half landed across, the starboard rail of the overhang. Letting go of the hook and its line, he shifted his left hand to pull himself over the rail in a tight roll. He came up—and there were two pirates already coming at him, their eyes wild and desperate.

Owen raised the pepperbox, aimed at the chest of the nearest pirate, and squeezed the trigger.

The front-heavy weapon blasted out a great volume of smoke—and pellets; loaded with a charge of .27 caliber lead balls, it emitted a cone of death that riddled the first pirate, and nicked the second one, spinning him around with a single hit in the arm.

Owen smiled as he heard the first of his Wild Geese clambering up behind him, and he drew his sword as the rest of the exhausted and widely wounded pirate crew turned, eyes wide. "Now, you bastards," he said in a voice that—even to him—sounded more like an animal grow, "let's be finishing this." He leaped forward with a shout, the Gaelic war cries of his men following right behind him.

Thomas North watched the close combat on the deck of the xebec; although still outnumbered about three to one, the six Wild Geese and their leader rapidly drove the remaining corsairs before them. Any who survived their hail of lead and attempted to close found themselves facing fresh, armored troops whose skills had been honed by a lifetime training for, and fighting on the battlefields of, the Spanish Low Countries.

As the last half dozen corsairs were driven back into the bows, some started dropping their weapons, and began making the strange prostrations of surrender common among the people from the southern shores of the Mediterranean. The gestures vaguely disturbed North, reminding him of the self-abasing postures of supplication that were the expectations of shahs, khans and beys.

Owen and his Wild Geese seemed to find nothing disturbing

in these appeals for quarter, perhaps because they did not notice them at all. The Irishmen made a swift, mortal passage among the remaining corsairs. Thomas grimaced: *not exactly a sterling display of Christian charity, but certainly no worse than these pirate dogs would have done had they won.* At least there'd be no torture or sodomy; the deaths were clean and quick, not cruel. Still...

Before North could give in to the temptation to pass harsh judgment on actions no different from those he'd taken many times himself, Owen looked up and waved wide and slow, repeating it three times.

So: Miro had his prize ship and a reasonable platform from which to operate his balloon at sea, if need be: the outsized poopdeck and overhang of the xebec made that possible, particularly if they lowered the mizzenmast. And, truth be told, North had to admit the xebec was a beauty that, from what he had seen, could sail as swift as a typhoon fleeing from the devil himself.

He turned to look at his adjutant. "Mr. Porfino, have you found your first battle edifying?"

"Eh? Uh...*si*, signor. I mean, yes sir."

"Wonderful. I suspect you might find yourself a tad closer to the action next time. But for now, signal the *gajeta* in the Cala Santa Maria inlet to make its way around this headland and bring the balance of the prize crew to the xebec." The young Piombinese swallowed and sprinted off to carry out his orders.

North set the safety on his rifle, leaned it against the rock behind which he had taken cover, and looked through his binoculars toward the *scialuppa*. Having chugged out to a safe range for the majority of the fight, the craft was now heading slowly back toward the inlet on oars alone, two of its crew readjusting the rigging of its lateen sail. When he finally found the right focus, he discovered that Miro and Lefferts were standing in the bows of their boat. And were looking back through their own binoculars; a moment later they both waved and grinned.

North returned their waves and felt the faint stirrings of annoyance at Miro. Yes, damn it, Estuban's bold plan had worked. Furthermore, with Harry's help and moral support, he had carried it out under fire, leading from the front because only he and Lefferts had all the necessary skills for this particular job. Miro was the only one who had possessed expert knowledge of the local waters, just as Harry had been the only one familiar enough with an outboard motor. Which, in turn, meant that he, Thomas North, veteran of innumerable campaigns across the continent, would now actually have to start acknowledging that intelligence amateur Estuban Miro was now in fact a genuine field operative. Which, North had to admit, was recognition he very much deserved.

But it was still very, very annoying.

# Chapter 38

Don Sancho Jaume Morales y Llaguno, governor of Castell de Bellver by appointment of the Carthusian monks of Valdemossa, was perplexed. And because he was perplexed, and hated being so, particularly in the presence of his social inferiors, he was angry. And growing angrier by the minute. He shook the sheaf of papers in his hand violently. "I ask again, what is this rubbish? Is it code?"

"It's runic," answered Frank Stone mildly. "An old Anglo-Saxon alphabet. Although, I think this is a little different. It's Dwarvish, you see."

Don Sancho goggled. "It is what?"

"It's Dwarvish. See, there was this author named Tolkien, and he took these runes from way back in English history—back from before the Viking invasions, I guess. He adapted those runes to represent the alphabet used by the dwarves, who are short, really broad, have long beards, and live under mountains where—"

The governor of Bellver leaned back. "You are here less than two weeks, and already suffering from delusions?" He glared at Giovanna. "Or has he always been like this? Has he bouts of insanity?"

"I wouldn't know," she answered airily. "I am often out of the house, grooming our unicorns."

Don Sancho's eyes widened, and then narrowed. "You mock me. You will regret this."

413

Gia smiled sweetly at him. "I doubt it." Then she looked out the window, drew her legs under her on one of the narrow alcove's courting seats, and enjoyed the breeze blowing in off the sea.

Don Sancho became red again and turned to stick a finger so directly into Frank's face that the up-timer was tempted to bite it. "I ask you again," snapped the governor, "what are these writings? They look demonic."

"No, no: it's just a novel. You know, like *Don Quixote.*"

The governor scoffed. "As I understand it, Cervantes constrained himself to writing his prose is an appreciably human script!"

Frank nodded, thought, *damn, this guy would have been really cheesed if I was writing in the elves'* Quenya. *He would probably have made me the main attraction at a human weenie roast.* "I'm sorry if it upsets you."

The governor stared, then threw down the papers in exasperation. "Señor Stone, I assure you, if there is sedition in these papers, or an attempt to somehow communicate beyond these walls, we will learn of it. One of the scholars in Palma indicated that the letters might be from an old Scandinavian dialect, so, although it may take some time, we will be able to decipher them. And moreover, no other person will see them until and unless you are freed."

Frank nodded again. "I understand." *And I also understand that even once you've deciphered the runic alphabet, you're still not going to be able to make any sense of it, because you won't have a single clue for understanding the other code in which it's written. Even if you somehow manage to make sense of all the terms I use from* The Lord of the Rings *and about a dozen fantasy games, you won't understand what it really means unless you know that the orcs are the Spanish, the uruk-hai are hidalgos, the Nazgul are inquisitors, and so on and so forth, all the way down to the Uttermost West being up-time Earth. So sure, you'll decode the alphabet in which the book is written, but you'll still have gibberish. Happy reading, asshole.*

"And we will take these documents whenever we wish, you understand."

"Of course," Frank agreed. *As if I'm stupid enough to make just one copy.*

"And we may have to take possession of it for extended periods."

"I would expect so."

Don Sancho dropped the papers. "You may have them back for now. Although I repent my agreeing to your request for the paper and ink. I would never have consented at all, but for the intercession of that annoying captain."

Frank felt his chest tighten slightly. "What annoying captain?"

"You know. The one who came with you. The one they stationed here with those arrogant brutes from Fort San Carlos."

Frank could feel Gia's eyes on him, both playful and recriminatory. "He did that?" asked Frank. "He helped me get the paper and ink?"

"Help you? Señor Stone, if it was not for his insistent meddling on your behalf, you would not have the papers, or the ink, or this apartment which, I will point out, was mine up until your arrival. It is the governor's privilege to enjoy the views and cool breezes of the top floor of the main tower. In Philip's own name, he forced me out, declaring it the most secure room in the entire fortress. Which it is, of course."

Frank frowned. "He—Vincente—did all that?"

"Why, yes, of course. Despite your refusal to take his visits. Frankly, I do not know why he tolerates such insolence."

"We, uh . . . we have a history." Gia was leaning over so Frank could not avoid seeing the way she stared at him with her twinkling "*told you so*" eyes.

The governor waved a dismissive hand. "That is your affair. But I suppose you are well suited for each other. You, a lunatic, will not be offended by his insufferable imperiousness."

Frank reflected that Don Sancho accusing Don Vincente of imperiousness was like an elephant criticizing a mouse for being too large.

The governor stalked toward the door, turned and looked back at the papers he had brought in. "So it is a novel, eh? What is this novel of yours about?"

Frank smiled lopsidedly. "Uh. A lot of things. But nothing in particular, just yet. It's a work in progress, you see."

"Hmf." Don Sancho looked down his nose at the papers that, when he tossed them down, had scattered across the dark wood surface of Frank's writing table. "It is all lunacy and sorcery, I'll wager."

Gia hopped down from her seat at the window and rose to her full height of just over five foot two. "My husband does not traffic in sorcery."

"He is an up-timer, is he not? That makes him a witch!"

"And you are an appointed official, are you not? That makes you an idiot."

The governor's eyes, darkened, kept burning holes in Giovanna even when Frank stepped between them. "Hey, hey, no reason for harsh words. You know how it is; wives hate to hear their husband's work being run down."

"Eh? So? This is work? It looks like rubbish to me. You can't even tell me what it's about. Maybe she can?"

Giovanna's eyebrows arched. "Maybe. Do not be so sure that I am not the muse that guides my husband's hand." She smiled at Frank. "Or at least his heart."

Frank smiled back. "Definitely my heart." He swallowed and felt butterflies in his stomach the way he always did when Gia looked at him that way. "And everything else as well."

Don Sancho Jaume Morales y Llaguno, governor of Castell de Bellver, scowled and began descending the stairs, down to the level of the lazarette that was flush with the roof of the castle. His griping grunt was clearly, and probably intentionally, audible. "Hmf. It's bad enough to be a warder for sorcerers. But sentimental ones? Bah. They are embarrassments to their own unholy profession."

"And you will inform them, Captain, that I will not suffer such insolence again—not from such villainous, demon-consorting, scum as them!"

Captain Vincente Jose-Maria de Castro y Papas managed not to roll his eyes. He kept them politely focused on Don Sancho, whose small form was almost fully hidden by his large desk. "Governor, do you seriously believe that Frank Stone is a companion to demons? Frank?"

The governor's haughty chin came down a bit, and he looked away, almost embarrassed. "Well...no, not him. He is too boyish, too stupid. But that wife of his! She could be half-devil, from the look of her!"

Now Don Vincente had to suppress a smile. Yes, judging from what the guards told him of some of the nocturnal noise-making she had perpetrated in Rome, he would not be surprised if there was at least a gill of diabolical blood in her veins. "Governor, I know the wife has a sharp tongue, if she is provoked. But if that is a mark of the devil, then fully half of us may be so branded. Besides, she is well into her second trimester and knows she will give birth to her first child in a prison. Taken together, I think these explain her testiness."

"Perhaps. And while we are on the topic of when and how

this bulging she-goat will whelp her offspring, the husband has been insisting that our local midwives are insufficient for assisting with the birth. He claims that the American ambassadora in Rome, this Nichols creature, is a physician, and that she warned them that, when the wife's time came, she should have a doctor."

Don Vincente wondered if he'd ever be able to display a genuine facial expression again; now he suppressed a frown. Odd. Frank had never mentioned this before. But perhaps this was because—

"I responded that they would have to make do with our midwives," the governor nattered on, "that our doctors do not address the delicate conditions of women. They are not perverts, after all."

Don Vincente nodded, wondering if the next thing the governor would reveal was that Frank had made a request for—

"So today Stone proposed that *xueta* physicians are the answer to this dilemma. Which I find surprising; to my knowledge, most of them have the same scruples and decency as true Christian physicians in this regard. Only a few of them will become involved with pregnancies, and then, only when there is an emergency."

Now Don Vincente was able to indulge in a genuine physical reaction: an affirming nod. But the affirmation it signified was not in relation to the governor's streaming complaints, only his own suspicions. On the one hand, if Giovanna did have any irregularities during her later pregnancy or delivery, a crypto-Jewish *converso* physician—one of the few willing to cross the implicit gender boundaries and treat a woman in dire need—was by far the best one to have. It was another dirty secret of Spain's nobility; they employed the services of *conversos*—who, it was uniformly known, persisted in the covert practice of Judaism—when their wives' pregnancies became too problematic for midwives to handle, just as they went to the *marrano* community to seek secret loans that were prohibited by Church's stern rules against usury.

But Don Vincente realized that the request for a true physician could also be a shrewd tactic for establishing a connection with the *xuetas*, Mallorca's own crypto-Jewish community. Beneath Frank's good-natured and idealistic exterior, there lurked a surprisingly canny and untimid mind that was quite capable of plotting deceptions and tricks. And in this case, it was very capable of considering the current situation and realizing that, if there was any way to send communications to, or receive them from, the outside world, it would be through Palma's "converted" Jewish community.

Grantville had become a haven for Jews throughout Europe, and had also evolved into the epicenter of their commercial interests, insofar as their far-flung involvements had anything vaguely resembling a center. Francisco Nasi, outgoing chief of Mike Stearns' intelligence network, was a leading member of that community. Stearns' wife, Rebecca Abrabanel, was the daughter of another. And in many of the places where the Wrecking Crew had plied their dubious trade, they had frequently relied upon the surreptitious support of Jewish communities. Don Vincente wondered if the up-timers would still receive such ready assistance after the debacle in Rome, which had led directly to the bloody reprisals against the Ghetto. On the other hand, Frank would be too smart—and too considerate—to request overt help from the *xuetas* of Palma; he would simply begin a relationship that he could groom into a conduit for news, and eventually, message sending.

Or, Don Vincente admitted, he might be just trying to secure the best possible care for a small wife who showed signs of carrying large. So he said, "Governor, in Stone's up-time world, most physicians, even those attending to female needs, were men."

"Perverts, just as I suspected," Don Sancho sniffed primly.

"From what little I have been able to glean, unholy lusts had nothing to do with it, Don Sancho. Up until the decades before the up-timers were taken from their world, most opportunities to study at universities and become doctors remained the province of men. The skills and sciences of saving lives—of mothers and infants, too—were thus entrusted to their hands."

"It is still a corruption of God's will, Captain. If our Savior wills that a mother and her infant be called to His Bosom in their holy innocence, then so be it. Our desire to save those lives is not merely an insufficient excuse for perversion, but heretical; if God wishes the company of these mothers and infants in His Heavenly Kingdom, who are we to challenge His Will?"

"I am no theologian," admitted Vincente in an attempt to placate Don Sancho. "But let us be practical: if Señora Stone's pregnancy is difficult, and either she or the child should be lost, what do you think Cardinal Borja's reaction would be? Or Philip's?"

Don Sancho blanched. "So you support the prisoner's request for a Jewish physician?"

Not wanting to look overly concerned with the decision, Don Vincente shrugged. "I cannot see how it would harm anyone to make the necessary inquiries in the *xueta* quarter. And let us not forget that the *xuetas* are, in fact, Christians, now."

The governor sneered. "In name only. As you well know." He seemed to frown down at the tabletop. "I suppose it is politically prudent to grant Stone's request. Although I must say I had expected a more manly resolve from you, Captain."

Castro y Papas stilled an impulse to grab the pasty-fleshed recipient of provincial sinecure by the neck and calmly ask him just what he meant by "more manly resolve." "I am uncertain what you are referring to," was what he said.

"I refer to your reputation among my men: that you are a relentless taskmaster. However, in the matter of the prisoners, you urge that we grant their request for Jewish doctors—yes, they *are* still Jewish—and that they be handled gently. Meanwhile, these soldiers you've brought from Fort San Carlos tell my men that the new rigid discipline, as well as the rigorous training, is all at your behest. And regarding your decision to reduce a man's rations when he fails to meet your standards: are you sure this will really promote superior morale and professionalism?"

"Actually, yes," was what Vincente wanted to say, but didn't. "These are effective training methods for the tercios, Governor Morales y Llaguno. I presume they will work here as well."

"Well, I am nowhere near so sure as you. In fact, I have a mind to—"

"To what?" inquired a voice from the doorway. Pedro Dolor's silhouette stood framed against the backdrop of white-pink groined vaults and delicate arches of the second interior story of Castell de Bellver.

The governor swallowed. "I—I was just saying. That...that we are unaccustomed to the style of training that Captain Vincente has instituted here. My men find it—"

"—what? Too strenuous? Then perhaps they should not be members of this garrison. Captain Castro y Papas is carrying out my directives, Governor, for we are all answerable to Madrid for the continued security of these prisoners. That requires constant vigilance and full readiness. Your garrison was deficient in both regards. I see improvement, thanks to the captain. And if I were to learn that he was encountering resistance in his attempt to meet those objectives—"

"There shall be no resistance," the governor said through a

loud swallow. "I was simply explaining why my men might not be improving as swiftly as desired."

"Yes," said Dolor after a moment, "of course you were." He turned to Castro y Papas. "Are you done here?"

The captain sent a polite glance at the governor, who nodded vigorously. Vincente made a short bow and followed Dolor out into the pleasant airs of the second story arcade. They walked slowly toward the stairs leading down to the ground level.

"I am returning to Palma this afternoon," Dolor commented.

*Thank God!* "So soon, Señor Dolor?"

"Yes. I have business there. Captain, you are not to allow the governor to obstruct you in the attainment of your objectives. The safety of the prisoners is ultimately in your hands."

Don Vincente raised an eyebrow. "After your own, of course."

"Only for now. Within the next two weeks, maybe three, I will return to Rome. Pope Urban has not yet been located. Until that task is completed, the Church cannot move beyond its current stalemate, which is in danger of becoming a true interregnum."

*What a nice term for that period of time after which an anti-pope will longer benefit from hunting down and killing the legitimate pontiff like a rabbit in a garden maze.* "I realize the urgency of that situation, Señor Dolor, but if left on my own here, I do not have enough legal authority to prevent the governor from—"

"Captain," Dolor turned at the head of the stairway; the eyes looking up at Don Vincente were as dead as a statue's. "I cannot confer more rank upon you, yet you must be firmly in charge here. You must accomplish this by the force of your personality and resolve. Do not fail me in this. I cannot tarry here; being in Palma does not move me closer to achieving my objectives."

And for the last time that day, Don Vincente Jose-Maria de Castro y Papas suppressed a facial reflex, in this case, a surprised blink. Dolor's words were innocuous on the surface, but his tone hinted at ambitions and desires that went far further, and were far more personal, than whatever skullduggery he had to settle for Borja in Italy. "I see," Don Vincente answered simply.

Dolor nodded. "I hope you do." Then he started down the stairs alone.

# Chapter 39

Just inside the entrance of the upstairs parlor that was rapidly becoming known as the Garden Room (the reference was to Gethsemane, not the barely visible vegetable plots behind the villa), Sharon put a hand on Larry Mazzare's arm as he passed.

The village priest-turned-cardinal started, noticing the ambassadora and her husband for the first time. "Oh. Hello, Sharon. Ruy." Antonio Barberini the Younger, with whom he had been talking, went on into the Garden Room.

Sharon kept her voice low. "Before you put on the gloves for round two, Larry, I just wanted to congratulate you on winning that all-important first battle. I'd have said so sooner, but we haven't seen much of you for the past week."

Larry smiled crookedly. "Trying to write a defense of up-time canonical doctrines from memory is pretty time-consuming, Sharon. Sorry I haven't been around too much."

"Not to worry, Larry; I'm just grateful that you proved we're not demonspawn. Of course, you put us all at risk of *auto-da-fé* in the process."

Larry's smile faded a bit. "Okay, now; let's not overstate the case, Sharon. Debating in every era, and particularly this one, recognizes a tendency to paint in broad strokes when making a big point. But yeah, I'm glad that one is over; it's tough walking the

421

rhetorical line between this century's presumed fire-and-brimstone literalities of Satan, and my own more symbolic beliefs."

Ruy nodded somberly. "I understand, but you are doing what you have to, Cardinal Mazzare. And that first victory was necessary for you to be able to continue this decisive war of words."

Larry nodded in return. "I grant you, I felt I was pretty much the favorite for winning round one. The judgment of the common people, and Urban's own actions, all point to an unspoken judgment that, whatever else we are, we are not infernal agents. But up until now, he's never proclaimed anything about our origins *ex cathedra*. If he does so, Urban will be committing the Church to a position that's going to earn him some real enemies."

"Yes, but most of those will be in Spain. Where he already has few enough friends, I think," appended Ruy with a smile.

Mazzare shrugged. "I suspect that's one of the reasons he's willing to let all this issue come to a head, now: all the people who will hate that pronouncement are already on Borja's side. But I think Urban's consciousness has become less political and more spiritual since the massacres in Rome. I think he wants to be sure—absolutely sure—that in trusting us, he's doing the right thing for the Church."

"Which makes him a good pope," averred Ruy.

"Yeah," interjected Sharon, "but like one up-time songster said, 'only the good die young.' And Borja certainly seems determined to use Urban to prove the truth of those lyrics."

"Ambassadora!" cried the delighted voice of Urban from the doorway. "I only heard the very end of your exchange—I can discern that I missed the best parts of it, alas—but I am still vain enough to relish the thought of one so vibrant as yourself considering me 'young.'" He beamed and winked. "I am in desperately short supply of such flattering opinions, so I am doubly glad that I did not have to declare you a devil. Now, let us take our places."

Vitelleschi began with his signature abruptness. "Today we resolve two issues. The first, that of the correctness of the up-time doctrine of papal infallibility. This has been conceded *nolo contendere* by Cardinal Wadding." The father-general's eyes sparked with what looked like amusement. "Of course, as he is a good Franciscan, I expected no different."

Sharon whispered to Ruy. "Huh?"

"He is referring to the dispute between Pope John XXII and the Franciscans that gave rise to the entire notion of papal infallibility."

Sharon, no more edified than before, simply said, "Oh."

Vitelleschi had not even stopped to breathe. "Cardinal Wadding has also inspected Cardinal Mazzare's documentation on the principle of the dogmatic infallibility of papal councils as articulated under the convention of the Sacred Magisterium. He also accepts this *nolo contendere*, conceding that it has been recognized, albeit less formally, since the time of Justinian.

"However, since Cardinal Wadding has already conceded this day's points of debate involving infallibility, he wishes to use his time to discuss whether the up-time ecumenical council known as Vatican Two, or the papal decrees which emerged from it, can be presumed to enjoy such absolute authoritativeness. He has asked to be the first speaker. Cardinal Mazzare, will you consent to giving him the first word?"

"He is as welcome to the first word as he is to the last," Mazzare replied with a thin smile.

Wadding rose. "Even the sparse documentation available here reveals that the convener of Vatican Two, Pope John XXIII, did not want the results of the ecumenical council to be perceived as having the impress of either consular or papal infallibility. Specifically, he expressly enjoined the council not to promulgate any dogma, but instead, to merely reaffirm the truths of the church in the idiom of that time, the mid-twentieth century."

Larry Mazzare smiled. "Yes—probably because he figured it was the best way to skin that particular canonical cat."

Wadding blinked. "I'm sorry; what do you mean?"

"I mean if the Council had been free to promulgate dogma, it would never have ended. As it was, Vatican Two went on for over three years, and its resolutions took eighteen years to emerge as a series of Apostolic Constitutions. John averted the possibility of a complete impasse by—technically—constraining the scope of the deliberations."

Wadding shook his head. "I take it that you are implying that even though John XXIII restricted the council to simply rewording Church doctrine, he was nonetheless hoping that this would produce *de facto* changes in how the doctrine was applied and practiced."

"Something like that," said Larry with a smile.

Wadding made a dismissive gesture. "Even if true, that still does not change the significance of his exhortation: that Vatican Two was to refrain from promulgating new, or revising old, doctrine. And insofar as that the council might believe itself infallible since it was convened by a papal injunction, John XXIII famously said of himself 'I am only infallible if I speak infallibly but I shall never do that, so I am not infallible.' How much more explicit could we ask him to be in indicating that the pronouncements arising from Vatican Two were not to be deemed infallible?"

Mazzare nodded. "John XXIII did say that about himself. However, although the infallibility of a papal council originally derives from that of the summoning pontiff, it does not continue to depend upon or defer to that imprimatur. More significantly, the pope who ultimately issued the numerous Apostolic Constitutions arising from Vatican Two—John Paul II—did not declare the same limitations upon his own exercise of the Extraordinary Sacred Magisterium of papal infallibility. Rather, he decreed new canon law and a new catechism from out of the corpus of Vatican Two. More significantly, in the bulls whereby he announced the Apostolic Constitutions, John Paul II repeatedly emphasized that the authority of the documents was also traceable to their origins in a papal council. Lastly, the language he used when issuing the relevant decrees leaves no doubt as to his intent."

Mazzare picked up a sheet from the small table in front of him. "In the *In Sacrae Disciplinae Lege,* he lists himself as 'The Supreme Pontiff Pope John Paul II' and writes: 'I order today, January 25, 1983, the promulgation of the revised Code of Canon Law.' And he clearly tells us by what authority he orders this. 'Trusting therefore in the help of divine grace, sustained by the authority of the holy Apostles Peter and Paul,...and...with the supreme authority with which I am vested, by means of this Constitution, to be valid forever in the future, I promulgate the present Code as it has been set in order and revised. I command that for the future it is to have the force of law for the whole Latin Church, and I entrust it to the watchful care of all those concerned, in order that it may be observed.'"

Mazzare put the document down. "In every particular, this wording fulfills the expectation of an *ex cathedra* statement of papal infallibility. It is absolute in its instruction, invokes the key terms of authority, and commands that it be retained as perpetually valid, along with an enjoinder for the Church to protect it against being either changed or disregarded."

Wadding held up a hand. "I will point out that the American cardinal Avery Dulles authoritatively argued that, although Vatican Two produced over eight hundred pages of commentary, there is not one new statement for which infallibility is claimed."

"He did write that," agreed Mazzare with a smile, "but he was, after all, only a cardinal like us. He was not the pope who initiated Vatican Two, nor the pope who issued the Apostolic Constitutions—who was the final authority on the matter of his own intents or exercise of his Sacred Magisterium."

Sharon held on to Ruy's arm and whispered to him. "It's getting mighty deep, here."

"The theological implications of papal infallibility are indeed as profound as the greatest trenches of the ocean, my heart."

"Sorry, Ruy, but when I said 'deep,' I wasn't talking about water."

"Dear heart! Can you truly be so scatologically flippant about matters so holy? Perhaps you are a demon after all; an infernal temptress, at least..."

"Ruy, you remove that hand right now. Yes, the one with your knuckle brushing against my—Ruy! There's a pope in the room!"

Wadding was nodding at Mazzare's last point. "As you say, neither we, nor your Cardinal Dulles, can know if a pope had unspoken intents. So it seems that there is insufficient reason for me to continue to question the infallibility of Vatican Two in your time."

Ruy's hand dropped away suddenly. Sharon looked at his face; his eyes, playful a moment ago, were deadly serious now. "Ruy—" she began.

"My dear," he interrupted in a tense whisper, "Wadding's concession means he is springing a trap."

Wadding stood poised, as if he had not completed his sentence. Then: "But I reemphasize: I constrain that concession of infallibility to *your* time. It is quite a different matter to assert that Vatican Two is an infallible teaching or dogma for *this* time," He picked up a paper from the small table on which he had his materials arrayed. "Paradoxically, my assertion—that infallibility cannot survive such a temporal and spatial discontinuity as that which brought Grantville to our world—arises from the text of one of the Apostolic Constitutions engendered by

Vatican Two itself. Specifically, in going through the end notes to the *Gaudium et Spes*, there is a directive as to how it should be read and understood. Speaking of its first part—*De Ecclesia in Mundo Huius Temporis*, or, "The Role of the Church in the Modern World"—the note explains that "Some elements have a permanent value; others, only a transitory one. Consequently... interpreters must bear in mind... the changeable circumstances which the subject matter, by its very nature, involves."

Wadding laid down the paper. "I have no argument with papal infallibility. And I am satisfied with Cardinal Mazzare's proofs that the Apostolic Constitutions arising from Vatican Two do, in fact, possess that infallibility. However, we must also pay heed to this passage, which is equally infallible when it explains that 'some elements have a permanent value; others, only a transitory one.'"

Wadding leaned forward over his table. "This, I assert, is the voice of the Holy Spirit, speaking across the vast gulfs of space and time, to caution us about what we might call the 'epochal provisional-ity' of canonical church doctrine. In short, it compels us to ask: does Vatican Two reflect God's intents across all eternity? Or was it specifically, and only, infallibly valid in relation to the up-time world, of that particular epoch, and at that particular moment?"

Vitelleschi made a cutting gesture in the air with his hand. "That intrudes upon the topic of our next session, Cardinal Wad-ding: whether the infallible doctrines and decrees of the up-time Church must be recognized as such in this one, as well. And so we are adjourned—and may rightly give thanks for the shortness of today's proceedings, for I note there is still light in the garden." Without further comment, Vitelleschi headed for the stairs that would lead him outside.

Sharon stepped over to Larry to offer her congratulations, but was stopped by the grim look on his face. "Why so glum, Larry? You won the day."

Mazzare glanced over at Wadding, who seemed unusually serene in defeat as he gathered his papers. "It's not today that concerns me, Sharon. Wadding pulled an exegetical judo move on me just now, one from which I may not be able to recover in the next session."

"You mean that he has used the rationale of your own defense of the infallibility of Vatican Two to establish a reasonable doubt as to its applicability in this world?"

"Exactly."

Sharon frowned. "And do you think he can prove that Two *is* inapplicable here?"

Larry shrugged. "He doesn't have to, Sharon. The burden of proof is upon me. I have to establish that its infallibility extends from our up-time land of never-never-when, all the way back down into this very real down-time world."

One of Ruy's eyebrows raised slightly. "And can you accomplish that, Cardinal Mazzare?"

Larry sighed. "Damned if I know."

"Do you really think they came this way, Valentino?"

Given the number of times he had now heard the question, Valentino would probably have slashed the inquirer across the face with his dagger—except that this time, the inquiry came from Cesare Linguanti. Quiet Linguanti, who was the only other senior—and therefore, trustworthy—man that Rombaldo had assigned to this search group, and who had not once showed any doubt in Valentino's leadership. Of course, he had yet to speak fifty words since leaving Venice. "Where else do you think we should search?" Valentino asked him.

Linguanti shrugged. He looked at the land humping up between the mountains that were rising ever higher around them as they entered the Asiago region from the south. "It's a lot of empty country and tall mountains, here at the gateway to the Dolomites."

"Yes," answered Valentino, surprised at Linguanti's relative loquacity, "but this is where the trail leads."

"Some trail," intruded a broad, brash Milanese accent behind him. "These days, there could be any number of groups on horseback with some English speakers. Since those up-time demons arrived, everyone and his father's whore is speaking English, it seems."

Valentino turned, schooling himself to patience as he did. The new voice in the discussion belonged to Odoardo de Mosca, who was so large that his horse looked like a pony, sagging under him. Odoardo was arguably one of the ten most dangerous—and contrary—men Valentino had ever met. It was an unpromising mix, and Valentino half-suspected that, after this job was done, he would have to preemptively, albeit surreptitiously, "retire" Odoardo from Rombaldo's payroll; the burly Milanese man-ogre was as indiscreet with secrets as he was with cheap, barnyard grappa.

"Yes, Odoardo, there are a lot of English-speakers abroad these days, but that's not the main reason we're on this group's trail."

"Oh, yeah? What's the big difference?"

"This group used an unusual method of victualing."

Odoardo spat; thick and phlegmy, the gobbet didn't carry as far as he intended. It hit his own horse square in the eye. The beast bucked; Odoardo smiled and wrestled it back under control, sawing at the reins cruelly. "That's bullshit, Valentino. From what we've been able to learn at each town this group visited, they bought the right amounts of food and drink for a big group. So what's so unusual?"

Valentino smiled and resolved to kill Odoardo in his sleep just as soon as the pope was dead. "Odoardo, you should pay a little more attention to the details. Yes, the men seen in the towns always bought the right amount of supplies for the group they claimed to be traveling with, but then why did that whole group never pass directly through any of the towns where they got their provisions?"

Odoardo frowned and shrugged a single shoulder diffidently. "Maybe they're shy."

"No one's so shy that they don't want to bring their horses or wagons to load up the provisions directly from the supplier, instead of dragging them off beyond each town's outskirts and *then* loading them."

"I thought you said that they didn't have wagons," Odoardo muttered, half annoyed, half confused.

"I was just trying to make a point—but you're right: we've not found much in the way of wheel ruts and the other spoor we'd expect if the group had any heavy wagons. So the reason they traveled so quickly is that they traveled light. And they took precautions so that no townspeople ever saw but a few of them, and usually not the same ones, from what we can tell."

"I thought the English-speakers always went to town."

"Odoardo, my boy," Valentino patronized, enjoying the rare opportunity to torture the insolent behemoth, "you really must pay more attention to the details. Yes, an English speaker—or several—were always in the group that went to town. But that might simply be because most of the party are English-speakers. Which would be exactly what we'd expect from a group of up-timers, don't you think?"

What Odoardo lacked in perspicacity, he made up for in stubbornness. "If this group is our target, then they'd have servants—from their Roman embassy. They could've sent them to do the 'victualing.' Then no one would have known there were so many people who could speak English. If they were trying to travel without being detected, that's what they'd have done."

"Yes. Of course they would. They'd send their servants. Servants who probably can't keep from inadvertently revealing their secrets any more than you can resist blabbing your own to anyone who'll listen. Not exactly the team I would send to buy provisions if I wanted to maintain a low, largely undetected, profile. And besides, although each provisioning group always contained English speakers, the shop keepers have reported very different accents: a few were genuine English, a lot used this Amideutsch that you hear Germans speaking these days, some say they heard genuine up-time dialect, and a few report strange accents, maybe from Ireland or Scotland. Which, when you consider the group we're looking for, matches the mix of expected nationalities."

"Merchants might be that mixed." Odoardo tried to sound confident.

It was Linguanti who answered. "If they're merchants, then where are their wagons?"

Odoardo's head went forward in a silent sulk.

Valentino had already forgotten him, looking at the northern panorama of mountains; far to the left, the Little Dolomites were leaning north, in the direction of the true Dolomites, whose distant peaks were painted bright pink and silver by the setting sun. "No," declared Valentino, "every other lead we found north of the Po checked out, made sense. But this one, this group—no. And what the devil would merchants be doing heading up into this country, anyway? If they wanted to traverse the alps from western Veneto, they would have gone via Lake Garda and then Trent, up toward Bolzano."

Odoardo's voice rumbled up from where his chin was tucked into his chest. "Maybe they're trading to the valley folk."

Valentino laughed heartily. "Oh, yes. Of course. How foolish that I didn't see it earlier. But I see it clearly now—thanks to you, Odoardo. In fact, we are actually tracking a multinational rabble of merchants who have journeyed all the way from the British Isles and Germany. For here, in PreAlpine Italy, they mean to set up a thriving trade going from one unpopulated valley to another, selling their big city baubles to the local troglodytes in exchange for riches such as smelly cheese, old goatskins, and the dubious favors of their cross-eyed daughters."

Odoardo was silent, except for the steady grinding of his teeth.

Valentino ignored him. He looked up at the failing light that was plunging the strange mix of both naked and pine-forested peaks into a rosy pre-dusk gloom. "No," breathed Valentino to no one in particular, "we've finally got the scent of these damned up-timers and their renegade pope. They're up here. Somewhere."

# Part Five

## July 1635

All venom out

# Chapter 40

Harry Lefferts sat in the stern of the boat. He was well-cloaked and, thinking back, reflected that the monk's habit that had been his disguise from Palestrina to Rome hadn't been so bad by comparison. The Piombinese fisherman-turned-sailor manning the tiller glanced sympathetically at him and offered a water skin that Harry waved away regretfully. All he needed to complete his collection of discomforts was an urgent need to relieve his bladder—because there was no way to do so without getting up. And getting up would mean having the cloak fall away. And that would be disastrous.

Because, against all odds, the three Mallorcan fishermen in the little ketch that they had spotted working only two miles off the Cap des Pins, were now engaged in animated discussion with Miro, who sat in the bows of the *scialuppa*.

The three fishermen had been leery of the close approach of the unfamiliar and bigger ship, and put hands to oars for a while before it became obvious that, with the newcomer approaching from windward, flight was useless. They had been pleasantly surprised to be hailed in the colloquial—and unintelligible—Mallorquin of a native speaker. Their attitudes had quickly changed from suspicion to welcome as Miro leisurely plied them—from a distance of about ten yards—for the latest news of pirates, trade, fishing, and coastal watches.

At least, that's what Harry was told by the fellow in front of him, a half-Corsican Piombinese who had sailed to the Balearics once or twice in the journeys of his youth. Harry could not make out any of the exchange, other than a few common nouns and verbs, here and there. Which annoyed him considerably. He'd taken high school Spanish, and had passed it, largely due to his innate facility for languages rather than any scholastic diligence. And so he had felt—with some pride—that his old familiarity with Spanish would prove to be a profoundly useful skill on this operation.

But here he was, sitting on a bobbing boat off the east coast of Mallorca, baking in the sun, straining his ears and hearing only indecipherable chatter. Catalan was not merely a "different form" of Spanish as one of the temporary teachers in Grantville High School had airily assured him years ago; it was a goddamned different language. Oh sure, you could hear the Spanish roots in it, but it was more like Spanish that had been hijacked by French, but also with some of those sloppy Portuguese vowel sounds blended in for good measure. And to make matters worse, the specific dialect used here was punctuated with buzzing z's and choppy x's and those hard, choked ch's he associated with German and Yiddish.

Although here, those phlegm-rolling ch-sounds were inheritances from Arabic. Mallorca had been in Moorish hands for many centuries, and afterward remained a prime hunting ground for North African pirates. The worst of the depredations had been carried out by the two Barbarossa brothers just a century earlier. Which was why Estuban had been so careful making his approach: the island was ringed by pirate watchtowers, and, although the last eighty years had seen a marked decrease in the size and frequency of the raids, they were still frequent enough to be a source of worry, particularly out here on the comparatively wild and sparsely populated eastern coast.

And now, yes, to make matters even worse, Harry Lefferts felt uncomfortable pressure beginning to mount in his bladder: he'd sipped too much water when the sun started getting truly intense at about ten AM. And now he was going to pay for it. So Harry gritted his teeth, tucked his knees tightly together and hissed a question at the half-Corsican in front of him. "What are they talking about now?"

"Signor Miro is asking harmless questions about the garrison at the tower just inland here." He jutted his stubbled chin toward the end of the rocky coastline hanging over them to the north like a pine-strewn shelf. "Then he asks about fishing. Then about the olives near Manacor. Then about the Torre de Canyamel."

"That's the big tower protecting the next bay to the north, right?"

"*Si*, although the tower is somewhat inland. It seems the garrison there is not large, and they do not mount many coast patrols. Which is good, because if they did, we would not be able to make use of the Caves of Arta."

"So the news is good."

"Mostly."

"What do you mean?"

The Corsican turned, looked at Harry's posture, and smiled sympathetically. "It seems that these fishermen worry about pirates, too. In fact, there seems to be an unknown fishing ship working these waters. Except they don't think it is a fisherman at all."

"A pirate?"

The Corsican shrugged. "They do not know. They do not want to find out. But they fear it is. Boats do not travel from afar to fish these waters. The catch in them is good enough, but they are not, how you say, with fish in teams."

"You mean, 'teeming with fish'?"

"*Si*; what you have said. So a new boat in these waters—a big *llaut*, carrying over twenty men—that stays five, even ten miles out?" The Corsican shook his head. "They are right; it sounds like a pirate."

"Lying off-shore while a small landing party looks for, and gathers intelligence on, some easy targets."

"*Si*. What else?"

Miro was waving farewell to the fishermen who at first refused a *real* as a token of his appreciation, but then, seeing he was not trying to press it on them, relented and accepted it when he offered it again. He moved back to the stern and smiled sadly, "You may urinate soon, Harry."

"That's the best news yet, Estuban. So, can we get into the caves, as planned?"

"Well, we can get into the caves. But not as planned."

"Huh? Whaddya mean?"

"According to these fellows, when pirates prepare for a quick raid, they land shore parties in advance. Those shore parties usually conduct their reconnaissance at night, and spend their days hiding out in the caves."

"So you mean we're not just going to be able to stroll into the caves and set up our first staging area and camp."

"I can't tell, but the odds are good that we shall find the Caves of Arta occupied."

"So if we go in and take the caves, will the pirates waiting off-shore just leave, or come to the caves, looking for their missing buddies?"

Miro shrugged. "They will probably not abandon their shore party without making some attempt to contact them."

Harry noticed that his left knee had begun to bob vigorously. "So, how long do you figure we have before the off-shore pirates arrive?"

"There's no way to even make a guess. If there is a scouting party in the caves, it may have put ashore today, or a week ago. And how long are they supposed to survey the area? A day? A week? Or perhaps there is no prearranged time; perhaps they will summon the completion of their reconnaissance with a small signal fire at the peak of the headland, Cap Vermell, and wait elsewhere."

"So, once we go to the caves, everything that comes next is a crap shoot."

"I do not know what firing guns at feces would achieve, but if you mean that subsequent events are uncertain, then yes, that is so."

"Good. Just one more thing, Estuban."

"Yes, Harry?"

"Are those guys far enough away that I can take a piss, now?"

Thomas North threw up his hands in exasperation and suddenly realized he had started reprising his father's trademark gestures. He dropped his hands quickly and glared at Miro instead. "First you go crawling around in these damn caves with Harry and almost get yourself killed, showing him where to find the pirates." North turned to Lefferts. "Good, clean job, that. Wish we could have taken a prisoner to get some intelligence on their ship."

Harry shrugged. "They weren't cooperative."

"I'll bet not." Turning back to Miro, North continued his gripes. "And now you propose to stroll to one of these little, one-eyed hamlets, these, these—"

"Because this is an old island, with old communities, and ties that were ancient before the Spanish ever set foot here. There are people who will know to watch over me once I step into their shops. They will pass word by channels swift, subtle, and still utterly unsuspected by the Spanish. They will be powerless to help me, but they will know everything that befalls me. Now, I must go if I am to be in Son Frai Gari by dawn." He turned to Lefferts. "Harry, in my absence, yours is the definitive word of the USE. You are in official charge, but—as I have done—you must allow Colonels North and O'Neill to command the operations you order or authorize."

"Yeah, sure. You just get your ass back here in one piece, Estuban—and hurry up doing so, okay?"

"*Alqueries*," furnished Miro calmly.

"Whatever. You propose to stroll into one, get a ride on the back of a wagon into Manacor where—with luck, as you say—you hope to find a horse for hire, and so ride on to Palma."

"That's the plan. About which you have questioned me at length, Thomas."

"Well, I have one more question."

"Which is?"

"Which is—are you stark raving mad, Estuban?"

The no-longer-ex-patriate *xueta* smiled. "I don't think so."

"Well, I do. You are in charge of this operation. You are the one operating at the direct behest of Ed Piazza to accomplish the military and political objectives of the USE here and in Italy. And now you are going to just toddle off into the night, without so much as an escort?"

"Yes, Thomas, that is exactly what I'm going to do."

"Well, that is—"

"Thomas, you asked me a question; hear my answer."

North silenced himself with an effort, but kept glowering.

"I am home, Thomas. I know this land and this people better—far better—than any other. I know where trouble lurks and where it does not. I have a hundred possible identities and stories at my fingertips to explain my presence here, and the odds are good that I know some of these peoples' distant relatives. An escort would only ruin my disguise." He smiled. "My greatest protection is that I belong in this place, am native to it, and everyone who meets me will know that immediately. My gear and dress announce I am a man with friends and not to be treated lightly, and that harm done to me will result in pointed—or, better yet, pointy—inquiries by those same friends.

"So be at ease, Thomas. My return will be much more swift than my journey to Palma, so I think you should see me again in five days, a week at most."

"At which point we will come looking for you, Estuban."

"At which point you will visit this man in Manacor," Estuban extended a written note to Thomas North. "He is a family friend—but his association with us is not known outside of a very small circle of us *xuetas*. If anything happens to me, he will already know what happened, where, and when."

"How?"

# Chapter 41

The soft, constant whirr and creak of the windmills lining the shores east of Palma had a soothing sound when mixed with a brisk wind, such as was blowing outside now. The cries of the gulls—distant grace notes, not raucous intrusions—added just enough variety to make it seem like a composition of God's own design, a subtle symphony to enjoy as Miguel Tarongi waited for—

"Hello, Miguel."

Miguel kept himself from starting as a figure brushed past him, evidently emerging from the supposedly secure rear rooms of the tavern. The figure drew out a chair at Tarongi's table—already laden with red wine, olives, salt sardines, and bread—and turned to face him.

Miguel nodded. "And hello to you, Estuban Miro." For, against all probabilities, it was he: the best-aspected son of the *xuetas* who had, for years, been their conduit to, and watchful eyes amidst, the commercial world beyond Palma. And who had seemingly fallen off the face of the Earth—and probably into the maw of Hell and perdition—almost two years earlier. "Nice to see you again," Miguel added with a laconic drawl.

Miro smiled at the understated tone. "Yes, it's been a while, hasn't it?"

"I suspect your mother thinks so," Miguel added a bit more pointedly.

Miro sighed. "Yes, I expect she does. Before I forget, Miguel, please give this to my family. But by indirect channels, you understand."

Miguel crossed his arms instead of accepting the sizeable parcel of letters. "You'll give them yourself—when you see your family."

Miro's eyes closed and Miguel had to work to maintain his gruff exterior; he knew the look of necessary, self-inflicted pain well enough. Living under the Spanish, no *xueta* remained a stranger to expressions as tortured as that one for very long.

"I can't deliver the letters myself, Miguel, because I won't be seeing my family. And you won't tell them I've been here until after I'm gone."

"This is nonsense, Estuban. You family deserves—"

"They deserve to survive, Miguel, which they won't if I have any contact with them while I am here. It would be the start of a new round of *auto-da-fe*'s. Trust me: I know."

Miguel sighed but took the letters. He also knew that tone: the voice of a man embarked upon a desperate course from which he could not deviate. Miguel looked around. After he determined they were alone except for the tavern-owner, who was, after all, one of them, he shifted into Hebrew. "So where have you been... Ezekiel?"

"Didn't you get any of my letters... Meir?"

"Not a one. Where did you post them, and when?"

"From Genoa, back in the spring of 1634, just before I went over the Alps and to Grantville."

Meir's eyebrows raised. "The Algerines were cruising the waters between the Balearics and Sardinia like schools of sharks, back then. Did you send it on a Spanish boat?"

"Genoese. I couldn't risk Spanish channels—for your sakes, here."

Meir nodded. "Which is probably why your letters never arrived; the number of Genoese ships that were lost to pirate-paid mutinies was very high. That only stopped recently."

"Because the Spanish antipiracy patrols have trebled?"

Meir nodded. "Yes. The African pirates are finding the waters a lot less profitable, and a lot more dangerous, now." He wondered at the small, satisfied smile on Ezekiel Miro's face. He would have liked to find out what it meant, but there were so many larger questions to be answered. "Grantville, eh? Have you met Nasi? Is the place as safe as they say?"

"It exceeds description, Meir. If there was any way to do it, I would encourage all the *xuetas* to relocate there, en masse. Or even to Venice."

"Why Venice?"

"Because the up-timer interests are very strong there. And where the Grantvillers set up permanent trading stations, they seem to insist upon a certain minimum of religious toleration. If conditions fall beneath that standard—such as preceded the Inquisition or the pogroms—they tend to leave. Or they effect what they call 'regime change.' That is the stick with which they beat oppressors, but their much larger influence is through the carrot of their commerce. Venice is booming, much stronger for its relationship with the USE. So, although they are not in any way sacrificing their autonomy, I believe the Council of Ten have realized that if they are to sustain their current surge in relative power, they must not antagonize the USE by ignoring the laws that give us Jews additional protection there."

Meir pouted, nodded. "Sounds promising. And you are doing well?"

"Quite well, but right now, I am not here as a merchant."

"No? So what brings you here?"

Miro told him.

Meir heard the finish of Ezekiel's story just as he finished the last of the wine. The olives and bread were already gone, as were half of the fish. The shadows had moved noticeably; their slant was more pronounced, their edges not so sharply demarcated. The sunlight was no longer the punishing white of morning and mid-day, but had become a bit more yellow. Meir dabbed the remains of wine and oil from his lips. "You are, of course, mad," he said.

Miro smiled. "And you are unchanged."

"I am realistic. Being of humble origins, I never had the luxury of grand schemes and flights of fancy. The life of an *orella baixa* is one of reason, you see."

Ezekiel smiled at the reinitiation of their old taunting ritual; they had become fast friends despite—or perhaps because of—the social differences between them. Meir, who was one of the *orella baixa*—or "low ears"—of the *xueta,* should have had little access to Ezekiel, who was the eldest scion of one of the most celebrated families of the *orella alta*—or "high ears." But Ezekiel early decided that these class differences were nonsense, and even as a boy, recognized the strong mind and strong, dogged loyalty of Meir—called "Miguel" in public—who was but a cobbler's son. "Thanks for your reminder that I am, in fact, a spoiled brat—intellectually as well as materially. Now, are the Stones being held in Bellver?"

"Of course. Where else?"

"And have you any news of them?"

"Until a few days ago, we were not even sure they were prisoners there. The Spanish were quiet about it. Word is that some factotum of Borja's oversaw the couple's transfer from Rome. Not much is known about him, however."

Ezekiel's face took on an expression Meir had never seen before—and for the first time in their long years together, Meir was scared of Ezekiel: physically scared. A man with such a look on his face might do anything....

"Does this factotum stay in Bellver?" asked Miro, his eyes still like a shark's.

"No. He mostly resides in the Almudaina."

"Not at the Black House, then?"

"Huh. This man of Borja's seems to have little use for the Inquisition. And they for him."

Miro's expression became a bit less ominous, a bit more thoughtful. "Interesting. But back to the Stones: any word of their condition, or where in the Castell they are being kept?"

"No, but the husband apparently pestered the governor to provide the services of one of our doctors until he got his way, if you can believe that."

"I readily believe he asked for one of our physicians. I find it very strange that the Spanish agreed, however."

"Well, it wasn't without some pressure. Apparently, an hidalgo who accompanied the couple here as a combination guard and overseer added his influence to the request."

"And why did the Stones want a male physician? Why not a midwife?"

"It is said that the up-time ambassadora in Rome, this female doctor Sharon Nichols, warned that there might be complications with the pregnancy, particularly since the woman is carrying twins."

Miro frowned and then, just as suddenly, he was smiling as broadly as when he had been a boy. "This Frank Stone is as shrewd as his father."

"What? Why?"

"Because I consulted with Ambassador Nichols before coming here. Giovanna Stone is not carrying twins. She is also as sturdy a woman as God ever made. It is her first pregnancy, true, so unexpected problems are more likely—but that only gives added credibility to her need for much help, and is all the the more to our advantage."

"What are you talking about?"

"Never mind, Meir. I am thinking out loud. Thinking flighty, useless *orella alta* thoughts, mind you."

"Of course. But—"

"So, they have not been provided a physician, yet?"

Meir shook his head. "No. All that has happened so far is that some inquiries were made in our community."

"Excellent. Is Asher still practicing?"

"Him? He will be doctoring from his deathbed. And he has too wretched a temperament to ever die, so we are stuck with him."

"He is also the best physician in the western half of the Mediterranean. Approach Asher and tell him he must accept this commission from the Spanish."

"Yes, but they might not go to him first. They might—"

"Then approach the other *xueta* physicians, as well. They are to refuse the Spanish commission, if offered."

"But, even if they agree, how can one refuse the Spanish? After all—"

"The others are all younger than Asher. They can refuse on the basis of modesty and that the forced intimacy with another woman is an insult to their wives, and to their duty as good Catholics. Lately come to the foot of the cross, they may protest their ardent desire to observe the highest standards of Christian propriety. The Spanish will accept that—readily."

"Yes, the bastards probably will."

"They are not all bastards, Meir. Believe me. Now, when the Spanish bring the commission to Asher, he is to haggle over the terms. Haggle hard. He must not look eager to take the commission. Which should not be difficult; he is old and travel to and from Bellver will genuinely tax him. And with his reputation for being cantankerous, the Spanish will not be surprised when he resists."

"But if he resists too much, they might seek one of our other physicians—"

"Which is why you will pay them to reject the commission. The job must go to Asher, but he must resist it. If he accepts the case too quickly, the Spanish may suspect it suits some purpose of ours and become suspicious and watchful."

Meir shook his head. "You were ever a deep one, Ezekiel."

"I was ever careful and thorough; you were deeper, more favored by the rabbis. You could have been a Talmudic scholar readily enough."

"I would have had to pay them to raise my ears higher, first. Speaking of the easy assumptions of snobs, just how do you propose I pay for the other physicians to refuse the commission?"

Ezekiel handed him another envelope. It was very thin.

"What is this?"

"Information that will give you access to funds held in the Rialto. You will find ample recompense there, as the accounting at the bottom shows."

Meir managed to keep his eyebrows from rising. "This is a most considerable sum."

"The USE is not without means. Nor is the very wealthy father of Frank Stone."

"Evidently. But Venice is far away, and the favors—and supplies—you need must all be bought here, right now."

"True. But I am not proposing this account as a line of credit against which you may draw. I am conferring it unto you; all of it."

Meir looked at the very large number once again. "So, we put up money equal to, say, half of this sum, and then are entitled to withdraw all of it from the Rialto."

"That is correct. You stand to make one hundred percent profit, but you must bear the risk of advancing the resources we need here."

Meir looked at his old friend. "Huh. There's some of your own money in here as well, isn't there?"

Ezekiel shrugged. "A little. Maybe. I don't recall."

"Breaking the commandments, now, eh, Ezekiel? As in 'thou shalt not lie?' I recognize the account number; this is the one you used to transfer profits to us when you were our counterfeit hidalgo trading from Lisbon to the Levant."

"Which simply meant that we already had an account that could be easily repurposed to support this operation, Meir."

"That's not a lie, but it is still an evasion. How much of your money are you spending to help free these two Gentiles?"

Ezekiel looked hard at Meir. "First, it is none of your business. Second, you do not understand what is at stake here."

"A man and a woman are being held captive under almost princely conditions; excuse me while I weep a bit."

"No, Meir, you are missing the point entirely. These 'Gentiles' as you call them are different. I do not mean different in terms of my personal association with them; I have never met Frank and his wife, although I know the father—and he is as good a man as God ever fashioned. That alone might make me part with some of my money to aid in the reclamation of his son, but that was not what makes him—all of them—different.

"Meir, they preach true religious tolerance and they practice what they preach. And when Jews in their territories were persecuted, they took steps—strong, even violent steps—to put a stop to the mistreatment and punish the offenders. And not so they could lean towards us for loans, as have the kings of Europe since we came to live among them. These up-timers protected our people because they believe it is the right thing to do, that it is their duty."

"Ah, so you have been dwelling among angels, then."

"Meir, don't be obstinate, not about this, and not now. Of course the up-timers are not angels; many are spoiled and impractical, and they are as susceptible to pettiness, jealousy, envy, and stupidity as all the other children of men. But whatever else we may wonder about their up-time world, I have seen this one truth with my own eyes: almost all of them despise bigots, and are incensed by the atrocities committed by them."

Meir shrugged, trying to hide his surprise; he had never seen Ezekiel this passionate about anything in his life. "And so?"

"And so virtue and prudence dictate the same course for us. In helping the Stones, we help those who will not fail to insist upon advancing the cause of justice in this world. And so, in helping them, we help ourselves."

Meir shrugged again, then tossed the account information down upon the table. "So what do you need?"

Ezekiel did not smile; he simply passed another piece of paper to Meir. Who almost gagged.

Miro was not done. "Obviously, I can't pick it up here in Palma, so I'll need you to contract a nondescript *llaut* with a reasonable cargo capacity. The master and crew will have to be discreet and available for at least two weeks. They are are to maintain the activities and appearance of fishermen; however they will ship these supplies out to us every other day, starting four days from now."

Meir nodded. "I know a *xueta*, fully 'reconciled' to the Church, who will be perfect for the job. Above suspicion and very clever, but not much of a fisherman: he'll be better at this. Where must he take the shipments?"

"You are familiar with Cala Beltran, just south of Cala Pi?"

"You mean, at the southern tip of the island—and right under the nose of the watchtower there?"

"Yes, the watchtower the Spanish still haven't finished building, from what I understand."

"You're pretty well informed."

"I try to be. With the tower still under construction, it does not have a full complement of guards and coast-watchers. But, more importantly, with all the *llaut*s going in and out of Cala Pi at dusk and dawn, who'll notice one more loitering near Cala Beltran?"

"Let me guess. My *llaut* will go up Cala Beltran, deposit the goods in one of the small, blind coves and then leave once your ship is in sight."

"Correct. Then my ship goes in to pick up the shipment before anyone can stumble across it."

"I forgot how many times you must have done this before."

"You have no idea, old friend. A few final details: Asher should be expecting to get messages from the Stones, but we must presume that he will be watched by the Spanish—both at the Castell and in his own home. Change his housekeeper now; make it someone who has helped us in the past, someone discreet and with whom we have routine, mundane contact."

"Obviously. And Asher will obviously immediately understand that he will have to bear our messages back to the Stones. Which he won't like."

"No, he won't, but he'll do it; he has to have something to gripe about, after all. But without his cooperation, we won't have any way to coordinate with Frank and Giovanna."

"And the communication between the two of us runs through the *llaut*?"

"Yes, they will carry my messages, as well as the personnel I will send to wait here with you."

Meir blinked. "Personnel? You mean military personnel who might attack Bellver?"

Ezekiel shrugged. "Anything is possible at this point."

"I suppose anything is, since you're obviously still trying to pull together the final details of your final plan." Seeing the look on Miro's face, he scowled. "Wait: do you even *have* a plan at this point?"

Ezekiel smiled faintly. "I have some basic ideas; nothing so firm as a *plan*, just yet. But trust me; we shall reclaim the Stones from their Spanish prison."

"You mean, by main force?"

"Well, yes, if it comes to it. What did you think?"

"I thought you were still sane. I presumed you would find a way to sneak them out, with maybe a rough moment or two along the way. But rescuing them by assaulting Bellver?" Meir stared at his friend. "Have you forgotten, Ezekiel? It's on top of a hill. It is a fortification with towers and a separate lazarette, surrounded by outlying battlements. The terrain makes it almost inaccessible, except for the cart paths up to the place."

"Yes, Meir; I remember all that. I know we won't rescue them simply by battering our way in."

"Well, what do you expect to do, Ezekiel Miro? Ask angels to pluck them out for you?"

Ezekiel started, stared at Meir and then laughed. "Yes. Something just like that."

# Chapter 42

Cardinal Antonio Barberini dipped his pen into the waiting ink as the other attendees in the Garden Room settled into their customary seats. Vitelleschi stood and raised his hands in something that looked like both a call for silence, and a benediction. "Today we resume our deliberations with the issue that Cardinal Wadding introduced last time: does the up-time ecumenical council known as Vatican Two reflect God's intents across all eternity? Or was it specifically, and only, infallibly valid in relation to the up-time world?" He turned to Cardinal Mazzare. "If you would be so good as to begin our discussions, Your Eminence."

Mazzare folded his hands in front of him and seemed to be collecting his thoughts. As he did, Barberini noted that the up-timer's posture was more studied, more implicitly cautious than usual. Antonio put his nose back into his note taking, but reflected that today's session might prove very interesting, indeed.

Mazzare began. "Today's topic troubles me more than any other, simply because the passage that Cardinal Wadding cited at the close of the last session seems implicitly contradictory. How can infallibility be transitory? Is the truth not the truth? Is the will of God not the will of God? We all agree that there is but one God and one Truth and they are the same. But then how is it that some of these timeless verities are 'transitory'?"

Mazzare spread his hands. "I would offer the following answer, which is not entirely unlike the one Cardinal Wadding seems ready to propose: in short, although God and his truth are constant and unchanging, humankind is not. Vatican Two was convened to make the Church more accessible. God loves his children, and as they grow, he wishes to communicate with them in a manner suitable to their new maturity. The delegates of Vatican Two understood this and merely included a reminder to future popes and councils that, as the ages accumulate and humanity grows in grace and wisdom, the same process will probably need to be undertaken again. Our Holy Father is truly our Holy Parent, who shows his love for us by adjusting his lessons, his language, and his challenges to our level of maturity and readiness. He does not give us more than we can handle, nor does he keep us frozen as infants: he expresses his thought and love to us as befits our needs, just as we aspire to a greater understanding of Him. Neither side of the human relationship with God is static; it is perpetually a dynamic equilibrium."

Vitelleschi's right eyebrow rose slightly. "Cardinal Mazzare, you have not yet spoken to the matter of papal authority, of how the doctrines and dogmas of up-time popes should be received in this world."

Mazzare shrugged. "I do not speak to it because the answer seems obvious; if they were popes, they were infallible in matters of faith and morals. And they *were* popes. On the other hand, they are dead popes. Their authority does not impinge upon the popes of this time any more than the popes who have died here in this world."

Barberini looked up for a moment, surprised by the falling tone at the end of Mazzare's statement. Clearly, this was all he intended to say on the matter. Which was surprising, because the final declaration sounded more like an evasion dressed up as an assertion, rather than a solid argument. Barberini was not surprised that Wadding was on his feet a moment later.

Vitelleschi glanced at Wadding, then back to Mazzare. "Cardinal Wadding seems eager to question you on this statement, Cardinal Mazzare."

Mazzare smiled. "I rather expected he might. I am happy to share the floor with my colleague."

Wadding wasted no time probing at the exegetical evasions that Barberini himself had detected. "Your Eminence, you say that the popes in your world are analogous to the prior ones in our own world, correct?"

"Insofar as their infallibility is concerned, yes."

"But how can this be?"

"How can this not be, if they are all popes?"

"Let us leave aside the issue of infallibility for just a moment. Let us instead remain focused on the issue of whether the popes of your world are so truly analogous to the past popes of our world. I question the accuracy of this analogy for the most obvious of all possible reasons: my world's long chain of prior pontiffs have exercised their Extraordinary Sacred Magisterium to establish dogmas and doctrines that are now binding upon the present pope, Urban VIII. Do you agree?"

"Of course."

"By which you implicitly agree that no present pope has the power to set aside that which was infallibly decreed by a prior pope?"

Mazzare cleared his throat. "Depending upon what you mean by the word *prior*, yes, I provisionally agree with that."

Barberini almost set down his paper to listen; he had never heard Larry Mazzare equivocate before.

Wadding smelled blood. "Unless there are additional meanings of which I am unaware, 'prior' means to come before, to precede in time. And that is the crux of the difference we must consider: the pontiffs who have gone before us in our world—the very same as those who went before Urban VIII in your up-time world— are 'prior' popes. But those who came after Urban VIII in your world are *not* prior to the papacy of Urban VIII in *this* world."

Mazzare smiled. "Yet we are even now discussing the infallible doctrines and dogma decreed by up-time pontiffs, which were first presented to His Holiness Urban VIII two years ago. Their presence in the canonical records of the Church thus precede these discussions and, as you have conceded, their perfection derives from the same Sacred Magisterium that is immanent in the current and prior popes."

"Yes—and as also manifested in the up-time popes who came after Urban VIII, who are *later* popes," corrected Wadding calmly.

"Yet here are their dogmas and directives, now; their existence precedes this discussion."

Even to Barberini, Mazzare's argument seemed somewhat ingenuous—and thus, desperate.

Wadding was pointing at Urban, "So you would have this pope constrained by the decrees of men who lived long after he died, and who you assert will now never be born, since the history of this world has been changed by your arrival in it?"

Mazzare spread his hands. "At no point did I say that this issue would be free of paradoxes. So allow me propose an escape from this one: God intends all things, yes?"

Wadding's voice and face were wary. "Of course."

"So it was known to God that Grantville would come back in time?"

"He is all powerful and all knowing, so this must be true."

"Then, if Holy Writ is divinely inspired, either it should furnish us with explicit guidance for how the Church should respond to such a paradoxical challenge, or it already contains an implicit answer for us. I assert the latter: no explicit guidance is needed because infallibility transcends all other considerations, including those of time and sequence."

Wadding smiled. "Cardinal Mazzare, do you really expect Holy Writ to include warnings about multiple realities and Churches? Should we really be surprised at the lack of specific injunctions to 'hold only unto thine own pope?'" He turned to face Vitelleschi. "Father-General, I agree that Holy Writ is not deficient, but not because of the insuperable nature of papal infallibility. Rather, we may look to its elegant reliance upon the common context of the word 'prior' to understand the relationship between the infallible utterances of this world, and Cardinal Mazzare's. Although we lack detailed documentation in this place—"

*God be praised*, thought Barberini with an irreverent smile.

"—I find that both down- and up-time constraints upon papal infallibility invariably stipulate that a prior pope's *ex cathedra* statements and doctrinal decrees may not be overturned, contravened, or ignored by later popes. Consequently, I do not see a paradox at all as long as we accept that 'prior' is not a term subject to recontextualization: it means 'to occur before.' Nothing more, nothing less.

"Cardinal Mazzare suggests, on the other hand, that we must eschew such a common-sense definition of the word and instead dive into a maelstrom of temporal paradoxes from which we cannot ever hope to emerge. He also proposes to resolve supposed 'contradictions' in the footnote in *Gaudium et Spes* which asserts that some of its own infallible elements 'have a permanent value; others, only a transitory one.'" Wadding smiled. "This statement neither contains nor engenders any contradictions. It is merely a reminder that the Truth that is God cannot be beheld by His children all at once. Indeed, as the Creator told Moses, no man may behold the face of God and live. Therefore, since we cannot survive exposure to the entirety of His Truth at once, we must have it relayed to us in successive parts, each new epiphany being withheld until our souls have grown enough to be ready for it.

"Cardinal Mazzare provided us with a most instructive analogy for this process: he likened it to the way in which children change. And what does the note to *Gaudium et Spes* say, really, other than this: that the basic rules we learn as spiritual infants are not tossed aside, but enriched and expanded as we grow. A five-year-old child might have a sense of right and wrong, and even justice. But would any one of us maintain that his understanding then will be the equal of that which he possesses when he is fifteen, or thirty-five, presuming he grows in Christ as he grows in his body?"

Father-General Vitelleschi was frowning. "Are you therefore suggesting, Your Eminence, that the population of the up-time world was more ready for complex truths than the population of our own world?"

Wadding nodded. "That is a distinct possibility. After all, the up-time world had three and a half more centuries experience in adapting to the complexities of religious toleration and political equality. The increasing phenomena of marriage between Catholics and Protestants, and then Jews and Gentiles, gave them ample opportunity to work out in daily practice what we down-timers see as unthinkably radical theological and social change."

"And how does this instruct us?" asked Vitelleschi.

Wadding bowed his head. "It shows us that our Lord is truly a kind, loving, and above all, foresightful parent. He waited for the up-timers to grow into these accomplishments before he set them the challenges implicit in Vatican Two. Allow me to illustrate what I mean in mundane terms: would you teach your little child to climb a cliff-face before he can walk? No, because it is imperative that, as a parent, you make sure that he walks, and then acquires other requisite skills, before he may confront the cliff-face. Similarly, God ensured the gradual maturation of the up-time world and Church, before sharing what was for *them* the infallible wisdom of Vatican Two. For Cardinal Mazzare and his peers, Vatican Two was an exhilarating new cliff to climb; for us, it would simply be a fast and fatal fall."

Wadding folded his hands. "Our wise and Loving God would not impose the same challenge upon both societies, without regard to their respective levels of readiness. And so I argue the term 'transitory,' as it is used in *Gaudium et Spes*, simply reminds us that the perfect parental wisdom of our Heavenly Father is both firm and flexible."

Wadding paused. "Popes—whatever else they may be—are still merely men, and are thus products of the time in which they live. They're born into the same reality as the flock in which they are raised, and ultimately, of which they become shepherds. Thus, you might say, each pope enjoys a special Temporal Charism. The inspiration of the Holy Spirit ensures that they are, so to speak, the right pope at the right time for the right flock."

Wadding turned toward Mazzare. "So let us allow that your John XXIII was such a pope, who called for ecumenicism in a world that teetered on the brink of man-made apocalypse. Let us assume that the same was true of your Pope John Paul II, who exerted his Sacred Magisterium to promulgate these infallible doctrines of tolerance. These papal actions may have played an essential role in ensuring the survival of your world, which was every bit as fear-filled and war-weary as this one."

"But it was also a very, very *different* world from this one. Yours was a world which had already resolved many conflicts that we are not ready to set aside, or maybe, more to the point, know that God does not yet wish us to set aside. Either way, I put it to you that your popes made the right choices for the flock of their time. But this is not that time, and this is not that flock. And so the same choices are not right for us—no matter how infallible they were in the context of your up-time world."

Wadding sat. Vitelleschi looked over at Cardinal Mazzare. "Your Eminence, do you have anything you wish to add?"

Mazzare shook his head. "No, Father-General; I am done."

As Antonio Barberini concluded his transcription and began dating and witnessing the document, he watched Mazzare rise more slowly than usual and thought, *Yes, Your Eminence, you were done about halfway through.* And then he realized, *If the up-timer has one more day like that, I suspect my immediate future will not include a papal Progress to a nice, safe haven somewhere in USE territory. Rather, I may be on the run in the provinces of Italy for the rest of my very short life.*

Cardinal Antonio Barberini found that thought not only unappealing, but downright terrifying.

# Chapter 43

Thomas North had to admit it: Harry Lefferts was not just a fine special operative, he was a fine field officer, as well. And nothing proved that so clearly, and so profoundly, as his ability to simply wait.

The pirate ship—an uncommonly large *llaut*, as the Mallorquin fishermen had claimed—had arrived and started its cautious approach to the Bay of Canyamel in the early hours of the morning. It put a small boat over its side when the sky was still goose-gray, and loitered behind while that skiff made its way into the bay just after dawn. Dressed as fishermen, the pirates rowed the small boat to the foot of the caves. Harry and North had watched through binoculars as they scrambled up the steep and craggy slope and then passed within, uneventfully.

That had been more than an hour ago. Many officers—both new and seasoned—would, by now, be fretting about what had happened. Under conditions like these, too many officers became convinced that it was A Bad Sign that none of their own men had emerged yet and so, started straining at the bit to go help—personally.

Not Harry Lefferts. He lazed on the stern thwart. If it was an act, it was a very good one. "Hey, owner-aboard and Captain," North said.

"What?"

"I suppose I should inform you that there's a movement afoot to name the ships."

"Oh? What are the names?"

"Well, the Ragusans have always had a name for their *gajeta*: *Zora*, or 'Dawn.' The Venetians felt that the old name for the *barca-longa* was a bit parochial and tepid, so they changed it from the *Maria* to the *Guerra Cagna*."

"*War Bitch?*" translated Harry. "Catchy."

"Quite. And I renamed the xebec myself: it's now the *Atropos*."

"What?...Oh, I get it. Bravo, Mr. Hornblower. I didn't take you for the nautical type." Harry patted the gunwale of the *scialuppa*. "And what have they decided to call this bucket?"

North shrugged. "They're leaving it with the name it always had: the *Pesciolino*."

"The *Little Fish?*"

"As I understand it, the context is more akin to 'the *Minnow*.'"

Harry's jaw fell open. "The *Minnow*? Really? The *Minnow*?" And without any warning, he fell backward in the thwarts, laughing so hard that Thomas was concerned that some delicate mental thread in the up-timer had finally snapped.

But upon rising to check on Harry, North discovered that the captain's malady was indeed nothing more than uncontrollable hysterics. "What in blazes are you laughing at? You're making the crew nervous."

"The *Minnow*?" Harry gasped. "Why didn't anyone tell me this was a three-hour tour?" And then he fell back laughing again.

"What the bloody hell are you talking about?"

Harry, tears streaming out of his eyes, propped himself up and explained, since they had nothing better to do, about the strange up-time TV phenomenon known as *Gilligan's Island*.

Hearing the return of calm to the back of his boat, Aurelio edged aftward to take a look at Lefferts. "He okay?" the Piombinese captain asked North.

Harry stared up at Aurelio, then pointed and chortled, "Oh. My. God. It's the Skipper—with a mustache and an Italian accent!" In an attempt to keep his laughing more quiet, Lefferts pitched over, head between his knees, his back quaking in time with his suppressed guffaws.

Orazio joined his uncle many times removed to look at the stricken up-timer. "The captain, he is not well?"

Harry looked up, and now the laughter was coming out as choked, wheezing spasms. He pointed again, this time at Orazio. "And Gilligan. Where's the Professor? He'll figure out the attack plan we need. And Ginger—oh, Ginger—" He bent over again, laughing so hard that he could no longer speak.

Aurelio and Orazio looked at North, eyebrows high, eyes wide. "The captain—is he—eh, that is, has he—?"

North sighed. "The captain is fine. Just very, very amused."

"Amused? While we wait to fight pirates?"

"He laughs in the face of death. Me too. Ha, ha."

The Italians' stares ping-ponged from North, to the recovering Lefferts, and back to North. Although they did not speak, their thoughts were easy to read: "Mad Englishmen." North couldn't blame them for thinking that; in fact, he was disposed to agree with them. Even if they did shamefully associate up-time Americans with their English progenitors. "You see, now; the captain is quite himself again."

Which was almost true. Lefferts sat up very straight, opened his mouth to begin what would probably be a very sane, rational explanation for his debilitating fit of mirth—when one of the Venetians who had been seeded on board the *Minnow* hissed, "The little pirate boat has started back from the caves."

The *scialuppa* was suddenly quiet. Lefferts' rapid, easy shift into complete tactical focus was, North had to admit, enviable. "Get yourself behind the sail, Orazio, and then scan the boat using the binoculars. Don't keep them out for more than a minute; we don't want the pirates getting a glimpse of the lenses. Tell me what you see back at the caves. Aurelio, start taking us to windward of the pirate *llaut*—slowly. Nothing suspicious."

"*Si*, Captain Lefferts." Aurelio did not like combat—he was a fisherman by both trade and temperament—but he seemed relieved at Harry's recovery.

"Orazio, what are you seeing? Tell me everything, lil' buddy." Harry snickered as the uttered the last words; North resolved to view whatever episodes of *Gilligan's Island* had made the journey back down-time.

If Orazio noticed Harry's strange form of address, he gave no sign of it; he was too intent on his job. "I see our men in the boat, dressed in the pirates' clothes and gear. The number in the boat equal the number of pirates killed in the cave, plus those who approached in the skiff. As you instructed."

"Excellent. Are they rowing or—?"

"Yes, they are rowing, but now they are also putting up the step sail. Captain, I am thinking they will be out here in ten, maybe fifteen minutes?"

"Except that the pirate doesn't seem disposed to wait that long," commented North. "Look."

They did: the pirate *llaut* had come about briskly, heading in toward the Bay of Canyamel, evidently determined to rendezvous as quickly as possible.

Harry smiled. "Guess they're getting antsy out here."

"Or don't want us close enough to observe what happens when they meet," offered North.

"Probably both," Lefferts replied with a grin. "Aurelio—"

"*Si*, Major; you want me to use the *llaut*'s change of position to work more to windward of them. And then close the distance. Slowly."

"You read my mind, Skipper. I'll have Mary Ann bake you a pineapple pie."

"Eh?"

"Never mind. Look to the sails. Thomas, it's probably about time for us to bring out the tools of our trade."

"Fishing rods?"

"Well—rods, I guess," commented Harry. Keeping it below the level of the gunwale, he unwrapped his SKS. "And appropriate for us fishers of men."

"My, that's awful grim for a Yank," commented North. "And improbably poetic. Are you sure you're not becoming English?"

Thomas, who had only been in a few shipboard fights over the course of his career, was once again struck by the almost surreal pacing of them.

First, there was a long cat-and-mouse game as each of the three ships tried to feign a false identity and purpose. The small skiff affected the appearance of being filled by busily rowing fishermen—or disguised pirates, depending upon the intended audience. The corsair *llaut* attempted to create the impression of a fishing boat lazily approaching the shore. And the *Minnow* mimicked the irregular course changes of a boat trying to find the best spot in which to let down nets. Throughout this ballet of deception, the skiff and *llaut* closed with each other slowly; the *Minnow*, having the advantage of the wind at its back, was able to approach indirectly and at a positively glacial pace.

But then, as the boats drew within a few hundred yards of each other, everything seemed to speed up. The skiff angled aside to bring the breeze more over its beam. This changed its approach to the *llaut* from a gradual yet direct rendezvous, to a speedier, but oblique course that would ultimately bring it across the bows of the larger ship: "crossing the T" as the admirals of later, up-time centuries had put it.

At the same time, the *llaut* had raised her yard a bit, putting more sheet to the reaching wind. The ship would call more attention to itself that way, but the pirates were probably preparing to abandon their efforts at mimicking a legitimate fishing boat. This close to the mouth of the bay, they probably wanted speed more than anything else; their goal was now to reach the skiff, take it and its men on board, and swing about toward open water where—if Spanish patrol boats put in a surprise appearance—the corsair could maneuver and evade.

Meanwhile, the *Minnow* began swinging slowly around to catch the wind from the rear starboard quarter. Given the way she was rigged currently, that pushed her forward at maximum speed. North heard the occasional, swell-cutting whispers of the prow mount into the hoarse, bumping rush that betokened speed great enough to generate a true bow wave.

Soon after, someone on the *llaut* obviously saw something suspicious in the oncoming skiff; wild gesticulations in its direction summoned two more observers into the bows, who hurriedly gestured to turn about.

The *llaut* veered off—but within moments discovered that it was directly leeward of the no-longer innocent looking *scialuppa*, which was now bearing down on them, its crew crouching low behind its gunwales. At approximately two hundred yards, the pilot of the pirate craft must have recognized the same speed and directness of course that he had set many times himself when attempting to intercept prey. Trapped, the corsair veered again, back toward its old course, simultaneously trying to cheat close to the wind, keep speed, and run out from between the two ships that were now clearly operating in concert.

But the prize crew on the skiff had foreseen and planned on this. Rather than giving direct chase when the *llaut* had first veered away from them, it had held its oblique course, continuing to push directly out of the bay, step sail raised high. And now the stratagem behind that maneuver became clear: when the *llaut* came around to avoid the *Minnow*, it found its prow aiming straight at the side of the skiff. The *llaut* no longer had enough room to avoid both of the ships; it would have to pass at close quarters with one of them, at least, or head deeper into the bay.

Seeing the small, overloaded skiff as the only thing standing in his way, the pirate captain made the predictable choice: to head straight for it. It was a sound tactic: on the one hand, it minimized the effect of the one volley its occupants might get off by making sure the spray of bullets came over the sheltering bow, rather than over the beam. Additionally, the ketch either had to move out of the *llaut*'s way, or be smashed by its almost vertical prow and then shattered under its rushing keel. For a vessel larger than a *llaut*, there would have been no reciprocal danger involved, but in this case, it was a somewhat bold move: the pirate hull was not so large that it was impervious to damage. But as it turned out, this calculated risk was in fact a fatal mistake.

Thomas North clenched the athletic whistle between his teeth and sent out a shrill blast that carried over the sound of the gentle swells and the hulls that were hissing and frothing through them.

From the skiff, the stentorian voice of Owen Roe O'Neill barked out orders. A moment later, the little boat nearly came to a stop, offering its waist to the onrushing *llaut*. When the separating range had diminished to seventy yards, six men rose up in the skiff, weapons snugged against their cheeks as O'Neill roared for the oarsmen to steady the hull as much as possible.

The pirates came on, confident that they would soon be past a single storm of lead and then smash the enemy craft to flinders. That was when the weapons of the six men—four .40-72 lever actions and the task force's two SKS-Ms—began their rolling torrent of sharp, percussive fire.

The SKS's alone pounded out fifty rounds in less than twenty seconds. The .40-72s fired at a slower pace, but there were four of them, and when one was dry, Owen handed that rifleman a fresh weapon. Fired from one moving, pitching, platform to another, the majority of the shots were misses, many quite wild.

But at least a score found their marks. Pirates kept sprawling, falling across their oars, under the thwarts, two going over the side. The one who had been heaving mightily on the yard collapsed; the yard tilted down, the sail sagged. The corsair captain, resolved to return fire, scrambled to the bow, raised his wheel lock—and had three bullets go through his chest before he could fire his own weapon. The man at the tiller stood to see what had happened, was shouting orders when a round hit him in the shoulder. It spun the steersman about, but he kept hold of the sweep and was still giving orders when a second bullet went in his left temple and emerged in a bloody gout from his right ear.

The *llaut*, tiller free and sail hanging, began drifting back in toward the bay, pushed by the currents and the wind. As the *Minnow* closed in on it, there was movement visible along the gunwales and then a few survivors rose up cautiously. A quick look at the bodies piled in their boat told them all they needed to know: that there were not enough crew left to man her. The survivors looked at each other, and then began to raise their hands over their heads.

Thomas felt his stomach clench, but did what he had to do: he gave two short blasts on the whistle. The four Hibernians with him in the *Minnow* lifted their weapons and shot the pirates down where they stood.

As the *Minnow* and the skiff converged on the *llaut*, no amount of rationalizing managed to untie the knot of guilt that was constricting North's stomach. He looked at Lefferts, whose face was not quite entirely impassive.

"We had no choice," said the up-timer quietly. "We knew it would probably come to this."

"Damned if that makes in any easier," commented North.

Harry nodded and watched the first of the Venetian sailors leap across the gap between the *Minnow* and the pirate *llaut*, carrying lines to make them fast together.

North cleared his throat. "Aurelio," he said, "go on board and tell me how fast you can get her crewed and ready to move. Owen?"

"Here."

"Any casualties?"

"Nary a hit, not even to the skiff itself. Shall we board the corsair and take inventory?"

"Stop reading my mind. By the way, how much food did you leave behind in the cave?"

"Dinner for twenty, maybe."

"Not worth the risk going back for it. Anything else?"

"No; every bit of gear—ours and theirs—is crowded into this wee boat."

"Transfer it all to the *llaut*, then put the skiff in tow."

"As you say, Lord Sassenach. And the bodies? What to do with them?"

Thomas glanced at Harry, who met his gaze and nodded. Thomas stood straight and called over to Owen, "Consign them to the deep."

Two nights later, Miro arrived at the Caves of Arta, found the skiff waiting for him, and made what was now a long journey over the horizon to the re-gathered flotilla. As the little boat finally approached the lightless *Atropos*, he grinned up at Harry Lefferts, who was awaiting him on poop deck. "Permission to come aboard?"

"Hell," drawled Harry, "near as I can figure it, you own this ship."

"Why, I suppose I might. But no: it's more proper to consider all the prize hulls common property for now, at least until we can work out the shares later on."

"You sound way too familiar with the conventions of this piracy business, Estuban. You sure you've told me everything about your past?"

"Never ask a question if you'd rather not know the answer."

"Huh. Figured. So: now what?"

North had strolled over with O'Neill and, seeing them approach Harry, Miro lost his train of thought for a second; they were truly, and naturally, comrades now. In his absence, these three very different men had finished forging the bonds that made them a team, a group of soldiers who worked well together, and even liked each other.

"Estuban? You okay?"

"Yes, Harry, just a little distracted. Tired from the journey, I expect. The rowers in the skiff briefed me on the way out, but some of the news seemed to good to believe. Did you really take the corsair without any losses?"

"Seems so," said Harry, who rummaged about in a deck locker and produced a bottle of wine and a fistful of small pewter mugs.

Miro looked down. "A victory drink? Isn't that a bit presumptive?"

"I think of it merely as a 'Hey! We're not dead yet!' drink," replied Harry.

Miro smiled. "Yes. We have been lucky. For a change."

"Let's hope that luck holds a little longer—long enough to grab Frank and Gia." Harry gulped at his wine. "So spill, Estuban: are the Stones where you thought they'd be?"

"Yes, in the Castell de Bellver. And we'll have all the help and supplies we need to get them out."

"And do you have a plan finalized yet?" Thomas sounded doubtful,

"I have a plan; you will all help me polish the details. And we'll need to do it tonight, in my cabin."

"Why so soon? And why inside?" asked Owen.

"It must be tonight because some of you will be heading directly to a safe house in Palma by tomorrow evening."

"Oh, and who would that be?"

"Well, actually...you, Owen. You and one of your men will be the first to go."

"Me and—?"

"Yes. Then you, Thomas; you'll head in a few days before the rescue operation is set to begin."

"And may I ask why I must be shipped into Palma?"

"So that you can lead the troops into Bellver."

"Wonderful. And how am I supposed to do that? By knocking on the portcullis and asking politely to enter?"

Miro smiled. "We'll worry about the specifics when we're done with the wine—and where none of the men can hear us talking."

Harry looked around at the black seas and up at the silver stars. "Huh. Doesn't look like a promising neighborhood for enemy informers, Estuban."

"It's not. But we'll be coming close to shore soon; I trust our men, but I don't know all of them well enough to be sure that, if they had a detailed plan to sell to our enemies, one of them wouldn't succumb to the allure of forty pieces of silver—or much more. And with all the pre-positioning, supply pickup, and transport that we're going to be coordinating over the next two weeks, they'd have plenty of opportunity to betray our plans to the enemy. So except for those groups who will train for the operation in separation from the others, we will not be sharing the details of the rescue with our men."

"So you *do* have the basics of a rescue plan," persisted North. "Does this mean you have also settled on a plan of escape?"

"I'm a little less certain about that part of the operation," confessed Miro. "It can be done of course, but—" Miro glanced around at the faint, moonlit masts of their small flotilla "—but it is difficult to see how we will get so many ships safely away, without any falling into Spanish hands."

Harry finished pouring out another round of wine. "Piece of cake. Do to them what they did to us in Rome."

Miro frowned. "What do you mean?"

"I mean, they had lots of vehicles too—carriages, there—but they still had us running a four-way wild goose chase while playing 'find the pea.'"

Miro realized he was the only one not drinking, but didn't care; Harry had shown him the answer, the way they could escape. In fact, if Miro's rapidly evolving calculations were correct, they'd not only be able to get out all the ships and their crews, but also—

"Estuban," Owen Roe seemed to say from a great distance, "what's wrong? Why the lunatic smile?"

"Oh, nothing. Just enjoying the genius of Harry's plan."

Lefferts had a sour expression on his face. "Just don't forget how my last plan ended up. Genius, my ass. If I was a genius I wouldn't have gotten so many people killed."

Miro shook his head. "*You* didn't get anyone killed, Harry. That was the work of a clever, deceptive, and well-prepared enemy, not you. This time, it shall be you—and the rest of us—who outwit them. And even if you insist you are not a genius—well, your escape plan most certainly is." Miro patted him on the shoulder. "It is genius. Pure genius."

# Chapter 44

Pedro Dolor looked from Captain Vincente Jose-Maria de Castro y Papas at one end of the table to Castle Governor Don Sancho Jaume Morales y Llaguno at the other. "You asked me to delay my return to Palma, Governor. Here I am, as you requested. Now: why did you ask me to sit in on this meeting?"

"To rein in your factotum, Señor Dolor." Don Sancho glowered at the captain.

Dolor sighed. "What now, Governor?"

"Ask him yourself."

"I am asking *you*, Governor, since, on the four prior occasions you asked me to intervene with the captain, the only 'fault' I could find was that he issued lawful orders that offended your inflated sense of self-importance. So you will answer my question and, in so doing, justify why I have been detained. Again."

The governor became quite red, but complied. "He has a Jew waiting outside the gate of my castle. A foul old Jew who has not reconciled to the Church. He does not eat pork, he—"

"A moment, Governor. Are you saying that Captain Castro y Papas has summoned a *converso* to sit outside your walls, simply to annoy you?"

"No, damn it! This Jew—David Asher—is a doctor, and foul-tempered to boot. He refuses to follow many of the requirements

465

placed upon *xuetas* in order to prove the earnestness of their conversion—"

Don Vincente sighed. "It is well known that in the matter of *conversos*, public display proves very little, either way. The Inquisition itself has said as much. Besides, I am told that he refrains from eating pork due to health reasons."

"Yes—those articulated by Leviticus, no doubt!"

Dolor folded his hands in front of him. "Governor, I did not ask for a character assessment of this David Asher; I asked why you believe Don Vincente has requested him to come here. Since you seem unable or ill-disposed to answer me directly, allow me to employ some deduction: since this *xueta* is a doctor, I presume he is here in a professional capacity. Consequently, I presume that he has been summoned to assess Giovanna Stone's condition."

"Yes—and without my permission! Captain Castro y Papas did not even bother to inform me of Asher's arrival today. I wouldn't have known the odious Jew was here if it wasn't for loyalty of my sergeants."

Which Dolor confidently translated as: *if it wasn't for the bribes I started paying my own soldiers to snitch on the comings, goings, and doings of the new captain and his men from the fort.* "I see. Captain Castro y Papas, although you are not formally required to clear such actions through the governor, why did you not do him the courtesy of announcing that this visitor was coming to Castell de Bellver?"

"I did, Señor Dolor. The governor elected not to acknowledge it. He simply countered that the man had already been invited here and had refused to come."

*Ah.* Now the scent of truth was starting to rise up beyond the ordure of the governor's righteous indignation. "Can you explain what you mean?"

"Of course. When the governor's efforts at locating a *xueta* physician began stalling last week, I inquired why. Don Sancho was not willing to explicate. I was compelled to, erm, seek independent explanations for this puzzling state of affairs."

Dolor nodded, understanding Castro's implication: *I had to speak to the* xuetas *themselves to learn what was happening.*

"From those sources, I learned that the governor was offering the physicians half the recompense we had agreed upon. The *xueta* physicians—who are, I point out, only *allegedly* Jewish—were unwilling to perform the task at any sum. Most of them were reluctant to become involved in the treatment of what the governor insists upon calling a 'true' Christian woman. The *xuetas* convincingly explained how involvement in such cases can often backfire upon *conversos* such as themselves.

"However, the best of these physicians—whose name I had passed on to the governor but whom, for some mysterious reason, he approached last—was the only one not to reject the commission outright. However, he was every bit as reluctant as his peers and had several stipulations—"

"Which were utterly outrageous!" the governor screeched, his jowls quivering.

Dolor might have sighed. "What were these stipulations?"

"He required at least two assistants to help him with medical procedures and getting up the hill and the stairs: he is in his late seventies. He also wanted an inordinate amount of spirits on hand."

"Spirits?"

Don Vincente nodded. "Yes; pure alcohol. He calls it ethanol. It is an up-time term, which signifies—"

"It signifies witchery, or I'll be buggered by a bull!"

"Ethanol is the up-time term for 'medical alcohol' is it not?"

Don Vincente shrugged. "Perhaps, but I think that may apply to what they call 'methanol.' In any event, Asher indicated that for now, he only has access to large quantities of ethanol. It is apparently quite effective at preventing infections."

Dolor had heard this before. "Did the *xueta* require anything else?"

"No, but the appearance—"

"Governor, I suggest you worry less about appearances and more about your responsibilities."

"I am, Señor Dolor—and I answer to the Carthusian Monastery for my actions, as you may be aware. So I elected to seek out a physician that was more pleasing both to God and the authorities of His Majesty. And I was fortunate enough to find one, residing for a time here in the Almudaina."

Don Vincente cleared his throat. "If I may, Señor Dolor?"

"Yes?"

"The physician to whom the governor refers was promoted to his current position after concluding his service to the aristocracy on the mainland, where, within the last year, he bungled three births, losing two of the mothers in the process. One was the niece of a prominent nobleman."

"A prominent nobleman who was well-known in court, I take it?"

"Very well known in court, Señor Dolor."

"I see. So, given the prospect of having this bungler from the mainland attending the prisoner's parturition, you decided to take matters into your own hand concerning the hiring of the *xueta* physician?"

Don Vincente shrugged. "Their doctors are quite proficient. This one is said to be the best."

"And also the most uncooperative," put in the governor. "At the captain's repeated urging, I finally relented and deigned to extend this signal honor to Asher. The heretic's response was so lacking in grace or gratitude that he deserved flogging on the spot."

Don Vincente shrugged. "I did warn the governor that we had to expect a measure of reluctance from the *xueta* physicians. They are most uncomfortable handling female medical matters."

Dolor shrugged. "However, is this case not made easier since it is not one of their own community?"

Don Vincente shrugged back. "Señor Dolor, let us speak frankly. Let us allow that many of the *xuetas* are still—to some degree or another—practicing Jews. They not only consider contact with Gentiles distasteful but dangerous—and in the latter regard, history vindicates their opinion. Frankly, I suspect that there are only two reasons they will provide assistance to Giovanna Stone."

"The money, of course," sneered Don Sancho.

Don Vincente's voice was sharp. "You mean, the money that was already insufficient before you decided to pocket half of it yourself?"

"What outrageous lie is this?" The governor's face deepened from red to purple. "I was holding the other half back, so that I might have something left to bargain with. You know how Jews are, how they will—"

Given the look on Don Vincente's face, Dolor was glad that the full length of the table was between him and the sanctimonious little liar who, it now seemed, was also an embezzler. The captain interrupted him again. "No, the money was not the motivation in this case: *converso* doctors usually receive ten times as much from the Christian nobles who sneak them in the back door when a delivery turns difficult. In this case, one reason was sympathy:

the woman is our prisoner and has no other recourse. In addition, this situation gives the *xuetas* an opportunity to quicken the gratitude of the Jews who are now in Grantville."

Dolor rubbed his chin. "Yes. If the rumors I hear are correct, the Americans have involved themselves deeply in the affairs of the Jews—and vice versa. The Nasis, for instance, have mostly relocated to Grantville itself. So you suspect that these *xuetas* will be eager to curry favor with their cousins by helping the daughter-in-law of the wealthiest of the Americans?"

Don Vincente shrugged. "In their position, wouldn't you? Since the Nasis left the Mediterranean, their use as trading liaisons for the other Jewish communities of the region has diminished. The *xuetas* here must be desperate to make new relationships. And with this Jewish cartel whispering in the ears of the Americans, whose influence is rising in Venice—"

Dolor shook his head. "Venice. The USE. The Nasis. All of them are our foes, Captain. And you are suggesting that this *converso* Asher may be part of a larger plot for the *xuetas* to make connections with those foes?"

"Yes. But where is the problem in that? We trade regularly with our foes. For instance, in the Low Countries—"

"Yes, I am quite acquainted with the peculiarities of that situation." Dolor held up his hand. "I leave this in your hands then, Captain. Governor Morales y Llaguno, you are to admit the *xueta* physician, and, presuming he will accept it, you are to offer him the commission at the full rate we discussed."

"Very well. But I do not like this. And I will have my men— my own men—present at all times. Even when the woman is giving birth."

"Of course. And I'm sure Captain Castro y Papas intends to have his own contingent present, as well."

"Yes," said Don Sancho, "so one would hope." His expression changed. "I can only hope that Don Vincente's conjecture is correct—that touching a Gentile woman will repel the old Jew. I will take steps to make sure that he must admit—in the presence of witnesses—that this signifies a further and final proof of his renunciation of Judaism: to touch, in an intimate fashion, a woman who is not of his race." His smile became smug. "And how delicious that, in so doing, he will simultaneously be degrading the little Italian she-goat."

Dolor rose, turned his back on Don Sancho, did not note if the man bade him a respectful farewell or not. All he could think was: *What a repulsive little swine.*

Dolor passed out through the portcullis, earning respectful nods from the soldiers from Fort San Carlos and averted eyes from the Castell's regular guard contingent. As he left the shadows and strode into the midday glare, a figure emerged from the bright, sun-dappling dust that had been kicked up by the *xueta* physician's donkeys. It was a representative from the viceroy's legal office, who doffed his hat and offered a prim bow.

"Yes?" Dolor did not even break his stride.

"A most unusual communication came to the viceroy this morning by way of the weekly packet from Rome, Señor Dolor."

"Oh?"

"Yes. It seems that a message arrived for you in Rome some weeks ago and has just caught up with you now."

"Oh? And from whom does the message come?"

The representative stood a little straighter. "No less a personage than the count-duke Olivares himself." The obsequious functionary smiled knowingly. "However, it seems to have met with impediments in Rome, delayed by inefficient bureaucrats, no doubt."

*You mean, by people like yourself?* But Dolor only nodded. The delay was not surprising. Borja would not know what to do with a private communiqué from Olivares to his own spymaster, particularly if it arrived without any communication to Borja himself. The pope-intendant certainly understood that his actions in Italy had aroused royal displeasure in Madrid, thereby costing him what few friends he had there. The preference—and greater trust—implied by a private communication to Dolor would have left Borja in a dither of uncertainty and anxiety. Unable to safely open the letter himself, but unwilling to let it slip out of his fingers, the cardinal had probably sat on the missive, hoping for some small sign as to its import. But when none had arisen, he had had little choice but to send it to Palma—by the slowest boat available, apparently.

The viceroy's representative cleared his throat histrionically. "Naturally, the viceroy would like to be on hand when you open the letter, since it may have news of import to him as well—news he would like to hear immediately."

*Rubbish. The viceroy is simply a nosy old cretin, wringing his hands, wondering why he doesn't get the favor of communications from the high and mighty any more.* But Dolor said "I will accompany you to the Almudaina immediately. I presume you have a carriage at the bottom of the hill?"

The representative bowed with a foppish flourish. "And a litter to convey us from this height hence."

"Lead," nodded Dolor in the direction of Bellver's outer gatehouse and began contemplating how to turn Olivares' gesture of comparatively overt favor into an exchange that could be parlayed into another personal meeting. Face-to-face contact would be the only truly safe—and effective—conditions under which he might reveal to the count-duke that he, Pedro Dolor, had possession of what had now been positively identified as the body of Lord John O'Neill, last earl of Tyrone, vassal of Philip, and traitorously fallen aiding the up-timers in Rome.

"Must they stay?" David Asher's tone was rough with age and annoyance. His glare was almost as damning as Giovanna's. Frank kept his arms folded, watching, terribly uncertain how to feel about the man who had entered the room at the head of four men-at-arms.

Captain de Castro y Papas bowed apologetically. "Doctor, Señora Stone, my apologies, but yes, they must stay. The governor insisted upon having his own men here. It seemed prudent—for a variety of reasons—that I should have an equal number of my own personnel present."

"Might as well sell tickets," grumbled Asher as he washed his hands in a bowl of water and ethanol, held by the smaller of his two assistants.

"Again, my apologies. I must leave them here, but I do not need to magnify the offense with my presence; I shall depart at once."

"Great," growled Asher. "We lose the only one with manners. Now, Señora Stone, try not to pay attention to the four men in the room."

"There are four men in here? I see only dogs."

Asher barked out a laugh. "You I will be happy to treat. What about your husband? Has he a tongue?"

"I do," said Frank.

Asher looked up, eyes narrowed but still surprised. "Huh. Some tone of gratitude from the nervous husband."

"I'm sorry, Dr. Asher. I have unfinished business with him."

"Who? The big hidalgo who just left? Take a word of advice, young man; leave that unfinished business unfinished, or he might finish you."

"It's not that kind of business. At least I don't think so."

Asher made a gruff noise as he testily rearranged the sheets his larger assistant had propped up to form a privacy blind. "Now I'll need you to relax, Señora Stone—and with your permission, I'll—"

"You have my permission, now and in all future times. You are a physician; I am your patient. If others imagine anything else, that is a product of their own backward low-mindedness."

Despite himself, Asher smiled. "I'm surprised your husband had the courage to marry you, Señora."

"So am I," admitted Frank. Then, seeing Giovanna's look, he amended, "I mean, she was so beautiful, I didn't think I'd have the nerve to ask her if—"

"Ah," interrupted Asher, who was evidently no longer paying attention to Frank. "It is just as your first doctor, the famous Sharon Nichols, suspected: there are at least twins. Maybe triplets."

Frank frowned. "No. Sharon said—"

"Yes, yes," grumbled Asher, "I know she believed it very unlikely that there were three fetuses, but I am telling you I disagree. And with your wife this much further along in the pregnancy, it becomes easier to discern them." He looked up hard at Frank. "So do not disagree with me, young man. When I say there are three here who will have to be brought out to safety, I know exactly what I am talking about."

Frank looked at the old *xueta*'s eyes, saw them flash—right before the one facing away from the four guards in the room winked.

"Yes," said the doctor slowly, clearly, "it appears that there are three Stones who will have to be brought out to safety. And probably sooner than any of us thought."

Giovanna sat upright and looked at Frank, eyes wide. Who got it now.

"Oh," he said to Asher, nodding. And keeping any hint of a smile off his face.

Captain Castro y Papas drifted in the direction of the impromptu mess that had been set up on the second gallery level of the Castell; the kitchen proper, having failed an inspection, was being thoroughly scoured. Approaching the cook laboring red-faced and sweaty over boiling pots and a field stove, Don Vincente had a sudden, almost nostalgic pang of recollection to his earliest years as a soldier—and then that moment of comparative innocence was shattered.

One of the Castell's regular guards belched and commented to his mates, "All this fuss about some Italian bitch and her demon spawn whelp-to-be is nonsense. I say asking for a Jew to deliver her is proof positive that she's a witch. So we should burn her, the devil-riding husband, and the Jew all at once and be done with it."

Grumbles of assent made Don Vincente's stomach churn; so, this was the flower of manly intellect in Imperial Spain? Centuries of war, conquest, and sacrifice had all been endured to produce this? He did not know whether to laugh, cry, or vomit. At any rate, he lost his appetite; he signaled the cook for a very small portion.

A more composed voice rose up in contention, speaking in pure Catalan, not Mallorquin. "You Mallorcan dolts understand nothing of politics. You might as well be capering around like a bunch of Moors, invoking the spirits of your ancestors to ward off ill omens."

"Is that so, Corporal? And what is your lofty understanding of this situation?"

"This is politics, fool, plain and simple. You bring the child into the world and use it to control the parents. They'll do anything to make sure it stays alive. Meanwhile, although you don't let them know, you give the child the best of everything. Bring 'im up in court, even."

"Why? So the demon-child can kill the king?"

"Yokel. The only demons and witches are the ones in your imagination and your grandmother's drunken dreams. Look: you bring the boy up in court to make him feel that it is his home. In time, you can use him as an agent against the USE, against his own grandfather, who's becoming wealthy beyond any one's dreams. Once the boy reaches the age of majority, a little intervention from a subtle assassin could put all that money at the grandson's, and thus our king's, disposal. That might even solve Spain's money problems in one fell swoop."

Don Vincente felt the food thump on his plate, did not see it. This voice—belonging to one of the soldiers he and Ezquerra had drawn from the garrison at Fort San Carlos—was far more learned, but no less horrific, than the first; the same grasping cruelty was there, simply converted into a godless format.

One of the other soldiers from Fort San Carlos was disputing the corporal's scheme. "That's bullshit, Enrique. The USE would never allow it: they'd seize Stone's firm, first."

The corporal's voice was unperturbed. "They may. But that has other costs. Political costs due to the hypocrisy of that action: so much for the vaunted up-time 'rule of law' and 'free markets.' Yes, they wouldn't stay very popular if they nationalized the company right after its new grandson-owner announces that the business will allow investors to buy shares in it."

The youngest of the Mallorcans—the son of a good family who had bought him a commission as an ensign—sounded dubious. "If it was to become known that we had so manipulated and twisted a child, it will make us—make Spain—more despised, even by our own allies."

"Nonsense," argued the corporal. "This is simply a matter of returning to more traditional and effective means of statecraft. This growing trend of considering children to be 'innocents' who must be shielded against the harsh realities of the world is a Reformation decadence, brought on by their fascination with Greek political debaucheries such as 'democracy.' All fueled by the up-timers. Who are already the basest of hypocrites, you know. 'Spare the innocents,' they all cried in their up-time world. And then their most civilized lands slaughtered millions of children with bombs dropped from flying machines.

"And besides, if the rest of Europe disapproves that we have groomed Thomas Stone's grandson to be both our instrument of vengeance, and our means of refilling our coffers, how does that concern us? We are Spaniards: the fate of the Church is in our hands. We have done harder things. We just recently removed countless corrupt cardinals and strove to accomplish the same with the heretic Pope Urban—my apologies: the anti-Pope Urban. So of what concern is a little old-fashioned hostage-taking to our accumulated reputation? Our lot is infamy among the decadent: so be it."

Don Vincente let his plate fall with a clatter. The soldiers looked up, stunned to see him at their margins. They never suspected that an officer would dine from the same pot, or come to the same queue to be served from it. "Acts that earn us infamy among the decadent is desirable—unless they also earn us infamy among the just. But of course, there are no just men or virtuous women beyond the borders of Spain, so my words are pointless."

The captain turned his back on them, stalked away, hands behind his back, head lowered in thought, trying—very hard—to rediscover the lost threads of righteousness he had once associated with both the nation and king to which he had sworn allegiance so many years ago.

# Chapter 45

When Sharon arrived at the Garden Room, Ruy was already there. Being married to him, she could see the telltale signs of—well, not anxiety, exactly: more like highly sharpened focus. The most noticeable physical sign was in his posture; although he always sat erect, there was also always a hint of serpentine fluidity about Ruy, even when he was perfectly still. That fluidity was not evident now; his spine seemed to be an inflexible vertical rod.

He moved to make room for Sharon as she glanced at the empty seats beside them. "Where is Sherrilyn? She planned on being here, this time."

"She is walking the perimeter. She fears laxity and so is making a surprise inspection."

"I see. And of course you didn't say anything that might have prompted her."

"I may have mentioned something about the danger of repetitive patrols without any surprises to test alertness. I do not remember."

"Sure you don't. You are just a forgetful old man."

"How very right you are, my dearest love. By the way, this morning, before I left to walk the perimeter at dawn, did I forget to—?"

"You did not forget to do anything. In fact, you did it twice. Vigorously."

"Ah. See the infirmities of age? Here I was, thinking I had

476

failed in my spousal duties to you, and was happily anticipating making up for them tonight. Making up for them twice, in fact."

"You know," mused Sharon with a slow smile, "maybe *I'm* the one who's forgetting. Maybe I'm remembering what you did *yesterday* morning—"

"Ah, so I may need to make up for a pre-dawn oversight after all? How wonderful. I assure you, dear wife, that when I make recompense three times for this oversight in attending to your wifely needs—"

"Three times? I thought you said twice?"

"Did I? See how forgetful I have become. It is—"

Vitelleschi entered and waited for the other clerics to find their places; their collegial banter diminished quickly. Although adversaries in the evenings, even Wadding and Mazzare had drifted slowly into a friendship, first based on mutual respect, but ultimately, growing out of a shared celebration of a life of the mind.

But there were no glimmers of that amity present this evening, and Sharon grasped Ruy's hand hard. "Here we go. I sure hope Larry's got his game on."

"Indeed," Ruy said, and she could tell from the way he said it that he was more interested in listening than talking—which was understandable: this night's debate might well define the fate of the papacy, and the immediate fate of the embassy, too.

Vitelleschi raised his hands once Urban had taken his seat before the fire. "Today we examine the present exigencies of the Church in light of the enduring mandates of God. We must answer this question: where should the pope go next? We already know the safest course of action"—Vitelleschi's eyes shifted to Sharon—"and we are in our hostess' debt for making further, better asylum available to us, merely for the asking. However, it is incumbent upon us to explore if, in accepting such a generous offer, the path of holy grace lies parallel to, or departs from, that mundane prudence. We must ensure that our concern for the physical safety of the Church does not lead us to compromise its autonomy and its spiritual survival. Cardinal Wadding, you shall speak first."

Wadding rose slowly. "In speaking of gratitude to hosts, Father-General Vitelleschi touches upon the core issue before us: not the nature of our prospective host, but of our responsibilities and duties as a guest. The first and foremost of which must be: never accept a courtesy which you must not repay.

"Note that I say *must not* repay. I choose the word *must* quite intentionally. A courtesy that one *cannot* repay implies a lack of adequate resources. I do not say *may not* repay, because this speaks to manners: we receive the courtesy of kings, as we receive the grace of Christ, knowing full well that it would be an insult to our host to even attempt repayment in kind. And I do not say *should not* repay, because the word 'should' indicates that this is a recommendation, not a dictum.

"So when might a prospective guest foresee incurring a debt of gratitude that he *must* not repay? Simply answered, when the host is likely to use the guest's sense of obligation to compromise his honor."

Wadding raised a hand, as if indicating an invisible heavenly multitude. "In every culture, the same wisdom is axiomatic: never be beholden to another. On occasion, this is presumed to be a reflex of vainglorious pride. It is not; it is a resolve to maintain absolute sovereignty over one's own priorities and commitments. This is why we should always ask ourselves this question before crossing a host's threshold: in this house, might my duties as a guest conflict with my original oaths and loyalties?"

"Consider our special quandary as the terrestrial children of God and the Virgin Mary: what *must* we be prepared to endure if we enter into the house of a known heretic? For surely, that host will question whether our virgin mother is worthy of veneration, will insult our pontifical ancestors, will challenge whether those forebears rightfully inherited the property they passed down to us, and ultimately, will contend that we do not therefore possess the holy titles, privileges, and duties which are our God-given legacies. What sane man—what moral man—would enter into such a house as a guest, no matter how warmly the invitation is proffered to him?" Wadding spread his arms. "How is our situation any different as we contemplate the invitation of the Swede to shelter in lands that owe fealty to him?"

Mazzare leaned forward; Vitelleschi nodded toward him. "You have something to interject, Your Eminence?"

"This is a false analogy, Father-General. Organizations are not people. Furthermore, rival sovereigns can host each other in amity, even though they maintain contending claims upon the same tract of land. Disagreement does not necessarily predict or imply disrespect, derogation, or conflict."

Wadding shook his head sharply "My analogy seems false only to minds so fixated upon the world of kings that they have lost sight of the differences implicit when one is discussing the King of the World. Rival kings are rival men; there is no perfection in their relations, nor their judgments. They struggle—even when it is for mutual justice—in the dark.

"Our Heavenly Father has illuminated our path with the Light of His Truth. Our pope is not merely a ruler; he is the living representative of Christ. He possesses the Sacred Magisterium of infallibility in matters of faith and morals. When he enters a house—any house—he should be considered its master; any who deny him this demonstrate, by that denial, that they are estranged from Christ."

Wadding raised a pausing palm in Larry's direction. "Save your objections, Cardinal Mazzare. Your time to speak is coming. For now, I would ask you to consider if your own analogy, which likens this matter to affairs of state among congenial kings, truly applies in this case. Can the Swede be considered an amicable monarch, given how his defamations of 'papists' have given aid and encouragement to his Protestant allies? Has he recanted? Has he apologized? Has he sent an envoy to the pope?"

Sharon cleared her throat very loudly.

Wadding could not help a brief smile. "I except Grantville and its representatives from these accusations. They speak no ill of Mother Church, have given us the inestimable Cardinal Mazzare as a colleague, and did us the signal honor of sending us their own envoy in the form of Ambassador Nichols, without whose kind intercession none of us would be alive to debate this topic. However, Grantville can barely compel the down-time natives of State of Thuringia and Franconia to obey its laws of religious toleration. Furthermore, the Swede did not send his greetings along with this embassy, or even give it his explicit imprimatur. So far as we know, and so far as we have seen, Gustav Adolf 'tolerates' the toleration espoused by his Grantville allies: no more."

Mazzare stood. "He has mandated the equal practice of religions, and enforced it throughout the United States of Europe in Germany."

"So it is said. But still: is he a Catholic king? Does he receive the sacrament of confession? Is he in a state of grace—and may he even return to one, should he wish it? Has he not made war upon the Catholic states of France, Bavaria, and Spain? And nearly so with Austria? Is this, then, a king that is in any conceivable way, congenial to our Church, its allies, or its interests?"

Wadding sighed and seemed to sag, suddenly tired and old. "I will assume that you, my brothers in Christ, are incarnations of the perfect will and resolve of the martyrs. I also assume that you would therefore be impervious to the subtle, as well as the great, seductions and coercions of dwelling with such a powerful host, who also has the power to derail or delay both the discussion and dissemination of whatever decrees our pope might make. For let us be frank: if you are Gustav Adolf's guest, it is the work of a moment for him to make you his hostage, instead.

"However, even assuming that he would not be a faithless host, I am still a weak man. I may be strong in Christ, but I am not so proud as to believe that I possess the moral fiber of the martyrs. What if, in Gustav's house, I falter in my resolve? What if I do not object to heresy when the Holy Spirit tells me I should? What if I once nod in agreement against my conscience, simply because my host has worn me down with an endless round of entreaties, arguments, and embargos? I ask you," urged Wadding, coming from around his table, "can the future of the Church be safely planned in such a place?

"For it is not enough that our pope survives this moment; he must rally the faithful to his banners. But how many of our brethren, summoned from the far corners of Christendom and traveling in constant fear of assassins serving a murderous anti-pope, will trust a host who is mostly known for hostility towards their faith? How many will stay away—or more tragically, will come to that place only to succumb to the same moral weakness that I fear in myself? Some? Many? Most? Whatever you respond, I ask one last question: is this path—one which places the heart of our Church in the terrestrial hands of one of its bitterest foes—truly a pathway to grace? Or are we prostituting sacred Mother Church for an old foe's dubious promise of temporary shelter against a storm?" Wadding resumed his seat amidst absolute silence.

Sharon looked at Ruy, clasping his hand even more tightly. "Damn, Wadding is good," she whispered.

"Distressingly so," Ruy agreed and fell silent, his eyes upon Larry Mazzare's back.

Mazzare, still seated, began quietly. "Our Savior unveils His Will in the examples of the Gospels. And what we discover in his deeds—even more loudly than his words—are lessons about the limits of strong places. Christ was born in a manger; he preached in open fields; he fished for souls in open boats upon rolling seas; he broke bread in a humble house nestled in the very shadow of the palaces of those who meant to kill him. Christ and his message did not require—indeed, they proved the prideful pointlessness of—strong places and great cities.

"Yet Father Wadding insists that the Church must maintain walls against any possible interference. Perhaps he can explain to us how his exhortation to protect and refurbish our terrestrial power does not also put us on the slippery slope of perdition, since if we must protect the Church absolutely, then we must have absolute power—which, of course, corrupts absolutely. The most recent proof of this is Borja himself, whose rule illustrates where unrestricted authority and an obsession with worldly power ultimately lead.

"Now, it is sad but true that sometimes, in order to follow the will of our Heavenly Father, a pope might have to take steps that will send some of his own lambs to slaughter." Larry rose. "But surely, a loving God would not be profligate with the lives of his sheep, nor urge his good shepherd to send multitudes of the faithful to needless deaths. Rather, is it not more likely that the Savior would whisper into each pope's mind: 'Good shepherd, care well for my flock, both in their souls and in their bodies. Do not forsake them in any way.'

"So I put it to you: in this dark hour, does 'caring for the flock' mean pursuing a course of action which not only commits this continent to further generations of sectarian strife, but will almost surely end in the martyrdom of the pope? For if he has no safe refuge while he labors to save the Church and end strife, it means nothing less than this: his death beneath the knives of assassins and the ascension of Borja, unobstructed, to the Holy See."

Mazzare's voice, usually fluid and pleasing, became sharp. "Is that grace, to have the butcher Borja seated upon the *cathedra*? You know him, Cardinal Wadding; you have seen him and his acts. Can any course of action which allows that man to steal the staff from the legitimate and loving shepherd of the Church be a course of action that is consistent with heavenly grace?"

Wadding closed his eyes. "I question not the will of the Lord."

"Nor should any of us. But tell me: do you claim to have the Charism of Sacred Magisterium, of direct inspiration from god-head, yourself? Is the humble Franciscan Luke Wadding not only to be the first Irish cardinal, but the first Irish pope?"

Wadding bristled. "I have neither intimated nor made such an absurd claim."

"Not directly, perhaps, but since you assume that it is the will of God that Pope Urban should shun the USE's offer, then tell me: by what special power have you divined His Will in this matter?"

Wadding became very still and very pale. "Cardinal Mazzare, do not construe my words of caution to be evidence of hereti-cal hubris. I simply point to what God *may* wish. Just as you are doing. Perhaps I am slightly more emphatic in my diction; consider that a sign of my ardor, not arrogance."

"Fair enough. But if that is so, if only the pope may rely upon the direct inspiration of God, then the actions and ideas of we lesser servitors of the church must arise from purely human insight, correct?"

"Unfortunately, yes."

Mazzare pounced. "So then, must we not employ our God-given powers of reason to protect our pope, preserve his flock, and provide for their future? Which is to say: is there to be no prudent preparation and self-guidance in a life of faith? Are we to sit motionless alongside the river of flowing events, stirring not, only accepting what the currents bring into our laps? And should we drown where we sit, when the waters of barbarous perdition rise? Is it God's will that we must not change our position—even if it means being swept to our deaths when the river of present events floods its banks? Faith in God may require acceptance, but does it necessitate apathy? Or rather," Mazzare's eyes glimmered with passion, "or rather, does it not, instead, *require* us to act? To *materially* nurture grace and defeat perfidy?"

Wadding raised his chin. "Just because I reject the comfort of Protestant heretics does not mean I support this anti-pope."

"No, perhaps you do not support him—but by doing nothing, you are still doing something. You are choosing not to acknowledge the need for human action. And Borja will not fail to teach you the error of inaction, both as a practical philosophy and as a pathway to grace." Mazzare sat.

Sharon, who had never seen Larry so emotional in this—or any—debate, was too stunned to react for a moment. But Ruy was able to. "They both did very well. I can tell nothing from looking at the pope or Vitelleschi; they could both instruct the Sphinx in the fine arts of impassivity."

"Yeah, and that means we need to talk to Cardinal Barberini before the next and last session."

"To see if he knows how Urban is leaning on this matter?"

"No: to see if the nephew can push the uncle in the direction of a USE fortress, no matter how he's leaning right now."


Sherrilyn Maddox leaned down to rub her aching knee just as a deep voice from the bushes behind her intoned, "Who goes there?"

Sherrilyn jumped, drew down on the bush. "The bitch who's going to kill you, asshole. Damn it, is that you, Hastings?"

The big English lieutenant emerged from the bush. "It is. My apologies. How is your knee?"

"Goddamnit, my knee is fine." Sherrilyn holstered her automatic, thought about resuming her walk around the perimeter, and then thought the better of it; the last thing she should do was walk where Hastings, or anyone else, could see her. "I don't have a limp," she commented unasked.

"No, ma'am; of course not," responded Hastings. He stared squarely at her knee.

Sherrilyn fidgeted. "What the hell are you doing out here, anyway? I thought you were off-duty now."

Hastings shrugged and hooked a thumb back toward the villa. "I was testing the alertness of our reserve force in the root cellar. Since the rest of us must walk around pretending they're not there, it also means that no one is checking in on them. I felt it best to—well, break the monotony. By surprise."

Sherrilyn grinned. "I'll bet they just loved you for that."

"Yes, for a moment I felt every bit as warmly beloved as my own, cheery Colonel North." Hastings' grin now matched Sherrilyn's. "But at least the hidden reaction force was relatively alert."

"Good to hear. The bad guys will try real hard not to give

us any warning before they strike, so everyone has to maintain peak readiness around the clock."

Hasting nodded and looked at her knee again. "For some of us, that might mean resting our knee instead of walking the perimeter."

"Look," Sherrilyn grumbled, "it's just an old sports injury. I'm fine."

"Yes, ma'am, I'm sure you are, but—"

"Shhh!" hissed Sherrilyn, ripping her Glock 17 back out of its holster. "Do you hear that?"

Hastings cocked his rather square head and listened. "Yes, I do. Music, from the house."

"Yeah, that's what I'm hearing, too. Damn it, what the hell is wrong with them?" Stalking back to the villa, she chose not to put her pistol away again; maybe seeing it in her hand would shock a few of them back to their senses. "If I've told them once, I've told them twenty times—"

"Miss Maddox, listen more carefully. Wait a moment, wait—there. Did you hear it? Do you know what that is?"

"A big, bad baritone voice."

"Yes. The pope's voice." Hastings looked at her patiently. "Tell me, Ms. Maddox, do you think you can get a pope to stop singing?"

"I can damned well try."

"You might find your efforts frustrated."

"You don't think this is a security risk?"

"On the contrary, Miss Maddox: I *know* it is a security risk. But given the current tensions among the priests, I suspect it helps them to relax together at the end of the day. And by having all the other folk in the house join them, sitting in a circle and shouting their hopeless harmonies—well, I imagine it helps to bridge the gaps across which they're arguing."

Sherrilyn glowered back at the villa, then up into the black and silent slopes rising steep and forbidding about them. "Yeah, well—I just hope it's worth the risk."

Sharon came into the villa's common room and stared. Fully two thirds of her staff, all the off-duty soldiers, and all the priests were sitting in a large circle, singing, playing an instrument, or clapping their hands. Only the profoundly nonmusical Larry Mazzare was not joining in, a bemused, even sheepish look on his face.

What surprised Sharon the most was that Ruy, behind her, began clapping his hands, too.

She turned to look at him. "Uh—isn't this the part where you step in and shush them all? For security reasons?"

"Dear heart," he said as the tempo increased, the players changing songs without stopping, "a few more minutes is unlikely to cause any more harm than may have already been done. They have been singing for five minutes, maybe ten. If any of Borja's villains are in earshot, they have heard it by now and deduced what they will surely deduce. The probability that one of them is just moving into or out of earshot at this very moment—well, it is also possible that lightning shall strike me dead every day I go out wearing a sword. But it has not happened just yet. And in the meantime, the good it does to let these people have a few more minutes of joy must outweigh the scant chance that they are doing any harm that has not already been done." And he went back to clapping his hands.

Sharon sighed, looked back at her staff, and saw that, for the first time in weeks, they were smiling. Wide, happy, unworried smiles—not the ones that signify willing obedience, or encouragement, or resolute cheer in the face of adversity. These were just folks enjoying themselves without a care in the world.

And they were enjoying themselves with a vengeance: instruments had materialized seemingly out of nowhere. Odo the radio operator was playing a well-worn cittern, two of the staff were keeping up with more traditional lutes, and no less a personage than Cardinal Antonio Barberini was putting a reasonably skilled hand to the strangest stringed instrument Sharon had ever seen: an oddly-fretted (was it almost double-necked?) monstrosity about the size of an overgrown bass guitar with a lutelike body and two sets of strings. The lower set, the ones Barberini was working currently, sounded like—well, probably what an electric bass guitar would sound like if someone could make it acoustic. Sharon shook her head at that inherent contradiction and was immediately struck by the powerful mezzo that rose up to meet the rollicking tune that had emerged.

The voice was coming effortlessly out of the wide mouth of the embassy's somewhat hefty cook: usually cheery, always passionate, and now saucily belting out lyrics that went too fast for Sharon to follow.

But it was, of all people, Pope Urban VIII who identified the song. "Ah!" he shouted, with a clap of his hands and suddenly bright eyes, "*A Lieta Vita!* As it was played in my youth!" And, from behind the cook, he commenced to roar out a harmony— more or less. Vitelleschi looked as though he was going to die of heartburn, but kept clapping anyway.

As Sharon stared, Carlo the messenger-boy came prancing into the circle that had been cleared for the cook and, like some upland sprite, twirled to the music, delighted to cavort about her skirts. And in the way she looked at him, eyes warm and her voice suddenly richer, huskier, Sharon understood: in her heart, the cook had adopted orphaned Carlo. And the little fellow knew it.

Ruy touched Sharon's elbow, whispered, "Shall I stop them after this song? It is a short one."

Sharon smiled. "Oh, I don't suppose another ten minutes will hurt."

When Valentino returned to the camp near Valsondra, it was three hours later than he had intended. His group had hit upon a new lead after scouting the skirts of Monte Campolon, and had actually hoped to find a sign of the renegade embassy, but it had been a dead end.

Consequently, Valentine was surprised when the camp, instead of being tense with worry over his tardiness, seemed to be quiet, waiting. Not that these men loved him—the nearly sixty cutthroats and ruthless mercenaries with him certainly did not—but they loved the notion of getting paid, and it had been made clear to them all that if Valentino did not come back alive and successful, the drink money they had been given upon signing up would be the only coin they would see from this venture.

"Linguanti?" Valentino called. "Is there news?"

Linguanti's long face turned toward him, painted faint yellow by the firelight. "Ask Odoardo. When he came back, I had to ask a lot of questions which he didn't feel like answering. Because he is not scared of me. And because he was sure it was unimportant."

Valentino turned toward Odoardo, who had his obscenely broad back to the fire. "Odoardo?"

"Yeah?"

"What did you see?"

"Didn't see anything." A long pause. "Heard something, though."

Valentino closed his eyes and counted to five. Extracting information from Odoardo was about as swift and interesting a process as watching a sliced apple slowly turn brown. "So what did you hear?"

"Recorders. One was really high pitched."

"Probably a sopranino," muttered Linguanti who kept his background as a failed musician fairly secret. Which was fairly easy, given how little he said.

Odoardo shrugged. "I don't know what they're called. It's just higher than anything I heard growing up. And then, when we got closer, there was singing. Lots of singing."

*Singing? Out here? And Odoardo didn't think that was impor-tant? I will truly enjoy killing him when this is over.* "Where?"

"We were near Laghi again, seeing if we could bypass it without being seen. It was coming from beyond there."

"Where there are two communes, yes? Menara and Molini?"

"Yeah, I guess."

Valentino took another deep breath. "Did it sound close to Laghi, or like it was coming from farther back in the mountains?"

Odoardo thought. "Farther. It was pretty faint."

"And there was singing. You are sure of that?"

"Are you deaf? Yes, I am sure."

"Lots of singing?"

"Yes, damn it."

"And any instruments other than recorders?"

"Uh, probably some strings. Lutes, I think. Like I said, it was pretty faint. Why?"

"Well, let's see, now: what would a lot of people be doing making noise at either a small hamlet like Menara, or at a poor, dilapidated villa like Molini, which we've been told is the only building back at the far end of the Val Lagio? And why are they singing? And accompanying themselves with expensive instru-ments?"

"So you're thinking—?"

"I'm thinking that the sound was too distant to have been coming from Menara, and that this old Villa Molini might not be as shabby or under populated as the shepherds down in Posina said it was. I'll bet they haven't actually been up that way in a year, rather than a few weeks ago, as they claimed. Just trying to make themselves sound worldly, I expect."

Linguanti nodded. "So what do you want to do?"

Valentino motioned everyone to rise. "If we start marching hard now, we can reach the caves south of Monte Cengio before dawn. That will give us a base camp only a half hour out from Molini. If it is indeed where the pope is hiding, they will have watch posts keeping an eye out for us. So tomorrow, we'll need to move in to observe it first. Only three of us are going to go ahead to do that; the rest of the group will stay behind in the base camp, out of sight."

"So when do we attack?" asked Odoardo.

"When I tell you to. You'll have tomorrow to clean your weapons while we go over the final plan. And remember, you have to remain silent: no shouting, no loud talking, and particularly"—Valentino smiled; sharks showed their teeth less menacingly—"no singing."

# Chapter 46

Frank and Giovanna, who were enjoying their fifteen minutes of daily freedom strolling around the lazarette's small roof, saw movement beyond the outer gatehouse below. Dr. Asher had arrived early, judging from the sound of the cranky mules and the equally cranky passenger. As usual, he had brought several sizable casks of ethanol with him.

Gia stood on the tips of her dainty toes to get a better look at the day's cargo, which was being offloaded by the same, dull-looking assistants who seemed incapable of speech. "He seems to bring more and more of the spirits every time."

Frank considered that observation, clucked his tongue, and smiled. "Yes, he does at that, Gia. Let's go and be ready for him."

Dr. Asher was approximately halfway through his exam when Giovanna's eyes opened wide, and she let out a yelp rather like that of a puppy whose tail has been trod upon. She looked over at Asher, alarmed.

Who soothed her. "There, there, do not fret. Just a little tenderness. There should be nothing to worry about. Not as long as I'm here to keep an eye on things."

He turned to Dakis, who had decided to observe the scandalous proceedings himself. Frank saw Asher's face change the moment he was no longer facing Giovanna. "Take me to the governor at once," he muttered.

✧      ✧      ✧

Don Sancho Jaume Morales y Llaguno frowned, his incipient glee dampened by his simultaneous worries of professional failure. "So the Italian she-goat will miscarry, you think?"

Asher sighed and closed his eyes. "It is possible. I cannot be sure."

"Well, what specifically did you find? How do you know this?"

Asher looked at the small man through thinned eyes. "I was not aware that you have a secret fascination with gynecology and obstetrics, Governor. Is your wife aware of these interests? If so, she must be a singularly open-minded woman."

The governor flushed, sputtered. "See here—I am not—not at all—but—well, these are prisoners, and I must ascertain if...if you are..."

"If I am lying?" When Don Sancho nodded brusquely, Asher folded his arms. "Respectfully, Governor, how could you tell if I *was* lying?"

The governor's mouth opened; no sound came out.

"Let me make this easy for you," grumbled Asher. "There are certain changes in the womb—of texture, more than structure—which can be signs that it will harden and expel the fetus early."

The governor leaned forward, listening and nodding earnestly.

"However, with proper care, such an event can often be averted, or at least delayed until such time as the child can be born with a reasonable chance of survival. That change in texture is how I know what I know. And now you want to know how you can be sure that I am telling the truth." Asher shrugged and sighed. "Let me ask you to consider this, Governor: what happens to us *xueta*s every time you Spanish become displeased with us?" Don Sancho raised his proud, if almost nonexistent, chin in silent reply to Asher's baleful stare. "So, Governor, tell me: if I fail you, would you treat me any differently than the other *xueta*s?"

The governor shook his head. "I would not."

"Then there is your assurance that I will do my very best work for you: fear. Fear for my own safety, and for that of my people. Plain and simple. Now I must leave."

"Leave? Why?"

"Because the trip back to Palma is long and I am old. But I shall return soon, Governor."

"Don't think you are ever welcome here, Jew," the governor grumbled.

Asher smiled. "Just because I was foolish enough to accept this commission does not mean I am a *complete* fool, Governor. I know my place—and now, I shall return to it."

When dinner was taken—and his manuscript along with it—Frank stared at Giovanna. "Well?"

"Well what?"

"What happened during the exam today? What did—?"

Giovanna reached into her skirts and produced a very small, smooth, oblong vial. It had a small scroll inside it.

"What?" asked Frank. "He put that in your—in—"

Gia smiled mischievously. "No. Asher is not stupid. He would not insert it there—for medical reasons as well as practical ones. After all, what if this beast of a governor had his own doctor secreted near at hand, to check me after Asher had? It could have been found."

"So then how—?"

"Dr. Asher was uncommonly thorough today, husband: he took the precaution of conducting a rectal examination, as well."

"Ah. How—inspired."

"Actually, it is. Now, let us see what the message is."

Working quietly, making other noise to cover their actions, they crushed the vial, which had been sealed with molten glass, and removed the small scroll. Giovanna ground the glass into a powder that she shook out the window to mix with the sand and grit in the dry moat.

Meanwhile, Frank puzzled at the brief message: *X3=10; X3=20.* "Huh?" he grunted. "How can 'x times three' equal both ten and twenty?"

Giovanna, dusting her hands off, came to stand behind him, looked over his shoulder for two seconds, and then turned to snatch up the one book they were permitted—were compelled—to have in the room.

"The Bible?"

"Of course, Frank. Asher has recorded book and verse in a manner that our idiot warders would not understand. Even the governor would probably see only an equation."

"And instead, you see—?"

"*Exodus*, chapter 3, verse 10, and *Exodus*, chapter 3, verse 20. It is a most obvious cipher."

"Uh...sure, if you say so." Frank wondered, as he often did, why someone as beautiful and intelligent as Giovanna had married someone as dimwitted and clueless as himself.

"So, here it is," she said, setting her shoulders to read forth—albeit quietly: "'So now, go. I am sending you to Pharaoh to bring my people the Israelites out of Egypt.... So I will stretch out my hand and strike the Egyptians with all the wonders that I will perform among them. After that, he will let you go.'"

"So Asher is Moses?"

"Or the representative of those who are intent on bringing us out of 'Egyptian' bondage."

"Yeah, by performing wonders among them first. Sounds like a high-tech rescue to me."

"Perhaps, or perhaps these were just the least ambiguous verses. I do not care. It means we are escaping. And soon!"

Frank nodded. "Yeah."

"And this does not make you want to celebrate?"

"Well, sure it does. Except, well...I just hope they bring back my book before we get rescued."

"Ah. The reluctant author has become attached to his work. Or perhaps it is just an excuse for spending less time with me? Am I growing too round for you, husband?"

Frank eyed his wife with a grin. "Not at all."

"Good. I believe you." She flopped down on their bed. "Now: entertain me. Tell me what you would have been writing about tonight."

"Well, I was mostly thinking about revisions."

"Such as?"

"Well—I thought that maybe I should change the name of where the hobbits come from."

"So? Not from the Shire, anymore?"

"No. I was thinking of 'Brigadoon.'"

Giovanna frowned as she mouthed the word silently. "It is a strange name. Besides, I thought you said that the original author—the one to whom you are making your homage—specifically used the name 'Shire.'"

"Yeah, well—consider it meaningful artistic license on my part. Trust me: the allusion works."

"The allusion to what?"

"To Brigadoon." Seeing the look on her face, Frank shrugged. "Maybe you're right; maybe I should just stick with the Shire."

"I think so. And have you written the manifesto we outlined?"

Frank kept from smiling; properly speaking, it was the manifesto *she* had outlined, but he let that detail slide by. Instead,
he affirmed, "Yes. And I kept the page hidden from the guards.
But you can't read it."

Giovanna reared back. "You would keep your writings from me?"

"No, no. I don't mean I *won't* let you read it: I mean you *can't*
read it. I wrote it in Tengwar."

"In what?"

"Tengwar is the alphabet of the elven language, Quenya. Except
I can't remember all of the letters. So I had to make some of
them up." Frank wiggled the rolled paper out of his trousers. "But
this kind of invented alphabet was the only safe way to put it on
paper, Gia. Otherwise, the Spanish might get hold of it and—"

"Yes, yes, husband; you are very wise. Now, quickly: what
revolutionary fire has burst from your pen?"

Frank held it up, cleared this throat and read: "We, the people
of Italy, solemnly declare our resolution to ordain and establish

    1) The unification of our country;

    2) The expulsion of the Spanish oppressors, and any
    other foreign powers that might occupy Italy;

    3) A democratic and secular state;

    4) Freedom of religion;

    5) The church to renounce its claims to temporal power;

    6) Universal suffrage for all adults."

He put the paper down and shrugged apologetically. "It's not
much. It's certainly not as important as the book."

Giovanna rose, frowning. "You may discover you are mistaken
about that, husband."

Frank shrugged. "I don't disagree with you, Gia. But the book
was what came to me first. I guess because it's what I'm familiar
with. You grew up as the child of a political firebrand. Me? I was
the child of a man who taught me and my brothers about ethical
behavior—and the perseverance of goodness—in the stories he
read to us. I'm just doing what I know best."

"I think you underestimate how famous you have become in
Italy. Coming from you, this proclamation will be taken seriously." She smiled. "First we have to smuggle it out, of course,
but I don't see any difficulty there. No one is likely to inspect
Dr. Asher that closely."

She walked over to his writing desk and laid the Bible down upon it gently. "So," she said, her voice shedding much of its prior gravity, "what happens in the last scene of your book? What happens to the hobbits?"

"Hey, never rush an artist! I haven't written that yet. And I don't want to talk about it; it might disrupt my delicate creative processes."

Her smile widened; she rubbed her belly. "I seem to recall that not all your creative processes are delicate, at least when it comes to *pro*creative ones." She looked at him from under very dark, and very sexy, brows.

Frank swallowed, trying to fight his instincts back to some semblance of prudence and self-control. She was pregnant, after all. Which he pointed out: "You're pregnant." He said it with all the conviction of a drinker denying the appeal of a tumbler full of whiskey.

"Am I? I hadn't noticed. I don't even know how I got this way." Giovanna's smile became positively demonic as she rose and walked toward him; the baby-bump was suddenly just another alluring curve in motion. "Perhaps," she said innocently, "you could show me how it happened in the first place."

# Chapter 47

The watchtower at Cala Pi appeared abandoned as the now-familiar *llaut* from Miguel Tarongi wound its way out of Cala Beltran. Once in open water, it headed straight toward Miro's larger *llaut,* the one his men had captured near the Bay of Canyamel and had named the *Bogeria*, or *"Folly,"* in Catalan.

The captain of the *Bogeria*—a Ragusan who had piloted similar boats before—cut an alarmed glance at Miro. "Don Estuban, what does this mean? Why is the other boat on course to meet us? Has the ship been seized by the Span—?"

"Steady as you go," muttered Miro, squinting into the distance. If only he could make out the deck crew, even one of them—

A loud bellow saved him the need of further squinting. "Heh, old friend; you look as blind as an owl at noon, screwing your eyes up that way."

"Miguel Tarongi, what are you doing here?" What Estuban wanted to say was, *"What the hell are you doing here, Meir? You and I are not supposed to have any further contact."*

But Miguel waved airily. "Oh, I thought we could chat while your fellows pick up the packages we left in Cala Beltran. Last load, you know."

*Of course I know!* What the devil was Meir doing, taking a chance like this?

Meir's *llaut* came close alongside the *Bogeria*. "Hop aboard," he called.

"Miguel, I—"

"Just do it, high ears. Don't worry about the Spanish; no one's home in the Cala Pi watchtower."

"Oh?" replied Miro, jumping aboard Meir's *llaut* as the two ships passed each other with less than a foot of room between their sides. "And just how do you know that—Miguel?"

A wave from Miguel and they were soon alone in the bows.

"You seem to forget," answered Meir as Miro recovered his balance, "that most of the Spanish troops west and south of Manacor depend on *xueta* sutlers."

"So it was easy to know how many need provisioning in the tower, and when."

"That, and it is easy to sneak inside when you know it is not manned. During which time one can infest the place with rats."

"You didn't."

"I most certainly did, Estuban. Since then, the Spanish soldiers discovered that swords are not good for killing rats."

"Still, to abandon a watch post simply because of rats—"

Miguel Tarongi shifted into Hebrew and a much lower voice. "The local militia—which provides at least eighty percent of Cala Pi's manpower—is all too ready to find any excuse not to spend the whole day, staring south, watching for pirates that no longer come. And the other twenty percent—the Spanish—had to find and hire locals with the right skills and tools to eliminate the rats."

"Huh. Pity you can't do the same thing with the staff at Castell de Bellver."

"True, but our *xueta* sutlers have been busy there, too; our plans are well in hand."

"And you needed to tell me that yourself? Is that why you came out this morning, Meir?"

Tarongi shuffled restlessly. "More or less. Besides, up until this point, staying at arm's length was prudent; we were simply exchanging cargos, not information. And the men you sent—well, they came with your instructions, which were all quite clear." He scratched behind his ear. "But now, we need to make sure that everything is in order, that nothing has been overlooked or forgotten. Because by this time tomorrow, you'll be bound back for Italy, won't you?"

"You know I can't tell you any more than I have, Meir. But you can rest assured that, by dawn tomorrow, I will either be bound elsewhere, or will be remaining in Mallorca. Permanently, I fear."

"Yes. So I gathered from your last message." Again, Meir scratched fitfully behind his ear and looked out to sea.

And Ezekiel Miro understood. "You came out today to see *me*. Because by this time tomorrow I'll be gone for good—one way or the other."

"Damn it, Ezekiel. Why did you have to get mixed up in this? You could have—"

"Meir." Miro lowered his voice. "The world is changing. We have always changed with it. That has often meant far travels. It has meant that some of us go ahead to prepare the way so the rest of our people can follow to a new place of safety."

"And is that what you're doing?"

"Who knows? I will send word when I know for sure. But that is all speculation for another time; let us settle matters. You need to be back in Palma before sunset."

Meir shifted his gaze west. "So I do. And I know you don't have a lot of time, either; you'll have to double back to wherever you're based right now. Which I'm guessing is on the Illa dels Conill?"

"That is not important," said Miro, who wanted to spit in frustration. Were his plans that obvious, that Meir could guess his remote hideout and staging area on the very first try? On the other hand, given the timing of their regular rendezvous at Cala Pi, Meir's only reasonable conjecture was to presume that Miro's base was located somewhere in the tiny Cabrera archipelago, just within sight of Cap des Salines, Mallorca's southernmost tip.

The island of Cabrera itself had a castle on it: insufficiently garrisoned, but a Spanish presence, nonetheless. But the Illa dels Conill, the next largest island, was rarely visited, had no natural water source, no useful flora or fauna, and was ringed almost entirely by forbidding cliffs. Also, the southernmost extent of the islet—that which was closest to Cabrera—presented a high hump to observers on the main island, thereby screening the islet's one, very small bay to the north.

"So, you are sure then: you'll make the attempt before dawn?"

Miro nodded. "The wind and tides are right. So is the weather: light low clouds and a thick haze coming up from the south."

"The *Llebeig*? Again?" asked Miguel quizzically, referring to the Saharan wind that blew out of the southwest. "We had a light storm from it just four days ago. It is strange that more clouds are coming from there, and so soon. This worries me; perhaps the earlier storm was just the harbinger of a heavier one following. If so, then—"

"Meir, I can't stop now. Besides, the skies over the cloud-tops are clear; there is no heavier weather following. And having the *Llebeig* blowing for us is an excellent bit of good fortune; we'll have the wind over our beam and our yards rigged away from it, to the starboard and north. Given our projected course, those conditions will make *Atropos* the swiftest boat in the water. Frankly, I would have preferred slightly heavier clouds, ones that would have given us a little rain, but this will have to do."

"You *want* rain? That would make it hard to navigate."

"It would also make it harder to see—and I would prefer to have the Spanish blind, particularly as we approach."

"Well, the moon seems disposed to hide herself until well after midnight. So it seems Fortune smiles on your venture."

"Let us hope it does—but that almost-dark moon is one of the reasons I'm willing to go without the rain or heavy clouds. And that's also why I had you re-pitch your *llaut*."

Meir smiled. "As I said, you were ever a deep one, Ezekiel." He looked over at the hull, newly coated with dark brown pitch. "I was wondering why you ordered that—and caused a three-day supply interruption. So it was to makes us less visible in the dark?"

Miro nodded. "And when you go out tonight, you'll no longer fly yellow banners and a white sail."

"Of course not. We'll set the black sail that you sent to me, along with North and his men, two days ago."

"Exactly. How are the troops holding up?"

Meir rolled his eyes. "How do you think? They're all stuck in a basement, going over the plans again and again and again, cleaning their weapons, reassembling them, then turning out the light, taking them apart, and putting them together again. O'Neill is at his wit's end, but doesn't complain as much as North—even though North is the one forcing them to go through all these strange actions."

"He's cantankerous," agreed Miro, "at least on the outside. But he knows what he's doing."

"And he's cursedly close-lipped for someone who talks and scolds so much."

"Ah. So you tried to trick North into revealing his part of the plans, then?"

Miguel looked out toward the rapidly sinking sun. "I don't like being so much in the dark on this operation, Ezekiel. What if something goes wrong and one of us has to improvise?"

Miro shook his head. "There can be improvisation only once we have all arrived at the destination. There will have to be improvisation then, for who can predict how all the details will actually unfold? But before that, no: there is no room for improvisation. That's why all of these men are with you beforehand, why they are hiding, why only a few of them know the whole plan: if something goes wrong, if one of my men should somehow fall into Spanish hands before we begin, then we might be able to cut our losses and try again. But only if the person captured has minimal knowledge. In fact, while you're standing here, North is briefing them on the final location and details."

"So all their planning—all the child's games played moving from doorway to doorway chalked out on the floor—they don't even know that they were learning the layout of Castell de Bellver?"

"Except for the officers, no." Miro smiled. "And the special casks? Are they ready?"

"Have been for a week. They were easy to build, since we've used something like them before. Just recently in fact."

"Oh? Why did you need them?"

"An informer who is a servant in the Black House told us that the Inquisition might be preparing to investigate a *xueta* family whose son was fool enough to have an affair with the daughter of a Gentile business rival. We sneaked them all out—even the idiot son—on a ship, using casks similar to the ones you asked for."

"Excellent. And O'Neill understands what to do?"

"He understood it well enough by the time he came to me; you seem to have drilled him no end on it. He's just eager to get it over with—and hopes he won't need that wondrous up-time watch you sent with him."

"Me, too." Miro sighed. "Because if he does, it will mean that something has gone terribly wrong. And lastly, were you able to find the—?"

"Yes, yes, those strange, large lanterns that float in the air when you light the candles at their center? It took many inquiries, but I located three of them for you. One was from a curio merchant who has apparently had one for years, unable to sell it. And an Ottoman merchantman sold several—copies from the Mughal

lands—when it put into port at the end of April; I found three
of those."

Miro smiled. "My friend, you are a wonder. Now, just one
last task: to guide Thomas North and his men to the Castell de
Bellver tomorrow night."

"Yes, well, I have someone who can do a better job than I can.
You remember Hayyim? He's one of the Castell's sutlers, now.
And his father helped build some of the newer fortifications, so
he knows the hills and quarries that lie around it."

Miro heard the evasive tone. "Meir, what are you planning?"

"What do you mean?" Meir would not look at Miro for more
than a moment.

"I mean, originally you had wanted to pilot the *llaut* that is,
right now, carrying North and his men over to Cala Pedrera.
Failing that, you were resolved to show them how to get up to
Bellver. Now you can't be there at all?"

"Oh, I'll be there; don't worry about that. But it looks like
it's time for me to go." He pointed to the *Bogeria*, wending its
way back out of the Cala Beltran. "This last shipment was a
big one, because of all that olive and fish oil. And between the
amount of pure spirits you wanted for Asher, and the amount
you wanted for yourself, I doubt there's a drop of them left in
Palma." Meir tried to smile as the boats drew closer together.
"So, begone with you."

"It has been good seeing you, old friend," Miro said, putting
a hand on Meir's shoulder, and then jumping the narrow, but
moving, gap between the two *llaut*s.

Meir waved. "*Viaja con dios,*" he said, articulating the Catalan
sardonically.

"*Shalom,*" Ezekiel Miro whispered earnestly over the rustle of
the sails.

"I think it is time, Frank."

Frank Stone looked out the window toward Palma; it was
almost dark. Asher would be waiting, by now. But if they started
too soon...

"Frank, everything is prepared. We can do no more. Now we
must act and trust in God. I am ready."

"Okay, then." Frank walked over to his wife and handed her
the vial that Asher had given them earlier that day. He waited

until she had finished with it, and then shouted, very loudly: "Gia! What's wrong? What—?"

Gia pushed over his writing table, went to the floor.

"Gia? Gia?" Frank turned and hammered on the door. "Guards! Guards! My wife is—she's—there's something wrong with her!"

The door yanked open; the face of the guard who came through showed a minimum of concern mixed with a maximum of annoyance. That ratio flipped when he saw Giovanna, balled up on the floorboards, a thin trickle of blood pointing the way back towards its source, high in her skirts.

"*Merda!*" the guard gasped. Then he shouted to his men to bring the governor, to bring Don Vincente, to bring the Jew doctor: to bring anyone, damn it.

Frank stole a quick smile at Gia. Who saw it. Then her eyes rolled back into her head.

That was when the shouting at the door became truly loud.

In the oilskin tent that his men had hidden in the folds of Illa dels Conill's rolling terrain, Miro leaned back from the map spread on the folding field table. Illuminated by a covered lantern, it was an enlarged copy of the bay of Palma, inexpertly but functionally reproduced from a *Frommer's Guide*, and heavily footnoted by Miro's appendations. Around the table, all the shipmasters, as well as Harry, Sean Connal, Virgilio, and one of the cleverest of the Wild Geese, Turlough Eubank, stared down at it intently.

"So, the plan is clear?"

Mumbled assent drowned out Virgilio's loud, nervous gulp. "Don Estuban, this journey could be worse than the Alps."

"Not for us. But for Harry—"

Harry shrugged. "Ah, this shouldn't be so bad. Anyhow, I do think I am properly equipped for the job." He patted his homemade web-gear, from which hung eight carefully handcrafted and slightly curved magazine pouches. "Eight thirty-round mags of Combloc 7.62 should do me just fine."

"I wouldn't mind having a few of those myself," muttered Turlough.

Miro smiled. "A point you have made several times, already. But they must stay with Harry. After all, he will be in a position to save your life, not you his."

The Irishman smiled crookedly. "Well now, if you're putting it that way..."

Aurelio was still frowning down at the map. "So after the rescue is complete, our ships do not stay together?"

"No. And I understand your reservations. Normally, there would be safety in numbers. But remember this: the largest of our ships cannot successfully fight theirs. Our advantages will be our head start, our speed in the wind conditions we expect—"

"—and base trickery," interrupted Connal; now even fretful Aurelio smiled. Miro suppressed a grateful sigh. From the very start, the Irish physician had proven as adept at raising spirits as he had at healing bodies, and both had been invaluable to the morale of the men. They might respect Miro, and hold Harry, North, and O'Neill in a kind of terrified reverence, but it was the young Sean Connal that they loved. Miro nodded at Aurelio, getting his attention once again. "Just follow the headings you've been given once we are on the run, Captain. First we'll confuse the Spanish, then we'll link up and make for home."

"Very well. Now, on the approach, it is the *Atropos* that leads us in?"

"Yes, but only to your loiter point, well south of Palma's bay. As indicated on the map, the *Atropos* will head farther west, leaving the rest of you to stay formed up on the *Guerra Cagna* until you begin to flee. Now, one last time: any more questions?" Silence. "Very well. Virgilio, are the burners at full?"

"Yes, Don Estuban. The crew of the *Atropos* signals that inflation of the balloon has begun."

"Are you sure you want to ride her on the way in? We have others who could now perform so simple a task as keeping her in true while being towed."

Virgilio shook his head. "She is my airship; I will be at her controls. And will be sure to supervise the correct loading sequence of the fuel casks. I don't want any of the gasoline containers mixed in with the regular fuel. I want all that gasoline reserved for our outbound flight. And I don't want to start loading until the last second: we must keep the dirigible as light as we can, as long as we can, to conserve fuel."

"We've given you a pretty good margin of error, Virge," drawled Harry at the nervous Venetian dirigible pilot.

"Yes, I have a good margin of error—but Fate usually eats it up. Particularly when she is tempted to do so by plans as auda- cious as this one." He shuddered. "So I will be a miser with the fuel, if it is all right with you, Captain Lefferts."

Harry shrugged, smiled. "Okay by me, Virge. Hell, I'm just along for the ride. Well, most of the ways. Which reminds me, Estuban; I double-checked the suspension lines and the wires for the airship's communications relay rig. We're good to go on my end."

"And I have checked the telegraph in the dirigible," added Virgilio quickly.

Harry frowned. "Well, if you really want to call what we've got a telegraph set, I guess you can, but—"

Miro held up his hand. "What I have just heard is that the suspension lines and the electric wiring we have secured to it are confirmed as fully functional, yes?"

The two men nodded.

"Excellent. Then we are ready. Aurelio, please have your men break down the tent. I will take the map back to the *Atropos* with me. Good luck to you all." He walked outside, glancing about at the flurry of activity: the tent being broken down, the last wind measurements being taken, and the captains moving purposefully to the small boats that would take them back to their ships, waiting dark and quiet beyond the low breakers.

Miro stepped toward the skiff from the *Atropos*, and nodded to the waiting rowers. "Let's be on our way," he said, as much to himself as them.

# Chapter 48

Linguanti rose to meet Valentino. "So, it is as we thought?"

Valentino nodded, came to the center of the dimly lit cave, and nodded for the man with the oil lamp to adjust the wick. The yellow glow brightened as Valentino scraped a quick map on the floor. "Yes, they are at the Villa Molini. We have seen their sentries—cleverly hidden—here, here, and here." He indicated the three compass points of north, east and south. "They may have one or two more that we missed."

"Probably behind them, to the west, too."

Valentino shook his head at Odoardo's suggestion. "No. They are shielded from the west by Monte Maggio. The only other way into the dell in which the villa sits—this very difficult pass from the Valle Terragnolo, up north—is where they might have another outpost. But for anyone to come at them that way, they would have had to travel by way of the Val Adige, almost all the way to Trento. And almost none of the news from this valley is going to pass over these high mountains to the other side, and vice versa. So no one on the Trento side of Monte Maggio would even know to come here, looking. So the up-timers and the pope can rest assured that their west is almost completely safe. And with their backs being up against that wall, we have no ready way to get around their pickets and come at them from behind."

"So what do we do?"

Valentino touched the point on the map that indicated his group's current position in the southernmost of the caves of Monte Cengio. "At dusk tonight, we start moving south, skirting Menara. Then, when we come to the low part of this arm of the valley, we turn west immediately, staying as far from Laghi as possible."

Linguanti looked at the map. "That puts us well within a mile of Molini. An easy walk."

"It would be, if the approaches weren't observed."

"So I ask again; what do we do?"

"We stay away from the most direct route, which they can observe from two points: the outpost they have just to the side of the path that leads to the villa, and the outpost they keep up north, on the western slopes of Monte Cengio. Instead, we will move across the path to the south, and sneak up on this small hill."

"Where they have an outpost, also."

"True, but we can get behind that outpost."

"So once we are behind them, then what?"

"We bait them out."

Odoardo guffawed. "What a great plan. If, as you suspect, they have a good number of professional troops, we're not going to be able to bait them out into the open."

"Of course not, oaf. We will be far more subtle. We will make faint noises to the front of their position. Nothing too provocative, but enough to get them to send out a scout. We will lead him on and, ultimately, into an ambush."

"Which the others see, or hear, and set up an alarm."

"No, because they will be dead by then."

"How?"

Valentino smiled. "I wasted part of my misspent youth hunting. But I was not very good with a bow, and we didn't have enough money for gunpowder. So I became quite proficient with this—" He reached back into his gear and pulled out the crossbow that all the men had noticed, commented upon, and apparently forgotten about. "These days," he pontificated, "the crossbow is an underappreciated weapon. What it lacks in killing power it more than makes up for in silence. And that is how we will eliminate the others in the south watch-post: one by crossbow, and the last by Linguanti, here."

"Oh? And what weapon does he carry?"

"Just this," said Linguanti, who produced a very thin garrote with lethal fluidity.

"And how will you get close enough to use it?"

"Odoardo, think back—if you can remember anything earlier than a minute ago—and ask yourself: have you ever heard me utter so many words as these?"

"No."

"And have you ever heard me make a sound when I move, or walk, at all?"

"Uh...no."

"Neither will the last sentry."

"Oh."

Valentino smiled and finished. "And once we are done here"— he drew an X through the southern outpost—"the way is clear to the villa, except for walking patrols."

"Which will see us and shoot."

"Not if we wait and pass through the gap in their intervals. And if they do happen to see us and shoot, we will shoot back. Some of us will be killed, but at this point, with all our force concentrated in one place, and with us charging over the flat ground to the south of the villa, we will be upon them quickly. Meaning we will only have the interior guards to deal with. With our numbers, we will finish them quickly—as well as everyone else in the villa. And I mean everyone."

Odoardo was frowning. "This still isn't as easy as you said it was going to be when you hired us, Valentino. A pope, a few priests, no more than a dozen up-timers and their retainers. This is a bigger job. More dangerous."

Valentino smiled. "You are welcome to depart now, Odoardo." Valentino straightened up. "Anyone is. After all, the fewer of us there are, the fewer ways there are to split the payment. *Reales* equal to a year's pay for Spain's best three thousand man tercio. So I thought a slightly difficult job would be good news, Odoardo. After all, are you—are any of you—eager to have your share reduced by having *too many* men alive to collect?"

Valentino watched the eyes of his hired murderers rove cautiously about, doing the bloody math of how many men were needed for the job, how many men might die, and how to balance between maximizing the odds of success with the minimum number of final survivors. He saw greed—growing—and no fear. Which was exactly what he wanted to see.

"We heavily outnumber them, we have the advantage of surprise, and we will strike at night. My only concern is that you don't get tempted to stick a knife in your mate's back, in order to get a bigger share for yourself."

Odoardo was still frowning. "There's only one thing that surprises me about this plan, now."

"And what is that?"

The huge man suddenly smiled. "That I like it." He stood. "Let's go kill a pope."

Cardinal Antonio Barberini started when Sharon and Ruy emerged from the further shadows of the Garden Room a moment after he started laying out his pens and parchment. "Ambassadora, Don Ruy, I did not see you—"

"You were not supposed to, Your Eminence," murmured Ruy. "Not until we knew you had entered alone."

"What? Why do you—?"

"Your Eminence," interrupted Sharon, "what I need to ask you is not something I want to share with the others."

"Why? What is it?"

Ruy and Sharon approached Antonio. He did not feel fear, exactly, but a vague sense of dread at the gravity in their expressions.

"We need to ask you to gather some information for us, Your Eminence. Nothing improper, but not the kind of request we can make to any of your peers."

"And what kind of information could you possibly want that you do not already have? You have heard all the proceedings as well as I have."

"Yes, but we lack a critical perspective on them."

Antonio Barberini frowned. "I assure you, I have no special *sub rosa* knowledge relevant to the proceedings."

Ruy raised a conciliatory hand. "No, of course not, Your Eminence. But you may make inquiries where we—indeed, where no one else—may."

Antonio shrugged. "It is strange you should think so; I am the only one who has no juridical role in the process. Mazzare and Wadding are advocates, Vitelleschi is the procedural judge, and my uncle listens. I simply take notes."

"Yes, of course, Your Eminence—which is why you are the person of whom we must ask our questions. You are an intimate of the court, yet not intimately involved in its official deliberations."

"Ah, now I see. Since I am the court's nonentity, you do not violate the propriety of the hearings by asking questions of me." Barberini smiled crookedly at Ruy. "Your diplomatic courtesy is impeccable, if somewhat depressing for me to hear. We all cherish loftier opinions of our importance than those warranted by our actual roles, I fear."

Sharon smiled. "I'm sorry we have to go about it this way, Your Eminence. But we have no choice; everyone's safety is at stake."

Antonio felt anxious heat across his brow. "How may I help?"

Sharon set her shoulders before asking: "I need to know if your uncle thinks he's going to decide to seek asylum with the USE or not."

Antonio laughed. "Again, I suspect your guess is better than mine. And guess is all any of us can do, for I assure you, my uncle has said no more about our proceedings outside of this room than he has said within it." ·

Sharon shrugged. "Well, for what it's worth coming from me, I think your uncle was wise to avoid taking a direct hand in the proceedings. But even so, he is a party to them, and that makes it impossible for us to ask if they've led him to any decisions, yet. After all, since we're personal friends with Cardinal Mazzare, that would be like asking, 'Hey, Your Holiness, how's our guy doing in the debate? Is he winning?'"

Antonio returned the smile. "Yes, I see your point. So you are speaking to me in the hope that I might whisper some favorable words in my uncle's ear?"

Sharon shook her head. "I thought about that, but realized that even if you did consent to say something on our behalf, that would probably just hurt our cause. We'd be doing exactly what Cardinal Wadding is worried that Gustav or his representatives might do: try to meddle in Church affairs. So, no: that isn't why we want to talk with you now. We just want to know what to prepare for."

"What do you mean?"

"I mean, after tonight's closing statements, your uncle is going to make up his mind pretty quickly. If he says 'yup, I'm going to seek protection from the USE,' we know how to proceed. But if he doesn't—well, that creates difficulties."

"Yes, I see that—but why did you wait to ask me about this until now?"

"Frankly, because we didn't want to impose, and because we didn't foresee how skilled a debater Wadding was going to be."

Barberini shrugged. "Cardinal Wadding has made some excellent points, but he has hardly won any of the debates decisively. He may not have won any of them at all."

Ruy offered a dubious frown. "Even if that is true, Your Eminence, Cardinal Wadding has always succeeded in adding a measure of doubt to whatever Cardinal Mazzare has asserted. And as your uncle said, if, at the end, there is any doubt remaining, he must consider those reservations to be God's own voice whispering in his ear, urging him to avoid compromising the Church by accepting any help from the Swede. And if that were to happen—"

"Yes. I see."

Sharon's voice was sharp. "Do you? Do you see all the consequences?" Her eyes were both hard and desperate. "The assassins wouldn't just come for him, or you: they'd come for all of us. And I'm not sure we have enough forces to protect us all, even if we're bunkered in behind these walls.

"But if your uncle decides to go on a walkabout, I'd have to split those already insufficient forces. One part would remain on defense here until we could be safely extracted, while another would travel with your uncle as bodyguards and escorts. But if we split our forces that way, we're just enabling the assassins to kill both groups, not just one. On the other hand, how can I *not* send an escort with your uncle? I can't let a pope just wander out my front door without providing any help other than a full canteen and our best wishes."

Barberini frowned. "Yes, that is a thorny problem indeed."

Ruy leaned forward. "And will you help us with it, Your Eminence? That we might know what plans we need to make in order to save as many of our lives as possible?"

Barberini thought: there would be no use approaching the topic obliquely with his uncle. The pope was too shrewd and subtle not to immediately detect the real reason behind such an inquiry. So it would have to be made directly, and Urban VIII might be annoyed that Antonio was trying to use their familial bond to access what was, currently, privileged information. But given what was at stake, that was just too bad; the time had finally come for him to—

Vitelleschi strode into the room. He nodded to the three of them; if he detected anything conspiratorial in their close huddle, he gave no indications of it. As the others filed in behind the father-general, he raised his hands in the fashion they had all come to recognize as the call to order. "Are we gathered, then?"

"We are all here, Father-General," replied Sharon, sitting down.

"Excellent. Then we shall begin..."

Mario Bianchi worked the handle of the flintlock pistol nervously in his palm, earning a sharp glance from the Marine corporal who had furnished him with the weapon. Mario crept to the edge of the shallow hilltop pit and looked into the darkness. "Corporal, I am worried about Private Cavendish. He has been gone for—"

"Hsst. Quiet, now, Bianchi. It takes a man a minute or two to investigate night sounds. But I think I hear him coming back, just there on our flank."

The corporal, who had turned to listen more closely, jerked, his head seemingly slapped sideways. As the larger man fell, Mario saw the fletching of a cross-bow bolt protruding from his head only an inch above his ear.

Mario gasped, scuttled backward; a simple porter like his father before him, he had no experience, no training, that would make his first reaction anything other than one of abject terror.

And so his rapid recoil from the site of the corporal's death brought him handily within the descending loop of Linguanti's garrote.

Wadding made his final bow and took his seat. Ruy and Sharon exchanged long glances; the Irishman had merely recapped his arguments, but that had been disturbing enough. "You're right," she said. "He didn't score any knockouts, but he might win on points."

Ruy raised an eyebrow at her boxing metaphor. "I think I understand your idiom, my heart. However, what I found most distressing was Cardinal Mazzare's silence."

Sharon nodded. *Yeah, why didn't Larry say anything?* Granted, the Irishman hadn't spun any new rhetorical wheels, but maybe he had enough traction with the old ones to—

Larry Mazzare rose. As if he had heard her silent questions, he answered them: "I suspect that everyone in this room—and perhaps Cardinal Wadding most of all—must have wondered at my silence this past half hour. Partly, I did not want to interrupt my colleague unless he raised a new issue—but he did not. However, I also did not want to tax my audience, knowing that I would finish on a note as new and provocative as Cardinal Waddings' were old and familiar."

Ruy and Sharon exchanged raised-eyebrow looks. "Uh oh," she whispered, "he's doing it again: playing for all the marbles."

Ruy nodded. "Yes; he is indeed swinging for the ramparts."

"Fences," corrected Sharon. "He's swinging for the *fences*."

"Did I not just say so?"

"No, you said 'ramparts.'"

"Oh, let us not quibble over that. Surely, mine is the superior phrasing: how can there be any courage, any heroism, in swinging at a *fence*?"

"Well, why is it heroism when one of *your* countrymen charges at a windmill?"

"Dearest, that is entirely different! In that situation—"

"Hush, Ruy: listen."

Mazzare's voice was very low as he began. "I have been thinking about grace, Your Eminences, about living in a Christ-like manner, as our Savior exhorts us to do. I have also been giving much thought to Cardinal Wadding's recounting of the ways in which possibly—*possibly*—the Church could be compromised if it accepts the aid of Gustav Adolf, whether directly or by proxy. And it is well that we have considered this, for if my colleague's reservations were wholly without merit, they would have been dismissed by now."

Barberini stopped writing and looked up, eyes wide. Vitelleschi's eyebrows had lowered. One of the pope's had risen. Only Wadding showed no response—other than a sudden rigidity in his unchanged posture and expression. Sharon studied him more closely: was the former Franciscan merely extremely attentive, or did she detect a hint of anxiety, as well?

"But, then," continued Mazzare, "I wondered: if we must follow Christ's example to attain grace, then must we not also consider the possibility that *rejecting* the aid of the USE might be an equal, or even greater, departure from behaving in a Christ-like manner?"

For the first time in the proceedings, a hint of a frown appeared on Urban's face.

"As I promised at the outset," said Mazzare with a smile, "I am suggesting a new—and provocative—perspective. But it comes to us from the life of Christ, himself. Specifically, it arises from his parable of the Good Samaritan."

Mazzare's voice seemed to expand. "We all know the parable: of a man—a Jew—fallen among thieves and left for dead. And we know of the priest who passed him by, and then the official of the temple who also ignored him, even though the stricken man was of their own faith. Instead, the person who stopped to help this dying Jew, the person who bound his wounds and tended to him at his own expense, was his enemy: he was a Samaritan, a group which was 'hated by the Jews.'"

"You would put Christ in the role of a beaten Jew who had no power to resist?" Wadding's voice had a slight edge in it.

"Well, that was not my point, Your Eminence, but yes, why not? What was Christ, as he limped to Golgotha, scourged and bent beneath the cross, but a beaten Jew who could not resist? The constraints upon his action were not those of physical limitation, of course, but of the requisite fulfillment of prophesy. But that difference is hardly significant, I think."

Vitelleschi's beard seemed to quiver in either anger or eagerness: Sharon could not tell which. "Well, if the parallel between the Church and the beaten Jew was not your primary point, Cardinal Mazzare, then please make your point clear to us all."

"I shall, Father-General. My point is this: I began reflecting upon this parable and asking, so who acted with grace? The Samaritan. And how did he show his grace? By choosing to help his foe.

"But then I saw that there was another, subtler lesson to be found in the parable, a lesson about the extraordinary grace of God himself. For it was by God's will that the beaten Jew came to be lying on the road in the path of the Samaritan, who then had a choice: to act in a Christ-like manner or not. If it were not for God placing that beaten enemy in the Samaritan's path, he would have had no chance to tangibly overcome the pettinesses, the selfishnesses, the fears that reside in all of us. Because of God, the Samaritan had the opportunity to exercise and embody the grace to which we followers of Christ aspire."

Mazzare paused, looked at all of his auditors. "So tell me: is it not hubris—the sin of pride—to declare that a Catholic priest, a church, even a pontiff may only play the part of the Good

Samaritan, but never the beaten Jew? If we refuse to acknowledge that, just like the beaten Jew and the scourged Christ, we might benefit from the charity of others, we are refusing to embrace the humility that Christ himself displayed. And in so doing, we deprive other men of the possibility of demonstrating their grace, by refusing to let them help us even as the Good Samaritan helped the Jew who despised him."

Mazzare paused. The Garden Room was utterly silent until he resumed. "The parallels to what we debate today are startling: the Church is in dire need of a Good Samaritan, but recoils when that assistance arrives in the person of Gustav Vasa, an enemy. Who, at this moment, could not only make us the beneficiaries of his kindness, but in so doing, perform a Christ-like act that would forever change the assumptions of antagonism that have existed between the two of us. God is providing both parties with a unique opportunity to grow in grace; all that remains to be seen is if we will embrace it."

If, as Sharon thought, Wadding was formulating an objection, Mazzare was too quick for him. "Our first response to this perspective is doubt and skepticism: we are ready to think, 'Gustav would only help us out of his own pride, only to indebt us.' But that suspicion flies in the face of logic. If it wanted to, the USE could undo the Roman Church this very moment, simply by giving the forces in this villa the same orders that Borja has given to his assassins. Or, even simpler, Gustav could have ordered the ambassadora to turn the pope and his party over to the nearest noble family that was willing to have them." Mazzare paused and looked around the room. "Of course, one wonders if the lords and ladies of this Serene Republic might fail the pope, just as the priest and the temple official failed their fellow Jew in the parable. Or, to put it another way, would the local aristocracy take the risks and be as steadfast as have the members of this USE embassy? With Borja's power growing in Italy, and noble houses unwilling to displease the new order in Rome, I am not not at all sure they would.

"And let us not forget that without the help of this Good—and yes, Protestant—Samaritan, the Church's present wounds could well prove mortal to not only its pope and its flock, but to the very basis of its authority. I do not exaggerate: consider the assured sequence of events if the rightful pope is lost. Borja refills the Consistory and forces it to name him the successor. He will be *called* pope, and believed to be so by the flock—which does not know that their good and true shepherd was murdered in a hidden place. And so they shall follow Borja—but to what end and what outcome? Will God provide an unlawful pope with infallibility in matters of faith and morals? Can he declare things bound, or loosed, in both Heaven and on Earth? And if not, then what power do the sacraments have? Are the new priests he illicitly ordains—and sends to preach bloody intolerance across Christendom—truly priests? And how is such damage to be undone, particularly when the Inquisition becomes the new model and *modus operandi* of the Roman Church?"

Mazzare looked up from under dark brows. "If the Church rejects the help of the USE, it must anticipate a future in which its name becomes an object of acrid hate upon every tongue. All Christendom will know and remember that, at this pivotal moment, our Church became an abattoir, that under Borja, it savagely corrupted the Gospels of love and hope to serve as twisted vindications for untold massacres, persecutions, and pogroms."

Sharon now understood why Mazzare had not spoken during Wadding's presentation: his sole objective had been to assure an uninterrupted space in which to summon forth this tidal wave of teetering cause-and-effect dominoes that were poised to fall one after the other in a tumbling chaos of culture-crushing consequences.

"Can we, in good conscience, refuse our non-Catholic brothers the opportunity to become our Good Samaritans, to reach out to us in this dark and dangerous hour? And if they do so, does it not signify that they deserve our love for all the days to come? For, in addition to being our rescuers, they will have shown that they, too, truly aspire to be Christ-like. And once joined by the undeniable proof of our common aspiration, by what reason would we resist the notion that the time is ripe for greater toleration among all Christ's children?

"But these Good Samaritans cannot help us unless we are strong enough to admit our weakness and need, cannot save us unless we give them the chance to embody the very grace we are trying to preserve."

Wadding stood without waiting for Vitelleschi to recognize him. "If you give the Protestants that chance, I say they will fail. And unless you are privy to God's Will yourself, Cardinal Mazzare, you must at least admit that the Protestants *may* fail. That is the nature of free will: no true test of virtue can have a guaranteed outcome. And if they fail, they will bring about not only their own spiritual downfall, but our terrestrial destruction."

Mazzare nodded. "That is true. And if they do fail and thus bring down the pillars of the temple, then let us trust that the Lord Our God will raise up His Church once again, just as He did His Son. But if they do *not* fail—tell me, Cardinal Wadding: how many millions, possibly billions, of lives might our act of hope save, on this and all future days? To risk such a choice is also to keep faith with what Christ tells us: that hope is second only to love—and so, to lose hope, is the greatest sin of all."

Mazzare waited for Wadding to respond, but the Irishman said nothing. Mazzare turned toward Vitelleschi. "In my century, it was said that people tend to live up to—or down to—your expectations of them. If you expect them to transcend temptations and adversities, they tend to do so. If you presume they will fail, likewise, they will not disappoint your sad prediction."

Vitelleschi's eyes were like chips of obsidian. "So to summarize your closing remarks, Cardinal Mazzare, you would have us put our hope in the 'good nature' of Protestants? Of those who 'protested' and separated themselves from God's Church?"

"No: I would have us put our hope in God. Because it is still He who moves within the good men who raise up their voices to Him in churches other than ours. They, too, have taken the indelible impress of their Creator's grace, so strong is its power. And so I say, yes, have faith that they will show us the grace they have learned from Him, just as the Good Samaritan showed grace to the beaten Jew. In doing so, we are not putting our faith in any mortal man, but in the power and love of God to touch all those who honor him, regardless of the different ways in which that honor is shown." Mazzare folded his hands and sat.

Vitelleschi rose slowly, staring back and forth between Mazzare and Wadding with an almost haunted look on his face. Then he swallowed, raised his chin, and declared: "These proceedings are concluded. Beginning tomorrow, I will consult with our Holy Father to determine how the Church will proceed in relation to the recommendations and counsel offered by the advocates. It is our intent to deliver a statement of—"

A ragged roar of muskets, coming mostly from the southern side of the villa, shocked Vitelleschi to silence—and Ruy into motion. "Gather the priests into our chambers," he ordered Sharon, "and keep them together. Your Eminences, it is well you finished your debate this evening."

"Why?" croaked Cardinal Barberini out of a dry throat.

"Because," answered Ruy as he raced from the room and toward the nearest duty station of the villa's security detachment, "it is unclear how many of us will be left alive in the morning."

# Chapter 49

As the dirigible came within thirty feet of the water, the surface breezes started playing with its trim. Virgilio, peering out over the front of the gondola, gauged the range, the rate of descent, and the distance to the water itself. He gave a thumbs-up.

Standing at the taffrail, Miro returned the sign, turned and announced, "Prepare to board the airship."

Standing alongside the *Atropos'* mizzen mast—its yard lowered to the deck to provide clear space abaft—Harry Lefferts moved forward to the boarding lines and the primitive bosun's chair they had rigged on them. Although the only gear he was wearing was his combat load and simple, black clothes, the lines still sagged significantly when he put his weight into the chair, which was also part climbing harness. Virgilio responded by juicing the airship's burner a little bit more.

That tiny increase in lift minimized the slack in the line, and Harry drew himself arm-over-arm to the dirigible, now thirty feet astern of the *Atropos* and only twenty feet above the gentle, lightless swells of the Mediterranean.

The rest of the team went up similarly: Sean Connal, then Turlough Eubank, then one of Thomas North's Hibernians—the only one that had been left behind with the boats.

Miro watched the chair come down for him. He glanced around the deck; Aurelio was beside him, the same worried look on his face that he had been wearing since they left the Illa dels Conill.

"Don Estuban, did you have to board the airship in such a—a complicated fashion?"

Miro smiled. Aurelio had tactfully used the word "complicated" but had really meant "hazardous." "Yes," he assured the Piombinese captain, "we had to do it this way. Inflating the balloon fully at sea is not easily or quickly done at night, so it was safer and faster to have it minimally inflated while we were still moored near land. But then, while we towed her, we had to keep as much weight—meaning us—out of the gondola to save fuel."

Aurelio looked at the airship with trepidation. "If you say so, Don Estuban."

Miro smiled at him as he belted himself into the bosun's chair. "I will see you at the Dragon before dawn."

"I will not be late, Don Estuban, if I have to row the *Atropos* there myself."

"Your dedication is worthy of legend, Aurelio."

"Dedication? *Fah!* I just want to be running well ahead of those Spanish bastards." He waved as the bosun's chair started up, drawn by hands already in the gondola.

Miro felt himself ascend. He looked down at the lights of the other ships in the tiny flotilla, and then up at the skies overhead: scattered bits of star-specked black peeked through gaps in the light clouds. It was a good night for a raid, although not a perfect night.

Either way, it would have to do.

The fellow who, until today, captained Miguel Tarongi's shipments out to Cala Pi, appeared in the doorway of the storm-savaged windmill that had been abandoned almost a year earlier. "It is time," he said.

Thomas North rose up out of the shadows and nodded for one of his Hibernians to check the surrounding area before they deployed. The Englishman trusted the *xueta*, but also trusted that fate would play a trick on his unit at some point during this operation: that was what happened when plans came into contact with reality. "Men," he said, "it's been a privilege working with you in preparation for this rescue operation, and I have the utmost confidence in you—mostly, because I prepared you myself."

A few grins rose up. The Hibernian came back in, nodded at North.

"Very well; our path out of Cala Pedrera is clear. We will travel in double column up the narrow valley that skirts the south slopes of the Puig de Sa Mesquida, the hill upon which Bellver is built. The ground near the coast is level, but starts rising after two hundred yards. That is also the end of any appreciable habitation; the next closest community is a hamlet of scattered farm cottages and goat-herders' huts called Bona Nova, less than a mile west of the Castell itself.

"If it becomes necessary to withdraw, and you are not in touch with command elements, you are to retrace your path here, and follow on down to the shore, where you'll find the black *llaut* that brought us over yesterday. That boat has a running crew waiting on board. Any questions? Very well. Mr. Ohde, if you would officer the men from the front, I will shepherd from the rear until we reach waypoint one."

Donald Ohde stood, moved to the door and waited for the fourteen other men to form in a column and hunch down. "Remember now; complete silence. We follow our guide precisely. No wandering off. The path has been checked and is clear—or was, thirty minutes ago. You do not engage any chance-met enemy until you are told to do so. Besides, we shouldn't see any Spanish before reaching our first waypoint—unless you consider occasional wayward goats to be subjects of Philip's. Now, double-check: gear secured with wrapping to muffle sound? All reflective surfaces dulled? Good. Follow me." Donald Ohde drifted out into the darkness.

North watched them go: three Wild Geese, two of the Wrecking Crew (besides Ohde), and nine of his own Hibernians. Two officers, fourteen men. Against a fortress as renowned and redoubtable as Bellver. Thomas smiled. *The poor Spanish bastards will never know what hit them.*

He followed the last man out.

The Catalan corporal sighed wearily as the two donkey carts struggled up to the gatehouse of the Castell de Bellver, having ascended the track that followed the slopes of the rocky spur upon which the fortification was built. The corporal squinted into the almost moonless dark and determined that yes, it was that Jew doctor Asher, finally arriving in the middle of the goddamned night—hopefully to settle that Italian bitch's screaming.

From atop the gatehouse, one of his comrades from Fort San Carlos called down: "Hey, Enrique, watch out for the latest invasion of Jews!"

Enrique sent a gesture over his shoulder that would have made even his harridan wife blanch and walked flatfooted and bored down toward the two creaking carts, each of which carried an immense barrel in their cargo bed. Either one was easily capable of holding more than a tun of wine.

"And what the hell are these?" the Catalan corporal asked.

"I'm sure I don't know, Señor Corporal."

Enrique narrowed his eyes at the cart driver, Roberto, second son of one of Bellver's chief sutlers. All of whom were Jews, of course. All of whom claimed to be *xuetas, conversos.* All of whom were affixed like leeches to the public teat, and all probably still practicing their Christ-murdering practices covertly. And always trying to get away with some new, money-grubbing chicanery. Well, not on his watch. "So, tell me, Roberto the Jew, why would you be bringing a shipment to Bellver of which you have no knowledge? Didn't your father sell it to us?"

"No, Señor Corporal. These are not provisions, but the doctor's supplies. We are simply transporting it for him. He said the need for it was urgent."

"And what is it?"

"Spirits," replied Asher from the side of the cart. "Which I've been bringing up several times a week, if you recall."

Enrique glared at Asher's acerbic tone. "Oh, I recall, Jew—all too well." He swiveled his eyes back toward Roberto, "I presume, though, that you've checked the contents of these tuns? And these smaller boxes along the sides?"

"Checked them? No, señor, we loaded all the goods and brought them here, for a fee. We are just teamsters, not sutlers, tonight."

Enrique rolled his eyes. "How wonderful. So now I have to soil my hands handling Jew freight." He called two of the local guards over. He pointed at the shorter one: "You, take the Jew's two assistants to the gatehouse and check them as usual. And you, open these boxes. One at a time."

The boxes held various implements that looked, in the lantern light, vaguely like a cross between medical implements and torture devices. "For aid in delivering infants," Asher supplied.

Enrique held up a long, wicked looking knife. "And what's

this for? Slicing off their tails? Oh wait, that's right: these infants aren't of your breed, are they?"

Asher closed his eyes. "What other questions may I answer for you, Corporal?"

Enrique went to the rear of the wagon, looked at the sealed bunghole at the head of each tun and pointed to one. "Tap it," he ordered.

Asher looked alarmed. "Corporal, I do not know how much of the spirits I will need, so I must not have you spilling it all out upon the—"

"Shut up, Jew. I am simply going to confirm it is what you say it is." He got a cup from the waiting guard. "Now, tap it."

Asher, the folds of his thin arms quivering as he wrestled to unseat the bung, angled it so that he could swap in the tap before the out-gushing stream became unmanageable. Wet and reeking of ethanol, Asher stood back.

Enrique tapped a finger's width of the fluid, sipped it, smelling the sharp odor of strong liquor as he did so. He swigged it, gagged, spat out the mouthful. "What shit is that?" he shouted, wiping his lips with his sleeve.

Asher shrugged. "That one is spirits infused with witch-hazel."

"Do you use it to heal your patients or torture them, Jew?"

Asher's face was set rigidly. "May I go now?"

"Yes. We'll join your assistants." Enrique moved toward the gatehouse; Asher poled after him feebly with the aid of his cane. "So you're expecting to deliver demon children, then—washing them with poison like that. And after all, anything but a demon child would die in minutes, if it was whelped this early in a pregnancy."

"We are here trying to prevent birth, Corporal. To delay it until—"

"God's balls, you think I'm interested in your sorcerous blatherings, Jew? Here, get in the watch room."

As the guards began stripping Asher unceremoniously and searching both his body and garments, he asked. "Corporal, about my spirits. I expect to have immediate need of—"

"They'll be in with the ready stores, as always. We'll have to move some crates to the long-term storeroom to make enough space, though." Spitting again, Enrique scowled. "You need all that? For one woman?"

"One woman who is carrying three fetuses. And I cannot know what will occur or for how long."

"How can you need an amount of spirits equal to many times her body weight? That just doesn't make sense."

"First, Corporal, the other tun simply contains boiled, purified water. Second, I was not aware of your expertise in medical matters. Shall I send word to His Majesty Philip, by way of Governor Sancho Jaume Morales y Llaguno, that his prize hostage's personal and obstetrical health is now being overseen by a corporal of the guards?"

Enrique glared, spat, and jerked his head toward the door. "Do your doctoring, Jew."

Virgilio called for another long burn, and Miro complied. The dirigible rose toward the lower extents of the cloud bank and would soon be up in it. And that meant it would soon be necessary to coordinate with the *Atropos* by means of the telegraph wire that had been slaved to the primary tow-cord. Miro checked one of his favorite possessions—a manually wound up-time watch that had cost him a small fortune—and confirmed the time: approximately an hour and a half past midnight.

There had been occasional chatter in the gondola up to this point, but as the feathery gray masses of the clouds seemed to descend toward them, the airship grew quiet. Harry was already loading his tools and weapons, piece by piece, on what he called his "web gear," carefully arranging it so that it would not obstruct the free play of the guidelines that were connected to the heavy black-leather harness he had shrugged into only a few minutes before.

Down below, the lights marking the boats of Miro's flotilla began winking out, one by one. They were coming closer to the coast now, probably within forty minutes of their target.

Virgilio snapped an order at the Wild Geese, who dutifully tilted two empty oil containers over the side and into the lightless waters below. "Turlough, tell me as soon as we need more fuel for the engines," he said with a nod of thanks. "We need to shift to gasoline soon. Doctor, if you would please man the telegraph; we need to coordinate our flight with the *Atropos* so we get the most power from her towing." It was not a difficult task for a pilot as experienced as Virgilio when he had a clear view of the ship pulling him. But once they ascended into the clouds, once they lost sight of their comrades below, they would have to accomplish the same objective flying by instruments and feel alone.

Miro looked over the side at the boats again—and with a feathery fluttering of gray vapor, they were gone. The crew of the dirigible fell silent as they forged ahead into what looked like the mists of Limbo.

Thomas North looked toward the head of the column: the local guide had stopped, and his men were crouching low, in the surrounding bushes. They were in the higher reaches of the valley just to the south of Bellver, just before its walls began pinching tightly together into a gully known as the Mal Pas. The men stood out slightly against the sun-bleached sandstone that was increasingly poking through the dark scrub growth.

Thomas tapped the two rearmost of the group—Hibernians—on their shoulders: "Rearguard," he muttered as he walked forward. They dutifully flanked well off to either side of the trail, crouching low into the scrub brush shadows, looking back down toward the dark bay.

As North arrived at the head of the column, the *llaut*'s master and current guide nodded to a crevice in the sedimentary rock. "Here," he said. "This is the cave."

Thomas nodded and looked around more carefully, mentally removing the undergrowth: yes, they were in an old quarry. "And you have scouted the tunnel?"

"My cousin did, three days ago. It is all clear. They have either forgotten or ignored it. After all, there is no way to open the door up into Bellver from our side. And except for the ancestors of the *xuetas* who were impressed to build this place, probably no one knows their way through the tunnels, anymore."

"Very well. We will travel with three bull's-eye lanterns: one at the front, one in the middle, one at the rear."

"Colonel, there are parts where only one man may pass at a time."

"Very well: single file. Stay close to the man in front of you." North checked his manual up-time watch, admiring the phosphorescent dot as it marched on its stiff, sixty-stepped circle around the miniature clock-face. "Let's not be late to our own party."

# Chapter 50

In the top room of the Castell de Bellver's lazarette, Frank watched his wife squirm in discomfort as Asher arrived, escorted in by guards. As usual, the medium-sized assistant followed the doctor closely, the larger, broad-shouldered one bringing up the rear with the more cumbersome boxes and paraphernalia.

As Asher's smaller assistant began setting up a folding trestle table and laying out implements, the doctor asked, "Now, are the pains regular or—?"

"Oh! Ow!" Gia exclaimed.

"Ah . . . irregular," Asher concluded as his assistants finished raising the sheets that would be used as a modesty blind.

Dakis emerged from the staircase that led down to the fortified walkway joining the lazarette to Bellver's roof. "So, what's wrong, Jew?"

"I won't know until I examine the woman," Asher snapped, "which is not helped by having three—now four—guards in the room."

"Just do your work. If you actually have any work to do."

Gia writhed as Asher turned away to look at Dakis. "And what does that mean, señor?"

"It means that I wonder if she really has any problems with her pregnancy or if they are all feigned."

"You suspect this is all just theatrics?"

"I suspect that this is a conspiracy."

"A conspiracy?" gulped Frank before he could shut his mouth or govern his panicked tone. "What for?"

Dakis stared at Frank, assessing. "Why to trick us, of course." He finished sizing Frank up and seemed to come to the relieving, if depressing, conclusion that the up-timer was too guileless and too overtly surprised to warrant suspicion. "Well, perhaps you aren't in on it, but your wife might be." Dakis darted a dark look at her and Asher. "I know fraud when I smell it. The Jew is getting a fat fee every time he comes up here, and charges us for all these pure spirits he claims will keep wounds clean and prevent infection. Probably a lie to justify the outrageous bills he tenders for the cost of his materials. And he's probably splitting the take with your wife, his accomplice." Dakis glared at Frank again. "But maybe you are in on it, after all: you certainly look nervous."

"I look nervous? Really?" answered Frank. "I can't think why—what with a doctor hovering over my pregnant wife, holding a knife, three months before she's due."

Dakis scowled, then blanched; Asher's hands had come from behind the sheets and were covered in blood. "Perhaps this is all part of our theatrics, señor?"

Dakis uttered an inaudible profanity and, crossing his arms, leaned his back against the inner wall of the lazarette. "Get on with it," he growled.

Asher glanced at his medium-sized assistant. "Fetch me more of the ethanol, quickly."

Virgilio angled the props to give a slight downward boost—and suddenly they were under the clouds again, with the xebec visible below and slightly ahead of them. Off to the right, watch lights showed where Palma slumbered at the far end of the bay to the north.

"Very well, we continue on our own, from here," announced Miro. "Dr. Connal, signal the *Atropos* that they are to release us. Aurelio is to signal the other boats to head south to their pre-chase loiter positions before he continues west at best speed. After you send the message, reel in the line quickly. Harry, are you ready?"

"Almost. Lemme double-check that my gear is attached good and tight."

"Virgilio, we have to be in the clouds again before you call for another burn; we can't show a flame any more."

"Yes, I know, Don Estuban. I will need more fuel for the engines now. Make it the best we have."

Miro turned to Turlough Eubank. "Gasoline into the engines, please. And since you will be otherwise occupied shortly, please fill the tanks to the brim, this time."

"Aye, just as you say, Don Estuban. Do I pitch the container if it's empty?"

Miro thought. "No, not any more. It's only a few pounds. We can keep the weight until we no longer have need of stealth."

Virgilio made a noise that suggested he would have answered Eubank differently. Miro smiled, turned to Connal, and saw the end of the main tow-line come up into his palm from over the side of the gondola; the wires protruding from the end of the narrow up-time electric cord attached to it were faint copper wisps. Connal handed it to Harry, who was waiting for it.

"Do you need help?" asked Miro. He had asked Harry this every time they had run the drill in preparation for this moment; Harry had never admitted needing assistance, and indeed, seemed not to.

But this time Harry said, "Sure, Estuban. Double-check each connection, will you?"

Miro agreed, tugged on and inspected each point where Harry had fastened the tow-line to his harness with D-rings. Then Miro took the device to which Lefferts had attached the wire-ends, which looked like nothing so much as a scissor with a spring resistor against easy closing. "The electrical connections look good, Harry." He handed back the odd scissors. "Test the handset."

Harry clicked through three long contacts, then a long-short-long combination. *Dah-dah-dah, dah-dit-dah* chattered the receiver nestled between Doc Connal's knees. He looked up and smiled, "'OK' indeed, Harry."

Lefferts nodded. "Then let's do this." He swung a leg over the edge of the gondola. "You have all the slack reeled in, Doc?"

"I do. Remember, we can let you down a lot more quickly than we can pull you up."

"Ain't that the terrifying truth."

"And remember: you have extra cable coiled in five one-foot spools at the first harness attachment point; you can give yourself a little more drop if you need it, Harry."

"Doc, you're starting to sound like my momma. Anything else?"

Miro simply nodded. "Godspeed, Harry."

He nodded back and swung his other leg over the side of the gondola. "Well, guys, it's been a slice." He turned slowly until he faced back toward the center of the airship, keeping his weight on his arms. He smiled, and said, "Geronimo!" And he let go—gradually.

Harry did not fall, but eased down into a position where he dangled four feet beneath the gondola; a smaller cable—just a cord, really—was attached lower on his back, which helped to stabilize him against spinning or tumbling.

"How are you, Harry?" Miro called down.

"I'm good to go," came the up-timer's reply, faint over the hum of the throttled-back engines. "Let's stop dawdling."

Miro smiled. "As you wish. Virgilio, can we get back into the cloud bank with engines?"

"Maybe," answered the pilot, "but a quick burst from the burner would be a great help. You can use the burn-shield to conceal most of it."

Miro turned back to Eubank again. "Do it," he said.

The Irishman, moving nimbly despite his cuirass, produced three pieces of thin tin plate and inserted them vertically in slots fixed along each side of the burner, leaving only the southern, seaward side uncovered. The panels had an excessive stove-piping effect, and had a slight tendency to overconcentrate the hot air flow up into the envelope, but they also reduced the visibility of the burner's flare considerably.

Eubank engaged the burner briefly; the airship climbed back toward the irregular gray fleece overhead.

Miro came to stand alongside his pilot. "We are on instruments only, now, Virgilio, so keep me apprised of wind direction and velocity. I will need that to revise our bearings if we are being pushed off course."

"Ah, Harry can always put us back on track," Virgilio pointed out as he throttled the engines back even more.

"I heard that," Lefferts' voice announced from ten feet below. "Just don't go too low, okay?"

"We will not, so long as you tell us what we need to do in order to keep you just below the clouds, and us just above."

"Count on it," the up-timer drawled. "Give me a little more slack; the top of the balloon is up in the clouds already."

Miro looked up; Harry was right. "Ten more feet of slack, please, Doctor."

Connal nodded. "Down you go, Harry," he said as he played out the line.

And then suddenly, they were encased in cool gray cotton again.

The tunnel had grown progressively narrower but now rewidened, opening into an irregular oval chamber with a low ceiling and detritus scattered about its dusty floor: ill-cut paving stones, half a belt, a forlorn and ragged shoe. In the shifting light of the lanterns, the men's bodies threw monstrous shadows on the wall.

The master of the *llaut*—ghostly from the gray-pink dust of the mining tunnels through which they had entered—pointed toward what Thomas guessed was the north end of the chamber. "We are here," he said quietly.

North squinted in that direction: stairs, leading up. They were not solid risers, but rather thin slabs of stone that had been set into grooves cut in the facing walls. They ascended toward a heavy-timbered, iron-bound trapdoor seven feet above them. North nodded, checked his up-time watch: they were on time—just. The summons could come at any time, now. "Weapons out," he murmured. "Check your actions; make sure there's no dust on or in them."

"Rearguard, sir?" asked Donald Ohde.

"Perhaps, but I—"

From behind them came the distant sound of feet slapping down against a wet section of the cave floor. Thomas North swung up his weapon; half a dozen of his men followed suit. But listening more closely, the Englishman allowed that it might be water dripping down through the porous sandstone. They had seen plenty of evidence of that on the way in. They waited, guns ready, for almost a minute. The regular sounds ended as a hasty patter, then nothing: water, certainly. "Stand down," muttered North.

"What was it, Colonel?"

"It was nothing, Hauer. Just water."

"Or maybe the witch," offered the master of the *llaut*, who suddenly discovered himself under the intense scrutiny of sixteen pairs of eyes belonging to heavily armed and already somewhat anxious men.

"I beg your pardon," said North sweetly, "but maybe it was the *what*?"

"The witch," repeated the master of the *llaut*. "*Na Joanna*. The one that inhabits these caves."

One half of the group—including two of the three Wild Geese—stared about balefully.

In contrast, Donald Ohde was grinning and shaking his head. "There just had to be something." He almost giggled. "There just had to be something we didn't learn about or consider. But an attack by a witch? Now, that will be a story worth telling."

"Yes," North agreed, "it will be a story worth telling—to scare naughty children. Now let me make a few guesses." He aimed his chin at the *xueta*. "First, the legends of this witch probably have to do with moaning on stormy nights, do they not?"

"Often, yes."

"You mean the kind of moaning that occurs when wind is forced through a narrow ravine, like at the head of this valley?"

The *xueta* shrugged. "Yes."

"And let me further conjecture that the witch's nocturnal harrowings are proven by sudden health afflictions visited upon wandering children and occasional disappearances of goats, followed by the eventual discovery of their skeletal remains."

"Yes."

"The former of which is simply parental terror-tactics, while the latter would be consistent with the action of wild dogs, wild pigs, poachers, or all three. And last, I'm going to go out on a limb here and make the wild surmise that the witch was responsible for the deaths of untold workers at the mines and the quarries, correct?"

The *xueta* smiled at last. "Yes, some stories claim that."

"And of course one couldn't possibly explain these purported deaths as being the consequences of mining accidents, malnutrition and disease, surreptitious murder by guards or rival workers, or missing persons who simply, in fact, escaped?"

"All true," said the *xueta*.

North finally smiled back. "And of course you, personally, don't believe in the legend of this witch at all, do you?"

"Not a word of the drivel," their guide affirmed with a nod. "But it is always worth a smile watching grown men shiver like little boys for a minute or two."

"Thanks for the entertainment, yeh barstard," growled Seamus Jeffrey, the youngest of the Wild Geese.

"What? Resentment? I have done you a favor."

Donald Ohde cocked his head. "How so?"

"Did I not divert you for a moment? Did I not take your mind off of the attack to come? And does it not now seem, in comparison, that the perils of men and steel seem small in comparison to the terrors your mind was building?"

Several in the group blinked; the veterans among them—the same who had taken no heed of the legend of the witch—tried to conceal amused grins.

"Yes, well," huffed North in an attempt not to smile himself. "Story time is over." He moved next to the stairs, produced his nine-millimeter automatic, and snapped the safety off. "Our next game is deadly serious."

Asher's smaller assistant looked over at the bored Mallorcan guard who had brought him down to the main ground floor storeroom to fetch a gallon of water and ethanol each. The guard was taking the opportunity to pilfer a few sausages hanging close to the door.

Asher's assistant opened the tap of the first tun. As the liquid started spattering noisily to the bottom of his waiting, empty jug, the assistant palmed a crude key wrench out of his sleeve. Judging from the angle of the guard's shadow, he was still facing out the open door into the courtyard; a sigh of contentment followed by earnest munching indicated that his attention was not on his *xueta* charge. After all, what mischief could the Jew possibly do with a guard standing within ten feet of him? The assistant grinned faintly while, using his body as cover, he inserted the key wrench in a well-concealed hole and gave it a sharp turn. Then he shut off the spigot, which squeaked. Then he half opened it, closed it again: another squeak.

The guard looked up. "What are you doing? Stomping on mice?"

"No; this spigot leaks. I have to ram it closed, hard. Here, one more time—" and his final effort produced a third squeak.

"You done yet?" asked the guard. He did not sound impatient, but wistful; his eyes strayed to another sausage hanging by the wall.

"One more," answered the assistant as he tapped the second tun. He repeated the process: when the guard wasn't looking, he inserted the key wrench in a similarly situated hole—just beneath, and concealed by the rim of, the tap. When he was done, the assistant scraped the key wrench across the handle of the spigot twice. Then he re-palmed it and once again tightened the spigot three times.

"What? Another squeaky spigot?"

The assistant shrugged. "Shoddy workmanship, I suppose."

"Just what a Jew would be willing to pay for," sneered the guard. He belched and pointed out the door. "Get going. If that little bitch dies, it's not going to be because you were late getting back."

Asher's assistant bowed slightly and walked out, a gallon jug hanging in each hand. He made his way up to the second level, and was about to start on his way to the roof when a rich bass voice called after the two of them.

"Guard, a moment."

The assistant's escort looked around dully, then snapped straight to attention; the hidalgo captain—Vincente Jose-Maria de Castro y Papas—was approaching from the governor's office. "I just heard about the prisoner," he explained. "I am going up. I will escort the doctor's assistant to the sickroom."

The guard spoke with his eyes fixed above the hidalgo's brow line. "Sir, I must continue to escort the prisoner. Señor Dakis' orders, sir."

"Ah. I see. Well then, I shall accompany you there."

"As the captain wishes."

Asher's assistant started up the stairs to the roof, wondering why this captain was concerned enough to accompany them, but he knew one thing very clearly: from all accounts, he was smart enough to be trouble.

Lots of trouble.

Inside the secret compartment at the core of the tun of purified water, Owen Roe O'Neill counted to fifty after hearing the three squeaks that signaled that the barrel's false interior was now unlocked and could be opened.

It was hard making sure that he did not count too quickly, but fortunately, the only light inside the hidden compartment was also the assurance that he did not succumb to the desire to rush his exit: the pale green phosphorescent dot of the up-time watch Miro had lent him continued in its orbit around the unseen center of the timepiece's face. The watch had not only been necessary to ensure that he waited long enough to emerge from the immense barrel, but was also a means of determining if the whole operation had gone awry. Had there been no three squeaks of the spigot within the next ninety minutes, Owen would have emerged anyway—but to withdraw as surreptitiously as possible: if the signal to come out was that late, it meant the operation was, as the up-timers put it, "busted."

Owen watched the second sweep hit the ten o'clock position and grabbed the handles on either side of the egress hatch from the secret compartment. He pushed them outward and heard the click that meant the spring lock had been pushed back far enough to allow the hatch to begin turning. He rotated it through ninety degrees and both heard and felt the flanges on the hatch clear the restraining tabs. Sliding himself forward, he got his arms doubled up behind the hatch, braced his feet against the back of the compartment, and pushed.

The head of the tun hinged outward at the first hoop, the water in the false reservoir there flooding out on the floor with a rush. Owen wriggled out, past the lead inserts that had given the barrel proper weight and rolled to his feet, dagger at the ready.

He was in a dark storeroom and he thought he smelled—sausage.

He turned toward the other barrel just as it, too, hinged open from the first hoop, the ethanol that had been trapped in the reservoir behind the spigot splashing out, mixing with the water.

Owen helped little Edward Dillon crawl out. Dillon clambered to his feet, reached back inside, and retrieved his pepperbox revolver. Owen shook his head. "No Edward, that's not the tool for this particular job. It's in here." He tapped the young man's temple. "*Como le va?*" he asked.

"*Bueno. Estoy dispuesto a hablar español.*" Dillon's accent was as convincing as his reply was swift and sure. Furthermore, being one of the "black Irish," he looked as genuinely Spanish as he sounded. His gear, like Owen's, had been carefully selected from among the pirate equipment that had originally been worn by troops on Spanish argosies. The disguise was very effective in Dillon's case; it was much less so for rangy, red-haired Owen Roe O'Neill, whose tip-tilted nose and plentiful freckles definitively marked him as a son of the northern Celtic peoples.

"Shall I lead, then, Colonel?" Dillon asked.

"Just a moment." Owen checked the handle of both spigots; he saw two fresh, lateral scratches on one of them: the 'go' sign. "Lead on, Dillon. You know the way." Twenty rehearsals on the chalk outline in Tarongi's basement ensured that.

Dillon nodded, went to the door, drew a deep breath, and fell into what he evidently hoped was a nonchalant posture. *A great actor he will never be,* thought Owen, *but he's good enough to walk fifteen feet to the left.*

Which is just what Edward Dillon did: pushing open the door casually, he wandered out to the left-hand side, not hugging the curving wall of the Castell de Bellver's lower gallery, but anyone on the opposite side of second gallery level would still have only seen him from the waist down. Owen shut the door behind them without attempting to muffle the noise and followed Dillon, who reached the door to the long-term storage room, located just to the south of the Castell's main entrance. The door was not open, but they had not expected it to be. They could not be sure if the room was occupied, either; their advance intelligence, while good insofar as layout and complement were concerned, did not extend to a precise knowledge of interior duty stations, or any others that could not be observed from the nearby slopes and low mountains just a bit inland.

Dillon looked at Owen, who glanced around the Castell's circular bailey or, "arms court": only two Spanish in sight, almost on the opposite side of the lower gallery, strolling. Were they walking a patrol of the interior? That hardly seemed plausible, since it was only one hundred feet in diameter. More likely they were simply off duty, bored, and glad for the freedom to be taking some of the comparatively cool night air. Owen turned back to Dillon and nodded.

The little Ulsterman opened the door without having to knock or fiddle with the lock; that much they had known—that this room was kept unlocked for ready access to routinely used tools and supplies. The dim light revealed a guard; before he looked up, Dillon muttered an informal greeting.

As the guard grunted his lazy response, Owen moved past Dillon quickly and quietly, noting that the Spaniard was portly, well settled into a snack of olives, cheese, and bread, and rather slow-eyed.

He looked up at Owen's approach, suddenly anxious at the sound of swift, decisive movement. "Sir, I wasn't—I didn't—" He stopped and squinted as Owen got within arm's-reach; the guard frowned, and his hand went to the short scabbard on his belt.

"Hey—" he started.

Harry Lefferts squinted into the murk and signaled on his handset for Doc Connal to lower him another ten feet in two intervals of five. The clouds had not risen as they approached the slopes on the west side of the Bay of Palma, which meant that they were damn near evolving into a ground fog.

Harry scanned under the thickening cloud bank to find the sea-level—and therefore, visible—landmarks he'd spotted during his approach. Using the lights at Fort San Carlos to the south, and Palma to the north as his points of reference, he confirmed his bearings. He looked at his compass, recalled the last time he had seen the dim outline of Bellver—probably about three minutes ago—and frowned. Unless he was completely screwed up on the numbers, he should be almost on top of—

Bellver's lazarette loomed out of the darkness at him the same moment that the line started playing out in response to his request for the first five feet of slack—putting him on a course that would carry him up against the battlements with a solid whack before he cleared them. Worse yet, he realized with a jump of his heart, the guys in the dirigible were about to lower him five more feet—meaning he was actually going to miss the roof entirely and instead splat full into the side of the tower at ten miles an hour. Not great, in itself, but then he'd either get dragged straight up the near side of the lazarette and be caught on its crenellations, or slide around curve of its outer wall, bumping as he went, his line possibly snagging one of the toothlike merlons, snapping, and dropping him one hundred feet down into the dry moat.

Harry signaled quickly with the handset and reached his other hand around to unholster his .357 automatic—a gun he was not particularly fond of, but was optimal for this situation. His signals—which were a three digit code for "emergency: raise me ten feet now: stop the airship now"—were evidently quickly received and understood; the second five-foot dip reversed into a hasty reascent that began as a lung-cinching snap. Wheezing,

Harry reached behind to release two of the small spools of landing slack affixed to his main wire and did the same to his "fanny
wire." As he approached the wall—a little too high, now—he
suddenly dropped two feet lower: his final altitude correction. At
the same time, his butt swung down, leaving him in more of a
sitting position as his course took his toes over the battlements,
his feet out to brace against an impact or land. His gun was up,
his eyes scanning for targets on the roof.

*Well,* he thought, *here goes nothing.*

Frank looked up as Asher's assistant came back with the water
and ethanol—and his heart sank. *Oh no.* Don Vincente Jose-Maria
de Castro y Papas pushed into the room ahead of the returning
guard, his eyes dark with genuine worry.

"How is your wife?" he asked, crossing to Frank in one stride.

Frank stared at him. So *it's just like old times, huh? Just like
that, all is forgiven. No hard feelings for the cold shoulder I've
been giving you for weeks, even though I* am *lucky that it was
you who beat me up. And I've never thanked you for the paper,
the ink, the niceties, and especially for Asher, because there's no
other way Morales would allow a* xueta *into his precious Castell.
So, despite my ingratitude and rebuffs, here you are, no resentment, just genuine concern. Probably ready to do anything for us,
for her. You poor sap.*

"Frank?" asked Don Vincente, the frown on his face deepen-
ing. "Are you quite all right?"

Asher's voice was loud and scratchy. "I need quiet. Here," he
said to his larger assistant, "keep this handy." Asher reached
out a long, wicked looking knife; it didn't look like any surgi-
cal implement Frank was familiar with, but then, he wasn't too
familiar with the doctoring tools of the seventeenth century. The
tall assistant reached out, took the blade carefully. Dakis and one
of the guards watched him closely until he set the knife down
on the table in front of him.

In the meantime, Asher had asked for his smaller assistant to
stand ready with two full quart-sized, long-necked bottles of water
and ethanol respectively. "I may need you to wash away a great
deal of blood and douse against infection," Asher said grimly
as his hands were busy behind the privacy blind. Giovanna, to
whom he had earlier given a draught that he identified as opiated

wine, murmured and moaned. "God help me," Asher muttered, "this will not be easy."

He seemed to be manipulating something gently when, suddenly, there was a splash of liquid on the floor: blood.

Castro y Papas flinched forward, clearly following an instinct to help, stopping himself as he inevitably realized that there was nothing to be done.

The smaller assistant asked, "Do you need the water or spirits, yet?"

"No, but have them ready. And you"—Asher looked up at the taller assistant—"be quick with that knife."

In the same instant that Owen Roe O'Neill took his last, long step to close with the slow-eyed guard, he drew his dagger and thrust straight forward.

The weapon's point entered the man's heavy neck just where the Irish colonel had intended: at the larynx. As the guard wheezed horror and dismay, Owen withdrew the knife at an angle, dragging its keen edge sharply across the jugular vein. Dark blood spurted and the man, in the midst of scrabbling after his own weapon and trying to rock up to his feet, suddenly grabbed at the mortal wound.

Owen knew the man was dead, but this way he would die neither quickly nor silently: in the time it took him to exsanguinate, the guard might tip over boxes, flail about destructively, and thereby, bring other soldiers to investigate. *Can't have that.* Owen, arm coming back from the exit slash, shot forward again into another thrust.

This time, the man was on his knees, moving feebly, when the Spanish dagger sunk almost four inches of its length into his temple. The guard's struggles ceased abruptly; he fell forward, face down on the paving stones, the blood leaking out of him in an ever widening pool.

Owen turned to Dillon at the door. "Have you locked it?"

"Yes, Colonel."

"Then get over here, on the double."

Dillon did, and together they quickly found the box of spare culverin balls that had been placed square atop the trapdoor into the exit tunnel. Lifting the balls out, they lightened the crate and moved it aside, exposing the trapdoor.

Locked. They could blow the lock off, but that was loud—and besides, this room was for storing tools, also, wasn't it? "Dillon, keep watch outside. Tell me when those late-night strollers are at the other side of the arms yard."

"They're over there now, Colonel."

Owen quickly found what he was looking for: a hammer and chisel. He set the nose of the chisel in place, tried a test blow.

Nothing more was needed. Evidently the trapdoor had not been used in many decades, nor cared for in the meantime; the lock, its securing arm almost rusted through, came flying off with a dull clatter. He tapped a sequence of knocks on the door's beams, a tattoo that the up-timers called "shave and a haircut." He got the "two bits" response—and yanked open the trapdoor.

Thomas North's dusty face looked up at him. "About bloody time, bog-hopper."

"Get your lazy *sassenach* ass up here and sort out the men. We have a lot of work ahead of us."

North came up in two bounds, swapped his nine-millimeter for his SKS, and stared at the locked door. "Any sign of the other element yet?"

Owen received his armor and the rest of his weapons from the oldest of the Wild Geese, Anthony Grogan, and shook his head. "No, we're still waiting for Harry's signal."

"And what is the signal?" asked North's *xueta* guide, looking up at them from his position in the secret tunnel.

*Surely there's no harm in telling the fellow now*, Owen thought, but North only said, "Even down there, you'll know it when you hear it."

# Chapter 51

Valentino led the main charge toward the villa, approaching it at an oblique angle to stay out of the sightline of the fifteen men who had volleyed at the external guards. That fusillade did its job, dropping the four enemy silhouettes all at once, like an invisible wave knocking over straw men.

At the head of almost fifty mercenaries and assassins, Valentino reached the side door into the villa, which he guessed was a secondary entry into a great room. Never having been inside, and not having dared pump local inhabitants for information, his attack depended upon overwhelming force, not advance intelligence. However, even his profound superiority in numbers would not be sufficient if the fight became a protracted gun battle.

"This group has up-time weapons," he hissed at his men, "so they will win if we keep our distance. But we will win a melee. So we volley and charge. Now, Arturo, take your group to the back of the villa; Ignatio, take your men around the front. Kill any external guards, keep anyone inside from getting out. Use any up-time weapons you find to hold off reinforcements from their perimeter patrols. Now go!"

The two units of half a dozen men rushed off into the darkness just as the fifteen musketeers caught up with the rest of the group along the southern wall of villa. "So if we're supposed to charge, why not charge in now?" panted Odoardo.

"Because we have to seal all the possible exits first. Remember, no one is to be left alive. No one. Now, Linguanti, let's give them something else to worry about."

Valentino's wiry lieutenant nodded and produced a ceramic bottle of olive oil about the same time a few shots spatted back and forth at the front of the house. He lit the linen wick jammed into the top of the bottle and nodded to Odoardo, who drew back his immense, trademark axe and smashed open one of the two shuttered windows along that stretch of wall. Two reports— pistols probably—boomed in futile retaliation the same instant that Linguanti lobbed the fire bomb inside.

Sherrilyn Maddox heard the volley, turned on her heel and started sprinting eastward, back toward the villa. Too focused on her job to be scared or surprised, she assessed the situation quickly: the attackers had infiltrated past, or eliminated, an outpost. Probably the southern one, since the sound of gunfire—and now, shouting—was spreading from the south of the villa.

She was about two hundred yards out and, fortunately, the root cellar lay right along her most direct approach to the villa's rear entrance, which opened into the building's great room. The four men walking the perimeter like she was might arrive in time to be useful, but not if they came rushing directly back toward the villa; whoever was attacking was professional, and would be sure to have set up ambushes to interdict reinforcements.

And damn it, she could already start to feel her knee stiffening like a rusted door hinge: unwilling to bend, threatening to break. But that was just too bad. Even if she was doing irreparable damage to it, she had to push it to the limit; the next five minutes could, quite literally, decide the future course of the Western World.

Refusing to limp, she glanced north toward the western skirts of Monte Cengio; two lamps burned brightly there. That signal meant Taggart had heard the attack and was even now collapsing inward toward the villa with most of his pickets. But there had been too little warning; he would not arrive in time, given how quickly the attackers were pressing their advantage. Sherrilyn could already see wisps of smoke rising up from the villa and heard gunfire at the front and then the back.

As she reached the root cellar and knocked a "shave and a

haircut—two bits" tattoo on the door, she calmly accepted that she was the only relief force in a position to rescue her friends.

The cellar's storm door banged back, and Rolf, the largest of the hidden reserve of three Hibernians emerged. She drew her Glock, waved it toward the villa, and resumed running. "Follow me," she hissed at the forms already trailing her at a crouch.

As soon as the defenders' two pistols fired pointlessly out the window, Valentino sent his men through the southern door of the villa.

Gunfire—flintlocks and one or two up-time weapons—barked a lethal salute as his men went through; three fell, a fourth staggered, but the next wave was in and firing back into a vast chamber seething with desperate, human chaos.

From what Valentino could make out as he entered in the third rank and dodged quickly to the side, they had been lucky enough to come directly into the villa's large, and surprisingly plain, great room—which, to his eyes, was appointed more in the style of a vast, well-to-do farmhouse. The long, plain tables were littered with trenchers, utensils, a few pewter plates, all in the process of pre-cleaning, the leavings mostly scraped into feed buckets bound for whatever livestock they had out back. A dozen—maybe a score—of domestics of all shapes, sizes, and sexes were now running to and fro, some focused and purposeful, most shrieking and confused. A few were pushing smaller trestle tables over for cover; a few more—workers who had no doubt been furnished with the weapons of off-duty Marines—were attempting to reload, their quiver-fingered haste and inexperience ensuring that they would likely be dead before they even got the wadding snugged down against the ball.

Valentino yelled, "Fire at will!" but hardly needed to: the murderous pack he had brought with him only needed the scent of blood to start killing indiscriminately. The second and third ranks had already fired their pistols into the milling crowd, many throwing the discharged weapons aside. Valentino conceded they were probably right in their implicit assumption that they would not have the time, opportunity, or need to reload them. Swords out, they began hacking through the mob. Men fell, the pink froth of their rent lungs exposed; women screamed, run through, their bodies' own weight dragging them off the swords that had mortally transfixed them. One, a heavy, sweat-stained cook, came roaring out of the press, a frying pan held ready behind her shoulder. Odoardo watched her approach with a sneer, and as she drew close, used one hand to casually flap his axe at her midriff. The woman stopped suddenly, stared down, saw her entrails coiling out, went down to her knees.

Screaming, crying, fists flailing, a young boy appeared from behind her, assaulting Odoardo, who barked out a laugh as his axe came down, hard.

The mortally wounded woman folded down over the small, ruined body with a great wail, and Valentino watched as Odoardo paused for the briefest of moments, clearly considering whether he should finish the job. An equally short-lived smile curled the left side of the ogre's mouth; having evidently decided to let her die in both emotional and physical misery, he moved on—just as the discharge of an up-time gun cut down the mercenary who had been standing behind him.

Valentino peered through the falling bodies. His men were doing a lot of damage, but not to the right people. There were at least four of the renegade embassy's Marines, now sheltered behind overturned tables near the base of the only obvious staircase to the upper level. As Valentino watched, the Marine with the up-time weapon put a bullet into any of the assassins who tried dodging through the thinning crowd to engage them directly. In the meantime, the other three were reloading their USE regulation flintlocks. If this went on—

"You men," Valentino shouted, beckoning toward the musketeers who had just followed them in, "look there: the Marines behind the tables. Volley at them on my command—"

Valentino watched another of his own men fall to the Marine with the revolver, who then ducked down, apparently preparing to swap a freshly loaded cylinder into his weapon. As he did, there was a momentary break in the press of running, falling bodies—

"Now! Fire!"

Four miquelet muskets roared just to Valentino's left. Two of the Marines went down, one trailing a rooster-tail of blood behind him as he fell.

Now almost deaf in his left ear, Valentino rose up, pointed with his sword, and screamed, "At them! Quickly!"

✧　　✧　　✧

Sharon, having led the four clerics into her suite, moved purposefully toward its large, rough-hewn armoire against the wall. "Larry," she said, "give me a hand, here." One of the two Wild Geese guarding the doorway hastened to help; she shook her head, jerked it back towards his post. "You keep protecting us; Cardinal Mazzare can help me move the furniture."

Larry Mazzare, deciding that the composure with which she made the odd request indicated that she was not succumbing to hysterical distraction, jumped over to comply—

—but was interrupted by the sound of heavy footfalls crossing the threshold. Looking up, expecting to see the approach of his death, he instead saw Lieutenant Hastings—in armor—with George Sutherland limping eagerly after him.

Sharon stepped away from the armoire at Hastings' gesture.

The lieutenant grabbed his end of the armoire and nodded to Larry. "Your Eminence, if you would be so good, on the count of three...One, two—"

Larry heaved at the wooden mass; it creaked away from the wall—

—and revealed a narrow, five foot high by two foot wide faded section of wall.

Sharon gestured toward the secret door. "Apparently put in by the first builders. Who never finished the job. But it should be enough to—"

"Ambassador," Hastings interrupted with an apologetic tone, "your husband sent me back here, in part to help you lead these men out to safety, but also to ensure that you did, in fact, come with us. He is concerned about your—"

Without a word, Sharon turned and ran—surprisingly quickly, for someone of her size—back towards the staircase and Ruy.

Hastings sighed, shrugged, went to the panel and pushed; it swung into the wall, revealing a black, narrow staircase leading down at a precipitous angle. "Your Eminences, you will forgive me if that is the last time I bother with formal titles; time is short. I will lead the way, Mr. Fleming will follow." The more plain-faced of the two Wild Geese nodded. "Then Cardinal Mazzare, His Holiness, the father-general, and Cardinal Barberini. Mr. McEgan and Mr. Sutherland will bring up the rear. We move until we are out of the villa. Once there, those of us who can will run north toward Lieutenant Taggart's outpost. Any questions?"

"Yes," said Larry. "Why weren't we told about this secret passage the first day we got here?"

Hastings looked at him squarely. "So you couldn't tell anyone else about it. A secret passage is only useful if it stays secret. Any other questions? No? Then follow me."

Ruy heard the two off-duty Hibernians he had awakened along with Hastings cursing at buckles and lanyards. "Can you equip yourself no faster?" he hissed in their direction, then leaned an eye around the corner at the head of the staircase to look down into the great room.

Drifts of oily smoke. Puddles and spatters of blood. The bodies of men and women with whom he had shared almost two months' worth of meals, laughter, and fear lay scattered about. Being a lifelong professional, he cordoned off the emotional consequences of what he was seeing with the suddenness of snapping down the safety of a gun. What remained was tactical data, all seen in a second.

The firebomb the attackers had heaved into the room had not been particularly effective at spreading flame, and several of the slain had fallen into the densest part of the smoldering olive oil, largely smothering it. Given time, it might start a house-threatening fire, but that was at least ten minutes off: an eternity, in a combat such as this one. Only two Marines of the ready guard in the great room were still alive, one of them armed with a Hibernian's black powder revolver. If it wasn't for that fellow, the whole band of cutthroats would probably be halfway up the stairs by now—but the Marines could not hold out much longer. Ruy could hear the rush of feet, some heading straight for their makeshift parapet of tables, others angling toward the staircase itself. Which was, of course, their ultimate objective. They—rightly—presumed that the pope would not be housed on the ground floor. The Marines needed some assistance—and right now.

As Ruy raised the heavy weapon in his right hand, he saw the Marines begin to fire in a panic, saw the leading edge of assassins come into view, two of them falling dead or wounded, but others preparing to push over the top of the tables. Another one appeared at the bottom of the stairs. *What fortuitous timing*, Ruy thought as he looked down the sights of the up-time weapon and began to fire.

Ruy was used to the kick of the S&W .357 magnum revolver
that Sherrilyn Maddox had forced upon him when she arrived,
and upon which she had trained him. However, having only shot
at targets, he had never seen what a lead hollow-point would do
to a man at a range of less than fifteen feet.

The two assassins who had been about to clear the table barricade, swords readied, went sideways as if hit by a battering ram.
The red crater each bullet punched into the side of a torso was
startling enough, but the wide spray of blood and tissue from
both of the exit wounds was more reminiscent of the effects of
grapeshot, to Ruy's mind. Still, he decided, as he tracked over
until his sights were centered on the openmouthed assassin frozen
in shock halfway up the stairs, it was a most inelegant weapon.
He squeezed the trigger and saw another red crater appear where
the base of the cutthroat's neck had been.

He leaned back behind the corner as the inevitable spattering of inaccurate counterfire from the rest of the blackguards
snapped and bit away at the mortar. Well, he reflected, that will
give them something to consider for a few moments—but only
a few moments. He calmly thumbed the release, swung out the
cylinder, fingered a readied speed loader out of his bandolier, and
turned at the sound of the approaching Hibernians.

Except it was not them; it was his wife.

Ruy was not often surprised, but this was the exception that
made the rule. "Sharon, you are back? I told you to run, sent
Hastings and George to assist you!"

She stared at him, her own, rather diminutive, revolver in
hand. "And since when do you tell me what to do?"

"That very spirit—which may now be the death of you—is also
why I adore you so. But if you refuse to leave, then you must
perform a crucial task." He shook his head when she raised the
revolver tentatively. "No, my heart, as ambassadora, you must send
word to our friends: you must rouse Odo and begin signaling."

That stopped her—as Ruy had knew it would. "But—but, the
staff downstairs—"

"Are beyond help, dear wife. Those who were able to flee, have.
The others are no more."

Sharon swallowed. "Then we don't have the time to send radio
signals. We've got to—"

"Dearest," he interrupted, "I am your chief of security, yes?"

From the corner of his eye, Ruy saw her nod as he snapped the cylinder back into place and strained to hear the orders being shouted back and forth downstairs.

"Yes," she allowed grudgingly.

"Then, wife, trust me in this," he said, as the two Hibernians finally—*finally!*—came out of their billet, lever-action rifles and revolvers ready. "Your superiors will want all the information you can send on this event. And any survivors among us may need help, or may be fleeing for our lives. The more your superiors know, the more swift and effective their first assistance will be. Now—and prettily I ask it—please go."

Eyes shiny, and without another word, she turned and ran back the way she had come.

Ruy spent a split-second appreciatively watching—savoring—her movements seen from the rear. Then he began giving orders to the Hibernians. "They will come again any second, attempting to overrun both the Marines down in the great room, and us at the head of the stairs. They may also try to send someone farther into the villa, down the corridor into the north wing. You, Corporal, see if you can get an angle on the hallway into the north wing; we need to keep all their men bottled up in the great room for as long as we can..."

"*Minge!*" swore Valentino as he surveyed what had become of the men he had sent charging forward toward the tables and the stairs. At least half of them were down, most wounded and so severely shocked that they could barely move or moan. "Linguanti, get another of those firebombs ready."

"*Si*, but—"

"Just do it." Valentino spent a precious second considering the claustrophobic battlefield. He could send more men to rush the barricade of tables again, but now that tactic had become very expensive—perhaps cripplingly so. Either the gunman hidden near the top of the stairs was very good, was not alone, or both.

Besides, men who fought for riches—even such as his had been promised—were more savage than stalwart. At this range, firearms could hardly miss and the damage they inflicted was shocking to see, even for hardened killers. True, far more of those who had fallen were wounded rather than killed outright, but here, in a villa at the ass-end of nowhere, those wounds were a death sentence, anyhow.

Which meant he needed to keep the men moving, fighting, busy—too busy to count their losses, and hear the keening moans of their dying fellows. Fortunately, the wailing would only start when the wounded tossed off the shock, by which time this battle would be over. Unless Valentino tarried here in this great room. So he had to act—now. Waiting for all his men to reload cost too much time, too—so the fire bomb was best. And once he got past the last two Marines...

Valentino measured distances: once his men reached the tables, the entry to the kitchen was only ten feet farther along to the right. About twelve feet directly behind the tables was the door leading out to the rear of the villa, where the firing had finally stopped; from the sound of it, Arturo's group had run into one of the revolver-armed guards.

Valentino needed to secure those two areas—the rear door and the kitchen—even though his ultimate target was probably up the stairs. However, once he cleared the Marines, he could, so to speak, turn the tables on the defenders; the trestle tops would not protect his men from up-time ammunition at that range but they would provide full concealment until they popped up to shoot. And if he could get a half dozen sheltered there to send a volley up the stairs...

"The firebomb is ready," said Linguanti.

"Good, get ready to throw it just short of the base of the stairs on my count of three."

"But, Valentino, there is no target there. And it might prevent us from assaulting up the stairs once we—"

"I don't want the bomb to kill people; I want its smoke to blind them. And don't throw it *on* the stairs, but a few feet in front, so we can still get up them. Now, Odoardo, look there—" Valentino pointed. "You see that corridor just to the right of the main entrance?"

"*Si.*"

"It apparently goes off into the north wing. There might be another staircase back there. At any rate, when you take a group in that direction, it will distract the bastards at the head of the stairs."

"I'm not putting myself in the sights of that—"

"If you go first, you won't be the one shot—not if you move fast enough. Just make sure the next man is close behind you."

He needed to get Odoardo out of there before he started balking at the casualties. If the big man did so then others would, too. Every man Odoardo took with him was one more who wouldn't be looking nervously around to see if his mates were fearful, if they were starting to think more about retreat than riches.

"Okay. And if there's no staircase?"

"Come back here, report, and prepare to assault up the stairs."

"I told you, I'm not going to—"

Valentino wished Odoardo was dead already. "Idiot. Listen: we will have the stairs blocked by smoke, and will have cleared whoever is at the corner. And you're not to be in the lead; you command from the second rank."

Odoardo smiled. "I'll get a dozen men." He turned to inspect the clutter of faces behind him. "Hey, you three, and you—"

Valentino turned to Linguanti. "On my count of three, you throw the bomb where I told you. And then, you follow the last of Odoardo's group. Two seconds after they've crossed the open area. Keep that oaf on the objective, do you understand?"

"I understand—enough to hate the task already."

"My sympathies." Louder: "Odoardo, stand ready. The bomb will be thrown in one, two, THREE . . ."

Half-blind in the darkness of the staircase, Cardinal Luke Wadding tried to control how rapidly he was breathing. Even back in Ireland, sought by English bounty hunters, he'd never been as close to being murdered as this. To keep his teeth from chattering, he muttered at Hastings' broad back: "Where does this passage lead?"

"There are two exits," the lieutenant explained. "The first comes out behind a wall-hanging in the hallway of the north wing, just beyond the stone wall of the kitchen. The other goes down into the kitchen's basement."

"What? There's no outside exit?"

Hastings' dim outline shrugged. "They never finished that part of the escape route. You can see, on the west wall, where they obviously planned to run a tunnel out into the back. But it's almost solid rock there."

Antonio Barberini's voice quavered in fear. "But we have no reason to go down to the cellar—just into the north wing and out the side exit, there."

Hastings shrugged as he neared the landing that would give them access to the first door. "If the north wing isn't secure, then we'll have to head down into the cellar, come up into the kitchen and run to get out the back door of the great room."

Wadding calculated, swallowed. "We'd have to cross about eight feet of open space."

"I know," said Hastings with a nod. "And I know you are all brave men. Now, quiet, all of you."

Odoardo ran across the smoky, blood-spattered room. He was in front of the main entrance when a new weapon spoke from up at the head of the staircase behind him: a deeper, powerful, spiteful report, followed by two more in rapid succession and a faint *click-clack, click-clack.*

The two mercenaries immediately behind Odoardo sprawled, one screaming, the other ominously silent.

Odoardo reached the northern hallway, which evidently led to the servant's quarters. He spun, leveled his short-barreled fowling piece at the head of the stairs, and fired. The gun sounded like a small cannon going off. The charge of pellets tore up the rude railing, the top step, caused jets of ruined plaster to gush sideways out of the landing's far wall. It killed no one, but his shot still had the desired effect: the gunman flinched back long enough for the rest of Odoardo's ten men to cross the open space to safety.

Linguanti, the last over, skipped an extra step when another round from the lever-action rifle roared at his heels. Odoardo looked at him. "Now what?"

"Now we check down the hall."

They hadn't gone ten steps before fire chipped divots out of the right-hand wall of the corridor; they threw themselves snug against the left-hand wall.

"Damn it!" Odoardo complained.

From farther down the hall, another spattering of small-arms fire went away from them, toward the door on the northern end of the villa. Odoardo thought he heard Verme, the Corsican, shouting about a lost finger. "They're holding off Ignatio's boys, too, from the sound of it."

Linguanti nodded. "Probably a very narrow doorway from the servants quarters to the outside. Easy to defend."

"Yeah," Odoardo sighed. "And I guess we can't get to them,

either. Unless we want to get slaughtered." He finished tamping the wadding down against the single-aught sized pellets with which he had reloaded his weapon. "So who do we kill now?"

Sherrilyn Maddox felt two aches in her legs: one came from the knee that now surged with pain at every careful step, and the other was a painful tautness in her calves that came from wanting to continue to sprint, flat out, to help her friends.

But that was the fool's move, despite the sounds of a firefight emanating from inside the house. The exchanges outside had been ominously brief, even though the Hibernian guarding the back doors had unleashed a steady stream of lever-actioned lead at the assassins who had been sent to neutralize him. Judging from the cries and fitful writhing of several indistinct shadows, he had killed or wounded at least two of them, but then a quartet of muskets had volleyed in the general the direction of his muzzle flashes—and all was stillness.

That had been only twenty seconds ago, so perhaps the murdering bastards had not yet sorted out their casualties and their next move, but Sherrilyn had decided to spend that time closing the distance quietly, not starting a running gun battle. With almost no moon out, and no light source behind the attackers, targets did not become distinct until you were within fifteen, even ten yards. And even then...

Sharon crouched lower, pointed to her eyes, then to the frontal arc across which the enemy was distributed. The three Hibernians, lever actions at the ready, nodded and raised their weapons slightly, ready to bring them up.

They got within twelve yards before the apparent leader of this group came walking out from the back of the villa. He scanned the surrounding area, and a moment later he must have spotted the four shadowy figures approaching in postures of stealthy menace. He brought up his gun, turned to shout.

Sherrilyn went down on one knee and brought her Glock 17 up into a two-handed grip. She squeezed the trigger twice; the leader went backwards—and around him, muskets fired off hastily into the darkness, murdering the air over the Sherrilyn's lowered head as her three Hibernians set to work.

The echoing cracks of the .40-72 rounds and the creak of the lever actions seemed to set the rhythm for the harvest of death at the rear of the villa. Working from the flanks to the center, noting where the wild-firing muzzle flashes had been, North's well-trained men cranked round after lethal round into their targets.

Six seconds later, Sherrilyn rose, charged the last ten yards, and found herself standing amidst the sprawled bodies of her attackers. She resisted the urge to spit on them. Instead, she hissed orders. "Corporal, find the man they killed back here and get his revolver. We'll need it. You and you; watch our flanks. And be alert; our perimeter pickets will be inbound as well."

"And what next, Captain Maddox?" asked the corporal.

"Next, we bust in there and save our people. So reload all your weapons now; you might not have another chance."

Valentino, who had just finished getting his men organized for another general rush at the Marines' table barricade, froze: gunfire at the back of the villa. And those were not his guns: the reports were too sharp and loud, and they came with the *bam-bam-bam* speed of multiple up-time weapons. Christ's balls, they had a reserve force, hidden somewhere near the building! So now, there was only enough time to—

"Charge!" he screamed, firing a captured flintlock pistol at the barricades. "We have to seize the back door now!"

Emboldened by their numbers, and the now sufficient volume of smoke roiling up from the oil fire at the base of the stairs, nearly twenty of Valentino's men rose and sprinted forward.

The Marines rose up to fire back, dropped several, were blasted down by the answering volley.

As Valentino's men reached the table, two lever-action rifles roared down the stairs at them, dropping the first two to reach the makeshift barricade, as well as two others who tried to assault up the staircase itself. From the look of the hits they might not be dead, but were certainly out of the fight.

Many more survived, though, to get behind the tables and turn one around to face up the stairs. Seeing that, the rest of Valentino's men dove for cover behind it, quickly grabbed hold of the other table and worked it around to match the position of the other. Within moments, one of his smarter mercenaries had found the unemptied revolver that had allowed one Marine to give them so much trouble; that fellow began snapping shots back up the stairs, where the volume of fire began to fall off.

The rearmost half-dozen who charged across the great room were now able to push past the tables and, without breaking their stride, they made it to either side of the back door, panting.

Finally, thought Valentino, feeling the sweat that ran along his brow and down his sides, they had control of all the villa's points of egress. "Reload!" he screamed at the top of his lungs. "Prepare to sweep the stairs!"

The firefight suddenly became so loud that Sharon could easily have believed it was going on right outside the radio room. She wondered if—how—Ruy could survive such a nonstop barrage of enemy fire—but then shut off the part of her mind that had spawned the question and the thousand mortal terrors she could feel clamoring behind it.

She looked over at Odo, who had frozen into immobility as the firefight surged. "Ambassador," he asked, "should we perhaps—?"

"Keep sending," she interrupted firmly. "That's our job, so we keep doing it." She drew her small revolver from her pocket and trained it on the door. "No matter what."

Larry Mazzare tried to force himself to remain calm as Lieutenant Hastings eased open the panel behind the wall-hanging in the north wing's hallway, but he couldn't keep from holding his breath. Within this stairway—built and hidden at the core of what, to external observation, looked like the villa's central, load-bearing stone wall and kitchen fireplace—the noise in the rest of the house had been dim. They had heard faint cries, and the dull, distant thrumming of gunfire, but it had been impossible to gauge how close, or how much of it, there was.

As the panel opened and light shone in, the answer became obvious to all of them: they were at the epicenter of a vicious firefight. Moans, smoke, surging spasms of gunfire, screamed orders, and running feet vied with the stink of burning oil, wood, and gun smoke—all of which drove home the point just how bad the situation was in the villa's interior. Worst of all, none of the voices they heard were familiar to them.

Antonio Barberini asserted, "I don't think it's safe to go out there."

"No," answered Hastings, "it isn't." He began closing the door. "To the cellar, then."

✧　　✧　　✧

Odoardo sighed again; he didn't really want to go back to the great room and charge up those stairs, no matter how much that asshole Valentino assured him he'd be all right. He looked over Linguanti's shoulder to determine if Valentino was readying such an assault—but suddenly forgot why he had decided to glance in that direction. He poked Linguanti, a sudden malign smile stretching from one well-tufted ogre-ear to the other.

Linguanti, looking up, saw that expression, saw Odoardo's eyes fixed gleefully on something behind their group. Linguanti turned around and saw what the big man had noticed: one of the smaller wall-hangings in the northern hallway had swung out slightly, as if it had been a narrow door opening. It was now closing again, soon to be flush against the wall.

"That," said Linguanti, with a demonic grin to match Odoardo's ogrish one, "is quite a piece of luck."

"Yeah," said Odoardo, hefting his fowling piece in one hand and his axe in the other, "let's go *that* way."

# Chapter 52

As his feet shot over the battlements of the Castell de Bellver's lazarette, Harry Lefferts heard the sound of the dirigible's distant engines go through what sounded like a split-second of dop-plering: *they've spun them about.* Sure enough, the balloon shed speed so quickly that, like the bob of an arrested pendulum, Harry did not travel all the way over the crenellated wall, but only swung forward, and—slowing—he could feel that he would start backward within the next few seconds.

*Damn it,* he thought, *I said "slow down" not "stand on the brakes."* But no use crying over spilt milk; the end of his forward swing had brought Harry well past the inner rim of the lazarette's battlements and into plain view of the two guards upon it.

They stopped, stared, mouths open as a black-suited ghost flew out of the dark at them.

Harry used that moment of surprise to hammer out rounds at the closest of the two, intending to use only two bullets. But the sway in his motion ruined his aim, and he had to track the target, firing as he did. The third and fourth rounds hit the Spaniard, who went down with a groan.

The other, startled out of his shock by the gunfire, had admirable reflexes: he had his miquelet musket up, cocked, and discharged almost before Harry could blink.

But the Spaniard's speedy reaction came at the cost of accuracy; the musket ball whispered off into the night.

Harry stretched his legs downward as far as he could. He popped off one round at the second guard—just to make him duck—and then the back of his boots and calves came into jarring contact with one of the merlons of the lazarette's battlements.

Harry flexed his legs, holding himself there, and released the rest of the landing spools. With an additional three feet of line, he was now able to pitch forward on to the roof, with slack to spare. Staggering ahead as the backward pull from the cable abruptly ended, Lefferts congratulated himself on a job well done—and looked up to see the guard almost upon him, sword drawn.

Since Harry was using both his hands—one free, one gripping his gun—to keep himself from falling nose-first on the roof, he knew he couldn't bring his weapon to bear in time. So, with his weight already forward, and with the Spaniard's backswept sword now arcing toward him, Lefferts did what he was best situated to do.

Harry's tight, forward roll took the Spaniard by surprise. Granted, the surprise did not last long—not quite half a second—but it was enough. And it was fatal.

Harry came out of the roll awkwardly but was still able to wobble up to one knee, spin and steady himself with his off hand as he brought up the gun with the other. He knew he was going to do some piss-poor shooting now, but that hardly mattered: the Spaniard had turned and charged again.

When Harry fired, the guard was less than three feet away. Just to be certain, Lefferts fired three more times, almost draining the magazine. It was essential that this particular fight was over *now*.

And it was. A second after the guard fell, Harry was up, using the handset to signal for Dr. Connal to belay the grappling hooks down the line. Soon the dirigible would be moored in place, the others could join Lefferts, and the real fun could start. And he now had plenty of time in which to accomplish that.

Why, he probably had a full twenty seconds.

"That's it," muttered Thomas North when he heard the up-time pistol roaring atop the lazarette. "Gate team, on me. Stair assault team, on Colonel O'Neill. Ground level security, with Mr. Ohde. Ready?" Nods. Thomas nodded back and pushed open the door of the long-duration storeroom.

He had expected troops running in every direction, meaning

a hard fight to even get to the gate. Or a score of them gathered in the arms yard, readying a skyward fusillade. What North had not expected was what he now encountered: a moment of absolute, stunned silence in the Castell de Bellver.

North did not stop to enjoy that second, or the striking architecture picked out by the torches flickering in their cressets; he sprinted to the left, and then turned left again into the wide passage that was the Castell's inner gatehouse and portcullis. Several figures had risen from a table pushed up against the south wall; two more were scrambling to put on their helmets and get their weapons.

North raised his SKS and started firing. At this murderously close range, he felt no need to double-tap any of his targets. The weapon barked repeatedly, each shot momentarily illuminating the crowded, falling bodies. He had killed three of the five when the rest of his team moved past. One defender charged out to engage and died immediately; another took cover behind the doorjamb to cock his musket. He never got the chance to fire it; a flurry of .44 Hockenjoss & Klott blackpowder rounds from two Hibernian revolvers chipped stone, and then clipped him. As the Spaniard came around, grasping his wounded arm, the next two bullets took him straight through the cuirass.

North scanned the gate area: no guards left alive. "Lower the portcullis and smash the gears," he ordered a large Hibernian who was already producing an iron-headed mallet. He pointed to another. "Corporal, we'll have company clustering along the moat soon. Pull up the drawbridge, and watch the Spanish closely. No reason to fire at them unless they're doing something productive. Keep a sharp eye out for them trying to turn the guns on the ravelins about to blow open this gate; shoot any who try it. Once we have the second floor in our control, you'll put two overwatch marksmen up there." The Hibernian nodded and moved to carry out his orders. Thomas turned, called back into the arms yard, "Gate secure."

As Frank had expected, the gunfire on the roof—because of both its suddenness and intensity—stunned the Spaniards in the room into momentary immobility. The infiltrators, however, had expected this signal and the shock it generated. They reacted with the surety of long training. Asher's bigger assistant swept up the knife that had been entrusted to him and, in completing that act, sliced through the neck of one of the guards. He started turning toward Captain Castro y Papas.

The small, average-sized assistant smashed one of his two long-necked bottles of ethanol full into the face of the closest guard; the guard fell to his knees, bleeding and dazed. Without pausing, the assistant swung the other bottle, cracking it less accurately against the side of the other's head. While that fellow scrambled from the room, holding his ear, the assistant spun toward Dakis, the razorlike shards of a broken bottle in either hand. But Dakis had recovered in that brief interval and leaped away, over toward Giovanna.

Frank could hardly follow Vincente's lightning reflexes as his arm shot toward his sword—which would be quicker to use, at this range, than his uncocked pistol—and jumped at him, grabbing at Don Vincente's sword hand. "No!" he cried.

Vincente looked down into Frank's eyes, wondering. Perhaps he had expected to see hatred. Perhaps fear. If Frank was sending the look he hoped, the hidalgo would see an appeal, even pleading.

Vincente frowned—just as the bigger assistant started closing in for the kill. Frank threw his hand out, turned to put his body between the long, scalpel-sharp knife and the captain's body. "I said 'no'—and that includes you too."

The large assistant stopped, stared, was about to ask a question—but was interrupted by Dakis' harsh voice. "Drop the knife."

They all turned, looked. Dakis did have his gun out. He was holding it directly against Giovanna's right temple.

Turlough Eubanks came sliding down out of the mists on the guide line—now lashed to an iron fixture in the lazarette's roof—with a humming noise. He made a wide-legged landing, breaking his forward fall with one hand, securing his gear with the other. "How're we doin', Harry?" he grunted out.

"Good enough. Get down to their room and secure the hostages, then out to the walkway to help me hold off the bad guys."

"As you say, but listen: the clouds are rising a bit. The balloon has to reascend and soon."

"Tell me something I don't know." He used the handset to signal that Eubanks was down and the line ready for the next man. "Are you still here?" he tossed over his shoulder at Eubanks.

But Eubanks was not there; he had already entered the small stone cupola that covered the tight, spiral staircase that ran down through the lazarette like a spine.

At the midway point of the passage that led from the gate to the arms yard, Thomas North met Owen at the foot of the staircase to the upper gallery. "Is your team ready?"

Owen looked at the four Wild Geese behind him—grim myrmidons in helmets and cuirasses, pistols and sabers held loosely but ready—and the two men carrying true up-time weapons: a Hibernian with an SKS, and Matija with another of those rifles and a shotgun for good measure. "Thomas North, the only thing that's holding me up is yer flapping gums. Now let me do my work."

North smiled. "Hop to it, bog-hopper."

"Eh, fek you too, *sassenach*. Lads, on me." And up the stairs he went.

Donald Ohde spent a moment watching him go. "He's heading straight into the worst of it."

North nodded, staying close to the wall as he edged back toward the arms yard. "Of course he is."

"My men are starting to go room to room on this level. We've hit a half dozen Spaniards who've tried to come out to see what's happening, but the rest have hunkered down behind their doors." He looked around at the thick walls that now kept Spanish reinforcements out of, but also trapped the attack team within, the confines of the Castell de Bellver. They heard rapid lever-action rifle fire contending with a short sputter of muskets as two of the Hibernians assigned to his team broke into another ground-floor room. "Like scorpions in a bottle, we are," Ohde observed

"Yes," agreed North. "But we sting a hundred times faster than they do."

Sergeant Alarico Garza exited the governor's office at a trot, crouching, his brows folded together tightly. His corporal tagged along. "What are the governor's orders?"

"I don't know; his voice did not carry well from his hiding place under the desk." A sharp report—much sharper than a musket—rang out in the courtyard; a bullet traveling at utterly fantastic speed took a divot out of the nearest archway. Garza reached up, pulled the corporal lower, and forced himself to think past his rage and ardent desire to throttle Don Sancho Jaume Morales y Llaguno until the coward's tongue came bulging out of his mouth and his eyes went blank. "Did Diego go to defend the stairs as I ordered?"

"Yes, Sergeant. But why do you presume they won't come up through the towers?"

"Because I wouldn't. They've obviously come in through the old tunnel—although God knows how. So they are already right next to the main staircase. Besides, the towers are tight spaces, with many blind spots and sharp corners on their stairs: hard to attack, easy to defend. No, the enemy must work quickly, and so they will press to take the main staircase, which is comparatively straight and wide. You must reinforce it now. I will get the other men to pull the torches from the cressets on this level and keep firing on the dogs in the arms yard whenever we get a glimpse of them."

"And what do we do about the enemies on the roof?"

"I've sent half our men there, going up through the towers. They should be enough to rush the lazarette and take it in close combat." *So you hope, Alarico, but you heard the speed with which that up-time weapon was firing. Still, what other choices are there?* "Now go."

Dakis, hearing increased noise on the roof, snapped an order at the man whose face had been savaged by the regular assistant's first bottle. "You. Bring all available troops here. Go. Now!"

Don Vincente drew his own pistol and went to stand near Dakis, who had to grab Giovanna by her hair to bring her to her feet. Frank started forward reflexively, saw Giovanna's warning look, held himself in check.

Obviously, Captain Vincente had not yet had the time to decipher the many layers of duplicity that now lay revealed: he blinked in surprise at Giovanna's sudden, easy movements. "But all the blood..."

"It wasn't hers," said Asher from along the wall. "It wasn't even human."

Vincente turned and stared at Frank while holding the room at gunpoint. "And *this* was your escape plan?"

"It was a fine plan—until *you* showed up, and ruined everything," Frank retorted. Then he jerked his head at Dakis. "And he didn't help either."

Dakis laughed—but stopped when two sharp reports of an up-time rifle sounded from just beyond the door. Outside, from the fortified walkway linking the lazarette to the main roof, there was a short, strangled cry: the guard—and the summons he had been carrying from Dakis—were clearly gone.

Dakis shouted toward the door. "If you enter this room, the hostages die." He snugged the muzzle of his pistol closer against Giovanna's temple; Frank felt as though he was going to pop straight out of his own skin. "And the woman will get the first bullet, right through her brain."

Castro y Papas looked at him sideways. "You wouldn't," said the captain, his gun still held steadily upon the others.

"I would—and you'd better be ready to do the same. We have to hold off whoever is on the stairs—and the roof—until some one comes to check the lazarette. And this little bitch"—he prodded his pistol deeper into Giovanna's temple—"is the only way to keep them at bay."

"Yes, but you are only bluffing. You wouldn't kill a woman—a pregnant woman."

"Idiot. Of course I would. And don't give me any of that *merda* about hidalgo honor, you ass; this is war."

"Is it?" asked Don Vincente in a strange voice.

"What the hell is wrong with you? Of course it is. Now draw your sword and take the husband in hand; if I'm forced to kill the bitch, you'll need to immediately threaten the other hostage to make them back off. You can do that, can't you, noble sir?"

Don Vincente Jose-Maria de Castro y Papas seemed to consider the order judicially for a moment. "No, I can't," he answered. He turned and shot Dakis in the head.

When Harry heard the two SKS reports, just beneath him, he dropped the handset and hustled over to the southern side of the lazarette's battlements, holstering his .357 automatic and unslinging his own SKS as he went. *Damn, but the party is starting early.* Peering around the merlon, he saw why.

Evidently a guard had escaped from Frank and Gia's room—where, now, he heard a single shot. That was not according to plan, but he'd handle that later. The escaping guard had been fleeing over the walkway when Eubanks had come down to the landing that gave access to it, as well as the prisoners' room. Eubanks had thought and fired quickly, bringing the man down. But in the process, he had further alerted the Spanish to exactly where their enemies were: a dozen of the men tasked to walk patrols on the roof and tend the bay-pointing culverins were now closing on the walkway, running at a crouch and drawing weapons.

*Oh well, I hate waiting anyway,* thought Harry as he snapped an AK-47 magazine into the SKS. He drew back the bolt, let it fly forward with a sharp *clack*, and leaned over the sights.

The light was not good, but with watch fires and cressets mounted on the other three towers, he could still see target outlines. He dropped the sights, leading the closest of the responding guards, exhaled slightly, and squeezed the trigger. He recovered and squeezed again. The running figure tumbled into a long forward slide and lay still. Which Harry only saw peripherally as he moved on to the next target....

Owen Roe O'Neil came to the top of the stairs, and paused; the basic lesson of fortress combat, particularly when one had the advantage, was to waste no time. Press a charge and take some casualties, particularly if it will allow you to take an important defensive position. But here, with so few troops behind him, and constant training in the duck-and-weave tactics extolled by the up-timers and that damned *sassenach*, he decided, *Let's spend a moment seeing what we're up against.* He swept the capelline helmet off his head, put it on the tip of his sword, and, raising it to eye level, had it "peek" around the corner.

The response was immediate: two discharges from the right and perhaps four from the left sang off the sandstone, sending chips and dust flying. His battered helmet banged down the stairs.

He smiled down the staircase at the dark figures behind him. "You know," he said, "That little volley means a whole lot of them are reloading now, or are down by one readied piece...."

Thomas leaned out of the Castell's broad entry passage to look around the entirety of the arms ground. North squinted across the arms yard. The men with Donald Ohde had now swept through all but three of the ground-floor rooms, one of the Hibernians getting wounded in the process. As he limped behind, Paul Maczka of the Wrecking Crew took his place as point man for entering the next room.

As they set up for the assault, one of the other ground floor doors banged open and several Spaniards came charging out.

"SKS's: supporting fire!" called North to the suitably equipped members of his team. They leaned over their sights, took hasty aim and fired, usually two shots per figure just to be sure. The muzzle flashes and crashing reports—intensified by Bellver's constraining walls—lasted only five seconds; by then the Spanish were all on the ground. One was writhing; the rest were still.

From across the arms yard, Donald Ohde waved his thanks and then gave Paul Maczka the signal to enter the next room. He and the Hibernians did so, one kicking the door as another went in low. Two flashes and reports, a moment of quiet, and then Paul came out, giving a thumb's up to Donald Ohde.

Which was the very moment that a clutch of muskets from the upper gallery fired down into the arms yard; two of the balls hit one of the Hibernians mid-torso; he went down backward, his blood spattering back into the room he had just cleared. Another one hit Paul, who twisted around and fell against the wall, either dead or stunned.

Donald and his men crouched and scooted to head back to the room they had just exited. North elevated his weapon, looked for targets on the second floor gallery, saw faint movement, and shouted "Suppression!" Long, bright up-time muzzle flashes led angry roars up at the place where he had seen the movement.

Using the cover fire, Ohde and his team charged out, one pulling Paul back through the doorway he had just exited, the rest making directly for the last room to be secured on the ground floor. *One objective completed,* thought North, *but if Owen can't take the head of the stairs, and we don't link up with the element in the lazarette . . .*

North decided he didn't want to think about that. He concentrated his focus on the second floor gallery and wondered if this might be a good moment to swap his current magazine for a fresh one.

# Chapter 53

Frank flinched as the door burst open. A man in a cuirass, equipped exactly like those he had seen in the courtyard of the Palazzo Mattei, came in at a crouch, a wicked-looking up-time rifle in his hands. Its muzzle swung swiftly, surely, in Don Vincente's direction.

Frank jumped in front of Castro y Papas, arms spread wide in a covering gesture.

The man in the doorway snarled "Shite." Then, louder: "You want to be rescued or not, Francis Stone?"

"Yeah, but you don't have to kill *him* to do it."

Don Vincente threw down his pistol in disgust. "Evidently not." He turned to Frank. "How well you have learned the lessons of Rome, Frank. Deceit piled upon deceit. You have outdone your enemy, in this. Dakis was right: this is war—and I was a fool. I may have been a fool for one second, and he may have been a brute and a monster—but I was still a fool."

Frank took a step toward the man he had once again started to consider a friend. "Vincente, tell me: is it ever right to kill a pregnant woman?"

Don Vincente frowned, then looked away. "No. Of course not."

"So you were not a fool; you were a man with a terrible decision to make. And you made the right one."

"Right for you, at any rate."

"Yes, it helps us escape. But it also lets you keep your soul."

Turlough Eubank shook his head in annoyance, shouted, "Two minutes!" and ran back out the door toward the fortified walkway.

Peering around a different merlon—no reason to give the bastards a consistent muzzle-flash to aim at—Harry Lefferts saw that Turlough Eubanks had at last arrived in his position just beyond the door into the lazarette. And just in time.

At some predetermined signal that Lefferts failed to detect, almost thirty Spanish rose up from behind the culverins, from out of the two closest towers, and from the cupola covering the stairs down to the upper gallery. A few paused to knock the torches from the cressets affixed to the towers; the rest charged for the fortified walkway that was the sole means of access to the lazarette. Lefferts measured their progress, assessed that he had maybe two seconds to spare, and spent it scanning the rest of his kill-zone. Sure enough, he spotted movement on two of the other towers: low, stealthy hints of arms, shoulders, heads over the edges of the battlements. These were the positions of marksmen assigned to kill him as he fired down at their charging comrades. *Good luck*, he thought, as he lined up the closest of the advancing Spanish and fired. The man went down, clutching his leg. Harry lined up another, got off a clean center-of-mass shot—and ducked, rolling behind the merlon and coming up on its opposite side.

At that same moment six, perhaps seven muskets roared from where Harry had seen the marksmen on the roofs of the other, lower towers. He popped up in his new position, took quick aim, and fired steadily at a spot on the east tower where dispersing gun smoke partially obscured motions consistent with reloading or exchanging spent weapons for fresh, preloaded ones. A surprised cry, a curse, sprawling bodies, moaning—and then Harry had to shift his focus back to swatting down the men charging the fortified walkway.

Too late: some had already arrived at the mouth of the narrow, stone chute—and Harry smiled as they discovered that it, too, was defended. Hunched low, and sheltering in the doorway of the lazarette, Turlough Eubank could not be seen beforehand—and could hardly miss the attackers: the walkway was hip high, and less than three feet wide. For a man to rush it, he had to enter that narrow tight space. And three of the Spanish did just that before the rest realized that not only was the walkway directly defended, but that the weapon doing so was like the one on the roof: it could apparently fire endlessly. Two more of the guards closed on the walkway, but with less eagerness than had those now piled up at its entrance. Harry took advantage of their hesitation: he put a round into each one's chest.

Behind him, Lefferts heard the cable-whine that signaled the approach of the third man of his element—the Hibernian—descending in the bosun's harness. The whine ended with a thump, a curse, and then the sound of a weapon being unslung. "Just in time!" Harry called over his shoulder. "Join the party."

On the Castell's main roof, the charge was wavering, particularly among the Spanish closest to the apparently unassailable walkway—and Harry knew he had them. Double-tapping each one quickly, he fired at those in the front, forcing them to either die or—in the case of the lucky ones who were not hit because of the darkness and his hasty shooting—flee. The Hibernian threw himself down into a crouch behind the adjacent merlon, raised his own SKS—a conventional model; no thirty-round clips for him—and began adding to the volume of fire.

It was impossible to know which finally broke the Spanish: their massive casualties, or the fact that there were now two of the demon-rifles spraying death down at them. Whichever it was, fewer than ten survivors managed to reach cover; perhaps an equal number lay on the roof, trying to stifle groans that would mark them for a second bullet. Harry could feel the lull in the action settle in, quickly swapped magazines, turned to the white-faced Hibernian. "Damn," said Harry, just to keep the mood light, "I sure could go for a smoke about now."

If anything, the Hibernian became more pale.

Sergeant Alarico Garza ducked as another bullet chipped away at the rim of the gallery. The nonstop thunderclaps on the roof above were not a good sign; there were a few musket discharges mixed in, but almost as afterthoughts. It sounded like a one-sided slaughter up there.

And for the first time in over twenty years, Garza hit a fork in his decision pathway for which he was not prepared: *What now? If our men lose the roof, then—*

Experience reasserted: *Do your job. And your job is to hold this level.* And right now, that meant holding the staircase that the enemy had just probed, and suppressing their activity in the arms yard.

But to counteract his enemies successfully, Garza needed to know more about them—and he knew almost nothing, other than that their weapons all seemed to be copies of, or actual, up-time firearms. How many were there? How much knowledge did they have about the Castell? How did the ones on the roof get there? Sergeant Garza was compelled to admit that each of these urgent queries was also utterly imponderable and so he lacked any hope of acquiring answers—which was not a good sign.

His corporal returned, crab-walking low with a small box.

"You found more grenades?" Garza asked.

"Four," replied the corporal.

"Good. Get them over to the men watching the staircase. Are they ready, otherwise?"

"Yes, Sergeant—but they were hasty responding to the probe. Too many of them fired."

Garza swore at himself: *Yes, because you weren't there to enforce discipline, to make sure that only two fired at first, and then two more when there was a clear target, and so on.* "What are they down to?"

"Two loaded muskets. But all the pistols are still charged."

Garza shrugged. "That is not so bad; pistols are better at these ranges. You'll never get a chance to reload, anyhow. So, pistols, swords, grenades." He mused. "Against these devils, knife range would be best, but we can't hope for that. Now, off with you—and remember: no quarter asked or given."

"No quarter," repeated the corporal with a gulp before he continued on toward the staircase.

Owen Roe O'Neill finished giving his men their instructions and made sure their assault order was precisely as he had directed. "Now," he said, "let's to it."

It had been a long time since he had uttered a war-cry—his Netherlands employers considered it a sign of irremediable Irish barbarity—but he loosed one now, to stiffen his own nerve. Because he had insisted upon being first around the corner—and knew exactly what that meant.

But his adversaries didn't, not this time. Before charging, he stuck his pepperbox pistol around the corner and fired blind; several muskets sputtered back. Cocking the pepperbox again he heard angry orders in Spanish about wasting ammunition—and at that very moment he charged out, heading to the left.

The firing resumed as he emerged from the staircase into a cross-fire from doorways to both the right and left. But the Spaniards' fire was ragged. And to add to the general confusion, Matija leaned around the corner to hit the right-hand doorway with his twelve-gauge shotgun. He fired without precise aiming, emptying the weapon with a rapid pumping action that made it sound like a long, pulsed roar of thunder. The incoming fire from that side—lively at first—tapered quickly. But probably not for long, Owen knew.

As he took his first charging step along the broad walkway of the upper gallery, he ignored the second, further doorway on the left—where most of his adversaries were—and instead swung tight to the left again, into the first stairway, which led up to the roof. As he did so, two weapons from the further doorway discharged; one ball rushed past his unhelmeted brow in the same moment he felt a deep, hot, pain in his right thigh.

But the events piled up too rapidly for him to keep track of; Owen did not bother to aim as he came around into the new staircase. He fired blind, then slashed his saber in tight, fast, serpentine arcs until a pistol roared. He saw the outline of a Spanish helmet as the hammer blow of the pistol ball crashed into his cuirass.

*Not the worst way to die,* he conceded, as his back smacked down on the paving stones.

Matija tossed the shotgun, swung the SKS off his shoulder and started hammering rounds back to the left, just as Owen disappeared into the stairwell that led to the roof.

As his shots reverberated in that tight space, more of the assault team emerged; the Wild Geese were running past, firing on the move and staying close to the wall. The longer they stayed out of Matija's field of fire, the longer he could suppress the defenders in the doorway that was their objective. But his magazine was just about dry—

He saw Spaniards going down as they exposed themselves to fire, saw one of the Wild Geese take two balls at brutally close range and topple over—and finally, saw two objects, each roughly the size and shape of a pomegranate, arcing out of the enemy-held doorway. He also noticed that they were trailing smoke and sparks.

"*Grenades!*" yelled Matija, charging forward, heading away from their probable point of impact behind him.

Apparently the defenders knew about counting down fuses: both grenades went off where Matija had been standing a second and a half before. He felt lancets of pain cut into his back, his buttocks, and the rear of this thighs. The shock of the blasts, while diffuse, shoved him sharply forward into one of the gallery's arch supports head first; he rebounded from it, the world spinning. His head was suddenly full of a strange coppery smell and he reflected, *Damn and shit, I thought death would hurt more than this. Why did I spend all that time worrying about it...?*

As Thomas North came to the head of the stairs, he almost tripped over the body of a Hibernian: the only man who had been killed outright by the grenades. He took a quick, professional glance at the walkway just beyond; two more of his men were down and motionless, Matija and one of the Wild Geese—little Dillon, from the look of his gear. The stairway up to the left was quiet, but that was not necessarily a good sign. Insofar as Owen had been bound that way, and was not in sight, it could be a very bad sign indeed. The further doorway—the one where they had expected the most resistance—was littered with Spanish bodies, and the last four Wild Geese were charging through it now, hacking, slashing and firing their pepperboxes at murderously close range. Those clunky revolvers had proven just the trick in a close assault. If the Spanish stopped to reload, the bog-hoppers cut them down with sabers, but if the defenders drew swords of their own, the Irish cocked the revolvers already in their hands and riddled them with lead.

But their toehold on this second floor was tenuous at best. More Spanish regulars—this had been the level on which they had been billeted, evidently—were coming around the gallery from the left, led by a short, grizzled fellow, probably the senior commander. Some were already beginning to aim at the Wild Geese. Meanwhile, on the right, North saw movement in the doorways that Matija had suppressed with his torrent of shotgun fire.

Two new threats. For which he had two different answers. Which had both better work...

North pushed forward to the low rim of the gallery's walkway, kneeling and aiming his SKS at the grizzled commander to the left. Feeling his group of Hibernians close around him, peripherally seeing the muzzles of their weapons matching the trajectory of his own, he then screamed at the top of his lungs, "Harry! HARRY! Southwest, level two! Southwest, level two!"

Then North and his three Hibernians leaned over their sights, training their weapons on the Spanish to the left.

Harry cocked his head. "You hear that shouting?" he asked the Hibernian with him.

"*Ja*, that is Colonel North's voice; I would know—and hate—it anywhere. Look."

Harry did, peering down at the far right-hand side of the second gallery, or, as per the prearranged codes, "Southwest level two." And sure enough, he could see Spaniards readying muskets and swords in the rooms closest to the stairwell. But from North's position at the due west lip of the upper gallery, they'd still be almost completely concealed.

But not from the top of the lazarette.

Harry braced the SKS, leaned so that the forestock was resting in between the merlons instead of monopodding on the banana-clip. He angled the weapon slightly, letting the tightly clustered figures drift into his sights. "Let's hit 'em," he said to the Hibernian and started squeezing off rounds.

Concentrated as they were in the doorways, probably preparing to volley and countercharge, the Spanish went down in bunches. Even from this height, and in the dim light, Lefferts saw black spatters on the floor, corners, doors. Two of the defenders managed to scatter back into the rooms to avoid the deluge of up-time rifle bullets. Other than one who crawled back through a doorway, there was only feeble, indistinct movement among the Spanish bodies left behind on the gallery.

"What now?" asked the Hibernian when there was nothing left to shoot at.

"Now," Harry answered with a grin, "we reload."

As gunfire roared on the roof and down in the galleries, Asher's medium-sized assistant picked up Castro y Papas' weapons. The Spaniard looked down, his feet wide, his arms folded. "And now what?" he asked Frank.

"Well, you have a choice. You could stay here and be executed by your buddies."

"Or be killed by you—which would be far more merciful, actually."

"Or you could come with us."

"What?" said Don Vincente.

"What?" said Giovanna.

"No!" said the regular-sized assistant.

Frank kept his eyes on Castro y Papas and shrugged. "It's your choice. But you don't have a lot of time to make it."

A new wave of fast, pounding up-time rifle fire from both overhead and below emphasized Frank's final point.

Sergeant Alarico Garza watched as half his men were slaughtered by the storm of fire coming down from above and cursed himself: *I should have thought of that. With those guns, from up there, of course they'd be able to see and shoot down at anyone on the south side of the upper gallery.*

But the entire attack on Bellver had been such a complete and swift surprise, and the effects of the up-time weaponry had been so shocking, that there just hadn't been time to think of everything. If only he had been as fit and alert and prepared as he had been when he was ten years younger—

No time for that; since the enemy fire from the lazarette was now stronger than ever, it was obvious that the attack he had ordered across the main roof had been a complete failure. That left Garza and his few remaining men little choice: they had to send a volley against the cuirassed intruders on this level and then charge to sword-range. It was not a pleasing prospect, but it was the only tactic that might succeed when fighting in close quarters against these positively satanic up-time guns. And the longer he waited—

"Ready on the line," Gazra said, and saw the muskets of his command come up sharply as he drew his sword. "Volley," he cried—but the guns that answered were not his own.

Thomas North did not stop firing until he had expended half his magazine. He simply fired, rode the recoil back down, looked for a moving figure, centered on it, fired again. Now, as he stopped and looked up over his sights, he saw the grizzled

enemy commander stagger, right himself, and then get shredded
by four more rounds—two from his Hibernians, two more from
the Wild Geese, who had finally cleared the room on the left and
had turned to add to the barrage that swept the last cohesive
Spanish unit away like dry leaves before a hurricane.

North jumped up, tapped the Hibernian to his left on the
shoulder. "On me," he said, as he sprinted over to the stairway
leading up to the roof—

—and found Owen Roe O'Neill on the ground, the lower left
side of his cuirass mashed and crumpled. Remembering the derelict cars he had seen being disassembled for parts and metal in
Grantville, a term came to mind: Owen's armor looked as though
it had been "sideswiped." But apparently not breached. The leg
wound, however—

Owen's eyes fluttered open, focused with surprising speed, and
swiveled over toward North. "Ah, Jayzus Christ. So I got sent to
hell, after all."

"No such luck; you're still alive, I'm afraid," said North, suppressing a grin and helping the Irishman stand.

"Not by much," commented O'Neill, looking down at the dead
Spaniard, who'd fallen back against the stairs, his head half
sheared away by a saber cut.

"No."

"Just enough," grumbled Owen, with a hand on his left side.
"The barstard's shot crushed my ribs, I'm thinking."

"Might have done for one or two, at that. Looks like his gun
was charged with small lead pellets. Lethal if fired into a mass of
unarmed men, charging around the corner. On the other hand,
a small pellet of soft metal like that is much less likely to get
through your cuirass—but it *will* hit you like a battering ram."

"Like two battering rams, if you please. Now, let's get up to
the roof and—"

"You are staying here, Colonel O'Neill. Take command of this
level; make sure our men go room to room. I'm going to the roof."

For once, O'Neill was either too tired, too dazed, too pained,
or too sensible to argue; he simply waved North on his way with
his pepperbox revolver.

North shouldered his SKS, drew his automatic, and, back flat
against the wall, worked his way upwards.

It was a short, uneventful journey. At the top, there were two bodies, one of a man who had dragged himself back under the high, narrow cupola that covered the staircase; he had since succumbed to the wounds in his torso. The other was a Spanish regular who had apparently been using the cupola as a safe spot from which to return the fire raining down from the lazarette. Apparently, the position had not offered quite as much cover as he had hoped. Beyond the two bodies, the roof was devoid of motion or sound.

*Well, we just might have pulled this off,* thought North, who, taking cover against the possibility of hidden stragglers, shouted, "Castle!"

Harry's answering cry of "Keep!" from the top of the lazarette was followed by one of the hillbilly's customary wisecracks. "What took you so long?"

Which meant that they owned the whole building.

# Chapter 54

Ruy did not have to look around the staircase to know what was happening in the great room below. The assassins were reloading and preparing to charge the stairs. Prudence dictated that he should cede his current position: all their adversaries were able to aim at the one corner around which Ruy and his two riflemen could fire, whereas the cutthroats now ringing the base of the stairs were in a variety of positions. There was no longer a safe way to take a peek, find a target, and fire: any sign of movement attracted the discharge of two muskets charged with smaller shot. Ultimately, those odds favored the attackers. Retreating down to the hall would give him and his two rifleman better cover, from which they could concentrate their fire upon the landing at the top of the stairs. From that position, a lengthy stalemate might easily evolve.

But not victory. And now, to complicate matters, Ruy was finally hearing what he had been waiting for: gunfire being exchanged through the windows—and perhaps the door—at the back of the villa. Which could only mean one thing: someone—Sherrilyn, probably—had brought the root cellar's reserve to the rear of the villa, and they were probably readying themselves to break in to relieve its defenders.

But if Ruy fell back from his position, she would have to fight her way through the door and into the teeth of more than twenty of the blackguards. Even if some of them attacked up the stairs, Sherrilyn's group would suffer considerable casualties against those numbers. Besides, doorways were an attacker's bane and a defender's boon: they forced those rushing through it into a predictable area, an area which a reasonable defending commander could quickly convert into a funnel of death.

So, no, thought Ruy. He could not surrender his position at the head of the stairs, because only from here could his force support Sherrilyn's entry into the room. And in order for her to be able to enter without all the assassins' guns and blades trained upon her, she would need a flanking attack—or a diversion, at least.

Ruy scanned what he could see of the staircase without poking his head around the corner. It was almost entirely obscured by bodies, appearing rather like a ramp of corpses. Hmmm. That might do. He made sure his swords were secure in their scabbards and nodded for his two men to aim down the stairs as soon as they were done reloading. *I am too old for this*, he reflected as he checked that his .357 magnum was fully loaded. *Then again, I was always too old for* this.

Ruy Sanchez de Casador y Ortiz sighed, crouched, and threw himself forward into a sideways roll that carried him down the stairs.

For a moment, there was silence at the base of the stairs—and then bedlam. Fortunately for Ruy, the assassins were all so startled that they delayed, and then discharged their weapons too hastily. He was hardly a predictable target, either; his downward roll was made uneven by the same stair-piled enemy bodies that cushioned him as he went.

At the midpoint of the stairway, he reached his arms out to grab the flimsy railing's sole balustrade with the flat of his palms, flexing his forearms and wrists against the sudden resistance and torque. The net effect was that his roll pivoted about that point: his feet and legs came around quickly as he clung to the balustrade, much as a fast-moving roller-skater might use the pole of a streetlamp to hang a fast ninety degree turn.

Ruy came off the side of the staircase, letting the momentum pull him all the way around so that he came down on his feet, facing out into the room and into the eyes of his attackers, many of whom had lost track of exactly what he was doing, their vision compromised by the greasy smoke guttering up from the base of the stairs. Most of them had fruitlessly discharged their weapons in his wake, unable to successfully predict his motion. Consequently, those few weapons that were still being leveled at him marked the primary threats. Snatching the .357 out of his holster, he fired at two of them and dove for the cover of a smaller, overturned serving table. Muskets roared after him—again, a split second too late.

Rolling up into a crouch and pulling his favorite rapier while bullets spat around and thumped into the tabletop, Ruy thought: *Whenever you are ready, then, Miss Maddox . . .*

Jerking back to avoid a musket ball that punched through the shuttered window through which he had hoped to access a target, Sherrilyn's senior Hibernian Rolf froze as a sudden spasm of gunfire erupted from beyond the door—but was not aimed outward at them. "What the hell was that?" he asked.

The next sound gave Sherrilyn the answer to Rolf's question: two distinctive .357 magnum reports. "It's Ruy! C'mon: pistols and swords. On me!"

Sherrilyn blasted four rounds blindly through the back door before she charged in. Between the bizarre events near the staircase, and the hail of nine-millimeter parabellum rounds punching through the timbers of the door they were hiding behind or next to, the entry's defenders were either distracted or flinching away when she came bursting in with the Hibernians right behind her. That split second of confusion was all the advantage the relief force needed. Sherrilyn's high-capacity automatic and the three Hibernians' cap-and-ball revolvers thundered and flashed in a tight arc around the doorway, often less than a foot away from their targets. Assassins sprawled, some clutching wounds, others suddenly motionless. Two tried to run, but were cut down. Sherrilyn's first post-entry order—"Down!"—didn't come a moment too soon; the other assassins who, a moment before, had been reloading to flush out Ruy, turned and fired at this new, more considerable threat. Musket balls whistled overhead, struck the wall or sang out into the darkness—where Sherrilyn distinctly heard Kuhlman, one of the Marines who had just arrived from walking the perimeter, mutter "*Scheisse!*" Well, thank God for reinforcements—even if it's only one man. "Kuhlman, covering fire from the door while we reload."

"Yes, Captain," Kuhlman shouted back, first firing his own flintlock and then the other undischarged enemy weapons that the Hibernians had leaned against the rear wall in readiness.

Larry Mazzare hurried into the kitchen's basement, glad to be out of the secret passage: the staircase had doglegged under itself after they bypassed the concealed doorway into the northern wing's hallway. A wedge of light slashed the dark ahead of Mazzare; he saw Lieutenant Hastings, still in the lead, gingerly raising the small storm door that opened into the kitchen, half a level above them.

"Is the way clear?" asked Vitelleschi's admirably composed voice.

"I'm wondering that as well, Father. McEgan, on me; we'll secure the kitchen and the way to the back door." Hastings glanced back at Wadding. "Keep an eye on us; if we wave 'all clear,' tell the others and then run for all you're worth." The gunfire beyond the kitchen suddenly crescendoed into a mad thunderstorm; it did not sound promising to Larry.

But neither did George Sutherland's calm comment two seconds later: "Someone's entering the passage behind us, back up at the eastern hallway, I think. Here, lad." He handed Patrick Fleming his prized, sawed-off double-barreled twelve-gauge, and quietly drew his preferred weapons for hand-to-hand combat: a short, broad-headed axe for his left hand, and a falchion for his right.

Fleming looked at the up-time weapon in his hands. "You're the better shot, Sutherland. I'm just—"

"Lad, you don't need to be a good shot with double-aught buck at spitting range. And besides, you may be a fine swordsman, but right now—no offense, lad—we need brute strength. We have to be sure that every one of them we hit goes down—and stays down."

Larry Mazzare thought that sounded like a very good philosophy indeed. He crouched low behind Fleming, who made sure his pepperbox revolver was out and ready, and his saber was loose in its scabbard. "Your Holiness," said Larry. He was surprised how calm he sounded.

"Yes, Lawrence?" came Urban's voice out of the dark behind Larry.

"Wherever you are, I suggest to move to the side wall and stay low. Very low."

"Thank you, Lawrence. You probably can't see it, but I have already taken that exact precaution."

And Larry, wondering if some part of him was becoming

hysterical, thought: *Evidently, the pontiff is also infallible in matters of faith and muskets . . .*

Ruy, feeling the change in the battle's tempo, popped up briefly from behind the table, fired once to pull the assassin's attention back toward him, and yelled in his combat-stentorian voice: "Riflemen: fire!"

Obedient to his command, the sound of the lever-actions resumed at the top of the stairs. A few of the blackguards who had grown incautious in their eagerness to get a firing angle upon Ruy paid for their forgetfulness: they fell, dark maroon stains spreading out from sudden holes punched in their sweaty leather jerkins by .40-72 rifle rounds. One stared at his wound, dazed; the other stared at nothing with lifeless eyes.

*Now,* thought Ruy with a smile, *you are caught between Scylla and Charybdis, you murdering dogs. And it is time for me to find some better cover—perhaps a slightly larger table . . .*

Valentino glared at the tableau before him. Twenty seconds ago, his forces had been ready—finally—to assault up the stairs, with plenty of men for the job. Now, with almost ten more casualties, and five more of the enemy in the room—one of which was a limping woman, strangely enough—the tide was reversing, and defeat was conceivable, if he did not do something immediately.

Fortune provided him with an opportunity: the older fellow— Ruy Sanchez, if Rombaldo's intelligence was correct—had risen, and staying low, was trying to get behind a larger table. At the same moment, one of Odoardo's group appeared at the entry to the north wing, shouting "A secret passage, leading to the kitchen. Don't let them get out!"

Valentino, seeing that Sanchez's course would put him briefly under the guns of the relief force that had come in the back door, screamed. "Volley and charge: attack into the kitchen!"

He grabbed two of his men as they prepared to pass. "But you two, come with me. We will hug tight against this wall and close on that miserable Catalan, the one giving the orders."

The larger of the two tossed away his spent miquelet-lock pistol. "Suits me fine," he grumbled, "Let's gut that old man."

Smiling to himself, Valentino let his two eager men lead the way, crouching low behind them.

✧　　✧　　✧

Sherrilyn heard the enemy bastard scream his orders, ducked as the volley of double-charged miquelet muskets sent smaller projectiles spattering around them, and heard a groan as one of her Hibernians took a ball in the arm. Back by the door, Kuhlman cursed again—but whatever his wound was, it left him alive enough to curse.

She raised her automatic, aimed into the charging pack—and flinched her finger off the trigger as Ruy's agile shape danced momentarily into her sights. "No, don't!" she screamed at her troops—and in that moment, almost two-thirds of the charging assassins veered off into the kitchen.

*What the fu—?* And then, eyes widening, Sherrilyn knew: they'd found the secret passage and hoped to trap the escapees in the kitchen cellar between two forces. She bounded to her feet, sagged when her knee almost buckled, and started firing into the rest of the sprinting cutthroats. "Up and fire! They're going for the pope!"

As Luke Wadding watched, Lieutenant Hastings, who had been moving stealthily toward the door joining the kitchen to the great room, suddenly found himself the apparent target of more than a dozen wildly charging assassins. A long, heavy sword now in his right hand for parrying, Hastings gave ground, firing his pistol as he did so. And, being armed with an up-time pistol he rained ruin upon those approaching agents of Satan.

They went down one after the other, sometimes requiring Hastings to spend two bullets to be sure of stopping them. And even then, about half them were not dead yet. Most were mortally wounded, but some even rose to fight again.

McEgan, similarly armed with a sword in one hand and his pepperbox revolver in the other, came alongside the lieutenant's left flank, his marksmanship a bit less precise, but he accounted for at least three, killed or incapacitated, before his weapon was spent. Two of the assassins still had charged pieces of their own as they entered; one missed wildly, slain as he fired, and the other put a small pellet through Hastings' left shoulder. If the Hibernian officer noticed, he gave no sign of it.

But then his own seemingly inexhaustible weapon was spent, and the press of attackers pushed them back.

Wadding's heart quickened with pride at the courage of the two men, but his throat was tight with the certainty of the outcome: there were too many of Lucifer's own servitors hemming them in, now. Despite their having killed several of the assassins with their pistols, their enemies now beset them to the front and flanks, and only their agility and training turned aside blows that would surely have slain them. Hastings took off an arm at the wrist; McEgan parried and pierced a lung before blades hammered him back even further, closer to the basement door.

A rapier went through Hastings' right thigh; a cutlass rang a glancing blow off McEgan's capelline-helmeted head. They did not fall, but staggering, gave even more, precious ground—which allowed their foes to press them even more closely.

From behind, Luke Wadding heard the voice of his beloved pontiff. "Can they win, Cardinal Wadding?"

"If God wills it, Your Holiness," Wadding rasped out. "If God wills it."

*What? They can approach us without making a sound?* Larry thought, when, from the secret staircase that led down into the kitchen cellar, there was the rapid *clack-flash-boom* discharge of a miquelet-lock pistol at startlingly close range.

Fortunately, George Sutherland had kept himself off to the side, partially covered by the edge of the doorway; the ball uttered a sharp screech as it clipped a chunk of the stonework off that corner.

With surprising speed for so large a man—and one with a weak ankle, no less—George was in the doorway, arms working like a bear that had been taught to thresh wheat ambidextrously. The sword hit the gunman with a leather-slicing sound that gave way to a scream—

—which ended almost as soon as it had begun; the axe landed with the sound of a heavy bone splintering. The exchange was conclusively punctuated by the thud of a limp body.

George leaned halfway back to his cover, said, "Be ready. There will be more than one of them creeping up on us to—"

Larry Mazzare saw a flash and heard a cannon go off just in front of him—or so it seemed, the sound shuddering savagely between the tight, rough-hewn stone walls. Intense pain in both his ears was accompanied by a ringing deafness. Then another gunshot went off—this was not nearly as loud. Something hit him in the legs and he was falling backwards.

And then the darkness of the secret staircase seemed to vomit out men with swords and axes, one after the other. Although hit several times, George seemed miraculously unaffected. The first attacker he caught on the point of his falchion, and with a lithe twist of the hips, re-angled the weapon so the groaning man slid off. That almost balletlike turn imparted extra force to the axe, which he brought around to cut deeply into the next assassin's ribcage, the blow flinging the man to the side.

More were coming—and George took a step back and to the side, exposing his belly to Larry's gaze. Mazzare hissed. The front of Sutherland's torso was a mess, spilling blood from a terrible wound in his belly. There was a bright, manic look in George's eyes. The man was already dead, for all intents and purposes—and he knew it, and planned to wreak a terrible last vengeance.

Mazzare snapped out of his fog. Grabbing Fleming, he yelled, "Shoot! Shoot! Why don't you—?" and only then felt that the arm under his scrabbling hand was utterly limp. Peering closely, Mazzare saw there was a bullet hole just above wide-eyed Fleming's left eyebrow.

That was when the next attacker that George killed—blood spurting vigorously—landed directly across both Fleming and Larry. "Trouble," grunted George hoarsely. And looking up, almost through the Englishman's legs, Larry could indeed see what had prompted his warning: three more attackers were coming down. The one in the lead was as lithe and spare as a weasel; George cut at him, the effort showing—and this blow was slow enough that the attacker was able to dodge low and roll. The weasel came up with a dagger, less than a foot in front of Mazzare, who discovered that he was coated with the last casualty's blood.

Behind him came another assassin with a cutlass, and behind him—

Larry was too dry to swallow but felt the reflex tug painfully at his throat: this man was as large as George and carried an immense, although somewhat short-handled, axe and a spent fowling piece. And he was smiling. Unscathed, somehow casual and contemptuous despite his swift approach, he clearly presumed that the next several moments would give him the pleasure of striking his immense adversary down.

George struck a falchion blow at the fellow with the cutlass, who parried and dodged sideways—but that move put him directly into the inbound arc of George's axe. His neck half severed, the assassin seemed to topple sideways—right alongside where the weasel-like assassin was preparing to lunge, dagger first, toward George's flank.

Mazzare, his throat too dry to speak, croaked out a warning that emerged as something less than a word; he flung out a hand at the little backstabber.

Who, stunned by Larry's glancing blow, recoiled—thereby putting him just barely back into George's field of view.

George, hearing Larry's sound, possibly perceiving the movement at the low periphery of his vision, wrist-snapped the falchion around into a backhanded cut, even as the little assassin jabbed his dagger into the only target he could reach in time. George's right knee.

The falchion cut into the murderer at the same moment he tore his blade free in the kind of swiping motion usually used to hamstring an opponent. Blood flew up at Mazzare again; the small body of the weasel crashed into him, rolling him off the right side of Fleming's corpse, where Mazzare felt his body bruised by a stone. Or a brick. Or maybe it was...Larry grabbed desperately at the object.

George swayed, his right knee quaking, ready to buckle, as the ogrelike axe man jumped down the last step, weapon high.

But George was not done; his axe came round sloppily, unsteadily, but with enough strength to force the ogre to draw up short and twist away, the edge of the English broad axe cutting a seam in the assassin's cured leather cuirass.

The ogre had his own degree of skill, however. Going with the angular momentum of the axe's glancing blow, he spun and brought his own axe around in an arc that, even in the dim light of the basement, gleamed like a lethal silver crescent.

Larry saw George try to parry, saw the contemptuous grin glimmer on the ogre's face as he cheated his weapon's angle down, and saw the head of the axe bury itself to the haft in the lower left side of Sutherland's torso.

Larry got his hands out from under him as George began to sway and his weapons fell from his hands and clattered on the stones. The ogre left the axe in the wound for a moment, then wrenched it around and then out, bone-splintering sounds accompanying the process. George Sutherland pitched backward and lay still.

The ogre seemed to gloat for a moment, peering at the pale clerical faces at the other end of the basement; Vitelleschi had found, and raised, a short sword in defiance.

The ogre guffawed, hefted his axe. "So," he said, "who's next?"

"You are," said Larry. He raised the object he'd rolled upon and finally grabbed up—the shotgun George had given to Fleming—and squeezed one of the triggers.

The flash and sound of thunder seemed to leap from the muzzle up into the ogre, battering into the massive body along its rear left flank. An array of broad, bloody pocks rippled into existence along his spine, lungs, and lower neck. The immense man whirled unsteadily, axe raised, gargling on blood; his unfocused eyes roved down, found Larry, lost him as the axe arm swung—

—and spasmed, dropping the weapon. The ogre emitted what sounded like a cry of irritated amazement as he fell; he quaked once and was still.

Larry's first thought was to apologize to the pope: some Christlike man he had become since the start of this evening—but what he did was spin around at the sound of stealthy feet on the stairs. And thought: *Please no, Lord. Not again. Not me. Do not make me choose between my vows and my pope—*

But as the steps on the stairs came closer, instinct took over. Larry sat up, braced himself, held the shotgun with both hands, and fired up into the darkness. Two screams, one short: a clattering tumble and a body rolled down, half obstructing the stairs. Larry immediately perceived the tactical advantage imparted by that corpse—it would be hard for attackers to find reliable footing anywhere near the body-choked base of the stairs—even as he heard a limping retreat heading back upward, then curses and a muttered consultation among an indistinct medley of voices.

As Larry began searching for Fleming's pepperbox revolver, he called into the dimness of the basement behind him, "Antonio."

"Y-yes?"

"Come over here and try to find the extra shotgun shells. George must have had at least three or four reloads. And do it quickly; we're going to have more company."

✧      ✧      ✧

Sherrilyn staggered in her attempt to run forward, felt her knee about to give, forced it to hold, felt something shift inside it—which triggered a starburst of pain that sent arcing flares racing all the way up into her groin.

—which she ignored. She snapped her eyes at Ruy in between shots at the assassins still trying to crowd into the kitchen; he was half obscured by smoke, and was now hopelessly mixed into a melee with three of the assassins.

*Good luck, boss,* she thought as, gun in both hands, she resumed blasting away at a handful of assassins who, unable to force their way into the kitchen, had rounded on her and the Hibernians, and were closing with swords raised and desperation in their eyes.

Valentino watched a handful of his assassins close with the up-time-armed mercenaries. His men would not prevail, but they did not need to—not for Valentino's purposes. They only needed to delay those reinforcements long enough for the pope to be crushed between the hammer he had sent rushing into the kitchen, and the anvil Odoardo was bringing in through the secret passage.

Meanwhile, his two men had jumped toward Ruy, who, sword trailing indolently, simply raised his immense up-time pistol and shot them down as they came. One fell limp, the other collapsed, holding his thigh and sobbing in a pitch as high as a woman's.

Spotting Valentino approaching through the smoke, Ruy raised his gun again, fired, and dodged—just as Valentino did the same. Both missed; both now had empty pistols. Valentino cast his away; Ruy reholstered his primly, and drew a main-gauche for his off-hand.

Valentino walked through the smoke, heavy rapier in his right hand. The Catalan's eyes flicked down to the assassin's empty left. Valentino watched two opposed forces war very briefly in the bantam hidalgo's eyes: practicality versus honor, he supposed. With something that might have been a shrug, Ruy resheathed his main-gauche. What Valentino thought was: *strutting idiot.* What he said was: "Are you ready to die now, old man?"

The Catalan now gave a true shrug. "I have always been ready to die."

Valentino did not let Ruy complete the word "die" before he leaped to the attack. A quick pass—lunge, parry, riposte, slash, and lunge back—confirmed what he'd been told; although the bastard was old, his vitality and skill was undiminished. So, now to end it quickly—

Valentino came in again, leading with a long athletic leap and a thrust that he wrist-rolled—*moulineted*—into a shallow overhand cut. The Catalan stood his ground—as his style and pride predicted he would—and met him, blade pushing up against blade. For a moment, they were locked almost side by side: exactly the position that Valentino had been attempting to achieve. He shook his left forearm sharply: the scabbarded dagger that was strapped there slid down into his hand. *And as the Catalan tries to stay at close range—with which he will attempt to diminish the advantage of my longer reach—I shall slip this between his ri—*

A bright light exploded in Valentino's right temple, staggering him. Peripherally, he saw the Catalan's sword moving out of his field of view, lowering. He understood; the old fool was not such a fool after all—and not such a creature of sterling honor as he had been told. Rather than working with the blade, Ruy Sanchez de Casador y Ortiz had fallen back on one of the most basic—and some would say base—tricks at the disposal of a swordsman: with his sword already raised point high, and close to his adversary, he had merely run it up along Valentino's own blade, maintaining the lock with it until he slid it off. And slammed his sword's half-basketed hilt into the larger man's lowered head.

Valentino, aware that he had less than a second to recover, tried to buy himself time. He cut at the Catalan—who was no longer there. But, to Valentino's great surprise, he heard movement behind—and then felt movement inside—himself. The point of the old man's weapon emerged from his chest, snapping the sternum as it came out.

There were other cuts after that—two, Valentino thought—but he barely felt them. He was only aware that, as his hidden dagger fell from his hand, and he saw the floor coming up at him, the Catalan snorted out a sharp, derisive laugh. "Once a street thug, always a street thug," he said a moment later, standing over the assassin. It might have been an epitaph.

At any rate, Valentino correctly conjectured, they were the last words he would ever hear.

Ignoring remonstrations and warnings from all around, Maffeo Barberini, who knew himself to be deeply unworthy of the office and title of Pope Urban VIII, moved quickly to the side of George Sutherland.

"My son," he whispered forcefully.

The Englishman's eyes fluttered open, moved about uncertainly: blind. The pale lips in his blood-clotted beard moved feebly.

"Who—?"

"It is I, the pope. I fear to ask it, that you might refuse, but—my son, would you take a blessing from me?"

"Why—why would I refuse, Father?"

"Because—well, what manner of Christian are you?"

George seemed to smile, brighten. "I'm a Christian of my own conscience, Father. I don't...I don't...I believe..."

And as George's coughing of blood suddenly returned, and whole-torso spasms began to wrack his body, Urban VIII, tears starting from his eyes, commenced the speediest, yet most heartfelt rite of extreme unction that he had ever carried out.

Luke Wadding clutched his crucifix, kissed it, and felt his heart explode into a hundred "Our Fathers" and "Hail Marys" for each of his companions, for surely, he hadn't enough time left to say even one such prayer. Anthony McEgan, whose sturdy defense of the left flank of lightly armored Lieutenant Hastings had kept that worthy from death at least half a dozen times, was slow coming back from a riposte that wounded an enemy. The adjacent assassin swept out his cutlass, opened a nasty cut across McEgan's right forearm. The Irishman snatched it back—at just the moment he needed it to protect against a hand axe wielded by a cutthroat who'd slipped into his left flank. The axe made a crunching sound as it caved in the lower left side of McEgan's cuirass. The blow did not penetrate, but over the wounded man's grunt, Wadding heard the snap of ribs. Hastings' protector was thrown sideways, writhing as he fell.

The other assassins rushed to get in at the lieutenant, so eager that they bunched up, knocking together. Hastings, dripping sweat and blood from almost half a dozen wounds, was still alert enough to discern which of the assassins was too hemmed in by his mates to effectively parry. The tall Englishman slashed with his sword; the targeted cutthroat staggered back, now weaponless and clutching the stumps of three missing fingers.

But the remaining assassins continued pushing Hastings back, and still more came behind them.

Wadding wanted to close his eyes while he gave his cross a final kiss, but would not do so. *I owe it to this man to watch his last sacrifice. I shall not look away; I shall not blink.*

Larry Mazzare fired, cursed himself, fired again, heard a groan up the staircase, winced when a pistol discharged down in his general direction. The balls chipped the stone less than two feet from where he'd positioned himself, kneeling half-covered at the doorway, with a firing angle all the way up to the bend in the staircase.

He couldn't see the bend, but he had a pretty good estimate of where it was. Like many priests and pastors in Appalachia, Larry was an experienced hunter—and in his case, an excellent one, especially with a shotgun. Hunting pheasant, quail and turkey to put meat on impoverished tables and charity dinners in his parish had given him a passing acquaintance with aiming by sound as much as sight.

The assassins had tried rushing down twice now, and he'd sent up two rounds each time, ready to fire more—but that had broken their spirit. However, his ability to drive them back was now reduced to one round in the pepperbox, which had only five chambers. He turned to Antonio, who was, in a ghastly juxtaposition of activities, rifling through George's pockets as the pope was gently sliding the big man's eyes closed with his palm.

Trying not to sound impatient, Larry asked, "What have you found, Antonio?"

"Eh . . . eh, not much. Maybe most of them are under him. But it would take two of us to roll him over so—"

"Antonio. What have you found?"

Cardinal Antonio Barberini held up two shotgun shells, one in either hand. "These."

Sherrilyn was already running for the kitchen door before Rolf had blasted down the last of the assassins who had rushed them, firing from a range of less than two feet.

Hobbling desperately, Sherrilyn pressed the magazine release, heard the empty box clatter down even as she had the other out, up, and into the grip in one smooth motion. She cocked the action, thanked the powers above for seventeen-round magazines, and staggered forward.

She found herself in a veritable obstacle course of enemy bodies: many motionless, many more writhing or crawling off in some deluded hope of escape. However, at least half a dozen live ones were preparing to carve up the last poor defender, who—*Good god, that's Hastings!* She brought up the Glock and started squeezing off rounds, aiming as best she could, praying she wouldn't hit the lieutenant, but knowing—knowing—that if she wasted one split second, he'd be dead anyway.

The bodies fell faster than she fired—and she became aware that one of the Hibernians had arrived alongside her, adding to her fusillade.

When the last of them fell, she saw Hastings on the ground. *Oh god, please no: please don't let me have been the one who killed him—*

But Hastings raised up on one elbow, clutching a leg wound with one hand, pointing toward the cellar with the other. "Down there," he gasped, "the pope—"

Larry got the two shotgun shells in the breech just as he heard the thunder of feet coming around the corner above him. There was a determination to the sound that he hadn't heard before; they had decided it was do or die, evidently.

Larry had come to the same decision long ago; he raised the shotgun, realized he'd never have the time to use the last round in the pepperbox, idiotically had a pang of regret for leaving any ammunition unexpended, and saw the first clear sign of movement in the dimness above him. He fired: screams, a man fell down the stairs, clutching his face and sobbing out his last breaths.

But they kept coming, Larry fired again, and this time, one actually staggered out of the darkness, still mobile enough to take a weak swing at him with a falchion before he collapsed. Larry jumped back, the pope and others clustered behind him.

More bodies came out of the dark rectangle that was the secret passage. Larry raised the shotgun one-handed, like a club; Vitelleschi moved to stand beside him, short sword out. Wadding was crying—evidently to God—"Help us; help us now!"

The assassins loomed out of the darkness—

—and Larry was startled by God's own thunder roaring over his shoulder and sweeping his enemies before him. Dumbstruck, he wondered: *Good grief, can Wadding actually call down God's wrath?* But then, a sideways glance showed him the visage worn by divine vengeance this day: it was the powder smeared, high-cheekboned face of Sherrilyn Maddox, whose pistol maintained its steady thunder of death and damnation upon the would-be assassins of God's own Pope. The last few of them turned and fled back up into the darkness.

Larry staggered forward as two of the Hibernians pushed past Sherrilyn and began edging up the staircase cautiously. Then he heard—very faintly from above—Ruy Sanchez de Casador y Ortiz addressing the last few cutthroats who apparently encountered him when reentering the hall of the northern wing. The Catalan's merry tone raised the small hairs on the back of Larry's neck: "Ah," he said, "do not leave yet. Tarry awhile." Then Larry heard the scuffling begin and the first body hit the floor.

Larry, oblivious to the Hibernians now charging up the narrow stairs to help Ruy, looked at his watch, wondering how many hours it had been since the first rattle of musketry had startled Vitelleschi to silence in the Garden Room.

He discovered that, all told, it had not quite been five minutes.

# Chapter 55

Frank and Don Vincente were still staring at each other, one in hope, the other in amazement when Harry Lefferts came pounding down the stairs and poked his head in the room. "What the hell are you still doing here? Evacuation is via the roof. So let's get going." He looked at Castro y Papas. "You too, if you're coming." And then he was gone.

Don Vincente Jose-Maria de Castro y Papas looked thunderstruck, probably not so much by the offer, but by the casualness with which it had been tendered—and by a man who had been sent to kill him, no less. He looked over at Frank and asked both the up-timer and himself aloud: "Should I? Come with you?"

Frank shrugged. "Why not?"

Don Vincente opened his mouth—and realized that he had no good answer to that very simple question.

Walking toward the south end of the main roof, North heard more outbound rifle fire—black powder lever-actions—from the second floor. As predicted, the Spanish were now trying to turn around the guns in the embrasures of the ravelins to fire at the castle door. Which meant they would destroy the raised drawbridge in the process. Not exactly an optimal strategy for reentering the fort, reflected Thomas, but he suspected they were now being driven by a frustrating need to Do Something, rather than by calm military logic. Just as well: it gave them something to do, and kept their attention off the sky, from which a dirigible would soon be descending.

"This half, all clear," called Anthony Grogan from the fortified walkway that marked the north end of the main roof. North signaled his acknowledgement; so far, only a few survivors had been found, and they were so badly wounded and semi-conscious that the only options were to leave them or dispatch them. North had decided that whatever dubious god there might be to smile, frown, or chortle over man's self-important follies should be the arbiter of these Spaniards' fates, not a humble colonel of mercenaries. Accordingly, he had given orders to leave the wounded undisturbed. North resumed walking toward the southern half of the main roof to finish his own sweep: they needed the security on the upper levels to be absolute before bringing the balloon down and exposing the hostages.

Evidently, the survivors who had been ambulatory enough to leave the roof had done so long before he and the Wild Geese arrived to begin their search for stragglers: there was no sign of any holdouts here, either. He turned to shout to Grogan, to give orders to start running fuses and powder trails to the roof battery's ready powder casks, when he noticed a white handkerchief protruding from beneath the carriage of one of the larger culverins. North, fairly sure he had not seen it before, swung his gun up—

Just as the handkerchief twitched a bit, and a voice said, "Señor, if I might come out?"

North wondered at the polite tone, consented: "Yes. But come out slowly."

A bit of scrabbling and grimy hands emerged, which in turn pulled out a man of small to medium height, who rose holding both arms in the air. "Sergeant Ezquerra, sir. At your service... eh, so to speak."

North cocked an eyebrow at the sardonic introduction. "Hmm. Rather strange to see a veteran under there. I'd have thought a man like you would have died leading the charge across this roof."

"It would be a stranger thing for a veteran not to understand that, in extreme cases such as this one, discretion is very much the better part of valor."

North smiled before he could stop himself; reflexively, he already

liked this man. Not that he was under any delusion that, given a
hair's breadth opportunity, Ezquerra would fail to cut him down:
that was his job, after all. But from the more detached perspective
of military professionals who could recognize each other across
the dividing lines of national boundaries and conflicting oaths
of fealty, North already knew this sergeant: a resilient career
NCO who was an inevitable fixture of armies everywhere and
a curmudgeonly blessing to any unit and captain lucky enough
to have him.

"So, Sergeant, now we have a quandary: what do I do with you?"

Ezquerra nodded in the direction of the lazarette. "Take me
there."

North frowned. "Why?"

"My captain—Don Vincente Jose-Maria de Castro y Papas—he
went in there. Does he live?"

North gestured with his left hand but kept his right firmly
around his the grip of his pistol. "Let's find out. After you."

Sean Connal turned to Miro, smiling like a boy. "Signal confirmed: all clear for descent. Hostages recovered safely."

Miro smiled back, started hauling in on the gang-line of
the mooring cables. "Virgilio, as soon as you have sight of the
lazarette, bring us around to the east side; there will be fewer
Spanish there, at first."

"They will come from the ravelins on the north and west
quickly enough," muttered the airship's pilot.

Miro reflected that the little Venetian, although barely older
than himself, was already well on his way to becoming a crabby
old man. "True enough, which is why we must still act swiftly."

Virgilio shrugged. "So pull harder."

Owen limped, stiff-legged, back to the staircase, and discovered
one of the Hibernians rousing Matija Grabnar, who blinked grog-
gily and swayed up to his elbows. "Damn, I thought I was dead."

"I'm acquainted with that feeling. D'you think you can walk, lad?"

"Uh . . . yes. But not well."

"Right. McDonnell, Jeffrey, move Mr. Grabnar up to the roof;
he'll be going with the balloon if they can manage it. Now, you
other men who aren't busy teaching Spanish artillerists how to
dance the lever-action gavotte, get yourselves downstairs in a

trice. Start spreading the powder kegs from the magazine, just as we planned. Remember, eight minute fuses. And mind you, listen for the whistle; you don't want to be left behind."

As Frank poked his head out onto the roof of the lazarette, Castro y Papas put a restraining hand on his shoulder: "No, stay low: the men at the ravelins will be scanning for targets."

"In this darkness?"

Castro y Papas shrugged. "Even without torchlight, a silhouette might be seen moving against the night sky. It is unlikely, but are you so eager to take a chance?"

Frank kept his head down as Harry Lefferts came away from the battlements, scooping up the empty magazines and counting the people on the roof. "Well, that's all of us. Nothing left to do here."

"Not quite," came Thomas North's voice from the bottom of the stairs. "Do you have a captain Castro y Papas with you? Or has he—erm, become a permanent resident of the tower?"

"It is not my intent to be so," Don Vincente answered, "but my intents count for very little this evening. Who asks?"

Before North could speak again, a smudged head popped up from the stairwell. "Going on a trip, Captain?"

Don Vincente beamed. "Ezquerra! I had prayed and hoped—hah! You lazy dog: sleeping when the invaders came, I'll wager. Snored in your bed while the rest of us fought nobly. It is the only reason you would still be alive."

"The captain's perspicacity is undimmed by the chaos of this night." Ezquerra's voice grew more quiet. "You are leaving, then?"

"Ezquerra, I—I killed Dakis. I cannot go back."

"Don Vincente, it seems that no living Spaniard has seen what you have done, so—"

"No, but I have seen it, and I will not lie. I must live with my shame. I only regret that my family—"

"—your family will mourn your passing, Don Vincente. Until such time as you decide to imitate Lazarus and come back from the dead."

At first Frank did not understand, but the shine in Don Vincente's grateful eyes made it all clear: Ezquerra meant to stay and claim that he had seen the captain die, bravely fighting for Spain. No disgrace would come upon House Castro or Papas, and no search would be mounted for a traitor against the crown. But in turn, that meant—

"Sergeant Ezquerra," said Frank, "I think you should know something. I just learned that, in order to leave as few clues as possible, our rescuers plan to uh...damage the Castell de Bellver."

"Indeed?" Ezquerra looked puzzled.

"Really damage it. As in *ka-boom*."

Ezquerra's eyes widened, then narrowed—and revealed to Frank, for the first time, how sharp a mind occupied the brain behind them. "How long do I have to exit the tower, Señor Stone?"

Frank looked over at Harry, who was waving for someone to come up the stairs quickly. Harry had evidently been listening to the exchange, though: "Call it eight minutes. At most."

"Ah. Good. That will be sufficient."

"For what?"

"For me to get down to the lowest level of the lazarette and go out through the eastern postern gate."

"Ezquerra!" exclaimed Don Vincente "That is still a long drop to the bottom of the dry moat!"

"Indeed it is, Captain. But I am a man who knows the value of rope—and knows where some is located, in that very room. I am off."

"Ezquerra!" Don Vincente called.

The round smudged head popped up through the hole again. "Yes? I *am* in something of a rush, Captain."

"Ezquerra, I...*vaya con Dios*, my friend."

"Captain, how unlike you to become maudlin! Besides, this is not farewell. I am sure to be a burden to you again some time in the future; the world is small, and our paths shall cross."

"Much to my annoyance, Ezquerra. Now go."

Ezquerra smiled. "Ah. Now, that is the true voice of my captain." His head disappeared.

Harry was glowering at the people on the roof. Frank wondered why; he cocked a quizzical head at him.

Harry saw the gesture and shrugged. "We're over capacity, now."

"What? Why?"

"Because of him." He pointed at Don Vincente. "And him," he added, pointing at Matija, who groaned up the narrow stairs, pulled and pushed along by two of the Wild Geese. "God damn it, that's a lot more weight than we counted on."

Asher bristled. "I will not stand for your blasphemy, Captain Lefferts."

"Okay, Doctor, maybe I shouldn't take the name of the lord in vain. But maybe you should be putting the name of the lord to good use."

"What do you mean?"

"I mean you ought to start praying."

"Praying? What for?"

"A miracle. We don't have enough lift to get everyone off this tower."

As the balloon came down out of the clouds, Miro was surprised to see that they were only forty feet above the roof of the lazarette.

The very crowded roof of the lazarette.

"Holy Mary and Christ on a crutch," breathed Sean Connal, "are all those people our passengers or a welcoming committee?"

Miro didn't respond; he was too busy counting the upraised faces that were drawing closer every second. Frank, Giovanna, Harry, Turlough Eubanks, one of the Hibernians, Asher, a prisoner, Matija—wounded, it looked like—and another face that seemed strangely familiar, dressed as one of Asher's assistants—

"Meir Tarongi!" Miro shouted, the headcount suddenly wiped from his mind.

"That's me," Meir shouted back up. "Just came to say goodbye and see what this fool contraption looked like. It certainly does suit you, high ears! Now, I'm off."

"Meir—"

"No time for goodbyes; we said those already. Besides, you might not have enough room as it is." Miro's friend started down the staircase—

"Meir—*shalom!*"

Meir turned. "Next year in Jerusalem, Ezekiel—wherever that might happen to be." He gave a crooked smile and was gone.

"They've seen the bloody balloon!" called Anthony Grogan from an embrasure overlooking the ravelin.

"Then let's show them some muzzle flashes," answered Thomas North. "All rifles to the embrasures overlooking the ravelin and the barbican. Your targets are men with long muskets. Fire at will!"

⟡     ⟡     ⟡

A musket ball zipped past the airship's gondola—which was fortunate, because the leather-and-wicker compartment would not offer much protection against bullets. "Drop the netting," ordered Miro.

Sean Connal complied; he pulled two slip-knots free and cast the triple-weighted net fringes outward.

As the bottom of the gondola came down to the level of the lazarette's battlements, a double-layered fishing net spilled out beneath it, suspended by two lines per side and one on each corner. Belaying lines led down into it from over the edge of the gondola.

"We're supposed to get into that?" asked Frank.

"Impossible," huffed Asher.

"Not at all, Doc," muttered Harry, who grabbed the old man around the waist, and in two long steps, went leaping out between the merlons of the battlement and into the net, which swayed a bit. Asher, after making sure he was alive and was going to stay that way, began berating Harry mercilessly.

Frank looked at Giovanna. Her eyes were wide, and he saw a look on her face that he did not recognize at first, but then did: fear. His fearless Giovanna was every bit as terrified as he was to jump off a hundred-foot-tall tower into a fishnet. So there was only one thing to do: he reached out a hand toward her.

She looked at it, then grasped it fiercely. Her eyes rose and locked on his.

Frank smiled. "Ready to go? In one, two, three—"

They jumped.

"The Spanish are moving again, damn it," cursed Owen.

"They might be, but you shouldn't," replied North. "You should be hobbling back down the tunnel already, so you don't hold us up."

The Irishman smiled. "You can't order me about, fellow-Colonel *Sassenach.*"

"Actually, I can. Colonel or not, I am in the direct employ of the USE. You, sir, are merely some baggage we picked up along the way. Meaning that I can indeed give you orders, and here is the one I'm giving you now: that you allow Mr. Jeffrey here to help you down the stairs into the tunnels and that you both start back to Cala Pedrera immediately. It's a long walk with a leg wound, and we have to be there fifteen minutes ago."

"Jeffrey's wounded too," objected O'Neill.

"Yes, which is why you both need to start moving—and helping each other along. Now don't make me send a healthy man to make sure the cripples do what they're told."

"*Sassenach* bastard," Owen grumbled.

"Yes, fine, I'm a bastard—just get moving."

Which the two hobbling Irishmen did.

North turned, looked up at the balloon, a black blotch against the almost black clouds overhead, and gave what he hoped would be his last orders on this operation: "Keep the Spanish musketeers under fire, men. Mr. Ohde, let's start lighting the longer fuses."

Miro scanned the remaining passengers. "You," he said, pointing to the tall hidalgo prisoner, "strip as far as decency allows."

"What? I am—"

"You are staying here if you do not do as I say; you are the extra weight we must carry." Miro thought again. "Turlough, you see that large leather case next to you?"

"Aye. What is it?"

"Something we are not going to bring after all. Toss it down the stairs."

"My instruments!" howled Asher.

"Doctor," said Miro in the most soothing tone he could manage, "where you are going, you will have the tools you've always dreamed of—and complained of not having."

"But those are my—"

"They are gone. I am sorry. And Turlough, leave your cuirass and sword."

"Maybe I should be getting a quick haircut, as well?"

"If I thought it would make a difference, I'd handle the scissors myself. Now, Virgilio, how many casks of oil can we dump overboard and still make it to Dragonera?"

"What? Dump fuel? That is not—"

"Virgilio, no arguments, not now. How many can we lose and keep a reasonable margin for error?"

"Two. Three at most."

"Virgilio..."

"All right. Four. But no more than that, really."

Miro nodded to Sean. "Four barrels overboard, then—and have them hit down inside the Castell. Let's give Palma a fireworks show it won't soon forget."

North lit the master fuse on the roof, stood hands on hips and surveyed the beautiful architecture one last time, reflecting that he might be the last human ever to see it in all its delicate, pristine beauty. A shame really, he thought, and then darted for the stairs.

As the last of the passengers on the lazarette's roof—the Hibernian and Turlough Eubanks—leaped over into the netting, Lefferts had finally finished hauling Asher up into the gondola, where he hung on the end of his belaying line like some limp, improbably bony fish. Frank and Giovanna were on their way up, and the net showed no sign of excess stress; Miro and Virgilio had tested it often enough, after all.

To the north, the bells of Santa Catharina began to chime. It was an alarum, of course, to warn the city that one of its defenses was under attack, but from here, it sounded like a celebration. Then, as if to remind Miro that they were not out of danger yet, a musket ball zipped through the floor of the gondola and carried on up to put a hole in the bottom of the envelope.

"Don Estuban," Virgilio gasped, "please; we must go."

Miro looked over the side, saw muzzle flashes aiming up at him, saw sharper brighter ones winking out the arrow slits along the northern and eastern faces of the Castell, saw several of the Spanish musketeers fall. He looked at the remaining men in the net. "We need to move," he apologized. "We'll have to pull you up as we travel."

"Fine," panted Turlough. "Just get us off this bloody shooting range!"

"Virgilio," shouted Miro over the revving engines, "take us home."

Thomas North counted the men as they went past. Many were wounded; Paul Maczka of the Wrecking crew was dead, along with two of the Hibernians, and one of the Wild Geese—little Dillon. Their gear had been carried out, but their bodies would be buried here, beneath the rubble of the storeroom that North now closed behind him.

He locked the storeroom door—mostly to intensify the effects of the impending internal blast—and checked the fuse on the two kegs of powder he had placed beside the trapdoor into the tunnel. It would burn down in four minutes, give or take.

North lit the fuse, blew out the match, dropped down into the secret passage, and closed the trapdoor behind him.

Virgilio had just completed a sweeping turn to the west, which would put them among the southernmost hills of the Tramuntana mountain range, thereby screening them from eyes in Palma. But as they slipped behind the crest of the Serra de Portopi, the passengers and crew of the dirigible heard a long, dull roar behind them.

Turning to look, Frank and Giovanna watched a column of white-yellow flame shoot up from the broad maw of the Castell de Bellver into the night sky. Large explosions pockmarked the blinding plume: those were powder kegs blown high before they, too detonated in mid air. "So long, fairy-tale prison," whispered Frank.

"And *saluti* freedom," sighed Giovanna.

The explosive jet settled down into a sullen orange glow; pretty at this range, it betokened an inferno trapped within the sandstone cauldron that were the walls of the Castell de Bellver.

Then they were behind the crest of Serra de Portopi, and both the flame and the sound of the bells were gone.

# Chapter 56

Thomas North tapped the Hibernian beside him, who left his position at the ruined windmill and fell back toward the black-hulled *llaut* that had raised its black sail. Back there, North also heard the sound he had been waiting for: the cough and steady growl of the extra motor that they had brought as an emergency back-up for the dirigible, now reverted to its original function: a small outboard motor.

A little more than half a mile to the northwest, the initially angry flames marking the Castell de Bellver had died down to occasional gutterings. From north and south, Spanish units were converging on the roads that led to the lanes that devolved into the cart tracks that wound up the slopes upon which the burning fortress was perched. What they would find when they got there was hard to estimate. On the one hand, there hadn't been that many flammables on hand, even counting the containers of fuel jettisoned by the dirigible. But, on the other hand, the castle was sealed and the Spanish had no way to get in to fight the conflagration. Given time, the wooden floors and beams and fixtures would catch fire, too—if they hadn't already.

"Colonel North, we're ready." It was Grogan's voice.

"Very well, Grogan. Back aboard, now." North followed the Irishman closely, and together they waded out to the *llaut*. They were hip-deep when they pushed it off the sandbar that its keel was barely kissing. As Ohde opened the throttle of the outboard slightly, North and Grogan hauled themselves over the side, receiving a hand from the waiting crowd hunkered low in the boat.

"No oars?" wondered Jeffrey, shivering.

"No, lad," muttered O'Neill, his leg out straight and stiff. "It takes a trained rower not to splash like a jumping fish—and if there's any light to be caught, you can be sure the Spanish would see it shining off the blades of the oars. And I think you'll agree that, just now, silence is all important."

Jeffrey bit his lip and nodded, looking over the bows.

The rest of them followed his eyes to the squat, blunt outlines of Fort San Carlos. Still under construction, this was a fortification in the modern style: low, sloped, thick walls, modern gun mounts—a far more ugly, and far more dangerous, structure than Castell de Bellver.

They stared at it as they approached, passing within four hundred yards. Everything was in their favor at this point: the almost lightless night, the black of the hull and the sail, the sound of the waves drowning out the persistent low growl of the engine—a sound which, whatever else the local down-time ears might make of it, would not signify "escaping boat." But they knew right enough that Dame Luck was a bitch goddess who refused to play favorites—because she didn't have any. So until they had passed out from beneath the cannons of the fort...

A musket fired into the night. They saw the flash, but could not tell, so far away, if it had been aimed at them, or just more generally out into the bay. After a few seconds, there were two other shots, one of which *plippshh*'ed into the swells twenty yards astern. But after that nothing.

Had it been a nervous new recruit firing at shadows? Had someone seen them, but not in time to bring any of the fort's impressive cannons to bear? Had it been a trial shot—meant to excite the response of suspected amphibious infiltrators who might fear themselves discovered? Or was there some other explanation?

They could not tell, and they would never know.

Which was, of course, the very fiber of uncertainty that comprised the bulk of all war, and was even more characteristic of it than the death and destruction for which it was rightly infamous.

✧　　✧　　✧

Using the lee of mountains to cover their long, altitude-sustaining burns, Virgilio brought the balloon under the clouds once they were safe in the uninhabited uplands north of the valley lake known as the Torrent de son Boronat, where they dumped half a dozen empty fuel containers overboard. Then they wound a bit farther to the north, staying high, often in the clouds, and estimating their progress and position by maintaining close running estimates of airspeed, heading, and wind.

After thirty minutes at twenty-two miles per hour, Miro ordered the burner be left alone and began to watch for the ground as the airship slowly lost lift. After five minutes, they came down through the lowest tier of clouds and discovered they were slightly lower than they thought, and only three miles away from the west coast of Mallorca. Which meant they were only six miles away from their ultimate destination: the oddly sloped island called Dragonera.

As they continued to lose altitude, it became evident to the occupants of the gondola why this island was called the Dragon. Although they were approaching its relatively smooth, southern side, its northern extents soared up dramatically. Creating a combined cliff top and crest that did invoke scenes of a sinuous dragon arising from the depths.

Virgilio conferred closely with Miro, now, whose experienced local eye guided them toward the level ground a few hundred yards north of the accessible part of Dragonera's coast, the inlet known as Es Llado. If the nearby watchtower had seen the airship, there was no sign of it; not even Harry's keen eyes could determine if the tower was occupied at all.

The landing was rough, the gondola scraping along the ground before enough of the heated air could be vented and the envelope began settling. Under Miro's and Virgilio's supervision, and with Harry's and Connal's trained assistance, those passengers that could began the process of breaking down the airship. The nosecone and partial back spine were separated and removed from the envelope, which was then hastily folded. The engines were dismounted, the rest of the gear packed and distributed to individuals. Miro was constantly checking his watch; the *Atropos*'s away boats were due within ninety minutes, and they had to have the entirety of the airship broken down and ready to move.

In order to ensure that they had not, and would not, be

spotted, Miro dispatched two of the group to keep an eye on the dark-windowed watchtower and the half dozen cottages of seasonal fishermen who worked the local waters. He chose Harry Lefferts for his extraordinary senses—including the sixth sense that always seemed to warn him of danger a moment before it became manifest—and, with some reservation, Don Vincente Jose-Maria de Castro y Papas, whose knowledge of Spanish military protocol was just as great as his ability to possibly deflect or at least confuse inquiries, if they were discovered by locals.

Sitting in the scrub only seventy yards from the cottages and fifty yards inland from the rocky southern shore, Harry was wondering how to start a conversation with a recent mortal enemy when Castro y Papas solved the problem for him—but in a most unconventional and unexpected fashion.

"I owe you an apology, Harry Lefferts."

"You do? I don't even know you."

"No, not exactly. But you have seen me—or my handiwork—before." When Harry remained silent, the hidalgo explained. "I refer to Rome. The courtyard of the Palazzo Giacomo di Mattei. I was in command there. I had the up-time shotgun. It was I who killed the man commanding those who attacked that part of the palace complex." His head drooped slightly. "It was hardly an honorable way to kill an opponent. That is the nature of war, I suppose—but I have long felt that our ambush upon you there was—well, particularly cowardly."

Harry felt the sea air rushing in his open mouth; he shut it. "It was you? You were the guy in the window of Frank and Gia's room?"

"I was."

"And so you knew that I was—"

"That you were in the belvedere atop the building near the Ghetto? Yes: who else but you would have been there?" He looked Harry in the eyes; there was much regret, but also much resolve in his stare. "I understand if you wish to satisfy the honor of your friend, the man I shot so many times in the courtyard, for his death was not befitting his station. I gather he was a man of some import."

Harry nodded slowly. "You might say that."

"Of course, we must wait until we are in a safe place before I may give you satisfaction."

"Satisfaction?"

"I refer to a duel, Señor Lefferts."

Harry considered. "A duel, huh?"

"*Si*—yes; that is how affairs of honor are usually settled."

"Well, I have a different way. But as I understand it, if I challenge you, then you get to choose the weapons, right?"

"That is true, but I am willing to waive that, in this case. I feel that my misdeed is such that—"

"Lissen, I don't need to hear any more. Here's the challenge: whichever one of us can drink more toasts to Johnnie—eh, my friend—he has to buy all liquor we've swilled. Deal?"

Don Vincente Jose-Maria de Castro y Papas was silent for a long time, frowning deeply. "You are challenging me to a...a duel of drinking to the death?"

"No, no. Jeez, you hidalgos are a real serious bunch, aren'tcha? Look: you seem like an okay guy. And there's been enough killing as it is—too much. So let's toast my friend with wine and spirits until one of us can't lift a glass anymore."

Castro y Papas looked long and hard at Lefferts. "You are mocking me."

"Dammit, Don Vincente, I'm not in the mood or place to do any mocking. Look: if I had been doing my job properly, I'd never have walked into your trap. But I was too sure of myself and my friend paid for that with his life." Harry looked away for a moment. "A lot of people paid for that with their lives. But it taught me a lesson—one I might not have learned any other way. So, yeah, you pulled the trigger—but I set up the target. You were just a soldier with a gun who had set a good trap."

Castro y Papas looked either like he was going to spit or cry—*damn, these Spaniards can get so intense!*—but then said, "Very well: I accept your terms, Señor Lefferts—and will happily toast your friend, whose name was—?"

"Eh...we'll talk about that later. That's a name to be shared in a safer place, okay?"

"Yes, this is acceptable. I must tell you, though, that the plan you speak of—the one which foiled you in Rome—was not of my design. I would not lay such a dishonorable trap, using a pregnant woman as bait."

"So, who *did* plot that ambush then?"

Castro y Papas smiled. "Yet another name for a safer place, Señor Lefferts."

"Harry."

"My apologies. Señor Harry."

*Oh, fer chrissakes...* "Yeah, fine; I can live with 'Señor Harry.'"
They nodded at each other, and Harry had the feeling that something had changed, separately, in both him and in Castro y Papas.
He had no guess what that something might have been for the
Spaniard, and truth be told, didn't have a much better guess of
what change had begun in himself, but it felt vaguely like a resolution of some kind, of a mistake owned, a debt paid, a new door
opened. Harry shrugged and put the incipient revelation on the
same shelf where he had left almost all the others he had experienced since he had been about seven—but this time, he resolved
to take it down and study it as soon as he got to a safe place.
Which kindled a small, unusual flame of quiet pride somewhere in
his chest. He smiled, liking the sensation, and looked out to sea.

—Where he saw, at the same instant Castro y Papas did, two
specks on the far southern horizon: the away-boats from the
*Atropos.*

Harry dug an elbow into the hidalgo's ribs gently. "Hey, lookit
who's early for a change. C'mon, Don Vincente; let's tell the others our ride is here."

Thomas North watched as the other ships of the flotilla headed
away and were swallowed by the dark. And he smiled. *Try to
catch us now, you Spanish bastards.*

When the black *llaut* carrying his troops had cleared Palma
Bay and reached the rendezvous point, she had blinked a signal
lamp into the darkness. A quick flash responded, marking the
precise position of the *Guerra Cagna*, which then relayed another
signal to the west: far off, a light had winked back. That was the
*Atropos*, confirming she had received the signal that announced
both the safe return of North's team at the rendezvous point and
that the dispersal of the smaller ships would commence as soon
as his men were on the *Guerra Cagna*.

That transfer was a quick affair. Although there were no Spanish in sight, and they were moving at night, the little flotilla
was still in sight of the shore and lighthouses (which was what
had made a nighttime sea rendezvous possible in the first place).
Consequently, they were not too far away from where the Spanish
would begin their pursuit. The flotilla's object was now to split

up and give their pursuers the same problem that the enemy had given Lefferts and North in Rome with multiple carriages: the need to chase a number of tantalizing leads simultaneously, thereby diffusing their search resources.

North's smile widened. *Your turn to play "find the pea," you bastards.* He looked back at his men, crowded on the deck of the *Guerra Cagna*. Some of them would later be tasked to tend to the oars if the pursuit got close, although they had also taken on the up-time motor from the black *llaut*. That local ship, along with the *Bogeria*, was heading due east and would not be part of the shell-game the rest were preparing for the Spanish. Instead, both ships would be swapped at a modest loss for equivalent hulls—probably on the northernmost Balearic island of Minorca—thereby removing these local boats from the area in which inquiries might be made, and hulls identified.

The other four ships now turned to follow their preassigned compass headings. The *Guerra Cagna* was to head southeast. Although a swift ship, she was carrying the heaviest load and was the largest, and so needed to veer in a direction that also gave her a head start to her actual destination.

Aurelio's *Minnow*—currently under the command of one of his seemingly innumerable relatives—would head due south, aiming her pert, responsive prow at Algeria. And the *Zora* would head southwest, directly opposite the course her master most wanted to go, but the crew of the little *gajeta* was eager for the bonus connected with the job, and this was their final obligation. Although the *Zora*'s crew would not be paid until they returned to Venice, they would leave the Rialto with enough money to support their families for half a year—more, if they were frugal.

North felt the *Guerra Cagna* come around to take the freshening southwest wind over her beam. That maneuver—positioning a ship sideways in relation to the wind—was still a novel experience for him. Having grown up around square-rigged vessels, for the most part, he remained surprised—and rather enchanted—by the almost mystical versatility of the lateen rig. Although inferior at getting speed from a following wind, they excelled at using a wind from over their waists. But they made reasonable headway with breezes coming from almost any quarter, able to sail so close to the wind that they could still make progress by tacking back and forth across a head wind.

This aspect of the lateen sail aided all the ships, now. For the *Guerra Cagna* it meant a maximally effective wind was already running into her two sails. North could already feel her speed picking up, and suspected that her master was going to need to slow her down so as not to overshoot their new loiter point, some ten miles southeast.

For the *Minnow*, her close-hauled heading meant less speed, but being light, she needed less wind; she'd still make the ten miles to her own new loiter point comfortably. And even though the *Dawn* was sailing straight into the wind, the skilled crew of that hull was doubtlessly tacking to-and-fro to make decent progress. If she didn't make enough headway, no matter. She could take a more westerly heading for a while, and in bringing her prow out of the wind, she would make better speed to her own new loiter point.

North looked east; no glimmers on the horizon, yet. Good, he thought, we'll make it to the new loiter points just in time to give the Spanish something new to chase. Why hunt down enemy ships alone, when you can hunt both a ship and an enemy balloon together? Yes, each Spanish pursuit boat—too separated from its mates to signal effectively—would certainly press on alone if they believed themselves poised to also capture the mysterious airship that had attacked the Castell de Bellver. And that is exactly what Lefferts' and Miro's escape plan would lead them to believe.

North's smile became unpleasant. "Happy hunting, you bastards," he muttered toward the distant lights of Palma.

From the stern of the *Atropos*, and with the *Llebeig* running in from the southwest, Miro watched the mizzen's lateen fill nicely. The *Atropos* herself had left Dragonera behind shortly before dawn, heading due north, almost out of the sight of the coast, and taking good, but not best, advantage of the *Llebeig*. With the yard mounted on the same side as the wind from that angle, the lateen was unable to work to optimum effect on that leg of their journey.

But that brief sacrifice was worth it, for ultimately, Aurelio brought the *Atropos* over hard-a-starboard and into a due east heading. From this angle, the *Llebeig* came full into the lateen, the yard being on what was now the leeward side of the mast. The xebec seemed like a suddenly spurred horse, leaping through the swells with speed that, according to the up-timers, they associated with powered boats or racing yachts.

That speed had been central to the overall escape plan: if the Spanish had not found the *Atropos* by the time it left Dragonera, it was very unlikely they ever would. Heading away from shore also meant heading directly away from potential pursuit. And now, with the wind at the most optimal position for the xebec's rig, there was quite probably not a single ship in the Balearics that could overtake them. This was one of the two reasons Miro had been willing to take the risks necessary to seize the xebec in the first place: it not only had a large enough stern to support balloon operations, but it was also the fastest getaway ship in the Mediterranean.

Miro leaned into the wind. Hours ago, the flotilla's four swiftest boats—each readying one of the large kongming lanterns that Meir had purchased for him—had, at the same time, gone to their new loiter points well south of Palma. There, with the first hint of graying in the east, they lit the lamps and sent them aloft, each tethered to its ship by a silken string.

Each lantern had been a flickering airborne lure, visible to one or maybe two of the Spanish chase ships. Being unable to communicate with the others as their search pattern carried them farther apart, the Spanish had been almost sure to follow whichever enemy ship-and-balloon combination they first espied. With the enemy barely visible upon the horizon, each Spanish captain would reasonably believe that he—and only he—was chasing the right ship: the one towing the balloon that had been seen during the attack on Castell de Bellver.

And right about now, if Miro guessed the position of the sun correctly, those captains would be discovering the final trick that had been played upon them: that the separate balloons they had each been chasing had been released from their tow ships at least half an hour earlier. And, more distressingly, that the balloons had actually been nothing more than aerial lanterns, common in the Far East but quite unfamiliar in the Mediterranean—and, as they had now learned, very misleading as to their size and range, particularly when seen at a great distance and against a uniform backdrop such as the sea. Miro smiled; there was a satisfying irony in having misled those captains by giving them exactly what they had expected to see—since that was just what the Spanish had done to the rescuers in Rome.

Shielding his eyes against the rising sun, Miro noticed that they had come back in sight of the shore; the dark gray coastline swept up higher to the north. The *Atropos'* course would parallel those peaks—the barren Tramuntana mountains that marched across the top of his home island like a wall—all the way until they reached the dramatic northeast promontory known as the Cap de Formentor. From there, the *Atropos* would maneuver to rendezvous with the *Guerra Cagna* and the *Minnow,* and let off a quick series of radio squelches that would signify "all well, hostages rescued, team returning." But even then, Miro would not presume they were safe—not until they reached the Ligurian coast, just north of the Golfo de Spezio, from whence they would relaunch the dirigible toward Brescia, one hundred and five miles inland and safe behind the Venetian border.

However, Miro conceded, leaning back against the taffrail and enjoying a sudden dappling of sunlight through the light overcast, it was reasonable to indulge in at least a small amount of satisfaction, even before they arrived in Italy. After all, the rescue plan that Harry and he cobbled together *had* worked. Miro smiled. In fact, it had worked quite acceptably.

Quite acceptably, indeed.

# Chapter 57

Larry was standing alongside Urban, looking out the rear window of the Garden Room, one of the few that had not been severely damaged during the prior night's combat. Out upon the villa's rear grounds—arrayed in rows between the herb and vegetable gardens—were all the dead. Mazzare swallowed, not having seen so many bodies since the Croat cavalry rode into Grantville in an attempt to slaughter all of the recently arrived up-timers.

"How many?" murmured Urban.

"Us or them?" asked Mazzare.

Urban closed his eyes. "How many of God's children, Cardinal Mazzare?"

Larry felt a pang of shame—not the first one he'd felt in the past day. "Er...eighty-four in all, Your Holiness."

Urban nodded, and after a time, opened his eyes. "There on the end, is that the boy who ran messages—Carlo? And is that the cook, the one with the lovely voice, beside him?"

"Yes, Your Holiness."

"I could not tell. They are almost completely covered."

"Their wounds—and dignity—demanded no less."

Somewhere, out near the small barn, a hoarse cry rose up and dwindled back down with a whimper. Larry closed his eyes. Even with Sharon here, there had been wounds too grievous to treat—and in the borderline cases, the preference had been routinely given to the staff and defenders of the embassy, rather than the attackers. Those whose wounds would ultimately prove mortal—and there had been many—had been moved to the barn, from whence screams and cries had emerged all night long. Shortly before dawn, the frequency and volume of the agonized screams had begun to taper off. Now, they were rare. If Sharon's triage assessments were correct, there would be final silence shortly past noon. And he, Cardinal Larry Mazzare, champion of peace, declaimer of war, had put at least four into that death house, himself. He felt a quiver start deep inside his body—

Urban put his hand on Larry's shoulder. For the first time in Mazzare's memory, the pope's grip felt almost frail, but it drove off whatever demon of guilt and remorse had been rising up in him. "This has been a hard night, Lawrence. How many assassins attacked us?"

"We're not sure, Your Holiness. There are fifty-one of their bodies out there. Some escaped, but not many."

"And how many of our own friends have gone to be with their Maker?"

"Twenty-one of the embassy workers, nine of the Marines, one of the Hibernians, and Fleming. And—" Mazzare paused.

"—and George Sutherland. Yes, I know. I think I will see his face for the rest of my days."

Someone cleared a throat behind them; they turned.

Sharon and Ruy stood just within the doorway. "Holy Father," she said, "I'm sorry to disturb you, but we need a moment of your time."

Urban sighed but put on a smile; it was arguably the saddest expression that Larry Mazzare had ever seen. "Of course, Ambassadora Nichols."

"I know it seems that, after last night, we should all have time to rest and recover, but we don't. We've got to move you again, Holy Father. We can't be sure that there is only one group of assassins.

"Tom Stone in Venice, and the USE leadership, both know our situation here. We just got a message from Venice that they are preparing our back-up site, have sent half of the embassy Marines—cavalrymen, every one of them—to reinforce us up here until we can move. They'll ride through the night and pick up an additional twenty troops along the way, mostly trusted retainers of four different nobles known to support you, and who are said to be incorruptible."

Personally, Larry wondered if there were really four such paragons of aristocratic virtue to be found in the entirety of this most materialistic of republics.

"I see," Urban said as the other clerics entered. "When will we be leaving?"

"That's just it, Your Holiness. We have to leave the second the cavalry comes over the hill."

Urban stood particularly straight. "So it must be. Can you tell me where we are going?"

Sharon sighed. "Actually, Your Holiness, that's the exact question I was coming to ask you."

"I beg your pardon?"

Sharon put out her hands helplessly. "We got a signal just a few minutes ago that Frank and Giovanna are safe and on the way back to Italy. So we have to make travel and security arrangements for all our 'at risk' persons as soon as possible. We don't want to give Borja another crack at you or them. But we've got one problem: we still don't know where you want to go."

Urban stared at the ground a moment. "I see your quandary. And I owe you that answer—now. Particularly after all of this. So, I assume we have some hours, yet?"

"At least a day, Your Holiness. And if there is another group of assassins who are able to reach us in that time, I'm not sure how much we could do to stop them—not if they are as large as this bunch was."

"Very well. Then here is what we shall do." He turned toward Antonio. "Cardinal Barberini, you will need your pen, ink, and parchment. I will give my judgment on what I have heard in the debates."

Vitelleschi raised on eyebrow. "Indeed? How soon?"

"In five minutes, my friend." He turned to a speechless Sharon. "Would you be so kind as to announce to those who can, and wish, to attend that they are welcome to do so?"

Wadding frowned. "Holy Father, is that wise?"

"I do not know, Cardinal Wadding, but I know this: no person who was in this house last night, sharing our peril, shall be kept away from our deliberations today. Now, Lawrence, let us go fetch a pitcher of cold water." Urban smiled crookedly. "Pontificating is thirsty work."

✧　　✧　　✧

The audience in the Garden Room was less than a dozen persons. After fetching water with the pope, Larry had sidled off to buttonhole Ruy and point out that it was defensive suicide to allow the security forces to attend. Ruy politely declined to undermine the pope's offer, but pointed out that all the security personnel were so deeply engaged in their duties, and so far away from the villa itself, that they could not possibly be summoned in time. Then, as three of the Hibernians walked by, not ten yards away, Ruy smiled at Larry.

Larry stared at the nearby soldiers, then at the ironic smile on Ruy's face, and said, "Oh."

If Urban detected, or was upset by the suspiciously limited audience for his pronouncements, he gave no sign of it. He simply stood and began.

"Time is short, so I shall not indulge in either a preamble or words of gratitude. Indeed, no words of gratitude could begin to express our deep debt to our hosts for what they have done, and what they have sacrificed."

Sharon nodded stately thanks and acknowledgment.

"Cardinals Wadding and Mazzare did their jobs with all the vigor and insight that can be asked of mortal men. Their part in this is over. The first matter for us to consider if there is any basis for a lingering doubt that—although the up-timers are not constructs of the devil—it is still possible that they have been called back to our time to work as his unwitting tools."

Urban folded his hands. "Much turns on this first matter—so much that I would be remiss to color the thinking of the most vigilant mind among us by expressing my opinion first. Therefore, Father-General Vitelleschi will share his personal judgment on this topic." Urban sat—and smiled at Vitelleschi.

The father-general stood rigidly for a moment; Mazzare couldn't tell if he was shocked or angry, or very possibly, both. But the Jesuit quickly schooled his expression to impassivity and folded his arms, staring downward. After almost ten seconds, he spoke, "I have heard only one credible reason that explains why Satan might choose these up-timers as his unwitting tools: that they might mislead us with new ideas for which we are simply not ready. This assertion presumes that it is perilous to embrace a doctrine for which men are not ready, or which ultimately distracts them from the salvation of their souls. Bellarmine rightly said that 'Men are so like frogs. They go openmouthed for the lure of things which do not concern them, and that wily angler, the Devil, knows how to capture multitudes of them.'"

Vitelleschi looked around the room. "What could be more tempting to us down-timers than the wealth of information that arrived along with Grantville? And surely, their record of societies which successfully embraced absolute religious toleration is a nearly irresistible lure for the war-weary people of this world. Satan would also foresee that, precisely because the up-time knowledge is so empirically sound, the principle of absolute toleration might acquire an unwonted halo of implicit truth just by sharing common origin with all the rest of the authoritative information they brought to us."

Vitelleschi's brows lowered. "This is precisely the kind of trap that The Deceiver would lay for us. Eager for the promise of peace, our multitudes might poison themselves by drinking in such spirits, Holy or otherwise, distilled during the up-timers' further centuries of strife and tribulation. As Cardinal Wadding argued, the up-time nations may have been prepared to healthily imbibe this potent liquor, but ours may not be."

Mazzare looked over at Wadding, expecting to discover him swelling at the scent of approaching victory, but the Irish cardinal was strangely quiet, listening carefully.

"However," said Vitelleschi, "we must now measure this hypothetical threat against the very solid—even bloody—reality of this moment. To be blunt, does it seem plausible that these up-timers—who have risked themselves for us, for our Church, our pope—could in fact be the Devil's tools?"

Vitelleschi shook his head. "The answer is obvious if we simply reverse the question: would we be alive this moment if they *were* the Devil's tools? Less than twelve hours ago, our survival and the future of the legitimate Church rested in the hands of these up-timers and their allies. That I stand here now, alive and speaking, is all the proof I need that they are not agents of darkness. Yes, I may be able to imagine fabulous plots in which Grantville is Satan's ultimate and pivotal conceit, but they all collapse under the weight of this momentous fact: if it were not for the up-timers last night, the Church would not exist this morning. Satan had his opportunity to strike a mortal blow last night, but instead, his hopes died along with Borja's assassins—all slain by up-timers and their allies."

Vitelleschi's proud neck went erect again. "And so I conclude—" he surveyed the up-timers sternly "—that whatever else they might be, the up-timers are not Satan's unwitting tools." With a brief glance at Urban—was it defiance, pride, annoyance?—the father-general sat.

Urban stood, and suddenly, Larry could hardly recall what Vitelleschi had said, because he knew he was about to hear history being made. And also, he was about to learn whether he was going to be traveling to the USE and living a while longer, or die very soon, because if Urban struck out on his own, Larry would have to—and wanted to—follow him. And they would all soon be found and killed, like rabbits beneath the teeth of wolves.

"I thank the father-general for his illuminating and instructive reasoning on the matter of our up-time friends, who, I now pronounce, speaking *ex cathedra*, to be found no different than the other children of God, possessed of the same graces, flaws, and origins as the rest of us. Now, let me speak to the other issues at hand.

"Since we have now accepted that the up-timers are neither satanic agents or dupes, then we are, de facto, accepting the reality of their future world. Which means that the later popes of their world are most assuredly popes. And this, in turn means that I acknowledge that they, too, enjoyed the grace of the Sacred Magisterium and thus were infallible in matters of faith and morals.

"Which brings us inevitably to the next point: by acknowledging them as true popes, one must also then acknowledge that God guided them to convene the council known as Vatican Two. And although God's instruction to them does not constitute instructions to me, His inspiration and intents were manifest in that council and the doctrines arising therefrom. And so I must bear in mind their decisions and deeds as I consider my own.

"However, let us now address the crux of the matter: are the decrees of pontiffs from a future world that will now never exist to be obeyed in this one? I cannot see how that could be. The papacy is not only a succession of men, but of interactions between man and God. Consequently, it is logical that a later pope may not question the charism of an earlier pope, whose deeds and relationship with God must necessarily shape those of his successors. But to obey the dictates of a pope who came *after* me? In this, Cardinal Wadding is certainly right: Vatican

Two's papal and consular authority must be constrained to your time, Cardinal Mazzare, because it was informed by centuries of history—both papal and global—that came *after* this century. How could the needs of your twentieth-century Church be no different from the needs of this one? The charism of perfection that attends the Sacred Magisterium made Vatican Two's doctrines perfect insofar as they reflect God's grace in answering the questions and quandaries that were particular to the Church in *your* bubble of time and space."

Urban made a small, circular gesture. "This bubble—*our* bubble—is not that bubble. So I must believe that, even if we asked the same questions that your Church did, the answers would be different. If Vatican Two was accepted without modification in this world, it would trigger far more schisms and wars than it would prevent, despite the fact that it provided timely and essential answers to challenges that had long vexed the Holy See of the twentieth century."

Perhaps Urban saw the worried eyes of his audience; he smiled and nodded. "However, it is also true that the mind of God does not change; man changes. And the way in which Vatican Two does apply to this time, and this world, is that it is a further revelation of the mind of God. And particularly important is its renewed emphasis upon one of the most fundamental truths Christ brought to us: we are not to convert others by the exercise of power, but by examples of perfection—by living in as Christ-like a fashion as possible."

Urban spread his hands. "When did Christ ever instruct us to do violence upon others? At what sermon did he commend our evangelical duty to the force of weapons, instead of words? He preached the tolerance and hope and charity that your popes reaffirmed through the Apostolic Constitutions that arose from Vatican Two. And although those Constitutions were not issued in or to this world, and are thus not specifically binding upon us, I acknowledge that they reflect the will and mind of God. Which leads me to conclude that, since we cannot accept the specific doctrines and language of your Vatican Two, it is incumbent upon me to convene one of our own."

Mazzare sneaked a look at Wadding, and was surprised to see the former Franciscan nodding thoughtfully.

Urban folded his hands again. "And so we come to the final

question I must answer: *quo vadis?*" Seeing uncertainty on the faces of most of the up-timers, Urban smiled and translated, "'Where are you going?'" He held up his hands. "I already knew the worldly, prudent answer—to reside in the USE while I rebuild our shattered Church. But Cardinal Wadding rightly pointed to the dangers of putting oneself in the house of another; one's freedom of choice will slowly, but surely, be compromised and constrained.

"But mostly, I was listening for My Savior's wise whisper. And it was Cardinal Mazzare who inadvertently pointed out how to listen for Christ's guidance in this matter. The story of the Good Samaritan is precisely the one I needed to consider at length, for among its many lessons, it shows us just what the up-timers own insistence upon freedom of religion truly reveals: that coexistence between faiths is not merely possible, but the only way to live a Christ-like existence."

Urban frowned. "As a pope, sitting safely ensconced in the Vatican, it is still all too easy to become distracted from the basic truths to be found in the Gospel. As protector of the faith, one is called upon to make—difficult decisions." Urban looked like he suffered a moment of indigestion. "With Gustav Adolf defeating our armies in Germany, and endless rounds of reprisals and massacres between Catholics and Protestants, my conversations with God become too focused on mundane urgencies rather than enduring grace. And with the Spanish cardinals always pressing the issue, the line between heresy and toleration was ever on my mind, ever a political issue, and often, a rationalization for the use of papal troops and authority, both to accommodate and thwart the policies of Madrid's coterie of cardinals. But now—"

The pope paused and stared out the back window; Mazzare wondered if he was looking at the sheet covering the last mortal remains of George Sutherland.

Urban turned back to the room. "Now, all those urgent decisions seem akin to the splitting of hairs. We can find all the truth we need in the Gospels, and at the danger of repeating myself, I find no place where Christ exhorted us to kill, rather than love, our neighbor. So how can I allow God's Church to fall into the hands of Gaspar Borja? And how can I prevent it but by remembering that God teaches us humility in many ways—and maybe, for this pope, at this time, that lesson comes in the shape of saying,

'Yes, I am the beaten Jew in the story of the Good Samaritan.' My God and Savior has had the infinite kindness and wisdom to place this lesson before me and maybe—maybe—help me to become a better, more Christ-like man than I have been up until now. So yes, I will gladly accept the help of Gustav Adolf, of he whom I thought was my enemy but who may now be my Good Samaritan. Assuming that is truly his will."

He looked directly at Sharon who, holding her breath, nodded twice, quickly.

Urban nodded back. "However, there is a one last, instructive detail of the parable of the Good Samaritan that wants mention. Although the Good Samaritan provided all aid to the stricken Jew, even paying for a room at an inn and a physician, he did not bring the injured man under his own roof."

Uncertain looks started ricocheting from face to face in the Garden Room; even Antonio Barberini paused in his writing and looked up with a perplexed expression on his face. But Larry suddenly knew what was coming—and scolded himself for not having anticipated it.

Urban raised a finger. "Let us not doubt that if the beaten Jew had *required* it, the Samaritan would have brought him under his own roof. But since he did not, we must ask why this was not, in fact, the best alternative?"

Urban clearly did not expect—and was not inviting—a response, but he let the rhetorical question dangle for a moment before answering it. "There are probably two reasons. First, although the Samaritan demonstrated his goodness by ignoring his community's prejudice against Jews, he could not have assured that the beaten man would have been safe had he brought him home. Indeed, his neighbors might have done violence against both of them for what they considered the effrontery and outrage of caring for an enemy in their midst.

"But perhaps the second reason is more pertinent. By taking the Jew to an inn—a neutral place—the Good Samaritan also avoided putting the recipient of his help under the obligations that accrue when one is a guest in another's home. Not only was the Jew rescued and healed, but his dignity was protected. What passed between them later, the parable does not tell us; we can only hope the Jew repaid the Good Samaritan with friendship and gratitude. But the free expression of such amity is only possible because he remained in neutral territory: he was never placed under any obligation to obey, or even thank, his benefactor."

Urban folded his hands. "And so it must be with Mother Church." He looked at Sharon again. "We are happy—and enduringly grateful—for the kindness shown, for our rescue, and for the promise of being carried to a safe, neutral place where we may recover our strength. But we may not enter your house, just as the Good Samaritan elected not to take the wounded Jew into his own. And in the better years to come, the Good Samaritans of the USE may thus know that the Church's future friendship and gratitude is given freely, rather than in the satisfaction of an obligation to a former host."

Urban crossed the room to stand before Sharon. "I hope this decision does not disappoint you, or those above you in the USE. It could not be otherwise, at this historical moment. After all, the faithful of the Church have accepted popes suspected of being murderers and liars; the record is sadly clear on that. However, to lead the Catholic Church from within the borders of a nation whose monarch is a Protestant?" Urban wagged a remonstrating finger and smiled. "No, *that* will not be tolerated. It is sad but true that if I did so, it would undo all we hope to accomplish by accepting your help: to make this the beginning of an open and full friendship between us, and to begin healing the wounds of sectarian strife."

"Your Holiness, I just heard you say you can't stay with us in the USE," remarked Sharon, who had made Urban-watching a near specialty of hers, "but why does it sound like you're trying to convince yourself of that, even more than you're trying to convince me?"

He smiled shrewdly. "Ah, Ambassadora, you are a most perceptive person. And of course, you are correct. There is no place I would rather visit right now than Grantville, and there is no place I would feel more safe. But at this time, it would not just be the Spanish cardinals who would declaim me for even visiting the USE. Too many of the moderate cardinals would be tempted to agree that I would only do such a thing if I had fallen under the spell of witches sent here by an infernal miracle.

"Yes, we have settled and put aside this issue officially today, but it will take time for many of the moderates to accept it. And beyond that, it will take my restoration to the Holy See before the suspicions of a distressingly large portion of the common folk are truly allayed. Consequently, the unfortunate realities of this political moment make a visit to your fascinating town completely out of the question. However, I promise you this—indeed, I request it of you as a further favor: that upon liberating the Vatican from Borja, and returning to my seat upon the *cathedra*, I may announce that my first official departure from Rome will be to visit my peerless friends in Grantville."

Sharon bowed. "We would be honored, Your Holiness."

"No, my daughter," he said with a solemn smile. "It is you who would be extending a singular honor to me."

And with a bow, he left. Vitelleschi followed. Wadding wandered out well behind them, hands behind his back, head lowered in thought. Larry Mazzare stayed behind, staring at the walls and realizing that, in regard to the Roman Catholic Church, *Now, nothing will be as it was before. With this, everything changes.*

As they walked out the front door—strolling in the back was unspeakably depressing and subtly disrespectful—Father-General Muzio Vitelleschi felt quietly pleased with himself as he primly asked: "So, I take it that this Council has been a help to you, Holy Father?"

"A help to me?" Urban laughed. "I did not require this Council's deliberations to help *me*."

"No? Then whom?"

The pope smiled. "It was to help you, my dear Vitelleschi."

It took Vitelleschi a second to realize that his mouth was hanging open. He finally sputtered: "Me? How? In what way?"

"Ah, Vitelleschi, old friend, how else could I know your true mind? And how else could you be free to know it yourself?"

"I do not understand, Your Holiness."

Urban smiled. "Without this process, you would have followed my decisions—as you always have—because that is your job. And you would have done so ardently and firmly, because of our long years together. But that is a very different thing from believing in something yourself. And I needed to know what *you* believed. That way, I could compare your conclusions with my own. But more importantly, I needed your *convictions*—whatever they might be—to be wholly and utterly your own. I did not want you torn between duty to me on one side, doctrinal doubts on the other, and with the middle-ground a mire of contending ideas and conjectures. No. You need to be as firmly committed to this new course, to our new policies, as I am."

"And had my conclusions been at variance with your own?"

Urban shrugged. "Then I would have restudied my tentative decisions on the matter." He smiled and glanced back at Wadding who was just emerging, squinting, into the sunlight. "After all, had your conclusions been different, you would then have been offering me the same counsel as Luke Wadding. And if the former Fathers Vitelleschi and Wadding can agree on something—if the epoch's leading Jesuit and Franciscan minds are in such unprecedented unison on any topic—then a wise pope must consider that true miracle a sign from God and take heed!"

# Part Six

*Early August 1635*

A sky grown clear and blue again

# Chapter 58

As Sharon watched, the second dirigible that the USE had leased for its Mediterranean operations appeared between the rounded crests of the northern Berici Hills, heading east. Other members of her recently reconstituted but still displaced embassy looked up to see it pass.

"There's our ride," murmured Larry Mazzare, beside her.

"Your ride," she corrected. "That one is only returning as far as Chur." She frowned. "I probably shouldn't ask, but do you have any idea where Urban is going to go after getting there?"

Mazzare shrugged. "No idea; I'll send a message from wherever we wind up."

Sharon put a hand on the small-town priest's arm. "And again I probably shouldn't ask, but are you sure you want to go with him?"

"Want to?" Larry's laugh was sudden and short. "Speaking as an individual, I most certainly do *not* want to. I just want to go back home, like you. But speaking as a priest, I want to go wherever he goes, come what may. Besides, Urban needs me, both as a cardinal in whatever Consistory he can summon to him, and as a radio-equipped emissary from the USE. At least he's arranged for excellent security—and is scooping up more all the time. And ever since Urban's survival was announced, and attested to by the priests who met us in Vicenza last week, most of the papal troops have stopped responding—even halfheartedly—to Borja's orders."

Sharon leaned closer and whispered conspiratorially, "Is it true that Urban made one or two of the bishops who came to see him in Vicenza cardinals *in pectore*?"

Mazzare glared at her. "Who told you that?"

"No one. Well, actually you did, by the way you just reacted." She smiled sweetly at Larry.

Mazzare muttered, "Remind me not to play poker with you." They shared a small smile and looked out over the small, remote valley just a day south of Vicenza; although sparsely settled by the standards of the Venetian Republic, the smattering of houses on the lush green hills produced a sensation of overcrowding after weeks in the almost uninhabited mountains around Molini. "Will you miss it?" Mazzare asked suddenly.

"Miss what? Italy?"

"No. Being an ambassador."

"Well, maybe a bit." *Sharon, you are such a liar; one half of you is dying to get home and get reacquainted with real honest-to-goodness running water, and the other half is screaming that it's like the old song says, "you can't go home again"—because what will ever compare to all this? Damn; I'm probably borderline PTSD now, but I've never felt so alive, and useful, and needed in my whole life. And how much is Ruy going to want a quiet domestic life? Hell, how much do I want it—if at all?* "It was a lot more dangerous than I anticipated," she added after a moment.

"Well, danger should not be a problem for those of us traveling with Urban, now. As soon the pope's personal friends heard he was alive, they started sending their most trusted retainers to join him. And the growing radio network north of the Alps has certainly accelerated the pace at which news of his survival has been spreading."

Ruy's voice rose behind them. "Yes, I have heard as much. I just finished decoding the latest messages from both the USE and the Low Countries. Given the guard contingents our pope's many friends are sending, it sounds as though the papal entourage may well be the safest place in Christendom. Also, the leadership of both the USE and the Low Countries have agreed to the pope's choice of a personal security chief."

Mazzare frowned. "Why was the consent of both states required?"

"Ah, because the poor fool Urban requested for the job has ties to both polities."

Sharon heard the odd emphasis upon "poor fool" and turned to face Ruy. "You? He chose you?"

"Ah, you see? My magnificent wife misses even not the subtlest hint! She is truly as quick-witted as she is beautiful."

"Ruy! Without even asking me? How could you—?"

"Eh. About that, my heart. The transmission from the USE had a few desultory lines included for your lustrous self as well."

*Oh. Great.* "And what are they?"

"You have been made the USE's officially appointed envoy to the papal entourage and its official political representative to the council Urban intends to convene."

*Well, did I speak too soon about not wanting to go home, or what?* And yet, truth be told, Sharon also felt relieved and perhaps just the tiniest bit excited as well. "So I guess this means we don't get to fly back on the repaired Monster."

"That is correct, my love. We will be in the balloon to Chur. But as I understand it, the Monster will fly along with us and oversee our safe arrival. Merely to provide assistance in the event of alpine mishaps and to show the flag to the Graubünders, as it were."

*Yeah, and to amaze and awe the natives. One of whom, come to think of it, was none other than*—"That guy that Miro met with—Jenatsch—wouldn't be so stupid as to think that he could deal a bigger hand for himself, what with a pope ripe for the plucking in his own back yard—would he?"

Ruy frowned. "He is too clever for that, I think—but, on the other hand, why trust to fate, or to the prudence of a man who left his mark on your history by employing a battle axe as readily as diplomatic nuance?"

"Exactly. So, the way I see it—"

Larry Mazzare rose. "Well, since good-byes don't seem to be necessary any more, I'll leave you two to your favorite pastime."

"Our pastime?" wondered Ruy.

"What are you talking about, Larry?" said Sharon.

But with an impish smile, the cardinal had started strolling down toward the small garden.

Larry Mazzare turned into the garden's largest, bee-busy arbor—and was almost run down by the big hidalgo whose sense of honor had overcome his oath of fealty to Philip and who had accompanied the rescuers back to Italy. And whose name he was always forgetting—

"Don Vincente," Larry said, relieved that the name had come to him at the last second, "I did not see you."

"A hundred pardons, Your Eminence. The fault was mine. I am—I am somewhat overwhelmed, I fear."

"Overwhelmed?"

"What he means to say," said Luke Wadding, coming up behind, "is that he just met the pope."

"I did, yes!" gushed Don Vincente, who looked as star-struck as a schoolboy and as harmless as a restless tiger. "It was—oh, if only I could tell my family. But alas, they believe I am—"

Mazzare stretched out a hand and touched Castro y Papas on the arm. "Don Vincente, I know you worry that the news of your death may be too hard for them to bear, particularly as they are older parents. But they believe your departure was with honor; they will endure."

He nodded. "True. And perhaps it is better that they do not know the truth: that in order to live, I forsook honor—"

"No," Mazzare's voice became firm. "You did not. You swore an oath to a 'noble and holy crown' did you not?"

"I did."

"And so tell me, were you not compelled by the duly appointed representatives of that crown to repeatedly act in ways that were the very antithesis of holiness or nobility?"

His head hung. "I was."

"Then, my son, it is not you who broke faith with them: it is our representatives of the crown who broke faith with you." Don Vincente looked sideways; Larry saw—as was to be expected in a man of his age and experience—that this had already occurred to him. But as a devout Catholic, he would not presume the authority to absolve himself; that had to come from a priest—as it had now. "I can well imagine your doubts, Don Vincente; the first tenet of chivalry is that one's virtue and honor is not contingent upon the virtue and honor of others. Just so. But your duty here was not just to yourself, but to the innocent. It may well be that we might have to pay a heavy—even an ultimate—price to abide by the oaths we swear. But should others—particularly an innocent mother and her unborn child—be compelled to pay for the keeping of our oaths, as well? The answer to that is 'No'—and you found that answer with great speed and clarity."

Don Vincente looked up. "Thank you, Your Eminence. This has troubled me—among other things."

"Oh, what other things?"

Wadding commented from over the big Spaniard's shoulder. "He's very much looking forward to meeting Ruy—a 'whispered legend' he calls him. But he is, let us say 'reluctant,' to share what he knows about Borja, and particularly, this Pedro Dolor fellow who has been his spymaster ever since Quevedo was—er, removed."

Don Vincente looked up quickly. "Is it true that Don Ruy slew Quevedo in single combat?"

Mazzare saw the gleam in the young man's eye, saw the opening there that Ruy would use to get him to share his precious insider knowledge of Borja's command structure, and simply said, "Why not go ask him yourself? He is just there, at the head of the garden."

Mazzare returned Don Vincente's brief nod, Wadding's knowing smile, and walked on to where he knew the pope had retired to meditate for a while.

But turning into the next long arbor, Larry saw Urban in solemn conversation with two of the Wild Geese—Owen and Sean, from the shape of the silhouettes. Rather than turn into that shaded tunnel of bright flowers and wafting lilac, Mazzare kept walking straight on. He considered returning to his own room to pack, but decided against it; as he had left, late-sleeping Frank and Giovanna had just begun stirring in the adjacent room. And if this day was like every other thus far, Mazzare would gladly miss their loud—and vigorous—celebration of the morning and each other.

Owen had not expected that Urban would bow his head in such an extended gesture of memorial respect, but he did, staring down at the small, flat stone under which they had buried those few personal effects of John O'Neill that had been carried back from Rome. All in all, they weighed only ten pounds, but they had to remain here: Franchetti had made it very clear that any balloon of his that got tasked with carrying the pope was going to have plenty of extra fuel, a spare engine, and no unnecessary weight.

The pope murmured something short and Latin, which puzzled O'Neill, because it wasn't any of he benedictions he was familiar with. As it was, Urban had already said a full mass for the fallen earl in Vicenza, for which Father Hickey had made the journey, looking so old and drawn that Owen wondered if he might not soon follow his dear Johnnie into the grave out of sheer grief. And here, Urban had murmured a familiar blessing and benediction when they first bowed their heads.

When the pope finally raised his chin, Owen asked, "Your Holiness, I'm sorry, I didn't catch what prayer you said there at the end."

"Oh," explained Urban, "that was no prayer. It was a line from a story—a story, and a line, which reminded me of your courageous—and I have heard it whispered, occasionally impetuous—cousin."

"Ah, he'd appreciate the truth of your words, Holy Father, and I doubt he'd dispute 'em. But what were they?"

Urban put his chin up slightly. "'But his strength and valor availed naught.'"

Sean Connal frowned. "I don't believe I'm familiar with that passage."

Urban smiled. "It would be truly miraculous if you were, Doctor. It is from a narrative called *The Romance of the Three Kingdoms*, a rather ancient work from China. Father-General Vitelleschi's missionaries in that land just sent back a translation in April. I had thought it lost—but it turns out the father-general had it all the time. He is a most resourceful man."

"As is His Holiness," replied Sean, "I understand that you have prevailed upon the ambassador—doctor, now, I suppose—to accept me as a medical trainee under her guidance. I am most grateful for this kindness, Holy Father."

Urban laughed. "Oh, it is no kindness, Doctor. It is pure, unadulterated selfishness. It is in my own interest to ensure that I have a doctor trained to up-time standards in my retinue."

Owen frowned. "What do you mean, 'in your retinue,' Your Holiness?"

Urban turned towards him with a look of such singular gravity that, for the most fleeting of moments, Owen was scared. "Colonel O'Neill," said Urban, "you are the Pope's Own Men."

Still frowning, unsure at the strange nature of the compliment, Owen bowed. "We thank you humbly, Holy Father."

Urban shook his head. "I doubt you understand what I mean...
because I'm not sure you would thank me."

Connal was the first to understood the implication. "Your
Holiness, are we to understand that your comment on our being
'your men' was not merely a personal observation?"

Urban smiled. "You are correct. My comment was official. I
will not command this, but I will ask it, for my welfare and that
of this troubled Church. Will you be known as the Pope's Own?"

"You wish us to become papal troops?" Although Owen tried
to keep the tone of his inquiry deeply respectful, even in his own
ears, he sounded as though he was choking on a chicken bone.

Urban shook his head. "No, no: not that. But until I may have
a Swiss Guard again—if I ever do—I would take great comfort
in being able to rely upon your kind and vigorous defense of my
person and the Church Militant. And I have already communicated my wishes to your employer, who has replied that my choice
honors him greatly, and that my trust is well and wisely placed."

"King Fernando said that?"

"He did—along with Archduchess Isabella. They have even
extended an invitation to visit there, which I might very well do.
I might even convene the council in their lands."

Owen spread his hands. "Your Holiness, how can you? The
Low Countries is not a purely Catholic realm anymore."

"Owen," commented Sean quietly, "tell me: which realms are,
at this moment, purely Catholic realms?"

The answers that first jumped into Owen's mind—all of Spain's
possessions and Bavaria—died before they emerged from his mouth.
"I see," he observed, with a pull at his newly trimmed beard.

"And besides," added Urban, "the Low Countries are one of
the few realms that have tendered such an offer to my troublesome self."

"Has France?"

Urban's smile was sly. "Of course. And they offered Avignon
as my papal seat—which, if I agreed to it, would be like declaring Borja the true pontiff and myself the anti-pope. No. I have
many friends among the French cardinals, but Richelieu holds
their reins. So I continue to consider one other offer."

"Which is—?" Connal wondered with a winning and far-too-
innocent smile.

"Which is best shared at a later time. Besides, I do not yet have your answer, Owen Roe O'Neill: may I indeed consider myself protected by those Wild Geese that you feel suitable for such duty?"

Owen Rowe O'Neill stood very straight. "Where the pope goes, we go. We are his men."

Urban smiled. "Nothing could please me more. Now I will ask one more thing of you: seek out Thomas North and Lieutenant Hastings. The USE has graciously offered to lend me their contracted services."

"A *sassenach* protecting a pope?" O'Neill smiled. "What is this world coming to?"

"It is coming to an urgent crossroads perched upon the edge of a yawning abyss, Colonel O'Neill. Over which I intend to build many such bridges before we all fall into it and are consumed. Now, please be so good as to tell the co-owner of the Hibernian Mercenary Battalion that their USE employers have decided to extend their current 'special contract' in a most uncommonly lucrative fashion."

Still smiling, Owen nodded his respects, and went in search of the damned *sassenach*.

Sherrilyn leaned back and tried stretching her knee out straight; it did not cooperate. *Damn it, what I'd give for a whirlpool right about now—*

"Quatrine for your thoughts?"

She turned and smiled in the direction of Harry Lefferts' voice. "They'd cost you a whole lot more than that, buddy."

He sat down on the bench beside her, but she could tell he wouldn't stay long: his body was bent forward over his knees, hands clenched between them. Obversely, when he meant to settle in, he slouched back like a cougar at repose. Feeling an awkward silence growing, she asked, "How's Matija doing?"

"Fine. Donald's in the sick ward with him right now." Harry looked out beyond the hills. "At least the two of them made it."

"Harry, listen," said Sherrilyn. "We're the Wrecking Crew; danger is our job description. Paul and George died doing their jobs as well as any of us ever have. And Rome is old news. What you and Miro pulled off in Mallorca—that was an extraordinary piece of work, and yes, everyone knows that most details of the close assault on Bellver came from you. You might be determined to play down your role in it, but Miro isn't; if anything, he's trumpeting your contributions while under-representing his own."

Harry looked off to the side. "Yeah, well—I'm not going to get all worked up about it. The last time I basked in the spotlight I got a little bit blinded. And that got some good people killed. Some really good friends, too. I don't need—or want—any credit for Mallorca. That was for the folks we left behind in Rome."

Sherrilyn put a hand on his shoulder. "Harry, listen to someone you trust—yourself. What you said in Venice was dead right: we had a good run, and had it as long as we could. When we first arrived down-time—when Mike Stearns recruited us—we were flying by the seat of our pants, and making up plans only seconds before carrying them out. And a good part of our success was because we were an unknown quantity; because the down-timers didn't know all the things we could do, but more importantly, they also had no idea about all the things we *couldn't* do.

"That was sure to change, Harry—and that's what happened in Italy. The job changed, not us, not you. We had our run, and we had no way of foreseeing just how fast and hard that run was going to be over." She rubbed her wrapped knee. "And I had no idea I was becoming an old lady."

Harry grinned. "Well, Sherrilyn, you should know—better than anyone else—that I have a thing for older women."

"Idiot," Sherrilyn said with a smile.

"Ya gotta hand it to me, at least I'm consistent."

"That you are, Harry," she said as he stood.

"Well, I'm off." He said brusquely—and then, his tone suddenly became serious, almost somber. "Every morning, when I wake up, I start the day by telling myself that the sacrifices we made were all worth while. We got Frank and Giovanna back, you kept the pope from getting killed, and we beat the other guys at their own sneaky games."

"Yup," agreed Sherrilyn, who rummaged around in her pocket and extended its contents up toward Harry: sunglasses. The weren't exactly like his trademark pair, the ones he'd broken in two and tossed in the Tiber, but they were close down-time copies that had come with an embassy worker out of Rome.

Harry looked at them and shook his head. "No, Sherrilyn, I'm through with them. I think I've gotten to that stage of my life where there's only one good reason to wear sunglasses."

"To shade your eyes against the sun?"

Harry nodded. "Pretty dull—but when the image gets in the way of the job, it's time to dump the image."

Sherrilyn hoisted herself up, wavered a bit, but finally stood firm. She snapped a clean, respectful salute. "It's been an honor serving with you, Captain; you are a hell of a soldier."

He returned the salute. "I'm going to live up to that, Sherrilyn. And—truth be told—the honor was all mine."

# Chapter 59

The sun in Barcelona was punishing, and Pedro Dolor had seated himself at the table with his back to it. This also gave his host—the count-duke of Olivares—the seat with the superior view of the harbor. If it also happened to make the older man squint and work a bit harder at maintaining a serene and superior composure—well, Olivares was an old hand at just these kinds of clandestine meetings, so Dolor thought it unlikely that he would be so easily rattled. However, Pedro was happy for any advantage he might acquire, no matter how small.

Olivares picked at his *camarones al ajillo* distractedly. "You seem to have done quite well for yourself in your new position, Señor Dolor." He nodded at the plain but fine clothes that Pedro wore, seemed to scan fingers and neck for any sign of jewelry. "Although you seem reluctant to make any display of it."

"Professional considerations, Your Grace. In my line of work, unobtrusiveness, not ornamentation, is key."

"But surely you can veer from this Spartan regimen when you are in private?"

Dolor shrugged. "If the lack of ornamentation remains an unexceptioned habit, then one cannot, in a moment of distraction, forget it. It is one's reality, one's sole reflex. Which is precisely what, in my case, it must be."

Olivares nodded slowly. He seemed to consider the shrimp he

held aloft on a silver fork, but Dolor knew that in fact, the count-duke was considering him. Measuring the increased confidence, the seemingly sudden increase in what Olivares and his aristocratic ilk would call "courtly breeding," congratulating himself on having had the foresight to promote this lowly lackey from bloody-handed work to the subtler requirements of the mission he had just completed. Which had, paradoxically, included the two most profitable failures of his career.

The paradox of the deeper successes implicit in those two superficial failures was evidently not lost on Olivares. "Despite recent outcomes, it seems that you are an indispensable man, Señor Dolor."

"Your Grace honors me with a compliment where I failed in both tasks?"

"Tsk. Nonsense—although your repeatedly expressed willingness to assume responsibility serves you well. What I—and others—note is that, as long as you were personally in charge of situations, they went quite well. In Rome, you did not merely defeat, but may well have shattered, the most famous group of military daredevils—so-called 'commandos'—on the Continent. In Venice, you crippled the USE's aircraft and designed a meticulous search strategy that ultimately located Urban. And given the restrictions under which you labored in Mallorca, and since you were not present when the USE's second task force of rescuers arrived, your responsibility for that outcome is, at most, marginal. As I understand it from independent sources, the viceroy had summoned you to the Almudaina to extort new threads of gossip from my letter to you, and to hold his nervous hand since he is no longer a favorite in Madrid."

"The Count-Duke is remarkably well-informed—and over-kind in choosing to see my merits above my failures."

"And *you* are over-modest, Dolor. Which I have always liked about you; it suggested your quality from the start. It is good—very good indeed—to have watched you grow into the full promise of your skills."

"Which I owe to your example and tutelage, Your Grace," Dolor lied.

Olivares may have actually believed that compliment, or taken it as another sign that Dolor was ready for advancement into direct court matters: flattery—as long as it was not excessive or untimely—was a prerequisite skill if one was to be successful in that rarified environment.

"You have come a long way, Pedro—and will go much further, if I am any judge of men. So tell me: what do you think happened in Mallorca?"

Dolor considered. "I think it illustrated why shattering the Wrecking Crew in Rome was not an unalloyed benefit."

Olivares held the shrimp frozen before his lips. "What do you mean?"

"Consider, Your Grace. By only breaking, rather than destroying, the USE's premier special operations tool in Rome, we actually pushed it to evolve into an even better tool, one that now boasts an even broader set of capabilities. Much of what occurred in Mallorca bears the mark of Harry Lefferts, but just as much suggests that he is now working with others who brought their own, unique strengths to the operation. And it seems obvious that this new whole is much greater than the sum of its parts."

The poised shrimp went slowly into Olivares' mouth. "There is much depth in you, indeed," the count-duke mused. "And before you left Palma to make this report to me, did you see to it that the responsible parties there were appropriately punished?"

Dolor knew that Olivares was asking about measures taken against the *xueta*. They were not directly implicated: the explosions and subsequent fire had destroyed almost everything but the stonework of the Castell de Bellver. The scant remains mostly defied identification. The deaths of Dakis, Asher, and Castro y Papas could only be inferred from the fire-scoured tools and weapons that had been recovered from the lazarette-crematorium. The governor's charred bones had been found amidst the scorched fixtures of his own armoire. Whether he had hidden there, or had been locked inside by attackers would never be known. And of the attackers themselves, there were almost no surviving signs. So if the *xueta* had been involved, there was no remaining evidence to suggest, let alone prove, it—no matter how very likely it now seemed.

But Dolor harbored no hatred of Jews—did they not bleed like everyone else?—and was unwilling to punish people for suspected crimes; he was happy to leave that brand of sadistic idiocy to the Inquisition. He decided to redirect the conversation into a more provocative—and, if carefully handled, productive direction.

"Your Grace, when you ask about 'responsible parties,' I take it you are referring to Cardinal Borja's political mismanagement of holding the Stones as hostages? Unfortunately, I lack sufficient authority to punish him—to borrow your own terminology."

Olivares blinked. "Be wary, Señor Dolor," he said in a severe tone. But Pedro saw in Olivares' eyes that the indirect remonstration was also insincere: Olivares' disdain for Borja, and delight at Dolor's question, was quite obvious. "I was referring to the parties responsible for what happened in Palma," Olivares clarified with a ghost of a smile.

But this was where Dolor felt the moment had come to play his well-established role of the ever-solemn professional. "With all respect, Count-Duke Olivares, I do in fact consider Cardinal Borja to be the architect of the disaster in Palma."

"How? He was not present."

"He did not have to be. The situation there was the direct result of his policy in regards to Frank and Giovanna Stone. How might everything have been different if the cardinal had been willing to conceive of them as useful assets, rather than scratching posts? One is tempted to think that it could have resulted in sustained dialog with the up-time powers—which, however noxious, would have been useful. Particularly had extended negotiations resulted in the repatriation of the pregnant woman."

Olivares' face became carefully expressionless. "And how would that have been beneficial to us?"

"First," Dolor explained, "I suspect that the up-timers would not have resorted to a strategy of forceful extraction so quickly, if ever. Had we repatriated the wife, they would have logically clung to the hope that the same could be achieved for the husband, with enough negotiation. And there was only one thing they had possession of that we would have been interested in negotiating for."

Olivares' eyebrows climbed. "The up-timers would never have turned Urban over to us in exchange for the husband."

"Of course not, Your Grace. However, once our requests were rebuffed, we could have sent an envoy to either Gustav Adolf or his adversaries within the government of the USE. They could have—legitimately, in this scenario—protested that, in the case of the wife, His Majesty Philip had made humanitarian accommodations desired by the USE. However, the up-timers had then autonomously rejected the reasonable reciprocal requests of Spain. Which was, simply, that the legitimate guardian of the fractured Roman Catholic Church, Cardinal Borja, be given the fugitive anti-pope. Or that the up-timers simply mind their own business and cease aiding and sheltering him."

Dolor ate, affecting not to notice Olivares' frank, admiring stare when he continued. "Would this have gained us access to Urban? Of course not—but it would have generated much political division in the USE. The almost autonomous activities of the up-timers against our forces and in our territories would have been brought into sharp relief. It is exactly the kind of issue that Stearns' opponents in the USE would eagerly build into a *casus belli*—and Borja missed the opportunity. Alas, he did not even see it—no more than he has seen the other situations in Rome that have severe international implications. Indeed, one such matter could send shocks of a most personal and unpleasant nature right into His Majesty's private chambers."

Olivares sat up sharply. "To what do you refer?"

It was now time for Dolor to play the card he'd been waiting for Fate to deal him his whole life. "You received my confirmation that it was indeed John O'Neill—son of the late Hugh O'Neill, the eldest of the two remaining princes of Ireland—who was slain in the courtyard of the Palazzo Giacomo Mattei?"

"I did," Olivares said, his eyes suddenly careful. "As you conjecture, that promises to be a thorny matter when presented at court. And I note that you made no mention of Cardinal Borja's reaction. Why?"

Dolor knew the time had come to turn the card face up. "Because I did not report it to him."

"No?" Olivares stared, and then, after a flash of what looked like both outrage and relief, an expression of careful calculation settled into his features. "Who else knows that it was O'Neill?"

"Others. Enough to make sure that the information is safe, that it cannot be lost by any collection of unfortunate accidents."

Olivares smiled. "Your prudence—against Fate's whims and my treachery—is duly noted, Señor Dolor. But it affords little flattery to our dealings thus far; they have been in good faith."

*Said the axe-wielding farmer to the Christmas chicken.* "That is true, Count-Duke Olivares. I mean no offense to you. After all, what if you were to pass this information to a less honorable subordinate this afternoon, but God called you to his kingdom at dinner this night? Kings have been slain by fish bones, after all."

Olivares smiled at Dolor's face-saving explanation. "Very well, so the information is safe. And not in Borja's hands. But why did you not share it?"

"I would have, had he asked, Your Grace. But he did not. He conducted no review of his own. Nor did he take note of the strange coincidence of Father Luke Wadding's apparent removal from St. Isidore's and the involvement of several Wild Geese at the *insula* Mattei. That alone would prompt a prudent man to begin a careful investigation. Which would have revealed O'Neill's identity quite quickly. And that, in turn, would have prompted an obvious question: why was the king in the Low Countries' best known mercenary commander in Rome? The obvious answer—that he was in Rome to kill his Spanish comrades and free the son and daughter-in-law of the wealthiest up-timer—has ramifications of singular import to His Majesty, King Philip."

Olivares' expression had become grim. "You are right, of course—in both your assessment of how difficult an issue this will be to raise with His Majesty, and Borja's failure to detect it." Olivares pushed the last shrimp around his plate in irritation. "This entire matter—of the Irish in Rome—makes matters more complicated in regards to evolving a suitable policy regarding the changes in the Low Countries."

"And I suppose it would become even more difficult to reveal that the Irish were also involved in the raid upon the Castell de Bellver."

Olivares forgot the rogue shrimp. His eyes widened. "The Irish were in Mallorca, as well?"

"Without doubt, Your Grace. We found these in Rome—" Dolor held up what looked like a strangely formed wooden ring—"and in Bellver as well. The two examples we have were badly scorched; they endured the fire only because they were apparently in or near a large tun of water, at the time."

"But what are these rings? Why do they signify the presence of the Irish?"

"These rings are used to hold the priming caps in place for a preloaded cylinder for this kind of revolver." And Dolor produced a battered pepperbox revolver from within the folds of his garments.

Olivares stared. "What is that?"

"It is a new design of pistol, inspired by up-time technology. After Rome, we found three of them, one near each of the bodies of the Wild Geese. I had inquiries made as to the weapon's manufacture. Do you care to guess where it is being produced, by privately contracted gunsmiths?"

"The Low Countries." Olivares tone was a statement, not a question.

"Precisely. The money came from the court, albeit indirectly. The design was conceived of—in general principles—by the last of the Irish princes, Hugh O'Donnell."

"I know him. And that only compounds the embarrassment." Dolor raised an eyebrow. "Why?"

"Because O'Donnell renounced his membership in one of Spain's most prestigious orders of knighthood, the Order of Alcantara, as well as his position as a Gentleman of His Majesty's bedchamber, within the past few months."

So. There was widespread disaffection brewing among Philip's long-neglected Irish allies. Hardly a surprise—but damnably awkward for Olivares. Which only made Dolor's hand stronger than he had anticipated. He played another card: "We found similar rings at St. Isidore's, but did not know what to make of them. And to return to the attack on the Castell de Bellver, one of the corporals manning the western ravelin heard a Gaelic war-cry within the walls, just before the shooting became most intense."

Olivares cocked an eyebrow of his own now. "I was not aware so many of our rank-in-file artillerists possessed expertise in obscure Celtic languages."

"Only those who served with the Irish at the siege of Breda and other Lowland campaigns, Your Grace. Our men have always noted that the Irish stir themselves up with such cries immediately before they make the most dangerous of charges or sallies."

Olivares actually rubbed his eyes with his hands. This was better than Dolor could have hoped for. "Do you have any idea of how many Wild Geese were involved in these attacks, Señor Dolor?"

"I doubt more than twenty, Your Grace. Probably more like a dozen. But the identity of one of their other leaders may be of greater significance than their numbers."

"What do you mean?"

Dolor spread his hands. "Several of my contacts in the south of France reported that, back in May, a person answering to John O'Neill's description was seen taking ship for Italy. Another notable was with him, and that person answered more closely to the description of Owen Roe O'Neill—whose tercio in the Low Countries is now reportedly under the nominal control of his arch-rival Thomas Preston. It is tempting to wonder if the redoubtable Owen Roe O'Neill was also present for the rescue attempts at both—"

"Enough!" Olivares held up a hand, shaking his head. "This whole matter becomes worse and worse. I had hoped to find a way of explaining Conde John O'Neill's involvement in Rome as a fluke, a personal aberration. But this begins to smack of a mission conducted with the blessing, maybe even at the behest, of Fernando himself. And with so much evidence pointing in this direction, I must reveal it now, or keep it forever buried."

"Perhaps there is a third option."

Olivares looked up, eyes narrow and quick. "What do you mean?"

And from the look in those eyes, Dolor knew he had Olivares. He finally had leverage over the man who could change his fortunes, even make possible the eventual supplantation of his father at court—who, being a figurative bastard, had long ago sired a literal, miserable one in the shape of one Pedro Dolor.

Olivares' tone was urgent. "What do you mean, a third alternative? Do you mean that perhaps the matter can remain buried, if only for a time?"

"Of course, Your Grace—if the evidence and the information is handled correctly. The inchoate reports from Bellver could take some time to untangle, naturally." Dolor smiled. "And after all, it will be sheer—and long-delayed—chance that leads me to eventually piece together the disparate evidence and physical clues that our own soldiers scattered in the aftermath of the combat at the *insula* Mattei."

"Yes, I see. These 'delays' would be most helpful, Señor Dolor." Olivares smiled.

Dolor didn't smile back.

Olivares' smile faded, then returned, sly but also an admission that his henchman had, in this moment, undergone a sudden transformation into something more like his vassal. "As I said, this would be most helpful, *Don Pedro*. Now tell me, what will it take for a complete report—and thus, news of the involvement of O'Neill and his Wild Geese—to be so unfortunately delayed?"

Dolor leaned back and savored the moment he had been waiting his whole life to savor. At last he would have a position from which he could begin to exact true and proper vengeance, the closest thing to justice he could acquire for all the little boys that Madrid's mighty and powerful had abandoned to cruel streets.

Little boys who had been abandoned just as he and his brother had.

# Chapter 60

Mike Stearns came into the headquarters tent of his Third Division, peeling off his gloves. As he did so, he bestowed an almost baleful gaze upon his two visitors.

"Ed Piazza, President of the State of Thuringia. Piazza, and my once-spymaster Don Francisco Nasi," he stated. "Come all the way here from such distant parts. No doubt you dropped by unexpectedly to bring me tidings of good cheer."

Nasi smiled. Piazza shook his head.

"Tidings of tension, I'm afraid," said Ed. "And it is rising everywhere."

Stearns sat down. "I take it you're referring to the backlash from Urban's rescue?"

"He most certainly is, Michael," answered Francisco. "The reactions have been pouring in over the last few days, and there are some twists that you should know about. The evolving situation could even catch up with you out here—particularly since you are getting close to Poland."

"What do you mean?" said Stearns.

"The latest information is that the leading clergy of Catholic nations have been much more swift in responding to the news of Urban's survival than we expected, probably because he is also calling for a papal council next spring."

"Well, I expected that eventually—but next spring? Where?"

"That's part of the kicker," Ed added. "Urban isn't saying where—yet. But he has already announced that one of the items on the council's agenda will be the state of relations among Christian nations, which will necessarily involve a close and critical assessment of the conditions that warrant having the Church declare other religious practices to be heretical, and more importantly, what conditions—if any—necessitate that it must take action against such practices."

Stearns looked at the other two. Then he took a deep, slow breath while he gazed out at the flat Saxon countryside visible through the still-open tent flap. The sun was setting. There was still enough light to see by, but his batman had already lit the lamps inside the tent.

He now understood why Ed and Francisco had come all this way to discuss the matter with him, despite the fact that he was no longer the USE's prime minister. He wasn't even a member of Parliament any longer, since he'd resigned from his seat when he accepted his commission in the army. They were probably violating at least twenty rules of political protocol, but...

Political protocol be damned. He looked back at his two visitors. "He's going to do a down-time version of Vatican Two." The statement was flat and certain.

Francisco nodded. "Which has triggered responses from the clergy of every major nation. Mind you, their statements are not always declarative—there are a lot of carefully muted reactions—but it seemed that no one wanted to remain silent."

Stearns leaned forward. "So how does it shake out?"

Ed scratched his head through his thinning hair. "Well, with the exception of a couple of whacko Calvinist sects that even the mainstream Calvinists avoid, every single major Protestant clerical figure or council has come out with either strong or guarded support for Urban's initiative. That includes most of the major voices in Switzerland and England."

"No surprise there," observed Mike, who eyed the small bottle of up-time whiskey that Ed was slowly edging out of his pocket.

"A similar level of support is looked for from Gustav, who we suspect will be in touch with you about a joint statement, given how prominently Larry Mazzare's name has figured in all this."

Mike rolled his eyes. "Make my day."

"Other regions declaring for Urban include the entirety of the Low Countries and, conspicuously, every one of the USE's Catholic provinces. Bohemia and Austria are being a bit more circumspect. They are careful to say nothing about Borja, but both express their relief to learn that 'the pope is alive' and look forward to his further messages."

Mike shrugged. "Still, that's about as overt as they can be without spitting in Borja's—and therefore Philip's—eye."

"Yeah," said Ed, "and while we're on the topic of spitting in Philip's eye, there was one real shocker among the Catholic nations: one of them made an almost militant statement averring Urban's legitimacy. The bishops who signed it even called directly upon Borja to vacate the *cathedra* which he had—and I quote—'brutally usurped from the true pope.'"

"Whoa. Dem's fightin' words. Where'd they come from?"

Francisco smiled. "Ireland. If you can believe it."

Mike frowned. "Not so hard to believe, really. As I understand it, with the prohibitions against Catholic colleges there, most of their clergy gets educated in Rome or the Low Countries. They used to go to Spain a lot, but not so much any more. Guess they got tired of being second-class Spanish citizens."

Ed nodded. "Yes, and some of them get educated in France now, too. Which brings up what might be the trickiest of all the reactions: the ones coming out of France. The French cardinals that really matter—the ones who belong to the Consistory—all welcomed the news of 'our pope's continued survival and future safety.' No surprises that they slipped in that affirmation of Urban's continued legitimacy; he has a lot of friends in that quarter. However, Gaston has rallied a lot of hard-line bishops to support his claim that, as a true defender of the faith, Borja's attack was justified because Urban destroyed his own legitimacy by tolerating and giving papal imprimatur to heretics."

"Meaning us."

"Among others—although with Urban's rescue and safety being openly attributed to up-time intervention, I think it safe to assume that we head the list of the aforementioned 'heretics.'"

"Along with Venice," added Nasi, "which also declared strongly for Urban. The papal lands that aren't under direct Spanish control are making similar, if less vehement, noises."

Mike nodded. "Okay. You've pumped me up with the good news. So hit me with the bad."

"Well, obviously Spain and all its associated satrapies and client states are firmly behind Borja. That includes Milan and

Naples—although the popular sentiment there is for Urban, building on the extant desire to evict Philip's tercios from Italy."

"As you said, no great surprise. Who else, Ed?"

"Poland and Bavaria are Borja country, also. Strongly so."

Stearns looked from one to the other. "That can't be all. I'm not saying it's not reason enough to come out here to update me—but I know you guys; you've still got something else up your sleeve. What is it?"

Nasi smiled. "Michael, are we really that transparent?"

"Entirely. Now, what gives? More trouble?"

"More detailed news from Venice. Including some new considerations that should not be communicated by radio," amended Nasi with a sly look.

"Okay, stop building the suspense, Francisco. What's the news from sunny Italy?"

"All good, except that the casualties at Molini have been confirmed: the number was not in error. Otherwise, the various parties have arrived in their various destinations safely. Our expanded papal envoy—"

"—you mean, The Traveling Pope Show?" put in Mike.

"—yes, them—are, according to Sharon's report from Chur, evolving nicely as a team. Tom Stone's report from Venice is one long paean of praise for how Estuban Miro handled his part of the rescue and protection planning. According to Tom, Miro apparently possesses—among other as-yet-undemonstrated skills—the ability to walk upon water, too."

"And Miro's own report?"

Nasi smiled. "As unpretentious and brief a document as I have ever seen. After itemizing the expenses incurred, and summarizing the actions undertaken—in which he indicates that Harry Lefferts was the prime architect of the final attack plan—he concludes with the most terse summary I have ever seen: 'Objectives were achieved; all operations may be considered nominally successful.'"

Stearns looked at Francisco narrowly. "Okay, Francisco, I know that smug look and tone of voice. What're you holding back?"

"Nothing—except that, as I suspected at the outset, Miro performed admirably. Most admirably."

"And you were right. So what?"

Ed coughed. "Mike, I really don't have a chief of intelligence, with Francisco gone. Cory Lang is a good field man, a good observer—but damn it, he's not cut out to run an intelligence—and counterintelligence—group. You need a chess master for that—and that's Miro to a tee."

Mike frowned. "You sound like this is an urgent decision."

"Mike, I think it is, because if Miro is the guy we ultimately want doing that job, we're going to have to commit to it now. Even if we don't tell *him*."

Mike's eyes went briefly to Ed's bottle as the former principal of Grantville High School produced three shot glasses as well. "Tell me why."

Francisco sighed. "Politics: what else? First, this council Urban is calling is going to be a powder keg of continental proportions. Anyone who goes to it is effectively drawing a line in the sand in front of Philip. I doubt Philip supports what Borja has done, but his pride and Spain's are now inextricably entwined with the would-be pope. And certain matters—family matters—are going to come to a head, as a result."

Mike nodded. "Ferdinand in Austria and Fernando in the Low Countries."

"Yes. Particularly the latter. Austria is a completely separate state, and its completely separate monarchs can agree to disagree; they have before. However, the Low Countries' position in relation to Madrid is nebulous, and this is going to the defining moment of Fernando's autonomy."

Ed picked up the thread. "So far, both brothers have been careful not to get into a show-down, but this situation could force them into it. And here's what could make it unavoidable: Fernando is going to send Cardinal Bedmar, Ruy Sanchez's old boss and a member of the Consistory, to the papal council. It's a cinch he's going to affirm Urban's legitimacy. And he's going to have to do it in front of the entirety of Europe. And everyone will know that he couldn't do so without Fernando's support."

Nasi shook his head. "Philip can't afford to have that happen, and does not want to go to war with his own brother. So we must anticipate that Philip will attempt to derail the council, and that he might even try to sabotage it."

Mike nodded. "And Ruy—although he will be an excellent security chief—should not have to wear the second hat of overseeing and planning the intelligence and counterintelligence activities both before and during the council. I'm sure Ruy is quite good at chess, but—"

Nasi nodded. "But it's not his game of preference, or his greatest skill. This job is for Miro. But we can't simply appoint him right away."

Mike nodded back. "Yeah, I see the problem. Miro's still pretty much an unknown quantity to our people in Grantville, and is a total stranger to the rest of the USE. So our people will have to get used to him, first."

Ed opened the whiskey. "It's a pain in the neck, but yes. And then there's the appearance—false—of nepotism if we appoint him: he comes to our attention through Francisco and then who replaces that selfsame outgoing spymaster? Why, his very own golden boy. It's not how it happened, but it's how it will appear."

Mike shrugged. "Look, let's not make a problem where none might exist. Miro's now got a business to run, right? Just before I left Magdeburg, I think you mentioned something about him and Tom Stone going into business together."

Ed nodded. "Yup. Building some balloons in both Venice and Grantville. And some related chemical processes, I think."

"Well," said Stearns with a shrug, "Let Miro tend the Grantville end of that garden for half a year or so. By handling purchasing and negotiation up in the USE, he'll naturally have contact with all the regional power-players through legitimate commerce. It will also get rid of any suspicions that his performance in the Mediterranean was solely because he had a huge home court advantage. Meanwhile, Ed, if any of your intel people feel that they just *have* to spend some time sniffing Estuban's ass before they let him into their pack, they'll have ample opportunity to get a nose-full while Miro oversees the case files on who's coming to the council. He'll be working up the operational planning on the intelligence at night, running his own business by day. And if he can handle all that, we'll know he's good for the long haul as our intel chief, and our people will have adopted him."

Nasi nodded as vigorously as Ed had ever seen. "It's a good plan. Simple and effective. If we help groom his contacts properly—make sure he is invited to the right parties, participates in the right negotiations—he could be present at Urban's upcoming papal council for completely legitimate reasons. It would be the perfect cover."

Mike Stearns leaned back. "That's what I'm thinking. And it gives Gustav Adolf absolute plausible deniability if anything goes wrong with Miro's operations. In fact, with the exception of a few of the folks under Sharon and back in Grantville, no one even needs to know Estuban is handling this for us."

Ed Piazza plunked his bottle down on the tent's small field table. "Mike," he said, "you are starting to sound like the people you always hated most, up-time."

Mike started. "What do you mean?"

"I mean, think about where terms like 'plausible deniability' come from; you hated those institutions and the entirety of the intelligence apparatus."

Mike shook his head. "No, Ed. I didn't hate the institutions; I hated what they became."

"Not to rain—or maybe piss—on your parade, Mike, but isn't that just a bit facile?" Ed cocked his head. "I seem to recall you asserting—convincingly—that because of what intelligence agencies are tasked to do, and therefore, how they must recruit and structure themselves, that they have innate tendencies to become exactly what you hated. As you said, 'Honestly, can you whelp a tiger and then hope it grows up to be a vegetarian?' Doesn't that worry you about what we're doing now?"

Mike looked at the hard packed earth between his feet. "It worries me every damned hour of every damned day. But do you have any better ideas?"

Piazza shrugged. "Not a one. Other than maybe we should all sit in a flower-power circle, passing around a jug, and singing 'We shall overcome.'"

"Huh. You've heard me massacre a few tunes, Ed, so you'll be pleased to know that I'm going to take a pass on the singing. But if you happen to have a jug with you..." Stearns eyed the up-time whiskey meaningfully.

Nasi smiled as Ed filled the shot glasses and pushed them to their respective destinations. "Actually, there was one last reason to come out and visit you here, Mike."

"Which was?"

Nasi lifted his shot glass. "To do this."

Stearns looked at his own glass before taking it up. "Yeah. Seems like old times."

Ed Piazza, raising the whiskey, reflected that, with Stearns soon to go into battle in the vicinity of Zwenkau, and Nasi heading off to Prague to help Morris Roth forestall one of the most infamous pogroms in history, it was all too possible that this time might be the *last* time they all lifted a glass of cheer together. Indeed, fate had been improbably kind to them, thus far.

Ed Piazza did not share this thought, but instead, joined them in sipping the whiskey in silence, as old friends often do when they reflect on the uncertainty and peril of coming days.

# Cast of Characters

| | |
|---|---|
| **David Asher** | *xueta* (crypto-Jewish) physician |
| **Aurelio** | ship captain from Piombino |
| **Antonio Barberini** | Cardinal and nephew of Pope Urban VIII |
| **Maffeo Barberini** | Pope Urban VIII |
| **Benito** | young scarred *lefferto* |
| **Gaspar de Borja y Velasco** | Spanish Cardinal, Anti-Pope |
| **Vincent Jose-Maria de Castro y Papas** | Spanish captain |
| **Sean Connal** | physician in the Wild Geese |
| **Dakis** | senior henchman of Pedro Dolor |
| **Edward Dillon** | soldier in tercios of the Wild Geese |
| **Pedro Dolor** | intelligence operative for the Count-Duke Olivares |
| **Turlough Eubank** | soldier in the O'Donnel tercio of the Wild Geese |
| **Ezquerra** | Spanish sergeant and adjutant to Captain Castro y Papas |

651

| | |
|---|---|
| **Fernando** | King in the Spanish Lowlands, Infant of the Spanish Hapsburgs, younger brother and nominal vassal of Philip II of Spain |
| **Luigi Ferrigno** | Borja's secretary |
| **Virgilio Franchetti** | Miro's senior airship expert |
| **Alarico Garza** | Spanish sergeant at Castell de Bellver |
| **Marzio Ginetti** | Cardinal of the Papal Household, Legate to the court of the Austrian Hapsburgs |
| **Giulio** | chief messenger and runner for Rombaldo de Gonzaga |
| **Rombaldo de Gonzaga** | chief of Pedro Dolor's assassins in the vicinity of Venice |
| **Matija Grabnar** | down-time member of the Wrecking Crew |
| **Gaspar de Guzman** | Count-Duke of Olivares |
| **Anthony Hickey** | Franciscan priest and teacher |
| **Hastings** | senior lieutenant in the Hibernian Battalion |
| **Ignatio** | assassin and arsonist in the employ of Valentino |
| **Isabella Clara Eugenia** | Infanta of the Spanish Hapsburgs, Archduchess of the Spanish Lowlands |
| **Georg Jenatsch** | Swiss military leader and statesman |
| **Felix Kasza** | down-time member of the Wrecking Crew |
| **Klaus Kohlbacher** | pilot of the *Jupiter Two* |
| **Harry Lefferts** | up-timer, leader of the Wrecking Crew |
| **Cesare Linguanti** | assistant to Valentino |
| **Paul Maczka** | down-time member of the Wrecking Crew |
| **Sherrilyn Maddox** | up-timer on the Wrecking Crew |
| **Melissa Mailey** | up-timer diplomat and advisor |
| **Dino Marcoli** | Giovanna's cousin |
| **Fabrizio Marcoli** | Giovanna's brother |
| **Giovanna Marcoli** | wife of Frank Stone |

| | |
|---|---|
| **Maria Anna** | princess of the Austrian House of Hapsburg, wife of King Fernando |
| **Lawrence Mazzare** | up-time priest, now Cardinal-Protector of the USE |
| **Estuban (Ezekiel) Miro** | intelligence operative for Ed Piazza |
| **Sancho Jaume Morales y Llaguno** | governor of Castell de Bellver |
| **Odoardo de Mosca** | Valentino's ogre-like assassin |
| **Franciso Nasi** | outgoing intelligence chief for Mike Stearns |
| **James Nichols** | up-time physician |
| **Sharon Nichols** | up-time EMT/physician and ambassador to Rome, wife of Ruy Sanchez de Ortiz y Casador |
| **Thomas North** | Colonel of the Hibernian Battalion |
| **Donald Ohde** | down-time member of the Wrecking Crew |
| **John O'Neill** | third Earl of Tyrone, exiled/attaindered |
| **Owen Roe O'Neill** | a Colonel of the Wild Geese |
| **Ruy Sanchez de Ortiz y Casador** | former Spanish officer and husband of Sharon Nichols |
| **Ed Piazza** | president of the state of Thuringia-Franconia |
| **Piero** | senior *lefferto* |
| **Orazio Porfino** | young relative of Aurelio |
| **"Romulus"** | code-name for a confidential agent of Don Taddeo Barberini, Duke of Palestrina |
| **Pieter Rubens** | artist and confidential agent for the court of the Infanta Isabella |
| **Arcangelo Severi** | factor for the influential Cavriani family |
| **Rita Simpson** | Tom Simpson's wife and Mike Stearns' sister |
| **Tom Simpson** | Captain in the USE Army |
| **Mike Stearns** | first president of the up-timers, out-going Prime Minister of the USE |

| | |
|---|---|
| **Frank Stone** | son of Tom Stone |
| **Tom Stone** | up-time magnate and chief envoy to Venice |
| **George Sutherland** | down-time member of the Wrecking Crew |
| **Juliet Sutherland** | down-time member of the Wrecking Crew |
| **Miguel (Meir) Tarongi** | *xueta* (crypto-Jewish) operative |
| **Valentino** | commander of de Gonzaga's assassins |
| **Muzio Vitelleschi** | Father-General of the Society of Jesus (Jesuits) |
| **Luke Wadding** | Franciscan theologian and Guardian of the College at St. Isidore's |